THE IMAGE MAKERS

To Vee and Bill —
— the very nicest
parents Susie could
possibly have!

Affectionately,

Bem

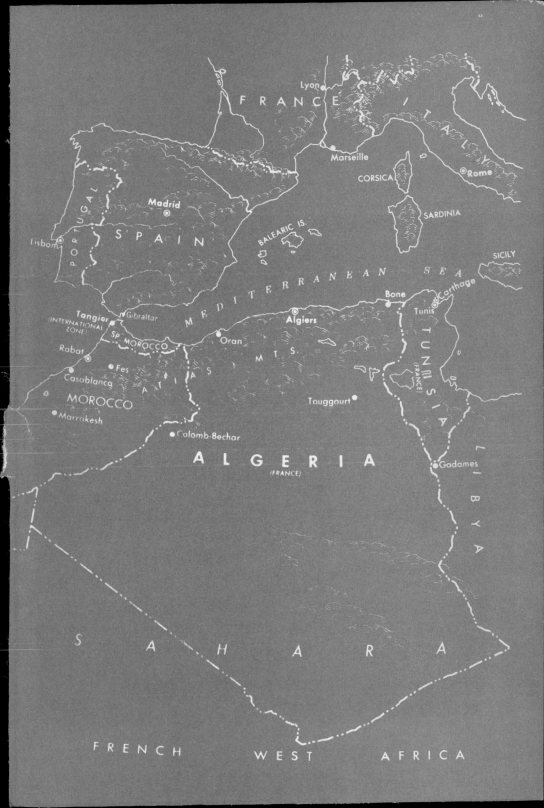

THE
IMAGE
MAKERS

A Novel by

BERNARD V. DRYER

Harper & Brothers Publishers

New York

Life is action and passion. I think it is required of a man that he should share the action and passion of his time at peril of being judged not to have lived.

JUSTICE OLIVER WENDELL HOLMES

CONTENTS

For
My mother and father
and Donna

BOOK I

Fortune's Wheel

(1)

ON OPPOSITE shores of the Atlantic, the global tides of the Western world followed the great astronomic tug of the moon. The lunar lamp hung in remote depths above the earth, ignored completely in a New York restaurant, admired extravagantly from a Mediterranean yacht, and cursed in whispers on a Moroccan hillside. The earth's shadow turned, following the solar procession, cosmic and indifferent.

In New York, Dr. Malcolm Adams and his wife Laura were winding up the evening at the Stork with several friends who were helping them celebrate their tenth wedding anniversary. They sat around a circular table with their guests: Mr. and Mrs. Carl Barkley of Greenwich, Connecticut, and Dr. and Mrs. Harry Scott of New Haven. Everyone was drinking champagne, except Carl Barkley, who said he could never stand the stuff, not even the extra dry.

Only five minutes ago an extension telephone had been brought to Dr. Adams' table so that he could take an urgent long-distance call from Washington. Laura Adams and their friends had lowered their voices courteously, but had talked just enough to pretend they could not hear the doctor saying carefully and obliquely, "Yes . . . yes . . . when? . . . I see, I see . . . not at all, don't mention it, thank *you*." He stared at the telephone for a moment, with his hand still resting on it, then he lifted it off the table and put it on the floor beside the wall, out of the way. Dr. Adams signaled their waiter to bring another bottle of champagne, but oddly, in a dampened way, just the opposite of celebrating. A well-known newspaper columnist came across the room and stopped by at the table to ask Dr. Adams, quietly, leaning off confidentially to one side, what the real story was on the Senator down there in Washington.

"The way I heard it," the columnist said to Dr. Adams, "the distinguished unnamed Senator from an unmentioned state checked into

3

Bethesda at the Medical Center just before you examined him. The way I heard it, the other consultants called it terminal throat cancer and you refused to operate."

"I don't know what you heard," Dr. Adams said to the columnist, "but all I heard about was a meeting of an Advisory Council at the National Institutes of Health in Bethesda. That's all I was called to Washington for."

"Then you didn't just go for a meeting, you were called down there?"

"Mr. Uh," Mrs. Adams said cheerily to the columnist, sounding like champagne but ladylike, "Mac shouldn't keep you standing. Please sit down and join us. We'll all be famous for a day tomorrow."

"Your husband isn't exactly unheard of, Mrs. Adams. This Washington business turns the spotlight right on him. The Senator's health is a key situation."

"Talking about Senators," said the man next to Mrs. Adams, Carl Barkley, "what's the inside scoop on the Democrats' income tax program?"

The columnist shrugged. "Taxes schmaxes, as they say. Just be happy."

"What good's happiness?" Mr. Barkley said. "You can't buy money with it."

"Please," the columnist said, "please. Forgive my barging in on the party. Well, Dr. Adams, I see you're not saying much. If they persuade you to do the plastic surgery on the Senator, happy landings."

"It's a fact," Dr. Adams said, "I've never exchanged a word with the unnamed Senator."

It was true. By the time he had reached Washington that morning the Senator, although conscious, had been unable to speak. The Washington call which had just come through to his table said the Senator had slipped into what looked like irreversible coma, and the men in Bethesda doubted Mac Adams would need to fly down to Washington from New York tomorrow. The Senator would probably need the last rites, not plastic surgery.

Dr. Harry Scott, a quiet-looking man on the Yale medical faculty

4

who practiced psychiatry, and who had not spoken before, leaned across the back of his wife's chair and said to Dr. Adams, "You look tired, Mac. Let's all call it a day."

Dr. Adams saw his wife Laura frown. He sat up straighter and smiled. "No," he said, with only a little effort, "we're just getting the ball rolling." In the back of his mind he had been planning the complex head and neck surgery the Senator might need, because he had been convinced he might give the Senator a few more years of life. The telephone call from Washington had changed all that.

The steam yacht *Hercules,* out of Monaco bound for Tangier, ran at a comfortable half speed over calm seas so clearly moonlit the water shone like ice. The moon which was remote and white over New York hung above the *Hercules* in orange voluptuousness, close and tropical.

Maia Obenpharo lowered her deck chair so that she lay far back in it, looking at the huge sky. The wide scattering of stars made a great celestial wheel. Occasionally one fell in a long glowing arc. Dreamily she half heard the Mozart concerto coming over the built-in wall speaker of the intercom and listened to her host talk to her and his wife about, of all things, Mediterranean piracy.

"During the war," her host was saying in French, leaning on the rail while slowly rotating his brandy in a big glass snifter, "they called it a bomber's moon. It's really a hunter's moon, especially here along the Barbary Coast."

"Theo," his wife said, "what are you drinking? Such romantic talk. Maia, take that glass out of his hand before he starts singing."

"Theo is never romantic just for fun," Maia said. "Are you, Theo? If he sounds sentimental he must be thinking about money."

Theo laughed and turned toward her from the rail, saluting her with his brandy glass. "I'm singing about a pirate's moon, my dear Xenia," he said to his wife. "Pirates have sailed these waters since my ancestor Hercules came this way to Mallorca, looking for the lost golden apples."

"Now I understand why he's moonstruck," Xenia said to Maia.

"I was just thinking the same thing." Maia murmured. "He's looking for lost golden apples."

5

Theo took a long swallow of brandy and said into the glass, "You see? My mind is just an open book."

"Theo, you've told that to everybody," Maia said. "On that oil tanker fleet investigation last year, I heard an American Congressman said, 'Yes, but your open book's written in ancient Greek. Who can read it?' "

"Hercules. The golden apples of Mallorca," Xenia repeated softly, as if saying it to herself. "Now I know why Theo raised anchor for Mallorca this morning."

"But we're going to Tangier first," Theo said.

"Of course, *chéri,*" Xenia said. "With you, two and two make five."

"Today's quotation," Maia said, "is six and a half."

"Maia," Xenia said, "please help yourself to the brandy. A lovely violet bouquet. It's bottled just for Theo, and you've hardly touched it."

"After all that champagne at dinner? Thank you, no. I've had enough truth serum for tonight."

"*Alors,*" Theo said, "while the truth is in you, my two mermaids, my happy harpies, read me the oracle of Delphi. What's on my mind? What's written there in ancient Greek?"

"Yours first, Xenia," Maia said. "You guess first."

Xenia got up, keeping her feet apart on the faintly moving teak deck, and stretched prettily, then went over to her husband and put her arms around him. "I don't know why I love him," she said. "He's really just a lost golden apple."

Theo tipped the brandy snifter back against his mouth to empty it, then, with no table within arm's length to put it on, he threw the glass overboard and bent to kiss his wife's classic Grecian nose.

"Theo," she said, "how Russian. Those glasses are expensive."

"Still the little girl from Athens, darling? Still the economical housewife? Right now, this minute, your own namesake, the *Xenia,* is bound this way. She's loaded with forty-eight thousand tons of crude oil out of Arabia bound for New Orleans, and she'll pay for enough glassware to stretch from here"—he pointed at the moon—"to that brandy snifter."

"I told you, Xenia." Maia stirred in the deck chair and sat up. "He *was* thinking about money."

6

Xenia laughed. "My mother used to say that a Greek loves a woman, but he's devoted to money."

The Mozart concerto ended with a flourish on the intercom speaker, and, in the silence, they could hear the faraway throb of their engines and the soft splash of bow waves. The glowing Mediterranean night seemed huge, beyond horizons, with a pressing sensual darkness.

"By George!" Theo said, saying it in English, then back to French, "I still haven't heard the temple virgins pronounce their Delphic oracle."

Xenia laughed aloud. "Did you hear that, Maia? If he really believes *that,* there will be no oracles tonight."

"Correction," Theo said. "Temple priestesses."

"My oracle," Xenia said, "is that we are going to Mallorca—"

"For a vacation—" Theo added.

"—for a vacation, because you have money in the film they're shooting at Deya. He has an investment in that Mallorca picture, doesn't he, Maia?"

"Banque Obenpharo never reveals a client's position," Maia Obenpharo said. "No gossip, not even from a lady banker."

"Money," Theo said. "Maia introduced me to a few very talented people in Paris, at the Banque Obenpharo in fact—"

"Ah," Xenia interrupted. "The few talented people. That's where the golden apples are buried. The star of the picture, that blonde Swedish tart with necklines down to here, *she's* the girl with the golden apples!"

"Thank you, my little oracle. This reveals more about you than me."

Xenia giggled. "If you go near her—!"

"Xenia, Xenia, save all this passion for bedtime. The evening is young."

Maia saw Theo's profile against the dark-bright sea turn toward her. "And you, Fortuna, what's your message from the gods?"

"You'll spoil the game, Theo," Maia said. "You can't call on Fortuna. She was a Roman goddess."

"No, no," Theo said, "my New York office cabled yesterday that

7

Chase National is financing our new shipbuilding program. Fortuna is now definitely one hundred per cent a Greek goddess."

"Such mythology," Maia said. "Chase is only financing half."

"Really? How did you know?" Theo was not actually surprised, because Maia Obenpharo always had all of Banque Obenpharo's information. Papa Obenpharo trusted her.

"Our New York correspondent, named Mercury, cabled *me,* in Olympus," Maia said, and they all laughed together.

"*Alors,* Fortuna, I offer sacrifices on your altar," Theo said. "I bring a nice piece of business into Banque Obenpharo—" Then he threw in casually, "By the way, does your Olympian father-in-law pay you a commission on my business, Maia—?"

"I'm Papa's partner, Theo," she said softly, "not a salesgirl." She was enjoying the little tennis match of information they were playing. "And our other clients may not be as handsome or rich as you, *chéri,* with beautiful Greek goddesses for wives, but as Papa Obenpharo always says, we make a living." That was a hard forehand drive down the center of his court. She liked him very much, but there was no need for his becoming lordly with her. Banque Obenpharo assets matched his.

"Your oracle," Xenia said. "You're not fair. I told mine."

"It's simple," Maia said.

"I told you," Theo said. "I'm really a very simple sailor, traveling by the stars."

"Swedish stars," Xenia said. "Excuse the interruption, Maia, but I couldn't resist."

"You see, Maia? My wife is a girl who just can't resist."

Maia stood up. "Well, my little ones, have your domestic fun. I'm going below to my lonely bunk and dream about Hercules."

"The oracle," Theo said. "By George, do we have to beg for it?"

Maia sensed immediately that Theo was really interested. Theologos never misses a trick, she thought with admiration, he's the smartest Mediterranean pirate of them all. Except Papa. Except Olympian Papa Obenpharo, who'll be so surprised to see me in Tangier tomorrow morning with Theo's golden loot, delivered dockside in Theo's own yacht.

"Well," Maia said, closing her eyes with her head thrown back,

8

stretching her arms out theatrically, "thus spoke the gods to me. Antaeus, son of Neptune, has built a city for his wife Tingis beside the Pillars of Hercules. In this city, called Tangier, a Phoenician seaman named Obenpharo has built a temple of worship called Banque Obenpharo."

"Wonderful," Xenia said. "She gets a commercial announcement into every oracle."

"Don't stop her," Theo said quickly.

"In this temple there stands an altar of pure gold—"

"—actually," Theo said, "it assays at ninety-nine point six per cent."

"—and to this altar will come a simple Greek sailor, who quibbles over decimals, in the good ship *Hercules,* bearing an Athenian goddess on deck with hair as black as the night sky, and in the hold below, pure one hundred per cent gold bars which really assay at ninety-ni—"

"—all right, I apologize—"

"—pure gold bars of great value," she said. "On the sea beyond the city of Tingis, which is now Tangier, there have always been Barbary Coast pirates searching for slave galleys or motor launches with contraband American cigarettes they could hijack."

Xenia looked up at her husband and saw him staring at Maia, smiling faintly in the dark. "Theo—" she began to ask.

"Don't worry," he said. "There isn't a chance in a million. Beside, we have the radar, the weapons chest is unlocked, and we have the speed if we need it."

"Is she right? Do we have gold bars aboard?"

"A few," he said. "Maia needs them for her papa's temple in Tangier."

"Why?"

"Who knows? Gold is a crazy hitchhiker. It rides with the law as far as possible. Then it becomes a stowaway. Legal, illegal, but it travels. Personally, I'd rather speculate in cemetery lots than bury gold in a bank."

Maia had dropped her arms. "Then why did you say yes when I asked for the gold, Theo?"

"Because Xenia and I have much admiration for you, Maia.

9

Xenia," he said to his wife, "you know that I love Maia secretly, don't you?"

"Of course, *chéri*. I never met a man who didn't."

"Good night, little ones," Maia said. "If any pirates board us to-night, send a big one in to me. There's something about the sea air that makes me hungry."

The cold downpour of moonlight on the hillside marking the border between Spanish Morocco and French Morocco threw long shadows from the crouching single file of Arabs. The first man bent forward, resting on one knee, and held up his hand. Each man at intervals all the way back down the hillside to the gully where the loaded donkeys of their ammunition train were herded held up his hand. The file stopped its advance while the first man lay flat on the ground, cradling his rifle across his elbows, and began to crawl slowly toward the border where they believed the French zone began.

At the end of the column, in the gully beside the donkeys with burlap tied on to muffle their hoofs, Roger Obenpharo crouched shivering in his *djellaba* beside Ahmed. The cold, and the silence, and the concern about French border patrols chilled him under the coarse wool. He placed his mouth near Ahmed's ear to whisper, smelling Ahmed's leathery odor of fatigue beyond fatigue. Roger Obenpharo knew Ahmed had been with the load of weapons all the way from Tangier to Ceuta, to Xauen, here to this damned lost hill with its damned bright moonlight. Ahmed had handled the loading and un-loading from open boats to the Spanish zone beaches, then to the trucks, then from the trucks to the little donkeys. Roger knew it had been heavy work, much of it under the sun, and he was grateful that Ahmed was as completely dependable in the slave labor of gun-run-ning as he was in courage.

"Why is the fool up there calling a halt?" Roger whispered angrily to Ahmed in Aïssowa dialect. "We are completely exposed here. We may be inside the French zone now."

Ahmed shrugged. His old bearded face was as wrinkled as a mummy's, and Roger knew he was worried, too. Until now they had run nothing bigger than rifles and ammo across the border; this was their first heavy shipment of machine guns and nitroglycerine. It was

10

of critical importance for their revolutionary work inside the French zone, and Roger was afraid these hill men would not be as skillful as with the usual lighter loads. That was why the Central Committee of the Istiqlal had agreed when he insisted he would go to the border just this one time, even though he was nominally a French citizen and that made the risks of capture by a French border patrol worth considering quite carefully. That made the risks so much greater that it became better to ignore them.

I was right to come, too, Roger Obenpharo thought. They need better guides and realistic tactics. I don't like bringing pack animals this far forward. A French patrol could easily hear a donkey bray. The sound would carry for miles in the still night, and the Legionnaires had four-wheel-drive jeeps, radio communications, and heavy weapon firepower. All we have is smallness and speed, and tonight our speed is gone.

"We should have unloaded from the animals to our backs closer to the trucks," Roger whispered. "We brought them too far forward."

"Ismael is a good guide, Sidi," Ahmed whispered back. "He must have stopped to crawl ahead. Think of the difficulty to find the border."

"I do not like it, Ahmed. He is not sure of himself. He should know if we have crossed the border. He does not know how to move heavy equipment fast."

"He has a great courage, Sidi."

"The courage I do not doubt. The thinking, I doubt. The having experience with so many heavy boxes, I doubt."

The real fault is mine, he thought. Ismael had the experience and the courage, so I trusted him, when I should have trusted my own critical judgment. But this is not exactly the same as committee meetings or making speeches, so I hesitated too long. From now on it will be different.

The donkey ahead of them shifted on its legs, making a sound dulled by the muffled hoofs. The animal was loaded with nitroglycerine in both wicker panniers and everyone near him felt uncomfortable. Roger saw Ahmed glance up at the sky, at a shooting star. The air had the incredible desert clarity, deeply blue-black, strangely luminous, and they saw another star flash down, then another. Roger

11

noticed Ahmed shake his head slightly, and knew that the old man considered this a bad omen. The lights in the sky were really fire spears used by the angels to hurl back the devils who spied on Allah, as any orthodox schoolboy knew.

Somewhere in the night a stone clattered, rolling and striking other stones at intervals, rolling, rolling, then silence.

Roger stiffened. "Which direction was that?" he whispered fiercely. "East," Ahmed answered.

He's wrong, Roger thought swiftly. All my Islamic brothers say *east* because Mecca lies that way. Even Ahmed knows no other point on the compass. And that sound seemed to come from due south, within the French zone. Was it Ismael? Or just one of their donkeys? Or a French sentry? Under the terrible moonlight there was complete silence now. The strung-out row of crouching riflemen looked like low rocks at intervals.

Here is where the weakness of our Moslem culture shows, Roger thought. These brave men are really children. They will charge into the muzzles of Legionnaires' machine guns to drive the French out of Morocco, because they know it is written: *Those who are killed for God and His laws are not dead but alive.* But they cannot tell what is real and what is not. Shadow and substance weigh the same. They say: Peace be unto you, using *you* in the plural because you are of course surrounded by several invisible spirit companions.

An experienced guide for foot traffic across the border tries a new route tonight because he takes it for granted that heavy loads should always be carried by animals, and now we are pinned down in the open while he scouts ahead to find his bearings. He wishes for the absence of the French border patrol, therefore, the patrol will be absent, *insha' Allah.* Maybe the time has come to pull everyone back, all the way back to the trucks safely waiting inside the Spanish zone, and make a new plan to cross the border tomorrow night. I can save the guide's pride by explaining no one doubts his courage, we only need to wait for a cloudy night. Everything is somehow off on the left foot, the guide's mistaken pride, my error in allowing him to go ahead, the shifty-hoofed donkey carrying nitroglycerine in the middle of our line, the cursed moonlight, everything is wrong. Each mistake compounds the next. If we weren't so close to the border, or across it already, I'd order a retreat immediately. Boldness and caution, caution and boldness, this requires a balanced act of decision, not dependence on the angels of the Faithful.

At that moment a star shell burst explosively in the sky above them. A huge phosphorescent ball hung over them, and simultaneously rifle and machine-gun fire began to sweep the hillside. Roger saw the tracer bullets begin at the head of their line and sweep downhill toward the pack animals. His own riflemen were pinned flat now, returning the fire in bursts, not daring to move under the terrible light overhead.

"Ahmed!" he shouted over the rifle fire and the fearful ripping sound of the machine gun. "Pass the word! All the animals back to the trucks! As soon as our riflemen can fire!"

He watched the machine-gun tracers rake up the hill and start down again toward their gully position with the loaded donkeys. The animal loaded with nitroglycerine was pulling its driver backward by its halter, braying madly, and Roger began to get off the ground to help lead the animal out of the line.

Out of the darkness the tracers reached closer and invisibly touched the loaded donkey, and the whole earth around Roger rose up into a towering shattering roar of rock.

In Greenwich, Connecticut, a short distance from New York, Dr. Malcolm Adams was at home now, deeply asleep, dreaming of rushing headlong through darkness. He threw his arm out against his pillow in defense against an attack from within, which a later awakening would wash away completely. His wife Laura slept peacefully in the twin bed.

Carl Barkley had driven him and his wife home from their New York party. Carl had one of his special cars, a Ghia Chrysler with Borelli wheels and Michelin tires, a four-speeds-forward gearbox and an exhaust-turbo supercharger and many other equally unique technical items, which Carl explained at great length while he drove up to Greenwich at his usual supercharged speed. Dr. Adams' wife Laura enjoyed the night drive, but Mac Adams did not. He knew Carl had a special supercharged approach to Laura, too, but Laura could handle that as well as she did everything else; also, it had been a long

13

day in Washington and a longer night in New York, and he was scheduled to operate at eight in the morning. The parkway had rushed like an illuminated trench toward his tired eyes, unrolling brightly into Carl's specially designed speeding headlights, and Mac had gone to sleep sitting up.

In her stateroom aboard the *Hercules,* Maia Obenpharo sat up in her berth smoking one of Theo's aromatic Papastratos cigarettes, trying to read a French picture magazine, but unable to focus, unable to sleep, watching the ladder of shadows cast by the moonlit blinds climb slowly up the bulkhead. The shining pile of Theologos' bar gold in the hold beneath her cabin was a diplomatic coup she had arranged without consulting Papa Obenpharo. How would Papa react?

The tension she always felt when she returned to Tangier drummed softly in her.

On the rutted road near the Ras el Ma in Spanish Morocco, rattling in a dust cloud away from the French border in the direction of Xauen, Roger Obenpharo lay unconscious in the back of a truck. His head was covered with a crust of embedded dirt fragments and blood, and they had placed him face downward so that he could breathe a little even though half his face was blown open.

From the top of the minaret in Xauen, the bearded muezzin waited until an edge of light ran in liquid fire along the eastern horizon, then he called out to the Faithful, *"Allahu akbar! . . . Night has fled with the darkness and day comes with the light! There is no God but God! Come to pray! Prayer is better than sleep! Arise and to God be the praise!"*

Above the sloping red tile roofs of Xauen a flight of storks rose bony-legged from their twig nests in the crumbling battlements built against the Crusaders; they flew upward, as they had for centuries, toward the rising sun.

(2)

MONSIEUR BENARI OBENPHARO sat in his high-ceilinged bedroom overlooking the tiled fountain courtyard of Villa Obenpharo in Tan-

14

gier while his Arab valet shaved him tenderly. He leaned back with closed eyes, listening to Radio Maroc broadcast the morning news from Rabat, the capital of French Morocco. He tried to repress the feeling which another night of fretful sleep and dawn awakening left in him, the feeling of disaster soon to come, the almost visual awareness of a sword above him.

"Louder, Mustafa," he said to his valet, opening his eyes and moving one hand slightly to indicate the table radio. Mustafa turned the volume control up.

Across the courtyard Benari Obenpharo could see the lattice shutters of Madame Obenpharo's bedroom swing open above her balcony. Her head appeared in the dim interior beyond the window, stationary, listening to the radio across the silent courtyard. So, he realized suddenly, she is sleeping as poorly as I. She is as much on edge as I.

". . . and in Casablanca," the French news announcer said smoothly, "Monsieur Dallant, the publisher of *La Presse,* was killed last night by a burst of thirteen machine-gun bullets as he stepped into the plaza before his apartment house. Two black Citroëns were seen racing away from the deserted plaza. Monsieur Dallant had been on his way to the airport, for a flight to Rabat. This morning the Minister for Tunisia and Morocco has been summoned by Premier Faure to Paris for urgent consultation. The killing of Dallant is linked by authorities to the bomb which exploded last week in the Rue Dumont d'Urville." He paused, then began a new bulletin. "Another border skirmish occurred last night when two platoons of a Legionnaire patrol surrounded a large group of Arabs attempting to smuggle guns. . . ." The announcer went on giving details, but Obenpharo hardly listened. These border incidents were daily affairs now, and hardly of real importance.

"Shut it off," Obenpharo ordered, and a moment after the radio clicked into silence, he saw his wife reach out and close the lattice shutters of her room. Even at this distance he could see that her hands were shaking.

As he leaned back and let his valet lather his face again to continue the shaving, with his eyes closed he said, "Mustafa, do you know the name Napoleon?"

"*Non,* monsieur." Mustafa continued in French, "Is the soap water too hot?"

15

"No, just right. Napoleon was a great European sultan, a conqueror before the time of your father's fathers. Once, in a conquered village, he dismounted dusty and incognito from his battle saddle so that he could be shaved by one of the conquered population, the village barber. The barber was so foolish he could not tell the difference between one uniform and the next. The poor ignorant barber thought himself honored to be shaving a great captain of his own country's army, not the enemy's. As his razor shaved skillfully over Napoleon's throat, he explained with great anger how he wished he could have the hell fiend called Napoleon in his barber's chair. Napoleon listened courteously when the barber, in his great anger, stopped shaving him for a moment and drew a line in the lather over his windpipe with the back of the razor. The barber was demonstrating his dream of how simple it would be to end the war with one quick razor cut. He, the village barber, could be a hero with one quick razor cut. His countrymen and the whole world would applaud his daring stroke. Napoleon sat pleasantly until his shave was completed. When he arose, clean and refreshed, he thanked the barber."

Mustafa had stopped shaving him. In a land where all can listen but most cannot read, Obenpharo thought, the ancient Mediterranean love of storytelling is strongest in the Arabs.

"Then," Benari Obenpharo said, "what should Napoleon have done?"

"Was this Sultan of Europe as great as the Sultan Moulay Ismail?" Mustafa wiped the lathered cuttings off his blade on a spotless towel.

"Yes, as great." Even educated Arabs spoke of Moulay Ismail's reign, a few centuries ago, as the Great Age.

"The Sultan Moulay Ismail would have first cut off the barber's hands. Then the barber's nostrils would be closed until his tongue hung out for air. Then the tongue would be cut off. Then, after a period of sufficient regret by the barber, in the Djemma el Fna, the Place of Death, the Sultan would himself cut the barber's throat with the barber's razor."

"Justice," Obenpharo said.

"Even so," Mustafa said. *"Insha' Allah.* Did the Sultan of Europe do the same?"

"No," Obenpharo said. He turned his head slowly from side to

16

side, inspecting his shaven face in the mirror Mustafa held up for him. He nodded approvingly, then said, "Napoleon told the foolish barber that he himself was the Emperor Napoleon and left the barber standing there."

Mustafa put the mirror down, frowning a little, puzzled. He bent over the table collecting all the shaving things and looked at Obenpharo for any further instructions. "Monsieur will go to the bank after breakfast?"

"Yes, have the big car at the side door today."

Mustafa started to leave the room, then turned at the door. "The story," he said, "I do not understand the Sultan of Europe. It weakens a country to leave criminals unpunished."

"There was no criminal. There was only a poor foolish little village barber with a heroic fantasy."

"But for the Sultan Napoleon to leave him there, and the poor barber fearing each day for years that he might be killed at any moment." Mustafa looked pained. "How cruel Christians are," he said.

Obenpharo attacked the iced melon on the breakfast table as if it were an enemy. He was impatient to get downtown to his bank. His office there was an island of order above the creeping edge of chaos. The silver monogrammed spoon in his right hand shook a little, and he wondered if the obnoxious shaking were due to a disease called Parkinsonism for which his Paris doctor had given him medicine which he consistently forgot to take, or whether it were due to the nagging feeling of a sword hung threateningly above him. You old fool, he thought fiercely, have you lived so long in Morocco that you can only think of concrete objects? An anxiety neurosis becoming a dangling sword? Fear of betrayal becoming Mustafa's razor? Shadows becoming assassins?

Ruqayya, his wife's personal maid, pushed Madame Obenpharo into the breakfast room on the aluminum wheelchair, then padded out silently. Obenpharo got up to kiss his wife.

"*Bonjour, ma petite.*"

"*Bonjour, chéri.* You look tired, Benari," she said in French. "Didn't you sleep well?"

"Like a babe," he lied, continuing in French. "And thou, my little one?"

17

"Fairly. There was a beautiful moon in the window," she said. "I walked too much yesterday and my ankles were swollen all night. Even now. I don't understand how a difficulty in the heart can cause a swelling in the ankles."

"Why do you walk so much, Mutirra? Dr. Moore warned you."

"It's so hard to sit still, Benari." Her voice had the faintest possible suggestion of tremor in it. As the servant placed the melon before her she waved her fingers nervously. "No, no, take it away," she said in Arabic. "I want only the British tea this morning."

"Tell me," Obenpharo said in English because of the servants, "will our son grace us with his revolutionary presence at breakfast?"

Her large dark eyes, the beautiful Arab eyes he had loved from the time he had seen her in her father's house in Rabat, met his. They looked enormous, pupils and iris equally dark and merging, pools of fear. "Ruqayya told me," she answered in accented English, "the butler mentioned to her that Roger's bed was not slept in last night."

"Servant gossip. That may or may not be true."

"I sent Ruqayya to see perhaps for herself. Ruqayya says to me, it is true. It is true the night before. And one of the cars is gone."

"Why didn't you tell me sooner, Mutirra?"

"What good would it do, Benari?"

"What good? Did you hear the radio news from Rabat this morning?"

"Terrible. Terrible."

"Forty-eight hours after Roger leaves Tangier."

"Benari!" Her hands came up to push away his implication. "Maybe the counterterrorists' *colons* killed their own countryman. Maybe the Presence Française wanted to silence Dallant. Any Frenchman who speaks for a liberal policy toward Morocco may be killed by other Frenchmen with machine guns. Don't blame every killing on the Moroccans or the Istiqlal."

"No, Mutirra," he said, "the Istiqlal are just a college debating club. Just friendly athletic philosophers, like our son, who unload small boats filled with smuggled weapons near Ceuta. And all the while the Spanish Morocco police turn their backs on the weapons traffic across their borders into the French zone. There, of course,

18

the weapons are used only for hunting small game. Like French newspaper publishers."

"Benari, please. Don't be obscene. Roger would never kill a man."

"No, because he's a leader. The leaders never kill because they can always order someone else to do the dirty work."

Mutirra Obenpharo began to cry soundlessly, forgetting the cup of tea on the table before her, with tears running in two lines down her face. "When you talk like that, Benari, I know you blame me."

"You encouraged him to convert to Islam, not I."

"You yourself say Christianity is filled with hypocrisy."

"All formal organized religions are. They all collect funds. They all forbid food and fornication at frequent intervals to force even the simplest humans to remember their rules. Roger has gone beyond Islam now. He's using the faith of the Faithful for political goals. He's making this revolutionary nationalistic movement a kind of new religion."

She sobbed once, and put the back of her hand against her mouth like an aged child. "What can I do, Benari? What can you do? Close the doors of our house to our only son? Tangier is his only refuge." She had gone back to Arabic now, as she always did when the teeth of the outer world beyond Villa Obenpharo began to bite through her silks. "Even the government calls part of French Morocco their *zone d'insécurité*. Imagine if they caught him inside their borders. Imagine the atrocity. I've heard the Foreign Legionnaires are mostly German. They have no pity."

"Only the Istiqlal has an exclusive possession of pity," Benari Obenpharo said. "When they kill one of their own Moslems for speaking of compromise with the French, they cut off his penis and force it between his teeth. A college debating club, your son's followers, all filled with gentleness and pity."

"Oh, Benari!" she cried. "Giving your bitterness to me like this helps not you nor me. We must keep trying to end this barbarism."

"We aren't omnipotent, Mutirra. In Europe, France is spitting blood. And here the Moors keep stabbing her above the heart. What can I do?"

Her voice went up. She was beyond tears now. "Where is the courage of the man who did intelligence for the Allies in the war, when

19

a knife or a bullet could come at any time? When twenty-five thousand people died in '37 during the Marrakech typhus epidemic, who was the only man to go there of his own free will to open his closed bank? The only one, going without sleep to be his own clerk and teller and giver of alms, so that people had money for medicines and food? When the officials died, and the nobles locked their gates, and the pashas fled to the mountains, who stayed in the city until his name was a legend in Morocco?" When he did not answer, she lowered her voice and said, "So he is *your* true son, not just mine. A leader. What you hate in him comes from yourself as well as from me. Don't blame only the Arab half that came from me. Our lives run together until we die. Don't abandon him, Benari!"

He looked across the table with great love and respect at the small sick dark-haired woman who was the only bond left between him and their son. He cleared his throat and said only, "Irra. . . ." It was the affectionate diminutive of her full name, an intimacy filled with memories of better years for them both, and when she heard it she put her face into her hands and wept.

A month ago he had tried to be the go-between, the peacemaker. He had gone to Rabat to see the Resident General. He had succeeded in getting a top French general staff officer sent quietly to Tangier, in civilian clothes, to meet with Roger. General Montret had known the Obenpharo family since the days of Abdel Krim and the Riffian war; he and Benari Obenpharo had captained rival polo teams years ago, and over all those years they respected one another.

A month ago, with the General coming to dinner, Madame Obenpharo had had the grand salon overlooking the Straits of Gibralter filled with fresh flowers. Every electric bulb in the enormous arched room was checked carefully, because each bulb had been hand-blown in Belgium, before the war, in the shape of a candle flame; special sockets had been manufactured for the special bulbs, so that now, as an electric light burned out, usually in the middle of a dinner party, it could not be replaced with a modern standardized bulb. As her heart disease worsened and an unhealthy puffiness struck her eyes and face like a fist, Madame Obenpharo welcomed each candle replacement for each mercifully burned-out light. Candlelight was kinder than electricity to a woman who once had a great reputation for beauty.

A month ago, she and Obenpharo had taken their seats at opposite ends of a long formal dining table in the grand salon. Roger had sat at his father's left, across from General Montret. As soon as they were all seated, Madame Obenpharo knew she had made a fatal mistake. The formal table was too big. They should have dined alfresco under the great umbrella of the fig tree in the fountain courtyard. A small outdoor table would have put them close together, able to chat casually. Now, with this great field of table linen and silver and glassware between them, informal discussion was impossible. The distance across the table required raised voices, declamation, she had immediately realized, and she had known at once they would end only by making speeches at one another. The salon virtues she had learned as a girl, the porcelain graces, were as useless now as a hooped skirt. Even their clothes were wrong. She saw that she was wearing much too much jewelry. Over one breast she had worn the decoration which Marshal Lyautey had pinned on her father's tunic so long ago, but now she felt Roger would interpret this as toadying to a French general. The General, who had just stepped out of a small airplane, had managed to change into dinner clothes to demonstrate this was only a dinner with a few old friends after all; but his iron face really required a uniform with starred shoulder tabs and rows of ribbons. Roger had worn a fine white *djellaba* over a business suit; Mutirra Obenpharo knew he had draped himself deliberately in a kind of nationalist Moslem flag. He'll probably even refuse the wine, she thought, just to make clear he's a true convert to Islam. The patriot was a good actor, like all leaders.

They had all tried hard through dinner to make small talk, but the length of the table made it difficult. It did not help that the General had known Roger when Roger was a law student in Paris, and even his most casual comment sounded faintly patronizing.

"Your present work is quite a change from your days as a junior executive in Banque Obenpharo," the General had said pleasantly.

"On the contrary," Roger had said. "I'm occupied with problems of finance all the time. The Istiqlal needs money. We do not have the French treasury. We do not have American foreign aid."

"Actually, we get very little aid," the General said.

"Little? Almost five hundred million dollars poured into American air bases? Even in the United States that much money is not considered little."

"And do you think, with five bases in Morocco, the Americans will let the French strangle?"

"They don't own the bases they paid for. We can rent the airfields to them as easily as the French."

"The Americans won't do business with revolutionaries, with Communists."

Roger had laughed a short soundless laugh. "You know as well as I do, General, we're not Communists. Revolutionaries, yes. Americans remember a revolutionary named Washington. The French should know better than anyone how sentimental Americans are about their own Revolution."

General Montret had turned politely to Madame Obenpharo to change the subject. "I always enjoy the Villa Obenpharo tremendously. Each time I come, I marvel all over again at this carved ceiling."

She had smiled at him gratefully for ignoring Roger's remark. "I'm glad you do. The craftsmen came from Fez and lived with us for three years until it was finished."

"By *us*," Obenpharo had added, "Madame means her father's palace in Rabat. The ceiling comes from his house."

"Looted," Roger had said calmly. "All looted."

Madame Obenpharo had thrown a quick begging look toward her husband, *tonight please keep self-control,* and Benari had kept his voice very correct. "Loot? It was a marriage gift."

"Not military loot," Roger had explained pleasantly to his father. "Cultural. The real economic looting was left for the French *colons*."

"Come now," General Montret had said. His voice was less casual now. "My father was a *colon*. He came to Morocco under Marshal Lyautey in 1912. When he came there was not a single bridge in the entire country. There was not one centimeter of railroad."

"Bridges and railroads. Transportation for loot."

"There was not a single hospital!" the General added quickly. "If you were sick and dying, it was the will of Allah. There was no printing press. The Sultan ruled inside a few cities, Meknes and Fez, but a merchant risked his life to travel a few kilometers beyond city gates. Agriculture was a wooden plow and a pointed stick. The country was a medieval slum. Casablanca was a handful of primitive huts. Look at Casablanca today!"

"Yes," Roger had said, "with the Bousbir, the biggest brothel in the world. A twelve-year-old costs half the price of a cigarette pack."

"You see," Obenpharo had said to General Montret, "the Istiqlal will forbid fornication under the slogan of national purity." He had ignored his wife's signals and plunged forward. "Then the girls who come down from the hills to earn their dowry in a few months will all die of boredom or starvation."

"Seriously," and General Montret was deeply serious because he was leaning forward intensely toward Roger, "my father was typical of the hard-working Frenchmen who lifted Morocco into the modern world. He worked morning, noon, and night. Just as the land began to yield, the drought crushed him. When he got on his feet, parasitic fevers knocked him down. There were six children in my family, and my father delivered the first two himself. We all worked. My mother and the children, until the farm was going well. When the villagers came to work for my father they were no longer at the mercy of the seasons. They had food the entire year."

"Yes!" Roger had thrown back, leaning forward now himself. "But your father's son grew up and went to a public school closed to the workman your father called *indigène*. When your father's son was sick he went to a hospital built by the French to help their own people in a land of strange diseases. He went to France, to school, to St. Cyr, to a career in life. The Moroccan tenant farmer's son became a tenant farmer. There were no schools for him. He had been kept illiterate so that he would remain docile while more and more land, the best land, fell into French ownership."

"Half truths. Exaggerations."

"Didn't Lyautey lay down the line? *'La force, la grandeur'*? He began with force in 1912, and we have been under the grandeur of continuous martial law since then."

23

"A half quotation," General Montret said. "Lyautey added *'le désintéressement, la simplicité.'* And he meant it. He loved the country. Your Moroccan streetfighters don't want liberty, they want only vengeance."

"More than that," Obenpharo had said in his deep voice. "They want the kind of war Cairo wants. You know, Cairo was named after el Karifa, the Arabic name for Mars, and since then Cairo has directed killing and more killing. A handful of angry blind intelligent men just like you, Roger, sit in Cairo on the Sherif Pasha Street—I even know the house number, Roger—and they order fanatics against fanatics."

"Better than the old diplomatic treachery. The dishonest *quid pro quo*. Negotiate, compromise, money under the table."

"Ugh. My jolly Roger, you sound like a street-corner agitator."

"Of course. Ask General Montret. That's what I am. But, thanks to your business training, on a big scale. On a thousand street corners. *Cedent arma togae.*"

Madame Obenpharo had raised both hands to her forehead, her rings sending out a hundred little diamond reflections of the Belgian electric candelebra in a miniature semaphore flicker of *richissime*. She spoke for the first time. "Both of you, stop, please. You give me a headache. This is fantastic rudeness to our guest, Roger. I hoped we could have dinner pleasantly for a change."

"Hope," Obenpharo had said. "Once I hoped when my only son came back from Paris with a Sorbonne law degree he would bring in modern ideas, modern business. But all I get are Latin phrases and the oldest, stalest, coldest bolshevik stews."

"Bolshevik is an old-fashioned term."

"I'm old-fashioned, Roger. I call things by their names."

"Please!" Madame Obenpharo had said.

"I've already said I'm not a Communist," Roger had said quietly. "I'm interested in Mecca, not Moscow. And if the Istiqlal party ideas are old, they aren't cold. Right now they're boiling. Ask the General."

"Brutem fulmen," General Montret had quoted with a thin deliberate smile.

"Certainly they're boiling!" Obenpharo clenched a fist beneath the table, in his lap, to keep it from shaking. *"You're the flame. You*

24

burn. You're cold, but you're burning yourself alive all the time. Wait until the Bolsheviks take over your fine naïve party. They'll do what your people did in Marrakech. Pour gasoline over you, one match, and *pouf! A chaque saint sa chandelle.* To each saint his own candle. Even Allah won't recognize your charred soul."

"Benari!" Madame Obenpharo had cried. "Please. Please! I beg you."

"Don't beg, my dear. Leave the begging to the street-corner boys. You know what they say the new slogan of the Moroccans is? 'Give us the job and we will finish the tools.' Hah!" He had swung toward Roger, and waved one hand widely. "Tomorrow let's assume it all comes true. Presto, change-o! You drive out the French. Morocco is free and independent. Your sultan comes back from French exile. Your whole dream comes true. Now then, what do you use for money?"

"Money," Roger said. "I knew we'd come back to money. *Sicut patribus sit Deus nobis.*"

"Must you play the medieval monk? Speak a language we all know."

Roger smiled faintly at General Montret. "Didn't they teach you, too, at the Sorbonne: 'Better good Latin than bad Latin; better bad Latin than French'?"

General Montret smiled back. "We've been speaking French all evening."

"Roger, don't change the subject with your little pedantic parades," his father had growled. "I hate to agree with you, but I do, about money. It's foolish stuff. But how will you run your fine free country without money? On camel dung? By squeezing pennies from the poor? By blackmailing high rent from the Americans for the air bases? By selling Sahara sand dunes?"

"That's why we need men like you," Roger had answered patiently. "You know finance and since the Marrakech epidemic the whole country knows you. You know the tremendous potential of Morocco. Every big investment you ever made created work and wealth."

"Except one," Obenpharo had said. "Except my deepest biggest investment." He had thrown his napkin on the table and stood up.

25

"Look into your mirror. You'll see my biggest failure." He had walked heavily out of the dining room, feeling his throat tighten with fury, and with a painful choking tension of unwept tears for his only, lost son.

Remembering the fiasco of the dinner party of a month ago, Obenpharo could understand very well why he had been sleeping poorly. A tide was rising. He knew he could make himself feel better only by going to the solid commercial world his father's fathers had created for their sons out of their cunning and their courage and their ancient belief that, after God, a man's family came first. Then the tribe. For them nations and national loyalties did not exist. Benari was the first of his line to think nationally and internationally. His father's world was one in which a clever man could rub one penny against another and always create a third, and now that world, Benari's, was Banque Obenpharo.

The Banque Obenpharo was a concrete cathedral on the Boulevard Pasteur devoted to the holy trinity of the gold dollar, the pound sterling, and negotiable securities. It rose skyward overlooking the Bay of Tangier and the Straits of Gibraltar, overlooking the distant horizon humps of the olive Spanish shore. It stared out over the world. At street level, at each side of the huge arabesque grillwork doors, two plaques announced in deeply carved letters: BANQUE OBENPHARO. The monumental doorway, the two gold plaques, the tall massive building; the bank was considered locally to be a new Pillar of Hercules. At the top of the bank, glittering greenly because of its special solar glass windows, was the penthouse office suite of Monsieur Benari Obenpharo.

Monsieur Obenpharo had bought the land the day in 1945 when he had seen an American destroyer drop anchor in the bay. The war in Europe had just ended, and the appearance of the tired gray nononsense destroyer announced to his agile mind immediately that, even though the Mediterranean was still a British lake, the wartime Spanish control of Tangier had really ended and the original International Administration would soon return. By his shrewd use of hard currencies, American dollars and Swiss francs, and a few kilogram bars of gold, Obenpharo had managed to persuade the panicky

26

Spanish owner of the land to sell out at a bargain. The seductive gold bars had really closed the deal, as he had guessed they would, because they were small enough to hide easily, move easily, hoard easily. A few years later in '49 and '50, when all the frightened money of Europe was fleeing the continent and pushing and tumbling and pouring into Tangier, Obenpharo was offered forty times his purchase price for the land, and decided the time had come to build a new Banque Obenpharo on it. Tangier was free, in a world of government restrictions, taxes, controls, and inflated currencies, and Tangier blossomed from a trading post into a metropolis.

Obenpharo's first architect for his new bank was a sensitive Frenchman who had been trained so agonizingly and so thoroughly in the classic arts that everything he designed was in revolt; completely modern, glass and stainless steel and aluminum, well proportioned and functional.

Monsieur Obenpharo had looked carefully at the architectural sketches and elevations and plans. "Beautiful," he had told the French architect, "beautiful. Slender, elegant. A subtle suggestion of Moorish Granada, but simplified beautifully."

The architect had been delighted, but like most artists in business he wanted to seem businesslike. "And as functional as a modern airplane," he had said. "See how the traffic flow of your clients is handled? The multiple doorways channel people immediately. No foolish marble pillars to block the way."

"Beautiful," Obenpharo had repeated softly. "But we will never build it because we are not in the temple of beauty business."

After shouting for some time, the Frenchman had quit on the spot. Obenpharo sent him his entire fee plus a bonus out of guilt and admiration, and then had spent the next two months looking for just the right architect. He needed a happy mediocrity. He finally found him, a South American youngster, wild-haired, with heavy hands and two gold front teeth. "He never knew it," Obenpharo explained to his former daughter-in-law, Maia, when he told her the story later in Paris, "but he really got the job because of those two terrible gold teeth. Any man as vulgar as that, a man who thought so much of gold that he advertised it in front of his mouth, that was just the man I needed for my bank."

27

"I don't follow that," Maia had said, amused.

"It's too simple. What's a bank except a hole in the ground? Or a box in a building? Or a hungry vulgar open mouth with a show-off façade of gold? That's what I wanted, and that South American boy understood it instinctively. With his whole heart he wanted to be like a bank, a big front of money success. Why do people put money in my bank? Faith, fear, and greed. They love to see gold nameplates. They like a few heavy marble pillars to show solid old-fashioned conservative management, and some good but not too good office furniture to show efficient economy. And two white-haired customers' men to prove old-line *bourse* and stock exchange experience. Three pretty girl tellers for visiting Europeans to joke with and ask out to dinner, and four quick young men to keep the real front office business moving briskly."

"And five golden pears hanging on a tree?"

"No, no, any golden fruit that grows in a bank is never hung in the open. Never, never. It's hinted at, mentioned, suggested, bought and sold by cable, but never displayed in the open. Never. Remember, that, Maia. Especially because you're at the Paris end of the bank and Paris requires subtleties. Gold is the most beautiful woman in the world. But take her out in the noonday sun and she looks shiny, with little blemishes here and there, and a little cheap perhaps, a tinsel whore. But only show a little of her, an ankle, a hand, and your imagination piles up the rest. Gold is every primitive want melted down to a permanent glitter, and when your bank shows a golden ankle, no more, say two simple solid gold nameplates at the doorway, then people will imagine tons of it in your vaults. Tons of love and power and lust and security and they will rush to you to give you heaps of money—give it to you, by the thousands and millions." He smiled his slow lion's smile. "Give it to you."

"What a wonderful fraud you are," Maia said.

"On the contrary, I'm one of the few remaining honest bankers."

"Because you lie to your clients, but never to yourself?"

So Obenpharo built the bank he wanted, higher than the Tangier Telefonica Building, as tall and square-shouldered and heavy as he was. On the roof he ordered a penthouse office walled with sheets of green-tinted glass under deep overhanging concrete visors to block the sun. At night the penthouse was always brightly illuminated, a miniature lighthouse of money. The shoreline of Tangier Bay below the bank curved far outward to the right and to the left, two sandy African arms embracing the Mediterranean, with a lighthouse on each extended hand: Cap Spartel on the left, Cap Malabata on the right. Obenpharo knew that his shining penthouse, when seen from below by a passing ship, sat higher than either famous lighthouse, higher, smaller, and directly between the other two, like a sultana's jewel hung on the barbaric forehead of the nighttime continent.

At first people were amused by the extravagance of an empty lighted office. "Spartel and Malabata warn you where the rocks are," they said in the cafés. "The bank penthouse warns you where Obenpharo is." But the laughter stopped when they saw most of the passing tourist trade trooping off the luxury liners directly to the famous beacon of the Banque Obenpharo to exchange their money.

Monsieur Obenpharo always made certain his bank offered a fraction higher rate of exchange than any other. He knew this added to the legend of his kingly generosity, and because he believed all the tourists enjoyed feeling they were getting—for the only time in their travels—something for nothing. Occasionally such a tourist would turn out to be a big financial fish, and another wealthy tax-avoiding account would swim as quietly as an eel through oil into Banque Obenpharo, bringing with it the commissions and percentages that paid the bank's bread and butter, and the deals and combines and partnerships that paid for caviar and champagne.

When the local branch of Rotary International met at the Hotel Velasquez, and a French speaker who happened to owe the bank money praised his ingenuity, Obenpharo modestly smiled and brushed aside the compliment with his manicured lion's paw. Actually he had picked up both ideas, the inexpensive advertising by an illuminated office and the inexpensive change-rate generosity, at a bank in New York renowned for clever modern ideas. That was when Maia suggested their new cable addresses: *Tangerpharo* and *Parispharo*.

There was a boldly lettered name plaque on each side of the bank's great doorway; the plaques were almost, but not quite, solid gold. The outer gateway between the plaques were twice as tall as a man, of iron grillwork coming to a blunted point. Obenpharo had purchased the double gate very cheaply from the palace of a young Moroccan prince in Marrakech who believed daily sexual activities were as basic as daily food, but found the belief expensive because of the number of women needed to prevent the boredom of repetition. Obenpharo had wanted the gates from the first time he saw them because the arabesque designs were intricate and beautifully wrought in traditional fashion. The fact that the upper edge of each gate was spiked for the once popular custom of impaling the heads of decapitated criminals only added to the apocryphal stories of what happened to Obenpharo's competitors. "Very few will notice the Fez craftsmanship," he told Maia, "so we can sneak in a little beauty. They're big and heavy and made of iron spikes, and that's just the façade of medieval protectiveness we need in this milieu."

The double gates were wide open when Monsieur Obenpharo's black Rolls glided with noiseless royalty down the Boulevard Pasteur toward the bank. A caravan of small donkeys down from the Charf with loads of squawking chickens and brushwood tip-tapped with their small hoofs along the gutter. One Riff countryman led the column. A second Riff, accompanied by a small barefooted boy with trachoma-blinded eyes like egg white, brought up the rear, all wearing identical burlap-sack-looking hooded burnooses covered with fringed tatters and patches.

Obenpharo's chauffeur blew the horn commandingly, but the donkeys and their masters ambled on at the same timeless pace they had used when the Roman chariots from Volubilis twenty centuries back had demanded the same imperial right of way. Allah is great, without beginning or ending: why hurry?

"Salesarabs," the French chauffeur muttered, making one word of *dirty arabs.*

"Stop the car," Obenpharo ordered. "Let them pass."

"One day I'll drive right over them," the chauffeur said. "They walk in the gutter like kings of the earth."

"Of course," Obenpharo smiled. "Aren't they the Sons of the Prophet?"

The chauffeur looked into the car's rear-view mirror and caught Obenpharo's little smile. "Yes, monsieur," he said, "and the sons of

30

sons." One of the donkeys suddenly loosed some droppings directly in front of the bank. The chauffeur added, "You see? Even the donkeys have the true faith!"

Hassani, the Arab doorman, stood before the massive spiked gates of the Banque Obenpharo quietly enjoying the scene. He was a sophisticated man from Fez who wrote classical poetry, a member of the nationalist Istiqlal party, and entitled to a respectful *Hadj* before his name because of his pilgrimage to Mecca. Obenpharo considered him a valuable addition to the bank's street façade, despite his Istiqlal membership. The doorman wore the usual red Moslem fez, but his shirt was of fine white linen with a pleated front, and his black Moslem pantaloons looked like enormous golf knickers of other days buckled at the knee; below his knees, over his bare calves, he plainly wore European elastic men's garters to hold up the short nylon ankle socks. He preferred shoes, but wore traditional yellow leather *babouches* with pointed toes because he felt his nationalist politics required nationalist homemade footgear. European tourists sometimes asked, or demanded, to photograph him, but he always refused with great dignity. Hassani liked Monsieur Obenpharo very much, which meant in the final analysis that if the Party should ever decide for some unexplained fantastic reason to demand that he shoot Obenpharo, Hassani would unquestionably obey, but with great regret. A year or more back, when a mob had run down the Boulevard smashing shop windows and breaking gates, Hassani had stood with his legs wide apart before the bank, and Banque Obenpharo had gone untouched.

At the moment he kept his face impassive as the donkey caravan passed and the Rolls pulled up silently before the bank. He opened the rear door for Monsieur Obenpharo and bowed.

"*Bonjour, Sidi,*" he said, using the Arab title for lord, or prince, which he truly meant. He always greeted Obenpharo in French, and Obenpharo always replied in classical Arabic, each paying the other a subtle civilized courtesy.

"The blessing of the day upon you, Hadj Hassani, Allah willing."

Obenpharo was a big man, well over six feet tall and heavily built, and he let Hassani help him out of the deep back seat of the Rolls. When he walked into the entrance of his bank, towering, Homburg-hatted, gloved and caned, with Hassani trotting along with his tooled leather briefcase behind him, he was like some admiral's flagship from the age of sail, a man-o'-war rigged under full canvas knifing through the narrow Straits followed by a rowboat. The lobby foamed away to each side of his passage.

And the blessing of the day upon me, too, Allah willing, Obenpharo thought as he entered the bank lobby. Today I'd like some news of Roger. Good news. I don't care a sou about the London or New York market today. All I ask is a small blessing, some news that my son is still among the living.

Nathan, the bank's general manager, hurried toward him across the terrazzo floor of the lobby, nodding right and left to clients as he came. *"Bonjour,* Benari," he said as he came up.

"Bonjour, Nathan." They then changed to English because of the public lobby. "Tell me, did you ever count your blessings?"

"Never. I'm so busy counting money." He glanced at Obenpharo and realized the old man was serious. He dropped his voice. "Roger again?"

"Yes. Yes yes yes."

"The bulletin from Radio Maroc this morning is no help."

"It is. In a negative way it is. You can interpret between the lines of French censorship. Dallant was almost surely killed by a French counterassassination group. Correct?" Without waiting for an answer, he went on. "When they say one Legionnaire sergeant wounded in a border incident that means an officer and six men hurt. Three trucks of Istiqlal arms and ammunition captured at the border is probably more or less true. Ten terrorists killed and fourteen captured means the Istiqlal was making a really big shipment this time. Facts, half facts, and lies. Without interpretation the radio means zero."

The two men, two old friends, stood silently together for a moment. Nathan thought of an ancient Hebrew admonition: *An ungrateful son should have his teeth set against the edge of the table.* To have only one son, Roger, and such a one. Disrespectful. Divorced. A revolutionist. A convert to Islam. The list only needed patricide for completion. And as a matter of fact, Nathan thought, Roger is killing his father little by little, the slow-drawn-out death of a thousand cuts.

Obenpharo thought: How I envy the Israelites. Family and family strength in a jungle world. Nathan's older son is solid, sensible, a good businessman married to an orthodox girl. The younger son was here in the bank, on his way up. No grandiose ideas of changing the world. No burning fanaticism to tear the world down. How I envy Nathan. He shook his lion's mane a little like a boxer clearing his head for the next round, and said, "Well. Let's get to business."

They crossed the terrazzo lobby side by side, with Obenpharo nodding politely in five languages to each passing good morning. At a glance Obenpharo saw how few tourists were at the exchange window—was tourist trade slacking off?—and the usual numbers of small local businessmen making deposits or petty cash withdrawals.

Small local over-the-counter services, Obenpharo thought, francs and pesetas, bread and butter. Just last week Nathan had said, "Benari, let's be what the Americans call a home-town bank. Let's expand our local credits and discounts of commercial paper. Push local saving accounts."

"Certainly," Obenpharo had answered, "and let's buy baby bottles for ourselves and sleep in cribs."

"Benari, listen to the conservative side for a minute. Local business brings in baby profits now, but if Tangier loses International Zone status in all this struggling, you can be the first to say we served the Moroccan people. It could save our necks."

"That's not conservative. That's dull."

"Two sides of the same coin. If you want to play the big plunger and run a private bank like a club for the polo playboys, then use our Paris office."

"You're preaching poverty. We're international, not a suburban branch. What would they think of us in Geneva and London?"

"You know what they think. We're a private bank. A rich man's bank. We don't publish a balance sheet. We never reveal sources of income or profits. They think we're really a front for your grandiose speculations, millionaires on Monday, paupers on Tuesday."

"Nathan, Nathan. Please. I'll build you a private wailing wall, but don't sing such sad songs to me. I dislike threepenny operas. The Obenpharos were bankers before the Rothschilds. The Obenpharos

33

were writing letters of credit honored in every Mediterranean capital when Marco Polo discovered all the rice in China."

"You sound like Winston Churchill. There will always be an England."

"Yes! Yes!" He sounded angry. "There will always be an Obenpharo."

"You're looking backward. I look ahead, with trouble coming."

"There's always trouble, Nathan. Without trouble in the world Tangier would be a financial flyspeck. Correct? You have to have faith."

"One faith is enough for me, Benari. Don't ask me to believe in magic."

"Hah! You're a magician but you don't believe in magic. What's this whole bank except a circus, with money for tricks, now you see it now you don't, in your pockets—oops! in my pocket. Isn't that magic?"

As they skirted the lobby they circled the huge ancient safe which was respectfully bounded by velvet ropes in the center of the terrazzo floor. The safe was a six-foot cube of iron now reddish-brown with age, a massive sixteenth-century contraption with foot-long keys, sliding bolts and bars and contraptions to deceive brigands. It had been sent full of gold bullion to one of Obenpharo's dimly distant forefathers for safekeeping by a prince of the ruling Alaouite family, and formed a link of trust to which each succeeding Obenpharo had added another golden link. When the new bank building had opened and Obenpharo had ordered the old moldy box cleaned and placed in the lobby, he waved away Nathan's protests about losing valuable floor space. "It's our proof of royal Moroccan faith," he had said. "Any pipsqueak politician from Cairo, and hot pants prince from Côte d'Azur who walks in here must bump into it. The box reminds them of all the stories about Christian girls in the Sultan's harem, with unspeakable delights. Concubines bought with Obenpharo gold is power and power means manhood to a man, and manhood means daily fornication to those boys. That safe reminds them that no Obenpharo has ever broken trust with the ruling house. It's our doxology: As it was in the beginning, it is now, and ever shall be."

34

"You're claiming a cost-free option on eternity, like all *goyim,*" Nathan had joked. "I believe that's a sin before God."

Obenpharo had patted his old friend's elbow. "I don't care what you believe, Nathan. It looks like their holy rock in Mecca, a miniature Kaaba. It's not what you believe, it's what I make *them* believe that counts."

Nathan recalled the days when Obenpharo was the mighty engine of the bank, a blur of spinning wheels throwing off ideas and sparks, pouring his electric energy into cables and transatlantic phone calls, leaving Nathan and his staff to scoop up the profitable shower of coins and count them. Now Obenpharo was an aging emperor, with a madman for crown prince, a sick woman for a queen, and loneliness for company. Only faithful Nathan, His Majesty's loyal opposition, remained unchanged.

Just beyond the mountainous iron safe was a railing with a low swinging gate which opened by an inner electric buzzer. The gate led toward the private little elevator which rose the full height of the building to Obenpharo's penthouse. Beside the elevator was the passage to Nathan's ground-floor office, and when Obenpharo turned into it while waving away the waiting elevator operator, Nathan realized that this was one of the days when the old man was not going straight up to his glassed-in eagle's nest, one of the bad days when he needed action, challenges, decisions, any busy work to help him forget his fears and pain.

Two things from Nathan's former office had been moved when they had transferred from the old bank in the Medina into this new building on the Boulevard Pasteur, the big rolltop desk with its dozen dusty cubbyholes and the little thumb-size metal mezuzah fastened at shoulder height to the doorjamb. Inside the little metal mezuzah like a small locket, was a piece of parchment on which were inscribed some worshipful phrases from the Hebrew Torah. Once when Obenpharo saw Nathan kiss his fingertips and then touch the mezuzah, orthodox fashion, he had asked, "Why do you do that when you leave your office for the day, Nathan?"

"To show thanks for God's protection all day."

"You're a rational man. Isn't that a gesture of superstition?"

"For some, yes, but for me it's a gesture of respect."

35

"Respect for whom, for what?"

"For myself, my parents, my religion. Maybe it boils down to self-respect."

Obenpharo had smiled. "It's a good thing, in a bank owned by an atheist, to have a religious believer for a manager. A bull and a bear on the celestial markets." He laughed aloud as he rarely did. "Obenpharo always plays both sides. *Faites vos jeux, messieurs et mesdames,*" he announced to the room, imitating a roulette croupier, "today we are playing both the red and the black. Nathan's God holds all the chips, the angel Gabriel runs a crooked wheel, and little Obenpharo climbs Jacob's ladder to Paradise to try to break the bank!"

"You're a madman," Nathan said, enjoying the whole extravagant sideshow. "Really *meshugeh*. You shouldn't be trusted with more than pocket money for cigars and a toy balloon."

"It's a circus, Nathan, how many times do I have to tell you? You're the magician. In Paris, Maia is our golden girl in spangled tights riding bareback and throwing kisses to rich Americans and snooty French and Greek artistocrats. The bank is a big tent, peanuts and popcorn, the wheel of fortune."

"And you? The lion? The king of beasts?"

"No, the trapeze artist. Swing high, swing low. And no safety net underneath. You take the risks. You feel the excitement in your bowels."

"You don't live any longer that way, Benari."

"No, but it *seems* longer!" And the short lion-growl laugh.

No, Nathan thought, this morning he's different, he's worried. Obenpharo touched the mezuzah on his way through the doorway into Nathan's office, and then kissed his fingertips. He looked at Nathan over his shoulder. "Do you think any of it will rub off on me? Today I need it."

This is bad, Nathan thought. Today he is worse than I have ever seen. He has a sixth sense, and a seventh, like birds before thunderstorms, and something inside is warning him of danger.

Nathan's younger son, Joseph, was working at his father's desk. He got up and smiled. *"Bonjour,* Monsieur Obenpharo."

"Bonjour, Joseph." He turned to Nathan. "In his father's chair.

36

When a boy sits in his father's chair, that means something. You bring them up on commodity quotations instead of milk."

"On responsibilities. How else does a boy become a man?"

Joseph held out a cablegram. "This is crazy. From Saudi Arabia." He read it. "Buy two hundred Esso current market." He looked up. "Can you imagine? Which Esso? American? French? Which?"

Nathan said, "Who sent it, Joseph?"

"Signed by a numbered account. Twelve zero forty-one."

"Saudi Arabia. The twelve zero series? It must be an American, either in oil or the construction business." He looked to Obenpharo for confirmation. Only Obenpharo had the ultimate code book in his personal vault, the code which matched the personal identities to the anonymously numbered accounts. No one, not even Nathan, had access to this holy of holies.

"Twelve zero? Yes," Obenpharo said, "an American account. He must mean American Esso."

"Buy at New York," Nathan instructed his son.

"And if we're wrong?" Joseph looked from one to the other. "A letter of apology, a check for any difference in the client's behalf, and begin again in Paris?"

Obenpharo tapped his stick on the rug, a little tattoo of applause. "Good, good. Joseph. A private bank always shows a friendly face. Personal service. Americans love it."

Nathan's eyes moved a fraction of an inch toward his door. Joseph understood immediately.

"I'll place this right away," he said. "Excuse me." He went out quickly.

"Like his father," Obenpharo said. "A born banker."

"No," Nathan said, "not born. Made. In my generation I wanted to be a rabbi. He wanted to be a doctor."

"No money in either one."

"Of course. And how can a young husband feed a growing family?"

"So you followed your father's calling, even after he lost his bank, and your younger son follows you." He paused, and added with his voice changing slightly, "A boy who loves his father wants to grow up like him. He sits in your chair."

This is bad today, Nathan thought. This constant chewing on the

37

father-son theme. Anything can happen today. If only that madman Roger would get caught by the French and exiled safely to prison.

A clerk came to the open door and knocked gently to let them know he was there. *"Pardon,"* he said.

"Yes? yes?" Nathan snapped, thinking: Careful, you're begining to sound on edge yourself.

"Monsieur Walker," the clerk said, pronouncing it Wall-care, "to see Monsieur Obenpharo."

"Walker?" Obenpharo said. "One of the R.C.A. transmission station people? I don't remember a Walker."

"He's one of those Wall Street journalists," Nathan explained. "He was here last week."

"Should I see him?"

"What for? He wants a front-page story for his editor, not facts. He never leaves the El Minzah bar. Yet he writes the authoritative standard *merde* about Tangier, city of sinfulness, city of smugglers. With the Moroccan crisis the banks are doomed. All our money is running back to Europe to hide in Switzerland. Et cetera, cetera. He'll cut our veins for his damn story."

"Well, isn't that about frightened money half true?"

"With all our problems? Do we need half truths now, too? This is the country of the straight from the shoulder half truth."

"How do you know what he's writing?"

"Take my word for it. I know."

Obenpharo saw immediately that Nathan had taken this journalist seriously enough to bribe someone behind the concierge's mail desk, or the messenger boy en route to Cherifien Post Office, or someone in the post office itself. There was a simple trick to open a man's mail which had been left over from the wartime days. A long hollow needle as thin as a hypodermic syringe needle with tiny holes along the shaft had steam pumped into it, like a tiny steam pressing iron, and this slender tool inserted properly into a man's sealed mail could melt the glue and open the flap without leaving the slightest visible trace. Obenpharo had introduced the device during the wartime years when the Nazis were everywhere in North Africa and it was a dangerous patriotic form of espionage. Now, like so many patriotic wartime tricks, including killing, inflation, and dishonesty,

38

it had stayed on. Banque Obenpharo even had a paper-slicing machine in the basement into which all the wastepaper baskets were emptied in order to chop to shreds any telltale office papers. Obenpharo knew Nathan hated the whole idea, and must be seriously worried about political affairs if he had told someone to tell someone else to stoop to such dirty little methods.

Obenpharo turned to the clerk. "Ask Joseph to come back here. Tell one of the girl tellers to offer to Mr. Walker the whole lengthy history of the iron safe in the lobby. Tell her to describe the Christian girls in the Sultan's harem."

"*Oui,* monsieur." The clerk went, and, after a moment Joseph came in.

"Joseph," Obenpharo said, "you know who this Walker is?"

"Yes, sir," Joseph said. "I know a good deal about him."

"What admirable communications. The family dinner table is a headquarters staff conference. If only your father had six more sons, we could challenge the Bank of England." Obenpharo sat down heavily in the antique mahogany visitor's chair beside Nathan's roll-top desk and began drawing circles and squares with his stick on the Kirghiz carpet. He felt the dark smoke of battle with this Walker fellow in his veins, only a minor skirmish this one, but still all the enjoyment of decoy and counterattack. "Joseph," he said, "get some men down to the vaults. Tell them to pile all our ingot gold into a wall as tall as your head at the front edge of the big vault." He swung to Nathan. "How much bar gold is there in Tangier?"

"You mean everybody's?"

"Yes. Moses Pariente, Hassan y Hijos, British West Africa, American and Foreign, Hispano Americano, Tangero-Suisse, everybody."

Nathan shrugged. "They say twenty or twenty-five tons."

"Divide by two for the truth. Ten or twelve tons."

"Fair enough."

"How much did we all together hold in '53? At the top, the month the Russians dumped gold on London?"

Again Nathan shrugged. "Perhaps eighty or a hundred tons. So they say."

"Divide by two. Forty or fifty tons at the top, ten or twelve now. Not exactly Fort Knox, eh?"

39

"Of course, Benari," Nathan said, "gold coins, eagles and double eagles and napoleons, and some gold dust, that would all push the total balance up a little. But you're right, entrepôt gold has been running back toward the Swiss Alps fairly quickly. It makes us all look frightened."

"That's bad. We should look confident, firm, not frightened. Faith is our business. How much gold do we hold?"

Nathan shrugged. "Ninety, maybe a hundred kilos in *entrepôt fictif*. Twenty kilos leaves by air today for Geneva."

"Who ordered that?"

"Jove, through Aphrodite."

Obenpharo swung to Joseph. "Do you know those code names? Do you know who they are?"

"No, monsieur."

"Your father neglected to tell you?"

"Not neglect, monsieur. I asked. He refused."

"You understand the moral, Joseph?"

"Yes, monsieur."

"I mean understand it completely, in your bones. The different levels of trust."

"I understand it. Completely."

"But do you believe he was right?"

"I believe it must be exactly so."

"Then I will ask your father to promote you. Aphrodite is my former daughter-in-law, Maia, in our Paris office. Why are you grinning?"

"Pardon, monsieur. The name is perfect for her. I should have thought of it."

"You see how simple the mysteries are when the veil is lifted? Another moral. Do you want to know who this Jove is, who can order twenty kilos of gold around?"

"No, sir. Not unless you tell me."

"Right again. Jove is none of your business." He rapped the stick on the rug. "Cancel the Geneva flight. Call my pilot and cancel it. Ignore Jove until tomorrow. If he screams by cable and threatens to take his business away from Banque Obenpharo, answer over my name that our plane broke down, a wing fell off, something mechanical, anything. I want a big high wall of gold bars at the front edge

of that vault, so that you can show it to Mr. Walker and convince
him the vault is full of it. Understand? Let him quiz you. After all,
you're the general manager's son, you have an inside line to headquarters, and Americans believe nothing except inside stories. Play
the bright boy, but a little naïve, a little puffed up with importance, a
little naïve. Convince him, Joseph."

"I'll convince him. He's smart enough to see I really am a little
naïve." Joseph smiled wisely. "A boy, in boy's clothing."

"Tell Mr. Walker, Joseph, that Banque Obenpharo will not sell
Tangier short. The Moroccan crisis—no, don't say crisis, say *events*
—the Moroccan events don't frighten us. A border skirmish does not
make a war. Our iron safe in the lobby proves that we don't run
away."

"A Rock of Gibraltar," Nathan added. "You almost convince me,
Benari."

"Go ahead, Joseph." But, as the young man reached the door,
Obenpharo suddenly raised his voice to stop him. "Joseph—"

"Yes, monsieur?"

"Two points. First: if one of the girls is telling this Walker the
history of the safe and looking into his eyes, don't interrupt. Let
her finish. If he invites her out for a drink or across the street to
that American place for a, what do they call that fantastic ice-cream
concoction—?"

"A chocolate sundae, sir."

"Yes, one of those. Anyway, if she is invited, she gets the afternoon off. Is that clear?"

"Yes, sir."

"Second: don't walk so fast. Walker won't run away."

"Yes, sir." Joseph smiled a little at the reverse pun and strolled
out casually, then poked his head back into the office like a jump-
ing-jack comedian. "Was that better?"

They all laughed together, enjoying the childish parlor game of
playing roguish buccaneers in the countinghouse, and Joseph vanished.

"Are you serious about the promotion, Benari?" Nathan asked.

"That's your business. You're the manager here. I can only recommend it."

"It's hard to decide."

41

"Why? Most boys are asleep standing up. This Joseph of yours is wide awake."

Nathan glowed proudly. "I don't like to move a boy up too fast. Next thing, he'll consider himself a financial hawk, a real *arbitrageur* or something, and lose us a fortune."

Obenpharo shook his head with mock sorrow. "Nathan, Nathan, when are you going to stop being so conservative? You want everything safe and solid, only the sure thing. You're so afraid of repeating your father's failure. One and three-quarter per cent on blue-chip top-drawer investments and you're happy."

The tide is turning, Nathan thought, he feels better now, the sun is shining again. "That's no joke, Benari," Nathan said, swimming with the tide.

"A poor man's joke, Nathan. That's why you're poor. You're such a fool that you never stole a penny from the bank."

"Don't believe it, Benari. I'm waiting until you make your next big killing, and I'll abscond with the funds."

Obenpharo got up and rubbed his back. "Even your client's chair gives a poor but honest backache. Worse than a bedpan."

"Of course. I don't want them to sit there all day. I have work to do."

"Don't push me. I'm leaving." Suddenly he sounded lonely again.

"No, no, I didn't mean you," Nathan said quickly. "It's just time to take a look at the Telex from New York with me. We'll see how the market closed last night." He spoke quickly, to make the old man feel needed.

The teletype operator looked up when they came into the cable room next to Nathan's office. He was startled to see Monsieur Obenpharo in the clickety-clacking cubbyhole and jumped to his feet.

"Monsieur—" he began respectfully.

"Sit down, my boy," Obenpharo said. "We don't want to interrupt you." He was watching the broad ribbon of paper come out of the machine. It reminded him of the last warning electrocardiogram he had had in the heart specialist's office in Paris, with the inky needle of the machine jiggling pathological hills and valleys on the paper to map the diseased geography of his heart. Except that this was the pulse and heartbeat of a whole country, the United States market, and of course that now meant the world.

"New York is just coming through," the operator said.

"I don't have my glasses, my boy. You read English of course? Would you mind reading off the paper, each word, but slowly."

The operator picked up the scroll of curling paper and read over the sound of the automatically typing keys. "Copyright by Manhattan Wire Services, Incorporated. Testing testing testing testing. Good morning good morning good morning—"

"Imagine what that penetrating bit of intelligence costs us," Obenpharo said to Nathan. "Copyright and all."

"Here," Nathan said to the operator, "I'll read it for Monsieur."

"Skip the good mornings, Nathan, please. Just the high spots."

Nathan slipped on his reading glasses. " 'Industrial production rose to 143 per cent 1947–49 average Federal Reserve Board reported. Two percentage points above last month.' "

"Yes," Obenpharo added sharply, "but the increase was seasonal. The index has to be adjusted."

"Bahrein Crude Sales Company Limited has raised prices seven cents a barrel for Arabian crude oil."

"That explains the Esso buy order from twelve zero forty-one that Joseph got. They're marketing affiliates. What's the new price FOB Lebanon?"

"Two forty-two a barrel for 34 gravity oil."

"What else is there? Just the high spots, please."

"Ah, Benari, here's your dear old friend, Sweeney of Continental."

"Read it. He's a thief, but he's never dull." Obenpharo indicated the teletype operator with one eyebrow, and Nathan told the man he could go until they called him. He went out.

" 'Huntington Sweeney, president of Continental Sales Company, said yesterday there is no foundation for any statement that the company faces a financial crisis.' "

"With his honest baby blue eyes and simple silk monogrammed undershirts," Obenpharo growled, "that's how he said it."

" 'Yesterday Continental Securities suffered sharp declines on the New York Stock Exchange. The 4 per cent bonds due 2007 closed off three points at 66¼ and the 4½ convertible income bonds due 2022 ended the day down 5¼ at 57¼.' "

"Skidding, skidding. I warned Maia in Paris about Sweeney. But she likes interesting crooks."

43

" 'There are financial problems of course, said Mr. Sweeney, interviewed yesterday in London, and there are serious operational problems as well. When I accepted the office of company president I stated I would not varnish the truth. That statement still stands. The facts in the case do not warrant—' "

"Enough, enough empty music, Nathan. He manages not to say one concrete thing he can be held for. I can't stand it." Obenpharo said, laughing, and enjoying it. "He can charm the stone gargoyles off the Notre Dame roof. I can see why Maia cocktails such a maestro."

"Maybe Sweeney cocktails Maia."

"Everybody in Paris tries to, why shouldn't he? Are you making a moral point or a business judgment?"

"Both. How can you separate them?"

"Judge by his books, Nathan, not by his bedclothes."

"You're angry because I comment on Maia."

"Yes. I'm angry."

"Why shouldn't I? Your daughter-in-law, pardon, your ex-daughter-in-law, represents us in Paris. I have to go over the books, and countersign checks for the bedclothes."

"Her private life is none of your affair, Nathan."

"Do you have a private life? Do I? Everything we do is noticed. With a private bank we pay the price of a public life."

"For the love of God," Obenpharo said, "stop it!"

Now it comes, Nathan thought, I knew today was marked. He walked in like a thundercloud, sooner or later the lightning strikes.

"Don't you understand," Obenpharo said harshly, "Maia's like a son to me? You have two sons, what do I have? My son's former wife, that's all. That's all! I don't really have a son. An intellectual boy who wants to be the new Jesus of Islam! A fanatic who thinks because Buddha was a rich man's son, he too can create a new nirvana in North Africa! The brightest brains in a decade, they told me at the Sorbonne, your son can learn anything, they said, and this minute he may be lying dead on the French Moroccan border. He's like no son at all, and Maia takes his place."

"I apologize," Nathan said with great dignity. "Forgive me."

"No, I need the forgiveness, not you. The gods punish *me,* not you. Why? What have I done, I don't know. One son. Your house is

44

full of grandchildren on Friday nights. I have one grandson with the name of Obenpharo who goes to elementary school in Paris and sees me twice a year. Maia's son, Nathan. One grandson. One cobweb to tie myself to the future, and Maia holds that cobweb. This is how the jealous gods hang a sword over my head. On one cobweb."

"Now it's you talking like a superstitious Greek."

"Not Greek. Phoenician. You forget. Two thousand years ago, when your people were building their second or third temple for the one true God, mine were unloading their purple dyes and cloth from their triremes and galleys right here in Tangier, and then sailing off to Britain. They knew the pagan gods forgive murder, but never pride."

"That's a Greek idea, Benari. *Hubris.* The sin of pride."

"A Phoenician will buy a Greek idea if he can sell it at a profit." He paused, and looked out the window. "But a very new and original idea occurs to me: what does it profit a man to gain the world if he loses his soul?"

"Benari, Roger is too smart to get caught by the French."

"Insha' Allah."

"Now the Moslem God? Before it was Jehovah. Then the Greeks'."

"When I'm in trouble I pray to them all. Even the Christian God. Your people made bricks without straw. I need a miracle without faith."

"Roger is too smart to go near the French zone. He's too high in the Istiqlal to be used in running guns over a border. Roger must sit somewhere in a back room with a telephone and give orders."

"Nathan, tell me something. You and Maia are the only ones who tell me the truth—" He paused, ready to ask a question, but Nathan interrupted.

"That's not true, Benari. She and I keep grinding private axes. She is raising the heir presumptive to the Obenpharo fortune, and I want partnership for my son in Banque Obenpharo."

"Good. Enlightened self-interest. A community of purpose. All the more reason for trust. I'm too old to ask for affection."

"You're too young to be so cynical."

"Nathan, you conservative croaking prophet, what would I do without you?"

"No thanks, Benari. I see one of your irresistible remarks about

45

prophets and profits coming. I refuse to be an accessory before the fact."

"Then tell me the truth. Where did I go wrong with Roger? I gave him everything. Where did I make my mistake?"

"You've answered it. You gave him everything." He added more softly, "Everything but yourself."

"He had his mother. She gave herself. Completely. Too much."

"She didn't have you, either. But she had him, so that's where she gave."

"Give, give. Always give? When does a parent take?"

"Never. It's all investment and no dividends. Taking is only for money. With people, with your children, you give yourself, not things. Not money. Not the Villa Obenpharo with troops of servants and French tutors, an oriental palace where a growing boy claps his hands for a glass of water instead of getting a drink for himself."

"I knew you'd say that, Nathan. It's a standard explanation."

"They're usually the true ones. If you want a complicated artistic answer, go down to the Carnivale and buy drinks for the types down there. They'll give you an artistic surrealist existentialist answer."

"This dirty talk is not like you, Nathan."

"No. And it's not like you, Benari, to come in to use me as a punching bag, a spittoon, a lightning rod, whatever you want to call it."

"I used you only as a friend."

"This isn't the time or place, Benari," Nathan said, making himself sound harsh. "I'm an employee. We're watching the market now. The owner and the manager. If you start acting like a courageous man instead of a frightened old father, maybe everything all around will go better."

"By God, I ought to fire you."

"Twenty years ago. It's too late now."

They smiled faintly together, and Nathan picked up the teletype paper scroll again. That was a gamble, Nathan thought with relief, not only a gamble but also very close. He's sick with exhaustion.

" 'Stock tape averaging three minutes late,' " Nathan read off the teletype. " 'Late profit taking converted gains in new crop cotton futures into losses at the close yesterday. Nearby months held rela-

46

tively well on further mill covering against textile operations. Singapore. Spot tin 385⅛ Straits dollars per picul versus previous 378 ⅜. . . .' " He glanced at Obenpharo. "Does this interest you?"

"No," the old man said, staring at the wall. There was a silence between them as the machine clattered indifferently, spooling great curls of market information from New York and Liverpool and Singapore into the wastebasket. "I'll be upstairs in my office," Obenpharo said to the wall, and when Nathan did not answer, he turned and walked slowly out of the little room, bending his great height slightly, burdened, a tired warrior.

Obenpharo was amazed, when he stepped out of the small private elevator into his penthouse office, to find Maia there. She stood at the far end of the room, copper-haired in silhouette against the green-tinted solar glass, half turned toward him at the sound of the opening elevator doors. It was the position of upstage center, for she made a stage of every room she was in, and she had walked there unthinkingly, automatically, when she had heard the little elevator coming.

"Maia! What a pleasant surprise!"

The high leather chair at his desk swiveled around and there sat young Henri Obenpharo covered with an eight-year-old's conspiratorial grin.

"Grandpapa!" he shouted as he jumped off the executive chair and ran to Obenpharo. The old man and the boy hugged each other, turning in a circle. "Surprise! Surprise!" Henri kept saying. "We surprised you!"

"You certainly did, *mon vieux!* No one downstairs said a word," he said, lifting his massive white head to Maia. He was still surprised and very pleased, and kept one hand gripping Henri's shoulder.

"We told them not to," she said. "It was part of our plan, wasn't it, darling?"

"Yes!" Henri said. "We planned the whole thing, Grandpapa. And then we waited and waited. We thought you'd never come up."

"Well," Obenpharo said, "you sit right back in the president's chair, Henri, like a real banker. I enjoy seeing you in my chair, and I want to say hello properly to your mother."

As he walked toward her, Maia held out both hands to him. He took them and kissed her on both cheeks and then moved back a step to look at her. "You look as lovely as always, my dear. The golden girl."

She wore a sheath of cool green linen that went with her eyes, with matching shoes, and a green belt with intricately worked gold threads in it to spell out letters of words. Against the solar glass of the penthouse her smooth helmet of hair looked more copper than gold. Her eyes were just faintly elongated, and made even longer in the current elfin fashion by make-up; porcelain eyes, almost blue, but looking green-irised now, and secret-smiling as a cat-queen of the Nile.

"Thank you, Papa," she said, giving him the little smile as a gift which beautiful women learn to give so they can pretend they are really pleased to be reminded of their beauty. "Were you truly surprised?"

"Completely," he said. He was. Usually he knew everything by wire or radio or telephone or messenger as soon as it occurred. He turned to Henri, who sat in the big chair, and he felt the familiar wave of love for the boy with Roger's thin face and deep eyes under a darker bronze version of Maia's hair. And sitting just where he belongs, Obenpharo thought happily. I have been humbled, and now the gods reward me.

"How did you manage to keep such a secret?" he asked the boy.

"Mamma did it," Henri said. "She knows lots of secrets."

Obenpharo's eyes met Maia's, and they exchanged a small complex smile. "Yes," Obenpharo said, "she does."

Maia looked down at Tangier Bay. "There's our secret just leaving the yacht basin on the way to Mallorca." Obenpharo came to stand beside her to stare down at the harbor, past the white gravestones and thin wall of skeletal cypresses edging the Israelite cemetery, past the big oil storage tanks and the crowd of little coastal fishing boats, past the freighter and the Gibraltar ferry and twice weekly Marseille passenger ship, out to where a single-funnel white steam yacht nosed toward the sea.

"Socrates Theologos in the *Hercules*," Maia explained. "He and Xenia brought us over. Xenia says Theo only wants to go to Mallorca to find the golden apples Hercules left there."

48

"Theologos?" Obenpharo said with surprise. "Mr. Knowledge of God himself? I haven't seen him since the Amsterdam days."

"Look, Grandpapa," Henri said, "look what he gave me!" He jumped off the big leather chair and brought a shining coin to Obenpharo.

"This is gold, Henri," his grandfather said, hefting it in his palm. "It's a beautifully faked napoleon minted in Milan for smuggling into France."

"Henri," Maia said, "Monsieur Theologos didn't really give it to you, did he? Tell Grandpapa what he said."

"He said he wanted to be able to tell his friends someday that he deposited the first gold young Obenpharo ever had." Henri grinned with Roger's thin Latin-scholar face, a sideways shrewd grin. "I told him we had a bank full already."

Obenpharo's great white eyebrows went up, then he threw his head back and shouted with laughter. "He did, did he? So it's not really given, just on deposit? And *we* have a bank full, do we?" The old man was enjoying this greatly. "Lord, lord," he laughed, "that was telling him! That put some snuff up his nose!" The tide of morning had turned, the sword above him was forgotten, and the gods were smiling because of the canny Greek shipowner's joke and the little boy's use of that wonderful word *we*.

He went to his desk and pulled open the bottom drawer and took out a small jeweler's suede bag. "Here, my golden apple," he said, "these are for you. If you're going into banking with millionaires for clients, you'll need some capital."

Henri climbed back into the big desk chair, laughing because of his grandfather's laughter and because it was all fun. He opened the drawstring on the bag and poured a small heap of gold coins on the desk top. "Look! Mamma!"

She paused in taking a Papastratos No. 1 out of a gold Fabergé cigarette case Theologos had given her as a farewell gift. "Pennies from heaven, darling," she said. "Never count them."

"There are American double eagles in there," Obenpharo was explaining eagerly to his grandson, "the ones that are marked twenty, and here, here now, here's a ten, that's called an eagle. And these are Swiss twenty-franc pieces. These coins are sovereigns, very good

49

in all Arab countries because of the English King's head on them, you see? This one here, with the Queen on it, they pay less for this one because having a woman on it makes it worth less."

"Papa," Maia said, "really now, don't carry Theo's joke too far, please."

"Joke? This is not a joke. Henri's a born banker. Just look at him in that executive chair counting out his money."

"I'm not counting, Grandpapa. I'm just making a pile out of each of the same kind."

"Well, count it, *mon vieux,* count it. Then take it downstairs to Monsieur Joseph and ask for a safety-deposit box and a signature card. Tell them to count the money in front of you and give you a written receipt."

"I can write my name fine, Grandpapa. But I'll never remember all that."

"Of course not. They'll do what they're supposed to do because you have the gold, they don't."

"Can I go down now?"

"If you wish. If your mother permits."

Henri looked at Maia. The first step toward empire, she thought proudly and a trifle sadly, and she came across the room impulsively to give him a light valedictory kiss. "Go down," she said, "but remember your manners. Speak French, not English, and don't interrupt anyone who looks busy."

One of the desk telephones rang shortly. Obenpharo ignored it. "You know, Henri," he said, "now that you're a new partner—" He paused as the phone rang again, and said to Maia, "I left standing instructions at the switchboard. Two rings, no more. If I don't answer after the second ring, it means I'm taking no calls."

"A very good system," she said. "Maybe we'll begin to use it in Paris."

"Where was I, Henri? What was I saying?"

"I don't know, Grandpapa."

"Annoying. Last few months. Begin a sentence and forget to finish it—" He frowned, trying to concentrate, then pretended to smile. "The eagle is turning into a cuckoo."

Maia changed the subject briskly. "Henri, you can take your coins downstairs if you like."

"If somebody talks to me in English, shall I answer in French?"

"If you think they're French, yes. It's more courteous."

Henri pressed the *Descend* button of the elevator on the interior wall of the office. A small green light went on, and a few moments later the wood panel doors slid open.

"Maia," Obenpharo said, motioning to the elevator man to keep the doors open, "shall I have the boy bring up some Perrier and ice for you? Forgive me for not asking sooner."

"No, thank you. We had late brunch with Theo."

"Brunch? English for lunch?"

"No, American for breakfast and lunch."

"Something new every day," the old man said, then as he caught sight of the waiting elevator, "Still there? Go down, go down." He and Henri waved good-by to one another as the panels quietly closed and the green indicator button changed to red.

Obenpharo lowered his heavy bulk into the regal leather desk chair and, very much the chairman of a meeting, motioned for Maia to take a seat. His eyes followed her as she crossed the room and sat down like an actress, fluent, effortless, and graceful. He saw her glance above him at the picture of Roger on the wall; Roger as he was years ago, after the war in Europe had ended, a slender dark-haired man in a well-cut expensive suit standing before the bronze doors of Banque Obenpharo in the Place Vendôme. Roger had been very much a wealthy Parisian intellectual then, newly married, a young banker with an interesting flare for monkish Latin phrases and otherworldly philosophy, and a golden-helmeted green-eyed secret-smiling wife. Life had glittered and sparkled jeweled promise for Maia then, with the great Obenpharo name to unlock every gate to every garden, and, inside, all that the ancient Greek poet had story-told of the apple tree, the singing, and the gold.

That was the time when Maia had found the stone house she wanted on the Quai de Bethune, the time when Henri was born, when the Obenpharo assets doubled and redoubled and tripled, and she had felt that special immortality of the young and the loved. Except that she discovered slowly and painfully that Roger did not love her; she had believed that for the first time in her life she meant more than a well-shaped vessel of usage, and now she discovered that the wealthier they became the more Roger filled their house with angry young

51

North African politicians, all drinking endless rounds of mint tea or wine—depending on how strictly they followed the Moslem injunction against alcohol—and arguing endlessly about Pan-Islam, the Moslem destiny, and the enemy called colonialism.

Maia had been shattered. She had loved him completely, offered herself completely, and now she had become neither unwelcome nor even troublesome; merely someone who was there. As Roger's nights became filled with debate, and his passion poured into politics, his trips to Cairo and Algiers and Casablanca and Tangier became times of lengthening tension for Maia. Some of their Parisian friends passed the word quietly that the Sûreté was compiling a dossier on Roger; when Maia spoke of this to Roger as a European wife speaks to her husband, he became furious and called her the typical *evoluée*, like his mother, more French than the French, turning their backs on their own origins, trying to leap from the harem to the salon in one clumsy jump. After that, Maia threw herself into the whole tinkling powderpuff idiot's-delight world of Paris, a dervish whirl of learning to fence and drive fast cars and talk the Thoroughbred Horses' Club crowd kind of talk. Roger detested her new friends and told them so pleasantly in French, English, Italian, Spanish, not forgetting Latin, thereby proving to them that he was completely but most interestingly mad. When she discovered that she had become almost professionally gay, and that sleep was impossible without pills, each morning a weight of tired emptiness, she asked Obenpharo to let her come into the bank. Under Obenpharo's encyclopedic tutorship, and by leaving the technical complexities of finance to the departmental experts in the bank, she had become Obenpharo's right hand in Paris within five years. Her punishment of Roger was complete. She had learned all the outward skills of an independent European woman. And most important, she had replaced him in the Paris office. She, not he, had become the true son.

Now, sitting opposite Roger's picture on the wall and Obenpharo, her eyes met his—still watching her—then slid blankly away and stared out at the intensely blue Mediterranean sky.

Obenpharo opened his tooled Moroccan leather cigar box and began tapping and sniffing for just the cigar he wanted, growling, "I asked the doctor if I gave up a sociable drink and my cigars, would

I live longer? And he said no, it would just seem longer." Then he added, apparently casually, "I don't believe Henri will mind if I sit on his throne, do you?"

"Henri is an Obenpharo, Papa. He's always generous with his junior partners."

"That has the faintest suggestion of propaganda from my favorite Paris vice-president."

"Banque Obenpharo Paris has no vice-president."

"No? What then are you there?"

"A viceroy."

"Checkmate." He saluted her with his cigar. "Maia, there's no one like you. No one."

"If you knew how hard it is to create that impression."

"And more beautiful than ever. Especially in green to match your eyes. The Venus of viceroys."

"That requires effort too, Papa. I don't know why, but red hair always fools the crowd."

"Such frankness. You and Nathan. The only ones who are ruthless and honest with me."

"How is yonder Polonius? Filled with sage biblical wisdom and conservative advice?"

"Maia, Maia. He is no threat to you or Henri. His loyalty is the rock I stand on."

She shrugged slightly. "He doesn't like me. In fact, he dislikes me."

"Must every man fall at your feet? Even the old ones?"

"Yes." She smiled her secret smile. "Dislike always makes me uncomfortable. I like to be liked."

"Theo liked you well enough, even with Xenia aboard, to cruise all this way only to drop you off at the dock like a load of coal."

She looked out through the great glass wall of the office. Far in the distance the *Hercules* was a white cork in a vast green sea made greener by the solar glass. "Papa," she said, "I came for several reasons."

"Certainly. And the surprise. Was that only for me and Henri to enjoy?"

"Partly. And you did, didn't you?"

"Everyone knows I'd give my right arm and my right eye for that

53

boy. But please don't try to manipulate my feelings. I'm too old for vanity now, Maia. The older I grow the more I return to simple virtues, like a small-town bourgeois banker. Family. Children."

"And how is your son, the new Moslem prophet of the down-trodden masses?"

"Gone again. And the radio filled with border zone trouble and shooting in Casablanca."

"He eats trouble like bread. In Paris they believe he's a Communist. The same old story."

"Only worse. But let's not pretend you care, Maia."

"No, no pretending. But remember, he divorced *me*. And in a Moslem court like a harem chattel. A two-dollar fee and the Koranic pronouncement: *I divorce thee*"—she washed her hands in the air —"and no more Maia. Until he left me, I was his faithful wife. I gave him a son. But no, he wanted to father a whole new political religion. He loves it when the little *fatimas* line the streets to wave at him and scream that *yuyuyuyes* of theirs. He wants to outfather his father by being father to a whole country. And if he survives you to inherit the bank, he'll pour every franc and shilling and dollar into the Istiqlal party."

"Leaving bare bones for you."

"Leaving bare bones for Henri."

"I beg you again, Maia, no iron hands in Paris gloves. Don't manipulate me through the child."

"I don't try to manipulate men I respect. But you said bare bones. All right, bare facts. I refuse to oversimplify or lie."

"That's why I respect you, Maia."

"And I love you. How can you believe I wish for your death?"

"Sometimes an old man with two coronary attacks—mild ones, but there they were—and just the beginning of Parkinsonism, sometimes an old man like that wonders."

She jumped to her feet and came to him and kissed his forehead impulsively. "You are my father and mother. Where would my life be without you? In the alleys of the Medina? Crawling with syphilis and begging under a street lamp?" Tears filled her eyes. "Do you think I will ever forget when I was a little Berber servant girl who came to Villa Obenpharo with the clothes on her back and nothing more?"

54

"Don't humble yourself, Maia. I've heard it said that the last con-cubine even the Sultan of Morocco married was a Berber servant girl. There are no better women."

"But did the Sultan give her European tutors? And the books, the teaching that was like food, and the music, and the encouragement most fathers never give their own daughters, leave alone another child?"

"Thank you, Maia. But we have this terrible agreement to be frank, and you know that was all done for Roger, for an only child. Mutirra wanted to help you, as a mother helps a daughter. She was Arab and understood you. But I wanted to help my son. That's the terrible simple truth, and yet not worth crying about now."

"I'm sorry. Whenever I think of my childhood, I cry. It's so ridicu-lous, because I can control everything else about myself, except this one thing." She walked back to her chair and sat down slowly. His massive calm always impressed her.

"You're tired, and here I am nagging at you," he said.

"No, no. Really. We had a lovely time crossing over, and I'm not tired. Theo's a wonderful host. Always considerate and full of jokes."

"Always clever and full of money."

"You owe him an apology. He came here to help me. To help us."

"To be sure. That's why he delivered you and Henri and sailed off without a word to me. Before the war, when he and his brothers owned a few rusty tubs, he used to run to me for advice. Benari, cable Niemayer for me. Radio Weber. Speak to Pilotti. Telephone McKit-trick. Now he gives my grandson a coin, and sails off without a word. As Roger would say, 'Timeo Danaos et dona ferentes.' "

"Be reasonable. They didn't want to miss the morning tide. And Theo really wanted to get to Mallorca promptly."

"Then why trouble to come here at all? Didn't you have your own fare? Why do I keep an expensive airplane and an American pilot at the airport, for show?"

"Theo delivered a hundred thousand in bar gold to Tangier this morning," she said strongly. "Henri and me and a little shining hun-dred-thousand-dollar pile, all in a row on the dock."

"Theo? Gold? Here?"

"Yes. Here. It's in the customs shed at this moment. You know how slow they are with copying identification numbers and assay per-

55

centages. But the gold will be in Banque Obenpharo before teatime."

The old man contemplated his cigar. Maia could see his pride was still hurt. He's very disturbed about something, she thought, and he has a big reaction to small things.

"To Theo," Obenpharo said, "a hundred thousand is a tip to the waiter, a bill for a fete. He loves soft currencies and inflation. He must have some need for gold certificates. Why else does he make token gold deposits in my bank?"

"Because it's *our* bank, Papa. Because gold is running like rabbits away from Tangier. I told him I wanted to show that Banque Obenpharo still stands for confidence. The lighthouse, no matter whether the Moroccans take over the International Zone or not. Tangier is a village. The word of gold arriving on the *Hercules,* and all that sort of frou-frou, it will be all over town in an hour. Who'll count it? Who knows the real owner?"

He bit into his cigar. "Customs."

"I took care of customs. Then the Reuters man all out of breath met me at the dock gate. I told him it was six hundred thousand belonging to Banque Obenpharo. I told him we want to show our confidence in the future of Morocco."

"I bow to you."

"To you, Papa. A pupil of a maestro. The impression we want will be on the financial page of the Paris *Tribune* tomorrow morning."

"Excellent. This helps with an American journalist from Wall Street who's snooping around the building right now. In the old days we'd show him the door, but the Americans have spoiled all their journalists with this public trust and public relations business, and we're stuck with it. Did you know Ballant et Fils has closed? Their bank building is for sale. The South American group has put itself into an *état de veilleuse.*"

"I heard that in Paris. And the Belgians?"

"Leaving next month. And the Transatlantique with all their New York capital a month later."

"Roger's mobs create a windstorm and the sand blows away. Only the lighthouse stands."

"And my old playmate from Athens helped out. Amazing. Absolutely amazing. Is it possible that loyalty still exists?"

56

"I spoke to him frankly, Papa. Nobody fools Theo."

"Of course. He has knowledge of God, and his God is money."

"And I helped him worship. We handle his Citröen and Saint Gobain, Rhône-Poulenc, Unilever, Royal Dutch, and Nederlandsche Handel Maatschappij."

"Small potatoes, a few exchange commissions. A rich man like that spreads himself in a dozen banks in half a dozen countries. Without him, Panama would starve only making hats, and the Swiss would choke on their cheese."

"You're forgetting our Paris house, Papa. Theo loves to come there, he loves the view of Notre Dame, and our paintings, the river going by. The whole *ambience* of the Ile St. Louis and Quai de Bethune."

"He loves the busty French and Italian movie starlets at your little soirées. Don't throw classic Greek culture or picture postcard Paris in my eyes, Maia."

"Why do you persecute him? He likes to make big money, but don't you and I? I invited him into a combine with that new independent American motion picture group, Ultima Productions."

"Maia, that's robbery! Ultima is using an American front. The money is Italian. I think of myself as a gambler, but you—you're a pirate."

"Where's the piracy? I put some of our own money into it."

"Maia, you know how speculative these cinema combines can be. If a film dies in the box office, we bury the body. Our clients lose fortunes in the grave and our name is on the tombstone."

"But if our client wins? And makes a fortune? Last time, Theo got back twenty dollars for every one he put in, all in two years. That's better than an oil well. And it's much more fun to order talented people around and have them to parties. Where else could Xenia meet Gregory Peck?"

Obenpharo stood up and stubbed out his cigar. "Let's finish this discussion of whether the Paris branch is a rehearsal hall for amateur theatricals at lunch. It's getting late."

"How can you tell?"

"As my forefathers told. And yours too. By the angle of the sun. It's over the yardarm."

"How astronomically simple."

57

"In the end, all the big things are simple, Maia. Love. Hate. Death. Money. Religion. Ask me. I see it all more clearly every day, on borrowed time."

"Only me, Papa. Not big and not simple any more. Still small and still complicated."

"Yes. But don't worry about it." He laughed. "Even you, you'll grow old and ugly and very wise."

"I'll never live that long."

He laughed again. "Come, my morbid Cleopatra, we'll go see Mutirra at lunch and let Henri tell her about his new senior partnership."

"Thank you, but you please run along home with him. I'll telephone Mutirra. I have to stop off at the American School and arrange for Henri to start classes."

"Why the American School? They're poor. They're always trying to raise money."

"But their teachers are good. The children come from every milieu and every country. And they don't try to make pale little professors out of the children, like the French."

"You're still sure you won't let me provide some tutors? They can be British, you know. Teach the boy snoblesse oblige."

She shook her head. "Still sure. Please don't ask me to raise a second Roger."

He frowned at her and said with an edge of anger, "Will we see you at dinner? You'll probably vanish to your intimate Arabic *pied-à-terre*?"

Her face stiffened. "Yes."

"Do you still keep your favorite Spaniard there?" He shook his head. "Jeanjean. What a moronic name. A typical Andaluce bum. A half-Arab professional Adonis pretending to be a noble Spanish grandee. I've seen his dossier. You know why he's such a sahib polo player? Because he was in Franco's Moorish cavalry. Do you know—"

She interrupted. "You swore you wouldn't interfere. We agreed that Paris was business, but here, Tangier is my private affair. Haven't I always been as discreet as a convent girl?"

"The affair offends me, Maia. It should offend you. Does his bru-

58

tality excite you? What is it? I don't ask you to live as a nun. But find a man, not an animal!"

"Same thing. But this time, such a handsome one."

"You're too young to be so cynical."

"I'm a Berber girl from the mountains, Papa. Roger called me his mountain goat. I'm ten centuries old. I was here before the Arabs."

"Today seems to be the day for pedigrees. I just told Nathan I was a Phoenician captain, twenty centuries old. A thousand years before the Berbers came with their Stone Age implements and their Stone Age morals."

"I refuse to be insulted. I like cavemen."

"I've seen this phenomenon before. Beauty and the Beast."

"He's really very handsome."

Obenpharo pointed his cigar at her. "There must be some book on abnormal psychology which explains it all."

She laughed. "You said the big things were simple. This is, too. He excites me like no one else. I can shut off my brain and turn on my body. Why read a book? It couldn't be simpler."

"In the end, it's my money that keeps him."

"Please. Please don't threaten me, Papa. It's not like you to stoop. I've handled the whole thing with discretion because of you and Mutirra. I hate hiding, and if I were independent I would live openly with him."

"I thought this had gone out of fashion, Maia. This high and mighty royal indifference to people's opinion."

"Now we're going in circles."

"Don't be impertinent."

"Ah. Before it was bare bones, the bold brave truth. Now it's impertinence."

He let his breath out slowly, then walked to the elevator and pressed the button. I dislike the fleshy romantic attitudes of this generation toward love, he thought. Love should be rapture given body by children; stable, a family processional. Without looking at her, sounding defeated, he said, "Well, if we don't meet at dinner, tomorrow then. I wanted to review our British position and sterling balances with you." The elevator doors opened just as one of the

59

telephones rang. "I ignore it," he said. "Just let it ring twice. Then it will stop. It's probably that journalist fellow."

She made a small mouth to mean a good-by kiss. "*Au'voir,* Papa. Dinner tonight."

He brightened immediately, sensing compromise. "Tonight, *insha' Allah,*" he said, and the sliding panels closed before him. As the floor of the elevator dropped beneath him he suddenly thought: She stoops to folly, but walks in beauty like the ancient Greek myths about her namesake among the Pleiades. What a fool Roger was to lose her, he thought, and closed his eyes against the downward-plunging sensation of the elevator shaft.

In the lobby, as he stepped off the elevator, he came face to face with Joseph and Henri and a stranger wearing a summer suit of American cut.

"Monsieur Obenpharo," Joseph said, "this is Monsieur Walker."

"That's the first time it's been pronounced right in days," Mr. Walker said in English to Joseph. "How do you do, sir?" he added in French as he shook hands with Obenpharo.

"Very well, thank you. Has Monsieur Joseph answered all your inquiries?"

"Not quite. My French," Walker said, "isn't exactly first class. I hope you'll excuse the mistakes."

"If you please, Mr. Walker. Speak English."

"You're very courteous, Monsieur Obenpharo."

"No, no." Obenpharo became courtly, expansive, as he always did with people whom he planned to brush off his sleeve quickly. "I only want your time to be productive, Mr. Walker." He nodded to Joseph, dismissing him. "Thank you, Joseph. Would you mind escorting Henri to the car?"

"I'll go myself, Grandpapa. Where's my mother?"

"In my office, Henri. You and I will lunch with your grandmother. But first I need a little time with Mr. Walker."

Mr. Walker put out his hand to Henri. "So long, Henri," he said as they shook hands. "Thanks for showing me your gold coins."

"We have lots more of them, don't we, Grandpapa?"

"Enough, *mon vieux.* Enough for our needs."

60

"*Au revoir,* Monsieur Walker." Henri gave Mr. Walker's hand a final pumping handshake and dropped it.

"*Au revoir,* Monsieur Obenpharo," Mr. Walker said solemnly. He turned to Obenpharo. "I enjoyed meeting your grandson," Walker said, watching Henri's proprietary march through the lobby. "European kids seem so grown up, with their formal manners, and the way they keep quiet. When I met Henri downstairs in the vaults, he greeted me like Baron Rothschild."

"Oh? Was Henri down there?"

"Yes. Making a gold deposit. Very tight-fisted, very much the young banker. Receipt and all, you know."

"Isn't that what you call a chip from the block?"

Mr. Walker grinned. "Yes, yes. Of course, I know you're not Rothschild. You're really John D. Rockefeller."

"Ah, if only that were so, Mr. Walker. You're talking to an old man who still has to work for a living."

"Actually," Walker said, "I've heard you're in the Rothschild tradition."

"You mean because this is a family bank, a private bank?"

"Yes. And the branch in Paris—or is this the branch?"

Obenpharo chuckled down in his chest. "The Paris tail wags the Tangier dog, but don't ever report that. I like to pretend I'm boss." He could see he was taking exactly the right approach with this Walker. Americans liked their tycoons to pretend they were simple straightforward fellows.

"Oh," Walker said, with his momentary boyish grin, "I got the idea downstairs that Henri was boss."

Obenpharo was delighted. "What did the boss say to give you that impression?"

"He said a large gold shipment was put ashore this morning from a yacht. Coming from him, the way it did, made it sound very impressive. Spontaneous enough and impressive enough to be true, in fact."

Ah, thought Obenpharo, this is one of the shrewd ones. Under the easygoing American informality there is an analytical brain. "Henri was indiscreet to talk so much. By the age of nine he will know better."

"Do you mind telling me about this new shipment?"

"Yes, Mr. Walker, I do mind. No rudeness intended, you understand. We have one major item from which to make our living: discretion. Financial anonymity. Professional silence, one might say, like an attorney or physician."

"That explains why gold can move in and out of here like bags of peanuts."

"Yes, but only partly. Actually the golden glitter casts no illumination on day-to-day banking, Mr. Walker. Don't let it dazzle you."

"But you're the only top banker bringing gold in. All the rest is headed out."

Obenpharo shrugged his great shoulders. "A little boy with a bag of coins from his foolish old grandfather. Hardly an international transaction."

Walker laughed. Now, for the first time, he began to believe Obenpharo was importing a sizable amount of gold. Maybe the goal was political, not financial. There was a son named Roger who was a big wheel in the complicated underground of Moroccan politics. Maybe that's where the gold was really going. For a moment he wondered if Obenpharo might be one of the rich anonymous men who helped finance the Istiqlal. But it was too early at the moment to probe this idea.

"Please remember, Mr. Walker," Obenpharo said, "and you may write in your paper I said this, gold is sterile stuff. Wonderful to fill a tooth cavity, but it bakes no bread for you or me. It produces no goods or services, really. It occupies space, and the owners pay expensive shipping and insurance and storage charges."

Walker enjoyed this. "You're anti-gold?"

"That's very American, if you'll permit me. You oversimplify. I mean this pro and anti *reductio ad absurdum*. I'm only realistic. Gold is like water. The right amounts in the right places can make the desert blossom. Too much, used wrongly, causes drowning."

"I don't follow your reasoning, monsieur."

"Look here, now, Mr. Walker. Most of the money of the world is soft, diseased. Most people in the world are denied by law from freely moving their assets from one country to another. Your own United

62

States, with a mountain of gold buried in Fort Knox, has the same disease mildly."

"You mean inflation."

"In the States, yes. With the disease of inflation comes a fever. The value of printed money goes down, the temperature of prices goes up. Inflation jumps off in commodities and lands with both feet in the stock market. In other countries it is worse than inflation. It is bankruptcy. The little man saves a hundred dollars, but when he turns around he can only buy fifty dollars' worth of goods. You know these ABC's, I'm sure."

"Of course. But I think you're making a point, monsieur. What is it?"

"My point is that a survival at any cost philosophy makes governments amoral. Although I must say that some of the bankrupt countries have shown a cynicism in currency manipulation which has wiped out the private assets of millions of people. The result is a fantastic global volume of illegal gold and currency transactions. The Chinese farmer buries a Macao gold coin under a pear tree. The Indian peasant with a good crop buys his wife a gold bracelet. This he will pawn next year when the drought strikes him. The Frenchman puts a few more napoleons into the mattress. A Balkan diplomat with diplomatic pouch privileges flies to Paris with some very heavy luggage—what's inside, olive branches?"

"Can I interpret you as saying what's illegal about gold transactions almost all over the world is legal here?"

Obenpharo's eyes closed for a quick moment, pondering all the gambits from this catch question like a great electronic computer, then he opened them. "Only financially. Tangier offers freedom. We're talking about governmental money, not private morals."

"You know Tangier's reputation about morals, monsieur. Sodom and Gomorrah."

"Yes, yes. Ridiculous. In such a big city as this, only one murder in years. Petty stealing, perhaps, but no robberies with gangsters and guns. Can your big cities compare, Mr. Walker?"

"I doubt it."

"We here are almost an international suburb," Obenpharo swept on. "The European colony is a small town, the few hundred Americans are like a village, everyone knows everyone. There is the usual cocktail folderol and gossip, like any suburb, but can vice flourish in such"—he searched for the word—"such, such *antiseptic* surroundings?"

"Well, I've seen quite a few pretty boys with bleached blond hair and hanky-panky."

Obenpharo brushed it aside. "That reflects the Arab acceptance of homosexuality, which reflects poverty, tradition, and the separation of women. The fringe people you see are mainly in a few bars, like Carnivale. New York and New Orleans and Paris, Marseille, Rome, Cairo—name any capital, Mr. Walker, and you'll find big-business vicious vice, not this open infantile fiddle-faddle."

"Well, how about drugs? No American newspaper publishes the daily market price of marijuana. That's unique, believe me. Yesterday somebody offered to show me some kind of candied hashish or marijuana called *majoun!*"

"Couldn't that happen in any big city? The difference here is that you'd be cheated. You'd be buying a chocolate bar in a plain wrapper."

"And the smuggling stories, monsieur?"

Obenpharo spread his hands slightly. "Half true for a short time after the war. One-hundredth true now. At this moment one of my clients can sell you a warehouse load of nylons, cigarettes, fountain pens, automatic lighters. All American made, excellent products. That would cost you, let us say, a hundred thousand dollars. Then you buy a speedboat, a big one to carry all these goods. Perhaps that costs sixty to another hundred thousand. Now you need another fifty thousand for maintenance and crew."

"That's a quarter of a million dollars, so far."

"Yes. And all this is completely legal. You sail out of Tangier harbor into the open Mediterranean legally. A properly purchased ship with a paid-for cargo. But when you enter European coastal waters with undeclared contraband, that's illegal. Would *you* risk a quarter of a million dollar investment trying to outrun the Italian gunboats and radar outside Naples?"

"I'd think it over."

"Mr. Walker, you come here with questions. I'm an old-fashioned

64

banker, not a smuggler. We may be a trifle unorthodox by your rules, but really there's very little excitement in a conservative bank such as this one. I respond to your questions with courtesy. Whatever I say I believe can be verified."

Walker recognized that he was being dismissed. "You've been very generous, monsieur. And more frank than most European or North African businessmen."

Obenpharo bowed his head very slightly. "A bank is a public trust," he said with every appearance of modesty. "But we've only talked about gold quite superficially, and about some sensational nonsense. Is a reputable paper like yours seriously interested in Tangier's dirty linen?"

"Moroccan air bases and Sahara oil and Tangier's position as the strategic cork in the Mediterranean bottle—none of those are dirty linen, monsieur."

Obenpharo's amiability began to disappear. He decided to be blunt. "Complicated subjects, Mr. Walker. Not sales material for the average sort of superficial news stories, wouldn't you say?"

"Well, I'm free-lance. Beside the newspaper stuff, I'm considering doing a think piece for *Harper's Magazine*."

"Ah, then the newspaper does not require you to think? Only the serious magazines?"

Walker grinned slowly. "For that, monsieur, I believe the word is *touché*."

"I pay you the ultimate compliment of being frank, Mr. Walker."

"Yes," Walker added quickly, "but also, to be frank, I have the impression of a lot of things left out."

"*Certainement.* Money is a very complicated subject."

"Yes. But the cliché is true: money talks."

"Always. To Banque Obenpharo first."

"And what is money saying to Banque Obenpharo right now, may I ask, monsieur?"

"It says the Mediterranean is the cradle of civilization, and some squalling brats are rocking the cradle dangerously. It says that Africa is the continent of tomorrow, Mr. Walker, as the Americas were the continents of yesterday. Those who use the Islamic religion as dynamite, with nationalistic issues for burning fuses—well, we could all blow up in a world explosion that will make the last one seem gentle."

Walker looked at him quietly for a moment, measuring his trustfulness. "You've hit an exposed nerve for me. An hour ago a friend of mine in Casa telephoned that the first American killing has happened."

Obenpharo's face closed like a door. He said nothing.

"A gang wearing native clothes," Walker said slowly, "stopped a jeep outside the air base at Nouasseur. There was an American Army captain driving that jeep, and they took him out and shot him in the ditch."

Obenpharo frowned sadly. "We hang together, as I said. That's the correct phrase in English, isn't it? We hang together, or we hang separately."

Walker nodded. "Can I get to see your son Roger, perhaps? Ask him a few questions?"

Obenpharo's jaw muscles bunched. After a brief second, he said tightly, "I cannot say. Only he can speak for himself."

Walker nodded again, looking much less boyish, much less casual now, and completely capable of writing something called a think piece. "Thanks for your time, monsieur," he said.

They measured each other with experienced eyes and a new mutual respect, then shook hands, long-armed, like tennis champions over a net. The game had ended in an even draw. Perhaps there would be a return match.

High above, in the penthouse, the telephone rang as Maia perched on the corner of Obenpharo's great desk. She ignored the ringing, and pulled the second telephone toward her to call the American School. The first one rang again, then again, with a prolonged insistence now. She picked up the receiver with annoyance.

"Yes?"

"Pardon," the switchboard girl said, "an urgent call for Monsieur Obenpharo, madame."

"He is not taking calls, Maria."

"Pardon, madame. I explained to them before, the first time. It is long distance, from Xauen, and the connection is bad and they speak Spanish bad, too."

"Xauen?" Who in the remote village of Spanish Morocco would

insist on being put through directly to Monsieur Obenpharo? "Did they say who was calling, Maria?"

"They refuse, madame. They only say it concerns Monsieur Roger."

A lightning shock passed through her. "Wait," she said quickly, "I'll try to reach him on the interoffice box." She leaned over the communication box, searching for the electric *On* switch before depressing the voice key for the doorman's phone. An instinct too swift for analysis made her pause, then turn back to the telephone.

"Maria, I believe he has left the building. Tell them Monsieur Roger's wife is on the line and wishes to speak to them."

"Yes, madame."

She held the receiver so tightly that the tips of her gripping fingers became pale, and there was a sensation of pounding within her ears. Xauen. Someone speaking argot from Spanish Morocco. About Roger. It could mean only one thing. I hope he's dead, she thought fervently. We'll all be happier.

The receiver clicked and hummed, and a faraway voice said in Arabic, "Lalla Maia?"

She strained forward to hear. In street Arabic she answered, "This is the Lady Maia. Speak. Where is my husband?"

"It cannot be said. But you must come here at once with a doctor." The receiver crackled and made electrical spitting noises, so that only a ghost of a voice could be heard.

"Speak. Speak!" To her amazement she was shouting. Her knees were weak and she felt dizzy. *"Speak!"*

". . . very soon," the voice boomed with startling suddenness in her ear. "We have an old corporal, from French service. He has bandages. But he says we must have a doctor today or your husband will die. Do you hear me, Lalla Maia?"

"Yes, yes!"

"It is very hard to hear you. Come quickly."

The phone went dead, followed by a second click and a different sound which she suddenly realized must be the Spanish listening on the line at the border *Controle.* Her hands were shaking a little now, and when she tried to replace the receiver it clattered to the desk and she had to make an effort to put it into place properly.

Her bones dissolved, leaving her limp. She held the edge of the

67

desk until she could lower herself into the big leather chair. In her chest her heart swung heavily, making her breathing come fast and shallow.

She looked at Roger's picture on the wall. I know now, she thought, that I can never truly love anyone because I will never surrender myself completely. But I came closer to giving myself to him than to anyone, and how strange it is that I hate him.

The possibilities which would follow Roger's death stretched before her imagination, an endless landscape of empire and victory. There was a prize for everyone. Henri got the bank, she would rule until he came of age, and Mutirra and Benari exchanged the agony of a son for the happy promise of their grandson. And Roger—she remembered the terrible night eight years ago when he had told them all he was rebuilding his entire life, turning his back on their empty materialistic world, and Obenpharo had shouted, choked with pain, "You hypnotized fool! You want to spend your life looking for death?"

"If that is what is necessary," Roger had said. "Better than living with the walking dead in Paris."

"You're a megalomaniac! You want to start a new religion!"

"I will if I have to, Father."

"Then make sure to get yourself crucified! And remember to roll back the stone and rise from the dead!"

Obenpharo had been awesomely right. The big things were simple. All she had to do now was remain silent. Roger had achieved his crucifixion. She doubted he would rise from the dead.

(3)

A HALF hour later Maia left the bank. She had washed her face in Obenpharo's private bathroom, letting the cold water run over her brows and eyes until the feverish feeling went away and her hands were steady enough to apply make-up skillfully. No matter how she tried, she could not control the growing tension inside her. Her legs trembled a little in the elevator going down, but she got off steadily and crossed the lobby gracefully, knowing she looked just the way everyone wanted her to look, cool and a trifle haughty.

Hassani had a car for her at the door. She gave him a five-hundred-peseta note, five times what he expected, knowing that he was of the old Arab school which believed in complete democracy between lord and servant, for all were equal in the eyes of Allah, yet his belief in eternal loyalty assumed without a doubt that gifts, money, and power would always come down from those above him. They both understood the money was not a tip, not a bribe, but only the rich sharing with the poor, the way of their world.

"May God bless thy hands, Lalla Maia."

"Thou too, O Hadj Hassani, remain under God's protection."

She leaned toward Raoul, the driver, and said, in French, "To the Carnivale." She had decided to let the American School matter go until tomorrow. Right now she felt as she never had before that she needed a drink. Jeanjean will be waiting for me, she thought, but he'll just have to wait. I feel like an escaped criminal and I need a drink all by myself.

There was no need to tell Raoul where the Carnivale was. Everyone knew, because sooner or later everyone in Tangier paid bacchanalian homage there. A vaguely Mediterranean refugee named Raïssa had begun it as a bar during the Tangier boom days when hard-looking guys from Marseille and Chicago were scouting deals in which they said a single motorboat load of American cigarettes could make a hundred-thousand-dollar profit in Tarifa or Naples. With prosperity, and a loan from Banque Obenpharo, Raïssa had enlarged the place with a mirrored Moulin Rouge *fin de siècle* décor and the famous circular carrousel bar in the center. The entire ceiling was a striped canvas tent which was reflected in a tall pillar of tiny flashing mirrors within the central space of the bar. Whenever someone ordered drinks for everyone, in a Klondike fashion strongly encouraged by Raïssa, the tall mirrored pillar would be set revolving to the recorded music of a steam calliope, and the reflections of the striped tent overhead would flash in a giddy kaleidoscope over the faces of the bar patrons. The well-to-do said that Raïssa was producing a three-ring circus without sawdust, but they came into her limelight because she offered them the best liquor between Casablanca and

69

Cairo. To help them play aristocrats in the grand manner, Raïssa gave them an audience of plebeians whom they could sneer at and carefully turn their backs on, and on-the-cuff credit and monthly bills which they could ignore. Raïssa also provided a tireless bawdy monologue and thrilling-willing boys and willing-thrilling girls who carefully observed good taste and decorum.

In addition to the well-to-do there were the other patrons, who came for exactly the same reasons.

Raïssa made sure everyone knew the real secret of her bar's name was not the carnival décor, oh no, how pedestrian that would be, but actually because Roger Obenpharo had told her once that Tangier needed a medieval *carne vale,* a farewell to flesh, before the inevitable jeremiad of purification in which she would become a pillar of salt.

Raïssa was a thin heat-hardened knifeblade of a woman, ageless because of her pencil figure, with very blond hair cut straight and close as a boy's. She murmured explanations about the phallic meanings of the circular bar with the shining pillar in its center, and the pubic Moorish archways, modestly adding that all this came from an Algiers woman psychologist friend. When the inevitable question came, she would stroke back her hair and throw away the line, "No, *not* a psychiatrist. My friend's a *lay* analyst." Psychology, she was sure, added a tone of intellectuality to her bar—"D'you mind if I call it my *salon*?"—and she kept a charitable eye peeled for bearded young artists willing to sit in a corner and explain existentialism in return for the extra free drink she always sent over with each full round his audience ordered. It was a cheap bonus. "Artists are sensitive souls," she would say blandly. "They need to be pampered." She let it be known that for old customers, or those tourists who became old customers in a single night away from their steamship hotels by spending freely enough, she would tell the Story of the Downward Steps, a sort of Thousand and One Nights tale diluted with club soda and ice cubes. Her current *amie* depreciated this. "Raïssa's only a cat o' nine tales," she said, "get it?"

The Downward Steps were arranged around the base of the tall mirrored pillar in the center of the circular bar. Like a sample display in the window of a store, a single woman's shoe stood separately on each step. There was a delicate shell of an evening shoe with a long rhinestone jeweled heel; there was a Cinderella thing, tiny, of

70

transparent plastic; there was a finely tanned walking shoe with a sensible heel and a fringed tongue; a slender black moccasin of the type called loafers; a flat Capri sandal with thin leather thongs; a rope-soled peasant girl's *espadrille*. There were rumors that one hollow step contained a unique contraption, of narrow straps and rubber, which Raïssa demonstrated only to the truly faithful. Raïssa encouraged this rumor adroitly so that she could deny such evil-minded whispering.

Raïssa would lift one of the shoes at arm's length like an actor, fondling it, playing Hamlet to the skull of Yorick, saying in what she considered an American Broadway accent, "This seven double A was Emily's, alas poor lass, an American college girl over to see the sights and maybe take a peeky at a cheeky-sheiky. A harem-scare'em type. Clean-cut, y'know? No make-up, just lipstick. Clean as Ivory soap—she floated, she was so pure—and cut off from home with a hatbox full of traveler's checks. Hair like cornsilk and blond, really blond, y'know what I mean, all over." Then the theatrical salacious sigh, and the Story of Emily's Downward Step would begin. "The fallen angel walked in here one night, no escort, lonely, y'know—"

Everyone said Carnivale was a *succès fou*. It was *sensas*, the Parisian slang for sensational. It was *fabulous*. "But of course," Raïssa would say, "we have them all, from rags and riches to bags and bitches."

When Maia walked in, Raïssa was leaning over one of the tables to sample something on a guest's plate. Raïssa saw Maia immediately and came quickly to meet her at the door. They detested one another, and so met smiling.

"Look, children, Salomé's back at the old stand! But where's St. John's head on a tray?"

Maia felt herself go pale, and the feeling of fever mounted instantly behind her eyes. "Raïssa, how are you?" she managed to say, letting Raïssa take her hands, thinking, what a dreadful bitch. The hardly disguised aggressiveness behind the greeting. The reference to sainthood aimed at Roger. The Arabic voice on the telephone from Xauen crackled again at Maia's inner ear. Guilt stabbed her. If Roger were to fall in battle, at least let him not be eaten by the jackals like this woman.

"Maia! Come closer to the fire, my little one. You look white as

71

a sheet and your hands are like ice. You're positively *frigid*! That's how you always manage to look so cool and green and lovely."

"No, no." Maia made herself laugh because the neighboring tables were watching. "It's done by prayer and fasting."

"Yes, and contemplating your naval escort. I saw you come ashore this morning from that monstrous *Queen Mary* of a yacht."

"How? How could you?"

"From my seaside terrace. With my beautiful Zeiss binoculars. I usually scan the beach for interesting tidbits, and this morning the bit tid was you, sweet. What in the world was in all those square wooden boxes coming ashore? Lingerie?"

Several people nearby smiled. Each one who recognized Maia quietly told the next the beautiful *poil de carrotte* was Maia *de la Banque Obenpharo,* Maia heard her name travel in whispers, so Raïssa's audience widened in ripples.

"Lingerie," Maia smiled. "I like that. A half million in solid lingerie." She felt the lapping of little waves of interest around her.

Raïssa leaned forward and put her bony hand on Maia's arm. *"Gold?"* she stage-whispered. "They say it's all going the other way!"

"You're too smart to panic, Raïssa. Smart money always swims against the current. Keep your little rainy day pile here. In our bank, of course." Her face had become warm again, almost flushed, and the weak-kneed feeling which Raïssa's extraordinary remark about Salomé had given her was gone. She sank into the chair an Arab waiter offered her. If I can only get a drink and keep talking about money I'm safe, she thought. The phone call from Xauen will stop running over and over again through my mind. One drink will brace me. Two will begin to blunt things.

Raïssa leaned over her. "Please be my guest today, Maia."

"Nonsense, Raïssa. How can you show a profit that way? How can you pay off your mortgage with us?" She felt her thrust touch bone. Raïssa's mortgage was of less than postage stamp interest to Banque Obenpharo, but to Raïssa it was the root of bitterness.

Raïssa's teeth met on edge for a fraction, then parted widely as she hooted with salon gaiety. "Wonderful, wonderful! Which of those lovely green eyes is the banker's glass one?"

"Both. Really, can't you tell?" When will this woman stop screeching?

"And those lovely green shoes." Raïssa leaned over her, scanning her completely as a street-corner *suiveur*. "You wouldn't have a spare shoe I can put on my steps?"

"No, dear," Maia said. "These two are all, and they're both nailed under my bed." Go, she thought, *va-t'en*. I need a drink, two drinks, not this lewd play-acting for the clients.

"And that lovely green belt. I just noticed that it has a motto worked into it."

"Nothing, really. Just some stitching."

Raïssa bent to read the belt. " '*Omnia—vincit . . .*' How quaint! It's in Latin!"

Maia tried to get rid of her. "Yes. '*Omnia vincit amor.*' May I order now?"

" '*Amor . . .*'! 'Love conquers all,' isn't that it? Fabulous! I love it! Another one of the noble Roger's noble comments?"

Maia closed her eyes and put one hand flat on the table to steady herself. Roger's thin dark face rose before her with mocking accusing burning eyes. Once more she felt the wave washing over her, her strength draining away in a riptide, the surf thundering behind her temples. "Please," she managed to say quietly, drowning in guilt, "please, the menu."

A cluster of small street boys closed in on Maia when she came out of the Carnivale an hour later. Maia stood in the full sun, triply bright after the dim womb of Raïssa's bar, and put on her dark sunglasses while her driver and the little street Arabs all shouted at once around her. I've had too much wine, she thought. Too little lunch, too much wine. But everything is under control now. What animals we are; when hunger goes, panic goes, too.

Raoul, the driver, waved his arms at the crowd of street children, shooing them away like flies. "*Va-t'en! Va-t'en! Emshi f'alkoum! Mashi n'ait polici!*"

"Nize fan, Chinee, see?" one youngster screamed at Maia, flicking a false ivory fan open and closed directly before her face.

"Her' Trib, N'ork Ti'," the newspaper boy was saying, holding up

73

last week's *New York Times* and yesterday's Paris edition of the *Herald Tribune* with a black headline: NORTH AFRICAN RIOTS KILL 33.

At the edge of the crowd of jumping shouting boys stood a girl whose body size looked six, with a face of twelve, and a sleeping baby slung on her back with its head lolling on her bony shoulder, its brown face covered with flies. Maia saw the girl just as she was about to step into the car, and went toward the child immediately, parting the pressing boys to each side like waves. She knew it was not her faintly alcoholic sense of well-being which pushed her forward; it was the subtle memory-tugging sense of walking toward her own ragged hungry childhood.

It was as if in a very real dream she were the child and saw herself as she was now, a rich European woman in cool green linen, walking toward herself and saying softly, "Thou, my little one. What is thy name?"

The child's deep eyes looked at her without love or hate, without hope or pity, without anything except a blind deep need to live.

"Flowers?" She held out toward Maia the small bunch of pink field oleander blossoms she clutched; by the grace of Allah the miracle of half a peseta might be forthcoming. Everyone knew the endlessly repeated tale of the beggar who went to stand before the Grand Mosque with one hand outstretched in just this way. His need for food was so great and terrible that he knew Allah would divine this and succor him. Across the thronging cobbled *souk* before the Mosque came a merchant who had owed a debt to the beggar for many years. Now, as the merchant saw the beggar there with a pious outstretched hand, he decided to pay the debt, and so placed in the beggar's starving palm the full amount. The beggar did not thank him, nor did he rejoice, for he had known with certainty, from that morning onward, that Allah would provide.

So the child held out the limp pink flowers to Maia. "Flowers?"

"Thy father and thy mother, little one, where are they?"

The child stared at her unblinkingly. "Flowers?" she asked.

Maia saw her own childhood before her, without the accident of her own pale beauty or unusual hair to help her escape; but the same dirty bare feet, the same torn coarse sack for a dress, the same fatalistic ability to accept blows, money, curses, food, kisses, famine, all face

74

to face and as they came. There was neither courage nor the face of courage, but only the world and things as they were. Those two drinks before lunch, Maia thought wearily, not just the wine alone; alcohol always makes me vulnerable like this. How I detest the stupid tears of drunks, yet I'm no different. The grimy little girl is as meaningless as one of the flies drinking at the lip drool of her infant sister's face, part of the crowding pushing life that crept from every crack in Africa. But Maia could not control the warmth which misted the inner surface of her sunglasses; it was her own lost childhood which made her want to cry.

Then she saw the fawn.

A half-naked Arab boy held a goat's-hair halter to a baby fawn no taller than his waist. It was toylike and spindly, as if blown in glass, speckled in shades of tan and brown, with alert anxious almond eyes and a quietly docile stance on tiny hoofs. They were a pair: a two-legged fawn leading a four-legged one.

The experienced street boys saw Maia shift her attention from the flowers to the fawn, and immediately began to shout, "Buy it! Buy it!" They enjoyed the suspense of seeing the grand lady begin to enter her car, step back, choose the country girl with the oleander blossoms, the implied promise of money in a moment, the sudden shift of interest to the fawn. And this red-haired woman of the great world spoke amazingly in their own street Arabic. All would yet be well, *insha' Allah.*

"Art thou selling the creature, boy?" Maia asked. As soon as she had seen the fawn she had thought of how Henri would love it. She could see his face as the fawn ran to him and licked a piece of sugar in his cupped hands.

"Yes."

"What is thy price on it?"

He shrugged, and the others shouted, "Fifty pesetas! Hundred pesetas! Two hundred pesetas!" The exchange rate of the day in the sidewalk *cambios* was under forty-three pesetas to the dollar, and none of them could imagine a price above two hundred pesetas.

"Shall we say thy price is two hundred pesetas?" Maia asked the boy.

He nodded. One hundred, two hundred, fifty; there was no meaning in numbers for him.

"I will buy it," Maia said, and at that moment, from behind her came the quiet hopeless word, "Flowers?"

She turned quickly. "Yes, little one. The flowers, too. Raoul, take the child's flowers." When her fingers trembled as she opened her green purse she realized that these were not purchases, not charity, but rites of gratitude before the altars of the gods who had lifted her out of this almost twenty years ago.

"A hundred pesetas for the flowers," she said, giving the girl the amount in a single coin, easy to hold. The girl's expression did not change. Today Allah had provided. Tomorrow, perhaps not. It would be as it would be.

"And five hundred for the small creature," Maia said, counting out five banknotes for the little boy.

"*Ai-yee-ee!*" the other children keened.

"Hold the money tightly," Maia warned the boy, "even if someone should push you or trip you. Take it home now." The boy nodded, and gave her the goat's-hair halter with his quick brown hand. The fawn moved back and forth on its toy hoofs, lifting its pointed ears, and Maia knelt to stroke the tiny furred slope of its neck. She looked over her shoulder at the biggest boy in the crowd.

"Thy name, O tall one?"

He was a city boy, and he grinned accommodatingly. "Ali."

"I will give you ten pesetas to be a guardian for this boy and his money. Take him to his house." Ali nodded quickly. "Tomorrow," Maia went on, "come with him to the doorman of the Banque Obenpharo who will question him. If all has gone well with him, you will be given a new reward. If not, the police will hear it."

"He will be my brother," Ali said, and seized the young boy's hand with fierce commercial protectiveness.

Even the driver of the car was enjoying Maia's display, and Maia gave him the halter to lead the fawn gently into the back seat of the car. "Now," Maia said, "to every child two pesetas for their good wishes." Carefully she gave each child some coins, and when several of the older boys ran around to the other side of the circle she gave them additional coins for their cunning. A babel of little voices rose around her. The children cried out and fluttered, waving their arms; they reminded her suddenly of the pigeons who surrounded the old lady in Paris who came each day to the Arc de Triomphe with a basket of crumbs in a winged aureole of chirping birds. By this time several of Raïssa's patrons, both grotesques and tourists, had braved the naked sunlight to come out to see a curbstone carnival so different from their own, indoors, and Maia knew that to the legend of the boxes of five hundred thousand dollars' worth of solid lingerie would now be added the one about how *La Belle Dame Sans Merci* made an incredible street purchase of a fawn. *La Belle Dame Sensas,* Raïssa would surely add.

Maia stroked the fawn's neck as she leaned into the corner of the back seat of the car. "To Banque Obenpharo first, Raoul," she told the driver, "then to the Bastinado Gate."

The fawn nuzzled between her knees as she stroked it, murmuring softly; its ears twitched, and once or twice it closed its eyes as she rubbed the top of its small-boned head. "Little one," she whispered, "oh, thou little one. Henri will love thee and feed thee milk and fruit." As I fed the lambs who were too weak to stand, she thought, remembering herself again much like the young street girl, but living far, far back in the highest range of the High Atlas, with city streets yet undreamed of and unimagined. The ragged little shepherdess of the Aït Hadiddou tribe beside the Dades River was five hundred kilometers and five thousand years away from this tailored woman of Tangier. She let her thoughts drift, siesta-like, because the morning had been crowded with so much intensity, and her lunch had been hurried to escape that harridan, Raïssa, and the half bottle of Chaud-soleil *glacée* and the two martinis had made her a trifle sleepy. Her usual iron self-control was weakened today, the fatigue of the journey to be sure, and something in the deepest down corner of her mind kept repeating a trifle drunkenly: *RogerRogerRogerRoger.*

In one lifetime I moved five hundred kilometers and five thousand years, she thought. It's all so strange as I look backward now, the strange journey from the pressed mud hut to the palatial Villa Obenpharo. Roger used to tell me the journey would never be completed and that I would always be the Berber shepherdess inside. "Five hundred kilometers is nothing in Europe," Roger had said, "but in

77

North Africa the distance to the High Atlas might as well be to the moon. Your little village of Aït Attiq is in such a Godforsaken mountain valley that even the French never knew it was there. Animal husbandry. Sheepherders. Spinning, weaving, crude pottery. Maia, do you realize you're a refugee from a Neolithic culture?"

By that time, early in their marriage, she had discovered he liked to parade his Latin and his learning, and she knew the timeless woman-wisdom of letting a man lead his own parade. "What is that?" she had asked.

"The Stone Age. Think of it." He ticked each point off on his fingers. "If your mother had not taken you with her to the market of M'Semrir, if the French priests had not come by with their medicine truck, if the English painter had not seen you in Marrakech, if my father had not known the painter in Tangier, if Mutirra had not always wanted a daughter, if all those ifs never happened, you would be climbing in the mountains now to gather a backload of brush for your fires and grinding corn between two stones."

She had shrugged calmly. "Whatever was to happen, happened."

"I don't believe it. Chance favors the prepared mind. You were quicker than the rest, brighter, tougher, or whatever the *élan vital* in you should be called. You're not honest or dishonest, or kind or unkind, or anything else learned out of books. You were a tiger cub. Or rather a mountain goat. So you climbed to the outside world."

"Food and warmth," she had said, "that's all I wanted. Whoever offered me food and warmth." She had loved him very much then, and wanted to forget the unutterable reason why her mother had brought a deflowered daughter of eleven, a marriageable age, to the market at M'Semrir; not only that, but also wanting to forget the English painter in Tangier who had used her when she was twelve, on canvas and in the kitchen and in bed.

Only Mutirra and Benari Obenpharo had been truly kind. Only the Obenpharos had ever thought of her as a person, not as a small slavey who crouched among the bleak mountain rocks to watch her flock on pain of beating if a lamb were lost; not as an impersonal nubile primitive with an unusual color of eyes and hair and cherry-nippled slenderness for the master's asking. Who but Mutirra would have said to her, "We are of the same family because we are both outcasts. You were violated by the man who lived with your mother and may have been your own father. My father sent me from his house when I said a woman was not property and I took off my veil. They called me the *evoluée,* a whore of the French and worse, and they scorned me. Soon the dirty wits of Tangier will smile at you, too, and say over cocktails, 'Did you know Berber comes from the Greek word for barbarian?' Ignore them. The mountain tribes have never been brought to their knees, and you are a mountain girl. I have been cursed because I cannot have more than just my one child, but you will be like the daughter every woman dreams of, with pride and beauty and intelligence." Mutirra had spoken to her in classic Arabic, and Maia remembered it had the sound of music.

"Food and warmth," Roger had repeated in his quiet intense way. "Is that what I give you, my little mountain goat?" And they had smiled at one another, because that was still in their smiling years, soon after Henri was born, before Roger had decided he could give his life meaning only by leaving his family and changing the world.

Maia was so deeply lost in thought that she did not notice her car had stopped before the Banque Obenpharo and that Hassani was opening the door.

"Ah, madame!" Hassani said in French, "you have missed Monsieur Obenpharo by just a moment!" His eyes took in the toy fawn with its little head in her lap, but he ignored it and would have spoken again except for her interruption.

"Tomorrow, Hadj Hassani," she said, "a small boy and an older boy will come here to you at the bank . . ." and she went on to explain about her arrangement with the boy who had sold her the fawn.

He nodded, then nodded again as she spoke, surprising her because this was as close to appearing impatient as she had ever seen him. When she finished her explanation his eyes flicked at the French driver's back and then he said in Arabic, "O Lalla Maia, the news is grave. A kinsman of my wife, a Party man, came from Tetuan on the fast Valenciana coach-bus a moment past. He told of Sidi Mohammed lying in pain, with half his face torn open by French gunfire."

"Who is this Sidi Mohammed, O Hassani?"

79

"Monsieur Roger. His Islamic name. He lies in Xauen near to death."

"And you told Monsieur Obenpharo the report of your kinsman?" She could hardly speak.

"Yes. Every telephone in the bank was closed by him in order that he could call, all at once, the doctor here, the Spanish hospital in Tetuan, the Spanish High Commissioner, the Teniente Coronel in Xauen. Now he has gone to Xauen like a storm. He took the Spanish Vice-Consul on the seat beside him to save time at crossing the border, and the doctor and a box containing bottles of blood covered with ice. He commanded everyone and everything, as in the old days."

"A thousand thanks, Hadj Hassani. Your fidelity is great. Your reward will be greater." She saw the driver watching her in the rear-view mirror for instructions, and she nodded for him to start. *"Salaam aleikum,* Hadj Hassani."

"Aleikum salaam, Lalla Maia."

She leaned toward the driver as the car entered the Boulevard Pasteur traffic. "Rue de la Kasbah," she said, then sank back into the corner of the seat. She lighted one of Theo's cigarettes. My hand is steady now, she thought with surprise. Maybe the hot feeling of guilt is gone, too. Maybe I partly wanted him to live.

Yes, she thought, I can sense that Roger will live. No Obenpharo surrenders to dying so easily. The Obenpharo family has seen too much history, the medieval famine in the streets, the Vandals pillaging and disemboweling the city, the Moorish scimitars flashing toward Spain, the screams of Christian captives under the lash as the slave columns shuffled in chains toward the Sahara, the frenzied mobs who poured by the truckload into Tangier from the Spanish zone a few years ago to smash shop windows along this same boulevard. The Obenpharos have seen it all and survived. No son of theirs can be killed so easily. Henri will have to wait to inherit his empire, and I must go back to being the woman who replaced an Obenpharo son at the viceroy post in Paris.

Suddenly Maia glimpsed herself as a captive on a golden rope, not the cool silken princess from Paris as she always thought of herself. Obenpharo holds me on a golden rope long enough for me to have

80

an illusion of freedom, unchained. He made that clear in his office this morning, about Jeanjean. *In the end, it's my money that keeps him.* He knows I do better with our Paris clients than his intellectual son ever did; yet he is an emperor because he knows better than most men how to separate what is true about me and Roger and the world, from what he wishes to be true, as he himself is so fond of saying. He holds me by his golden rope because he knows I will do anything, anything, so that I will never go back to poverty. He holds me by my love for Mutirra, and my unique fear and love of him. Her eyes narrowed as she looked into the little cloud of cigarette smoke before her, thinking: And I hold him by his son's son, his first mortgage on immortality. The accounts balance.

Then she thought: I must stop this thinking. They have over-civilized me. My weakness today was the weakness of a hothouse-bred European. But I grew on rocks. They wanted me to bring them sons and strength, a new birth of mountain men with city learning. Roger knew it. He knew exactly what his father wanted. Roger knew I was his family's choice, the classic concubine brought in and raised as a princess; the emperor's never spoken but clearly understood choice for his son, and Roger knew that beneath the coiffure, and the glowing emerald ring from Van Cleef, and the Balenciaga linen dress, was a forever frightened fawn, a small-boned creature who needed both nimbleness and strength to survive.

Everyone has used me, she thought with quick furious insight, everyone has filled his own need with me, and now what of my own needs?

Her driver honked his car's horn angrily at the strolling pedestrians who ambled along the gutters and in the center of the road with equal casualness. Two men directly before them in the road, bearded and turbaned, walked side by side holding hands in the Moslem manner of friendship, ignoring the car behind them. A French storekeeper standing in the shade of his doorway with a green parrot perched haughtily on his shoulder shouted at them, and, after a brief kingly glance backward, they moved out of the way toward the sidewalk.

Maia stared through her sunglasses at the Arab *fatimas,* women veiled completely from head to foot in their white or blue *haiks,* walking by with only eye slits exposed to the world. Many wore sunglasses, like Maia's, which blocked even the eye slits. Some of them were *femmes d'occasion,* amateur or professional, announcing their availability despite the laundry heap of their draperies by the semi-transparent veils over their faces, pink and black veils with sequins or elaborate lace edges, like lingerie. They should be wearing my belt with the Latin motto, Maia thought. My love has never conquered. I'm always the loser.

The great graying stone walls of the ancient Portuguese Kasbah, the Fortress, cast a whole geometry of angled shadow and fierce tropic brightness over the crowding gently pushing bargaining watching eating strolling throng. The car ground along in low gear now, finally defeated like every invader, by the oceanic swarm of African life.

An Aïssowa snake charmer came alongside her window with a wicker basket under the crook of one elbow while he held stiffly outstretched toward her his other arm. It writhed and coiled with three or four snakes. Beside him, his blank-eyed blinded partner played a flute softly, ululating with sounds in a minor wailing key Maia remembered from her childhood. A youth in a caped *djellaba* held a large goatskin tomtom above his head like a parasol, tapping out an endless rhythm, the pulsebeats of fever. The snakes rose and fell obscenely in a tortured invisible captivity of sound as the snake charmer called for money through Maia's window. He would never have dared to approach so boldly, with the faintest subtle suggestion of threat, a year or two before the nationalist disorders began. Maia hurriedly held out some paper money, and he nudged his young tomtom-playing partner to approach her, crouching, turning, so that she could fold the paper note and tuck it into the pocket made by the hood of the cape hanging down his back.

"Go now," she said in street Arabic, which in Tangier was part Spanish, "go with thy snakes. May the Prophet guide thee."

The blind flute player took the instrument from his lips and toothlessly mumbled a few guttural sounds. He was dumb, as well as blind, a leprous gargoyle of the *souks.*

Near the site of the Catherine Gate, at the junction of Rue des Siaghines, the jewelers' street, and Rue Senmarin, a Moorish wedding party appeared suddenly with musicians piping loudly into the pressing amiable crowd, the bride's family following the drummers and the tambourine players. Behind them the *amariyah*, a covered palanquin carried high on shoulder poles, swayed dreamily above everyone's head. Silk cloths of many colors flew from the great peaked box. Maia had a sudden vision of its interior, hot, closed in until the bridal feet could step down directly, without ever touching ground, into the groom's bed. Later, in an hour, or a day, whenever his bachelor feast ended, her master would come to take her. For a moment she, Maia, was the hidden bride under a brocaded cloak heavy with pure gold needlework. She was the bride, stiff-faced lest the spirits resent a proudful smile, certain of her purity so that tomorrow morning her maidservant could throw from the upper bridal chamber to the assembled family below the blood-spotted bedsheet, proof of virginity. Deeply, remembering without thinking, her own first encounter came back to her; the tall bearded man whom her mother sometimes said was her father, sometimes not, and the manner in which he had found her tending flocks alone, and there, between two walls of rock, had fallen on the eleven-year-old girl with a primitive lust. There were other times, later, with other men, when the wave of this memory washed over her so that she did not recall the details of what had happened but only that in this or the other bed, with this or the other man, she found herself struggling shudderingly, searching uselessly for completion, cold as the mountain stone under her bony eleven-year-old shoulder-blades.

She had never mentioned this to anyone except Mutirra, who came into her room one night when Maia was thirteen because she had heard Maia cry out in a dream, and afterward Mutirra told her of a passage in the Christian Bible: "If a man find her in the field and force her and lie with her, nevertheless the damsel has not earned death, for she cried out and there was none to save her."

"You can do what I did," Mutirra had told her. "Don't be a slave of the old way. Become a European woman. Read as much as you can. Learn languages. Sit with the men when they talk. Decide matters for yourself." And yet, there is a kind of trap for women like Mutirra and me. We are never completely Europeanized, meaning French of course, and yet we can never go back to the childhoods we wanted

83

to escape. We hang between two worlds, like the legend of Allah's punishment of Az-Zuhra.

Far above her the shaft of the Mosque rose into the glassy blue bowl of sky like a square-edged mosaic finger, dominating all the squat white labyrinth of buildings and alleyways within the *ville ancienne,* the Medina quarter of the city. At the peak of the Mosque, several large signal balls the size of Chinese lanterns hung on a pulley from a flagpole. Maia saw the Friday midday ceremonial dark blue ball being lowered; its dark color symbolized the mourning of the Faithful for the loss of Granada in 1492, Roger had once explained to her, adding: In Islam nothing is ever forgotten. As the usual white ball was hoisted in the other's place the muezzin began his call: *"Allahu akbar . . . God is most great! I bear witness there is no God but God! Mohammed is the Prophet of God! Come to prayer! God is most great! There is no God but God!"*

The muezzin's voice rang out high and thin in the transparent air, rising and falling, rising again over the swarming humanity far below him. Submit, submit, submit to a will greater than your own.

Enough, Maia thought with sudden intensity. A white heat rose in her. I've had enough of all this ant heap for today, and now I'm smothering in it! I want my own little house, with the cool inner garden, and a frosted cold glass in my hand. With this sudden impulse she lifted the little fawn in her arms and said to the driver, "Enough, Raoul. I will do better walking today. Open the door."

"Oui, madame."

"Tonight at seven," she said, as he took her elbow to help her step out of the back seat, "come through the Bab Haha and wait for me at the Bastinado Gate." She did not want him near her door because she always took precautions for no one to discover the location of her little Arab house, buried in the ancient quarter.

"Oui, madame. At seven. You will be going to the Villa Obenpharo?"

"Yes, and returning later."

"Au'voir, madame."

" 'Voir, Raoul."

The cobbles under her high heels, and the rising stone steps through the twisting alleyways, made walking difficult. Because of her impatience she decided to go through the Rue Zeituna, a passage she disliked because it was a narrow tunnel in which the upper stories of each house jutted outward to touch its opposite neighbor, and the sun never penetrated past the overhang to reach street level. It stank of centuries. Once a metal craftsman in a tiny open basement shop paused to look up at her, his bearded sweating face lighted from below by an iron pot of glowing charcoal through which he was forcing air with a crude leather bellows. For a moment they stared at one another, and then she hurried on with the fawn lying in her arms like an infant.

No one except Obenpharo and Jeanjean and her servant Yacoub knew of her little house. Obenpharo purposely avoided knowing its location, and she knew Yacoub would never tell anyone. It was a Moorish house built halfway into the ancient Portuguese stone of the massive Kasbah walls, showing only a small arched doorway to a passage so narrow that, if she stretched her arms out to each side, she could place her palms flat on opposite walls. Her door was of solid mahogany, copper-studded, and above the door, lighting a majolica tile with the Arabic script for *Allah is great* hung a Fez lantern of many colored squares.

The English artist who had remodeled the original house wanted nothing so much as to leave the world outside behind him; the complex turnings to find the house, the childish pirate game of having first to walk slightly bent through a donkey's-width arched tunnel in the great stone walls, the sudden turn into the unnamed cul-de-sac at the end, the lantern-lighted doorway to an inner world . . . it was all just what he wanted. Maia had spent the twelfth year of her life there, and many years later, when she bought the little hideaway house, she had made over its interior into a jewelbox.

The fawn stirred in her arms as she raised the green copper life-size hand of Fatima which served as a knocker. She murmured softly to the little creature, stroking its pointed ears, and knocked again. There was no sound from within the house. Our buildings are as we are, she thought; they show an impassive outer face to the world, all private life and feeling restricted to the interior. In the distance there was a faint mumurous public humming, the ten-thousand-voiced Medina street life, the fruit vendors and water carriers, the children

85

and donkeys, the trinket peddlers and bracelet salesmen, the snake charmers and storytellers, the noble Arab *sidis* in fine white-hooded *djellabas* and yellow leather heelless *babouches,* the hawk-faced bearded Berber Riffs in coarse brown cloaks and battered sandals, the Spanish and French and Israelite shopkeepers with their unveiled wives and daughters hovering palely in the background, the wandering tourists with cameras slung from a shoulder searching for souvenir bargains, the arrogant horn-blowing Cadillac convertible coupe of some local grandee creeping in low gear toward a cocktail in the suburb called California, and the backfiring tough-snorting motorcycles of the white-belted white-gauntleted white-crash-helmeted white-holstered Sécurité Police who would be pushing their goggles up with sweaty exasperation at the mob, pigeons fluttering, asses braying, sparrows twittering, laughter, lamentations, tambourines and tomtoms, the perfumed smells of display basins of henna for the hair and palms and soles, small sacks of antimony for eyelash coloring, dung and gasoline, oils and essences, cones of white sugar with the little brass hammers to break them, pistachios and melon kernels, pepper, poppy, saffron and aniseed, curry and cloves, thyme and ginger, smell into sound into sound into sight and smell again, forever and ever, the whole juggernaut turning wheel of fecund pulsating Mediterranean Africa beneath the sky-arching benediction of the Mosque of Islam. . . . *Allahu akbar!*

The entire day had left Maia more vulnerable than ever before in her life to the snarled web of ancient city sounds, and she repressed a little crawling shiver of fatigue. Angry now, she swung the copper knocker hard just as the heavy door opened slowly. As soon as Yacoub saw her he opened it more widely and gave a small bow. As she walked by him she noticed pleasantly he had changed into fresh clothing since leaving the yacht that morning. Bless him, she thought, I'm home at last.

"Madame," he said, as she came into the cool stone-walled foyer. He held out his arms for the fawn, showing no surprise, but she did not move. She stood for a moment, letting the stillness flow into her, the whole pattern of this blue faïence entrance which was hers alone, with its wall niche for the fragile priceless Carthaginian vase Obenpharo had given her, now filled with Iris Tingitana from her own garden, and the opposite niche for a hammered bowl of Fez copper containing floating petals, and the nerve-cooling splashing fountain sound of water from the courtyard. Tranquillity stroked her; for this she had come from Paris, for Henri and the American School, for Obenpharo and their bank position—but actually for this and for Jeanjean.

"The *bagages,* Yacoub?"

"All delivered from the dock, madame. Shall I run your bath?"

"Yes. Is Señor Rasa here?" With Yacoub she always called him Señor Rasa, never Jeanjean.

"In the court, madame."

"What is wrong, Yacoub? Did you tell him I would be here about noon?"

"*Oui,* madame. This morning when I came. As the afternoon went by he became very angry. That's why I was late answering the door."

"Your voice. What is wrong?"

"He has a visitor."

She looked at him. "A woman?" Not now, not now. No, not now. The day is crushing me. Not another blow while I am vulnerable. He wants to punish me for my lateness, like an irritated baby.

A scale of a woman's laughter came from the court, then a light giggling shriek. Without a word, Yacoub opened the door of the foyer closet for Maia. In it, on one of the wooden pegs, hung a *fatima's* cloak with a flimsy black-lace tinsel-sequined face veil draped loosely on top. Maia's calm vanished. The white heat of the last hour became volcanic. She strode furiously through the foyer out to the shaded courtyard.

There, at the far side, Jeanjean stood beside a pretty unveiled Arab girl of about fourteen. She lay back on a pile of cushions, a tray of dark candied squares beside her which Maia guessed immediately must be *majoun,* and she was laughing like a child while Jeanjean exercised his peregrine falcon. Bébé, the falcon, was a wild-caught haggard Jeanjean had trapped himself near Valkenswaarde. He carried it everywhere, even traveling, placing it in a screened cage within a wicker basket. Now its talons were clinging to his heavy gauntlet, legstrap cords of leather jesses dangling below their attachment to its feet and making tiny jinglings with the attached Indian bells.

Jeanjean was allowing Bébé to tear at a piece of red meat attached to a pigeon-feathered leather lure held in his gloved hand. With great patience he kept returning the bird to its flat wooden perch, patting its gray feathers with the fierce comradely gentleness of an excellent trainer. He walked off a few paces, trailing a long leather leash to the falcon's leg, then, when he whistled sharply, Bébé stretched her wings effortlessly to sail with a fluttering attacking *thump* to his out-stretched gauntlet and begin tearing and raking at the bloody meat. Each swooping rush of the bird to the meat lure was so single-minded and plunging that its striking force against the gauntlet rocked Jean-jean on his heels. It was this that made the Arab girl laugh, the sight of a strong tall man almost unbalanced by the bird.

Maia stood rooted, rigid with anger. Both the giggling girl and the gray falcon had been forbidden to come here, and she knew this was Jeanjean's boy-brain way of pretending his independence of her and her money and her house and her body.

The Arab girl saw Maia first, across the courtyard, and her laughter stopped. Jeanjean turned, lithe, languid, and sensuous, and smiled widely with the strong white teeth, the red-lipped olive Spanish-Arab face, smiling with the high cheekbones and the coiled look of panther readiness that never failed to turn Maia's heart over.

"Aha," Jeanjean said, "the lady has finally condescended to come. The Sultana visits her serfs." He saw the fawn raising its head, tensing under the lewd hunger of the falcon, ears quivering slightly and pawing at the air with its hoofs. "And look, fresh meat! All the way from Paris!"

"Hood your bird!" she said quietly and when he did not move, she repeated between her teeth, *"Hood your falcon!"* The hurrying sound of Yacoub's slippers came toward the court from the inside stairs.

Jeanjean laughed and stepped lightly across the Arab girl's legs to pick up a Dutch falcon's hood of green and gold leather with a feather-tufted peak which he dropped and fastened over the unwink-ing fierceness of the falcon's head. He put the bird on its flat-surfaced perch, stroking its wings and saying gently, "Back to sleep, now, Bébé, back to sleep."

Maia turned to Yacoub as he came into the court and held out the shivering fawn to him. "Feed this little one some milk in the kitchen."

"*Oui*, madame. I have left your bath ready upstairs."

"Good. I'll attend it in a moment."

With one quick look Yacoub sniffed the charged air between Jean-jean and the girl and Maia, then hurried out with the fawn held stiffly in his arms.

Maia walked across the tilestones of the court, trembling a little with anger. As she came closer, the Arab girl rose from the cushions to her feet. Her eyes were painted with *kohl*, and she was very pretty. She sensed what was coming and began to raise her arms defensively, but Maia swung openhanded with all her might, striking the girl's face sharply.

Jeanjean laughed again, throwing his head back and laughing loudly, *"Olé!* What strength! What a royal diet of meat can do!"

The girl stood still, holding her henna-palmed hand up to the angry red splotch on her cheek, then she darted suddenly past Maia, across the court and out of sight.

Maia turned as the girl ran past, then began to walk away slowly. Jeanjean caught her elbow and swung her back, trying to put one arm around her waist, but she pushed him away.

"Is this how you come home, Maia? After two months in Paris?"

"Let go, stupid. You act like a stupid child." She pointed at the tray of candied drugs near the cushions. "You're feeling tall as a house, filled with *majoun*. One day I'll find you smoking *kif*. You're in another world, and I'm too tired to talk to you."

"Yacoub said you were coming here for lunch instead of going to Villa Obenpharo. That must mean you wanted to see me very soon."

"I did."

"Where were you, with the hand-kissers?"

"What's the difference? I had to change my schedule."

He put his long arm around her waist again, but she shrugged it off. He laughed. "So angry? Not even a hello yet, Maia? The street boy did not obey the Sultana?"

"This has nothing to do with obey. For a change you can act civilized."

89

"Like Paris, you mean."

"Yes, I mean Paris."

"I don't like to be insulted, Maia. Even Spanish peasants have very much pride."

"And I? No pride for me? You swore there would be no more girls in my house whenever I am away in Paris. Have them, play sultan to a harem, but not in my house."

"The truth is—"

She raised her voice over his. "Your twin, your hungry falcon, so magnificent for hunting on the Charf! But not in my house!"

"You hate Bébé. Too much champagne living, Maia. You don't appreciate the wild heart of the champion any more."

"I don't appreciate training a bird to kill, not in my house. For the noble sheiks to hunt in the open, yes, but not in my house. I don't appreciate that your boy-brain wanted to punish me for being late. I kept you waiting all afternoon and your great Spanish pride was insulted. You think I don't understand your little Moorish comedy with the giggling girl and the falcon?" The word *Moorish* stung him, she could see by his eyes, just as she had meant it to sting, because of his pretense of being pure Spanish.

"I'm glad you call it a comedy. Throw me a coin. The Sultana is amused."

"And you're the clown. A big clown with muscles who wants to show he doesn't care whose money he lives on, who pays his bills, who buys his sports cars and polo ponies, what bed he sleeps in."

"The bed. I knew we would come to the bed."

"There is no bed for savages."

"And you came all the way from Paris. For a savage. For a real man, Maia."

"For my son. For the bank. For a dozen other things."

"But mostly for the bed." He tried to kiss her, but she arched herself away. "Stop it," she said. "I've had a long hot day and I want no nonsense. My bath is running."

"It can wait. Yacoub will tend to it."

She pulled herself free and took a deep angry breath. "If you ever do this again—" she began to say.

"Maia, Maia, such excitement! Over what?" He spread his brown

90

muscular hands. "A little girl. A neighbor's child who is amused by the bird."

"But I am not amused. Not by your child whore. Not by you. Not by your bird."

"And I was not amused when you went to Paris for two months. Maia, you know how I need you every day, and you left me here to rot for two months."

"Left you here? I left you? If you break the law, is that my fault? If the Judiciare scheduled you for trial, am I the magistrate? Did I take your passport away?"

He held his hands up, curling the fingers, and smiled whitely. "Next time I'll kill that Frenchman. Nobody calls me *salesarab*. I'm Andaluce Spanish."

"Let's not discuss your pedigree again."

"Didn't you miss me? Two months is a long time."

"Miss you? In Paris? With not a man to be found anywhere?"

"Men? Those fancy señoritos! Handkissing and conversation. They think a woman wants talking."

"Sometimes a woman wants a bath." She tried to pull herself out of his arm, but he tightened it.

"Yes," he said, "you come to our little Moorish house all the way from Paris just to take a bath."

"Let go, you savage. I'm serious."

"Such struggles. Such delicate bones. I like to feel the struggling."

"And I do not!" She swung her arm to strike him as she had hit the Arab girl, but he caught her wrist in mid-air hard, sending a stab of pain up to her shoulder. He held her forearm and rocked it slightly. "What tender white meat. What tender little bones. If you try to spit at me, you cat, you'll get a fist in the face."

She spit at him, and he hit her with the back of his hand, using a flick of his closed fingers, stinging the skin like a whiplash. He twisted her wrist gently and leaned forward to kiss her, then dropped her arm. "Go, my Sultana," he said. "Your Arab eunuch has your precious bath ready. You can wash off the stink of Paris."

She walked away unsteadily, weak with fury and fatigue and a wild feeling without a name, then turned back to where he stood, still watching her. "Get out!" she threw at him. "Get out, you filth! Go

91

paw in whores' beds! Get out!" She ran from the court to her bedroom upstairs, her heels clattering up the narrow curve of marble steps until she reached the cool dimness of her room. She kicked off her shoes and tugged so angrily at the zipper fastening of her green linen sheath that the metal jammed tight. The tiny frustration, heaped on the entire day, was more than she could bear, and she tore the seam loose so that she could throw off the dress. A secret agitation drove her.

In the full-length mirror she saw herself, and went over to inspect her hotly stung cheek. Years ago, she remembered with piercing suddenness, the English painter had struck her the same half-hard contemptuous way for much the same reason. What in me finds such men? something within her cried. Why am I still an Arab concubine now, and in my own house?

She ran toward the sanitary perfumed sanctuary of the bathroom, with its mirrored French fittings and bath salts and monogrammed things laid out neatly by Yacoub beside the filled tub. It was Paris here, orderly and cool and sophisticated, no sun-hot savagery. No flocks to tend, no fears of tribal punishment, no mountain rock pressing painfully against her shoulder blades as a bearded face rose and fell above her.

Maia stepped into the bath and let herself slip into the water, a sun-scorched traveler melting into an oasis of coolness. She closed her eyes and lay back in the peaceful water, stretching her back and fingers and toes, consciously letting her tense muscles ease into relaxation, until a small sound made her open her eyes.

Jeanjean stood smiling there, his bulk filling the doorway. Their eyes held, locked together as he walked in slowly, and, leaning forward, lifted her as easily as a dripping child and carried her out to the bedroom.

When she began to struggle wordlessly on her bed he pulled both her arms behind her and held them in one hand while he used his free one cunningly for insolence and pleasure. For a brief time, with her breath growing shorter, she continued the sick bittersweet struggle, against the deep wants which had driven her here as much as against his tender violence. Once more she felt the mountain rock against her childish back, the rush of nothingness across her eyes, until her knees fell apart mindlessly.

92

BOOK II

The American Surgeon

(1)

THE entire geometry of French earth could be seen far below his plane through open spaces between the clouds. France was a green-blue world down there, an abstract painting of squares and rectangles and almost-triangles, blue-green, gray-green, purple-green, yellow-green, sometimes surprisingly green-green. The sun was at an angle behind their private plane, so that they seemed always to be flying toward a collision with their own shadow on the white towers of cloud formations. At the moment, North Africa seemed very far away, remote as the planets, not at all their destination beyond the horizon.

Dr. Malcolm Adams leaned back away from the window, letting himself relax in the deep foam rubber seat, swiveling the custom-built chair to watch the young beardless Arab steward make a ritual of preparing *thé à la menthe,* mint tea, in the plane's stainless steel galley. We're ten thousand feet over France, Mac Adams thought, cruising along at something less than two hundred miles an hour, and Yacoub stands there in his medieval *djellaba* and yellow leather *babouches* making Arab tea as if Saladin were still Sultan supreme in Jerusalem and the Moorish sword now lay in a steel crescent across the Barbary Coast to Spain.

"Yacoub," Mac Adams said quietly.

The Arab turned, holding several delicately shredded mint stalks. "Monsieur?"

"What time will we reach Tangier?" Mac asked in French.

Yacoub hardly moved, but his smooth beardless face and his entire body expressed a shrug. "Today," he said, *"insha' Allah.* God willing."

Clearly, Yacoub's idea was that whenever they arrived in Tangier, they would be there.

When Obenpharo had made arrangements for his private plane to fly Mac down to Tangier from Paris, he had said, "Several hours, Dr. Adams. A nothingness. A long siesta during the flight, if you wish. The boxes of your surgical equipment with the *bagages* will not be heavy enough to slow down your air speed."

Yacoub's shrug was right, Mac thought. What's the difference when we arrive? Time isn't a wristwatch with these people, time is astronomy, and by astronomy we will be in Tangier sometime today. *Insha' Allah.* Let's not forget *insha' Allah,* because that's even more important than the astronomy. Even the word Islam meant submission. God was willing or not willing and it was acceptable either way, not just because one accepted, really, but actually because one did not even think about it. No Christian questions of conscience, no Hebraic heroism wrestling on mountaintops with Jehovah. Just acceptance.

He began to feel a little drowsy listening to the monotonous engine drone and thinking about Islam and watching the endless cloud valleys. To keep himself awake he held up to the window one of the large X-ray films Monsieur Obenpharo had given him with all the other clinical data about Roger Obenpharo, but he could see nothing in the zygomatic bone, and sphenoids, the left orbit, or the missing segment of the left maxilla he had not seen before, so he slipped the large skull film back into its heavy envelope with all the other X-ray pictures. It would not be simple surgery, but they never really were, were they?

The Arab steward came toward him down the aisle of the plane carrying a hammered copper Fez tray. Yacoub had put on a white steward's jacket with brass buttons carrying Obenpharo's monogram and he set the tea expertly down on the low taboret of inlaid wood beside Mac. The aromatic tea, the mother-of-pearl table, the Kairouan rug, Yacoub himself—even aloft, Mac suddenly realized, Obenpharo had made his private plane a flying Moroccan living room. Mac suddenly remembered the sixty-foot family cruiser his father had owned many years ago in Connecticut; each stateroom aboard was a little non-nautical replica of the bedrooms in their house. Obenpharo and his father were of a generation which always wanted to feel at home, even when traveling, and the worship of streamlined

96

function above all else, and aerodynamic shapes, had not yet begun. But why do I connect Obenpharo and my father?

"Your tea, monsieur." As Yacoub handed Mac the glass, his eyes scanned Mac's face as quickly and lightly as a blind man's fingers estimating character by touch. "Monsieur le Docteur—" Yacoub began, then stopped.

"Yes?"

"You will permit a question?"

"What is it?"

"You will not be angry?"

"That depends."

"It is said you are a great American surgeon."

Mac did not answer. It might also be said by the uncharitable that he was off on a fool's errand in a strange country for the wrong reasons. It might also be said that he would soon be risking his patient's life, and part of his own reputation, and all of his peace of mind, for reasons that weren't reasonable. It might also be said, and this made as clear as when Oliver Wendell Holmes had said it, that a man who does not live with action and passion might be said never to have lived at all. Well, if these were the only requirements, action and passion, then he was very much alive, very aware of the difficulties he would find in Tangier. And now there was no turning back.

"It is said," Yacoub was murmuring, "that kings and pashas come to you when their faces have been hurt and they wish no scars to show."

"Not the scars," Mac said. "The scars do not matter as much as how the face functions and eats and speaks again. The scars are of less importance." Cosmetic surgery versus reconstructive surgery, Mac thought, must I debate the subject here too? Even doctors persisted in thinking plastic surgery was mostly a complicated way of prettifying breasts and noses.

Yacoub and I are both here, Mac thought, but I'm in the twentieth century and he's in the sixteenth. The same words mean different things. So time is not astronomy, either. Time is an attitude of mind. Lesson number one for your sojourn in Tangier.

"What do you want to ask?" Mac said.

A little frown came to Yacoub's face. He was offended by such

97

directness as much as if Mac had clapped him on the shoulder. Conversation should be a long slow spiral, not a short straight line.

"You want to know if I can repair Monsieur Roger's face?" Mac asked. "You want to know if he will look like a man again?"

Yacoub bowed slightly, but this time did not raise his head. "No, monsieur," he said in a low voice. "There is no doubt of your skill, *insha' Allah*."

Mac waited until Yacoub looked up.

"Monsieur—" Yacoub began.

"Tell me," Mac said quietly. "No doctor can help unless you tell him. Are you in trouble?" Venereal disease, probably, or a pregnant girl. In his clinical experience this kind of halting speech often went with sexual difficulties.

"Monsieur," Yacoub said and began to cry. He covered his eyes with both hands like a child. "This is my last chance to see you alone, monsieur, to speak to you." He knelt before Mac and touched his forehead to the rug.

"To prostrate yourself is not necessary," Mac said. Such oriental gestures made him vaguely uncomfortable. "Sit up and speak."

"It was an injury done with a knife," Yacoub said in a muffled voice. "Where it should not be done."

"Yes?" Now Mac began to see with new understanding the dark beardless skin, the slender delicate hands.

"Many years ago. In the desert, by the black-robed marauding Regouibat, may they be accursed a thousand times. My father was killed, *en silo*. My mother and I were made slaves." His voice was trembling a little.

"Slaves?" Mac was amazed.

"The injury, Monsieur le Docteur," Yacoub said in the same low voice, "it is a very private thing." He placed his hand between his thighs and began to rock slightly back and forth, as if the wound were new.

Slaves. Eunuchs. It was too fantastic to consider. They had just come from Paris and Orly Field, over the railroad tracks lying parallel like iron pencils in a box going into Villeneuve-St. Georges, a world of engines and people and civilization and policemen. They were in an airplane, silver emblem of the century. Slaves? Killed, *en silo*—what was that?

"You do not speak, monsieur. I have offended you."

"No, no. A doctor is not offended to hear of injury."

The doctor's dilemma, Mac thought. Wherever you go, these curbstone conferences, the hidden human pain. And to whom do you bring your own different kind of injury? I came to Paris from my own kind of Sahara. Maybe the idea is farfetched, but actually there was nothing left for me but wasteland. Why did I agree to leave Paris to go now to Tangier?

Yacoub sat up. His face was wet now as he looked into Mac's eyes hopefully.

"It is said you know the human body, monsieur," Yacoub whispered. "Can you make me a man again?"

The door to the cockpit opened and the American pilot, Bud Williams, came into the cabin, stretching and yawning and scratching his seat. Yacoub lifted his tray quickly and almost ran back toward the galley.

"How goes it, Dr. Adams?" Bud said, and without waiting for Mac to answer called in English, "Brandy soda, Yacoub. Chop chop, boy." He turned back to Mac. "Got to keep these wogs hoppin'. They think they can take all day."

Time was a wristwatch again, an alarm clock ringing. "What's the hurry?" Mac asked.

"My tin book gives our E.T.A. in two and a half hours. Attaboy," Bud Williams said to Yacoub, taking the glass. He saluted Mac with it, "Here's mud in your health, sir," and put away half the drink in one long gulp, then stopped to shake his head in mock ecstasy while making snorting sounds. "Old man Obenpharo sure stocks the best," he said. "The Frenchmen say it slides down your throat like a god in velvet pants." He finished the glass in one more lengthy swallow and handed it back to Yacoub. "Encore, boy, hit me again. It almost makes life bearable."

"Bearable?" Mac repeated. "Then why do you stay in Tangier?" he asked, thinking: Maybe I'd better cut this conversation short. After all, even though the weather is clear, those are clouds down there with occasional crosswinds, and the co-pilot at the controls now is probably really a mechanic, and this man is a drinker.

The American pilot leaned toward him slightly. "I know what you're thinkin', Doc," he said. "I can tell." He stopped long enough to take the fresh glass Yacoub handed him, then turned back to Mac. "You think: He's an American in the tropics, and they don't live there unless they have to. Unless they can't go home. Or if they want to play sahib like the British, or aristocrats like the French." He took another of his remarkable swallows, his throat working up and down like a plunger.

Mac decided to remain silent. People never minded a silent doctor because they knew he could not fail to be fascinated by their unique explanations of themselves, given objectively, of course, detail by detail.

"That's what you think," the pilot repeated. His face was beginning to show a slight flush now, and he tipped his visored cap further back on his sweaty forehead. "Well, you're wrong. You think I sit on my duff out at Boukhalf Airport playin' dominoes and waiting for Obenpharo's crappy little messenger boy to call me?" He imitated Joseph, Nathan's son, speaking English. "Monsieur Obenpharo will fly to Paris di-*rect*-ly after the lunch. You will please to be ready with the aircraft at fourteen hours." Bud Williams let his breath out contemptuously. "The jewboy knows it all," he said.

"Air's getting a bit bumpy, isn't it?" Mac said. "Don't let me keep you from your work."

The pilot did not respond to the suggestion, and Mac recognized the slightly glazed inward look of his eyes.

"You're a fellow American and you're a doctor," the pilot said, "so you oughta get the straight poop on Tangier before the *merde* hits the fan."

He's entering the zone of the broad gesture, undying friendship, and the big ideas, Mac thought. A ham hero. If the jagged Pyrenees were not ahead of us on the horizon this might be interesting. How pointless it would be to crash into the mountains. I'm committed to a course of action and passion now, so that living is preferable to dying. *Insha' Allah,* he added in his mind, feeling faintly amused.

"They'll tell you Tangier is two towns," the pilot said, pronouncing it Tahn-jay, like the French. He held up two fingers. "They told me there's the Arab town, and the European town." He shook his head. "Uh-uh. There's the third." He raised another finger. "The American. We're not like the others. We're babes in the woods. We come down to Morocco with our diapers full of foreign aid dollars and buy into the diplomatic poker game the wogs and the frogs and the limeys have been playin' since Columbus. We dig up millions, hundreds of millions by God, to build Moroccan air bases at El Djema Sahim, Sidi Slimane, Benguerir, Nouasseur, and Boulhaut. And what happens?"

Wearily, despite himself, Mac said, "Well, what does happen?"

"They rob us blind!" the pilot said furiously. "The Moroccans are fighting to bring back the Sultan and for independence, and as soon as they're free they'll beat the French at stealing the shirt off our backs."

"I thought it was diapers."

"Hell, they steal your eyeballs if you fall asleep! They *live* off our money. They say we bribe or we bully. The French hate us because the Arabs talk about George Washington and how the American colonies pulled the first successful overseas revolution. And the Arabs hate us because we give the French so much money and military equipment. And the Spanish hate the French and help push a little more gunpowder across the border of their zone into the Moroccan firecracker every chance they get. And the Spanish hate *us* because we're Protestant and we don't like Franco and his fat-assed Falange."

"Sounds terrible." Mac decided there was no stopping the pilot now. "Is that what makes you so angry?" he asked. "Just the money and the cheating?"

The pilot leaned forward and tapped Mac's knee. "Listen," he said, dropping his voice as if others beside Yacoub were eavesdropping. "Tangier is one of the last free ports in the world. It's an International Zone. You know what that means? It's wide open. *No income tax,*" he said reverently. "None. You keep what you make, Doc. You can buy gold by the kilogram bar or in special little sizes that fit your pocket."

"You sound like a man who wants to get rich quick."

"Sure, but with my own money. Individual ruggedism, you know? Not like the cruds who sit there with our tax dollars and make fortunes in their own stage money."

"Does that really happen?" Mac said, more gently. Pyrenees or not, the conversation was becoming interesting. *I might even learn something about my invisible patient, Roger Obenpharo.*

The plane lurched suddenly and Mac's glass of tea slid off the

101

taboret to the floor. The pilot swung angrily toward the cockpit, then back again to Mac with an afterthought as the plane immediately trimmed level and Yacoub came forward with a small cloth to wipe the rug.

"Doc," he said, "I hear chitchat you're charging old man Obenpharo fifty thousand iron men to fix his son's face." He stopped, his eyes narrow and shrewd, waiting for corroboration, but Mac was silent. "Anytime you want to take your fifty grand and parley it up to millions," Bud Williams pointed to himself, "let Buddy know. I've got lots of friends in Tangier. Most of the smuggling stories you hear, strictly bull, don't believe it. I'm talking about business, legitimate. No cops and robbers. No kid stuff. We load a boat with everything, nylons, cigarettes, electric shavers, fountain pens, any damn thing they want in Spain, and then the boat heads across the Straits from Tangier to some little Spanish port."

"Isn't that smuggling?"

"Hell, no. Because it's all fixed. It's on a business basis. We wire the Spanish authorities and tell them when and where the boat is landing."

"You inform on your own boat?"

"No, no. It's a system. You hedge your bet, like any business. The Spanish cops meet the boat and confiscate everything. That gets all the stuff into Spain."

"Very efficient."

"And with no risks. The Falange boys handle the whole deal for a cut, and they're worth every damn peseta. We still clean up. One hand washes the other."

"Does Monsieur Obenpharo know all this?"

"Does one and one make two? Everybody knows the system. Even Madame Obenpharo. The *young* Madame, I mean. Maia Obenpharo."

Mac could sense how closely the pilot was watching him as he mentioned Maia. Until now, Mac thought, I've been doing a good job of not thinking about her, or those nights at the Quai de Bethune, or that slow silver afternoon on the Seine, or all the rest. I've been cool, rational, a surgeon on his way in an airplane to do a difficult piece of work in another country, knowing all the while that I was

102

getting myself into something big enough to risk becoming painful.

Mac realized the pilot was still talking, and even though his own mind was thinking, *Maia, Maia,* he twisted himself back to the present, back to the pilot and reality.

(2)

OBENPHARO'S airplane droned above Spain toward Tangier at nine thousand feet. The pointed stone pile of the Pyrenees was behind them now, and off to the right, pock-marked into the tan monk's cloth Spanish landscape, Mac Adams could make out the stubby earthen buildings of a town. "Yacoub," he called, pointing downward, "what city is that?"

Yacoub peered down for a moment without interest. "Bilbao, perhaps, monsieur. Or San Sebastian. From the air all Spanish cities look the same." He balled his fingers into a fist. "Many houses close together"—he raised his thumb—"with a church sticking up in the middle. Almost like our Medina with the Mosque in Tangier." He pointed in the opposite direction, toward the distance. "That way are the Cantabrian Mountains."

As recently as six or seven months ago, Mac thought, I would have considered this present flight to Tangier as remote a thing to do as taking a trip to the moon.

If anyone had mentioned Tangier to him a half year ago he would have been uncertain about its location at first; immediately afterward he would have remembered the distant shore lights of the city while it was under temporary Spanish control during the war, and he was a young military surgeon at the rail of a blacked-out troop transport slipping through the Straits of Gibraltar toward an unknown North African port.

Six or seven months ago, if he had met either Obenpharo or Maia back home in the States, he would have found them strangely exotic, costumed corsairs from the Barbary Coast swaggering between continents for plunder and buried treasure.

Mac had met wealthy bankers before, but no one with so much

—to use the American pilot's phrase—individual ruggedism as Obenpharo. And Maia? Ah, Maia. It wasn't the too-elegant elegance which set her apart—he had seen a good deal of that—it wasn't the open sensuality or the obviously golden good looks, or the uncomplicated childlike directness of her pains and pleasures. It was—well, what was it? And why try to be objective and analytical about her, instead of accepting her as a natural phenomenon—a summer sunrise would be as good a choice as any—morning warmth with the bright promise of blood heat by high noon and thunderstorms by nightfall. Their last month together in Paris had had its share of both, the warmth and the storms.

Six or seven months ago in the States he had been hard at work in his practice, with only an unusual consultation like his trip to Washington to see the Senator, to change his daily rhythm. Occasionally he had told himself it would be good to get away from the surgical grind for a little, to Paris say, where he had friends with interests far from plastic surgery, and then promptly had reminded himself that if he insisted on launching dreamboats he ought to pick one that would float. It was out of the question. He was too busy, too involved. To spend all his time at sculpture just didn't make sense. Yet only a few months ago he had come to Paris after all, unexpectedly and blindly and absolutely sure that he would stay there at least a year or two without interruption.

And then Maia had interrupted him.

So much had happened during those months in Paris, and so much had happened during the period just before them, while he was still in the States. It all reminded him, in some obscurely oblique way, of one of those old-fashioned movies shown for comic effect on television with all the silent action speeded up. People walked jerkily along at sprinting speed, doors flew open and closed, cars whizzed around corners, a spinning wheel of distortion. And clearly, he might just as well face it, something must have been seriously distorted in his orderly-seeming life at home for it all to have whirled him here to Obenpharo's plane.

Six or seven months ago seemed as remote to him now as six or seven years ago. Here and now he was going to Tangier and it was his former life in the United States which seemed at the wrong end of the telescope, diminished, a trifle unreal because of its small faraway scale. When he thought about his old life in the States he decided he had not been equipped for everything which had happened at home in Connecticut during those six months.

He was surprised, looking backward now, that he had traveled through the eye of a personal hurricane, surrounded by wreckage, and yet retained enough balance to adopt, half humorously, a slogan, any slogan, leave alone the romantic bugle call of Oliver Wendell Holmes for action and passion.

Suddenly, a door opened in his memory, a recollection of surgery which he had refused to do, of anger because his patient was vulnerable and no one cared. He had completely forgotten it until now. It was a simple matter; the circumcision of a frightened seven-year-old boy, a simple five-minute procedure he had accepted because two old friends who were parents of a tense only child insisted that, for the boy's sake, it needed to be done with more than the usual routine ease and understanding. Why am I irrationally recalling a minor thing like a circumcision now, he thought. Because I wondered about Yacoub's loss of manhood in the desert? Or is a general preoccupation with manhood something men developed whenever they sensed the pattern of their lives beginning to emasculate them—the soft suburbs, the unloving wives, the exhaustion of chasing success?

Back home in the States, he thought, in a way entirely different from Yacoub, maybe I had had my own feeling of injury. Nothing obviously genital, no pathological behavior, only a much more subtle underground sense of anger for unknown reasons, of big reactions to small frustrations . . . and then in his memory he came through the double doors of the operating room trying to control his annoyance. . . .

. . . The two young surgeons in green O.R. suits who were scrubbing up were amazed to see Dr. Adams come out through the swinging doors from the small operating room. He walked stiff-armed through the O.R. doors, letting them swing closed behind him, then stood still and began stripping off his rubber surgical gloves so fast that one tore. The two young surgeons at the scrub sink let their glances cross above their masks, and turned back deliberately to the swish-scrub swish-scrub rhythm of antiseptic wash-up technique.

Instead of turning toward the doctors' dressing room, Mac auto-

105

matically carried his torn rubber glove to the discard bin near the scrub room. In that extra moment Miss Perkins, the chief O.R. nurse, came in while pulling her face mask angrily down around her neck, her rimless glasses shining with battle. She stopped short and spoke to Mac's back.

"Dr. Adams, we can't delay this circumcision case. The small O.R. is scheduled for a breast biopsy at nine."

Mac flung his glove into the bin and turned to her. "Delay? It's canceled, Miss Perkins." Control, his mind said, control. It's not her fault the little boy is hysterical and the anesthetist botched the job. She runs a clean, taut ship here, bless her, so don't blame her.

"Canceled?" Miss Perkins' voice had gone up.

"Look, Miss Perkins," Mac said, "you run your show. I'll run mine."

"This *is* my show, Doctor. We can't hold that O.R. indefinitely until you decide when—"

"I've decided. It's canceled."

A flash of the front office reaction to all this lighted Miss Perkins' mind, so she tried once more, trying harder because Mac had taken off his face mask and cloth cap. "Couldn't Dr. Varnum slug the youngster with some quick I.V. amytal—"

Mac's voice was so tight with anger that even the two young surgeons stopped scrubbing up for a moment. "Damn it," Mac said, "nobody, Dr. Varnum, nobody, *slugs* my patients with anything. Understand?"

Miss Perkins' face had become pale and pinched-looking.

Mac said, "Don't they have that boy out of there yet!" He stepped quickly to the O.R. doors, just managing to slow his pace down to an apparently casual entrance as he went in with Miss Perkins a pace behind him. Easy does it now, easy with the boy.

A seven-year-old boy lay in the cool glareless circle of light on the operating table. He was crying quietly from beneath closed eyelids, with an occasional convulsive heave of his chest as he gulped air. Dr. Varnum, the anesthetist, was still sitting on the stainless steel stool at the head of the table beside the complex anesthetic gas machine, sitting with his arms folded and looking withdrawn. The scrub nurse was still in her sterile O.R. gown, mask, and cap, hovering over the

106

instrument tray until Dr. Adams' decision to operate or not was made.

Mac put his hand on the boy's shoulder.

"Take it easy, Tom. I know how you feel. We're going to take you out now—" He went on talking quietly, letting his hand move gently down the boy's arm and gauging the tension in the tautly straining thin muscles until suddenly, at the wrist, he found the heavy leather cuffs still locked in place. Without changing his quiet tone or raising his eyes from the boy's, Mac added, "—and Dr. Varnum will open these things on your wrists so you can wave your arms around—"

Dr. Varnum moved quickly to unfasten the leather restraints at wrist and ankle, mumbling, "Sorry, Dr. Adams. Don't know why it slipped my mind. . . . I guess I . . ."

Mac said over his shoulder to the young scrub nurse, "If you'll just cover those completely," indicating the tray of shining instruments beneath her, and then, to Miss Perkins, "And we don't need all the overhead illumination—" and the huge surgical light went dark. Suddenly the entire room looked less formidable.

"Now," Mac said to the boy, "you can sit up." The boy opened his eyes, wary and hostile. "Sure," Mac smiled, "we thought you ought to take it easy for a while. We're not going to do anything now."

The boy said unbelievingly, "You're not gonna do it—?"

"No, not now. Later, yes. But not now. You remember I promised you we'd put you to sleep in your bed, and you'd wake up there with the whole thing finished?"

The boy nodded. He was watching Mac's face intensely.

"Well," Mac said, "the other doctors were so busy this morning they weren't able to do what I promised. They brought you in here wide awake and you got scared, just like my own boy would. Or anybody." He could feel the stiffly flexed muscles begin to relax a little.

"But you're still gonna do it?"

"Sure, Tom. But real gentle, the way I promised."

The wheeled stretcher was pushed into the room, and Mac picked up the boy in his arms and carried him over to it. The boy spoke

107

with his face against Mac's chest, muffled and ashamed. "I didn't want to cry—"

"You cry all you want, Tom. I've seen grown men do it, and soldiers. Brave people. I know how you feel." The doctor's benediction: *I know how you feel.*

He put the boy on the stretcher. "You can sit up, Tom. You're not sick or anything like that."

The boy pulled himself up to the sitting position. Mac kept his arm around his shoulders. "Look, Tom. Dr. Varnum over there will come to see you later, just the way I promised you yesterday. He'll put a small rubber tube—"

"I know. Like an enema."

"Sure. It'll feel a little bit uncomfortable for a minute, but it won't hurt. Then you'll fall asleep."

"Will I have a bandage on my peter when I wake up?"

"Sure. But not half as big a bandage as when you scraped your knee. Just enough covering to let the outside skin heal in a couple of days."

A nurse put her head in at the door and said to Miss Perkins, "The breast biopsy still going in here? Patient's coming down now."

"Right." Miss Perkins looked through her glasses at Mac.

"In one minute," Mac said. He turned back to the boy. "You know, you don't have to ride that stretcher, Tom. You can walk back to your room like a young man." The boy looked up at him. "Sure," Mac said. "You're okay. Pop off that stretcher. The aide will walk with you. And I'll see you pretty soon."

The boy climbed off the stretcher and Mac gravely watched him put on the terrycloth hospital robe. "See you later, Dr. Adams," the boy said.

"See you later, Tom."

As soon as the swinging doors closed behind the boy, Mac swung back to Dr. Varnum and Miss Perkins. "Got five minutes for a scuppa scoffee?" he asked them both.

"Dr. Adams," Miss Perkins said, "don't try to butter me up."

"Lots of butter," Mac said, "because I'm going to fry you to a turn. How about it, Dr. Varnum?"

108

They sat hunched over three coffee mugs in the little diet kitchen near the nurses' station at the end of the corridor. Silently they passed a fourth mug filled with sugar, using wooden tongue blades as spoons to measure out the sugar and to stir. Miss Perkins sat stiffly apart; she was a combat veteran and would play this by the book, Mac knew, with no other goals except to maintain her dignity and her status. Her hair was neatly bundled beneath her green surgical cap and coif, giving her a nun's look. Seeing her that way reminded Mac of how often she had driven herself beyond what was usually known as the call of duty when hell was breaking loose in surgery.

The page box overhead suddenly spoke. "Dr. Adams. Dr. Malcolm Adams." It was an ordinary double page, and she had used his first name. That meant there was no hurry. The call could wait the five minutes he needed with Dr. Varnum and Miss Perkins.

Dr. Varnum, the young resident, took a swallow of coffee, then set his mug down solidly. "Let me apologize, Dr. Adams," he said slowly. "I remembered your telling me how sensitive and scared this kid was. I had him down in the book for rectal anesthesia in his room before surgery, but I got there too late this morning. They'd wheeled him over here already."

"What's all this about?" Miss Perkins said. "A dinky little five-minute circumcision, and all of a sudden the roof caves in."

"It's about two things," Mac said. "One: the boy's only seven. He needed this circumcision when I first saw him, two years ago. But you know as well as I do that it's not the minor surgery at all. It's the idea a kid has in his mind about his genitals and what we're doing to him. It's as simple and as complicated as that. I put off doing the circumcision two years, till he was old enough to understand some kind of explanation. Not only understand, but accept the idea."

"Well, hush my mouth," Miss Perkins said. "You don't believe that castration complex crap, do you?"

Mac looked her in the eyes. She knew just what he was thinking. For a moment she held, then her face and neck and throat became flushed with pink.

"Perky," he said, "Dr. Varnum is new here, but you and I have known each other a long long time."

"Please, spare me the soft soap, Doctor."

109

"Wait a minute. You were up until six o'clock this morning helping me on that truck driver with the massive skin burns."

"Why did you have to call me? I was off duty."

"Because I thought we'd lose him unless every single last detail was right. I needed you, Perky, not some of those new kids."

Dr. Varnum spoke quickly. "As a matter of fact, both my own youngsters were sick all night. Strep throats. That's why I got in late—" He stopped.

"Okay," Mac said. "So we're all sleepy and a little irritable."

"And dog tired," Miss Perkins said. "And there's pie in the sky."

"And," Mac added, "I've really always loved you, Perky."

"As of the last half hour," she said, "if you'll pardon the expression, I hate you." She took a swallow of coffee and stood up. "Town meeting over? All souls saved?"

"No," Mac answered, but before he could go on the page box overhead suddenly interrupted. "Dr. Adams, Dr. Adams, Dr. Adams." It was a triple repetition, meaning emergency, call Telepage switchboard at once. Miss Perkins pushed the phone across the table toward Mac as he began to dial T-E-L. He lifted the telephone closer. "Telepage? Dr. Adams speaking."

"Thank you, Dr. Adams. Greenwich, Connecticut, on the line. One moment, please."

Dr. Varnum stood up. He looked more relaxed and friendly now. "We'll take good care of the kid, don't worry."

"Thanks," Mac said.

Dr. Varnum started out of the room but paused at the door. "Coming?" he asked Miss Perkins.

"No," she said, making it clear she meant no.

An electrical buzz in the telephone, then a pleasant woman's voice sounding quite close. "Hello? Hello? Mac?"

It was Laura, his wife. What's happened, he wondered. I hope Stan hasn't pulled some boyish stunt and hurt himself. "Hello, Laura," he said. "Is something wrong?"

"Well, dear, I paged you before and there was no answer."

"I was busy. Is Stan okay?"

"Of course. The floor nurse said you were out of surgery and having a cup of—"

"I was." Try to explain the difference between just having a cup of coffee and really having one. "But this was a triple page, Laura. You know. Emergency."

"Well, I just wanted to make sure we had our signals straight about tonight."

"Tonight?" The fatigue of the preceding all-night surgery was still with him, and now the annoyance of Laura's having used the emergency call system to reach him—about what? What was happening tonight?

Laura's voice sounded amused. "Your show in New York, dear. Your biggest one-man show so far. Don't tell me you forgot!"

"No, no," he said. "Of course not." But he knew and she knew that he had.

"The pickup truck from the gallery just loaded the bronze head of the blind boy. I watched it like a mother hen."

"Good." The bronze head was his best piece of sculpture, and worth fussing over. And Laura knew just how to do it—the folded ten-dollar bill for the pickup man from the gallery and his helper, the cold beer waiting in the kitchen, a pretense of rustic simplicity. In fact, Laura had really pulled together this entire one man show, running into New York several times a week to make sure all the little details were just right.

"Are you taking the train from New Haven, Mac?"

"No, it's such a nice day I thought I'd put the top down and drive in." He looked forward to the two-hour auto ride from New Haven to New York in the clear sun. He felt wide awake now, with the tension and fatigue of the painstaking all-night surgery on the burned truck driver just barely tapping at his consciousness. That's why he'd forgotten the New York show, he realized: because he didn't want to go. But Laura would be very annoyed if he didn't, and maybe riding in the convertible with the top down would brighten the situation. "Do you want me to pick you up on the way, Laura?"

Now the conversation was on familiar ground, because most of their phone calls these days seemed to be concerned entirely with transportation schedules: who would take the station wagon, who would pick up Stan and some Cub Scout friends, which train from Grand Central to meet at the Greenwich station, or whether to take

111

the express to Stamford, whether he was going to stop at his office or drive directly into New York, and how about those two visiting French doctors from the United Nations—shouldn't two pairs of tickets to Mac's show be held at the door of the Erve Galleries on Fifty-seventh Street for them? Did Laura want him to pick her up at home on his way down the Merritt Parkway from New Haven to New York?

"No, dear. Carl offered me a lift into town. He has some new super-charged gadget on that fancy Chrysler, and he's rarin' to roll."

"Carl's getting to be practically your chauffeur these days."

"Do I detect a green husbandly eye over my shoulder?"

"No. Passing observation." Carl had a big garage filled with English and German and Italian and French sports cars, trading in one against another, always searching for the perfect car. Jaguars and Ferraris and Porsches and Alfa-Romeos came and went. Now he had a Ghia-Chrysler. Mac knew Laura liked riding in Carl's cars, and wearing the clothes people usually wore when they rode in them, because it made her feel like a North Shore girl again, carefree and young and a little wild.

"I'd rather drive in with you, dear," Laura was saying, "especially if you're in a top-down convertible mood on this nice day—but I've got to stop early at Abercrombie's, then Brooks, then uptown to Jensen—"

"Laura, please don't buy me any more modern Viking cuff links."

She laughed. "No, this is that Danish silver whosis. It's your secretary who's getting married, you know."

"Oh, yes, yes." He had completely forgotten about the gift for his secretary. He used to remember those things, but Laura was so completely efficient that he had gradually allowed his ability to recollect dates and places to atrophy like a useless muscle. But Carl, his mind suddenly said, and then immediately added: Don't be a damn fool. Carl didn't really have to work for a living and had lots of time, and everybody knew Carl's wife had migraine headaches which came on suddenly, leaving Carl high and dry and probably lonely in a perfectly understandable way. Everyone understood Carl was a speed demon behind the wheel of one of his sport cars, but otherwise completely sensible and well balanced.

Miss Perkins had taken off her glasses and sat with her head bent forward, resting her brow against an upraised hand. As the telephone receiver crackled near his ear, Mac realized she could hear Laura's voice in the small room almost as clearly as he did. Laura was talking about the newspaper reviewers who were invited to the show and how the *Trib* man was sure to disembowel Mac's sculpture for being in the classic tradition of realistic forms instead of abstract, and, as she went on suggesting possible rebuttals to possible questions, an O.R. nurse hurried into the room and spoke quickly and quietly to Miss Perkins.

Miss Perkins glanced at Mac, then got up and started out after the other nurse. She paused at the door and came back in. Hastily she scribbled a note on the top sheet of a pad of hospital patient history-taking forms, paused, added a few lines, then walked out without looking back.

"We'll stay in town with Carl and Erve and the Campbells for dinner," Laura was saying in the phone, "so I've arranged for Stan to have his with the Hutchins."

"Who're they?"

"Mac, really. You met him two weeks ago at the Turf Club. He's that athletic New York banker who bought the Palomino. His wife's being analyzed and wears her ego on her sleeve, remember?"

"Never met 'em."

"Mac, this absent-minded professor approach is getting worse. The boy who's always coming up the drive to see Stan on that fancy English racing bicycle—"

"Oh, sure. Perry."

"One gold star for memory, dear. Perry has a last name: Hutchins."

While Laura was talking he reached across the table for Miss Perkins' note, and, by balancing the telephone receiver against his ear with a raised shoulder, he was able to free both hands to tear the top sheet off the hospital pad. The first blank space on the printed form to be filled in by the examining physician was headed: PATIENT'S CHIEF COMPLAINT.

Under it, in the space, Miss Perkins had scrawled: *Excuse. Gotta go.* And then she had added: *I don't really hate you, Mac. I'm sorry for you.*

For a moment he didn't listen to a word Laura was saying. He re-

113

called for no reason at all the last staff conference lecture of Dr. Kleiner on the subject of the biological tempo of modern life, and Kleiner's having said something like, "Doctors burn themselves up faster than almost anyone else in our technologic society. From personal experience they should be first to recognize in their patients the predisposing, precipitating, and perpetuating factors of the syndrome I propose we call Trackus Rodentia. The rat race."

Trackus Rodentia. A scholarly joke. But the *Dr.* in front of Kleiner's name was a Ph.D. in sociology, and many of the medical doctors in the audience felt his data were fuzzy, subjective, and not really convincing.

"Mac," Laura's voice was saying, a trifle insistently, "are you there?"

"Sure," he said, "sure." Are you there—sure, I'm here.

"What's the matter? You didn't answer when I—"

"Laura," he interrupted, "would you mind if I didn't come down to the opening?"

Pause.

When she spoke again it was softly and quietly. "Mac, it's your biggest and best one-man show. Doesn't that ring a bell?"

"Sure it does, but not awfully loud. You know once I finish a piece of work, that's it. I don't really care what the newspapers say." It occurred to him at that moment for the first time that the show had not even been his idea. It had been Laura's. Erve had mentioned it at a party, just an idea, and Laura had taken it from there. It was a one-woman show.

"But, Mac, you follow up on *patients.*"

"Now wait a minute. They're people."

"Don't you suppose these are people coming to the show? Richardson's driving in from New Hope only because I told him you'd be there. I talked Erve into talking Willy into putting off his flight to Rome until tomorrow, just to see you. And our dinner guests—"

"I know." He made a rude Scottish bagpipe sound. " 'The Campbells are coming, ta-ra, ta-ra.' "

"Mac, that's a foul blow. I don't care how much money they have. Ellen Campbell was at school with me—"

"Sorry," he said. She was right about the whole thing, as always.

114

He felt a little guilty because she had really gone to so much effort and was enjoying it as a change from suburban routine and he was letting a little feeling of tiredness put him off. "I'll be there, Laura," he said.

"Not in that tone of voice, Mac, please."

"I'll be there. Better?"

"Much."

Pause. A silence of electrical telephone noises swung between them, the thematic background noise of a noisy century.

" 'By, dear," Laura said.

" 'By."

He hung the receiver carefully on its cradle, as if it were fragile, and sat still for a moment. He reread Miss Perkins' note then crumpled it into a tight ball and tossed it across the room toward the wastepaper basket. It fell just short, and he methodically went to pick it up.

After changing from his surgical gown to street clothes, Mac walked quickly down the corridor of the surgical suite to the elevators. He glanced at his wristwatch. About a quick hour left to see his patients, a quick stop at the laboratory to check on the microscopic skin sections using the new fluorescent cellular staining technique, then a quick lunch at the University Club with the other members of the medical library committee, then a quick two-hour trip down the Parkway to New York. . . . He stopped ticking off the items as the elevator doors opened before him.

"Good morning, Dr. Adams."

"Morning, Mrs. Brownlee." He didn't mention which floor he was going to because the elevator operator knew. "How's Margie's hand?"

"Jus' fine, Dr. Adams. She's holding her bottle by herself now, and her fingers bend real nice."

Margie Brownlee was about a year old, and had managed to put her hand in the wrong place when her older brother slammed a car door closed. Mrs. Brownlee had telephoned Mac at his home in Greenwich, and he had told her he'd be up in New Haven to take care of Margie within an hour. It had been a Sunday afternoon, and he had just put on his swimming trunks, taking the call at the ex-

115

tension phone beside the pool and looking at his boy Stan splashing around. He had hardly seen Stan all week, except at breakfast, and he had been looking forward to this Sunday afternoon; it was the only time he had for a quick swim with Stan, and then a few hours in his garage studio, woodcarving or modeling in clay.

That had been many months ago; two complex operations had been done on Margie's hand. Mrs. Brownlee had absolutely insisted that he send her a bill, so he had, for twenty dollars. She hadn't managed to pay anything on it yet, but one of these days her ship would come in, or something would turn up, and maybe she'd be able to pay the fee. In the meantime she was effusive with gratitude.

"I remember you in my prayers, Dr. Adams," she said, as the elevator stopped at his floor.

"Thank you, Mrs. Brownlee," he said gravely, and stepped out. The metal doors of the little lighted cave closed between them.

He entered the private wing and stopped at the nurses' station to go over the chart of his patient, Porter Bradford. The nurse at the desk didn't stand up as he came in, because that had gone out of fashion during the nursing shortage years, but she smiled and held out an enormous box of candy.

"Loot, Dr. Adams," she said. "Have some chocolate calories."

"Never touch 'em, Miss Cantrell," he said, choosing one. "They stunt your growth."

"I know," she said. "And the vitamins are all in the wrapping paper. Please take another one. This will probably be your lunch, the way you dash around. This is from your patient, by the way. Does he print his own money, or what?"

"Sure he does," Mac said. "Right there on his Long Island estate. He asks the government how much it needs and sends them some, and then budgets himself to live on the rest."

"Why wasn't I born rich," Miss Cantrell said, "instead of just beautiful? Which reminds me, one of his Broadway girl friends came up to see him this morning. With a big covered steamer basket. Full of fresh fruit, she told me. The only fresh fruit, I guess, was the young lady herself."

Miss Cantrell handed him the clipboard holding Porter Bradford's chart. Mac scanned the most recent doctor's order sheet, particularly

116

the antibiotic dosage. Porter's hand wounds were healing too slowly, and Mac was wary of destructive inflammation by some of the penicillin-resistant staph infections patients picked up in hospitals. Hand reconstruction required every bit of tissue which could be salvaged, and infection at this stage would be disastrous.

"Those last incisions aren't healing very well, Miss Cantrell."

She glanced at him quickly, preparing herself for criticism until she recognized he was merely commenting. Dr. Adams had a reputation for working with nurses, not above them, so she decided to be frank and co-operative.

"I don't understand it, Doctor."

"How's he sleeping?"

"So-so."

"Chart shows seconal every night."

"You ordered it, P.R.N., Doctor. He says he can't sleep without the pill."

"Does he eat his meals?"

"So-so. Sends the tray back. Says he's not hungry."

"Seem depressed?"

"Depressed? Mr. Bradford?" She laughed. "He's the life of the party. Jokes and wisecracks all the time."

Then he is depressed, Mac thought swiftly. And his protein intake must be too low for good healing. The part about his not being hungry—Mac wondered if Porter had managed to smuggle in a liquor supply. That steamer basket. Porter might even have a subclinical cirrhosis due to a long-standing enthusiasm for alcohol.

"Dr. Adams," Miss Cantrell was saying, "why did you ask that, about if he's depressed or not?"

"Well," Mac said, "if I were thirty-eight and rich and *toujours gai* and busy at polo and yacht races and boyish games and I went up in my plane for a little ride and cracked myself up into lots of little pieces—I think I'd be slightly depressed. Maybe I'd manage to smuggle in some liquor, enough to get myself out of the blues, just enough so that I didn't care whether I ate any real food or not."

Miss Cantrell nodded. "I see. Two and two makes four, now."

"Uh-uh." Mac shook his head. "Never four. Not with people.

117

Five or six, maybe. But never four." He put the clipboard down. "Did you remember to buy the sponge rubber ball for me?"

"Oh, yes," she said. She opened the desk drawer and took out a small child's ball. "That's ten cents you owe me."

He took the ball. "Sometimes I believe I owe you more than that," he said, smiling to take the heavy-handed weight of seriousness out of the comment.

"Why, Dr. Adams," Miss Cantrell said. "Have another candy, please. Have the whole box."

Mac knocked at the open door of Porter Bradford's corner room. "Stay out!" a man's voice called. "Go away."

"It's Mac, Port. The Greeks come, bearing gifts."

"Good! Stromberry poy! Enter, Aesculapius, and be recognized!"

Porter was sitting up in bed when Mac came in, with one arm around a very pretty blonde girl who sat sideways against the pillow beside him. A bottle of Scotch and two half-filled glasses were on the night table, and even from the foot of the bed Mac noticed the faint lipstick on Porter's mouth.

"Malcolm!" Porter crowed. "This is my youngest son," he said to the blonde girl. He turned to Mac. "Meet Bettina, Malcolm. She's restoring my will to live."

Bettina looked capable of all kinds of therapy. The neck of her dress was cut in a deep V, and the space between was supposed to be filled by a scarf. At the moment, Porter was wearing the scarf wound around outside his head bandages like a turban.

"Gee, Doctor," Bettina said in a high schoolgirlish voice, "when're you gonna let my Porter pie out of here?" She turned and rubbed the tip of her nose against Porter's cheek. "It's awful lonesome in New York without him."

"Eight million people there," Porter said, "half of them at the Copa to see her dance, and she's lonesome."

"Oh, I didn't tell you, Port!" Bettina said. "I signed yesterday with the Ballet Group."

"Bless you, Betts. On long cold nights there's nothing like a good ballet."

Bettina wrinkled her pretty little nose at Mac. "Isn't he brave, Dr. Adams? Always joking."

118

Porter and Mac looked at each other the length of the bed. Porter's face was pale and gaunt, and the thin scar line from the corner of his mouth across his cheek looked too brightly pink.

"My buddy," Porter said. He turned to Bettina, and gestured toward Mac with one bandaged hand. "My college roommate for three years, my anchor man on the swimming team, my number two man in the national polo finals, I was best man at his wedding, and now—" he turned to Mac, "Dr. Jekyll, when can we ship the body right the hell out of here?"

"It won't be long now, Port. Our orthopedic friends showed me your last set of X-ray pictures yesterday and—"

"Oh," Bettina said, "I'd love to see Port's X-rays. I've always wondered what was inside of him."

"Tell her, Mac. Tell her you saw a big valentine heart with the initial B carved on it."

"The ribs are healed," Mac said. "The fractured vertebrae are healed. Both legs are solid. Humpty Dumpty's all back in one piece."

"There's nothing like one good piece," Porter said.

Almost everything in Port is healed, Mac thought, except the big empty loneliness which nothing has ever filled, not the governesses and tutors and instructors and coaches, not the roommates and teammates, nor the thoroughbred horses and polo championships and girls and big mechanical toys like airplanes. From the age of ten onward, Porter had been in and out of courtrooms while his lawyers fought his mother's lawyers over the mountain of money in the Bradford estate.

"If he's all healed, Doctor, why does he have to stay here?"

"Until he's walking again. Until his hands are strong enough and flexible enough to hold things." He took the sponge rubber ball from his pocket. "Here's the gift, chum. Finger exercise ball. Catch."

Porter caught it neatly between his good hand and the bandaged one. "If this ball is as useless as my other two," he said, "you might as well take it back."

Bettina giggled.

Porter looked hollow-cheeked suddenly. "Betts," he said, "get off the bed."

"Oh, honey, I didn't mean to laugh."

"Get off, I said."

"But you're always joking," she said plaintively. "Sometimes I can't figure you out."

"But I can figure you out. I'm nailed here in bed while you dish out one good ballet after another on the town."

"Port, I swear—"

"Betts," Mac said, "will you please go ask Miss Cantrell to send an aide down for that steamer basket?"

"Now wait a minute, Mac, old boy—! Not that basket!"

"Too much fresh fruit ruins the appetite, Port. Will you, Betts?"

She stood up and smoothed her dress down, then walked toward the door with a special voluptuous gait, as if the floor were uneven.

"Betts—" Porter said.

She stopped at the door and turned artificially to look over her shoulder like a girl rehearsing badly in a play.

"Come back here," Porter said. "But slower."

She walked back toward him slowly, using the same gait until, when she stood beside him, she unwound her scarf from his head. "I'll need this," she said with dignity. "It's getting chilly here." Porter put his hands on her arms, the good hand and the bandaged one.

"Betts," he said, but she shrugged his hands off and turned and walked out.

"The only hips in the world that rotate in a complete circle on ball bearings," Porter said. "There's a patent pending."

"Can we hold off on the jokes for about one minute, Port?"

"Okay. One minute for station identification."

"For practical purposes, Port, the only thing those X-rays didn't show was a pile of empty bottles inside you. Not enough solid food in there to help heal a mouse."

"Mac, not you of all people. You're not going to lecture me about liquor."

"Sure I am."

"If a man can't have a drink—"

"Sure he can. But you're not having a drink, Port. You're drinking. And you aren't getting the food you need."

Porter sat up straight. "Now let me tell you something. The medical care here is tops. But the food and service are garbage warmed over. As a hotel, this place is a barn. Why can't I check out right now, Mac?"

120

"Because you're so close to complete recovery I don't want to gamble that you'll go downhill. You need physical therapy gradually built up. You need blood tests to go along with the drugs we give you. Lab work to check your blood protein levels and the white cells. And you sure need better nutrition."

"I can get all that, and done better, right at home."

"Sure, but done by people you pay to do what you want. And you won't want the whole dreary routine. Not very long. You'd drop it. Here, you can't."

Porter stared out the window. "Mac," he said, "you wouldn't kid me along, would you?"

"No, Port, I wouldn't."

"I mean, it's been a long time, Mac."

"Sure, Port."

"You wouldn't lie to me, I mean."

"I might."

"I'm glad you said that. But just not this one time, Mac."

"What is it, Port?"

"Not this one time. Promise."

"It's a promise."

Porter turned his head to look at Mac carefully. "You said when my spine healed, and I could move my legs, and I had bladder control and all that, I'd be as good as I was before I crashed."

Mac spoke slowly. "I brought Jerry Mendelsohn up from New York, Port. He's one of the best neurosurgeons in the country. He confirmed every detail. Our orthopedic consultant and the radiologist, everybody, we all agreed."

"Well, all the king's horses and all the king's men are wrong." Porter paused, and when he spoke again his voice had changed. "Everything's come back, except one thing. I can think all the right things up here, especially when Bettina's around, but nothing happens down here. A woman wants a man, not a dead soldier."

"Maybe it's not dead. Just wounded and recovering."

"You said you wouldn't lie. This is one goddam time I want to count on you, Mac."

"I know how you feel. This is as straight as I can make it, Port. There's a complicated set of nerves from the lower part of your spinal column that control the erection. We know those nerves are

121

healed because all our tests prove it, but we don't know what messages your brain is sending down there."

"Don't tell me I'm impotent just in my mind."

"Maybe. Partly."

"But I've always been one hell of a swordsman."

"Those are the guys most worried about losing it. And when they worry too much, they drink too much."

Porter looked at the bottle beside his bed. "I thought alcohol was an aphrodisiac."

"In small amounts, maybe. After that, it's just a wet blanket."

Porter sat up straighter, watching Mac carefully, then swung his legs over the side of the bed, and paused. "I get dizzy if I do this too fast. Feel a hundred years old."

"You'll be flying a new plane in a month, Port. You'll be buying new polo ponies in three months."

Porter stood up and kicked his feet into slippers and walked toward Mac, trailing one hand along the bed. "And Betts? How long for that?"

"Well," Mac said, "in the words of a great medieval poet: Why put off until tomorrow what you can do today?"

Porter gripped Mac's elbow with his good hand. "Mac, you're *sure*?"

"No, I'm not. If not today, tomorrow, maybe. But one day pretty soon, I am sure."

"By God, I'm going to send you a check—"

"Not me, Port. No, thanks. You'll drive my tax people hysterical. I'll give you the names of a couple of worthy research projects, including my own."

The bedside phone rang. Porter shuffled over to answer it. "Yes?" He listened, then said, "Hold on," and put his hand over the mouthpiece. "It's the nurse at the desk. The aide is here to pick up the steamer basket."

"How many bottles are in it, Port?"

"Four. All Scotch."

"Well, there're four house officers on duty in this division, two interns, two residents. Comes out just right, don't you think?"

Port looked at the open bottle on the bedside table. "And that one? Just pour it down the sink?"

"Hell, no," Mac said. "Keep it around for long cold nights and imaginary snakebites."

Port grinned widely, looking more alive with the little tense lines around his eyes smoothing out. "Miss Cantrell," he said into the phone, "thank you, but we won't need the aide. And will you ask my young lady visitor to come in, please?" He put the telephone down with an enthusiastic bang.

"I've got to shove off," Mac said. "I'm going to leave new orders for you in the book. Eggs and steak and a new antibiotic and vitamin pills. And absolute privacy this afternoon. Especially the privacy."

"You can't scare me any more. I'm on your side now."

There was a gentle tap at the door and Bettina came in. She stood in the door, posing only a little with one leg forward and bent slightly for modeling, looking from Porter to Mac and back again. Slowly she began to smile as Porter did—like two high-school kids at the senior prom, Mac thought, and here's hoping my clinical assumptions are correct.

"I've got to hurry," he said. "So long, Port."

Porter didn't answer. He was watching Bettina as if he had never seen her before, smiling in a gently sensuous one-sided way.

Bettina came in, taking off her scarf as she walked across the room with her special gait.

Mac decided to leave quickly, and as he closed the door behind him he heard her say, "Port . . . *darling*. . . ."

He looked at his wristwatch as he hurried down the tile-lined hospital corridor, aware suddenly that he was hungry and that he had put off going to the men's room, then—automatically—repressing both sensations because Porter had used all his morning's reserve time and more, and there was still the medical library committee meeting at noon at the University Club and before that time he needed to stop at the laboratory to check on the last group of experiments and the corridor paging speaker overhead was saying, "Dr. Adams, Dr. Malcolm Adams."

He stopped at the next nurses' station and called Telepage.

123

"Your laboratory called, Dr. Adams," Telepage said.

"Thanks." He dialed his lab. One of his technicians, Dorothea, answered.

"Plastic surgery research," she said mechanically, sounding like: Go away, don't bother me now.

"Hello, Dotty. Dr. Adams."

"Good morning," Dotty said tonelessly. "Is it morning?"

"You sound sleepy." He reached heavily for jocularity. "As the British say, are you there?" No, not the British; it was Laura who had asked: *Are you there?*

"Only in body, Dr. Adams. Are you coming to the lab this morning?"

"On my way over now. Start the coffee and stop loafing." I'm being awfully jovial this morning. Is everybody I talk to really depressed? Or is it that I'm trying too hard?

"Aye aye, sir. You've had some calls. Greenwich—"

"I've taken that one."

A gray-haired pipe-smoking doctor wearing a white clinical coat over tweed trousers came down the hall and stopped when he saw Mac. He stood still, waiting for Mac to finish the telephone conversation, holding one bent elbow in his opposite hand while he smoked slowly. "No hurry," he said to Mac. "I'll wait." The bow tie he wore with a blue oxford cloth button-down collar shirt made him look very youthful, in a New Haven way.

"And a Dr. Varnum called," Dotty was saying over the phone. "He's on a T-and-A right now, but will you call him at eleven sharp?"

"I'll be in the lab by eleven. I'll call him from there."

"Well, that's it. Finished and over."

Finished and over. Airplane pilot's language which might ordinarily be part of Dotty's manner of talking somehow seemed offbeat and forced at the moment. "Dotty," he said, glancing out of habit at his watch, then at the waiting doctor, "what's wrong?"

For a moment she didn't answer. "I had a late night," she said in a flat voice, "and an early morning. That's all."

He considered quickly: Money? He had given her a raise two months ago. Some freak lab accident that destroyed a year's research?

124

"I'll be over pronto," he said. His wristwatch drove him; and generous concern took a lot of time.

"*Sí, señor. Hasta luego,* no yes?" The phone clicked. Now he was certain something was wrong at the lab.

The waiting doctor stepped forward. "How are you, Mac?"

"Want the chief complaint, Harry? Or a full clinical history?"

He was thinking of Dotty's voice. Joking. Porter had been joking, too. Maybe it wasn't a personal thing, but a national habit: pack up your troubles and smile, smile, smile.

"Got five minutes, Mac?" Harry was asking.

"Will you take two? I'm headed for my lab, and then—"

"Good. I'm going that way, too." Harry fell into step beside him as if neither Mac nor he had anything else to do except stroll down the corridor.

Harry Scott had been a year ahead of Mac in medical school, they had been elected to the same Greek letter medical honor society, Alpha Omega Alpha, and they had been attached to the same outfit in North Africa during the war. Now Harry was a full-time associate professor of psychiatry at the medical center, deliberately restricting the number of patients in his private practice so that he could do some intensive research on schizophrenia in children; he also carried a heavy load of non-paying staff consultations as well as medical student and resident staff teaching. His income was one quarter of Mac's, which always made Mac feel just a little guilty.

Mac remembered Laura talking about Harry Scott one night as they were driving home from a party at the Scotts' in New Haven. "I don't see what's so special about him," she had said. "Maybe he doesn't have that smart-aleck know-it-all look of the New York head shrinkers, which is a pleasant change in psychiatrists I must say, but that foul pipe and those tweeds and that slow way of talking are pretty corny, Mac. Admit it."

"If he just acted tweedsy and pipe-ish," Mac had said, "you'd be right. But he lives it. He's really homespun. If he went into private practice full-time he could triple his income."

"He wouldn't know what to do with money. His forefathers were ministers and now he's a man of the cloth, too, except that now it's

125

tweed. He's a small-town professor who learned the technical mumbo-jumbo and became a psychiatrist."

"More than that, Laura. He was analyzed."

"So what? Is that supposed to be equal to baptism?"

"For a psychiatrist, yes. It makes him aware of his own motivations. It makes him a psychoanalyst."

"It makes Harry Scott a tiresome bore."

"Because he doesn't know music, or pictures, or the latest books, or funny stories, and doesn't give a damn whether horses are thoroughbred or not?"

"Yes," she said, "all that. He's like most doctors, a nice middle-class boy without much imagination—"

He interrupted fiercely, "Who was tops in his college class, intercollegiate chess champ, tops in med school—"

"Who always beat you at chess, which always impresses you out of all proportion—"

"Oh hell, Laura, Harry Scott saved more men from cracking up in North Africa—"

"While we're on that, you just wouldn't happen to be one of his grateful patients—?"

"Hell, no. I'm just the nice middle-class boy who married the rich girl and never had enough imagination to crack up."

"I'll ignore that one."

"Well, I don't ignore the fact I was in a nice safe steaks and cold beer surgical post in Algiers while Harry was up with the infantry against the Afrika Korps and eating mud."

"Harry Scott," she had said. "Great Scott."

"Not great, pun-wise or otherwise. Just very good. Just one of the very few who are very good."

"It wouldn't be because he's like you, Mac, long and bony with one of those authentic solid rock maple early American faces—?"

"No, it wouldn't. Please don't give me the last Puritan song and dance. He's not puritanical. He's just disciplined."

She had thrown her head back and laughed. "Oh, Mac, that's priceless!" She was really laughing now, with the annoyance gone and the spontaneous burst of laughter filling the car. "Can't you see that as a *New Yorker* cartoon? A man in tweeds, with a pipe, stretched out flat on a bed of nails like an Indian fakir, and the well-dressed lady in the foreground with a fussy hat on is staring at him while her husband in the same tweeds and pipe says, 'No, dear, he's not puritanical, just disciplined.' "

He had looked at her in the faint glow from the car's instrument panel. She was very attractive with her head back, looking as quick and clever and youthful as when he had first met her at the Seawanhaka-Corinthian yacht club on Centre Island. Miss Laura Woodring of Oyster Bay and Aiken. At that time he had told her she was a North Shore sea nymph made of sugar and spice and nothing else nice and a generous portion of vitriol, and she had called him a pleasant peasant filled with out-of-this-worldliness. The mutual insults were required under the rules of the game then accepted, and were understood to convey affection, just as it did in glossy films and magazines. When Boy met Girl and they insulted one another, everyone understood that it must be love.

His headlights had picked up an approaching roadside park, and on impulse he had swung the wheel to bring the car off the road, under the trees.

Laura had glanced at him. "Stopping?"

"Yes," he had said, turning off the engine. "If we're going to fight I'll need both hands free, like this. Like our first summer."

She had been genuinely surprised. "Mac! Of all the high-school boy tricks—," and then her face was suddenly next to his, "Oh, Mac!" —and he kissed her hard, feeling tears on her face. "I hate myself when I get going," she had said against him, "but I can't seem to stop and when you're so damn patient that just makes it worse—"

"I know I'm a pleasant peasant," he said, "and I'm hardly ever home, and even then not on time—"

"And I'm just a rich bitch from the word go, but, Mac, I try so hard not to flaunt it or pressure you—"

"I'll pressure you," he had said. "Like this. Right here."

Later, after they had driven down to Greenwich and turned off at Round Hill, Laura had said, "While we were dressing tonight I looked into the mirror and all of a sudden it hit. You're thirty, I said

127

to myself, and you'll never be twenty-nine again. I guess that started it."

"Don't sound so tragic. We'll never be nineteen again, either, thank God."

"And then to top it all Harry Scott sounded so, I don't know, so *secure*."

"Sure. He knows who he is and he knows where he's going."

"And we don't?"

"Do we?" The yacht club dances and the sea nymph were far away now. They were a man and his wife driving home from a Saturday night party, and discussing the other people until inevitably they realized they had been looking at themselves all the while.

"I suppose we don't," she had said. "I suppose I wanted to be a pretty girl all my life, and keep busy playing games—"

"Now, Laura, don't go to the opposite extreme. Don't hit yourself so hard."

"Well, I promise not to tear into Harry again. I never meant to hit him at all."

No, of course not, something cool and deep in his mind said, you meant to hit me.

Mac always had time when Harry asked for it, and it was obvious Harry wanted to discuss a clinical problem.

"Do you remember Mrs. Saunders, Mac?" Harry asked through his pipestem as they walked down the hospital corridor.

"Mrs. Saunders?" Mac tried to place the name in his memory. He knew Harry would not say anything to help him for at least another minute, out of professional habit rather than perversity, because Harry was one of those psychiatrists who believed you remembered what you wished to remember and forgot whatever you wished to forget. Out of habit he was testing Mac's attitude toward Mrs. Saunders by learning whether Mac would remember her or not.

"Mrs. Saunders," Mac repeated, then his mental card file opened to the right place. "Saunders. About forty-five, born in Ireland, widowed five years ago, stormy menopause, carcinoma of right vocal cord. The tumor was pinhead size with healthy tissue on both sides, so we didn't touch the left cord. There was an unexpected single

128

malignant node in the cervical chain, which was why we did a wide en bloc neck dissection. Took a whole morning. My damn left foot went to sleep."

Harry saluted him with his pipe. "Not bad. That's almost total recall."

"Almost? Wait a minute. I left out the endocrine therapy and the E.N.T. consultation and X-ray work at each checkup."

"And you left out the strict religious background and the suicide attempt."

Mac smiled. "I was blocking, Dr. Freud. Thinking too much like a surgeon. Sure, Mrs. Saunders had a hostile superego, an aggressive ego, and a really primitive id. I didn't like the lady."

"Maybe," Harry said, "maybe. You gave her about a year to live—"

"Not so fast. There was a big *if*. If additional metastatic nodes appeared in the cervical lymph chain, about a year."

"Did you tell her that?"

"Of course not. I told her oldest son, mostly to make sure he understood the importance of clinic checkups. I put it on a statistical basis, and kept emphasizing the exceptions to the rule. Everything was in her favor, actually. But routine checkups were the key to survival."

"I'm not pushing you, Mac. No need for a speech."

"I'm tired. I feel like being aggressive."

"Why did you dislike her so much, Mac?"

"Because she was an anti. Anti-life, anti-love, anti-everything."

"I agree with you. But why should you dislike her?"

"I don't know. I never analyzed it."

"Please don't get sore, Mac. I need to know."

"Why?"

"She's in my office now. Even with one good vocal cord, she hasn't been able to speak since her suicide attempt. After she got the complete battery of tests we decided it was a psychological problem and I got her." Mac glanced very quickly at his wristwatch, but Harry Scott caught it. "Mac," he said, "this is important. Yesterday she spoke for the first time, and today again. Just two words."

"I know. 'Damned forever.' "

"No. 'Dr. Adams.' "

129

Mac stopped short. "Seriously?"

Harry Scott put his pipe between his teeth and said nothing.

"So now I'm supposed to see her?"

"Yes. It's important. Cancel something else."

"You're a dog."

"At regular intervals. Always in a good cause, though."

"What am I supposed to say to her?"

"Whatever you feel."

"Well," Mac said, "I'm glad she's speaking again."

"Okay, tell her so."

"I'd feel guilty if I didn't feel glad."

"Don't tell her that."

"I'm telling you."

Harry looked him in the eyes. "We all feel guilty about all kinds of things, Mac," he said quietly.

"Even you?"

"Yes. But I forgive myself."

"I don't," Mac said. "I just realized why I never liked Mrs. Saunders." He paused, but Harry was silent, waiting, as always. "I suddenly remembered my grandfather. The Reverend Mr. Benjamin Maccabee Adams. He lived with us in Greenwich at Adams Farm while I was a boy. He was always praying and always making me pray, standing up, you know, in the old tradition. He had a halo of white hair and a white beard, like an Old Testament prophet, and gray eyes like bullets, all with that rock-ribbed Calvinist pulpit manner. He hung a motto on the wall in my bedroom, I remember it was a sampler my grandmother had stiched by hand. It was linen with a double black border and it said: *In Adam's fall, we sinned all.* When I was a youngster I used to believe our whole Adams family were direct descendants of Adam, and doomed. I really did."

Harry took out his pipe and rubbed the bowl with his thumb. "Another anti?" he asked mildly, "or just a dignified old gent you never understood?" Then he jogged Mac's elbow gently. "Let's go, you sinner, and tell Mrs. Saunders how happy you are the good Lord has restored her voice."

Remembering that day in New Haven, sitting now in a private plane bound for Tangier and remembering clearly and accurately

130

that particular day, Mac decided it was only the accident of hospital scheduling and meeting Harry Scott which had crowded so much into one morning. He spent most of his time in his own private practice in Greenwich, with only one day a week at the medical center in New Haven, and it was inevitable that the string of little crises which most staff doctors saw spread out during the week would be concentrated into a single knot on the one day he was available in New Haven to untie them.

He was an associate clinical professor of plastic surgery at Yale, and drove up to New Haven from his home in Greenwich every Thursday morning for surgery and staff conferences and, time permitting, some research work. The word clinical in his faculty title meant that he was not a full-time on-the-spot salaried member of the hospital staff, like Harry Scott, and that his operating work and consultations and his teaching of the surgical residents and interns were all done without payment.

Of course, his being given a laboratory and two technicians and a small research budget for equipment was an indirect and impersonal form of payment, and his staff privilege of bringing occasional private patients like Porter into the hospital was supposed to be of direct and personal benefit. Also, an associate was only one rung in the academic ladder below a full professorship, like a colonel who needs only one step up to become a general, and at a big medical center like Yale's there were not many men in their thirties who were associates. They were demonstrators, fellows, instructors, assistant professors, but not associates. Mac knew his promotion was based mostly on his serious teaching of the house staff. His research on skin grafting was like so much other clinical research, put and take and catch as catch can, so different from the religious intensity of the basic scientists and some full-time staff men, but it *was* research and saved him from the usual University Club lunch table slur of: "Him? A body mechanic. One of those *very* successful surgeons. You know, them what's got gits."

Actually, he had become so interested in the biological glue that held the human body together, the mucopolysaccharides in the ground substance and the question: Was this where the body's tissues really aged?—that only his distaste—or was it fear?—of living on his wife Laura's money prevented him from going into research full-time.

131

Since the end of the war, with inflation climbing and academic salaries stumbling behind, everyone pretended to respect the poor scientist, but always the prevailing winds of the world blew ashes into the ivory tower. Now, even Mac bowed before the unspoken academic judgment: By his income shall ye know him.

And, Mac knew, the fact that his father had been a clinical member of the Yale faculty for twenty years had not exactly held him back, either.

—Mac Adams? they would say, especially if they'd had one martini, now that the one-martini-type lunch had invaded New Haven, you mean old Mac's boy?

—You're becoming antediluvian, sir. Old Mac's gone, and his boy's been a man quite some time now. Married Laura Woodring—remember Professor Woodring at Sheff and his petroleum processing work? Laura inherited all the oil patents, and they're living happily ever after in the green-dollar pastures in Greenwich.

—Well the greener the pasture, the higher the hay. Saw his name with Korey's on a research paper. Read the summary. Something about skin grafts. How's it going?

—Well—then the little deprecatory smile—you know how it is with clinical skin research that ignores basic biochemistry. All descriptive, nothing explanatory. Yesterday it was calamine lotion, today it's X-rays, tomorrow cortisone. In the skin game you can't kill 'em and you can't cure 'em.

—Mac will probably come up with the cure of skin allergies one of these days. He must be smarter than we are. Married a rich girl, didn't he?

—Um, yes. Indeed.

For several reasons, then, he was an associate clinical professor who spent every Thursday in New Haven.

During the rest of the week in Greenwich he usually had breakfast with Stan, his eight-year-old son. Laura hated getting up before nine or ten o'clock—"I hate people who rise and shine," she said; "I'm no farmer. What's there to get up *for*?"—so Stan and Mac pretended they had a kind of austere masculine breakfast club. Secretly, they both missed Laura's vitality and quick laughter.

After breakfast, every day except Thursday, Mac drove from

132

Round Hill down across the overpass above the Merritt Parkway and around past the Country Day School to drop Stan off, and then to the Greenwich Professional Building where his name was painted on the pavement in one of the most convenient reserved parking spaces behind the building. He had heard that in these traffic-congested days a reserved personal parking space had become a more valuable symbol of social status than such commonplace display items as Cadillacs or mutation mink coats, and he often wished patients would stop parking their cars in his space to prove it.

Thursday mornings were different because he had to be in New Haven to begin his operating schedule at eight o'clock. On Thursday mornings the housekeeper, Mrs. Baker, would have breakfast on the table for him when he came quietly downstairs at six. Mr. Baker always brought the Ford convertible around the curved drive from the garage to the side door of the house and held the driver's door open, leaving the motor running warmly, just as Mac came down the fieldstone steps ramming his hat on askew and juggling his briefcase. There was a smooth precision to it all that Mac liked, even though it occurred to him at least twice a year to wonder why he needed to live so efficiently.

"A good morning to you, Dr. Adams," Mr. Baker invariably said in his silver-haired dignified slow way that would have been ridiculous in anyone else, and somehow reminded Mac occasionally of his grandfather, the Reverend Mr. Benjamin Maccabee Adams.

"A good morning to you, Mr. Baker," Mac always replied, because ever since he had been old enough to speak he had called the dignified man Mr. Baker by his father's instructions, and when he had married Laura after the war and brought her to Adams Farm it had taken some elaborate explaining to her.

"Well, at least *I* wasn't brought up on his knee," Laura had said, "so there's no need for me to." After that Mac made sure his son Stan remembered to call the couple Mr. and Mrs. Baker.

Mr. Baker would close the door as soon as Mac was behind the steering wheel. Once Laura had asked Mr. Baker why he never brought her Jaguar sedan or the Chrysler station wagon around for Mac and he had said quietly, "Country doctors never drive such big cars, Mrs. Adams."

133

"But Dr. Adams isn't a country doctor!" she had said vigorously.

"No, ma'am," Mr. Baker had said, "but his father was until the end of his life, and I believe Dr. Adams is one at heart."

Neither Laura nor Mr. Baker had ever mentioned this to Mac.

Wednesday afternoons were originally set aside for golf with Laura at Wee Burn, weather permitting, or squash or handball with one of the doctors in his building. But during the past five years, as his practice had become very large, and his research took more time, and the Governor appointed him to the Rehabilitation Commission, and the United Nations people asked him to accept two young French doctors for some postgraduate plastic surgery training, and he became a Special Consultant on the Plans Committee of the new County Hospital, and he accepted a medical liaison membership in the Nursing Shortage Study Group, and a trustee appointment for the Little Symphony, with two nights each month at Stan's Cub Scout meetings, one night a month for the Medical Society meeting, one night for *Time* Magazine each week, two nights a week for trying vainly to keep up with the flood of professional journals and correspondence from the American Society for Plastic and Reconstructive Surgery, Saturday nights out with Laura at the Hunt Club or Tokeneke or the Yacht Club in summers, or a neighbor's house, or into New York for a play, and Sundays set aside for sculpture in his studio over the garage.

Sundays. Even his closest friends respected his Sundays, when the only interruptions he accepted were either emergencies or calls from any of the hospitals in which he had patients. During the past five years he had had two one-man shows at Erve Galleries on Fifty-seventh Street, both well attended but drawing mixed reviews. Just as much serious writing of criticism in the arts had deteriorated into hit-and-run reviews calculated to amuse the reader at the artist's expense, much sculpture had become something called abstract either because the sculptors had no ideas about the world around them or else lacked the technical skill to represent in solid forms the world within themselves. When Mac found the rare fine piece of abstract sculpture he envied the ability and talent which could put human feeling into non-realistic forms, and occasionally he wondered why he always took the traditional path of realism. He worked entirely with life-size human figures, or heads, or hands, and some reviewers

134

allowed themselves a respectful mention of the meticulous knowledge of underlying anatomy which one recognized in each of his sculptures. He had sold several pieces, but the only one which had attracted wide attention even before it was exhibited was the bronze head of a nineteen-year-old boy thrown backward in pain with the ropy cords of his neck stiff with agony. It was called "Vision of April, 1945," and Mac had done it from the memory he had of the last sporadic fighting during the springtime months before Germany surrendered. He had been operating on wounded men continuously for twenty-two hours in a tent hospital, and had just rolled himself into his sleeping bag, stony with fatigue, when his technical sergeant had shaken his shoulder gently. "Major Adams, there's an eye case just come in."

The eye case had been a boy of nineteen lying on a stretcher in the shock ward with the plasma bottle hung above the needle into his arm vein. A bullet had hit the boy at a right angle, entering one eye socket, crossing the bridge of his nose, and then out of his head through the other eye. When Mac saw him first, the boy's head had been arched back, and where his eyes should have been were two large monocles of blood. Despite the morphine the boy kept repeating, "My eyes, I can't see . . . my eyes, I can't see. . . ."

The orbital enucleations and facial repair had taken several hours, and, when Mac finished and stepped out of the long corridor of the bare-bulb-lighted operating tent for some air and a quick cigarette, the forested German hills around them were coming alive at sunrise, dawn walking barefooted through the April trees, and Mac's vision became suddenly acutely aware of every grass blade and the horizon glow of morning.

He had never told this story behind the bronze head to anyone except his son Stan. Stan often worked beside him on his own boy-size modeling stand, usually doing Whitey, his pony, or their comic Dachshund, Herr Tannenbaum, in great lumps of enthusiastic untalented clay.

"War is bad, isn't it?" Stan had said.

"It's terrible, son," Mac said.

They had both worked silently for a while, then Stan had asked him, "Do I have to be a doctor when I grow up?"

"Only if you want to, Stan."

135

"You did, like your father."

"Well, I wanted to."

"But you wanted to be a sculptor too, didn't you?"

Mac had put down the wood chisel he was using and looked at Stan. "I did, but I didn't think I could be one of the great ones. That's when I left the art school and started to study medicine."

"Are you a great doctor, Dad?"

"No, not great. I'm good at it."

"Mr. Baker told me you're one of the best plastic surgeons in the country, Dad."

"Well, he's pretty fond of me, Stan."

"I thought you were one of the champs. No kiddin'. That's what I told 'em in school."

"I never discovered anything great, Stan. I'll never be in one of the history books."

"Well, gee, Babe Ruth never discovered baseball and *he* was a champ, wasn't he?"

Mac had laughed. "Okay, if that's the way you look at it, Stan, I'm a champ."

Stan had grinned. "I knew it," he said.

. . . His life had been orderly, pleasant, successful. Like the world in which he spent most of his time, the air-conditioned office, the air-conditioned operating room, the air-conditioned home, he and his life and his wife seemed to have built-in thermostats which prevented temperatures from rising to the heat of ecstasy or dropping to the freezing point of despair. There was no need to be prepared for disaster.

After Mac had talked to Mrs. Saunders in Harry Scott's inner office, and to Mrs. Saunders' son, and to her parish priest in Harry's outer office, he hurried back down the corridor to the nurse's station and telephoned his office.

"Plastic surgery research," a woman's voice said in the receiver.

"Dotty? Oh, Wilma. Where's Dot?"

"Stepped out for a while, Dr. Adams."

"Something serious?"

"No. Just low-grade chronic frustration. Engagement-itis, with no marriage date set."

136

"Anything we can do?"

"Sure. Don't notice a thing. You were supposed to be here twenty minutes ago, weren't you?"

"I'm on my way, if I can make it."

She laughed. "That's what you always say."

"Will you call the University Club, Wilma? Ask for Dr. Barney and tell him I can't get to the committee meeting."

"Okay. There's a note on the pad here about calling Dr. Varnum at noon."

He looked at his watch. Noon had passed five minutes ago. "I'll call him right now. I'll be going back into surgery, Wilma, and then I have to make a dash for Greenwich and change and then down to New York."

"Do we have your New York phone, Doctor?"

"It's in Dotty's desk book under Erve Galleries. Fifty-seventh Street."

"When are you having lunch?"

"I'll grab a chocolate bar on my way up to the O.R." And he suddenly remembered there was also a long-delayed stop to be made at the men's room.

"You do this all the time, Dr. Adams. Aren't you stopping in the lab at all today?"

"Can't do it, Wilma. This has turned into one of those days."

"Dr. Adams," Wilma said, "take some advice from your old family doctor—"

"Yes, Doctor—"

"—slow down, Doctor. You'll live longer."

"I can't," he said. "It's a disease."

"Not money-itis," she said. "Not with you."

"No," Mac said. "Trackus Rodentia."

Three hours later he was in New York, swinging his car off the elevated highway down into the crowded traffic of Fifty-seventh Street. In those three hours he had managed to get back to the operating room for the circumcision on Tommy, the seven-year-old boy, then to drive from New Haven to his home in Greenwich to change his clothes and to have a glass of milk standing in the kitchen and pretending it was lunch.

137

Mrs. Baker told him his son Stan had felt very much left out of all the excitement involved in his father's one-man show in New York, so Laura had finally taken him with her when Mr. Carl Barkley had come by in that fancy car of his. Mac's immediate reaction, which startled him because it came so fast, was to think: Then I was wrong. If she had wanted to be alone with Carl she wouldn't have taken the boy. He felt faintly ashamed that the idea should even have occurred to him. Carl wanted to show off one of his high-powered cars; it was as simple as that.

As soon as he had finished at home, he drove hurriedly back to the Parkway for the final half of the trip into New York. He was late for the opening at Erve Galleries, and he knew Laura would be faintly annoyed but not showing it except by a certain very subtle remoteness, a kind of punishment by withdrawal.

The late afternoon truck traffic and the snaking swarm of taxicabs on Fifty-seventh Street slowed him to an exasperating crawl. He noticed that some of the passers-by strolling along the sidewalk were able to get to the next corner before he did. For a moment he felt his lack of sleep during the previous thirty-six hours and the frustration of big city traffic combine into a knot of anger in his stomach; he knew his anger was no one's fault but his own, because he had never adapted himself to the scurrying hornblowing snarling grinning kind vicious foolish brave purposeless ant heap, and at mid-century it was high time he learned that *A* stood first for Atom, then for Adaptation.

After twenty minutes he reached the front of Erve Galleries, near the corner of Park Avenue. Erve had put a canvas archway out to the street, and Carl's Ghia-Chrysler was parked directly beside a *No Parking* sign at the entrance, with a half-dozen teen-age boys inspecting it with religious awe under the eye of the doorman. It must have been Laura's idea to park the car in such a convenient illegal place, and only Carl and his unusual car and his open athletic tip-flourishing manner could have arranged it with the doorman. Another twenty minutes went by before Mac was able to find a parking lot which would condescend to accept his car, and ten minutes to walk several blocks back to the gallery.

Erve met him as he went up the steps to the second floor. "Malcolm my boy!" he said. "Why so late?" He grasped both Mac's elbows and gestured up the steps with his head. "Listen to all that enthusiasm up there!" A deep interwoven hum of voices came down the steps sounding exactly like what it was, a cocktail party.

"And listen, Malcolm," Erve was saying, holding Mac's elbows and leading him up the steps, "there's a chance the Met will buy the bronze head of the blind boy. Isn't that wonderful?"

"Sure," Mac said.

"What do you mean, 'sure'? You sound like a farmer. This doesn't happen every day, Malcolm!"

"Well," Mac said. "I'm just a little sleepy, and it's kind of hard to get excited, if you know what I mean. Besides, I think I'm a farmer at heart, Erve."

"Then help me spread a little manure around here, Malcolm. I've been telling everybody that if you weren't such a fancy-schmancy surgeon you ought to chuck cutting people and do sculpture full-time."

"That's occurred to me once or twice, Erve."

"You're a natural, Malcolm, a real natural. You ought to think about it." He shook Mac's elbow. "Now, let me introduce you around."

It was hard to think about anything just then because the gallery at the top of the steps was filled solidly with people. A thin cloud of smoke hovered in the warm air, drifting through the overhead spotlights Erve had arranged to illuminate each piece of Mac's sculpture in the long room. The voices had reached a pitch which Mac recognized as being approximately after the second martini, which meant he was really quite late.

Laura came toward him, followed by Stan and Carl, all three of them working their way carefully between clusters of busily talking people. Mac went to meet her, and, as he bent to kiss her, she said, "Watch my martini glass, dear."

Mac put one arm around Stan's shoulders and shook Carl's outstretched hand with his free one.

"Absolutely terrific opening, Mac," Carl said. He looked very handsome with a high outdoors-looking flush. His enthusiasm had a thin martini edge on it, but he was obviously sincere. "Mary Ann sent

139

her love, Mac. Sorry as she can be about missing this. If she didn't have another one of those migraine attacks, she'd be here too."

"How do you like it, son?" Mac asked Stan.

"All the statues look so different here, Dad. Over our garage they looked one way, and here they look different."

"I know what you mean, Stan."

"He insisted on coming, Mac," Laura said. "I told him it would be like this"—she gestured with her glass at the crowded noisy room —"but you know Stanislaus Adams, your number one fan."

Mac could see Stan's small face turned up to him, so he squeezed the boy's shoulder lightly and said, "I'm glad you came, Stan."

"Laura," Erve said, "tell him what the man from the Met said about the head of the blind boy. I've got to see a dog about a dog. Be right back, people."

"Laura," Carl was saying, "wasn't I supposed to remind you about the telegram?"

"You got a telegram on the phone, Dad," Stan said.

"Hold my glass, Stan," Laura said. She tumbled a few small objects in her little purse and pulled out a square of folded paper. "It's from New Haven to Greenwich. Mrs. Baker referred them here. The operator said it was signed 'Port,'" she said. "That wouldn't be Porter Bradford in the hospital, would it, Mac?"

"We'll see," he said as he opened the folded sheet. Laura had written the message in a quick scrawl, but it was clearly legible: I LIE IN GREEN VALLEYS. MY CUP RUNNETH OVER. BOY MEETS GIRL WITH HAPPY ENDING. THANK YOU DOCTOR AESCULAPIUS. PORT.

"What's so funny?" Laura asked. "It sounded very mysterious to me. Is it some kind of code?"

"Yes," Mac said, still laughing. "You know how Port is."

"I know how he is, dear, but I never dreamed he read the Bible."

"Usually he doesn't," Mac said, "but he was praying today."

Laura realized this was one of those things known as a confidential communication and that Mac, unlike some of their friends who were physicians, never discussed his patients with her. When they were first married she had told him it was sort of too bad doctors couldn't talk about their work at home, like most people, but, if that was how he felt about it, it made sense to her.

140

Two short dark-haired men who looked like brothers came up to Mac. "Oh, Dr. Adams," one said, "there you are." He spoke with a distinctly French accent. "We 'ave look for you for congratulation." He shook Mac's hand briskly.

"Yes," the second said, "you are really a fine sculptor."

"Many thanks," Mac said in French. "I'm glad you could come. You've met my wife and son, I believe."

Everyone nodded pleasantly, both Frenchmen murmuring "Madame" politely to Laura, while one shook hands solemnly with Stan, saying, " 'Ow are you, Dr. Adams, junior?"

"Okay, thanks," Stan said, grinning.

"This is Mr. Barkley, a neighbor of ours," Laura said. "Dr. Lescamp and Dr. Patric."

While the handshaking began again, Carl said, "Oh yes, you're the United Nations doctors here to study in Greenwich with Dr. Adams. I remember now."

Dr. Lescamp said, "I believe I remember to hear your name, too. You are the owner of the car, the special one."

"The Ghia-Chrysler?" Carl asked happily. Mac had noticed Carl enjoyed discussing cars more than anything else, although Mac had never quite figured out why high power and speed should have such fascination. He knew the usual glib psychological explanations, but Carl seemed much too normal to fit the textbook reasons.

While Carl began to tell Dr. Lescamp about his last trip to France to see the Le Mans auto race, the one in which a car had spun off the road into the crowd, Dr. Patric said quietly to Mac in French, "Dr. Adams, may I speak with you a moment? Excuse," he added in English to Laura, as he and Mac stepped to one side.

"Is something wrong?" Mac asked, because Dr. Patric had a worried little frown.

"Yes, I think so," Dr. Patric said. He looked over his shoulder at the people crowded near them, then back at Mac. "I'll speak French, if you do not mind it, Dr. Adams."

"Of course not."

"Mr. Stacey, you remember the patient Mr. Stacey you assigned me to do?"

"Yes. Certainly. We had some difficulty with the debridement.

141

We were concerned about possible infection of the face wound, I remember."

"Yes. We were right, because he has had a high-spiking fever for two days now. The blood culture grew out staph, penicillin-resistant." He paused. "To bother you now, at the opening of your one-man show—"

"The patient is more important," Mac said. "We're beginning to see more and more of these resistant infections."

"The trouble now, just before we left the hospital to come here," Dr. Patric said, "is the patient has developed a psychosis, a toxic psychosis I believe. He shouted and imagined people coming into his room through the window. And then he tore off the bandages and began to hemorrhage. He had been typed and cross-matched, of course, so we were able to give him blood immediately. I made sure hemostasis was good before I left." He paused, then added, "I told the resident I would speak to you about this as soon as I saw you."

They looked at one another, weighing and balancing the critical little details of Mr. Stacey's age, surgery, infection, antibiotic therapy, blood loss replacement, and nursing care. To add up the medical arithmetic was not difficult, except for the X factor in every such equation, because X was the unknown unexpected one-chance-in-a-thousand every doctor fears or pretends he does not fear even though he knows X is always there. In this particular case, there was the added complication that Dr. Patric had done the original plastic surgery without a fee as part of his advanced training under Mac's direct supervision at the operating table, but the legal responsibility for the patient's welfare lay with Mac. If anything happened to Mr. Stacey, the explanations and the final signature would be Mac's. Dr. Patric knew this; it was critical enough to force him to discuss the problem immediately with Mac even here and now in New York. Suddenly there was a subtle change in both doctors; Dr. Patric was no longer the pleasant French visitor at Mac's show. The semi-authoritarian codes used in medicine to determine precisely who was responsible for what, and at which level of responsibility, senior or junior, were now in effect, and Mac had the kind of invisibly isolated quality sometimes referred to in military matters as command decision.

"Let's call the hospital in Greenwich right now," Mac said, with

142

the unhurried ease which was also part of the code. Dr. Patric's frown smoothed out; he looked very relieved. Mac had taken him off the hook.

Mac went back to Laura. Carl was still talking about cars to Dr. Lescamp, analyzing the new Citroën design now, and Laura brightened hopefully when Mac approached. "Laura," he said quietly, under the chatter of voices all around them, "there's a little difficulty in Greenwich, at the hospital—"

"—oh no! Don't tell me you're going to—"

"—hold on, wait a minute. I'm just going to phone the resident about it."

"Mac, the Campbells just arrived. I hope you remember we're having dinner—"

"Sure, sure, I remember."

Laura had seen too much of this sort of thing before and was realistic about it now. "But what if you have to run back to the hospital, dear?"

He shrugged slightly. Even though there was no saluting or barking of orders or any other obvious show of discipline in medicine, you did what you had to do. That's all there was to it. Without thinking, he rubbed one hand across his forehead, feeling quite sleepy now. "If I have to go back to work on this patient," Mac said, "maybe I can get back into town in time for coffee."

She saw the weariness in his face, and put her hand on his arm. "Mac," she said, "that's silly. All the driving back and forth. All night in New Haven, then down here, and back up to Greenwich now. It doesn't make sense, dear."

"If I have to leave for Greenwich now, I can take Stan with me."

"Oh, he's enjoying this too much, Mac. He's beginning to see his father as a real no-kidding sculptor."

"I wish I could see it," Mac said.

"It's all around you, Mac. If the Met buys the bronze head we'll have a real celebration."

"You know, Laura," he said in the quiet intimate way a man sometimes talks to his wife, even though they were being jammed from each side by people, "I think I'm so tired that I don't really care."

They looked at each other in the twilight smokiness of the noisy

143

gallery, Laura having had enough to drink to drop her arms and armor for a moment, Mac having been stripped to the bottom rock he stood on by the fatigue he breathed like air.

"Don't say that," Laura whispered. "Don't say you don't really care. Why are you doing all this if you don't enjoy it?"

"Look, Laura, I've really got to get to a telephone. Dr. Patric is waiting over there for me."

"Mac, you always run away as soon as we get to the point."

"No, I don't." A coil of anger tightened in him. "There's been one demand after another on me all day, Laura. And last night. And yesterday. And for the last ten or fifteen years. I'm not running away. I'm always running toward somebody else's fire alarm to put out the fire. Do you think I *want* to drive back to the hospital now?"

"Maybe you do," she said, beginning to look at him in a steady unwavering way. "Maybe you're so driven because you've gotten things set up that way."

"Maybe lots of things, Laura."

"Yes, dear. Maybe."

As he made a move to go, he said, "You know everything may be under control at the hospital. Maybe I won't have to leave."

"Don't worry about Stan and me, dear. Carl's coming to dinner with us and he can drive us home. But please try to stay if you can."

"I'll try," he said, even though both of them realized he had almost no choice.

For some reason he glanced back over his shoulder as he walked away. Laura was standing there looking very sleek and fashionable, holding her martini glass and turning already back to Carl and Dr. Lescamp. She put one arm around Stan's waist as the little group stood talking together, and Stan stood beside her looking interested in everything, like a boy at a circus. Later, Mac was sorry he had not thought of going back to say good-by to Stan.

About a half hour before midnight, the telephone beside Mac's bed rang and rang again. He was so deeply asleep that he had no idea how long it had been ringing before he recognized the sound and awakened enough to answer it.

The call was from the Parkway police. There had been a very

144

serious high-speed accident on the Parkway. Mrs. Adams looked badly bruised, probably that was all, but the driver of the car and the boy were both very seriously hurt. The officer's official-sounding voice seemed to keep repeating the words *very serious,* and Mac snapped awake instantaneously. He turned on the bedside lamp and carefully wrote down the road directions to reach the little suburban hospital where Laura and Carl and Stan had been taken by the ambulance, and the name of the intern on duty in the emergency room, and he managed to tell the officer quietly that he was sure he could get there before midnight.

For a moment he sat with his hand resting on the telephone. The officer had said both Stan and Carl had been found unconscious. The information chilled him, because that suggested possible brain injury. Suddenly he remembered the neurosurgeon Mendelsohn. He and Laura had known Jerry Mendelsohn for at least ten years. A good doctor, a good surgeon, one of the quiet thorough lifesaving good ones.

As he lifted the telephone and began to place his call to Mendelsohn, the receiver fell from his hand and clattered on the floor. Until that moment he had considered himself always rational, always in complete self-control no matter what the stress, and now for the first time, when he was needed most, he discovered he was as vulnerable as everyone else.

He hardly remembered how he reached the small, out-of-the-way hospital. There was only the feeling of a deep lighted hole drilling into the night as his car raced over back-country short cuts; that, and the muscle-clenching fatigue, the weariness upon fatigue of the last twenty-four hours, fatigue piling silently higher in the centers of his brain which needed rest, judgment, critical control, precision. The always-awake part of himself noticed that he drove as if he were a little drunk. His car took the corners too widely. Distances to an approaching crossroads stop sign seemed distorted and he had to use his brakes too hard and too often.

He remembered this sensation of bone-weary lightheadedness from the war years, when he and his anesthetist and two technical sergeants made up a mobile plastic surgery team roving freely in their

145

own truck, on call, from one field hospital to the next. There was the same rush through darkness over unfamiliar roads, the same slack-bodied fatigue which was the stage before exhaustion. At the end of every road was a tent hospital and the long canvas corridor with a row of operating tables beneath a hanging row of naked bulbs under one of which he would stand for eight hours, twelve hours, sixteen hours, then the coffee and the cigarette and the quick handshake from the medical officer in command, then to try to sleep in the bed roll in back of their six-by-six truck, trying to sleep in a bone-breaking bouncing oblivion filled with strangely distorted dreams while the truck raced through another darkness down another unfamiliar road toward another field hospital.

At last, when he turned into the emergency entrance of the small brick fifty-bed hospital and parked beside the police car, he had to make a conscious effort to do as simple a thing as unclench his hands from the wheel.

As he walked toward the brightly lighted doorway under the sign, EMERGENCY, he thought: I hope Dr. Mendelsohn gets here soon. I hope he gets here really soon. Good neurosurgeons aren't easy to find, and he's the best. He trains all the rest, and if he gets here soon we're in the clear. On the phone, when Mac had awakened him at his home in New York, Mendelsohn had said immediately, "Of course, Mac. Of course. I'll be there in little over an hour. Yes, I know the hospital, yes, off route 220. Yes, I know it. And, Mac . . . if Stan or this other fellow has actually had a period of unconscious-ness, maybe you'd better have their heads shaved and prepped, just in case we need to operate, you know . . . of course . . . maybe just exploratory burr holes, though I hope we won't need to go in. . . . After all, nighttime in a little backwoods hospital, so to speak. . . . Yes, good idea, I'll bring some of my own instruments. . . . And, Mac, you know all this, but you sound awfully tired so let me remind you—yes, exactly what I wanted to suggest, get a good base line. Not only the vital signs, you know, but pupillary inequality, un-equal or pathological reflexes, you know, any signs of trouble. Do they have X-ray service out there this time of night? Well, we'll see, I'm talking too much, I'm still half asleep, you'd better hurry along and I'll see you soon. . . . Don't mention it, please, not at all, not at all. . . ."

146

Stan and Carl were lying on adjoining high-wheeled cots when Mac entered the small emergency ward. A police officer was talking to Carl, and a nurse was washing the dried blood off Stan's face. As Mac crossed the room he could feel a sense of relief spread through him when he saw Stan turn his head to answer a question the nurse was asking. Stan was awake, not unconscious. It was a difference which made all the difference, and he took a deep breath. The nurse looked up and said, "I'll bet this is your father."

Stan saw him and began to cry. Mac put his arms around him, feeling the small-boned body through the sheets, and said, "Everything's going to be all right, Stan. Everything's going to be all right, just don't worry." He stopped because there were tears stinging his eyes and because he realized he was trying to reassure himself as well as the boy.

"Your wife's down the hall, Doctor," the nurse said. "The doctor on duty just went down to give her a shot of morphine."

"How is she?"

"Lucky, mostly. Lots of superficial abrasions and raw areas, but nothing broken." She stopped, then said, "I guess. Our X-ray department is closed for the night. And our surgical chief is getting married at some hotel in Manhattan, and practically our whole staff is down there gettin' looped right this minute. Wouldn't you know it? Of all times."

"My head hurts, Dad," Stan said. "It really hurts like the dickens." Both his eyes were swollen almost shut, and one side of his head looked bad.

"He's vomited once," the nurse said.

"Projectile type?"

"No."

"Good." Projectile vomiting, when there was head injury, pointed to brain damage.

The police officer beside Carl stood up. "Are you Dr. Adams?"

"Yes, I am."

Carl turned his head slowly toward Mac. His hair, like Stan's was completely matted down with blood, and dark red areas of coagulated blood lay in his ears and in the corners of eyes. He put out one hand slowly, and Mac took it. It felt hot, and Mac sensed the first small needle prick of warning in his mind.

147

"I'm sorry, Mac," Carl said slowly, his voice sounding drowsy and slurred. "Awf' sorry, Mac. All my fault. Awf' sorry. I mean about Laura and everything."

"Laura's okay, Carl. Just some painful skin burns. I'm going down to see her in a minute." Carl's eyes had the sick shine of fever and Mac moved his hand out of Carl's to feel Carl's pulse. It was slow. He turned to the nurse, feeling more confident with each minute now. After hearing the police report that Stan and Carl had been found unconscious he had somehow expected disaster, both of them in coma, all the risks of major emergency surgery without a trained neurosurgical team, without the entire armamentarium of special diagnostic equipment, without experienced surgical nurses, without the whole apparatus of a big modern hospital.

A young doctor wearing hospital whites walked in quickly, and came directly over to Mac. "Dr. Adams? I'm Dr. Behrens, the intern on duty tonight." He had the young, intelligent look of any of Mac's own house officers, with the same faintly beginning lines of sleeplessness around the eyes. Mac looked at him carefully, because Dr. Behrens might turn out to be a vital man very soon. As they shook hands, Mac said, "Before we review your findings, Doctor, has there been a chance to draw bloods for typing and cross-matching?"

Dr. Behrens shook his head. "Haven't had a chance. Our chief is getting married tonight. We're left with a skeleton crew, and one resident and I have to cover all our beds and E.W. here. Our second-floor nurse can run the bloods in the lab while we—" He stopped because he saw Stan listening hard. "Of course," he said, "our blood bank supplies are sort of limited. We're a pretty small outfit."

The police officer snapped his accident report book shut. "You going to need me for anything, Doctor?" he asked Mac. It was clear that both he and the young doctor assumed that Mac was now in charge.

"Can you stand by just a few minutes, officer?" Mac asked. "Thanks. Nurse, you're—?"

"Miss Stepany."

"Will you start a vital signs chart, Miss Stepany? Blood pressure, pulse, and respiration recorded every fifteen minutes. Temperature on the half hour." He felt his voice becoming more brisk, and both

Miss Stepany and Dr. Behrens began to look a trifle more confident. He put his hand on Stan's shoulder. "I'll be right back, son."

"My head hurts, Dad," Stan said. He was trying not to cry. "Can't I have an aspirin or something?"

"Son," Mac said, "Miss Stepany can rub a little water over your lips, but we can't even give you a drink for a while." Actually, it helped that Stan had vomited, because if he needed surgery they would have to empty his stomach anyway. "Miss Stepany is going to take good care of you for five or ten minutes while I'm gone. I have to see your mother, and I'll be back as quick as I can."

Carl's hot fingers grasped his wrist. "Mac, Mac, I'm awf' sorry about Laura, Mac—"

"Don't worry about Laura, Carl. She's doing fine."

"I'm awf' sorry—"

The level of warning rose in Mac's mind. Carl's slowing pulse and rising temperature, this stumbling repetitiousness, all typical of some forms of brain injury. The wave of confidence he had felt a moment ago began to recede, and once again he thought: I hope Mendelsohn gets here soon. He's a neurosurgeon and he'll know exactly how to interpret what he sees, and exactly what he's doing if we have to go in. Central nervous system symptoms were usually among the most subtle and trickiest to diagnose, even for men who practiced neurology exclusively.

"Carl," he said, trying to talk distinctly to test Carl's sensorium quickly before he walked away, even for a few minutes, "Carl, can you hear me okay?"

"Sure thing."

"Know where you are?"

"With you."

"But where? Where are we?"

"Hosp'l, isn't it? Isn't this a hosp'l?"

"And what day is today?" Pause. "What's your phone number?" Another pause. Carl tried to remember, his face showed it, but there was no answer. Mac looked across him at the police officer. "You're sure he was unconscious when you found him?"

"Out like a light. Both of them. Only the lady was conscious."

"Awf' sorry 'bout Laura, Mac—" Carl sounded sleepy.

149

Mac glanced at Dr. Behrens. "Any rhinorrhea? Any fluid in the ear canals?"

Dr. Behrens understood Mac was asking obliquely about signs of a hidden fracture at the base of the skull. "No, sir. No signs of a basal fracture. I sure wish we could get skull X-rays. Maybe we'd better phone Portchester or Greenwich—"

"Maybe very soon," Mac said. "But let's hope Dr. Mendelsohn gets here sooner—" In this part of the country doctors never mentioned Mendelsohn's first name because it was like saying Einstein in mathematics. "Let's get our blood types. Then, if we have the time to spare to put in a call and wait, maybe we can get the extra blood to come out with their X-ray man." He looked down at Carl. "Rest easy, Carl. I'll be right back."

As he and Dr. Behrens and the police officer walked toward the corridor, he asked the officer, "How is it you brought them here? They need big hospital facilities, and they can't be moved now."

"Well, Doctor, headquarters assigns districts to each part of the highway. Any accident in my district comes here."

"And what happened on the highway?"

"Near as we can figure, your friend must have been burning up the road in that fancy car. He barely sideswiped a station wagon, just enough to swing off balance, and he plowed off at an angle into the side of the road. He was going so fast he snapped off a steel light-pole and plowed up a whole stretch of safety fencing. Just tore the bejasus out of it. You ought to see that car of his—" He squashed his two hands together tightly. "They're lucky to come out of it. The lady was a hundred feet away from the car. I guess she got thrown out first and rolled. You going to need me any more?"

"No, that's the picture we needed. Thanks." Unconsciousness. Now they were lucid. Direct brain contusion? Or epidural hemorrhage? Or both? Make sure to check for skull fracture—

A nurse came hurrying down the dimly lighted hospital corridor. She stopped. "Dr. Behrens, did you want two bloods typed and cross-matched? I just got the call—"

"Yes, in the E.W. I haven't had a chance to draw them. Stat, okay?"

"Okay. I sure hope they don't have anything real rare." She hurried through the swing doors into the emergency ward.

150

Mac said, "Can you give me your positive findings in a nutshell, Dr. Behrens?"

"Well, I think it boils down to obvious acute head injury in both cases, with questionable and probable neurological damage. No apparent skull fractures. Your wife is okay. I gave her some barbiturate, but she was too hopped up and complaining of pain, so I just gave her a quarter-grain of morphine."

"Good. Now this neurologic problem—you know how tricky these diagnoses are—"

"You're telling me!" Dr. Behrens sounded like a worried boy for just a moment, then became precise and scientific again. He ticked his examination findings off on his fingers. "The history of trauma and unconsciousness in both of them. They were both awake and responsive when they arrived here, but I noticed just now the man's sensorium seems a little depressed."

"Right."

"Multiple body abrasions and lacerations about the head in them both. Your son has an avulsed area, looks like, in the left temporal-parietal area. Maybe it's a good thing you're a plastic surgeon, sir."

"Right this minute I'd rather be a neurosurgeon. What else?"

"Well, you saw your son's eyes. The periorbital edema and ecchymoses make it pretty hard to check his pupils or extraocular muscles. That's a pair of real shiners, those eyes. And I think the man may have a couple of broken ribs at the costochondral junctions, maybe third, fourth, and fifth, but it's hard to be certain. I sure wish we had X-ray. I feel lost without it. They both have elevated respiration, blood pressure, and the man has a slow pulse that worries me. Motor ability and strength, and sensation, intact in both of them, but there's a suggestion of weakness on the man's right side—"

"We'll have to watch if it's progressive—"

"—and a suggestion of a Babinski on the right. Your son's deep tendon reflexes were all hyperactive. Cranial nerves all seem intact in both patients, but I wish we could see your son's eyes better."

"No sign of unequal pupils in either one?"

"No. Are you thinking of epidural bleeding, sir?"

"Epidural or subdural, or maybe both, God forbid. Bleeding inside the skull should give us eye signs pretty quick, usually."

"I hear," the young doctor said slowly, "that usually neurological

151

problems are not usual. That's always the trouble. Each one is a jig-saw puzzle of its own. I sure am glad Dr. Mendelsohn is a friend of yours."

"I'd like to see my wife for a minute, if I may."

"Corner room, end of the hall." He looked at Mac for a moment, then said, "What do you think, Dr. Adams? Do we sit on them and watch, or do we go in?"

"We don't go in unless we have better evidence for surgery," Mac said, "unless Dr. Mendelsohn overrules me. But I wish you'd get the O.R. ready, instruments autoclaved—" Mac paused. "Have you ever assisted in neurosurgery, Doctor?"

Dr. Behrens raised his hands slightly, then let them both drop. "Just a one-month clerkship in my senior year. And even that was mostly as second or third assistant, not even holding an idiot stick. And the resident's upstairs delivering a baby." He shook his head. "Jesus, Doctor, excuse the expresion, but of all times to be running a hospital with a skeleton crew!"

"Don't worry," Mac said. "We'll manage."

The young doctor glanced at him, and when he saw that Mac meant it, he nodded. Mac added, "I'll be in my wife's room just a few minutes. Call me if anything changes, will you?"

Laura was stretched out flat in bed with one elbow bent over her eyes. When he came in, she put her arm down painfully and stared at him in the dim light from the corridor.

"Mac?" She had the faint sound of fearfulness, like a child awakening tensely and irritably from a terror dream.

He took her hand and held it between both of his. "How do you feel, Laura?"

"I don't know what drugs that young doctor gave me, but I ache all over and my head's going around, and I feel so long ago and far away—"

"He just gave you something to ease the pain and help you sleep—"

"Sleep! I've got skyrockets going off inside. What in the world took you so long to get here?"

"I came as soon—"

"—typical doctor's family," she swept on angrily. "Shoemaker's

152

children. Every Tom, Dick, and Harry gets instantaneous loving care. But when it comes to your own—"

"—Laura, take it easy, now. You're hurt and the drugs have you half dopey—"

"—everybody always tells me what a wonderful doctor you are—and now, here, what have you done for any of us—?"

"—actually, Laura, I'm waiting for Mendelsohn—"

"—Jerry Mendelsohn? The neurosurgeon—?"

"—yes."

"—but you're supposed to be so super-duper—"

Patiently he said, "But I'm not a neurosurgeon, and when there's really a complicated neurological problem—"

She wasn't even listening to him, he could see. "Good God! A surgeon is a doctor, isn't he!"

"Laura, for Pete's sake! Quiet down. There're people trying to sleep next door! This isn't 1925, or the movies, where the family doctor does everything. There's a reason for men like Mendelsohn because some problems take a lifetime of special training. If it were his family, and plastic surgery, he'd wait for me."

"—but a neurosurgeon! Just to sew up a few cuts and bruises!" Suddenly she stared at him wildly. "Or has something god-awful happened—?" Her eyes shut tightly—because of pain, or the sedation, he couldn't tell which—then opened with effort.

"Let me take care of everything, Laura. Everything's under control. Don't talk or fuss about it."

"—if I don't, I'll explode!"

"You won't. You'll sleep like a log and get up better."

" I know," she said with sarcasm, "it's all a bad dream."

"Try it," he said. "Just let yourself go."

"I can't. I can't. Can't you understand? I just can't!"

"Don't talk now. I just wanted to make sure you were—"

"—Carl and Stan—" Her fingers tightened between his hands. "How are they? Tell me the truth, Mac—"

"Stan's holding his own pretty well. Carl's a little off the tracks. Keeps talking about you and how sorry he is—"

"Oh, God!" Laura arched her head back into the pillow and pulled her hand free from his. She put both her hands over her eyes and

153

rolled her head in pain. "Oh, God. I didn't want to tell you till later, Mac—I wanted to explain the whole thing about Carl—"

"—Laura—"

"—oh, God, God almighty, if this is punishment for Carl and me—"

He stared at her. People became children when they were sick and hurt, and the drugs removed even more self-control, but this went screaming off far beyond pain alone. . . .

Automatically he said, "Laura, don't worry—don't talk now—"

She threw her hands off her face. Even in the dimness her eyes looked large and shining white. "Don't hush-hush me now, Mac! I've had it for ten years, your damn Christian forgiveness and sweetness and light, and I'm sick of it! I'm sorry Carl told you I want a divorce, because I wanted to tell you myself—"

"—Laura, Laura—"

"—you were never there when I needed you, never! Even tonight you took forever to get here while we were all in agony—!" She began to push herself up to a sitting position, but he held her shoulders down. She struggled against him furiously. "Take your hands off me!"

"Laura, you're hurt all over—don't thrash around like this—"

"—let go of me!"

He took his hands off her shoulders and she fell back, sobbing hysterically. He stood beside her, rigid, watching her whole body shake convulsively. It was impossible to believe this was all happening to them. It couldn't. Not to them. He had seen hysteria and agony a thousand times, but for the first time he felt the sword turn in his own bowels. A minute ago he had felt there were only the practical and technical problems of an extremely difficult diagnosis, especially in his fatigued condition, and possible surgery under completely inadequate circumstances. He had been threading his way between a hundred little pressures and judgments, balancing compromise against compromise, the absence of X-ray against the minutiae of physical diagnosis, the concern about whether the blood bank had supplies of the correct types of blood Stan and Carl might need. The visit to Laura had been only to cheer her briefly and reassure himself before going back to the really serious problems—and now the earth had opened before him. The entire day's fatigue came roaring down on him all at once, and his hands began to shake. He was horrified. His

154

hands suddenly had a life of their own, shaking like fools, and he rammed them into his pockets.

Dr. Behrens came into the room quickly. "Dr. Adams, I'm sorry to—" He stopped when he saw Laura. She covered her face with her open hands, crying. Mac turned toward Dr. Behrens, unable to speak. "The man," Dr. Behrens went on, "his right arm is getting weaker and his right pupil's enlarged. His systolic pressure is climbing while his pulse drops. It sure looks like"—he glanced at Laura, and his voice slowed— "like we'll have to decide about going in or not."

"Yes," Mac said. "Yes." He patted Laura's arm mechanically, feeling numb and remote, and followed the young doctor out into the corridor. In his pockets, his hands were still shaking.

The small operating room was very quiet. One of the night-shift floor nurses was acting as a circulating nurse, carrying covered trays of sterile instruments to Miss Stepany, who was the scrub nurse now in a sterile cap, gown, and gloves. Their shoes made soft rubbery sounds in the silence, with only the little click of the metal clips on their heels to drain off static electricity and the clatter of hemostats being racked together on a Mayo stand.

Standing in the scrub room, glancing through the window of the swing door to the operating room, Mac saw the whole room reflected in the large sheet of plate glass which separated the O.R. from a small observation gallery. In the center of the reflection, Carl lay under white sheets in a halo of light. Mac thought he saw two figures move dimly behind the glass—observers? curious nurses? At this hour of the night?—then he forgot about it in the rhythm of the scrub brush on his hands and wrists and forearms. Don't think, don't think about anything, just keep going.

Beside him, Dr. Behrens said through his face mask, "Miss Stepany has your friend's head shaved."

"What?" Somehow, his hearing seemed dulled.

"Miss Stepany has his head shaved, Doctor."

Mac repressed a wave of shivering in his arms by scrubbing more briskly. "Better ask her to go over his scalp with Scotch tape to pick up all the stray bits of hair." He shut his eyes, trying hard to keep steady, the calm even steadiness of good surgery.

"We don't have Scotch tape in the O.R.—"

"—adhesive tape will do it. . . . I'd like his head on an occipital type of stand just in case I need bilateral access." Mac felt the muscles around his eyes tighten, and thought: Depend on the ritual, stop the thinking and depend on the ritual, stop the weakness and depend on strength—*you were never there when I needed you!* —no, no, don't exaggerate, don't remember, don't make judgments, maybe she's hallucinating, maybe a reaction to the drugs, everything seems bigger and worse at night when people are tired, just depend on the ritual, hold on until Mendelsohn gets here—he may disagree with the occipital headrest, the usual horizontal position might be better. . . .

"Look," he said to Dr. Behrens, opening his eyes, "we won't have much chance to talk in there. Almost surely he has a hemorrhage from the middle meningeal on the right, or one of its branches. If he doesn't—well, he doesn't, and I'd rather run the risk of a negative exploration than miss an epidural hemorrhage—and we've got to decompress his brain immediately if he does—did you get his blood type—?"

"B, Rh positive. We have four units in our bank."

"Good. While I drill the burr holes in the skull, you'd better get an I.V. going slowly in an ankle vein. You're sure he doesn't have any other source of bleeding—?"

"—I checked, I don't think he has."

"How about my boy?"

"His blood type?"

"Yes."

"AB, Rh negative. Pretty unusual."

"Never needed to know it before," Mac said, feeling guilty.

"Only one unit in the place."

"Phone Greenwich for more. Tell them it's for me."

"Our second-floor nurse is on the phone now."

"Are those people in the observation gallery nurses?"

"People? In the gallery?" Dr. Behrens stared past Mac, past the lighted operating room at the dim sheet of plate glass reflecting Carl lying on the table under the great shadowless circle of the surgical light. "I don't see anybody. Can't be nurses. The girls are really hopping tonight, God bless 'em all."

A thought struck Mac. He had been badly negligent not to think of

156

it before. He must be in worse condition than he realized. "Did you do a lumbar puncture? What'd the spinal fluid show?"

"I didn't want to try one, Doctor. I was afraid if the pressure was too high—well, I saw a guy die real sudden once. Autopsy showed medullary compression. As for cisternal puncture, I'm afraid to try one."

He's a good man, Mac thought gratefully. He's young and inexperienced, but he's capable and everything he's done has been intelligent and fast.

"If you get the blood going, I'll finish prepping him," Mac said, "then I'll rescrub and join you and drape the skull—remember, let's use an occipital headrest. D'you have one?" He heard his voice going on, improvising, planning ahead, Dr. Behrens listening carefully and nodding. The training and the discipline and the ritual and the discipline—he had stopped shivering, even though the armpits of his surgical suit were soaked through. He was much steadier now, and he desperately wanted to keep himself that way.

The night-shift floor nurse, who was acting as circulating nurse in the operating room, came running to the swing door of the scrub room. She pushed it open quickly and said, "His heart just stopped!"

Mac and Dr. Behrens dropped their scrub brushes and ran into the O.R. Mac tore the sheet off Carl and saw immediately that he lay in a pool of his body's wastes; both bowel and bladder sphincter controls were gone, a sure sign of decerebration. Carl's back was arched stiffly and the palms of his hands were turned outward. As Mac felt for a pulse, he raised each of Carl's eyelids with his free hand, at the same time snapping out, "A syringe of adrenalin, nurse. Dr. Behrens, get an ampoule of levophed going into a vein," noting as he spoke that there was no pulse and that one of Carl's eyes now showed a greatly dilated pupil. It was just what he had feared, the slow invisible rise of pressure due to bleeding over the brain during an hour's time, then, like an avalanche started by a single shout, the whole final complex of cerebral compression occurring within a few minutes. Now he was sure there had been an epidural hemorrhage under the skull, pushing downward on the brain. With quickly increasing pressure against the brain the thin-walled veins would flatten and close and the vital nerve centers controlling the heart and breath-

157

ing would be forced downward until their own blood supply was squeezed shut. One moment there was life, then, immediately, death.

He grasped the neurosurgical drill lying on the Mayo stand in his ungloved bare hands, sterility and good technique meant nothing now. Any single burr hole was a gamble, because he had only a minute or two to create an opening—in exactly the right place— through which the pressure of the hemorrhage under the bone could escape outward. As the drill ground through the layers of bone his hands began to shake slightly and he bit down on his teeth unthinkingly until they hurt so that he could steady himself. Carl's skin was bluish-white. "The gas machine," he spit out, "give him pure oxygen! Use pressure!"

Suddenly his drill eased, and he was within the skull. As he pulled the instrument out it was followed by an oozing gush of dark clotted and fluid blood. With his other hand he took the syringe of adrenalin the nurse was holding ready and plunged the needle directly through Carl's chest into the heart muscle. Miss Stepany set the earpieces of a stethoscope into his ears and held the bell of the stethoscope directly over Carl's heart, so that he could listen yet keep his hands free. Dr. Behrens had put an intravenous needle into a leg vein and was injecting part of an ampoule of levophed directly into the plastic tube where the fluid from the hanging bottle entered Carl's body.

He's dead, Mac thought; immediately, as if he had been struck with hammers, his head began to pound violently at the temples.

In the observation gallery overlooking the operating room, two men were busily photographing the entire operation. The man with the Leica aimed, shot, advanced the film, aimed and shot again. Quietly he said to his assistant, "Load the Speed Graphic, Larry! Hurry up!"

"With Tri-X?"

"Yeah. That surgical light is terrific, and I don't want flash." He shot a frame, and then said, "It's the documentary look I want, all highlight and shadow."

As he loaded the larger camera, the assistant said, "I slipped the cop ten bucks."

"Five'd be plenty, Larry."

"For a tip-off like this? This is bigger than that Post Road smash he called us on, and you gave him ten that time."

"Remember, we gotta say thanks to the nurses with nylons or some damn thing."

"We'll hit every wire service for top dollar with this one. One gift more or less won't hurt us. The cop said the guy on the table is the buddy of the doctor. And that's his own kid in E.W., remember."

"Did you get some establishing shots in the E.W.?"

"Both outside and inside. Half a roll."

"The kid I'd like to save for one of the picture magazines. Y'know, a real spread. C'mon, Larry, don't take all night to load that thing."

"Can I help it? I can't stand watching him drill into that big guy's skull."

"Give it here. I'll do it, schmoo."

"Here. And don't forget the ten bucks I get back."

"You'll get it, you'll get it, you leech." He loaded the bigger press camera with high-speed film and then carefully aimed his viewfinder toward the operating room, like a gun.

"Mac," Mendelsohn said, "it could have happened to anybody."

"I waited too long. I should have gone in sooner, Jerry."

"Of course, you should. That's happened to me, too. It's easy later to say what one should have done."

"I waited too long. Just too damn long."

"No, you were right to wait. But of all the critical situations in head injury, epidural hemorrhage heads the list, Mac. I'm not saying this just to make you feel better. I've watched patients for hours, then, in the three minutes I've stepped out into the hall to write the orders, I've had them suddenly go out."

"Jerry, you don't have to be kind—"

"Kind, hell! Mac, this is clinical common sense—"

"I made a mistake and he's dead. You call that common sense?"

"Mac, stop walking around. Stop knocking yourself out. Anybody could have made the same mistake—"

"Not you. You would have gone in sooner."

Mendelsohn shrugged. "Maybe so. Who's to know?" He was sitting up on the edge of the desk in the little office off the emergency ward,

159

smoking quietly and watching Mac pace the room. "Mac," he said, "you don't know how exhausted you look. If we have to operate on Stan I'll need you, and I'd rather have you rested a little."

"Jerry, I can't. I feel as if I've been shot between the eyes."

"I know, I know, Mac. I know he was a friend of yours."

"—and Laura's," Mac added tensely, remembering: *I didn't want to tell you till later—I wanted to explain the whole thing. . . .*

"It's never a good idea to treat your own family or friends," Mendelsohn said. "Obstetricians don't even deliver their own wives. You can't possibly be objective."

"That's why I'm glad you're here, Jerry." He stopped pacing. "You're sure we're wise in waiting with Stan?"

"If he were a stranger, what would you say?"

"Well, he's pale and sleepy now, but he's not in shock—"

"Not so fast. If I've learned anything in twenty years, Mac, it's that the usual shock picture of injury to the extremities or viscera doesn't hold true for the nervous system."

"Well," Mac said, "his pressure is 90 over 60. Pulse was 120 when you came. It's 76 now. Respiration's 18. His pupils are equal and react to light."

"Right. All not so bad, so far, wouldn't you say? Did you feel there was any deviation of the left eye?"

"No. But when I took a look inside I thought I saw some mild venous pulsations behind the retina and minute bilateral subhyaloid hemorrhages."

"I agree. For a tired man, you've got a sharp eye."

"The borderline suggestion of bilateral extensor plantar reflexes bothers me."

"Me too, Mac. Now you see it, now you don't."

Jerry Mendelsohn swung his legs off the desk and stood up. It was clear to Mac that Jerry was being very kind, taking him through the examination findings on Stan step by step, very objectively, so that Mac could do for himself what no one else could do for him—recover his nerve. Or, at least, recover enough to help Stan.

"All right, Mac," Mendelsohn said. "If Stan were my boy, what would you tell me?"

Mac hesitated. "I'd—" and somehow he heard: *you were never there when I needed you* and he again saw Carl's blue-white body arching backward in the spasm of dying. He tried to wipe his mind clear to answer Jerry Mendelsohn. "I'd say it was borderline, Jerry. Fifty-fifty. Maybe a subdural hemorrhage."

"I agree. Probably a few of the bridging veins are torn. It's a reasonable diagnosis."

"If we wait, a clot might form and organize. You can remove it later, when he's in better shape for surgery and you can do a completely detailed workup on your own service with your own team."

"So what would you tell me, Mac?"

"To watch him, and wait a little longer."

Mendelsohn stubbed out his cigarette. "All right, Mac? Isn't that what we're doing? But let's scrub up and stand by in the O.R., just in case."

At the door, Mac stopped. "Jerry—"

"What's the matter, Mac?"

"I can't even begin to thank you."

"Don't try. Tomorrow, when Stan's better, we'll both be thanking God."

They were both wrong. An hour later Stan suddenly became very pale, his heart and pulse slowed, and his sleepiness began to slip toward stupor.

Mac stood beside him in the operating room. "Stan," he said, "how do you feel?"

Stan's voice was weaker now. "—head hurts—"

"We're going to take care of that, Stan. Tomorrow you'll wake up feeling fine. Can you hear me all right?"

"—sure—"

Mac turned to Jerry Mendelsohn, who was swabbing Stan's shaven scalp with an antiseptic solution. "What's your choice of anesthesia, Jerry?"

Mendelsohn glanced briefly at Stan, then up at Mac. "All things considered, I'd prefer local."

"Good enough, with adrenalin."

The circulating nurse nodded at Mac to show him she had heard and went to the supply cabinet. Mac bent over Stan again.

161

"Stan. Stan, are you listening—?"

Stan's eyelids fluttered open. "Yes—"

"Scared, son?"

"Not with you here—"

"Well, I'll be here all along. Stan, we're going to put some more medicine in the skin on your head. You'll feel noise and everything up there, sort of like when the dentist filled your tooth, remember? Stan—remember?"

Stan's eyes opened again, sleepily. "Uh-huh."

"Don't let the noise up there bother you. You'll feel as if your head is made of wood."

"Okay, Dad."

The brain itself had no pain sensations, so that after Jerry Mendelsohn got through the anesthetized layers of the scalp and through the bone, there would be very little problem of additional anesthesia. It was wonderful to have Jerry as the operator, because his years of experience meant skill, and skill meant speed, and speed meant they might be able to handle the whole operation with local anesthetics without the risks of putting Stan to sleep. It meant that Mac might be able to talk to Stan during the operation, to reassure him, to give him the transfusion of courage he needed as much as the bottle of blood suspended above his right ankle for replacement transfusion. Other patients had told Mac what it was like, to be half conscious while the surgeons attacked the bony fortress of the skull.

Jerry had finished prepping the scalp and was changing into sterile gown and gloves. Miss Stepany moved the tray of instruments closer to the head of the table while the circulating nurse reached up high to adjust the huge surgical light into precise focus on the operative field.

"Stan," Mac said, "now I have to put your hands into these leather cuffs so you won't wave them around while you're sleepy. Hear me?"

"My head hurts worse, Dad—"

"We'll fix that real soon."

As he put Stan's thin wrists into the heavy leather restraints, a tremor ran through him. The boy looked very small under the sheets, and, with his swollen eyes and his shaved head bathed by light, so

162

vulnerable. As Mac looked down at him another tremor racked him and he had to stand tightly still for a moment to regain control. Stan closed his eyes. In sudden terror, Mac quickly lifted each eyelid. Both pupils were normal, and Stan stirred his hands. Mac sagged with relief. It seemed impossible that Carl had lain dead on this table two hours ago.

Suddenly Mac bent forward and kissed his son's cheek. Fear locked in his chest so that he could hardly breathe.

"We're ready, Mac," Jerry Mendelsohn said calmly. "I'll drape him and start the debridement while you get into your gown. Unless you'd rather debride yourself."

"No, no, Jerry. Go ahead." He turned away from the shining table, feeling broken.

A half hour later the scalp wounds had been cleaned completely and Mendelsohn pointed to the four key points on Stan's scalp for the exploratory burr holes. There was no need to speak, with Mac as his first assistant. Everything was running smoothly. Their team was adequate, with Dr. Behrens as second assistant and Miss Stepany as the sterile scrub nurse to pass instruments. The circulating nurse adjusted the drip-drop rate of the blood transfusion Stan was getting through an ankle vein and then returned to recording his vital signs. There were only the tiny metallic clicks of instruments and the even glareless flood of light. Mendelsohn picked up the drill.

"Stan," Mac said, "you're going to hear that noise now in your head, but you won't feel it. Stan, d'you hear me?"

Very sleepily and quietly, Stan said, "Dad—?"

"Yes, Stan. Did you hear me? Don't mind the noise. You won't feel anything hurt, just the noise." He nodded to Jerry Mendelsohn and, when the burr entered, he felt it as if it had struck his own body.

After the last burr hole, Jerry inspected the sheet of tissue inside which covered the brain itself. "Mac," he said, "there's a dark bulge near the coronal suture. Want to check it?"

"No, Jerry. Go ahead."

"I'm going to turn back a bone flap and incise the dura. It's a subdural hemorrhage, just as we thought. With better exposure we can get it all out."

163

As Jerry slid the slender metal saw back and forth to make a small window through the skull, Mac thought: We're almost there now. Everything has gone just right. We didn't even have to risk general anesthesia. Stan is still conscious. We're ahead. The odds are on our side. He moved his gloved fingers slightly, feeling the circulation return in them. Without his realizing it, he had been holding his hands rigidly to keep them from shaking.

Jerry turned back the newly made bone flap and exposed the bluish protrusion. They were near success now. Expertly he made a star-shaped incision in the tough sheet of tissue which was bulging, and dark blood spurted from it immediately. Mac quickly inserted the vacuum sucker tip to evacuate the hemorrhage and relieve the pressure on the brain beneath.

"Not too fast," Mendelsohn said warningly. "Decompress slowly." Just as he spoke, one of Stan's hands began to tremble beneath the sterile drape, then his whole arm and shoulder began to shake violently. Mendelsohn and the nurse checking Stan's heart and blood pressure spoke at the same time.

"Jacksonian seizure!" Mendelsohn said.

"Doctor, his heart just stopped!"

Mac dropped the vacuum tubing, and everything began to happen at once. "Endotracheal tube!" he shouted to Dr. Behrens. Mendelsohn said quietly and quickly to Mac, "I think we'd better open his chest, Mac. It's cardiac standstill. You intubate him while I go in."

Mac nodded numbly and swiftly reached for the endotracheal tube which would keep Stan's lungs inflated with oxygen while his heart was massaged back to life.

Mendelsohn felt for the space between the ribs and with a single forceful scalpel stroke went cleanly through the intercostal muscles. He forced the small ribs apart to insert his gloved hand past the lungs so that he could grasp the heart. A moment later the collapsed lungs began to expand slowly as Mac got oxygen flowing through the tube in Stan's mouth and throat.

Jerry Mendelsohn's hand was pumping, squeezing, pumping, squeezing, with a pulselike rhythm. Mac seized the nearest syringe and swiftly injected blood-pressure stimulants into Stan's arm vein. He felt Stan's pulse. There was a slow beat in it now as Mendelsohn's

164

hand tightened repeatedly around Stan's heart, imitating the heart's own pumping action.

Fifteen minutes went by in complete silence. A half hour. Mac knelt beside Stan, hardly noticing that his surgical suit stuck wetly to his back. He felt a great coldness come over him. He looked at Jerry Mendelsohn. "Maybe if we open the pericardium—"

Jerry grunted agreement. His forehead was beaded with sweat and the rim of his surgical cap was dark with it. He paused in the steady cardiac massage just long enough to take the scissors Mac handed him, and opened the tissue covering the heart muscle with a single cut. Mac leaned forward and very carefully dripped some procaine on the naked central muscle of the body. Jerry immediately reinserted his hand and began the artificial heartbeat again. "Mac"— he said, breathing hard through his mask—"my hand—my fingers —tired—"

Mac swung to Miss Stepany. "Let me have some new gloves—" and, when she opened a fresh sterile package of gloves, he quickly rammed his hands into them and knelt again beside Stan. The moment Jerry removed his hand from the interior of Stan's chest, Mac leaned forward and plunged his own hand past the lungs to grasp the boy's heart. It was startlingly warm and firm in his gloved hand and he opened his mouth widely beneath his face mask, breathing with pain, as he tried to wring life back into his son's body.

How much later it was he did not know, but suddenly the fistsized muscle in his hand took on an inner life of its own and began to beat. He pulled his hand back, trembling.

"Going—?" Jerry whispered.

He nodded. Together they looked into the rib cage, with the pink lungs rising and falling slowly, watching the dark meaty ball of muscle at the center, beating again. They watched it carefully for ten minutes, twenty minutes, until Stan's color improved. Stan half opened his eyes and looked at his father.

The surgeons stared at each other. "I think I can close the pericardium now," Mac said. His mouth was so dry he could hardly speak.

Miss Stepany passed Mac the needle threaded with a suture to

165

begin to close the sac of tissue around the heart. Just as he took the first stitch, the heart stopped again.

"Oh God—" He groaned aloud, and threw the needle aside to grasp the heart again. From that point onward he had no recollection of time, because he became a machine with a hand which opened and closed around Stan's heart. He did not remember refusing Jerry Mendelsohn's offer to take over the cardiac massage. He remembered nothing and knew nothing and felt nothing except that life must flow from his body into his son's.

Two hours later his arm and hand suddenly no longer obeyed his will and he fell forward on his face.

He sat in Laura's room at the end of the hospital corridor, sitting stiffly in one of the two visitor's chairs in the room. The faint light of dawn sifted between the tilted blinds.

They had all been very kind. They had tried to give him coffee, some orange juice, anything. He had refused. They had untied his surgeon's gown and peeled off his rubber gloves, and then he had pushed them aside, completely without speech. He did not know how he came to be there, but now he found himself in Laura's room, staring sightlessly at the thin rim of light rising in the sky.

Laura slept immovably, hardly seeming to breathe. He wanted to throw himself beside her, to weep, but he could only sit and stare at the light. For the first time in his life he felt the ultimate human condition. He was completely alone.

(3)

EVEN now, sitting half asleep in Obenpharo's plane flying to Tangier, with Spain a faraway cashmere landscape beneath him, he could look back with complete recollection at that one particular time because it marked such a clear-cut ending and such a definitely new beginning.

It was not that he was trying to forget his life at home. Auto accidents, and infidelity, were more commonplace and tiresome than daily weather reports, as any newspaper would prove, and that was why his idea was to look squarely at the memory and honestly recognize the pain attached to it and then to chip away at the part which hurt until all that was gone and only the memory remained, mute and manageable.

He had tried very hard to be sensible, not to think of Laura or his son, Stan, or of Carl, or even of himself as the sort of person he had been only six months ago. During that period he had had a good deal of time for introspection, something he once had disliked in others and never considered possible in himself. Living alone did that, he had heard, and now he believed it. You thought to yourself, almost as if it were a conversation.

Go ahead, he would think, run downstairs into the cellar of your mind and feel around in the dark for something interesting we can look at. Something that will explain your failure with your wife, or hers with you, or of this century with its citizens, or the price of potatoes in Idaho.

No, why go to the trouble? Freud was able to do it, playing blindman's buff in his psyche, but you're not that smart, friend. You don't have that mittel-Europa training in philosophy. And you're not that tough.

Tough as nails, friend. To survive the past half year, to come out of it on your feet, not crawling, that wasn't easy. A little tremor of the hands, occasionally, especially after a sleepless night, but after all that had been a rough ride, these last few months, a really rough ride.

His last day in the States, before he had left for Paris, was one of those remarkable days possible only in the middle of the twentieth century. He had had breakfast in Connecticut, lunch in New York, and dinner over the Atlantic Ocean en route to Paris. Each meal was unique because of his awareness that everything in his life was changing overnight and would never be the same again. It was a little as if he had decided on a special kind of exile, and each last contact with each room of the home he had lived in all his life, except for the war years, was magnified in feeling. He seemed to experience everything more intensely and notice little things which he could not remember ever having noticed before.

He had had breakfast in the glassed-in alcove off the kitchen of his

167

home in Greenwich. In the distance, he had been able to see the water of Long Island Sound glittering like blue ice between the trees. It made him remember the morning about a year back when he and Laura and Stan had sat at breakfast and Laura had said without any preliminaries, "Those three big elms will have to come down. If they're out of the way we'll be able to see the Sound from here."

"What for, Mom?" Stan had said. "You can see it from the library and from upstairs."

Laura had looked across the lawn and through the trees as if they were cut down and gone already, as if the Sound could be glimpsed in the distance like her memories of her childhood at her father's shore place. "I just like the idea, I'd like to see the Sound from anywhere in the house," she had said. "I like a room with a view, with some kind of vista."

"*Hasta la vista*," Mac had said, then regretted it immediately because he suddenly realized she was recalling the years when her father was living and he and Laura did so much sailing together.

Laura made a face. "Your taste for puns, really, Mac."

He put his coffee down. Stan said nothing because he sensed there was something larger here between his mother and father than three trees or a view of the water.

"Laura, those elms are over two hundred years old." Mac looked at the trees, wondering why she suddenly wanted to cut down something. "Hell's bells, I fell out of that near one when I was Stan's age and fractured my fibula."

"Is that the name of a leg bone or an arm bone, Dad?"

"Do we have to take a medical approach to this, too? We have hundreds of those elms all over the place, Mac. And you yourself said two weeks ago the biggest one might have Dutch elm disease starting in the crown. If it does, we'll do ourselves a favor by getting rid of it now." She sounded pleasant and sensible, perhaps because Stan was there.

"It's hard to explain, Laura. They were there for generations while this was a farmhouse. They've had a lot of growing."

The Hutchins boy from down the road had come pedaling into view just then on his new lightweight English racing bicycle, and Stan had dashed outside with greyhound speed.

168

"Mac, you sound so cloistered. You're usually the first to laugh at ancestor worship."

Mac looked at his watch. He was sorry they had started on this. He was scheduled to operate on the Minelli baby whose hand had been caught in a laundry wringer, with some tricky tendon grafts which would delay Mrs. Grayson's operation. And ward rounds at eleven, and senior staff conference at twelve-thirty, and office hours all afternoon, and the two young French doctors training under him on a U.N. grant were coming for dinner. It was one of those days that seemed to be coming along almost every day now.

"Mac," Laura was saying, "you're always so protective, so cozy and fix-it-up and make-it-last and don't-cut-it-down. So middle class, dear."

"I was sort of afraid we'd get around to the middle class, Laura."

"Oh, dear, you're becoming such a successful stuffy doctor."

He stood up. "If you need a new vista, Laura, go ahead and cut them down."

She looked up at him suddenly. "You sound like the voice of doom, like what's his name in *The Cherry Orchard,* Mac."

"Never heard of it." He was putting on his vest and coat.

"Chekov, and you know it. Don't give me your gee-I-only-know-medicine act, please. You must have learned something at Yale besides boola-boola."

"He was a good doctor, Chekov. I've read his stories. I think he'd let the trees stand. Just on general principles."

"Must you wear that vest? Why don't you wear that cashmere pullover I just bought you?"

"What for, Laura?"

She smiled a little to herself and shook her head tolerantly.

"Because a sweater is so *casual,* dear. You're being so, so I don't know, so *untouchable* this morning."

"Now when do I have a chance to be *casual,* dear?" He knew he sounded childish, aping her intonation, but he was annoyed by a vague feeling of being boxed in, how or why he didn't know. Laura was a lovely girl, but every so often this kind of thing happened even though there was hardly anything tangible enough to lay your hand on and say: This is where it began.

169

Laura was standing now, her eyes looking larger. "Mac," she had said, "do you feel I'm sort of cutting down your childhood?"

"Do we have to be Freudian?" he had said. "Now? Right after Chekov and breakfast?"

"But do you know what I'm talking about, Mac? Don't you feel closed in sometimes? You used to like to look at distances as much as I do, and now you just look at your watch."

"Good thing I've got one. I'm late at the hospital." He knew he sounded banal, but somehow he couldn't match her mood of suggestive recollection. He knew he should have talked to her then, right there that morning, but he didn't have the time, and after all they were waiting for him down at the hospital. Or maybe he could have found the time, but he did not have the courage.

He had kissed her lightly on the brow. "You're right, Laura. Cut 'em down. I'll enjoy a view of the Sound at breakfast as much as you."

The whole conversation had come back to him that morning as he sat finishing his last breakfast in the house before leaving for New York and Paris. The letter from Laura's Reno lawyer lay on the table in front of him in a long tricolor-bordered airmail envelope. He could see the water of the Sound shining clearly through the trees, but he turned away from the sight of it.

The real estate people were outside and he could hear the furniture appraisers upstairs finishing their inventory. Mr. Grimmett, senior, of Grimmett and Sons, Realtors, had said, "I know you want to make a clean sweep of everything, Dr. Adams, but no kidding, it's a whole lot easier to move a house in today's market if prospects see the place while it's still furnished." Mr. Grimmett had been in Greenwich so long he no longer sold anything. He *moved* them. Mr. Grimmett, and a man and woman in identical tweed sport coats, came around the corner of the house, with Mr. Grimmett talking and making alternate sweeping gestures with one arm at a time. He was probably calling attention to the new clover-leaf pool Laura had put in two years ago, and the stables, and the smaller outbuildings where the land sloped toward the meadows, and the unusually fine view of Long Island Sound. Mr. Grimmett's advertisement in the *New York Times* had read: "Famous historical home—Revolution-

170

ary period background—reflecting throughout a rare taste in studied informality."

If his family had not owned the farm for a long time, Mac would not have purchased it as these real estate clients probably would. He had seen so many "charming" farmhouses being "done over" that when Laura's friends in New York talked of doing over a charming farmhouse he consciously had taught himself to keep quiet.

And now, there he sat while the whole place, right down to the clothespins, was being sold out. At first he had thought of keeping some of Stan's things, Stan's first electric train, and the little microscope, the Cub Scout pin, and then he had realized how morbid a clinging it was and he had made arrangements to give everything away.

It was not until he was driving through the entrance gates without looking back, going past the small white-painted board sign, ADAMS FARM, which Laura had wanted to change to a wrought-iron HILLTOP HOUSE, one of the few disagreements on which she had surrendered, it was not until then that he realized that he was beginning to feel sorry for himself, and that he would probably never come back. He had stopped the car suddenly and turned to look at the house through the green elms of spring, and with a sudden impulse—he who believed he could never be impulsive again—he stepped out to lift the small farm sign off its hooks and lay it face downward on the back seat.

He had met Evelyn Desmond after a late lunch at the United Nations Secretariat in New York that same afternoon. He hadn't seen Evelyn for years, and meeting her again that day somehow changed time in his mind so that past and present became one. It was all part of that very special twenty-four hours.

The feeling of the morning had remained with him on the drive all the way into New York, and Professor Turneau of the World Health Organization had been very patient with Mac's absent-mindedness during lunch. The Professor had even tried being hearty.

"*Alors,* Dr. Adams, you will manage like all the Americans to arrive at Paris in the springtime."

"Arrive when?" Mac found the quiet professorial voice hard to

171

follow with three different languages being spoken at the same time on each side and directly behind him.

A man's voice said pleasantly, *"Je peux vous offrir quelque chose à boire?"*

An intense woman's voice said, *"Que cosa mas mala es la guerra."*

"Springtime. *Printemps,*" Professor Turneau was saying.

"Well, actually," Mac said, thinking of the airmail letter from Reno that morning, "I just waited until my decks were clear of all lawyers' letters and such legal matters."

"Ah, Dr. Adams, you take my saying too serious. I was making a little joke, you know? Actually, I have too much respect in your—" He searched for the English word. "I mean what you are doing, taking time on your last day in the U.S.A. to see me directly about our postgraduate students."

"Patric and Lescamp are both good men, Professor," Mac said. "They will be excellent plastic surgeons when they go back to France to practice."

Professor Turneau bent his head slightly. "Thank you." Now that they were on an official subject he was quite formal.

"They show great ability, both of them," Mac said. "Before leaving I wanted to do one thing, to see you, personally, about them."

"You could have written from Paris."

"Would that have been the same?"

Professor Turneau smiled a little. "No, it is better that you come."

"I'm glad to hear it. No letter can really tell about a young doctor's promise. His honesty with a patient who is dying, his dishonesty when he needs to be dishonest with another patient who can't last another day. His intelligence to consider the choice, his courage to make the choice. You see what I mean? Both Patric and Lescamp have this, and I can't put it into a letter."

"The surgical part, the cutting, you make that part sound not so important, Dr. Adams."

"It's important, but any intelligent man or woman can learn how to handle the knife. It's making the decisions about the patient, the patient as a human being with fears and doubts and a demanding job and debts, making the decisions before the operation, and all the watchfulness about infection and pain afterward, not just in the

172

hospital, but until the patient is home and living and working again—"
He stopped. "My favorite subject. I always bore people with it."

"No, no. No, really. Please finish."

"Well, I'm finished. Some doctors have that invisible thing, some others are very skillful but they just don't have it. Patric and Lescamp do."

Professor Turneau waved one hand to indicate the whole modernistic multilingual room. "But we are a big organization. A bureaucracy complicated by a hundred languages. We need something, as you say, in black and white."

"Hell's bells," Mac said.

"A letter over your signature," Professor Turneau said persuasively, "that could mean funds for another year of study for both young men. Send it from Paris."

"I'm going to vanish in Paris. Just disappear," Mac said. "That's half the trick. I'm not even going to a hotel. A friend of mine is loaning me his houseboat. No more reporters, no more flash pictures. No more schedules or committee meetings. And by God no more surgery."

"No more surgery? Is that possible?"

"Not possible. Definite."

"But you are an active man, not a Left Bank loafer."

"I'm going to do what I haven't had time for since medical school. Sculpture. In the last generation there've been Horatio Stone, Theodatus Ganlick, William Rimmer, and Robert Tait McKenzie. They were all surgeons and good sculptors. Not great, not Maillol or Rodin, but good. Well, I'm going to make healthy faces. If my hands can still control the clay." He could feel the mood of the morning running through him with the view of the blue water through the newly green elms, and he suddenly recalled taking the worn board gate sign off its hooks. Maybe that was why he was talking so much; he wasn't explaining to Turneau, he was simply reassuring himself. "Today's a special day for me. I'm starting all over while I can and before it's too late. This is my last chance to do as I please. I'm going to learn human structure and function as a sculptor does, not a doctor."

Professor Turneau smiled a little. "For a plastic surgeon, is there

173

any difference? Aren't all plastic surgeons artists at heart?" He was too intelligent a man to expect Mac to answer that, so he threw his napkin on the table and pushed his chair back. "How many hours do you have until your flight time?"

Mac glanced at his watch. "Two hours and twenty-five minutes."

The Professor stood up, smiling more broadly. "How precise. An American answer."

"Take off one hour lost in afternoon traffic. You're not going to insist on that letter, are you?" Mac asked as they began to walk between the tables out of the vaulted room.

"No, of course not. But it will be needed if you recommend we get funds for these men to stay in the States one more year." Professor Turneau thought for a moment. "Look here. Come to my office. Dictate the letter in twenty-five minutes. We hold a car for you downstairs. *Voilà,* you are on time at the International Airport."

"As we say in Brooklyn," Mac said, "you just got yourself a deal, Professor."

Professor Turneau's outer office was a luminous carpet-hushed air-conditioned cube overlooking the stone pile of Manhattan. A man and woman, both in uniforms carrying a good deal of gold braid, were silhouetted against the sky at the side of the room. Several typewriters were mutely tip-tapping away in different languages, and Mac wondered which of the girls would be interrupted to take down his hurried letters of recommendation for Patric and Lescamp.

Just then the uniformed woman turned. Mac stared at her, a memory beginning to stir quickly. She stared back too, until the man with her stopped what he was saying and looked at Mac.

At the same moment they recognized one another.

"Mac! Maccabeus the Adams!"

"Eve! Well, I'll be damned!"

Dr. Evelyn Desmond and Dr. Malcolm Adams met in the middle of the room in a bear hug that was all arms and talking at once, and the young secretaries stopped typing to watch and smile at such an unusual exhibition of feeling in older people, people as far along as their mid-thirties.

"Mac, of all the pleasant surprises!"

"I should have saluted, Eve! You look like a general!"

174

"Colonel, sir. Star rank in the Reserves comes only with senility."

The tall man behind her smiled broadly and said, "Now, Eve, Congress keeps all the stars in its own pockets. Don't blame the Public Health Service."

Eve turned. "Mac, let me introduce my temporary boss, Surgeon-General Steele." As the men shook hands, Eve said, "Dr. Adams was my first big collegiate crush."

"Collegiate! Eve, you were in medical school by then."

"The way I mooned and swooned," Eve smiled, "that was collegiate. Lordy, this makes me feel ten years younger and five pounds thinner!"

Professor Turneau was feeling left out. "Adams and Eve," he said hopefully, "if you will permit a joke, Dr. Desmond."

With Evelyn Desmond there things had begun to move more and more quickly. Sitting now in Obenpharo's plane, Mac smiled a little to himself. Looking down at the brown Spanish earth, he found himself remembering it all clearly. It had been a unique twenty-four hours, from start to finish. Eve's vitality and directness, the bright-eyed schooltime period of his life she represented, gave him a roller-coaster sensation after all the pedestrian days and years of scheduled living. His solitary breakfast in Connecticut and its feeling of farewell and remembrance of things past had left him feeling detached, elegiac. Eve had changed all that. The shy and silent caterpillar of medical school had sprouted wings, not of a butterfly, but of an eagle.

"Paris!" she had said. "What luck! I'm leaving for Paris too! Tomorrow. See you there the day after."

"Oh no," he had said, "we're having dinner together tonight on the Paris plane."

Her eyes began to gleam. "But my reservations—" she began.

"Give me your tickets," Mac said. "Gregory at Pan-American is a former patient, and he runs the joint."

"But my housekeeper. I mean, you know, packing things and—"

"Give me your phone number. She shall be persuaded by a tongue of silver and a voice of brass."

She clapped her forehead. "My orders, my official travel orders. They're dated tomorrow."

Mac swung to the Surgeon-General who by this time had begun

175

chatting with Professor Turneau. "Doctor," he said, "may I interrupt? If I loan you my pen, can you change the date on Dr. Desmond's orders to today?"

"I don't see why not," the Surgeon-General said. "I signed them in the first place."

Mac swung back to Eve. "See? Simple."

"Brass," she said, "you were right. But there's a but. We have a conference at four with the U.N. press and radio people."

"Call them right now. Ask them to come right up. Or meet them downstairs. Will that be possible, Professor? Fine. While you and the Surgeon-General straighten out the reporters on international health, I'll get your housekeeper started packing, and change our tickets, dictate a letter I came here for—"

"I'll loan you my car to the airport," the Surgeon-General said. "Barrens used to drive a taxi, so you can imagine the rest."

"So," Eve said, "you're in this plot with him, too!"

"No," said the Surgeon-General. "I only want you to arrive in Paris with that look in your eyes. I have selfish motives."

"Mac, I'm overwhelmed," Eve said. "I'm just a simple country girl, you know."

The Surgeon-General laughed. "Not at the Paris Conference, please, not on our time. You're supposed to make vigorous noises, sort of a ladylike time bomb." To Mac he said, "Thanks for lighting the fuse, Dr. Adams."

"Synchronize your watches, men," Eve chortled, "we attack at dawn."

Changing the plane tickets had been more difficult than Mac had expected, but Gregory at Pan-Am had finally managed to do it. The remaining arrangements had gone smoothly, with everyone catching Mac's wave of fast-talking enthusiasm. He even managed to dictate the letter for Patric and Lescamp. Aristotle was wrong, Mac remembered he had thought as they came out of the U.N. Secretariat. Give me not a lever but a hyperthyroid and I will move the world.

The U.N. press and radio people had hurriedly interviewed Eve and the Surgeon-General on the wide curving plaza below the heroic procession of national flags. The green-glass marble honeycomb of the U.N. Secretariat Building hung in the sky overhead behind them,

176

its windows offering a thousand mirrors to the stone city, clean-lined, air-conditioned, hopeful.

"Dr. Desmond," the Surgeon-General was saying rapidly to the reporters, "is a pediatrician who has made a subspecialty of respiratory illness in children. She is an assistant professor of pediatrics at the Cornell School of Medicine and was promoted today to the Public Health Service rank of Medical Director. That's the equivalent of Colonel, as you may know. Suppose you take it from there, Dr. Desmond."

"Yes, sir," Eve said. She was smooth, efficient, precise. "Tuberculosis is the problem which concerns my current assignment. Even with our new so-called wonder drugs, tuberculosis is still a common and serious disease in the United States. In Europe and North Africa a preventive vaccine called BCG has been given to millions of children. In this country we have not given it to our children, for many good and very technical reasons. I will visit the countries in Europe and North Africa which have kept careful statistics of their results. What are the criteria of giving or withholding the BCG vaccine? Has the incidence of tuberculosis really gone down in some countries, or is any decrease more apparent than real?"

As she went on, Mac glimpsed a world of medicine which he had never thought about and which the public hardly knew. Eve had become one of the new breed of physicians, doctors international, preventive medicine experts whose decisions affected millions of children and adults. They treated whole continents, and instead of little black doctor bags they carried shiploads of DDT and penicillin and calculating machines to check their astronomical statistics and diplomatic passports so they could drop in on Paris or Geneva or Casablanca as busily as family doctors making house calls. It was like the food distribution system of a big city—so basic to human life, so complex and organized and impersonal that no one noticed its hugeness any more than he noticed the enormous ocean of air he breathed each day.

I've been dealing with one patient at a time, Mac thought, as he listened to her cool non-technical explanation of BCG, the Bacillus Calmette-Guérin vaccine, and to her diplomatic references to this French bacteriological achievement, just one patient at a time while she thinks in terms of entire populations. He had been a little startled

177

when she had said, in answer to one of the reporters' questions, "Tuberculosis of the bone? Well, luckily, an old friend is going to Europe with me, Dr. Malcolm Adams, gentlemen. Dr. Adams is a plastic surgeon who can tell you what bone destruction does." She swung toward Mac, smiling, pleased that she had made him a participant.

Suddenly, standing there on the breeze-swept plaza beneath the parade of flags, he was the center of attention. As he quickly put together a brief description of bone repair he could sense what was coming.

One of the group of reporters, an American, asked the inevitable. "Are you the Dr. Adams up in Connecticut who was—?"

"Yes," Mac interrupted. "But shall we stick to the subject?"

Eve was even smart enough and disciplined enough to know when to slow down and stop. On the Pan-Am plane that same evening, sitting beside him in a handsome gray suit and bright silk blouse that made her seem like a different person than the uniformed woman officer of the afternoon, she had let herself lean back with a little sigh. "Do you mind ordering dinner, Maccabeus? I'm numb with fatigue."

"Why do you call me Maccabeus? That's the second time today."

"Didn't I ever tell you in school?"

"Never."

"Maybe you never asked me, Mac."

"Maybe it never occurred to me."

"Oh, Mac, you make me feel a little sad. The things that never occurred to you then. You were such a clean, intelligent, promising *fool!* The last Puritan. The dreamer and the doer all mixed up."

Mac couldn't help smiling a little. "Spare the rod, madam. You're talking about my best friend. He means well, just misguided." For a moment—especially the phrase about the last Puritan—she had sounded just like Laura, and a thin sliver of distaste had scratched him. Perhaps it was inescapable that American women were character carpenters who thought of their men as lumber, good raw material, but in need of some hammering and sandpapering before becoming satisfactory.

It wasn't until after she had finished her second cocktail that she asked him quietly, "Mac, what's been happening to you?"

"We really did lose track of one another, didn't we?" he evaded. "What happened to you these last ten years?"

She looked out the window without answering, twisting the stem of her glass back and forth. It was dark outside now, and, despite the absence of sea or landmarks, the closeness of the stars gave a feeling of being very high, no longer earthbound. "Look," she said suddenly, "isn't that Nantucket?"

Mac leaned forward. Far below them he could barely make out the outline of Nantucket Island, a darkly glinting crescent against a darker sea. For a strange moment his day-long feeling of time compressed swept over him; past and present experienced at once. His father and he had sailed up from Greenwich to Nantucket so many times, a thin serious boy and his serious father talking medicine constantly. "These new sera for pneumonia, Mac, next time you're at the hospital with me remind me to show you the Quellung reaction. Remarkable! D'you realize if the time ever comes when we can lick pneumonia—!" The world was fixed in its orbit then, the stars over Nantucket rotated in their great endless circles, and the boy lay flat on his back looking upward and listening to the hiss of their bow wash and responding to his father's enthusiasm, a fence rail of a boy filled with a huge mysterious ache to be a man and a physician. And now he was both, man and physician, and his plane to Paris was one of the shooting stars above Nantucket.

The huge humped plane engines on the near wing threw faint reflections of intense blue flames within their explosive guts, and the continuous muffled sound had a remote and faintly hypnotic quality. The hushed dimness of the long cabin, the patterns and pools of light with occasional bursts of laughter, the swift and silent movement of the air stewardesses, gave Mac the sense of intimacy of a good restaurant in which two people can talk to one another on an island of their own in a busy room.

The stewardess was suddenly there, bending toward them to take their dinner order. When Mac finished, Eve said, "Very much the boulevardier. You didn't learn about Châteauneuf-du-Pape at New York Hospital."

"Laura knew a lot about those things," Mac said. "I guess some of it rubbed off."

179

"Oh, Mac, don't sound so harsh." She put her hand on his arm lightly. "Forgive me. I know I've had two drinks and all that, but really, Mac, when will we ever see each other to talk like this again? Laura helped you, Mac. You were honest as the day is long, but you were fierce and adolescent about it, and you were crude to the point of being cruel. She polished you smooth, Mac."

"She polished me, all right."

"Does it still hurt that much, Mac?"

"Hell, no," he lied. "But you know about me. Anybody who can read a newspaper knows every bloody item about me. You were going to tell me about you."

"No, about you," she said. "I know I sound terrible about this, but I really want to know."

"Eve—"

"Dr. Desmond to you, sir. I'm taking a professional history."

"Why? What good will it do?"

"Lots of good, Mac. That hunted look you got today when the reporter spoke to you. You shouldn't look hunted, Mac."

"Those guys gave me a hard time during the past couple of months, Eve. Some of those pictures of me in the operating room while Carl was dying. The ones the picture magazine reprinted. I don't know how they ever sneaked into the O.R. balcony with their cameras."

"It's their job, Mac."

"I know, I know. I know all that."

"And you and Laura and Carl and his wife were prominent people. That's news."

"Eve, let's not be so damn logical about it. There's no logic to pain."

"Fine talk from a doctor. Pain tells you something hurts. It tells you to *do* something."

"I have. I've wound up my practice—not a single patient who wasn't completely taken care of. I finished my teaching today at U.N. with some letters of recommendation. I've sold everything I own except the clothes on my back."

"I went through all this," Eve said, "after Bill was killed in Korea. Somehow I decided I'd never marry again and that I'd better do something to fill the hole in my life with a new kind of work. So I wound up my practice, too, and went into academic medicine." She

180

paused. "Mac," she said softly, "you wouldn't be running away the way I was, would you?" When she saw the look on his face she added quickly, "I'm sorry. You don't have to talk about it."

"You're wrong. I do. I haven't until now, and I suppose that's unhealthy. You've said out loud what I've said to myself. Am I running scared? Eve, I went through France and Germany during the war and I've been scared down to my bowels, but I was rigid with fear that night."

"Oh, God. It sounds like such a terrible mixup between unhappiness and tragedy."

"You know, I had that same odd feeling of unreality during the coroner's inquest. Newspaper stories about people's lives getting messed up always sounded like stupid soap opera to me before. You know: Highway Death Toll Rises. Crash Kills Two. Not now. Not any more. When Mary Ann swore that I knew about Carl and Laura, that I'd known about them as long as she had—I guess she knew all along about the affair—and that I had let Carl die on the operating table—well, it was as if nothing of our real lives was real any more, do you know what I mean? Only these fears and hidden agonies under the everyday surface were real. You know what I mean?"

"I know."

He leaned back in the seat, suddenly realizing his fists were clenched. "Even now it doesn't seem real about Stan." He paused, then added, "His signs and symptoms in the emergency room were so shifting it was hard to decide—and I—"

"Mac—you don't have to explain—"

"—well, I called Mendelsohn to come up from New York. There isn't a better neurologic surgeon anywhere. Remember Dr. Mendelsohn with that wonderful gentle way?"

"Bless him, yes."

"Well, he finally got there at four in the morning, driving those country roads like a bat out of hell. We watched Stan, and waited. When he took a turn for the worse, Mendelsohn decided we'd operate. I assisted. It was a subdural, massive, and I should never have delayed the operation. Maybe that's what pushed him over the edge." He stopped. Eve turned away. They sat silently watching the darkness gather in the sky.

The stewardess came a little later to say dinner would be briefly

181

delayed and would they care for more champagne. Eve said yes, yes indeed, the sooner the better, and wiped her eyes when the girl left, and powdered her nose and put on fresh lipstick.

"Forgive me," he said. "I haven't talked about it before. I got started and couldn't stop."

"I was the one, Mac. I insisted."

"I know, but after a minute it's a kind of abuse. Laura used to say I was an upside-down snob, and maybe I am, because if you weren't a doctor, Eve, I don't think I would have talked so much."

"You didn't finish, you know. Laura left and got a divorce, the paper said."

"Final papers three weeks ago. Her Reno lawyer just wrote me."

"Three weeks ago. If I remember my brief surgical experience, aren't twenty-one days needed for scar tissue to form?" She smiled faintly to assure him it was a special kind of joking, then looked up. "Ah, here's dinner. Just in time, too. I don't know if we're maudlin, or just in hypoglycemic starvation. I was about to bite you." She lifted her empty glass. "If you please, Dr. Adams. The patient badly requires additional medication."

As he poured, he said, "You're asking for treatment without a diagnosis. That's not fair."

"Who wants to be fair?"

He smiled. "That's a primitive comment, coming from a lady colonel."

"And that's the first time you've smiled at me, you great stone face. The first time since we met at U.N. this afternoon."

"Do a good deed, meet a pretty girl. There's a moral in it somewhere." He recognized she was trying very hard to change their mood to something more gay, and he wanted to try, too. Diving deep to dredge up the past felt like a form of drowning. Let it rest in peace.

Eve finished her glass and held it upside down to prove it was empty, then lifted it toward him for refilling. "I'm shameless tonight. I've heard that conscience is the alcohol-soluble portion of the personality, and tonight"—she paused to sip her fresh drink—"tonight I want very much to feel younger and brighter than I have in years. Maybe the specific remedy for unhappiness is happiness."

182

"Sure, and it comes so conveniently in bottles."

"Oh no, on hot plates. Mm, just taste that fillet! You know, I don't sound even the least little bit drunk to me, but I must sound disgraceful."

"You sound fine, Eve."

"You lie so gracefully. What worldly success does for a man."

"You sound champagne-ish, Eve. Nice and bubbly."

"Mac, you amaze me. Such fancy uninhibited talk from strong silent you."

"Maybe I'm more soluble than I realize."

She raised her eyebrows at him. "And maybe you forgot that good champagne is served cold."

"Are you one of the cold ones, Eve?"

"Do you think that's likely?"

They paused and looked at one another across the small, charged space between them. "No," he said, "but my old friend and cracker barrel colleague, Malcolm Adams, reminds me that all things are possible."

"I thought your old friend and colleague had left."

"Definitely gone. But not far."

"Leave him be. Three's a crowd."

He put his hand under her chin and turned her head toward himself so that he could bend forward to kiss her very lightly.

"Don't go away," she murmured. "That one took me by surprise." She took his face between her two hands and kissed him slowly.

"Adams and Eve," Mac said, "if you will permit a joke."

The passenger in the seat diagonally across from them nudged his wife beside him. "Look at that, honey. They think they're in Paris already."

(4)

EVE was as unexcited as a suburban commuter when they arrived in Paris the next morning. When their plane had touched down at Orly Field and taxied up to the unloading ramp, Eve said, "Look at the little crowd waiting at the gate. Do we have somebody special on board?"

"They're probably waiting for you," Mac said.

"Me?" She was surprised. "Why me?"

"My friends and countrymen," he said oratorically, "these last few months your Uncle Malcolm has learned a thing or two about news while it is news. I learned the hard way. You're news because you're a very pretty lady doctor fresh from United Nations headquarters to save the children of Europe."

"If you only knew how corny you sound," she laughed.

"The guys who interviewed you and the Surgeon-General yesterday, remember? They didn't think it was corny. You underestimate yourself."

"Yesterday. Seems like a week ago."

"That BCG stuff and the bow to French bacteriologists was on the wire to Paris pretty soon after you said it. The American Embassy must have gotten it, too, and they'd be the first to notify the press."

The stewardess was coming down the aisle in their direction, looking at them expectantly as she approached.

"Here it comes," Mac said. "You'll see. If you want to do right for God, your country, and for Yale, powder your nose for the flash cameras."

"Phooey," she said. "I'm no chorus girl." But she whipped out her compact mirror for a swift inspection, throwing him an ironic sideways smile as she did.

The stewardess was beside their seats now and leaned forward with a combined air of respect and conspiracy.

"Dr. Adams?" she said.

"Oh-oh," Eve said, and began to grin. Mac looked startled.

"The tower has requested us to hold up everyone until you can leave the plane," the stewardess explained. "A group from the American Embassy and the newspapers are waiting."

Eve was laughing at Mac now, to the girl's amazement. "You're trapped," Eve said, "hoof in mouth disease."

"I won't do it," Mac said.

"Just be thankful you shaved this morning, Mac, and don't be stubborn."

"I won't do it."

"With only one exit you have no choice. This is for God, for country, and for Yale."

Her amusement about the situation made him feel a trifle pompous, but dammit, he thought, even the friendliest reporters have made me gun-shy.

Everything had begun to happen at once as Mac left the plane and came down the steps toward the ground. Flash bulbs went off brightly, and the loose group of people waiting nearby tightened into a knot at the foot of the ramp. A short man with crew-cut hair and heavy-rimmed glasses pressed forward with an air of authority.

"Dr. Adams," he had said. "I'm Warren Ross, press officer at the American Embassy." He shook Mac's hand, which was difficult because of the tightly packed small crowd.

"Mr. Ross," Mac said, "you haven't organized one of those Lafayette we are here welcomes, have you?"

"No, no," Ross laughed, "nothing like that. Just a few of your patients from the war years who—"

"Mr. Ross—" Mac's voice was angrier than he intended.

Ross interrupted him quickly, soothingly. "I know. I know how you feel. But here they are. They'll be hurt if you rush off."

"Docteur Adams—" a French voice said behind Mac.

"Later, Lescaut," Ross said over Mac's shoulder toward the voice. "Press conference at noon at the Embassy."

"I won't have it, Ross—" Mac was saying at the same time, but Ross had turned away already to a cluster of three men wearing French military uniforms and a dark-haired girl carrying flowers. She was enjoying all the attention and the picture-taking, Mac could see, and then as she held the flowers out he noticed her stubby not-quite-fingers and the missing thumb. He glanced swiftly at the Army men. Of course! Plastic surgery patients, every one. The first man in uniform had a glass eye set into an excellent repair of the orbital socket, the next was a cheek and mouth multiple excision reconstruction, the last had a forehead built up from a tubular flap and two rebuilt eyebrows in both of which the hair, transplanted from the same area of the scalp, sloped the same way.

"We wish to zank you, Dr. Ah-dahms, *mille mille merci,*" the girl

185

said as she gave him the flowers, then, as his hand touched her stubby repaired fingers, she burst into tears.

Mac let her kiss him wetly, a little hysterically, on both cheeks while the flash bulbs began to pop quickly. He stood very still, feeling the frown of the past half year of tension soften on his face, feeling a wave of relief sweep through him. These people didn't care about his troubles back home at all. It had filled his own mind, night after night and day after day for months, and he suddenly realized how distorted and personal a nightmare it really was, how many people there were who had never heard of the coroner's inquest and all the rest.

He could feel himself once again becoming the successful, friendly doctor, the kind who remembers small personal details to reassure the patient she really matters. He held the girl at arm's length. "You're little Thérèse. I remember now."

"Leetle!" she cried, "I am *maman* now. I 'ave baby, 'usband!" and then she began to laugh again and cry.

It all came back in a rush. The hospital at Neuilly, the little French girl with the crushed hands, the letter from French Headquarters about people who were complaining that Dr. Adams had been loaned by the American Army to work only on French generals and could not a civilian patient, preferably a child hurt during the street fighting, the daughter of a wounded veteran, be given plastic surgical care as a special favor?

Mac moved toward the line of men standing at attention, hardly realizing Ross was expertly shepherding his elbow. Everyone around was smiling a little, the plane's passengers had enlarged the crowd, everyone was talking in English and French at the same time, and Mac knew the whole ceremony was in the best and warmest tradition of French and American camaraderie. The top side of the golden coin that ignored the underside of cheating, gouging, the suspicions and resentments. If all this airport reception had started out as a press officer's public relations idea, it had changed now into something real.

The first man in line saluted as Mac came up to him. He was in the uniform of an artillery captain. There was only a rosette of the Légion d'honneur in his buttonhole, and an oblong faded patch over his chest pocket where he had removed all his other decorations.

186

"I am Captain Emile Champon," he said in excellent English. "I was your patient from October, 1944. It is a pleasure to meet you in France again."

Mac held out his hand to ease the military stiffness into something more friendly. As he and Captain Champon shook hands, Mac said, "Weren't you the liaison officer to the Fifth Corps?"

Captain Champon began to smile—and Mac noticed professionally and pleasantly that the ocular prosthesis and the eye socket were so well done that it was a very good smile. "You remember, Doctor! It is remarkable." They stood there for a moment shaking hands, saying nothing, remembering much, then Champon added suddenly, "I remember the government gave you the Légion d'honneur. You are not wearing it."

"Well," Mac said, "if I had known about this warmhearted welcome—"

"Please," Champon said, "please." He took his own decoration off his uniform and began to fit it into the buttonhole of Mac's lapel and the camera flash bulbs began to make a miniature chalky lighting around them. In the crowd a woman called, "Bravo!" and some people clapped. The top side of the golden coin, hands across the sea, the Statue of Liberty, the last time I saw Paris, all the myths and hokum and the reality of plastic surgery and wartime suffering somehow mixed together.

Mac ducked his chin to look uncomfortably at the rosette in his buttonhole. "Captain Champon," he said, "this really belongs to a commander of the Légion d'honneur. I'm only of chevalier rank."

"On the spot," Champon said, loudly, so that the reporters could hear it, "I promote you!" Then, as Champon embraced him cheek to cheek in the grand tradition, Mac thought: Lafayette, I'm really here.

Mac's interview by three reporters from the *Tribune* and *Paris-Soir* and *France-Presse* went quickly. The reporters held single-page biographical fact sheets which Ross had given them, Mac noticed, and they seemed to think they had enough for their stories after a few questions. It was a pleasant change from the sort of grilling newspapermen had given him recently. And then, somehow, they were in the long black Embassy car and threading their way out of the airport in low gear. Eve and Mac sat in the back seat with Mrs.

187

Warren Ross, and Mr. Ross sat sideways on the folding seat so that he could face them. He tried to disarm Mac immediately.

"You're a PR natural, Dr. Adams," Ross said. "You handled that like a maestro. But, Judas priest! I never dreamed you'd take it so hard at first, Doctor. I guess I owe you a number one apology."

"Must you say Judas priest, Warren?" Mrs. Ross said. She was as small as Ross was, but as blond as he was dark, with that alert birdlike brightness the wives of diplomatic personnel learn to play upon their constant stream of visitors like a searchlight beam.

"Where are you staying, Dr. Desmond?" Mrs. Ross asked.

"The Royal Monceau," Eve answered. She was sitting back, pleasantly relaxed, Mac noticed, just letting everything happen and taking it as it came.

Ross said, "We've gotten a suite at the Georges Cinq for you, Dr. Adams. Four star. Veddy plush, but not gaudy."

"Wait a minute," Mac said. "This is going too fast. A friend of mine is loaning me his houseboat. All I have to do is track down his sister-in-law who has the keys."

"A houseboat!" Mrs. Ross said. "How romantic!"

"How private," Mac said, looking at Ross.

"Well," Ross said, "you'd probably end up in a hotel tonight, anyway. And Georges Cinq is convenient for interviews."

Mac stiffened, but as he felt Eve's leg move in warning against his, he managed to say with controlled patience, "I appreciate your putting me up in style, but I don't want the hotel and certainly not the interviews."

Mrs. Ross sensed the gathering storm and clapped her hands suddenly. "I know!" she exclaimed. "Come to our apartment. It's huge. We've got all the room in the world. And we haven't had a distinguished visitor since I don't know when! If you're a good bridge player we'll *worship* you. And you can shave and shower and track down your boat keys while I prepare the finest onion soup and *Chateaubriand* steak you ever—"

"It's all she can cook," Ross interrupted, "but Judas, she really can make it."

"—and real hot coffee, not that tepid *filtre,*" Mrs. Ross was saying.

188

"Cindy, stop showing off," Ross said mildly.

"I think it's a wonderfully generous idea," Eve said diplomatically to Mac. She turned to Mrs. Ross. "The poor man really needs a home until he tracks down his incredible boat."

"Mrs. Ross—" Mac began to say.

"Mrs. Ross," Mrs. Ross said, "that's Warren's mother. Please call me Cindy."

"Cindy," Mac asked, "are you from the South?"

"Charlestown, Dr. Adams," Cindy said. "Oops, I almost called you honeychile."

Ross looked at Mac, grinning a little at his wife's transparent blitzkrieg of hominy grits and hospitality. "See?" he said. "I never had a chance. Under the whalebone corset beats a heart of solid corn pone."

"Hush your mouth, you lil' ole Yankee," Cindy said, purposely using an exaggerated Deep South accent. "I'm on your side. Don't you know the way to a doctor's press conference is through his stomach?"

Warren Ross told the driver to take a roundabout route through the city, exposing them to the muffled drumbeat of history in Paris street names: Austerlitz, St. Michel, Henri IV, de la République, and Mac remembered again the 1944 look of the 28th Division marching without bands and the thousand-footed sound of boots past the Arc de Triomphe toward Saint-Denis where they would be fighting by midnight, and the weary little Negro soldier with his arm in a crude sling right behind General de Gaulle as the French came battle-proud up the Champs-Elysées. And now it was as if a century had gone by since then. A deep gulf of years, atoms and anxiety for breakfast, and the slow iron wheels of history becoming electronic, turning faster. For a moment's flash, like a landscape glimpsed by lightning, he saw his own driven journey not as an act of free will as he had believed, but as decided partly by impersonal and larger forces. But the idea was too complicated to follow at the moment, too grandiose a posing of a single man against the middle perspective of his personality and against the towering historical background of his place and time, and the thought slipped beneath the surface and was gone. For a moment he sensed that the idea was very important to him, that he needed

189

to think about it later, alone, quietly, but it was gone like an elusive handful of smoke.

"What is it, Mac?" Eve said quietly beside him. "You look sort of long ago and far away."

"Nothing," he said. "Except that I keep remembering things."

She looked at him alertly. "Will you remember to remember to tell me later?"

"Let's lunch at the Ritz gardens," Cindy was saying to her husband. "I just love those cute flat blue sun umbrellas."

"Sure," Ross said, "but does your cute flat figure take to those *fines de claires* you also love, honeychile?"

"I prefer the Belons or the Marennes. The *claire* is too Portugaise-ish and too deep-sea-ish for me."

"Listen to them," Eve said loudly to Mac, behind the pretense of a lifted, shielding palm. "Americans in Paris debating about oysters. Perish forbid!"

"A houseboat," Ross remarked to himself. He turned on the cramped folding chair to Mac. "Where'd you ever dream up an honest-to-blazes houseboat?"

"I bet it was the Paris housing shortage!" Cindy exclaimed. "What a clever idea!"

"It wasn't my idea," Mac said. "Boisson dreamed it up after waiting six years for a studio apartment."

"But the red tape! Lord sakes, you need one lil' ol' permit to get another one to get a big one with an official red wax seal that says: Nope. And if you're not a permanent resident, just one of those Americans who has to cross the Belgian border every three months to keep your tourist status legal—"

"Boisson," Ross murmured respectfully. "They say he's the next Rodin. Best sculptor in France. Didn't he do that famous fountain in Copenhagen? He must be a real buddy to loan you his dreamboat."

"Well, we both share the same ideas about sculpture. He thinks my surgery and the sculpture I've been doing for years make a good beginning. A couple of years of hard work here and I'll be on my way."

"What do you mean about the same basic ideas?"

Mac realized Ross was drawing him out, but he didn't mind. "Well,

190

we both want to present the world as it is, with some disciplined craftsmanship. Neither of us want to use the trick of the second-raters, you know, exploiting our own personalities to amuse or shock. No clowning, that's what I mean."

"Discipline? Craftsmanship? No clowning!" Ross snorted ironically. "What old-fashioned ideas!" Mac's opinion of Ross began to rise.

Their car swirled the fallen chestnut blossoms into miniature pink and white windstorms along the gutter while they talked about sculpture, with Warren Ross surprisingly knowledgeable about Mestrovic and Brancusi and Epstein, and Mac suddenly had the feeling of having really returned to Paris, the oldest truest cliché of them all.

The feeling had begun as they crossed Pont Neuf, with the Seine stretching calmly into the bridge-arched distance. Mac remembered the legend about luck coming to anyone who saw a white horse, a priest, and a red-haired woman all crossing Pont Neuf at the same time, and when, as they turned off the bridge into Quai du Louvre, he saw a horse, just an ordinary wagon-pulling horse, he couldn't help being amused. He found himself responding to the sense of openness, the sunlit air, the flower sellers, the grayed stones of history on every side, the whole visual vocabulary of the ancient city which in reality was a river of time flowing through a place and a way of living.

The streets of Paris did for him what the last view of his lifelong home through the springtime elms had done, what meeting Eve in New York had done, the view of Nantucket from the air. He experienced an expansion of time, as if he stood at the peak of a pyramid looking down simultaneously on past, present, and future, and with this, an enlargement of feeling so that little things he would ordinarily never have noticed were heightened in scale, and even a horse seen fleetingly at the end of a bridge suddenly had the status of an obscure symbol.

The Parisian hodgepodge of the big guidebook things, the beauty and vulgarity, meanness and magnificence, the large public grandeur, came toward their moving car in waves, and Mac tried to see it all with a cool perspective, and yet the warm clean wonder of a child, or an artist.

191

Warren Ross did not mention public relations until after they had had an excellent lunch of *truite au bleu* with a fine bottle of Pouilly. Mac became annoyed with himself because he felt he was surrendering subtly to Ross's purposes, and those had nothing to do with all the work he wanted to do in Paris. Perhaps he was becoming co-operative because he did not want Eve to consider he was being tense and defensive again. He knew she would say, "But Ross was only doing his job, Mac, and you've got to admit his wife was awfully cute helping him out of hot water, wasn't she?"

Also, even though he knew he was somewhat too anxious to be liked these recent days, he could hardly shake off the training of a lifetime which said: Do the decent thing. Gentleman. Manners, Malcolm, manners, boy. Our family sets examples. A good doctor almost never says no. A good doctor understands, he's not a judge, d'you see the difference? Your father, Malcolm, is the one man in the whole town whom everybody, yes everybody, trusts, you can't say that about most men, y'know, and that's something you should be proud to live up to, boy. The Adamses have always led the parade, not with pride, no, no, not with pride, but doing their duty as they saw it. They didn't leave Somerset in 1638 and settle around Braintree and Dedham and Woodstock just for the winter sports of New England, you can be sure of that. Why, son, if you go out to the old burying ground over behind the high meadow, you'll find the coat of arms empty on every stone. And why, d'you suppose? Because the Adamses picked the lead out of their own family gravestones to make bullets for their muskets in the Revolution, that's why. Courage, Malcolm, plain humble courage to see the right and courage to up and do it. Remember that.

They had talked to him at home, quietly, intelligently; and at the Country Day School and the Academy, quietly, intelligently, with all emotions under cool control; and at Yale, where his sudden temporary detour into the School of Fine Arts and the sculpture had been understood, quietly, intelligently; while over in Europe, in Germany, there were street fights and smashed store windows and some mad clown named Hitler, and the world was becoming noisy and fury-driven.

And today, because he had been shaped by many forces, inner and outer, he found himself angry with himself because doing the decent civilized thing somehow meant doing what Warren Ross wanted.

192

With coffee, after their lunch, Ross shook an American cigarette out of his pack, offered it around, lifted it to his mouth without touching it, and lighted it by scratching one thumbnail expertly across a wooden match. "Dr. Adams," he said, letting the smoke curl out of his mouth as he talked, "you don't know how important you are to us right now." Crew cut, cigarette, match, and smoke made a little self-conscious hardboiled charade of the manly frontiersman. Mac decided Ross must feel very insecure indeed. Under the tough important job must be a highly intelligent good-natured frightened boy.

"Right now," Ross was saying, "we're catching hell in the French press about our middle of the road policy in North Africa. Bomber bases, dollar diplomacy, Coca-Colonization, atomic warmongers, all the old rotten tomatoes are being tossed at us. But you, you represent us at our most humane and scientific and non-political best. And your war record in France. And the two young French doctors you had in training with you. And wait until the papers print those shots at the airport! Get the picture from my angle?"

Mac glanced down at the Légion d'honneur rosette Champon had put into his lapel. "I've got it," Mac said, "but I don't like it."

"Oh, by the way," Ross said pleasantly. "I'm arranging with the French to get you a special one-year resident's permit. That'll save you from the usual three-month deal, and all the red tape and *paperasserie.*"

Again the soft encroachment, the unasked favor. "Thanks," Mac said. It was the only decent thing to say.

By his second day in Paris, Mac knew he would end by compromising with Ross.

Boisson's sister-in-law, the possessor of the houseboat keys, had no telephone; her concierge said Madame Boisson had absented herself from her apartment for weeks. *Tant pis.* Mac became a guest in the Rosses' enormous apartment overlooking the Bois, and he found himself relaxed by their excellent bridge games and amused by Cindy's pretense that her hospitality was really a cynical trick. Actually, she and Warren Ross enjoyed having Mac stay with them because he was so unlike their conventional picture of a doctor and because they could understand him when he talked about art or sculpture as one form of human expression, without the usual pretenses about capital

193

A type Art, or the usual nonsense about Paris as a mysteriously creative place unmatched elsewhere. And Mac liked being there because of the flavored blend they had mixed together out of two jiggers of youthfulness, an ounce of Paris, liberally garnished with American suburbia, with a dash of sophistication. Daily he was brought up to date on Paris goings on through what Warren called a Cindy-eye view.

"When I heard," she would say brightly, "that you had to be a *member* at the Cour et Jardin, and that it was the *coqueluche,* and that that really literally meant *whooping cough*—well, sir!" She was able to refer to various parts of the body in the accepted casual modern manner, but occasionally the little girl inside her would be confronted by the straightforward French approach to biological matters and she would retreat hastily, saying, "Honestly! And they talk so much about being civilized!" Or, "I'm no prude about sex, honestly, after all women are the best thing that ever happened to men, but when they go at it so open and *raw!*" Mac realized that she confused civilization with automatic laundries and immediately available hot water in a sumptuous bathroom. Husbands were a sometime bedroom thing, but mainly providers of pleasant needs like homes, cars, clothes, and paid-up life insurance. All this gave her play-acting at continental worldliness, the American Diplomat's Wife Abroad, a doll-like innocence and charm.

"Mac," Warren Ross said apologetically at dinner one night, "would you give two brief talks in your excellent *parlez-vous-Français* to two local meetings?"

"Two?" Mac asked suspiciously. "What kind of meetings?"

"One is a group of *chirurgiens,* or whatever they call surgeons here." He flipped through the pages of a little notebook. "Here it is. The Société de Chirurgiens de Paris. Their chairman said they'd like to hear from you about American advances in plastic surgery. It's their big annual meeting. Very important. Gets top coverage in all media." Ross sounded very boyish, very enthusiastic. "The other is Boisson's old gang. Sculptors of the Maillol-Boisson school. More old-fashioned than you are, lots of beard-stroking. Everybody will bring his latest girl friend to see the odd-ball American doctor without a beard and with a yen to make like Michelangelo."

194

"Top coverage in all media?" Mac asked, keeping a straight face.

"So-so," Ross answered seriously. "It's the culture angle we're after."

"What bait," Mac said. "What a double trap."

"The surgical meeting is really a big thing." Ross was very anxious for Mac to accept the invitation, but he had learned not to push too hard.

Mac glanced at Cindy. She made a small mouth at him. "Warren hasn't quoted the President at you," she said. "You know: Every American represents his country abroad. I think he asked you very nicely, and—" she turned to her husband, "I'm proud of you, sweetie."

"I won't talk to the sculptors," Mac said. "Even the best artists in the world are impossible when they get together. And besides, dammit, a sculptor ought to show his work and keep quiet!"

"How about the surgeons?"

"Who else is on the program?"

"I'll show you the list tomorrow. First-rate men, they tell me. In your case, our Ambassador will introduce you. He was hot as a two-dollar pistol on the whole idea at staff conference today."

"All right, I'll do it. But that's all, Warren. *Fini.*"

Warren grinned widely. "What a relief! I'd said yes already!"

He did not tell Mac that the Ambassador had enthusiastically cut twenty minutes from his own opening address to make room for Mac's scientific report; nor did he mention in specific detail that everything would be televised and broadcast and filmed. Only Mac's complete grasp of the subject, and his clear French, and his frequent references to the French pioneers of plastic surgery, Denonvilliers and Morestin, changed a possible disaster into a new success.

Two young doctors at the meeting came up afterward and introduced themselves as friends of Patric and Lescamp, and would Dr. Adams do them the honor of coming to the annual Interns' Ball next week? If he required introductions to a lady friend, there would be no difficulty. Not the slightest. Mac immediately thought of how little he had seen of Eve and how much she might enjoy it and said yes quickly, yes, he had a lady friend. It was a costume ball, the young doctors said, and it was required only to come in something minimum. Human anatomy was the major course of study at the Ball, functional topographic anatomy, *seductio ad absurdum* one might say. Perhaps Dr. Adams and his friend would be most comfortable if they came dressed as American Indians, eh? Wearing a feather here and there? It would be *formidable*.

The newspapermen covering the surgical meeting knew who he was, now, and treated him in a friendly way. One evening newspaper even went so far as to spell his first name correctly.

The next day a taxi driver recognized him, and Mac realized he would have to accept being mildly well known for at least a week. He also had to accept the daily questions of Cindy's maid about a vague abdominal complaint; and the cautious probing of the massive concierge downstairs, who was only asking for a friend you understand, concerning the price of having one's nose given a cute little retroussé tip; and the unexpected phone calls from unknown Americans who always began with, "Thank God there's a real American doctor in town, I'm up to my whosis in these French antibiotics, and if you could come right over—" and lastly, a few days after he had finally gotten his keys and had moved aboard the houseboat, he had to accept what Cindy called his farewell party from *chez* Ross.

Maia Obenpharo awakened slowly at noon in her Paris house, moving from sleep to wakefulness like a diver returning from sea bottom to the sunlight, gradually, gradually, through shifting depths, with the light becoming lighter until suddenly there was the surface and reality.

She lay half awake, drifting upward, wisps of a dream beginning to vanish, a dream of love, dallying at first, then she felt she was running barefooted through a palm grove, hair streaming, green-sleeved and wild with youth, playful, secretive, and then, with her senses alert for fierceness and consummation, the anonymous pursuer was gone, the sensuality evaporated, leaving her vaguely unsatisfied and cheated, unaware even that she half dreamed all this. She often had this disembodied sensation before awakening, and she knew it had some significance she could not puzzle out, but she never mentioned it to any of her Parisian friends who would have enjoyed analyzing it

196

for her at great length, and, she knew, entirely in terms of their own distortions.

Suddenly the light flooded her closed eyes and she was at the surface, awake. The tulip-shaped antique Huyghens watch at her bedside read close to noon, and she stared for a moment at its enameled case with fat Cupids encircling a robust nude Venus pretending to be a shepherdess. It's just the other way around for me. I'm the shepherdess who became Venus. Then she shrugged off further recollection—after all, what was past was done with, what was future was written and unchangeable, so only the present really mattered—and opened her door wide to the day by ringing for breakfast.

She swung her legs over the side of the bed, enjoying the pleasant silken slide of the sheets, and walked barefooted—again remembering her childhood for a moment, re-enacting the unshod Berber poverty on the safe luxurious rug—and went into the bathroom. The walls and ceiling here were solid sheets of mirror so that no matter which way she turned she approached herself from a dozen viewpoints. She had slept without nightclothes and saw herself now, nude with a heap of disordered golden hair tumbling over her shoulders, slender and small-hipped as eighteen with only something around the eyes that would never be eighteen again. If only I were young and hopeful-looking again, she thought, a believer in the future—but then I would not have all this, and it is better to have all this here and now than to be young and a believer in the future.

She never took her shining hair or fluent body for granted. Together they made her feel she had a passport across any boundary, into any country, sometimes even a ladder to mount the walls of heaven, and she guarded herself like a precious possession. She put her hands flat against her ribs, watching the red-haired girl in the mirror do it, and ran her palms down to her hips, taking a deep breath all the while and raising her breasts up into points. For a moment she admired the figurine, then let her breath out suddenly with a tiny self-conscious smile. I must be lonely, she realized suddenly, lonely and needing reassurance.

When the maid knocked and came in with the tray, Maia called out of the bathroom, "I'll have it on the terrace today, Marie. And tell Yacoub to come up with all the Paris papers."

She had seen some pictures and articles about an American plastic surgeon in Paris, and she wanted to get all the details accurately before telephoning Obenpharo in Tangier about him. He seemed to have all the qualifications Obenpharo demanded that she find: great skill, freedom from a local practice, and none of the prejudices a French surgeon would have toward Roger's explosively revolutionary status in Morocco.

"All the Paris papers. Yes, madame." The maid smiled because she liked the terrace as much as Maia. Actually, it was a little room on the roof, completely enclosed top and sides by glass, with shelf after shelf of opalines through which the sun filtered, casting blue and yellow globular shadows. There was almost a feeling of being airborne, because most of Paris lay at their feet from that height, with the Seine and the Ile St. Louis directly beneath them, Notre Dame so close it seemed near enough to touch, the Tour d'Argent just across the river, the Panthéon marking the center of the horizon line, the Eiffel Tower far off, and the Tour St. Jacques and St. Eustache to the right.

As she broke her *croissant* and began to sip the hot chocolate, Maia surveyed the world which she had always dreamed of reigning over as all hungry girls do, the difference being that she actually had now everything she had dreamed of, except of course the subtle always-escaping something of her awakening half dreams.

The terrace had been her idea. A year after she and Roger had been married, and she found the Rue du Faubourg St. Honoré a disputed passage to the top, she looked everywhere for a Paris home to which the world would say: That's where *she* lives. It would have to be convenient, for comfort always came first after so many years of discomfort; it would have to be fashionable, not just for a season, but always; it would need to capture the imagination, because worldly success could be bought by any *nouveau riche* and she knew that she was *nouveau* yet so unbelievably *riche* she could even purchase the aristocratic patina which only time gives, and time covered the Ile St. Louis and Quai de Bethune like a worn parchment skin.

"That house on Quai de Bethune!" Roger had said in that early year of marriage. "A house on an island? Where did you get such an idea, Maia?"

"It's fascinating, Roger. I want it. The view of the river. That owl's-eye window, and those iron balconies." She became encyclopedic here, because she knew his intense respect for book learning was flattered by having a beautiful wife whose mind was unexpectedly alert and factual. "It was built by Louis LeVan, the designer of Versailles, for Nicolas Sainctot, Master of Ceremonies and Introducer of Ambassadors to Louis XIII. Imagine all that!"

"Imagine all the architect told me," Roger said, pretending to be logical in his best Sorbonne law manner. "The building leans sideways. The floors slant. The cellars are so water-logged you can catch fish from the Seine just by going to the basement."

At that time Roger still believed that logic alone could persuade people to change their minds. She knew this, and had prepared her case with a defense attorney's care. She knew how much it would cost to build a new level water-tight foundation and tear out the Bonaparte froufrou some nineteenth-century owner had installed, and—this caught his imagination—to remodel the servants' quarters on the top floor to give them a unique penthouse overlooking all of Paris, perhaps with a heated glassed-in terrace so they could go out even during dramatic thundershowers, poetic under a transparent tent, and yet comfortably dry despite the elements, Olympian.

But it was the great cost which had persuaded Benari Obenpharo to back her project. He was impressed by the cost when he came up to Paris from Tangier. The whole undertaking sounded both regal and imaginative, fashionable above fashion and an excellent real estate investment. The cost was no problem because it was 1949, Macao had become the center for unrestricted world bullion because Portugal had neglected to sign the Bretton Woods monetary agreement and the troubled people of Asia were desperate for gold, and bullion-rich Banque Obenpharo was a financial skyrocket.

Roger had explained it to her while apologizing once for having been gone so long on his trip to New York and Calcutta and Macao. "It's simple," he had said. "Every ounce of gold in New York is at the pegged price of thirty-five dollars, and a frightened Chinese businessman pays about fifty-five, almost twenty dollars more for the same ounce in Hong Kong. Beside," he had said, frowning, because this part offended his legal mind, "the gold arrives as 99.6 per cent pure bullion, and Chinese standards let us dilute it with silver to just 99 per cent. There's five hundred thousand ounces entering Macao each month, and fifty thousand ounces of that is Banque Obenpharo Tangier. Add it up for yourself."

Those were the days when Roger was giving only money to the Istiqlal, before he had decided to give himself completely, the way an idealistic young man leaves his family to go off to a war.

Now he was back from his personal war, lying in a private Tangier clinic and being fed by nose tube and by vein because of his Face. How could she ever forget his Face? She had been in Roger's room with Benari when the nurse came in to change the bandages. Obenpharo had risen to his feet heavily, using his cane.

"Maia and I will wait in the hall, Roger."

Roger had aimed his one burning eye at his father like a spear. "There's no need to leave, Father." He swiveled his eye at the young Spanish nurse. "We're not afraid of the evil eye, are we, señorita?"

"No," she smiled, "but only, please, monsieur and madame, remain over there and do not cough or sneeze while the dressing is off." She put on a face mask and sterile gloves and began cutting away Roger's mummy hood of bandages.

"My real enemy is the staphylococcus," Roger had said, changing from Spanish to French. "Clever infiltrators. Wonderful partisans."

"Your real enemy is you," Obenpharo had said, flinching a little in spite of himself as the nurse's surgical tongs lifted off one wet gauze pad after another.

Maia knew Roger had wanted her and Benari Obenpharo to stay there during the dressing of the wound to punish them with the sight of his injury, and she was determined not to change her expression no matter how terrible his face was. Yet, when the final soaking gauze strips were lifted off, and Roger closed his one eye tightly in pain, she drew her breath sharply at the sight of the horrible excavation on one side of Roger's head and face. Tears came involuntarily as she saw Roger's head press back into the pillow while his distorted new voice said, "Ah . . . ah . . . ah-h-h. . . . Nurse . . . *despacio, mas despacio*. . . ."

"A moment," the Spanish nurse said sympathetically, "only one more moment."

Maia had grasped Benari's elbow, feeling sick. Benari Obenpharo had been staring, agonized, at the grotesque anatomy of his son's face; now he turned slightly toward her and put his great hand over her tight fingers. He had realized as well as she what Roger was doing to them, but his hand was shaking.

In the silence, Roger's eye had opened to look at them both.

"Man is made in God's image," he said. "Remember that."

"Stop talking like a fool, Roger," Benari growled. "You're not getting any better here."

"I'm holding my own."

"You're risking your life."

"Well, that has its political advantages. Just ask my friends at the door."

His friends were two Istiqlal bodyguards who alternated with others on a twenty-four-hour watch. One stood at the door each day while the second went outside to the small crowd of gaunt cloaked men at the outer gate of the clinic and admitted one person at a time. The visitor had probably come sixty miles on foot to visit the terribly wounded leader, but he would be frisked for weapons from head to foot by the guards. They were afraid of an assassination attempt by the French, or pro-French Moslems. Then the visitor would remove his slippers in the hallway, as if entering a mosque, and walk with small reverent steps into Roger's room to bow and touch the corner of the bedsheet with his lips for the *baraka.* The nature of Roger's injury, and the manner of his getting it in the great tradition of battle, gave him great *baraka,* the quality of benediction, making him a kind of secular Pope who can shed holiness on others as a lamp sheds light. Roger had grown from a political leader into a hero, and now hundreds of people came and went in the narrow street outside the clinic, constantly watching his balcony, praying five times each day toward Mecca, crouching over little charcoal braziers to brew tea on the sidewalk, sleeping huddled against the clinic gates.

Roger had turned his single eye to the Spanish nurse. "You have a light hand with those tools. Many thanks."

This is how he builds the legend, Maia had thought. His quiet gentle manners with little people who go away and tell others: How simple he is!

201

"A good patient," the nurse had said. "That makes it easy to be a good nurse." She had looked at Obenpharo and Maia. "If only the infection would stop, we would all be happier."

"My friends," Roger had said, "my little staphylococci."

The nurse had smiled briefly at them and had gone out briskly. A man's voice spoke a guttural Spanish question to her in the hall just outside the door, and they had been able to hear her answer. "Like a steak, a raw steak."

"If you'd only allow me to fly you to Paris—" Obenpharo had begun to say.

"Yes," Roger had interrupted. "Paris. First there would be French medicine. Humane. Skillful. Witty. Then would come the French police. Not humane. Not witty. But very skillful at flying people back down to the Sahara, to one of their nice healthy open-air concentration camps. To them, I'm a French citizen who breaks the law."

"Rome, then. Or we could go to Madrid. Copenhagen. London." Obenpharo had waved one arm to indicate all Europe.

Roger shook his head.

"The surgery you need does not exist in Tangier," Maia had said. "You need the facilities of a big medical center."

Roger's eye had pierced her. "Thank you for your concern, Maia. I'm sure it impresses Father."

"The longer you use your hospital bed as a religious throne, Roger," Obenpharo had added, "the longer you risk having this infection get into your bloodstream or your brain. The doctor tells me that the usual antibiotics are useless in your case."

"Everything is a risk," Roger said quietly. "One kind or another."

His quietness reminded Maia of the way intellectual little boys fought underground their arrogant fathers, by a deep polite quiet manner with which it was impossible to grapple. They're both exactly the same!—Maia thought with a blinding realization. Roger is as imperious and demanding as his father, but Benari's generation permitted and encouraged fathers to be all-knowing, all-powerful, so that was what Benari had become, a kind of generous Jehovah. Roger's generation had revolted and only turned the mirror around, and in their quiet bookish ways they were more cruel than their

202

fathers' worst tyranny in pursuit of an Idea which would improve Life, not for this man nor that man, not this year nor next year, but Someday. My God, thought Maia, they're both so wise, so intelligent, so gentle when loved on their own terms, so charming when obeyed, so understanding when you surrender—so completely self-centered and ruthless.

Obenpharo had snorted. "Nursing care keeps you from dying, you fool, but only surgery will cure you."

"Let the surgeon come here. I'll stay in Morocco, believe me. The French may capitulate any day now, and the Sultan will come back to Rabat. The day the Sultan begins his independent rule, I want to be in Morocco."

"I thought you wanted a democratic government, not a return of medieval monarchy."

"One step at a time, Father. To move Morocco from a sixteenth-century colony to seventeenth-century independence in a few years —not such a poor acomplishment, agreed?"

"And your health?" Obenpharo had asked. "What if the Sultan comes back? What if he makes you the Foreign Minister of a new independent country? What of your health and your face?"

"Let me show you what the people think about that," Roger had said. Slowly he sat up at the edge of the bed, rising sideways and shifting his weight slowly as if his head were a bandaged metal pendulum. "Ahmed," he said. "Ali."

At once both men appeared in the doorway. Ahmed was an ageless Riff, with wrinkled leather skin, a scraggly beard, and a countryman's loosely wound white turban. Ali was a young city boy, in patched trousers, a too-tight sharp-shouldered jacket, wearing a red fez. The city and the country, Maia had recognized at once, Roger makes sure to balance his support.

"My *djellaba*," Roger said. The younger man went to the clothes closet stiffly, rather self-consciously militaristic, and took out a long white cloak with a hood. The ageless Riff helped him lift it over Roger's head. Roger got into it with his arms held high, like climbing into a great pillowcase and then he stood up, keeping his feet apart for balance. Neither Maia nor Obenpharo had spoken during this performance which so clearly had been rehearsed.

"Now," Roger said, "the face veil."

Then Maia had understood. It was the dress of a desert tribe, the face covering of a Tuareg nobleman, the blue-veiled Saharan warriors who, in contrast to most in North Africa, veiled themselves, not their women. It was said the Tuareg were too proud to let their women see their facial battle scars and so had begun the tradition of indigo face veils, and Maia had immediately seen how Roger would use the heroic tradition. His fundamentalist followers believed he was one of them, directly inspired by God and His Prophet; to them the face veil would be a reminder of his battle with the heathen French *faranji*. To his politically sharpened city followers, like this young tough-looking Ali, his Tuareg dress meant a truly native warrior caste as well as a complete break with European clothes. And always, to be sure, the face veil would hide that Face. From every viewpoint, the Tuareg face covering was a clever device.

Roger's single eye looked at Maia, a kind of challenge, then at Obenpharo; then he had walked slowly to the tall French balcony doors which Ahmed pulled open for him. From below, at the grill-work gates to the clinic grounds, a shout began, with separate voices coming through more loudly than others. But when Roger stepped out on the balcony, with the offshore breeze from the bay molding his hood against his head, letting some of the white bandages show through, the voices ran together into a rising roar upon roar.

Roger turned to look at his father once, with his single eye blazing above the veil in a triumph that was like a victory in physical combat. Obenpharo's cane clattered on the floor. Then Roger turned back toward the balcony, and when he raised both his arms skyward in an almost ecclesiastical greeting, the sound became non-human and enormous within the narrow street.

Only Roger could do it, Maia had thought in hate and admiration. Only Roger could follow Voltaire's recipe so well—first to become crucified, then to rise from the dead.

Yacoub came onto the terrace carrying the Paris newspapers, both English and French. He bowed. "May God lengthen thy life, Lalla Maia," he said in Arabic.

"Ahlan wa-sahlan," she responded. The Arabic words were,

"family and plain," which meant: You may be at ease as if within your own family and may your feet walk as easily as upon a level plain. The ancient and gracious greeting would please Yacoub, she knew: also, since the trouble with Roger, and Henri's staying with his grandfather and grandmother at Villa Obenpharo, she went out of her way with the family's Arab servants. Their good will eased the complicated domestic arrangements in Tangier.

"The man who designs the clothing at Dior is downstairs with the gold cloth," Yacoub said, using French now.

"For once, on time. He can wait."

"You will want the car today, madame?"

"I don't know yet. As soon as I finish with these papers, place a call to Tangier. Try to get Monsieur Obenpharo at his office."

"Yes, madame."

"Before that, telephone Madame Warren Ross and when she comes on the line bring me the instrument."

"Yes, madame."

She turned to the newspapers. There was a closeup picture of the American surgeon, Dr. Malcolm Adams, addressing a scientific meeting. She looked at the strong serious face, the long fingers holding the edge of the lectern, and then began to read the article carefully, noting his war record, his research, the recent scandal in his personal life, until Yacoub returned trailing a cord and put the telephone on the table.

"Madame Ross," he said, "on the line."

" 'Allo!" Maia said into the phone, trying to say the *H* and sound American. "Cindy, you thief in the night, where have you been hiding?"

"I'm home day and night," Cindy's voice crackled in the receiver, "what with our new guest. You must have read about him this week. One of those fabulous surgeons."

Maia kept her voice easy. "No . . . sounds interesting. . . ."

"He's fascinating! I haven't enjoyed anybody so much in years. And my maid is staying on because he solved her stomach trouble. Would you believe it?"

"Send him right over here!"

"You wouldn't like him. He's not gay or smooth, and he keeps pretending he's a real nature boy, you know, very simple and know-nothing about anything except medicine and sculpture."

"Sculpture!"

"Don't get me started. He's a sculptor, too. It's a long story."

"I'd like to hear it. Sounds twice as interesting."

"Well, there's a lot of unhappiness in it, a dead son and a broken marriage. Warren made me *swear* not to breathe a word about it."

"How is the Ross these days?"

"Oh, Maia, you know Warren. Still fighting Communism single-handed."

"A solitary man with a mission. I'm familiar with the type."

There was a pause, which was unusual for Cindy. Maia knew Cindy had no information about Roger, and was trying to guess what she meant.

"What are *you* busy at these days?" Cindy asked. "Still seeing Laurance Ingersoll?"

"He haunts me. He insists he'll make me immortal if I let him do a nude."

"Immortality, here I come."

"Why? Who wants to live forever? Right now I'm going to look at a new gold dress."

"Not that one they were fitting at Dior's two months ago!"

"Yes, yes, yes, the same one. Can you imagine? I've been to Tangier and back twice, and they're still fussing."

"You mean they actually went ahead and tried to match the gold thread to your hair *exactly*!"

"They tried. We'll see today. Otherwise back it goes again."

"Oh, Maia, if only I had your looks and your courage. And your beautiful money."

Maia laughed. "I know you think I'm crazy. But for a red-haired woman, anything in red that doesn't match absolutely exactly looks like a *poule,* and not very de luxe, either."

"Maia! I just got a wonderful idea! I've been thinking about a fare-well party when Dr. Adams moves out next week, and if Warren says yes, and if you promise to come—"

Maia moved the telephone earpiece a little further from her ear and Cindy's enthusiasm, and signaled Yacoub to bring her a fresh cup of chocolate. Things were going well, but she knew it would be a long conversation. The only interruption she would permit was her call to Tangier. She could hardly wait to tell Obenpharo she had found the right man.

(5)

"THAT'S Maia Obenpharo over there," Cindy said over her champagne glass to Mac.

He looked across the room filled with Cindy's well-dressed party guests. "The redhead?"

"Uh-huh. She came tonight just to meet you."

"Really? Why?"

"I don't know. Probably has a friend with a mole on her whosis. Heaven knows *she* doesn't need any plastic surgery!"

Mac looked between spaces in the crowd at the redheaded girl in the gold dress. Her hair was bound up in an elaborate Psyche knot, and she looked extravagantly beautiful. Her *haute couture* elegance was very Parisian, very simple, giving the impression of effortless flawlessness.

"*Sensas,* isn't she?" Cindy asked.

Mac had learned that word meant sensational, and he nodded, still watching the girl. There was hardly any point in meeting her, because beautiful women were usually either stupid from lack of effort, or so self-consciously on display they became waxen mannequins. In either case there was no warmth, and he disliked being roped into the admiration of icebergs.

"Believe it or not," Cindy said, "the gold thread in that dress is really gold." She took his wrist and shook it gently with each word for emphasis. "And would you believe it, they took three months to match her hair exactly! Three months! Just to match the thread to the exact shade of her hair! Isn't that *sensas*?"

"Sounds like a South American heiress or a Texas oil baby."

"No, no. She's even more *exotique*. She's Berber."

"She's what?"

Cindy caught her husband's sleeve as he went by. "Warren, honey," she said, "come here. We need your intelligence."

"How d'you like your little clambake, Mac?" Warren asked. Warren was enjoying the talk, the pleasant party noise, the hand-tailored crowd, the diplomatic confidences, the proprietorship of a distinguished guest. "I," he said, "am feeling no pain."

"Didn't you say Maia was Berber?" Cindy asked.

"My oh Maia," Warren said. "Just her name makes me drool."

"Isn't he *awful*, Mac?"

"The Berbers, my little one, are sort of but not actually Arabs," Warren said. "They're *the* Moors. I've heard they're Celts, they're this, they're that. They came from Europe centuries ago. They were Christian for a long time until the Arabs beat them back to the mountains, and lots of them are whiter than I am, and blue-eyed and blond." He turned to look over his shoulder at Maia, then back again. "Her family is in some kind of international banking in Tangier. One of the oldest old families. Here in Paris, they've got a fabulous seventeenth-century house on Quai de Bethune on the Ile St. Louis on the edge of the island overlooking Notre Dame. I guess she does the Paris end of the family's bank entertaining there."

"Her house is real real casual," Cindy said, "like the Louvre." She paused because she realized Mac was still watching Maia, and not listening to her.

When Maia moved, Mac noticed, it was with a light-footed dancing-walking way. Or she was completely still, grave-eyed, with an unmoving tranquillity. She was out on the balcony now, with a man on each side, looking from one to the other, leaning on the stone rail with the room light catching the glittering metallic outline of hair, shoulder, hip, and thigh. When she turned slightly with a gleam of little highlights she appeared in bas-relief against the evening darkness, golden, sculptural. All Technicolor, he thought, but Cindy was right. *Sensas*. Women like her made one myth about Paris come true, because they played the game of elegance with the seriousness and precision of ballet.

"Even her nail polish and her eye shadow are gold." Cindy sounded like an awed little girl. "I'll bet you never saw anything like her back home, even in New York."

208

"New York!" a British voice said behind them. They turned. "Maia's a handmade European custom design, not one of your bloody New York assembly line beauties!" It was Laurance Ingersoll, a thin man with a thin pale face and a mop of uncombed curly hair, who had brought Maia to the party. Mac had seen him toss down several straight Scotches as soon as he arrived.

"You're the nice clean-cut American hostess," Ingersoll said.

"I hope so." Cindy sounded unsure.

"We met while I was running toward your bar sinister."

Mac could see that the man's abrupt manner had confused Cindy. She took courtesy for granted, and Ingersoll had managed to sound discourteous.

Ingersoll half turned and pointed at Mac. "And you're the famous Dr. Adams Maia wants so much to meet. Has she told you why?"

"No."

"And if she had told you, would you admit it now?"

"No."

"You know, you sound just as doctor-stuffy as I thought you'd sound."

"If you're desperate for a witty two-way conversation," Mac said, "maybe we can find you a small fly-specked mirror."

Ingersoll raised his glass. "Salute. Well said. Bravely spoken."

"The hors d'oeuvres—" Cindy muttered, "excuse me—" and fled.

Ingersoll took another drink and glanced at Maia, then back at Mac. "I came here to bury Caesar, not to praise him."

"You're barking up the wrong toga. I just met the lady an hour ago."

"But you don't know Maia as I know Maia. If she wants to know you better, that's it, chum. She's a girl who always begs, borrows, or buys what she wants." He took another drink and looked at Maia over the rim of his glass. "She's the lady who makes you think you're the tiger. But when she comes back from the ride, you're inside."

"That's mighty picturesque." Mac said.

He had met this type before, the clever talented ones who were so afraid they weren't clever or talented enough that they spent all their time at downstage center, posturing and making speeches, damning themselves if they did, damning themselves if they didn't, and completely incapable of ever being simple or direct or really friendly with another person.

"Don't sound bored, M'soor le Docteur," Laurance Ingersoll said. "She came here tonight for one reason, and my prophetic soul tells me this is going to be a smashing heave-ho for our mutual friend, Laurance Ingersoll."

"I'm an innocent bystander," Mac said.

"She eats strong silent bystanders for breakfast. And while you think you're sailing safely by, Ulysses, old boy, she'll sit on the shore combing her golden hair and singing till you hit the rocks." He raised his glass. "The Scotch on the rocks." He drained his glass, leaning backward, and rattled the ice in it with his tongue. He had sounded argumentative, drunk not only with drinking but also with the effort of trying to talk as if he were quoting a not yet written biography of himself. He looked up under his eyebrows sideways at Mac. "You think I'm afraid of losing a meal ticket?"

"I've heard about boys who get so worried about their girls they try diving to the bottom of the bottle."

Ingersoll stumbled and caught Mac's elbow. He looked haggard, and the boyish Bohemian clothes somehow made his face aged and sick.

"Why don't you go home," Mac said quietly, "before you fall down."

Ingersoll shook his head. "The best planned lays of mice and men," he said, "and it's tally-ho for Ingersoll. And everybody thinks the British peerage has an exclu-u-sive patent on the goddam girl mantrap with ivory skin. Ho! This girl has twice the selfishness and ruthlessness and three times the beauty and brains of any damn English aristocrat. She's built a better mantrap and the world beats a path to her boudoir."

Mac saw Maia coming toward them across the room, suddenly aware that she wore nothing more than the golden sheath and golden shoes and a cool golden smile, and that the total effect was designed to emphasize the total effect. Her hair was a blond yellow red gold he had never seen before. Maybe Ingersoll was right. A gold and ivory girl.

"You're talking about me," she said to them in French as she came up. "I can tell, even from across the room."

"Dr. Adams," Ingersoll said in English, "doesn't think you're really real."

The startlingly blue-green eyes under the flyaway eyebrows met Mac's and held them levelly. "But I am," she said in accented English. She raised one arm. "Here, Doctor, feel my heart. Excuse," she laughed, turning her wrist, "my pulse I mean. Is that what they call a Freudian slip?"

He took her wrist, as Ingersoll watched them frowning a little, and put two fingers professionally over her radial pulse. "It's the best pulse I've felt in years," he said. Her skin had the same warm-cool quality as her smile, and he moved his two fingers very slightly over its texture.

"Now it's a little faster," he said.

"Tango tempo?"

"I'm just making a clinical observation," Mac said.

Her eyes still held his in the level half-smiling way. "You see?" she said. "I'm really real. Dull and normal."

"Doctors are heathens about reality," Ingersoll said huskily. "They're so rational they don't believe anything. No faith. The triumphant barbarians."

"Go away, Laurance," Maia said. "You look disgustingly drunk and noisy, and I want to talk to Dr. Adams. Can't you see we're holding hands?"

"Now look here, Maia. I brought you and I'll be damned if you—"

"Barbarians," Maia said to Mac in French, letting her hand rest now in his. Mac sensed the subtle beginning of excitement. She was neither stupid nor a wax mannequin. "Did you hear this man mention barbarism?" Maia asked calmly.

"Goddam you Maia!" Ingersoll's voice had gone up like that of a hysterical child whose hysteria spirals upward with the excitement of its own performance. "This is the last dirt I'll swallow—"

Mac turned to him. "Maybe if you did go, old boy," he said very pleasantly, "we'd all be happier, including you."

Ingersoll's face was white with flared nostrils now. He put his glass down unsteadily. "If you'll just step outside a minute—!"

211

Maia laughed. "Huff puff! Huff puff! The courageous drunk!" She took Mac's arm and began to walk toward the opposite side of the room. "Let's escape the part that comes now about the manliness and the fists. I detest fighting. What a bore. Can you understand my English?"

"As my grandmother used to say, it's good enough to eat with a spoon."

She threw her golden head back and laughed as completely as a little girl. "Oh, the lies! The lies one hears! Not you, I don't mean what you said. I mean they told me you were a very sober doctor from the New England part of America."

"I am."

"But such people are not supposed to say such extravagant things."

"I never have before."

"Why not?"

"It would seem ridiculous. With you it seems right."

"Be careful," she said in French. "Don't drink your own words, like Laurance. He's a painter and a writer, you know, so you mustn't mind him or the way he dresses. You know, the kind that never lives or does anything, only writes very cloudy stories for American magazines about English boys. Always he refers to Freud, but he has never read a single page of real medical psychiatry. They tell me some American critics have made him very much the vogue with your intellectuals—"

"I admire your dissection technique," Mac said, "but I've never heard of him."

"Because you are not an intellectual."

"Sure I am," Mac said, "in disguise. The Americans who invented the United States were all hardboiled intellectuals. It's just that I'm trying to be as old-fashioned as some of my ancestors."

"Strength?" she said. "Not weakness?"

"Maybe. At least I hope so."

"Your hand feels strong."

"Would you like yours back?"

"No, hold it." She moved her fingers along his. "Yes," she said, "strength."

"Pianists, carpenters, and surgeons," Mac said. "Once an Ameri-

212

can poet wrote there was more in the turning of a wrist than in the whole journeywork of stars."

"Nice. Was he a doctor?"

"No. A very fine poet. The best ones understood more than most doctors, you know." That's enough speech-making, he told himself. Party or not, Technicolor or not, let's sober up a trifle, my friend.

She gave him a long look. "Shall we sit in this corner? I want to talk to you with no interruptions."

He sat down, thinking: Interruptions? I'd completely forgotten we weren't alone.

Around them the party was moving in little circles, coming and going, talking, drinking, the inevitable pianist playing Chopin quietly in the corner, and an occasional high laugh coming with surprising suddenness. Mac ignored it all. From across the room this girl had seemed haughty and unapproachable; now it was as if they had met before.

"So," she said, stretching one arm along the back of the little sofa in a gesture which somehow seemed to extend itself to include him in the bend of her elbow, a kind of intimacy. "So you read poetry?"

"No. Not for a very long time, since college days."

"Why not?"

"Well . . . the war. Then the postwar."

"You sound very French, blaming everything on the war."

They laughed together. He discovered that she never took her eyes from his. There was no coquetry, only something level and direct in her which he had rarely seen before. Very fine and experienced nurses had it, or very fine and experienced mothers of grown children, the serene look of women who had seen many troubles and knew now who they were, why they were here, where they were going, and what their reserves of strength were if there should be need for strength on the journey.

"You're staring at me," Maia said.

"I just remembered out of no place a line from my college days. For some reason you're making me remember quotations I haven't thought of in years."

"A Laurance Ingersoll kind of words? The kind that try so hard?"

213

"No," he said, "a strong sensitive man, not a weak sensitive one. 'Wherefore, O Pyrrha, dost thou bind thy golden hair?' "

"*Là, là,*" she said, using the Parisian derogatory equivalent for *what nonsense,* "now comes the troubadour. I've heard many compliments, including Latin quotations by my former husband from ancient poets, but never that one."

"I'm putting my best literary foot forward." She did say *former,* didn't she? he asked himself.

"But not in your mouth, like Laurance."

"Never. I'd like you to sit for my first sculpture in Europe."

"This too," she said. "This I have heard before. But never from a sculptor."

"Sculpture is out of fashion. The work is too hard. It's easier to drip paint in circles and call it abstract."

"But this sculptor is really a surgeon."

"People remind me every day."

"Forgive me."

"It's nothing."

"You must admit it's odd. Like Gauguin, who was a stockbroker."

"It's not odd. The only difference between plastic surgery and sculpture is that the clay the surgeon works on bleeds."

"Quite a difference! But I see what you mean."

"Every great sculptor has tried to overcome the difference, to make his clay bleed, and every one knew he never could. And all the great ones kept trying and failing and never stopped trying."

"I have never heard this before."

"I've never said this before, either."

She sat looking at him. "Maybe I will," she said suddenly. "Maybe I will sit for you. What do you see in my face?"

"Your orbicularis oculi and corrugator supercilii," he said, "with the almond shape in the corners. The invisible pterygoids under the surface. Lovely zygomatic arches. Your buccinators and masseters, and the neat little risorius muscles you're using now."

She was laughing, half puzzled. "All that?"

"All that, and the frontalis and levator labii superioris, too."

"You see me so—so *stripped*? How could a woman resist such an eye?"

"How could a woman stand it?" he asked, because she was taking the medical joke a bit too seriously.

"Ah," she said, "so you're willing to leave a little flesh here and there for covering."

"Willing?" he said. "Enthusiastic. If I weren't so shy, I'd say I've never met anyone covered as nicely as you." Hell's bells, he thought, I'm still making speeches. But in a good cause.

Their eyes held. "I never thought we would talk like this," she said. "Not from the way the newspapers—"

"Don't believe them," he interrupted. "Unless they're very good, everything comes out too simple."

"I thought I would meet one of those doctors, you know, with a little bit of gray here and here on the temples, very suave, immaculately tailored—"

"If you insult me, I'll know we're friends."

"But you know what I mean? A type."

"Which one? You may not know all the standard American types. There's young Dr. Kildare in the little farm town. Ever hear of him?" She shook her head. "He's a friend of good old crusty old Dr. Jones, the musty old country doctor who never charges fees or sends a bill. Kildare had a one-year internship and Jones none at all, but they do cardiac operations and brain operations and Caesarian sections on the farmhouse table by a kerosene lamp."

She smiled uncertainly, because the American names were strange, but she knew he was saying something serious in a joking way.

"And I'm not Dr. Twyeffort, the Park Avenue psychiatrist with a low voice and low opinions, in a Twyeffort suit, with an office filled with antique furniture and modern heiresses who want to jump off the couch into bed."

"So you're not Twy—how did you say it?"

"Doesn't matter. And I'm not the brilliant Dr. Arrowroot with heavy horn-rim glasses and a white lab coat and test tubes, telling his beautiful wife to go home alone because he has to spend the night with his microscope and guinea pigs."

She was laughing out loud now, and someone passing said in English, "What's so funny ha-ha?" She waved her hand. "It's too long to explain. Go on," she said to Mac, "don't let them stop you. Tell me about your friend, the American lady doctor who came in with you, which type she is not."

"Well, she isn't a lady doctor. She's a lady who is a doctor, and that isn't the same. And she doesn't have the heavy horn-rim glasses that Dr. Arrowroot had—go ahead, laugh—but she really doesn't, and she never wears her hair pulled back tight and she never wears mannish suits and when she's tired she sounds tired, just like ladies who aren't doctors."

By now there was a small circle of people around them listening to the show Mac was putting on. When he finished, Eve's voice behind him said, "That's the nicest thing anyone ever said about me."

As he bent back to look up at her, she leaned forward and kissed him lightly on the mouth. Several people applauded. Eve looked across the small space at Maia. "Has he said nice things about you too?"

"Yes. Fantastically exaggerated, but nice. All my muscles, in Latin. I like him very much."

The women's eyes met and locked. "So do I," Eve said.

(6)

UNEXPECTEDLY, proofs of the research paper on skin metabolism he had submitted to the *Journal of Plastic Surgery* a year ago came in the mail from the States, and Mac had simply put it with all the pile of his other unopened American mail on the side shelf of the houseboat cabin. He was a little surprised that he seemed to have no feeling about the *Journal* paper into which he had once put so much work. Heterologous skin-grafting research seemed like a faded letter from his youth now. It was only that the proofs of the *Journal* paper said certain things to him just by being there in its manila envelope. *Malcolm Adams, M.D.,* it said, a name on a brass plate shined once a week by Henry, the Greenwich Professional Building custodian, a brass plate with little traces of the abrasive cleaner along the edges of the raised letters.

Hospital trustees' meeting, mail from the States said, *in the Hunt*

216

Room at the Greenwich Club. And all the other memories that went with any mail from the States. It was very simple not to open the mail, even, but to let it gather in a pile on the shelf.

A phone call for him from the American Embassy came to the tobacco shop on the quay above the houseboat. As he crossed the plank from the boat to the coping stones of the quay, the two *clochards,* Parisian tramps who had set up housekeeping under the bridge nearby, saluted him; the man with two fingers halfway toward his brow, the woman with a smudged alcoholic smile.

"*B'jour,* madame, monsieur," he called to them.

They were probably eating tomato soup. Recently they both had been working nights unloading food crates at Les Halles, and if a dropped crate scattered a few cans of tomato soup or heads of lettuce, why leave good food lying in the gutter?

"*Bonjour,* Monsieur le Docteur," they called back. "We are saving some fresh duck's eggs for you. And some pumpernickel *à la russe*."

"A thousand thanks." Incredible. Tomorrow they might have caviar. A day later they would starve.

"Tomorrow," Mac called to them, "the launch comes to tow me up to Neuilly-sur-Seine. This is my last day here."

"Ah, no," they said. "Why?"

"The authorities. The boat repairs are completed. Now I have to go back upstream."

"The authorities. So always with a Frenchman. He has a beard, he wears a decoration, he asks for more bread, he is an authority. *Bien manger, bien boire, bien dormir,*" they quoted, "*après, fini.*" They shrugged, both in the ragged classic of bravado, Charlie Chaplin versus the police.

During the two weeks he had been living on the houseboat, putting it into shape, the *clochards* had drifted by, amiable in the warm weather and interested in the repainting of the houseboat's deck and the sound of hammering and calking below.

Once Mac heard them explaining his activities to one of the women of the *quartier,* one of the innumerable dog owners who walked her dog each evening along the quay.

"The boat is a studio," they said. "He works on it."

217

"Oh? A painter."

"No. A sculptor."

"Unusual."

"Well"—listening to them Mac could imagine the explanatory shrug—"he's American."

"He must be a great success. There is a very chic brunette."

"A brunette? Yesterday I saw a redhead arrive on the quay." The dog owner probably made a gesture with her free hand, because Mac heard a special faint whistle meant to express the ultimate in admiration.

"Yes. She too. Formidable, no?"

"*Ah, là là.* Truly a success, this sculptor."

"In the tobacco shop one says he is a surgeon."

"No, truly?"

"Truly."

A giggle. "With only two women patients. He must be rich."

"An American."

"But very rich. The redhead arrives in one of those enormous British cars."

The *clochards'* voices sounded as if they had shrugged. "But the brunette comes in a taxi."

The dog owner's voice added, "Ah, yes, but nobody comes by bus or Métro."

"But he goes everywhere on foot." This said triumphantly by the *clochards,* proof of his proletarian integrity. They were on his side. . . . He leaned out of the nearest porthole and saw that the owner of the poodle had allowed herself to be towed on a taut leash toward the next tree. "One never knows," she said over her shoulder. "Here on Rive Gauche even the rich play the game of being poor."

They saw it all in the Left Bank tradition, Mac thought, as he mounted the stone slope which led up to the street level of the quay, the whole operetta climate of *la vie bohème.* The scenario was perfect in their folklore, including a brunette and red-haired triangle. They'd soon have him wearing a beard and a decoration, and asking for more bread, and becoming an authority. *Après, fini.*

Halfway up the stone steps, Mac noticed the *clochards* had put a torn square of rug on the stones and had hung a broken mirror

218

on the wall above a shelf which held a geranium in a tin can. They had discovered a special kind of illusion of freedom, he thought, and even though they pay for it by being winos and outcasts you can't help wondering for a moment, like a boy watching gypsies, how it must feel. Was that a twinge of envy? Haven't I become a gypsy, too? A kerchief, a guitar, and one gold earring, and the picture would be complete, my wayfaring friend.

He reached the landing by jumping the last two of the worn stone steps and crossed the newly watered-down cobblestone street to the shop under the sign *Café-Tabac* to answer the phone. I'll have to tell Maia about the conversation of the dog owner, he thought suddenly. It will amuse her. But not Eve. Eve would not be amused, not by the conversation, not by the gypsy idea.

"American Embassade," the proprietor said in his own personal English as Mac came in the door. He jerked his thumb toward the phone. "I say you work down on boat, but no—" he shrugged, "with Americans everything queeck, queeck."

From years of habit Mac said into the phone, "Dr. Adams." The scratching electrical noises in the ancient telephone earpiece seemed worse than the usual Parisian service.

"Mac? 'Allo! 'Allo! Warren Ross. How goes it?"

"It goes, after a fashion."

"Don't sound stiff-nosed, man. Only reason I've interrupted your creative sculptural whosis is because I've got an important visitor in my outer office. He insists on seeing you."

"Warren, look, you and I talked about this before."

"Is it my fault if the French papers played you up? The European subconscious is hypnotized by plastic surgery. Think of their millions of wounded. Just—"

"Warren, we've been through the European subconscious. Last time with boots on. I can't operate on an assembly line. And no more bigshot medical speeches."

"I really picked the right time to call, didn't I?"

"I'm not blaming you. Well, hell yes, I do blame you. I—" He stopped, almost having said I was thinking about this girl with the name Maia, and remembering about the States; remembering the constant activity that always managed to stop you from doing what

219

you really wanted to do, then he realized that Warren Ross was in a swivel chair, in a government office overlooking the Place de la Concorde, with the background sound of typing heard faintly, and this was no time for reverie or remembrance of things past or capsule conclusions about the hurry up and get it done world he had left behind. I've become one of the *clochards* of the world, he thought. Less alcohol and better fed, but one of them.

He began again, gently, as he did with patients who sometimes telephoned after midnight. "What is it, Warren? What can I do for you?"

A moment's pause while Warren Ross digested his new tone. Ross's voice came down too. "The Ambassador just brought in Monsieur Benari Obenpharo. He's *formidable*."

Mac leaned against the tobacco-smelling wall and closed his eyes. Everything in Paris was *formidable* or *sensas* this year, the prices, the girls, the new pictures, everything. Keeping his cool-but-warm professional voice without realizing it, Mac said quietly, "Yes?"

"Mac, this guy is the J. P. Morgan of North Africa, plus the U. S. Treasury. No kidding. When he blows his nose, the price of gold falls in Zurich. He had lunch at Quai d'Orsay with the Foreign Minister today. That was his *tuyau,* you know, his channel to the Ambassador."

"And now you're his channel to me."

"Now you're getting sore again."

"And I'm his channel to his mistress's sagging *mamelles* or his daughter's nose. Right?"

"Wrong. Look, Mac, dammit, if I didn't get goosed from upstairs do you think I'd bother you? I know how you feel. This Obenpharo flew all the way up here from Tangier just to see you, nobody but you."

"You're a diplomat, Warren. Briefly tell him no in three hundred words."

"He knows where you live."

"Okay, Warren, I'm down. Kick me again, this time in the teeth. I might as well live in a hotel with a switchboard."

"I honest to God did *not* give out your address, Mac! I promised you that, and by God—!"

"All right, all right. So I say yes and he comes polite, through channels, or I say no and he comes anyway. . . ."

"That's about the size of it, Mac."

"Well, then I say no."

Silence, then, "Mac, this guy is the father-in-law of your friend and my friend, Maia Obenpharo."

Mac suddenly realized that during the past weeks he had never once thought of Maia's last name. It was so different from anything he had ever heard that he automatically ignored it. "Father-in-law? But she's divorced."

"Okay. Ex. But she's still in the family like a daughter. Her husband was—well, actually, he *is*—one of those bush league Nehru types. You know, the rich man's son who loves the downtrodden masses. He's raising hell with the French in Morocco right now."

"Warren, if you don't mind, that little problem belongs to your friend and my friend, the State Department." So, Mac thought, she's still in the family like a daughter.

"Mac," Ross was saying, "I'm on the spot with upstairs. All they know is Obenpharo is Mr. Big who wants a plastic surgeon and you're the miracle man from the Oo-Ess-Ay who makes human faces out of wrecks. Go fight City Hall, y'know? Don't let me down. Say yes, man."

"No. But let him come. He'd better be like the other Ali, or Aga, you know, worth his weight in gold."

"No," Ross laughed, "gold hair."

"You're bribing me. You're striking at the soft underbelly of Europe, Mr. Churchill."

"Thanks for the memory." Ross laughed again. "So long, maestro."

Mac turned away from the phone, and saw the proprietor watching him. Yes, the man is right, Mac realized. Life is hard for the small shopkeeper, his telephone has been of service, a token of appreciation is indicated.

"Cigarettes, please, monsieur," Mac said.

"Certainly, monsieur. Lookie Streak? Cahmel?"

"Laurens Khedive."

"Ah, only two packs left. Very few Americans ask for them."

Mac paid for them, then remembered to pay extra for the matches,

221

thinking: Maybe very few Americans know girls like Maia who smoke aromatic Greek and Egyptian brands I never heard of. I asked for Khedive without thinking. Now I'll have to remember about Chesterfields for Eve. As he zigzagged back across the street between the Italian motor scooters and Citroëns, he smiled a little to himself. The *clochards* and the dog owner were correct. It had become a triangle, but a four-cornered triangle with his deep unwillingness to become involved in anything, anything, standing in the fourth corner.

So Obenpharo had come to the quay an hour later and the manner of his arrival was such that all Mac's planned barriers were completely outflanked.

Obenpharo had his chauffeur park the Bentley up along the quay, across the street near the tobacco shop, where it could not be seen from the boat. Mac had been chipping away at the life-size mahogany figure of Maia, one stroke of the mallet after another, watching the wood curl back with satisfaction, feeling the image emerge from the imprisoning wood, and he did not hear Obenpharo come down the stone steps with his cane and across the plank to the houseboat.

A deep voice spoke from the cabin door, in English.

"Is that Maia, Dr. Adams?"

He turned to face an enormous man who filled the doorway. Mentioning Maia was the most businesslike thing Obenpharo could have said under the circumstances, but it was not until much later that Mac learned Obenpharo always said the most businesslike thing under any circumstances.

Obenpharo stood in the doorway of the houseboat cabin only long enough to lay aside his cane and Homburg and gray mocha gloves.

Directly behind him was a smaller dark-skinned man in a chauffeur's uniform and wearing a turban, who had suddenly appeared carrying an elaborately tooled Moroccan briefcase. The chauffeur put the case down so quietly beside Obenpharo's cane, and was gone so quickly, that Mac hardly had time to recognize him as Maia's chauffeur.

It was hard for Mac to continue toward Obenpharo the hostility of an interrupted sculptor, an attitude he had planned after the telephone conversation with Warren Ross at the Embassy. Obenpharo's ponder-

222

ous formality reduced his annoyance to a passing irritation. The man was huge, perhaps two hundred and fifty pounds and three or four inches over six feet tall, immaculately dressed in a dark business suit whose color had sensibly been called banker's gray when Mac was a boy—why do I recall that now? Mac asked himself, and only later did the answer come—because Obenpharo made him feel as his father's sudden dignified entrances once had: like a boy, vulnerable. Little lights winked as Obenpharo came toward him, and Mac noticed the diamond rings on both hands, the discreet diamond tie-pin, the square diamond cuff links.

Obenpharo's hair was completely white, cut closely *en brosse*. Head, clothes, voice, diamonds—all were so imposingly leonine Mac considered it almost a pose. But it was Obenpharo's face which Mac watched as he went to meet the big man. Above the heavy jaws and cheeks, and beneath two white jungles of eyebrows, it was as if there were no eyes, but only a slit between eyelids with a spot of bright blue behind. It was a face for a Roman sculptor working in Caesar's imperial bronze.

"Monsieur Obenpharo?" Mac had put down his mallet and wood chisel, wiped his hands on the sides of his corduroy trousers, and had come forward to shake the big man's hand. It was a friendlier gesture than he had intended for someone who insisted on interrupting his work, but the mention of Maia had set something vibrating which he could stop only in the stage business of conventional gestures. Her gloves lay on the sideboard beside the terra-cotta head, one of them with its leather fingers still curved in the shape of her living hand. Obenpharo's herculean face changed a little, as if a glacier shifted on a mountainside. It was a smile, but the slits which guarded the bright blue eyes remained the same. He took Mac's hand. "Dr. Adams. You look younger than your pictures in the newspapers. It was good of you to see me."

"Mr. Ross was very persuasive."

"He was very kind."

"He's very busy these days. You must be very influential."

Obenpharo shrugged. "I have a few friends. Shall we sit down?" His almost invisible eyes behind their slits flicked over the completed terra-cotta head of Maia and the incomplete mahogany figure of

223

Maia which Mac was working on, perhaps over the gloves, but he did not mention Maia again. "My English is only fair, not good. I'm relieved you speak French so well, Doctor."

"It gets better each day, fortunately."

"You learned it during the war?"

"Before, during, and after. I've been here many times. Let's sit out on deck." The cabin and the mahogany figure were somehow Maia's, and he preferred Obenpharo outside.

As they went out of the cabin and Mac unfolded two canvas chairs, Obenpharo said, "*Sequana*. The name of this boat. Does it have a meaning?" He sounded casual, like a man who had nothing to do but make conversation.

"Sequana has been the goddess of the Seine for two thousand years, since Roman times. My friend who owns the boat liked the idea."

"And those eyes painted on the bow. What are they?"

"My friend borrowed that from the Portuguese fishermen. An *apéritif,* Monsieur Obenpharo?" I was going to get rid of him in two minutes, Mac thought, but there's something special about him and now here I am, ye olde host pouring drinks. I've come all this distance to be alone and work, and somehow I've been continuously surrounded by people, usually with a drink in one hand. I need to cultivate a ruthless unfriendliness.

"The eyes," Obenpharo was saying. "They are to help the boat see where it is going, Dr. Adams?"

"That's the idea. Sort of spiritual radar."

Obenpharo glanced up the Seine, at the stone embankment walling in the slow silver curve of the river, at the massive steps leading up to the quay and the cobblestone street above, at the two fishermen on the opposite bank, at the homey little alcove of the two *clochards* under the bridge. The slow controlled ponderous quality of his movement reminded Mac somehow of the turret of a tank seeking out a target.

"May I ask a personal question, Dr. Adams?"

"All questions are personal, Monsieur Obenpharo."

"I deserve that riposte, Doctor." But he did not pause. "May I ask where *you* are going?"

224

It caught Mac unprepared and he repeated foolishly, "Where am I going?"

Obenpharo put his *apéritif* down solidly and looked at him. "Forgive the directness of an old man, Dr. Adams. It is easier for strangers to exchange intimacies, is it not? And doctors are accustomed to seeing exposed the dirty linen and passions we all keep hidden even from our best friends. Ordinarily I do my business through deputies or by cablegram or telephone. But this morning I was up at dawn to fly here, and it has been a busy day. Fatigue makes old people impatient, you know. You see, I do not conceal my strong desire to see you." He said it as if conceding a bargaining business advantage in advance to clear the air.

"Mr. Ross at the Embassy made that point."

"Obviously, I wish to ask you to do some surgery. You guessed as much."

"Yes." A ruthless unfriendliness, that's what I need. Mr. Big can peddle his problem elsewhere. There are lots of other surgeons.

They were both silent a moment. From the quay above street sounds drifted down, and across the Seine the two fishermen were sharing a bottle of wine while their fishlines dripped into little concentric circles on the still water. If they catch no fish, Mac thought, they've at least caught some of the calm of the river, which must have been the idea in the first place.

Obenpharo got to his feet heavily and went to the cabin to pick up his elaborate Moroccan briefcase, and came back. He opened it to take out a folder labeled—Mac could read it even upside down—*Adams, Dr. Malcolm.* Obenpharo's eyes scanned a typewritten sheet which was clipped to the folder like a summary memorandum, holding it at arm's length, then he looked up.

"Adams is not an uncommon name in America, or among doctors. You are *the* Dr. Adams?"

Mac couldn't resist laughing. "My father was *the* Dr. Adams, Monsieur Obenpharo."

The glacier shifted slightly; it was a smile. "I bow, sir. Filial respect. As vanishing a virtue as virtue itself." Mac wondered if the huge white-haired old man always talked this way, as if he were on a platform looking down. And then it occurred to him that Obenpharo's

225

height, his physical and financial and political size, together made exactly such a platform. Obenpharo must see everything in scaled-down perspective, as from an elevation.

"More precisely," Obenpharo was going on, "you are the Dr. Adams recently acquitted of manslaughter charges in—ah—" He consulted the typewritten page.

"Greenwich, Connecticut, U.S.A.," Mac said, recognizing himself how his voice had changed. This was not necessary. Mr. Big was knuckling him in the solar plexus.

"A tragic affair," Obenpharo said. "My information is that not only civil action was taken because the man's wife accused you, but also your right to practice medicine was threatened."

"The Medical Society cleared me completely. It is no longer a subject for discussion." Hell's bells, now I'm talking the way he does. This is not necessary. He is purposely making a point in his private poker game way.

"Ordinarily, Doctor, one does not discuss it, you are correct. I respect your right to privacy. I deplore what the newspapers have done to you." Obenpharo spread his hands slightly. "But what can I do? I must make sure you are"—the smile again, "—*the* Dr. Adams. I am the head of a family. In business, with all modesty, in all weariness, I have very wide interests, yet I take pride in my family. The future of both family and business will someday depend on one man, my son, and I think his future depends on you."

Mac stared at him. Obenpharo had said it all so simply. It was as if a steel door to a bank vault had swung open to reveal a little lighted candle burning in its cavernous metal heart. Clearly, he was not a simple man. Under that glacial formal manner, he might even be capable of feeling human pain.

"My son," Obenpharo added. "Roger. My only son. Roger Obenpharo. You have heard the name here in Paris?" He seemed to be watching Mac very closely as he asked the question.

"Only the name." This Roger had probably been one of those standard-model low-slung Riviera rich boys, who played games with girls and cars and horses until suddenly they were sixty, sexless, with an enlarged prostate. Ross's description fitted a man in search of confession and absolution.

"It is possible you will hear more of him, Dr. Adams. Roger is active in, ah, North African political affairs." The eye slits were a trifle narrower now. "His terrible facial injuries. Didn't Maia tell you about this?"

No matter how much he tried, Mac still reacted to her name. I must learn to hear her name as if it were a thing, or a day of the week. Maybe it's because she was here such a short while ago and I haven't leveled off yet. . . .

. . . Maia had come to the houseboat a few hours earlier, during the morning of that same day. He had heard her heels clicking down the great stone steps of the quay and he had walked out on deck to watch her, a slender descending curved line made tiny by the huge Seine embarkment, her red-gold hair shining in the sun like a helmet. Carrying a wicker picnic basket a few steps behind her came her turbaned Arab chauffeur. Mac had gone forward to help her step in her higher-than-high heels from the shore to the boat, and she had allowed herself to fall lightly against him as she jumped down to the deck.

"I came after all, darling," she had said. "You thought I wouldn't."

"You didn't yesterday. I lost a day's work."

"I'm doing penance today for that sin, darling. Can't you see? I'm all in black and wearing no lipstick."

He had held her at arm's length looking at all of her, the beautifully molded mouth certainly without lipstick, the light black woolen sheath which said nothing and told all, the little necklace and suspended crescent of diamonds which made a delicate exclamation point at just the right place.

"Penance," he had said. "Just a simple Christian maiden in a Christian Dior dress."

She laughed and moved under his hands. "Your fingers hurt, you American monster." If she professed any faith, Mac knew it would be Moslem; the little expensive Parisian version of the crescent symbol of Islam was part of the costume. And with Maia every detail of every costume counted, perhaps even when she wore nothing.

The chauffeur had put the wicker basket in the cabin and came out to stand at a respectful distance. Maia turned to him and said a few

227

words in rapid-fire Arabic. He bowed his head slightly and stepped ashore and went up the stone steps.

She had swung back to Mac. "It was such a lovely morning I thought of you, darling. So clear-eyed and strong and wholesome." Her long blue-green eyes smiled a little, smiling, but looking deeper, more serious. "So *healthy*. I couldn't resist making a little *pique-nique* with a loaf of bread and a jug of wine."

"And thou," he had said, using the French *tu*, "my red, white, and blue-eyed girl, hast thou ever been kissed standing in the middle of the Seine?"

It was hard to realize that Obenpharo was now sitting where Maia had sat, asking him whether she had told him about somebody named Roger. It was a curious sensation, because her quality was so intense that whenever he thought of her it was as if she stood beside him for a moment. The phrase, *she's in my blood*, he once considered ridiculous; now it seemed sensible.

"You are thinking of Maia." Obenpharo said. It was a statement, not a question.

"Yes," Mac said. Damn my voice, it always gives me away.

Obenpharo looked upstream at the two *clochards* cooking a pot over a small charcoal fire, then across the river at the two tranquil fishermen, then back at Mac. "She has the third of the three beauties St. Thomas Aquinas once wrote."

"I'm a typical scientific barbarian, monsieur. I have never read much outside of medicine."

"A pity." Obenpharo closed his eyes and said in French-accented English, " 'For Beauty includes three conditions . . . wholeness . . . harmony . . . and radiance. . . .' "

"The third only?" Mac said, using French without realizing it. How does he know so much about her? Does he have another dossier labeled, *Obenpharo, Madame Maia?* "Not the wholeness? Not the harmony?"

It was only when he thought about it afterward that Mac realized that Obenpharo must have been deeply disturbed despite his mountainous stillness, because his thumb and forefinger were rubbing, rubbing, in the characteristic pill-rolling tremor of early Parkin-

228

sonism. At the time Obenpharo had seemed rock-bound, unmoved.

"Maia," Obenpharo said, "is my daughter-in-law here in Paris. But not at home in Tangier."

"That sounds like a riddle."

"No riddle. There were two marriages. In Tangier first. Then under French civil law Maia married my son Roger here in Paris."

"You were against the marriage?"

"No. Both my wife and I hoped for it. Roger had become a Moslem convert, and like all converts he was twice as faithful as the Faithful. He insisted on a Moslem ceremony at home, in Tangier. Understand, Dr. Adams, that Moslem marriage is not a sacrament. It is a civil contract. Either partner may begin divorce proceedings."

"I thought only the husband could divorce his wife."

"By custom it has become difficult for a woman to use the rights the Prophet recorded for her. That is why it was Roger, not Maia, who made the break when it came." He sighed deeply. "I am not sure I understood either of them. They are both unique people, both living in that uncomfortable place in the middle of the bridge between Arab and European cultures. Maia tries to out-French the French, in elegance, in the grand manner. You know her. Isn't that true?"

It was true enough, although Mac had never thought of it in just that way. In New York, San Francisco, Rio, and Rome, there were women with the endless time and money to play mirror mirror on the wall, and in Paris they played it more skillfully than anyone else. He had taken Maia's flawlessness for granted, and it had never occurred to him that she was a girl from the colonies out to capture the capital.

"They were fire married to storm," Obenpharo was saying. "Unfortunately, as a Moslem, Roger could get a divorce simply by making a declaration to the local pasha in the Mendoub's court and paying seven hundred francs. It's as simple as tearing up a dog license, under Islamic law."

"Maia would not appreciate a dog license."

"To be sure."

"That makes two strikes against your son, monsieur."

"How so?"

"Three strikes and you're out. That's American baseball."

"Oh, I see. Maia being Maia, perhaps she awaits the third strike. She has won every game she ever played, so far, except this one."

"So Maia is divorced in Tangier, but married in Paris, so to speak."

"Yes."

"Do many people know this?"

"Very few, even though we are a prominent family. We have some pride. Also, you will understand more than most, we seek for privacy in our lives like water in a desert."

"Then why do you tell me so much that is intimate?"

"Does anyone do anything for only one reason? Perhaps, as I said before, because we are strangers, because you are a doctor, and I need your help. I believe there was an Englishman who said that man is the only animal who laughs and cries because he is the only one who understands the difference between things as they are and things as they should be."

"And how are things? How should they be?"

"My son should be in business with me, that is how it should be. He and Maia should have remained together to have a large family. Then I could feel my life had some meaning for the future. Do I sound like an old-fashioned bourgeois banker? I hope so, because that is what I am. My work, my family—these give a man a rock beneath his feet."

"That is how things should be. But how are they, actually?"

"Actually, my son is a broken man. He may be slowly dying from his injuries, and malnutrition and infection. His father weeps beside the waters of Babylon, because Paris *is* Babylon, and begs a doctor from another country to bring his skill to Tangier. And this man gives his skill to clay and wood instead of people because he wishes incredibly to be a sculptor."

"No. He wishes to be a happy man, with time for a little thought and a few friends. After that, everything follows."

"There is greater happiness in art than in healing?" Obenpharo sounded genuinely incredulous. "How is that possible?"

"Only the artist can be his own master. The healer is a public utility. A fool can call the doctor anytime, and command him. An hysterical woman who sees the whole world distorted by her own fears can call him into public court to guillotine his reputation."

"That is how you feel now?"

"Yes. I'm not inventing. These things have happened to me."

Obenpharo reached into the pocket of his coat and pulled out a long slender gold-tooled wallet. From it he took a monogrammed check blank on which he wrote his signature with a quick flourish. He waved it in the air for a moment. "This is a check on my bank." He held it out to Mac, and, when Mac did not take it, he put it with his pen on the table near Mac's chair. "Please fill in your name and any amount you wish. I am serious about this."

Mac did not move. "You are very generous."

"I am trying to make it clear how serious I am, Dr. Adams. Forgive me if I raise the question of your fee so abruptly, but I want the best in modern surgery for my son."

"There are at least a dozen excellent plastic surgeons in Europe."

"Yes, yes, of course, of course. But has any one of them your record of hundreds of maxillofacial operations within the past several years? With results as good as yours?"

"One?" Mac held up his hand. "I can name five. Ten."

"Perhaps. Will any one of them leave his practice for six months or a year, come to Tangier to live as my guest, explain to my son each operation step by step, train the nursing staff and the operating assistants and the anesthetist, and do each operation properly without too much hurry because he does not have to rush back to a busy practice in Paris or Rome? You don't answer because you know that only a nomad, a wandering surgeon like you, could do it." He paused, watching Mac closely. "Are you listening to me, Dr. Adams?"

"Yes. Why can't Roger come to Europe?"

Obenpharo's eye slits closed almost completely. "Is that good treatment? To move a patient back and forth while new skin is growing here and there?"

"Not the best, but a possibility. Or he could move to Paris for a year or so, and be finished."

"He has refused to leave his political work for such a long time. I confess I seek to bring Mahomet to the mountain. I have come to where I am in the world because I recognized the possible combinations of people and events before most of my colleagues. In you, when Maia told me you were here, I recognized a unique opportunity for my family which will not occur again. If you fear inflation

231

and wish to be paid in gold, I can arrange it by noon tomorrow." He tapped the check lying beside Mac. "My New York informants estimate your gross income last year as close to six figures. If you write a year's income on this check, I will thank you for your generosity."

Mac picked up the pen and handed it to Obenpharo. "Put it away, monsieur."

"You are not serious."

"The money makes no difference. Your informants exaggerated. I am alone now and I have enough for everything I need. If I accepted your request, my fee would be the same as I would charge anyone at home."

"Please. I know you are not one of those money-grabbing surgeons who cuts with a gold knife and sews with silver thread. Forgive my talk of money. It is the only language of give-and-take I know. I am too old to beg in a new language."

"Let me think about all this, monsieur."

A small persistent mechanical sound began inside Obenpharo's coat. For a moment he did not hear it because he sat sagging with defeat. Then, finally, he pulled a large watch from his pocket and shut off a miniature alarm on its side. "I must leave for the Place de Puits-de-l'Ermite. The Great Mosque is there. I must see one of the Moslem leaders before it's time for his Maghrib prayer," he explained. He sighed massively. The glacier was gone now and his face was working with pain and self-control.

"May I see that remarkable watch, monsieur?" The watch had at least six little dials set within its face, as well as a calendar and the phases of the moon, and was a convenient conversational diversion from Obenpharo's anguish.

"A clever toy, is it not? Here is the time in Paris now, here on this dial. Here is New York time. This is Zurich. Beirut. Singapore. Macao. Buenos Aires."

"You do business in all those places?"

"And more. I have one department which specializes in arbitrage, another in commodities. In each world capital the exchanges open at different hours." He got to his feet slowly. "It has been a pleasure to make your acquaintance, Dr. Adams."

232

Mac stood up and shook hands in the formal manner of the French. "It has been for me, too."

"You resented my interruption at first?"

"Yes. But not now. It was very interesting."

"But a little too complicated all at one time, perhaps? Like my Swiss watch, perhaps, too many wheels within the wheels?"

Mac smiled. "You are not simple, monsieur. You remind me of those remarkable clocks in Geneva. Very complicated. Never wound with a key. They run forever on atmospheric pressure changes."

Obenpharo's eye slits opened a little more. With the glacier gone a new lion's smile appeared. "I'll tell you a secret. I am wound with a key. A solid gold key." The smile widened. "Even my competitors say I have a heart of gold. And you, Doctor? Tell me your secret."

"There is none," Mac said. "No secret. No key. No heart."

"What a pity. You are a child of the century. No secret, no key." That is not true, Obenpharo thought, Maia is his secret, Maia is his key. "Come to dinner at my house, if you please."

"Thank you. I already have an engagement."

"If she is a woman of the world she will forgive one indiscretion, no?"

"Perhaps. One never knows."

"We dine late. Simple people, simple food. My chef is Cordon Bleu. Maia will be with me. Come if you can. Maia asked me to ask you."

Wheels within wheels, Mac thought. He began our talk by mentioning Maia and he ends the same way. He uses Maia like a rope lasso of silk. This will be a command performance for her, I'm sure. But the gold key has stopped winding and the old man looks weary and humble. He had planned to buy a doctor for his son, like a shipment of banknotes, but there was no price tag and no sale.

"Is your house—?" Mac began to ask.

"Yes," Obenpharo interrupted. He gestured with his cane at the nearby bridge, pointed at the great twin towers of Notre Dame. "You have been there. Quai de Bethune, eight o'clock?"

"Eight o'clock," Mac said, and then, grinning, *"Insha' Allah."*

Obenpharo threw his head back and laughed aloud for the first time. "You *faranji* heathen!" he laughed, and shook Mac's hand

233

ponderously again. "*Salaam aleikum.* Peace be with thee. Did Maia teach you the response?"

"*Allah 'aník,*" Mac said. "And with thee be peace and the grace of God."

At seven o'clock Mac picked up the lobby telephone at the Royal Monceau. When the operator answered, he said, "Give me the suite of Dr. Evelyn Desmond, please."

"Moment, please."

After a brief buzz, "Hello?"

"Eve. This is Mac."

"What a pleasant surprise! Long time no see but lots hear."

"Don't punish me, Eve."

"I won't. It just feels odd to be speaking English to someone. Those rolling Parisian *r*'s have my tongue in a square knot. I'll prove my affection if you dash over for an *apéritif* before our dinner date."

"I've come over on my hands and knees to break our date, Eve."

"Mac! I've seen you only three times since that party Cindy and Warren Ross gave. And each time I had to taxi down to your dock, like a sailor's girl friend."

"I know, I know. And I've come to explain."

"This had better be good. Not funny or cute. Just good."

"I'm in the lobby downstairs. I want to see you, Eve."

"You will please to ascend, m'sieu. You remember the number. Better wear a bulletproof vest."

When she opened her door for him she was wearing a silk scarf around her hair and a quilted robe. "Come in, come in. Black tie and all!"

"Hell of a thing to barge in on you, Eve."

She gave him one of her long sideways looks. "It's always good to see you, even on a disaster basis. Did you know you're all the rage in Paris?"

"I know. Sort of like Lindbergh in '27, but with only one cylinder."

"Sit down, Mac. Let me give you a drink. I'll take the quickest shower in the world and become radiant."

"Good. That's the third of the three beauties."

"What?"

234

"Wholeness, harmony, radiance. The three beauties."

"Mac, my strong silent conservative friend, there are just some times I wonder about you. Where did you of all people ever pick up this poetic fragment?"

"From the John D. Rockefeller of Morocco, Monsieur Obenpharo."

Eve put her hand on her forehead. "And I thought you were spending all your non-working time with that exotic Arab redhead, what's her name."

"You know her name. And you promised no punishment."

"Tell the truth, Mac, if you cut off the red hair, what have you got left?" She raised both hands. "All right, all right. Ignore my fantasy. Don't say a word. That's the most lascivious grin on the mouth of a vulgar male I've ever seen." She started out of the room, but turned at the door briefly to purr, *"Meeoow,"* and then disappeared. A minute later Mac heard the shower splashing as vigorously as an angry little rainstorm.

BOOK III

Action and Passion

(1)

Maia stretched out flat on the deck of the houseboat, offering her face to the early morning glow, a sun worshiper's sacrifice. "You," she said to Mac, with her eyes closed, "you must have hypnotized me with your invitation last night." She covered a small yawn. "I haven't been up this early in years."

Mac looked ahead, at the tow launch pulling them upstream in the Seine at the end of a taut line. "Those fellows on the tow launch said early, and I knew they meant it."

"It's so barbaric. It's almost American."

"Flattery, always flattering me." The early departure had really been the idea of Monsieur le Pilote, the French owner of the tow launch. He had said he wanted to move Mac's houseboat from its Paris location up the Seine to its berth in Neuilly in a single day; he explained to Mac that he had a deep belief in taking a long slow lunch hour, therefore logic required an early start. Mac recognized this variety of take it or leave it logic, and took it.

Maia held up one hand to shade her face as she raised her eyelids to look at Mac. "Really," she said, "what's the use of hurrying about anything?" She frowned. "What's so funny about that?"

"Nothing. It's a profound thought, straight from the Koran, I'm sure."

"I'm not Moslem, you know."

"Yes, I know."

"Then why do you smile?"

"Well, you reminded me of something. There's an actress named Mae West in the States. Years ago she became famous for saying, 'I like a man who takes his time.' "

She smiled in the thin transparent mask of shadow under her hand. "You see?" she said. "A man should take his time. What's the hurry?"

239

"You know," he said, "stretched out on the deck like that—"

"I know," she said, "I know. But it's comfortable, too."

"Cleopatra. On her royal purple barge, sailing up the Nile."

"Why Cleopatra? Why not somebody who had a happier ending?"

"Well, I take it back. But the books say she had red hair."

Her hair lay loosely in a fan beneath her on the deck, the ends curling in the breeze, shining in the sun. This loose schoolgirl coiffure was the latest in a series of hair-style changes he had seen, each different from the last. The Psyche knot, the coronet, the thick-coiled bundle all off to one side, the stubbed bullfighter style, the center parted with knotted side braids, the high topknot and curled tendrils of the Napoleonic era . . . each time he saw her she looked different. Mac considered it an astonishing performance, and today's golden wind-touched looseness was one of the most casual, the most attractive of all.

"My hair," she said, "always that, and never me."

"How could you tell?"

"Your eyes. I was watching them."

He bent forward and kissed her lips. It began as a caress, but the warmth was there, warm and alive with a moving softness, and when she put one arm around his neck to pull him closer, opening her lips and beginning to use her tongue, he felt the hard shaft of wanting her stir in his loins. In the near distance he could hear the quay traffic on both banks above them; all the gear-grinding buses and the wasp-buzzing Vespa scooters and the racing car exhaust sounds of a thousand French drivers giving vent to their thousand dreams of being Grand Prix racing car champions. Mac felt pleasantly primitive, with the slanting morning sun from behind Notre Dame's twin towers warm on his back; this pink warm kissing blur beneath his lips, and all the warm busy world noises around them to enfold their excitement within a kind of open innocence.

"Now," she said, with her lips against his, "you're smiling again."

He kissed her again, briefly, and sat himself up, cross-legged. He waved his hand to indicate the stone walls of the Seine embankment, the sidewalk strollers glancing through pages at the bookstalls, the Quai des Grands Augustine on the left, the grim stone pile of the Palais de Justice on the right, the purposeful traffic crossing Pont Neuf just ahead of them. The corners of her mouth lifted in a tiny

240

smile as she caught his unspoken meaning; they were a moment's beat, a pause, in the whole surrounding symphonic clamor of the city. They were as public as the sky, yet private and apart.

"The first day I arrived in Paris," Mac said, "we crossed Pont Neuf, driving into town. I remembered the old legend: If you see a white horse, a red-haired woman, and a priest crossing the bridge at one time, you're sure to have good luck."

"Did you? All three? The very first day?"

"Well, there was a not quite white horse."

"And here's your *poil de carrote,* your redhead," she said. "Except that we're going under not across the bridge."

He put one hand on her arm. "And I won't even look for a priest."

"You mean," she asked, "there's nothing yet to confess? You know," she added, sitting up to face him, crossing her legs tailor fashion the same way as his and holding her hands in the lap of her skirt like a child, "do you remember last week? When we were walking back to my house after dinner at Lapérouse?"

"Sure I remember. What about it?"

"We crossed Pont Neuf and came along the Quai des Orfèvres and stopped to lean against the stone wall right there." She pointed upward at the wall.

"No," he said, "it was down a little further."

"No," she said, "it was just opposite that big gate in the Palais de Justice where all the big *panniers de salade* drive the prisoners in."

"Salad baskets?"

"Oh, you know. That's argot for the big black police trucks."

"Black Maria, we call them."

"Okay," she said, pronouncing the American word as *ookay*. "You remember that platoon of police who came by while we were leaning against the wall under the street lamp and you were kissing me and one of the *flics* said: Bravo!"

"I remember. Right across the street from the city jail and the French F.B.I. and police headquarters. It was definitely a bravo situation."

"Well," she said, "I loved it. It made me feel gay again. Carefree and open, walking along the river, being kissed by a handsome stranger while the police force marched by."

"So. That's what I am."

241

"The handsome part, darling, that's just flattery. Anybody can look handsome. You look interesting."

"Thanks for nothing. Those are fighting words."

"How?"

"In the States, when someone says, 'That's very interesting,' it means that it's not."

She made a quick flinging movement with one hand. "I just threw interesting overboard."

"Fine. Now we're back to handsome again."

"No, Mac, we're back to stranger again."

"Impossible. Me?"

"Yes, darling, you you you."

"I've never been good at riddles. Why 'stranger'?"

"Simple. We've never slept together."

He saw that beneath her small bantering smile she was serious. Strange, he thought, I never know what this girl is going to say next. She's so different from anyone I've ever known that she seems just a little unreal and closed off, yet she's so direct and honest that she's actually an open person. Eve, who seems so straightforward and open in the frank American manner, is actually a closed woman. He said nothing, thinking this over.

"So quiet, darling? You're offended, Mac?"

"No."

"You're so quiet. Maybe in the States a woman is not supposed to be so direct."

"Well, Maia, usually they aren't. At least, I suppose not. My experience isn't exactly a Gallup poll."

She put one hand on his arm sympathetically. "Mac, you don't have some kind of trouble, do you? You know what I mean?"

He couldn't resist laughing. "My trouble," he said, "is I love them all. The long, the short, and the tall."

Her careful smile became more spontaneous. "I deserve that kind of answer. Foolish questions, foolish answers, no?"

"Yes," he said, "and now I want to ask you something." He got to his feet. "Don't move," he said. "Just sit right there, just like that."

"Like this?"

"Yes. I'll be right back." He went into the cabin and returned in

242

a moment with his sketch pad and a Conte crayon; without saying another word he sat on the deck opposite her and began to draw very rapidly. He wanted to capture the carefree pose, the cross-legged casualness, the left hand dropped into the lap of the skirt while the right was lifted to hold back the wind-blown ends of her hair from her eyes. This was not the elegant Maia, the voluptuous Maia of his unfinished life-size mahogany figure; this seated Maia was a river sprite, as gay and golden-shining as the sun on the water.

"Sie kämmt es mit goldenem Kämme," he quoted to himself as he sketched, *"und singt ein Lied dabei."*

"What does that mean?"

"The Lorelei," he said, "combing her golden hair with a golden comb, singing to the river sailors."

"What makes you think of that, Mac?"

His hand was moving in quick strokes over the sketch pad, tipping the crayon back and forth to get heavier and lighter shading. In the corners of the same sheet he did a few detailed sketches, the hand holding back the hair, the head half lifted, the hand lying in her lap. "I don't know," he answered her, hardly taking his eyes off the pad. "The connection is obvious, isn't it?"

"Is it? Didn't the Lorelei sing men to their destruction?"

"I apologize. My mistake. You don't even have a comb and you certainly aren't singing me onto the rocks."

"I wonder what made you think of it," she said slowly. "First Cleopatra, now Lorelei. Did Laurance Ingersoll say something fantastic like that to you?"

He put the pad down after a quick final stroke. "That's the way I like to catch a figure," he said. "Alive, and with the wind blowing."

"Mac, I have the feeling you're avoiding every question I ask you."

"About Ingersoll, you mean?"

"Yes. He was very fond of the Lorelei idea."

"It's just a highbrow way of calling a girl names. Forget it."

"I have, Mac. Have you?"

He took her face between his two hands and said, "Maia, your barbaric American stranger can't talk seriously on an empty stomach."

"I can't tell if you're joking or playing for time."

243

"Half and half. If you want to talk now, we'll talk. If you want my special three-course breakfast and some real coffee, hot coffee, I'll have it ready in a minute."

She put her hands in two smooth warm cuffs around both his wrists. "I love it when you're foolish and practical and, and . . . I don't know the right word—"

"—hungry?"

"No, you clown. Not hungry." She jumped to her feet, still holding his wrists, pulling him up, too. "It's the coffee that seduces me. Nothing else could do it. I'm not human this early in the morning until I've had coffee." She stretched as luxuriously as a cat and, in the middle of it, collapsed into a huge yawn.

"You see?" she said. "I'm so completely relaxed, my bones have melted. It must be some kind of yogi, getting up so early."

"This isn't early any more, Duchess."

"Anything before noon is early, isn't it?" They walked toward the cabin. "What's the first course? American canned fruit juice with ice in it?"

"No. A duck egg."

"And the second?"

"Duck egg."

"And the third is duck egg?"

"Of course."

They went into the cabin laughing aloud like children.

She stacked their empty breakfast plates in the tiny galley while he poured another cup of coffee for them both.

"What a wonderful chef you are," she said over her shoulder. "That was excellent. Now I'm completely willing to be cast ashore on a desert island with you."

"After that little six-course effort your cook produced last night, I had to try my best."

"The cook always creates wonders when Papa Obenpharo is in town. Papa has that effect on everybody."

"Sugar?" He wanted to talk to Maia about Obenpharo, but this didn't seem to be the right time. There was a good deal to be said about Obenpharo.

"None." She came back from the galley and sat down opposite him.

"Cigarette?"

"Mac!" She took one from the pack he offered her. "They're Khedive! You incredible man, you'd probably even remember my birthday."

"If I knew it."

"I have a sort of birthday party every year on Bastille Day."

"Can I come this year?"

"You must. I always bring in a Moroccan orchestra and dancers." She laughed. "We'll have to get you a turban and a *djellaba*."

"Is Bastille Day really your birthday?"

"Of course not. I just like the idea of having the whole city celebrating all around me. I have no idea when I was born."

"Is that possible?"

"My American, from the land of vital statistics. Don't you know that millions of people have no exact idea when they were born?"

"That's fine," he said. "You can be seventeen every year that way."

"I intend to remain twenty-six forever. Does that seem too old?"

"Old? No, an infant. Until I met you, Maia, I felt as if I'd reached the biblical limit of a hundred and twenty."

It sounded heavier than he had intended, but once he heard himself say it, he knew it was true in its own way. She was a new world. Before Maia had walked toward him across the Rosses' living room he had expected difficulties in settling down in Paris, a sort of slow non-working warmup period during which he'd visit the museums, the galleries, the magnificent collection of Rodin at Hôtel Biron. It was only meeting Maia a few weeks ago which had made him want to begin to sculpt immediately, without the mystical preliminaries many artists need to prepare themselves for that wanted, yet somehow unwanted, plunge into new work. Usually he approached his sculpture as if it were a research problem: selection of subject—the head alone, or the entire figure? material—wood, metal, or stone? emphasis—on character, sensory texture, or symbolism? This cool technical approach had always troubled him faintly, it seemed so flatfooted and plodding. He considered himself a professional, a sculptor no longer dependent on ritual or mood in order to work. Yet Maia had triggered

245

an impatience to begin new work based on swift intuitive judgments so different from anything he had ever felt before that he was amazed. Stone or wood—it didn't matter. Wood mallet, stone chisel, or carving knife; what was the difference, if only he could capture the level steady eyes, the secret smiling mouth, the look of worldly wisdom yet childlike openness, the slender voluptuous line of her figure? Clay, mahogany, terra cotta. He'd try them all! He couldn't remember ever having enjoyed his work and such a sense of freedom before.

She held her cigarette quietly, looking at him steadily through an aureole of smoke. Each of them realized something of what the other was thinking. He glanced out of the small curtained window beside him, squinting against the flickering water reflections which struck his eyes in sharp glints, hardly noticing that the Seine was much wider now, and its traffic of *péniches,* the broad-beamed river barges, was heavier.

How does a healthy man explain a complicated set of ideas about the aspects of love to a girl like this one, he thought. Eve must have wondered about it, too, and probably he owed an explanation to her first. With Eve, explanations would be easier, because their upbringing was so similar; she had had the same intelligent rational parental climate, the same severely self-analytical discipline of medicine, the same final acceptance of guiding conduct by an intellectual code instead of instinctual gratification alone. How easy and childish it was to label his viewpoint about love as puritanism, a label which even intelligent Europeans used constantly about Americans, as if an exaggerated, oversimplified, and derogatory-sounding word explained anything. Even the intelligent French physicians he met accepted the idea of a rotisserie of *affaires,* each gently browned and basted but rather meaningless, each demanding an elaborate parlor game of phone calls, rendezvous, lies to the previous woman, explanations, maneuvers, a daisy chain of narcissism. He had met Parisian doctors who were just like their slick American counterparts, hand-patters, casual purveyors of antibiotics, diagnosticians by magical fancy, and he took it for granted that such men had not the faintest idea of modern medicine's reasoning about the nature of promiscuity. But that the others, the first-rate men, should accept the amorous merry-go-round after the adolescent years—when the search for manhood and the screw-'em all bedroom trophies of conquest were such blazing goals—that even they should accept this as a rational daily occupation for mature people was a surprise to Mac. And, he thought, I must surprise them as some sort of primitive cowboy who ignores the basic facts of life.

Maia blew a stream of smoke into the air. "How nice to be with such a quiet man. It's been so long."

"Now that I've had breakfast," he said, "I'm grappling with my soul."

"Yes. Remember how Obenpharo quoted Thomas à Kempis last night? 'Who hath greater labor than he who hath combat with himself?' Not bad, I'd say."

"I'm not in combat with myself."

"That's not true, Mac. But what's the difference? It's one of Obenpharo's thousand and one favorite lines."

"Another cup of coffee? The cup that cheers."

"Thank you, no. It was very good."

"You think I'm avoiding a discussion."

"You said that. I didn't." She put her hand over the back of his on the table. "It's so peaceful, this little room. The sound of water going by beneath us. The river and the sunlight. I haven't felt so tranquil in years. There's really no need for talking, is there?"

"Maybe not, Maia. But I think I'd like to."

"All right then. But only about us. Nothing else interests me."

"I like your honesty."

"And I like yours. I liked the way you didn't pretend the night we met at the Rosses' apartment."

"You bowled me over, Maia. At first I thought you were a movie star, or a top model."

"A model? Did I look so artificial? I'm not thin enough for the photographers, and not fat enough for the painters."

"Sounds just about right for a sculptor."

She glanced up at him quickly from beneath her eyebrows. "Is this an American habit, always saying serious things in a half-joking way?"

"I'm not joking, Maia. I've never met anyone like you."

She wrinkled her nose. "Don't say that, please. So many men

247

have said it to me. First, that. Then the invitation to dinner. Then the invitation to bed." She stubbed out her cigarette carefully, then pointed at the words glazed into the little café ashtray. "You see? Even the ashtrays." She turned it so that he read the phrase around the pottery edge.

Love makes time pass, it read. *Time makes love pass.*

Maia pushed the ashtray aside. "You see? Very Parisian: how do you do, tip your hat, *enchanté,* let's go to bed."

"There's nothing in that, Maia. You must be saying something else."

"I'm trying to say I liked the way you were when we met. Not complicated. But not too simple, either. I even liked the Latin names of the face muscles, even though I have a reason to hate Latin. That's why I said yes when you said you wanted to do that terra-cotta bust. Usually I say no."

"It came out very well, too. I'm going to call it Maia Terra Cotta, like a name, because it sounds good."

"You sounded good. You were serious when I came. You really worked. The good ones are always serious at work."

"If you're giving me credit for not making a pass at you, don't. I thought of it every time you came."

"That's what I mean, Mac. I've never seen a man hold himself in that kind of balance. After all, just admiration is not exactly new to me."

He quoted her. " 'The red hair fools everybody.' "

"Well, I take some trouble with it, and it does. I thought at one or the other of our modeling sessions you'd finally come to the point—"

"—and all I did was kiss you once or twice—"

"—which can be a very dirty trick, Mac—"

"—apologies—"

"—no, how do they say? Better a crust—"

"Maia—"

"Please. Don't be angry, Mac."

"I'm not. Only—"

"You looked it. You looked angry."

"I'm not, Maia. But let me tell you something."

"At last. Another cigarette, please. It helps keep my mouth shut "

248

He put two cigarettes between his lips, and after lighting them both passed her one. "I don't know how to start. I feel clumsy and self-conscious."

"How nice. Everyone else in Paris is convinced he's brilliant, and doing you a favor by talking to you."

"Well, that's just it, Maia. I haven't had years of practice sitting on the terrace of some café and yakkity-yakking—"

"What's that?"

"It means talking, talking, talking about little things on and on."

"This?" She raised her eyebrows. "This is little?"

"Good God, no. Let's not stumble over American slang."

"Talk French, then. It's easier for me, too."

"I don't have the precision in French."

"Good. Only the French have. Just say what you mean."

"Agreed," he said in French. He paused, then said, "I've wanted you from the minute you walked across the room at the Rosses' place."

She watched him for a long minute, searching his face in a way he could not understand. Finally she said, "Ah, progress. So, you wanted me. We're making progress in French."

"If you start joking now—"

"Forgive. Am I forgiven?"

"Always."

"Isn't it terrible, Mac, that exactly those words have been said to me before?"

"I'm saying what I mean, in simple French. Take it or leave it."

She picked up his hand and put his palm against her cheek, keeping her own over his. "I'll take it. Tell me more."

"When I began to work so well, Maia, it was a feeling of—well, like a small miracle. Before that, it was like living underground so long I forgot the light outside. And then coming out into the sun. You follow me?"

She turned and kissed his curved palm which she held against her cheek and said, "Yes," muffled against his hand. The gesture was so simple and spontaneous, so different from her usual pretense of sophistication, he was deeply touched. He could not imagine one other woman among those he knew capable of it.

"Maia," he said, "I wanted to leave well enough alone. I didn't

249

want to begin a new set of complications in my life. I was as super-stitious as an aborigine. Just leave well enough alone. I felt a little guilty about Eve—"

"Of course. She's charming. I respect cool intellectual women like that tremendously."

"Put down your dagger. She's a warm wonderful girl."

She bit into his thumb.

He pulled his hand back and rubbed the painful teethmarks. "You need a muzzle."

" 'Warm.' 'Wonderful,' " she said. "That's what I thought. You're her lover."

"No," he said. "It could have happened, but it didn't."

"Why not? Two doctors. You could get into bed, sterilized sheets of course. Rubber surgical gloves. You could discuss diagnosis and therapy. You could listen to that steady intelligent heart beat with a stethoscope—"

"You're really a cat. Cleo, the cat."

"Of course," she said calmly. "No conscience. Just claws."

"Well," he said, making a move to get up, "that's that."

She caught his arm. "No, no you've just begun."

"Maia, when I hear myself out loud it sounds—" He gestured with one hand, not finishing his sentence.

"Don't be such a barefoot bashful boy. Let it sound as it sounds."

"I don't want to make it clinical, Maia. Outside of a hospital meeting, medical talk sounds offensive to people."

"My God, Mac, will you stop running away! Talk like a doctor. Talk like a man. What's the difference how you talk?"

"Okay," he said in English, then returned to French. "More than wanting to keep this new way of living on an even keel—more than knowing that one step with a woman leads to another and then all your tranquillity and work vanishes—"

"Someone told me, Obenpharo I believe, that continence makes intellectuals out of men."

"I'm glad you mentioned him. I'm coming to him in a minute."

"Obenpharo?" She was really surprised. "Where does he come into this?"

"I told you it was complicated."

"Maybe I ought to keep quiet."

"No," he said with a straight face, "don't do that. There's no one else here to interrupt, if you don't."

She threw her head back and laughed heartily. He enjoyed the complete way she did it. "Oh, Mac, Mac, I never dreamed I'd hear a man have such a hard time telling me no."

He slapped his hand flat on the table, making the cups jump. "You redheaded fool, I'm telling you yes!"

"But you sound so mixed up. You've read too many books. You're too complicated!"

"I'm not." His self-consciousness dropped, and he began to say what he meant. "I only have a dislike for the infantile running around I see. The into bed and out of bed, like shaking hands. There are medical explanations for promiscuity"—his voice rose slightly—"and personally I'm not in a constant frantic search for new vaginas!"

"Yes," she said quietly after a moment, "you were right. That does sound clinical."

"Sure," he said in English, unthinkingly. "I knew it. But that's what it is."

"Personally, I know very little psychology from books."

"Thank God. Nobody else who isn't a professional does, either, but everybody pretends he does."

"But I think I know what you mean. It's like the woman who can't sleep with a very exciting man unless first they are friends. It's hard to understand. If you ignore the excitement until you are friends, the excitement may never come back." She shook her head slightly. "You believe first there must be a relationship, no?"

"Yes. That's part of the idea. I think the hit-and-run boys are frantic. Doctors see it every day, men pushing themselves to prove to themselves what men they are, women who climb into the hay like taking a department store escalator. They've never grown up, and there's no real happiness in it."

"Over here," she said, "people consider sex a need, like food. Or a pleasant game, like window shopping."

"For those that do, fine. It's just true enough to work for simple people."

"But many of these people are not simple. They're quite worldly."

251

"Then they grew up accepting those values, and it's as natural as eating tons of olive oil in Spain or drowning in *pasta* in Italy. This gets us from medicine into anthropology, and I jump the track. I'm not that smart."

"So," she said, with her voice changing, "it depends on how one grows up? And where?"

"Much of it, yes. Why do you look like that?"

"I'm thinking, I'm just thinking it over. I feel very thoughtful when I think about how I grew up. In the hills of Morocco nobody talks or thinks about such things. Everything is done as it has been done for thousands of years. I—" she began to say, and stopped.

"Tell me about it. It's just about your turn to confess."

"Some other time. Not right now."

"Now I'm really curious. Where did you grow up?"

"Please, respect the lady's privacy."

He chuckled. "Go to bed with the lady, but respect her privacy."

"Somehow that sounds insulting."

"No," he said, "it just illustrates the café society attitude I've been talking about."

"After all," she said hotly, "an interesting evening, a little *affaire,* that's one thing. But to know another person's mind and thoughts—"

"Yes," he said triumphantly, with an edge of ironic anger, "like sharing toothbrushes, that's really carrying intimacy too far, isn't it?" Here was the root of it, he thought. Suddenly he remembered Warren Ross saying: *She's a Berber. That's sort of but not quite, Arab.*

Maia turned the ashtray round and round, not reading the glazed motto on it, not speaking. Finally, she said, "A cigarette, please. And light two, the way you did before."

He did, and gave her one of the lighted cigarettes. They smoked silently together, as he watched her eyes narrow in thought.

"I think I'm beginning to see what you mean," she said slowly. "I've never heard it expressed before."

In English he said, "Even after years of yakkity-yak? There's really nothing new in it."

"Perhaps not to you." She shook her head a little, smiling, and repeated, "Yakkity-yak. What an odd word."

"There's really nothing new in any of this, Maia. Monogamy has

252

been a religious idea in the Western world for a long time, but I don't think I'm talking about monogamy." He glanced quickly at her. "Did Obenpharo show you his complete little dossier on me?"

"My office assembled everything about you from our New York correspondent for him, darling. I confess."

"You know, I keep forgetting you work in a bank."

"Let's call it a gilded cage and forget it, darling."

"Yes, except now you know from those file clippings that monogamy didn't work very well for me. My wife divorced me."

"On that subject, I live in a glass house, Mac. I never throw stones." How deeply it still hurts him, she thought, remembering the information in the file. In this moment the impersonal file became human for her; the whole dreary account, everyday newspaper misery and therefore dull, now became Mac's frown, Mac's eyes, the remembered pain, real and human. I must remember to get rid of that file dossier. He needs every bit of privacy he can get.

Mac was looking out the window, past the Seine embankment, past the tall apartment houses, over the riverside iron cranes and chimneys, past the far-off Eiffel Tower, all the way back to Greenwich. "I still don't know what went wrong," he said, as if talking to himself. "I think it bothers me. I think it's one reason I came to Europe—to see myself the way I was, from a distance." He glanced at her. "You see? I warned you this would be complicated."

"I hope you're not saying that the present means nothing to you, you're in cold storage, until the grass grows over all the graves of the past."

"Well, I felt that way for a little while. But I realized how morbid and unhealthy it was. But I'd rather face it all in my memory than pretend to bury it."

"What is there important to face?"

"I was a complete failure with my wife, obviously. I don't want it to happen again, and I suppose that's why a woman like Eve—"

"—an American woman who reminds you a little of your wife—"

"—a little, yes. A little. That's why—"

"—but I'm from a different planet—"

"—yes, and so damn beautiful—"

"Don't call me that. Beauty is so troublesome."

253

"Good God, why?"

"To begin with, I'm not really one of nature's flawless pearls. I have to work at it."

"But so do most women. Except you're off to a head start."

She shook her head impatiently. "Shall I share my toothbrush with you?"

"Beauty is one of the great human goals. Why is it troublesome?"

"Everyone wants to handle this kind of beauty. Own it. Use it. Destroy it. Fill their emptiness with it."

"Even me? I thought I was explaining that I didn't want just to use you."

"But you have. I'm your stimulant, your escape into sculpture."

He was amazed. "Maia, what's all this? The old twist? Reverse psychology?"

"No. I couldn't be more serious. When a man calls me beautiful, I know we're doomed. You never called me that before."

"Now you're the superstitious aborigine," he said.

"I resent that!"

Her reaction was so far out of proportion to what he had said that he became immediately wary, professionally alert. "Maia," he said gently, "we all believe in magic. All of us, really, inside. But when you start talking nonsense about doom—"

"You began it by talking the usual nonsense about beauty," she said with more annoyance than he had ever seen in her before. "A month ago, when you joked about the medical names of face muscles, then I thought: He sees below the surface."

"But, Maia, muscles—they're just raw meat."

"Raw meat is better than hors d'oeuvres."

"But you're being so damn contradictory, Maia! First you want a casual affair, play with the toy doll, that's the way it goes. Don't go any deeper. Invasion of privacy. Now you turn it around the other way. Now it's to hell with champagne, just give you raw meat."

"And you? You're too logical and reasonable ever to be contradictory?"

"Hell's bells," he said in English. "Hell's goddam bells. How did we ever get into this? If you're going to straddle the fence, with a foot on each side, you're sure to be right."

"Of course. Obenpharo taught me that in banking. Hedge your bet whenever you can."

A shout came from the stern of the tow launch. "Alloo-alloo-alloo!"

Maia raised her head. "Is someone shouting?"

"Monsieur le Pilote," Mac said, pointing at the man on the tow launch who held his hands up to his face like a megaphone. "Alloo-alloo!" the launch pilot shouted.

Mac got up and opened the cabin door. When the pilot saw him, he shouted, "Twelve o'clock! We're going to tie up ashore for lunch. Agreeable?"

"Yes," Mac called back, "agreeable." He came back into the cabin and stood over Maia, bending forward a little with one hand resting on the table, the other on her shoulder, feeling the skin warmth through the cloth. "Agreeable?"

"Twelve o'clock! Where did the time fly to?"

Mac moved his shoulders up and spread his hands apart, deliberately exaggerating the traditional French shrug. "Who cares?" he said.

"But you were going to tell me something on your mind about Obenpharo."

"We've talked enough," he said. "Maybe we've talked too much," he added, bending closer to kiss her upturned mouth. She put her hands up and pulled his face toward her.

Mac helped the pilot and the pilot's helper secure the houseboat side by side with the launch, which had in turn been moored by bow and stern lines to the landing dock of a riverside *mariniers'* restaurant. At the end of the dock a short stone path of steps under arches of roses led to a shaded terrace before the little restaurant. The *patron,* wearing a long white apron and shirtsleeves, stood at the top of the steps waiting for them. Behind him several groups of men sat at the tables on the terrace eating lunch seriously among a cluster of wine bottles.

As Maia crossed from the houseboat to the tow launch, she mounted the rail and stood poised there, ready to jump down to the launch deck, her hair on fire in the hard noon sun, seraphic against the sky. She looked down at Mac standing there on the deck below her, still holding his helping hand, sensing his admiration. "You down there," she said. "What are you looking at like that?"

"Not beauty," he said. "Just some raw meat."

He caught her lightly as she jumped, then carried her across the short space of the deck, and swung her over the polished rail of the launch onto the dock. "Bravo a second time," she said, laughing a little, and pushed back the hair ends blown into her eyes by the river breeze.

Mac jumped over the gleamingly varnished rail, up to the dock. "Think nothing of it," he said, taking her elbow as they followed the pilot up the path. "The movement of a load of meat."

With her elbow she squeezed the hand which held it against her side. "So," she said, "I opened my mouth before, and now I must pay for my sins."

"Crime and punishment," he said. "I hereby sentence you—"

"—don't be vulgar, now!"

"—how could you tell what I was going to—"

"—by your voice, Mac. And that wicked look."

"Well, I've been surrounded by so many sterile tools and sterile ideas for so long, I think I'd enjoy a nice long healthy dose of vulgarity."

They had reached the terrace now and exchanged polite little nodding bows with the *patron*. He looked at the pilot, then at Mac and Maia. "A table for all four?"

Mac looked at the pilot. "May we join you?"

The pilot said politely, "Our pleasure," but his assistant scowled.

"If you and Monsieur, your assistant, will be kind enough to be our guests—"

"On the contrary. Monsieur and Madame will be ours."

Here we go again, Mac thought. The whole French-American vaudeville act. He does not want it thought that he is poor, that France is poor; that he needs American generosity, that France needs American generosity; that he is not my equal as a luncheon host, that France is not a first-rate power. Since the end of the war—no, before that—since the liberation of Paris, even the most sensible French seemed to catch the epidemic disease of disliking the United States while, at the same time, they liked individual Americans.

"Monsieur?" the *patron* was saying questioningly. Mac suddenly realized that Maia and the others were seated and that a chair was being held politely for him.

"Pardon," he said. "Thinking. Didn't hear you." He looked across the table at the pilot and his young assistant sitting there a trifle stiffly. "Permit me," he said, "should have made introductions sooner, Monsieur le Pilote, Monsieur Solbert——"

"Robert Solbert," the pilot said, bowing in his seat to Maia, "and my assistant, Maxime Quinet." Maxime blinked and stirred uncomfortably; this was clearly a new experience.

"——Mademoiselle Obenpharo," Mac finished.

Maia beamed at the pilot. "What a clever idea to stop here," she said. "A stroke of genius."

"We had such an early start, only time for a quick coffee with a little something in it to give it body——"

"Not me!" Maxime said. "I can't stand cognac in my morning coffee," then looked surprised as the others laughed.

"Anyway," the pilot said, patting his belt where his beret was tucked into it, "there comes a time to put some solid fuel on the fire."

The *patron* brought the menu while a green dragonfly came to hover with vibrating wingtips over their table and white butterflies danced unevenly in and out of patches of sunlight around them. A barge loaded high with firewood sailed downstream slowly; the whistle on it blew once, and a man in the wheelhouse leaned out to exchange waved greetings with the *patron*. At the neighboring tables, people had politely gone back to their omelets and bread and *vin ordinaire,* only taking a quick appreciative look at Maia now and then.

The gauze of morning mist had been burned off the surface of the waters, and along the banks of the far shore a kingfisher followed by a squadron of sandpipers flew zigzag over the yellow patches of ragwort, the climbing belladonna, and white convolvulus. Mac realized the quiet he had noticed when he had first come ashore was really filled with a hundred tiny early summer sounds, and the name, *la vielle Seine,* almost the equivalent of Ol' Man River, made good sense.

"May I suggest," the *patron* said, folding his hands across his apron, "*Maquereaux au vin blanc,* with just a trace of thyme and bayleaf and peppercorn?"

"The *marinade* is excellent here," the pilot said.

"And some Sancerre. Or a little glass of our own wine, flavored with mirabelle. And later, for Madame, *Salade d'oranges* with some kirsch?"

"What's your preference for lunch?" Mac asked Maia. "The mackerel sounds good." Across the table the pilot and the *patron* were discussing *potée champenoise* in great detail, using gestures.

"Darling," she answered in English, "don't ask me to use my brain, even for food. I'm drifting like a cloud. Whatever you wish."

"What I wish," he answered in English, "isn't written on any menu."

Within the dark little circle of the pupil of each of her eyes he could see himself reflected clearly, as if in miniature mirrors, with his hair tousled by the wind, looking carefree. That's how I look to her, he thought with surprise. She could not see the intensity of his feelings, the complicated self-questioning he had recently acquired, the attempt to see each action and idea in three dimensions—an attempt which he was beginning to feel was his growing strength and most threatening weakness—no, he thought, looking deeply into the little twin mirrors of her eyes, she sees that open, laughing, athletic-seeming American.

She smiled her slow secret smile. "No menu? And now you wish it?" she said very softly. "You think opportunity knocks twice on one day?"

After lunch, over coffee, Mac reached for his American cigarettes, but the pilot must have been watching him because he immediately offered around his pack of Gauloise *bleu*. Maxime did the secondary honors round the table with a match, for which Maia gave him a thank you that made the boy blush from the throat upward. They sat smoking the pungent dark tobacco, slowly drinking the small cups of equally pungent dark coffee.

"If you will permit," Mac said diplomatically to Monsieur Solbert, the pilot, "it would be my pleasure to buy a round of armagnac."

The pilot combed his broad fingers back through his short gray hair, once, then a second time. "Armagnac would put the cork in the bottle just right," he said, and the deep creases in his face eased into something like a smile.

258

Finally, Mac thought, that did it. That turned the key in the lock. Obenpharo had a golden key. This man's was made of armagnac.

The pilot leaned back in the wicker chair, combing his iron hair with his fingers once or twice, and loosened his belt. He looked across the table at Mac. "If all our jobs were like this."

"If every day were like this," Mac said.

"One says you are a famous American doctor."

"Not at all famous," Mac said.

Maia spoke in English. "No escape, is there, darling?"

"It was in the newspapers," the pilot said.

"There was a coincidence because of my wartime experience in France. Such things are not forgotten here."

"No," the pilot said, "they are not."

"That was why it was a big thing in the papers. But now it can be forgotten."

"Are you a specialist in the liver, monsieur?"

"Ah," Maia said, "the liver. In America, the heart. In Britain, the stomach. In France, the liver."

"No," Mac said, "the liver is of interest to any doctor, but it is not my specialty."

"Sad. We have many sculptors, but not enough liver specialists."

"Not enough anything!" the silent Maxime said loudly. "Not enough houses or apartments. Not enough tractors. Not enough political stability. Not enough new ideas."

"Don't look so surprised, monsieur," the pilot said to Mac. "He's like all the silent ones," he added, making a repeated circular motion over his chest, "lots of things going around inside."

Maxime looked bitterly at Mac. "We're in the middle here. You don't realize. None of the Americans realize. When the atom bomb drops, we're the ones who will be pulverized, not big countries like yours and the Soviets'."

"It won't drop," Mac said. "You'll live to be a grandfather and light your house with current generated from the atom."

"Monsieur," Maxime said intensely, shrugging aside the cautioning arm the pilot put on his elbow, "such incredible optimism is either politically naïve or American propaganda!"

"Maxime!" The pilot was angry now.

Maxime raised his voice over the pilot's. "He's an intelligent man! I pay him a compliment. I'm frank."

"Are you a Communist?" Mac asked.

"Ah! Always the first American question! The poison label. I'm left, but not red, something Americans can't understand."

"I'm not labeling you, Maxime. I'm interested in your viewpoint. You've labeled me: American. Next comes the part about the capitalists, the military, the mistreatment of Negroes, and our crazy wish to drop the atom bomb. Is that right?"

"What's going on here?" Maia asked, sitting up straighter. "A minute ago we were having lunch."

The pilot jerked his thumb toward Maxime. "His class of reserves has just been called up for duty in North Africa."

"I'm not going," Maxime muttered quietly. "To hell with the jingoes. It's a dirty little kind of a war down there."

The *patron* came beaming toward them with a tray. He set it down on the table and set out four glasses proudly. Then he stopped and said, "Something wrong, gentlemen? Changed your minds?"

"A political discussion!" the pilot said.

"On a day like today? After such a meal?"

"I agree," Maia said. "Barbarism."

"If we want to shut our eyes to the world," Maxime said fiercely, "opium would have been better than mackerel."

"Ah, ah," the *patron* said wisely. He lifted the bottle in his other hand and wiped the dust from it with the edge of his apron. "Here's the opium." He pulled the cork, and began the ritual of pouring.

Maia's hand touched Mac's beneath the table. In English she said, "Poor darling. No escape. No place."

"I'm not sure I wanted to escape," he said. "Did you?"

"Yes, Mac. I accused you, but I'm the one."

"Why, Maia?"

"It's too complicated." She sighed faintly. "Such a nice day, too."

"There you are!" the *patron* said, stepping back. "Taste it."

"No," Mac said, "a glass is missing."

"But, monsieur, there are four."

"We need five. One for you."

"No, no, monsieur. After all—"

260

"I insist. In the name of your grandfather."

The *patron* made a quick little pleased bob of his head and hurried back into the inn. The terrace was empty now except for the butterflies, the pools of light and shade, and a bearded old man at the next table smoking a long pipe and scanning an open newspaper whose front page headline read: CASABLANCA TROUBLES CONTINUE: STERN REPRISALS. The high sun was at an angle now and the morning coolness was gone. Maia opened the top buttons of her blouse, smiling a trifle when she saw Mac watching her.

The *patron* came back to the table with another glass and poured himself a finger level.

The pilot raised his glass. "To long life and a happy future," he said.

"Impossible," Maxime said.

"Truthfully," Maia said, looking around the table, "we should drink to the cameraderie of the mackeral."

She quoted the old country saying. "*Mon petit ventre, console-toi, tout ce que je bois c'est pour toi.* My little belly, console yourself, all that I drink is for you alone."

Everyone laughed a little. Even Maxime smiled. "That's a non-political central position," he said, "and very true."

Mac raised his glass. "To present company, present laughter," he said. They all nodded and drank the toast. Mac swung sideways in his seat and raised his glass to Maia, saying in English, "To present company, present love."

She touched the lip of his glass with hers and they drank together.

After they said good-by to the *patron* and went back down the stone path beneath the arches of roses, the pilot said to Maia, "Do I remember correctly, mademoiselle? The name is Obenpharo?"

"Yes," Maia said.

"I ask because just yesterday I won a little pile at Enghein on a beautiful horse named Pharaoh. It was a two-year-old from the Obenpharo stables in Chantilly."

"There is no connection," Maia said shortly.

"A pity. One always hopes for an inside tip."

"Yes," Maia said, "a pity."

261

She and Mac helped the pilot and his assistant cast off their lines and tie up the long pair of tow ropes. Within a half hour they were moving upstream again. Maia went into the cabin to freshen up, then came back up to the bow where Mac stood watching the green banks slide by. He put his arm across her shoulders lightly.

"That stupid boy, Maxime," Maia said, looking straight ahead at the launch. "Everything was fine until he blew his horn." The light wind was whipping her hair in strands across her face; with a quick gesture she brought both hands up to her temples to control it. "I suppose," she added, "you think I'm like Marie Antoinette at Versailles, playing at being a simple milkmaid on a manicured toy farm."

"No," he said, "I thought you were very understanding with Maxime."

"Europe and North Africa are filled with Maximes. Hopeless. And angry because they're hopeless, and ready to blame the world around them for their own failures."

"Why take somebody like Maxime so seriously?"

"Obviously, it's not Maxime. It's the man he reminds me of."

Neither spoke as a string of barges pulled by a tugboat passed them. On one of the barges a woman was hanging out children's clothes to dry on a line, and, when Mac waved toward her she waved back. A child and a puppy played together on the deck beside her, both tied around the waist with safety lines to the railing.

"You're feeling friendly toward the world today, aren't you?" Maia said, looking up at Mac. To see him better, she lowered her nearest hand from her temple, and the wind immediately waved her loosened hair across her face like a small flag of silk threads. She stepped back, turning her head aside, laughing. "I'll go put it up in a scarf," she said.

"No," he said quickly. Until today she had always seemed too well put together, the kind of art which needs gilt salon settings to seem natural; her remarkable series of coiffures was the symbol of her effortless-seeming efforts, so that somehow, today, her casually loose and tossing hair was a break toward naturalness.

"You'll be sorry, if I don't," Maia said. "So will I. When my hair's a mess, the whole illusion is lost."

"Well," he said, "I've been losing quite a few of them lately."

"What do you mean?"

"Nothing in particular."

"But everything in general. It had a special sound to it."

"Well, the pilot asking you about the racehorse reminded me."

"It's true," she said quickly. "We sold our stables in Chantilly. Obenpharo's father began it, and after the war Obenpharo sold most of our stallions abroad, in the States and Great Britain, to raise our dollar and our sterling balances. Papa is older now, and he's lost interest, and I'm bored by the whole religion of breeding thoroughbreds, so we sold it to a combine. They keep the Obenpharo name for prestige."

"I keep forgetting you're an executive," he said. "I suppose it's because I've never seen you at your bank office."

"I'm just a girl on a raft," she said. "Today the game I'm playing is being a castaway on a desert island."

"In France," he said, "everything is a combine, isn't it? Buying a stud farm, building a steel mill, starting an art gallery."

Her eyes searched his face. His voice was going in a direction she preferred not to follow. He had deliberately ignored her obvious remark about a desert island.

"There's another word I've heard," Mac said. in the same even tone. "*Tuyau*. The pipeline. Jacques is a pipeline to Pierre, who knows the first secretary in the Ministry of this or that, and if you want to do business with the Ministry you have to go through Jacques and Pierre and the first secretary."

"Mac," she said, speaking quickly, "instead of talking about French business methods, why not put on bathing suits and lie out in the sun? I brought a Bikini which has a written guarantee to stop river traffic for a kilometer in each direction."

"Maia, Maia," he said, sounding faintly sad, "you're trying too hard."

"Could we—could we sit down, please?"

"Here? On the deck?"

"No. That puts the wrong end of me to sleep. Maybe we'd better go inside."

They went into the cabin. We came in laughing to breakfast, Maia thought, the morning was like a new bride, shining and full of promise, now something has happened. Why is it always like this?

They took the same seats they had had at breakfast, and Mac

263

reached for the small glazed ashtray holding a pack of Maia's preferred cigarettes.

"No smoking for me," she said, then smiled warily and added, "how does it go: 'Smoke gets in your eyes'?"

"I don't know quite how to say this—" he began.

She was quiet. She had learned that he always ended by saying just what he meant, but for some reason he always began with a declaration of not being able to speak well. It wasn't a pretense, she decided, so it must be part of his personality. Like so many Americans, he might be afraid to talk in a way which seemed bookish or self-conscious; most of those whom she knew wanted to sound like tight-lipped pioneers of a hundred years ago, in a way that would have embarrassed a true and learned woodsman named Lincoln.

"You don't have to look at me like that, Maia. I'm not going to throw anything."

"Of course you are, darling. That's why you say not. What is it?"

"Well," he said, "you're the nicest *tuyau* I've ever seen. You're Obenpharo's pipeline to me."

At last, she thought. "That's a harsh thing to say, Mac."

"No, I don't mean to sound harsh. But at dinner last night, I realized it. Whatever Obenpharo needs done in Paris, you do it. Clients. Selling thoroughbred stables." He paused, then, "Buying a thoroughbred surgeon."

"Mac, darling. It's so clear you can't be bought."

"Yes, I can be. But not for money. So that's when Cleopatra comes in."

The edge of bitterness in his voice cut her. "Mac," she said, "I went out of my own wishes to Cindy Ross's party."

"Why, Maia? You always say no when somebody wants you to model for him. You said yes to me immediately. Looking backward now, it's so obvious. All you knew about me at Cindy's party was the hoopla in the papers. The great miracle man who can restore human wrecks to God's image on earth." He stuck a cigarette into his mouth and pulled it out again, stabbing it forward in the air between them like a little paper weapon. "Well, I can't! There are no miracles! Obenpharo with all his brains is as much a child as everybody else—wish on a star, hire a well-known name, pay an exorbitant

264

fee, and a godlike medical miracle will pass over the face of the waters."

"Over the face of his son," she said. "Don't make a villain of him, Mac. His only son, in a world of father and son family traditions like iron. And he doesn't want a miracle of handsomeness. He just wants Roger not to die from that big wound in his face."

"You don't need to sound annoyed. We're just talking about this, Maia."

"We're not just talking, Mac. You're accusing. You infuriate me."

"Go ahead, attack. That's the best defense."

"There's no defense needed, Mac! You're God's right-hand repairman on earth, aren't you? Because of some tragic things in your life, because you've run away from the operating room—"

"Now wait a minute, I haven't run away!"

"You're not the first in the world who's had something terrible happen! Don't fathers have a right even to *ask* you to heal their sons?"

"I let him ask me. And I told him."

"But your pride hurts because he thought a redheaded girl could persuade you!"

"Damn it, Maia, that was more than persuasion this morning. That was—"

"—don't say it, Mac!"

"Know a better name?"

"Yes. Maturity. I thought you were a man in a world full of boys, but you're the same crybaby as the rest."

"If you think this is crying—"

"What else is it? Maybe you've spent too much time in big hospitals, and you don't know the little everyday facts of life. You were offered enjoyment—but no, Monsieur le Docteur must have a big true love or nothing!"

"I told you before, Maia. I meant it. I'm not in the enjoyment business."

"Yes. Certainly. Of course. Stop eating. Don't breathe. What a joke, Mac."

"What a pipeline. And it almost worked."

"I don't care if it never works!" she flashed. "I don't care if Roger dies tomorrow!"

265

He was startled into complete silence.

"Don't you believe me?" she said, leaning tensely across the narrow table. "It's true. He's destroying our lives in his own quiet fanatical way. Mine, and my son's, and his mother's, and Obenpharo's. It's all so invisible, but it's as real as cancer. He thinks he's another Nehru, or Nasser, or Sun Yat-sen, another one of Allah's prophets. They even gave him the Moslem name, Mohammed. He'll fight the French, bring back the Sultan from exile, put his country into a place in the sun. Personal life means less than nothing. He lives in Tangier. To see his mother? His son? To be with his family? Oh no, only because he's safe under the International Administration and yet close to French Morocco. He bleeds the Banque Obenpharo indirectly for political cash by working through dummies, old clients, Moroccan business people who come to us for legitimate-looking loans. And his father knows it, but what can he do? Roger is his mother's life, but she lives in a bedroom now with heart trouble and can hardly sleep nights. Why do you suppose we sold those Chantilly stables? After all, they used to bring almost a half million in dollar exchange alone every year. Because Obenpharo exhausts himself with tension, and wherever he looks he sees darkness and no future. If not for my little boy there would be no light anywhere in his life." She had said so much, speaking so rapidly, she had to stop and catch her breath.

"So you wanted to help him."

"Yes."

"Whatever helps him helps you and your boy."

"Yes. And Mutirra."

"Who's she?"

"Obenpharo's wife. Better than a mother to me."

"You love her?"

"Completely. Helping Roger helps her."

"And this is why you came to me?"

"At first. But you were not what I expected."

"What was that?"

"Oh, you know. The usual doctor. A little huffy, a little puffy. Remember how you joked at Cindy's place about those make-believe doctors with all those names?"

"And I turned out to be a little cracked, instead? Not huffy or

266

puffy. Just a little foolish about being a sculptor. A little foolish about money and vulnerable enough to fancy red hair to be persuaded into doing surgery free."

"Do you think you sound like the last judgment? I think you sound vulgar and contemptible."

"The arrogance of the very rich. So *I'm* the one who's vulgar?"

"The arrogance of the very brainy. So clever at seeing everything from all sides that they never see what's in the middle."

"You're in the middle. I could have kept quiet. I could have taken you and Obenpharo's money, too. You wouldn't call that brainy, just what's called these days smart. Sharp."

"Yes."

"But what Maxime called a dirty little war."

"I knew that moron started this one."

"No, Maia. I almost told you what I thought about Obenpharo this morning, before all that lunch talk."

"Oh, Mac, Mac, you sat right there this morning at breakfast, so clear and clean and listening to me and talking—" She stopped, then began again, "And all that time you had this in your mind."

"You seemed to be enjoying yourself so much—"

"—I was, you'll never know how much I was—"

"—and I was, too, and I didn't want to end it."

"And all that holier-than-thou talk about women, one true love at a time—"

"Nothing holy, Maia. True enough to be true enough."

"And do you think it's the truth when I say I came with you today for myself, not for Obenpharo?"

He shook his head slightly. "You're not that simple, even if you wanted to be."

"You'd be amazed at how simple I really am. I'm annoyed when people call me primitive because it's the truth."

"You? Primitive? With those elaborate Parisian hair arrangements? With the high-fashion clothes?"

She bent her head back so that her uncombed hair hung away from her neck and she swung the tawny mass lightly, then sat up and looked at him. Her uniquely unwavering level look was back now, the steady look, and the secret-smiling mouth. "See?" she said. "This pile of loose hair, you call that an *elaborate* coiffure? As for the high-fashion clothes—" She stood up and began to unbutton her blouse. "I can get rid of them, too."

He watched her without moving. "What's this, the final assault? If you warned me, I could have gotten drunk at lunch."

She took off the blouse and stood naked to the waist. "I don't care what you call it." She began to get out of her skirt.

"What's the idea, Maia? A strip tease? Am I supposed to go wild like a boy?"

"No, like a man." She let the skirt drop.

"You pull a stunt like this and I'm the vulgar one?"

She stood there, grave and nude, her skin brightly touched by the reflected water lights. "This isn't vulgar. Just primitive." She stepped toward him with her steady secret look and grasped his shirt and calmly ripped it open from his shoulder to his waist. At that he stood up and pulled her toward him roughly.

"Maia—"

She put her arms around him, moving against him.

"How I've wanted you—" he said thickly.

"Of course, darling. We mustn't ever fight like that again."

Their hands and their mouths were wild as they joined in the cabin bunk, trying, meeting, clumsy and eager. She held him tightly as if afraid to let go, faster and faster, tossing, murmuring his name over and over, attempting sensualities he had never experienced, laughing in her throat when he arched back in sudden feeling. Her belly and breasts were burning in the soft secret struggle, her mouth became greedy and carnal, and she began to use Arabic words in quick little gasps. She was far more than wanton, frenzied. He entered, and she worked hard against him with her eyes closed, her flanks closing in a hot vise, all with a frantic shamelessness that startled him into doubting her pleasure. Suddenly, strangely, she began to withdraw in spasms, throwing her hands against him as if struggling to escape, making inarticulate sounds on the border of fear. He grasped her shoulders, strongly, pushing her back flat against the bunk. He sat up.

"Maia, stop acting!" he said furiously. "Goddam it, stop acting with me!"

She tore at his shoulders. "I'm not, I'm not!"

"You are, damn it! I'm not fighting you."

"I'm not fighting, darling!"

"You act as if you're afraid of being raped, Maia! You make me feel like a damn gorilla!"

She stared at him so blindingly that he was amazed, then turned herself toward the wall and began to cry soundlessly, with her whole body trembling, holding one hand over her mouth like a girl afraid to cry out her pain.

He leaned over her. "Maia! Maia, what's the matter with you!" He shook her shoulder a little, but she threw one elbow across her eyes, shaking as if she were freezing. He kissed her forehead, her shoulder, stroking her as if she were a fevered child, and, when her terrible quiet weeping continued with spasms of shivering, he stretched his body along hers and held her quietly against him in his arms. "It's all right, Maia," he kept repeating, "Maia, it's all right."

The moving water outside cast wavering lights like fire on the roof of the cabin. The arterial pulse of the river beat softly beneath them, flowing quietly toward the great heart of Paris.

(2)

HE SAW no one for the next two weeks. He threw himself into a continuous blaze of work, eating and sleeping irregularly, modeling a new one-quarter life-size figure of Maia from the sketches of her he had made. The unfinished life-size mahogany figure stood ignored in a corner of the cabin, while he set his turntable modeling stand in the center of the room where the illumination from the skylight was best. He knew exactly what he was trying for, and put together a wood and wire armature for the original clay modeling without the slightest hesitation. Even the clay itself was obedient and plastic, not too soft for the beginning layers over the framework of the armature, not too dry and crumbling as he went along, building up the form with a sureness and precision so complete that he lost all track of time.

The figure he worked on continuously was that of a seated girl, with one hand lying in the open lap of her skirt between parted knees, ankles crossed, the other hand held up to brush backward from her eyes a cloud of wind-blown hair. Her head was bent slightly back, and she was laughing, her whole figure captured flexibly in a moment suggesting movement and happy spontaneity. The clay melted and molded under his hands as it never had before; torso, shoulders, arms, the delicate arch of the back, even the technically complex masses of face, head, and the skewed halo of hair; everything was caught at just the right moment. For the first time he subordinated realistic details to achieve a mood of simple gaiety, suggesting the skirt's folds rather than modeling them precisely as he might once have done, letting the facial planes and curves suggest subtly the underlying fine-boned slenderness, letting his highly technical knowledge of anatomy dissolve itself into a living fluidity.

It was good, and he knew it.

It was much better than the bronze head he had done of the blinded boy. He had just seen the wax figurines of Degas' ballet dancers, and, when he looked at this seated laughing river sprite of a girl, he thought: The old maestro would have liked this one. This is one of the good ones.

Day after day went by without interruption. The move from the heart of Paris out to the suburban berth in Neuilly-sur-Seine had been useful. His houseboat was moored along a bank with about ten others in a row; most of them had electric lines run down from the top of the embankment. There up at the summit of the sloping grass riverbank, a paved street slumbered in the summer sun, and the parallel rows of chestnut trees stood placidly in pools of their own shade all day long. There was no hurry here; the trees and the river had seen everything before, the days flowing by with the water.

At night he would wash up before dinner like a stoneworker, and throw on a fresh shirt and a clean pair of trousers. He would cross the plank to the shore where his friend Boisson had dug a small terrace into the side of the bank, in the center of which a circular field-stone pool made a little gray-blue water world for a half-dozen goldfish as long as his hand. At the bottom of the pool lay a small stone comical whale Boisson had carved to amuse himself. Where the plank from the boat joined the shore, a brass ship's bell with the name *Sequana* etched in it hung on a post, and as Mac left the boat for his nightly walk to a nearby restaurant he would swing the clapper on its short rope and listen to the pleasant nautical sound of the brass bell. From the small riverside terrace a flight of wooden steps with a rope handrail led steeply up to street level; it ended at a swinging gate which even had a thin mail slot at the center of a circular life preserver nailed to the wood. Suspended from two hooks at the top edge of the gate was a white-painted wooden sign with simple hand-lettering which read: ADAMS FARM. The mailman had asked Mac about this, and after some discussion concerning the translation and the meaning, he had walked off, shifting his leather sack impatiently. A *farm*? Boisson's orderliness and country childhood had one final expression: a row of green hedges at street level, beginning at each side of the gate and stretching out in both directions for a hundred feet. The hedges were thick and well trimmed, and the sidewalk stroller who casually enjoyed staring down at each houseboat in the little colony found the hedges enough of a barrier to provide Adams Farm with some privacy.

Each night, after dinner, Mac walked back along the quiet suburban street beneath the trees. Across the street, opposite the riverbank, was a row of three-story modern apartments, and he caught glimpses of people moving within their rooms, a man lifting a little girl high into the air, a mother leaning on the sill of her window to watch a boy down below—just about Stan's age, Mac thought with a stab—ride his bicycle toward her. Mac would push open his gate, hearing the minutely wooden *plunk* of the signboard swinging against it, then hold the rope rail as he went down the steps. After a day or two he no longer rang the ship's bell as he stepped onto the burlapped surface of the gangplank; it sounded too loud in the still air, and besides, no one ever answered. Once aboard, he would light a few kerosene lamps, then sit out on the deck, smoking slowly as the water slapped idly against the hull beneath him.

Tranquillity. Exactly what he had come for. A world which made no demands and let him work at his own pace; sleep, eat, work, whenever he wanted. Out of habit alone he shaved each day, seeing a sunbrowned clear-eyed stranger in the mirror whom he hadn't seen in years. At night he sometimes dove off the bow into the quiet river, plunging into a cool liquid dark world, floating on his back and trying to identify the close intimate stars, feeling the sensuous velvet movement of water against his skin, thinking of Maia. He thought of Maia every day and every night.

He was lonely.

Russo, the foreman at the Thodier Foundry, rotated the turntable before him slowly. On it stood the original clay model of the seated Maia. Mac stood beside him in the tall peak-roofed foundry shed, leaning on a long wood table to check the plaster cast of the clay, the negative gelatine mold of the plaster, and the final wax mold ready for metal casting. Around them the high foundry shed had the busy clutter of a medieval workshop; a heavy crane overhead running on steel tracks to a melting furnace in the corner, the sand pit and drying oven nearby, the long pipes along the wall from the forced air blower to the furnace, wall racks of metal tongs and bars and casting tools, and the twentieth-century additions of acetylene blowtorches hung from tall cylindrical metal gas tanks with pressure dials at their heads like mechanical eyes.

Boisson, the owner of the houseboat, had introduced Mac to Russo soon after the end of the war, and now, with information from Boisson saying that Russo was still at the Thodier Foundry, Mac brought the clay model there immediately. He had planned to use the French sand method for the final metal casting, but with a craftsman of Russo's skill available, he immediately decided on the more finely detailed lost-wax method. He wanted this work to come out flawlessly, and there would be a nicety of detail achieved by the wax method which the French sand process could not approach. Especially the wind-blown hair; that required delicacy for reproduction in metal.

Russo ended his inspection on the turntable and looked toward Mac. He was a short wide-shouldered man with hair which had whitened since Mac had last seen him, with a bright-eyed intelligent face. He had lived in Philadelphia for many years before the war, and had gone back home to Naples for the traditional triumphant return just in time to become stranded on the continent in the legal snarl of Italy's Army draft call, and now he remained in France because

272

no other place met his standards of metallurgy and casting. His English was all his own; it was like a vaudeville imitation of an immigrant of years ago, but he insisted on using it instead of French with Mac.

"Hey," Russo said approvingly to Mac of the figure on the turntable, "prett' damn good. I say so myself."

"It's good," Mac said. It was.

"The hair worry me, know it? Alla fine lil hairs the wind blows out." He held his thumb and forefingers in a pincer's grasp to indicate very small space tolerances. "Ver' fine. It'sa secreta whole thing. She'sa laugh, but because a wind blows her hair, so the hair mus' be good."

"I'm not worried," Mac said. "If you can't make it good, we all might as well quit."

"Alla men in shop," Russo said, "ever' one say that'sa good work." He nodded toward an old man in the corner who was welding two sections of a monumental bronze horse together with an acetylene torch. "He'sa maestro *patineur* here—good as the Limet *frères,* know it?—he knowsa great sculptor, Despiau, Bourdelle, Saupique, Darde— he looksa this one, he saysa good. Ver' good." Russo dropped one eyelid confidentially and lowered his voice as if the newspapers were eavesdropping. "That'sa more bett' praise thana critics in paper, know it? They don'ta care, good work, bad, your friend, my enemy, like, hate, they don'ta care. But whena maestro *patineur* likes, that'sa best."

Mac was more pleased than he could say. Russo was right about the critics. There were only a few of strong independent judgment and learning; the rest followed current fashion as slavishly as shoe salesmen. The *patineur's* praise was really worth accepting. Mac made a new decision on the spot.

"Russo," he said, "I've got a surprise."

Russo shook his head. "Too long in thisa business. No more surprise."

"Well, I've decided not to cast it in bronze."

"No? What'sa mat', Doc, scare?"

"No. I just decided. We'll use gold."

Russo whistled softly. "Gold! Lotsa gold for this one. This lil baby needs more thana wed' ring, know it?"

273

"I know it. She'll get more than a wedding ring," he added, thinking: That about the ring will amuse Maia—and it was then that he realized he wanted to break the silence which stood like a wall between them since that afternoon coming up the Seine.

"Lotsa gold to get quick, Doc."

"Why quick?"

"Bastille Day holiday soon." Russo waved his arm to indicate all the men in the foundry. "Ev'body. Three weeks' vacation, you know, the *grand vacance*."

"Where do you hide your telephone in this barn?" Mac asked Russo. "We'll button down the gold right now."

"Banque Obenpharo," the switchboard operator said.

"Mademoiselle Obenpharo, please," Mac said into Russo's telephone.

"May I tell her who calls, please?"

"Dr. Adams," he said without thinking.

"Thank you. Do not quit the line, please."

The moment she cut out of the connection Mac jiggled the receiver rapidly to call her back. That *Dr. Adams* was all wrong; it came from years of telephone habit, and he knew how it would seem to someone like Maia, someone who was unusually direct about the big things and endlessly subtle about microscopic nuances.

There was a click and a cool formal voice he hardly recognized as Maia's said, "Good afternoon, Dr. Adams."

All wrong, he thought; she took it as the declaration of an attitude. "How are you, Maia?" he heard himself saying inanely. Suddenly he hardly knew what to say first. The mood of a moment back, when he had dialed her number so enthusiastically, was completely gone.

"Where are you, Doctor?" she was saying. "A wind tunnel? What's that noise in the telephone?"

"That's an acetylene torch close by," he said, shutting off his open ear with his forefinger. "I'm in a foundry."

There was a silence, then: "That's reasonable. After two weeks of silence you're in a foundry. So you decide to call me. Some people's minds work that way."

"Well," he said, sounding even more stupid to himself, "I want to open an account."

274

"Always welcome. Ask for the assistant manager when you come in."

"Hell's bells, Maia! We don't need red tape, we need some gold."

"The same man can handle that for you, too."

"Damn it, Maia! You sound as if you're putting off a hoarder. I've been working night and day like a dog on a new figure of you, and we're ready to cast it at the foundry, and the only way I can get that much gold in a hurry—"

"Of me? A new figure? In *gold*?"

That's better, he thought, this new voice is a definite improvement. "Yes," he said cautiously.

"The gold. Is this some new philosophical idea? An upside-down slap at my money, et cetera, cetera?"

"Maia, will you relax? The gold is because I want the best for the best."

"So, this is a good one?"

"Yes. Even the men in the shop here like it."

"What's the pose?"

"That's a new surprise. Wait until you see it."

A new silence, then: "Oh, am I going to see it?"

"For the love of God, Maia!" he said angrily into the blank black little telephone mouthpiece. "Of course you'll see it! I've been sleeping, breathing, and working you into this figure for a couple of solid weeks! Don't give me a hard time!"

"Oh, Mac! And I thought you were so angry we'd never see each other again. I counted the days. If you knew how I listened when the telephone rang."

"Angry? Why should I be angry?"

"I thought you hated me."

"You're a fool, Maia, the prettiest redheaded girl fool I've ever met. If I was down there now, I'd prove it."

"Don't stop talking, Mac. After all these days you don't know how glad I am to hear you talk like this."

"I've got to stop. I'm practically kissing this damn plastic telephone."

She laughed, and it sounded like a fine one. Better and better, he thought, realizing that this girl thought silence was a form of living burial.

275

"Look," he said, "Signor Russo would like to get ready for the casting before Bastille Day when everybody goes off on vacation. If we could come down there—"

"Come down," she said quickly. "Come down, come down. We'll give you whatever gold you need."

"I just thought," Mac said. "He and I are both not exactly in Place Vendôme costume. Your door man may be snooty because we're in our working clothes."

"No matter," she said, "so am I."

"I can just imagine," he said. "I can just see it in my mind's eye."

"Stop talking, you foundryman," she said, sounding happy, "and get yourself down here by special delivery."

When the little taxi circled the Place Vendôme and stopped in front of the tall bronze doors of Banque Obenpharo, Russo said to Mac, "Hey, Doc, in *here*? You can jus' walk in, say I wanna coupla thousan' gold, walk out just lika this?"

Mac paid the taxi driver and they started across the sidewalk toward the bank entrance. "Well," he said, "I'm going to open an account. But I thought you wanted the metal right away—"

"I do. Do a job while she'sa hot. Before Bastille Day."

"Sure. So I called my friend who runs the bank." He looked sideways at Russo. "Don't worry about how we look. We'll get it."

The doorman was polite but firm. First there was a call to the assistant manager, who came after a dignified interval to the door, wearing his badge of a hairline mustache, eying Mac and Russo with a pantomime of suspicion until another call, this time to the office of Mademoiselle Obenpharo, changed the look on his face as if a bright key had turned inside him. Russo had been shuffling his feet with embarrassment, watching a Hispano glide up to the curb to accept an amazingly dandified man, wearing spats and a boutonniere, from the bank. "Hey, Doc," he said in a low voice, "you sure you gotta' ri' place?"

But now the assistant manager was asking for the privilege of escorting them to the office of Mademoiselle Obenpharo. Russo hitched up his dusty corduroy trousers and plunged courageously into the lobby behind Mac and the dapper manager.

The lobby was tall and dimly cool after the heat outside, with a

276

discreetly muffled sound of adding machines here and there, and well-dressed people at marble counters handling interesting little piles of banknote paper. An enormous crystal chandelier hung above them, shining with a disembodied glitter in the lofty upper spaces of the lobby. Straight ahead there was a partitioned customers' room with deep green leather chairs, a wall of stock and bond exchange quotations with a marking clerk busily chalking in new prices, and an optical enlarger to flash the ticker tape numerals on a glass screen like a miniature motion picture. Several men sat in the leather chairs smoking cigars and watching the big board.

The assistant manager indicated the curved staircase which led gracefully with its wrought-iron balustrade up to a mezzanine floor above. "Docteur, maestro," he said to Mac and Russo, "this way, if you please. After you, please."

As they went up the steps, Russo whispered quietly in English to Mac, "If I'da know you got frien's lika this, Doc, I'da raise my price fora work, double!"

Ahead of them, on the mezzanine floor, Mac saw Maia hurrying toward them, already smiling and holding out both hands. Russo stared at her, then, when he saw the direction of her smile, turned to Mac and said, *Mamma mia!* This youra frien'?"

Mac saw Maia was really in her working clothes, once again the elegant Parisienne of *haute couture.*

She met him at the head of the steps. "My dear dirty darling!" she said, taking both of Mac's hands. "Consider thyself kissed on both cheeks."

"Thou likewise, Cleo," Mac said. "This is Signor Russo, the maestro I told you about."

Russo took the hand Maia held out to him and kissed it gallantly. In French he said, "If the doctor had told me his friend in the bank was a *principessa*—!" He grinned at Mac. "And I was imagining a potbelly in a stiff collar."

Now that Russo had begun it, they all continued speaking French.

"I'm delighted you came, maestro. The doctor tells me you are of the best."

"After so many years, Principessa, there are no more mistakes to be made. So now I know the work."

Maia nodded over his shoulder, indicating the respectfully hovering assistant manager. "If you will tell Monsieur how much gold is needed—"

Russo rolled his eyes at Mac. He was enjoying this more and more, Mac could see. "Doctor," Russo stage-whispered to Mac in French, clowning it, "can we name any amount we wish?"

"Within reason," Mac said. "Without the double price, my maestro of inflation."

Russo shrugged as if ordering a pack of cigarettes, the game of pauper playing prince, "Oh, about ten kilos should do it," he said, then looked startled when the assistant manager said, "Certainly, maestro. I'll bring them right up." He skipped off down the steps.

"This way," Maia said to them. "We can wait in my office."

They followed her along the mezzanine past a row of opaque glass doorways on which were lettered gilt departmental titles.

"It's interesting to see you in your working clothes," Mac said.

"This is the new Fath *trompe-l'oeil* silhouette," she said. "Like it?"

"I'm dazzled, Maia. I feel like a bull in a china shop."

"The bird in the gilded cage, you mean?"

"Some cage," Mac said, looking at the well-lighted paintings hung on each wall, the wainscoted wood paneling and somberly glowing Savonnerie carpet. He had never imagined Maia in a bank so much like her own home. There's the air of a private club here, he thought, then it occurred to him that the club atmosphere was just what the Obenpharos wanted.

The pair of glass doors at the end of the corridor opened, framing a tall Spanish-looking man who kept his long arms stretched out to grasp the edge of each door as they approached. If it had been intended as a theatrical spread-eagle gesture, it was successful.

"Ah," Maia said, surprised. "Jeanjean. I thought you had left."

"I wanted to meet your friend from America first," the tall man said. His deep dark eyes flicked between the two men, then decided on Mac, and scanned him from head to foot.

This big guy must be a ballet star, Mac thought; he has the overly muscular looks, the alligator shoes and too-expensive clothes, and he uses his face like an amateur operetta to project what he's projecting right now: the lifted eyebrow for interest, the eye corners wrinkled for almost-smiling sociability, the nostrils flared a trifle to

278

go with the faintest curl of the lip corner to show scorn, the folded chamois gloves rolled in one palm like a small baton to dramatize, no doubt, that he attempted no more serious kinds of work than driving a sports car.

Jeanjean dropped his outstretched arms from the doors, as if removing a barrier to Maia's office, and held out his hand to Mac.

"Dr. Adams," Maia said, with a faint change in her voice, "Señor Rasa. And Signor Russo."

When the handshaking and nodding and bowing were completed, Jeanjean stepped to one side and made one of his arm gestures. "Come in," he said, "come into the parlor."

That has an odd sound, Mac thought, proprietary and scornful at the same time. Just who is this guy? I don't know him, but I dislike him already, with a pleasant unreasonable dislike so primitive that Maia would be delighted.

Russo stepped inside the glass doors and looked around, holding his beret in his hand. "Principessa," he said, "this little jewelbox, this is your office?"

Maia looked very pleased. "You like it, maestro?"

Tall figured green silk panels were inset at intervals around the walls, alternating with mirrored oblongs that created a half-dozen Maias from every angle of the room. A long glazed tile fireplace dominated one wall with a magnificently baroque antique bronze bust of a girl mounted above it; in the metal pedestal supporting the head was mounted a large complex dial showing the season of the year, the day of the week, and the phase of the moon. The metal girl's strangely contrasting white eyes were clocks, too; by looking straight into her mechanical stare the minutes could be read in one eye, the hours in the other.

"You like it?" Maia asked. "It's one of Lepaute's best clocks. He spent three years making it for the Cabinet du Roi at Versailles."

"Now I've seen everything," Russo said. "The bronze has a very good patina."

"It's no good," Jeanjean said. "It never keeps good time, and there is no alarm."

Maia put the room on parade with a spontaneous enjoyment Mac found charming. Her simple pleasure in Russo's admiration was the

279

only real thing in the room; everything else had been created, polished, inlaid, woven, designed for intricacy and illusion. There was no desk, only a low polished cabinet holding two white telephones beside an ash-white damask-covered Louis XVI armchair.

Maia put her hand on it. "Riesener did this writing desk for Marie Antoinette. The bronze decorations and all the inlay work, he did it all himself. A real artist."

Russo crouched before the desk, running his fingertips delicately over the joints and the bronze work. "I couldn't do better, not even with all our modern tools at the foundry."

"How do you like that tapestry?" Jeanjean asked, directing their attention to the wall hanging behind the desk and chair. It covered the entire section of the wall, and showed a stylized Asiatic figure in the manner of the Hindu god, Siva, with eight arms all bent outward, each holding a different object; only a moment later did the objects become clear—a telephone in one hand, a mirror in the next, a dueling foil in a third, a champagne glass in the hand above it. The tapestry managed to be delicate and beautiful and humorous at the same time.

"Bretonvier did it to show Maia at work," Jeanjean said. "We almost died laughing the day he hung it in here."

"What's so funny about it?" Russo asked. "The texture is a dream, just look at it. Nobody else but Lurçat could even touch it."

Maia clapped her hands lightly. "Bravo, maestro. Some people are so afraid to admire modern artists."

Jeanjean raised one eyebrow at Mac. "Maia tells me you're an artist, Doctor. One of those rare birds, a doctor-artist."

"A sculptor," Mac corrected. "Sometimes, with a little luck, the art appears."

"This time, yes," Russo added quickly, almost protectively. He added to Maia, "Wait until you see this one. In gold, especially."

"Why the gold, Mac?" Maia asked. "Isn't bronze good enough?"

He looked at her. "Not for you, Cleo."

Jeanjean tapped his rolled baton of gloves against his leg. Each of his gestures seemed to be acted out to make clear his feelings, as if they were needed to guide everyone else to consider them. "Cleo? What is this Cleo?"

"Not Cleo," Mac said. "The Lorelei."

280

Jeanjean caught Maia's wicked little intimate grin and began tapping his gloves harder. "Cleo? Lorelei?"

I'll let buddy-boy here have it, Mac thought. *"Sie kämmt es mit goldenem Kämme,"* he said, making the quotation sound like an explanation, *"und singt ein Lied darbei."*

The gloves were beating a tattoo now. Jeanjean said, sounding annoyed, "What language is that, German?"

"High German, señor."

"High? Is there a low?"

"Of course, didn't you know?"

Jeanjean's nostrils flared slightly. "Pure Castilian Spanish is my native language. We have nothing low."

"In English," Mac said, managing not to smile, "we have much low. You speak English, of course?"

"No." Then Jeanjean added, "There was never a need."

"A pity," Mac said. "It's a useful tongue."

"Castilian serves, Doctor."

Maia broke in quickly, as if stepping between antagonists. "Jeanjean speaks Arabic like a native, though, don't you, Jeanjean?"

Jeanjean frowned at her. Suddenly he said, using Arabic, "Your friend in the dirty clothes here is baiting me. I do not like it. Get rid of him."

In French, Maia said to Mac and Russo, *"Pardon,"* and then spoke in rapid Arabic to Jeanjean. "Go yourself. No one asked you to stay."

"This thin fool in dirty trousers attracts you? This friend of an Italian workingman?"

"Yes," Maia said. "Yes yes yes. He has much learning. If you try to insult him he will twist you into knots."

"What good are his schoolbooks? A man has to be a man."

Maia paused deliberately, then said with different emphasis, "Don't worry. He is a man."

Jeanjean frowned at her, then suddenly shot out in French to Mac, "You play polo?"

What a child our little bully-boy is, Mac thought, with a child's one-and-one-makes-two craftiness. "Polo? Not for some time." . . . Not since the days before he married Laura, the days when he and Porter Bradford had played on the same Long Island team.

"Ah, you used to play?"

"Yes." For a moment he remembered Port lying in the hospital bed in New Haven, and the girl with the Broadway name who had brought the steamer basket filled with Scotch.

"You no longer play?"

"No."

"Why not? Too expensive?"

"That's one of several reasons, señor."

Jeanjean did another of his scanning enactments, taking in Mac's working shirt and denim trousers. "What kind of mallet do you prefer?" he asked cleverly.

Mac paused just long enough to recollect the information, not only because it had been a long time since he had played, but also because he wanted time to aim properly at Jeanjean and fire both barrels. "A 53-inch," Mac said, making a show of precision. "With a Parada handle, a Moonah short-jointed cane shaft, with a 9½-inch R.N.P.A. 7-ounce vellum-bound bamboo head."

"So?" It had worked. Jeanjean was impressed. "And your bridle?"

"Half-moon Pelham." Mac decided to shift from defense to attack. "Do you play enough to care about the finer points of the game?"

"I'm scheduled to play in the championship match at Deauville next week. On Obenpharo ponies," he added, to Maia.

So that's it, Mac decided. Bully-boy must be a de-luxe client around here, with ultra de-luxe treatment.

"Have we finished?" Maia said to Jeanjean in French. "Is the discussion of the length of sticks and types of bridle finished?"

In Arabic, Jeanjean answered, "I thought at first he was lying. He looks like a workingman in those clothes."

In Arabic, she said, "He never lies. Never. About anything. And he works with his hands in ways you will never understand."

"I work with my hands, too, Maia," Jeanjean said, continuing the Arabic, "especially in ways you can understand."

Maybe I'm wrong, Mac thought, listening to the throaty language rattling back and forth. This has the look and sound of a lover's quarrel, and bully-boy doesn't want to lose his favorite kewpie doll.

A little light flashed at the base of one of Maia's telephones, and she lifted the receiver. " 'Allo?" She listened, then said, "Good— yes, at the door, and order the car—just a moment, *ne quittez pas*—"

282

She looked up at Mac and said in English, "With all that gold, wouldn't you like a lift back to your foundry?"

"Thanks, we'll catch a taxi."

"But I hate to see you disappear. And I like your craftsman here very much."

"Be careful," Russo said, grinning hugely, using his special pronunciation, "I speaka English, Principessa."

"All God's chillun speak English," Mac said; and when Maia and Russo stared at him he explained, "A private joke. Excuse it." Stupid remarks, Mac thought; maybe bully-boy annoys me more than I realize.

"Jokes," Maia said. "For the last fifteen minutes the room has been full of jokes."

"Look, Maia, we don't need an armored car. We'll take a taxi."

"Please, Mac, I have only one quick errand and then I can drive both of you back to work. I'd love to see your foundry, maestro."

"You invited thisa minute, Principessa." Russo chortled, "Leta Doc take taxi, we take-a gold your car."

"Okay," Mac said, "okay, you two. We'll do this thing in style."

Maia's eyes flicked over the room, then back to his. "You've had a little too much style for one day, Mac?"

"Well, yes and no. I have a lot of respect for antiques and games like polo, but a man can breathe just so much pure oxygen. Then he needs a little ordinary street air again."

"I agree, darling. We're going out to the street right now." He was touched by her wanting to agree so quickly. She spoke into the phone. "The big car, yes—" She glanced at Jeanjean, "Do you want to ride with us to the Bourse?"

"No," he said sulkily, "I'll drive myself." In Arabic he added, "The stableboy always follows behind."

As Maia continued giving directions into the telephone, Mac said quietly in English to Russo, "How did you keep yourself from adding Italian to all this?"

"In one minute more I will," Russo said. "I don'ta believe this macaroni here speaka 'taliana. He'sa phony."

"Now, Russo. You're just sore because he cuts such a fancy figure."

283

"You talka me, Doc?" Russo said shrewdly. "Or you talka you-'self?"

Maia finished her telephone conversation and stood up, looking at the time in the eyes of the bronze girl. "They're holding your gold downstairs," she said to Mac. "Shall we go?"

They made a small procession down the corridor. One of the glass doors leading to a side office opened and two men came out talking excitedly together. "Ah, Maia!" the shorter one said. He took her hand and kissed it, completely ignoring everyone else. "I'm so glad to catch you before I leave for Washington."

"George, you poor man! Washington? In July, of all times."

"This time it's worth it. My New York partner says Senator Whelen is ready to talk about sponsoring a higher U.S. Treasury price for gold."

"Oh, George, the heat has really done something to you! Raising the U.S. price for gold is the oldest dream of them all."

"Look, Maia," the short man she called George said excitedly, "this is the logical time. Thirty-five dollars an ounce perhaps made sense back in 1934, but now——"

"I know, I know your line. With an inflationary trend the price of gold should rise with other commodities, no?"

"Precisely. That's precisely our line of reasoning."

"George, stop fooling yourself." Her brisk voice was entirely new to Mac. He listened to this latest facet of her, wondering if there were as many Maias as in her office mirrors. "George," Maia was saying, "face the fact that gold is not a commodity. It's a monetary metal. In the last analysis, gold is really worth only what the U.S. Treasury will pay for it. No more, no less."

George frowned at her. "You sound more American than French, Maia."

"I only want to sound like common sense. Don't confuse your wishes for a bonanza in the States with the reality of the situation. And don't believe the sterling area crowd with all that talk of not enough gold to go around. Ignore them. Really, George, who would benefit if gold went up to, say, fifty dollars an ounce?"

"I pray for the day, Maia."

"Get off your knees and use your head. The nations who lack the international liquidity the sterling people shout about, really, they would hardly benefit from revaluation. The hard currency countries would benefit, but they don't have a balance of payments problem anyway, am I right?"

"Right." George sounded reluctant and deflated.

"And the Soviets would benefit because who knows how much slave labor gold they have. Am I right?"

"Right, right."

"So revaluation is a temporary bandage, not a cure."

"You sound like Obenpharo now, Maia."

"Of course. Where do you think I learned this?"

"Maybe from the American Embassy."

"Come, come, George. I know it's fashionable to dislike the Americans. Don't be chauvinistic. And now that you mention the Americans, imagine what raising the price of gold would do to them. Their dollars would be devalued, and probably there would be a new boost to inflation, a drop in sales of U.S. savings bonds, a rise in redemptions, and a hedging of capital. In the short run, you and your partners may make a few million francs, but in the long run everybody else gets hurt."

George turned around to the taller man behind him, who had remained standing silently in the door to his office. "Your chief," George said, "she's pinned my shoulders to the mat."

"I warned you she would," the taller man said.

"Now what am I supposed to do?" George said, spreading his hands toward Maia. "My plane leaves Orly in three hours."

"Take it," Maia laughed. "Go and have fun."

"After all your discouragement?"

"Don't be foolish," she said. "Get an air-conditioned suite in Washington. Entertain the native girls. I've heard it's a bachelor's paradise. Tell the Senators France is in the front line fighting Communism and to keep sending over dollars. Spend money like a sailor and convince your New York partner you're a wonderful lobbyist."

"You know, Maia," George said slowly, "sometimes I wonder about you."

She put her hand on his arm sympathetically. "Poor George. Because I always tell the bitter truth?"

285

"Yes," he said. "It's a form of cruelty."

"No," she said, "I just remember what Papa always says: Remember the difference between what is true and what you wish to be true. Your gold project is a good example, George." She turned to Mac and Jeanjean and Russo. "Let's hurry" —then back to George— "forgive my hurrying like this but I have a really mad rush appointment with Socrates Theologos, and I'm late." She began moving down the corridor.

"*Alors,*" George said after her, "so the big rich ones get the beauties and small fry like me are left with a canceled ticket!"

"If you stay in Paris," Maia called over her shoulder, "come to my Bastille Day party."

"Those Arab girl dancers again?"

"Yes, again."

George moved his clenched hand downward, like a gavel. "That settles it, I'm staying here!"

As they went down the curving staircase into the bank lobby, Maia said quietly in English to Mac, "Just one stop at the Bourse, then off we go to your foundry. I hope you don't feel you've become tangled in a revolving door."

"It's interesting to see you at work, Maia. You really wanted me to see you here, didn't you?"

"Maybe I did. Oh, Mac, you know I don't always analyze my motives, the way you do. Maybe I wanted you to see that you're not the only one who lives in three or four worlds at the same time."

"I'm living in only two, Maia. Yours and mine."

"But mine is an intruder, darling. I disturb you, don't I?"

"Talk French!" Jeanjean said from behind them. "You sound like a couple of tourists!"

The assistant manager met them at the bottom of the steps and escorted them across the lobby floor toward the tall front doors. "The doorman just put ten kilo gold bars into the back seat of the car, madame."

"Thank you."

As he stepped out of the building Mac saw Eve coming toward them, walking slowly, pausing now and then to look into the glittering shop windows. She was dressed as fashionably as the women strolling past her, yet there was something calm and simple about her

286

which made the others seem anxious and gaudy. She was what every woman wanted her daughters to grow up to be, warm, wise, and self-contained. It suddenly occurred to Mac that it was Eve's quality of balance which set her apart, in a world of seeming adults who were actually frantic children, so that her very strength became her weakness; it isolated her because she gave the impression of needing no one.

He came up beside her and said, "Dr. Livingstone, I presume."

Eve glanced up quickly at his reflection in the shining plate glass of the shop window, then turned. "Why, Mac! What a nice surprise!" She sounded so pleased that he felt a twinge of guilt. "I've been thinking about you," she said warmly, then, as if she did not want him to misunderstand, she added, "You know, wondering how your work was going in suburban solitude."

He appreciated her delicacy; she did not want him to feel grappled at, wrapped and swathed like a papoose in the silk bindings of a hovering motherliness. But her mention of solitude—was she suggesting subtly that he had ignored her these past weeks?

He looked evasively at the jeweler's shop window beside her. "Are you in the market for a bucketful of diamonds, today?"

She laughed. "No, no, I couldn't afford a paper clip in one of these places. My office is practically just around the corner here, and usually I come by this way after lunch."

He took her arm and led her toward the group waiting for him in front of Banque Obenpharo. Maia stood between Jeanjean Rasa and Russo, watching him and Eve curiously.

"Maia," he said as they came up. "you remember Dr. Evelyn Desmond."

"Of course," Maia said in English. "The lady who is a doctor. How could I forget? How are you, Doctor?"

"Fine, thank you." Eve surveyed the group. "Is this a costume party, or can anybody come in?"

"Eve," Mac said, "Signor Russo, descendant in spirit from Benevenuto Cellini, and this is—" He stopped short, realizing he had forgotten the handsome Spaniard's name.

"Señor Rasa," Maia said, completing the introduction, adding in English, "descendant in spirit from Don Juan."

Jeanjean Rasa took Eve's hand and kissed it. For him, it was a

287

natural gesture, but somehow he seemed to give it the slight exaggeration he gave everything else. *"Enchanté,"* he said as he straightened, using his eyes and making it all seem like an intense experience.

Maia motioned toward her car, where the driver was holding the rear door open. "If you're shopping, can we give you a lift?"

"No, thanks, I'm due back at the office soon. I'm just window shopping like a kid at the five-and-ten."

"What is that, the five-and-ten?" Maia had a thin frown line as she caught the quick glance exchanged between Eve and Mac.

"Excuse me," Eve said in French. "Woolworth's. It is a particular kind of store in the States. Children love them."

"Yes, Woolworth's, of course. But children don't have offices near Place Vendôme," Maia said coolly. "Are you at the Embassy?"

"No," Eve smiled. "That's too grand for doctors. We're just in back, on the Cité du Retiro."

"Permit me," Jeanjean said. "Let me drive you. I can go by there easily." He motioned to the red Ferrari coupe behind Maia's car. It looked like a blooded bullet, hard and tense, filled with locked power.

"Thank you," Eve said to Jeanjean in French. "I've always secretly wanted to ride in one of those."

"Jeanjean is the answer to every woman's secret wishes," Maia said smoothly, in English. "He gives a fast ride."

Jeanjean was smiling aloofly, recognizing his name only and pretending to follow the English portions of their conversation. He tapped his rolled gloves against his leg and looked into Eve's eyes. "The fastest way into a pretty girl's heart," he said, "is in a red racing car." He turned to Mac. "Why don't you buy one with those gold bars, Doctor?"

"No, thanks!" Mac bit off. "I've been through this before." There was such a bitter snarl in his voice that he was as startled as the others to hear it; he was so accustomed to a continual self-control, a never-sleeping gyroscopic steadiness, that naked anger in himself was always a complete surprise.

Jeanjean grinned with pleasure. "I think I touched a sensitive spot with you. Even with a Ferrari, you can't win every race, Doctor."

Mac caught the obvious reference to Maia, and this time managed his voice better. "This has nothing to do with races or with winning." No, he thought swiftly, only with losing. A broken child lying in coma on the sterile catafalque of an emergency room operating table. Give us this day our daily bread and forgive us our neurotic responses to buried memories, and damn all the speed-mad bastards in the world.

Jeanjean interpreted Mac's new, courteous tone as a sign of retreat, and swooped to the attack. "If you're afraid of the speed, or handling the wheel, Doctor, I'll be glad to teach you."

"It is not the fear," Mac said. Only hatred, he thought, an overwhelming unreasoning completely primitive hatred. For a moment, Carl stood in front of him, not Jeanjean; the same muscular charm, the same curly-haired puppy let's-play-together charm, the same irresistible up-into-my-saddle and we're off. And Eve, even Eve the wise and warm and self-contained, had said: *I've always wanted secretly—*

The assistant manager was beside Maia, murmuring deferentially, "A call just came from Monsieur Theologos at the Bourse, madame. He's in his private box in the gallery overlooking the Parquet."

"Did you tell him we were en route there? Women are not allowed inside until two-thirty, anyway."

"Yes, madame. I begged him to be patient. He said he would need an additional hundred thousand in coins because the Arab price was going up."

Maia put her fingers gently to her head. "That man will exhaust us. Did you tell him we have combed the Mediterranean market from Beirut to Tangier? That we now hold in his name the largest collection of gold coins in the world?" She turned to Eve. "Pardon me. It's just that I'm very annoyed with a good friend who insists on dealing with Arab kings who own oceans of oil. Some of them are so medieval they will not accept royalties in anything except gold sovereigns or napoleons or louis, did you ever hear of anything so fantastic? Ordinary dollars and sterling aren't good enough!"

"I'm sorry," Eve said. "I can't even balance my checkbook sometimes. I don't really know what this is all about."

"Sixteen million dollars in gold coins," Maia said. "Can you imagine finding that much in *coins* within a one-month period? Like finding sixteen million eggs in one basket."

Eve smiled. "I'll stick to medicine. It's so much easier."

"I accept the reprimand, Dr. Desmond. Medicine requires brains. Money only needs cunning."

That little mention of the five-and-ten, Mac thought; it made Maia feel like an outsider, a foreigner, and now she's hitting back.

Eve was nodding her head slightly from side to side, as if shaking off Maia's comment. "I disagree," she said. "Medicine needs money. If your oil friend decides to throw a few of those coins away, consider me at the head of the line. I'd like to buy one of those." She pointed at Jeanjean's red Ferrari.

Jeanjean immediately opened the little car door for her. "Jump in," he said to Eve. "I'll take you wherever you're going."

"Fine." Eve held out her hand to Mac. *"Au 'voir,* Maccabeus. I'll see you in a few months."

"A few months?"

"I'm leaving on a survey trip next week. A swing through Europe, two weeks in Copenhagen at our tuberculosis statistical center, then down to North Africa, and back to Paris via Spain."

"Before you rush off to all those places," Maia said quickly, before Mac could speak, "let's meet for lunch."

"Well—" Eve began, uncertainly.

"Oh, please," Maia said. "I know how busy you are, especially with so much travel coming. Please, come to my house. We'll have some Moroccan specialty, just to put you in the North African mood." She put her hand on Mac's arm with the faintest suggestion of possessiveness. "Mac, why don't you bring Dr. Desmond?" She turned to Eve, still talking quickly, still holding Mac's elbow gently. "Mac knows exactly where my house is. He'll pick you up, won't you, Mac?"

"If Eve—" he began.

"Fine," Eve said. "I'll be delighted to come."

"Tomorrow?" Maia asked, then stopped short. "Oh no, tomorrow we're pouring Mac's new golden statue—"

"Statue?" Eve asked. She looked at Mac. "Gold?"

Mac suddenly recognized what Maia's purposeful little gambit had done, but he carried on. "Yes," he said, and motioned toward the paper-wrapped parcel lying in the back seat of Maia's car, "there it is."

"Sixteen million," Eve murmured. "Gold statues." She looked amused, and took a step toward Jeanjean's car. "I'm losing touch with reality. I'd better get back to the office."

"How about lunch this Thursday?" Jeanjean asked Maia. "Then both our doctor friends can watch our little fencing exhibition and we can all have lunch afterward together."

Maia said something quickly in Arabic, and he answered her just as quickly in the same language, smiling widely. "Thursday?" Maia asked Eve. "Can you make it then? Jeanjean gives me fencing lessons on Thursdays, and we'll try to put on a good show." She sounded slightly reluctant now, but unable to dodge Jeanjean's suggestion gracefully.

Eve smiled. "Fencing? I'd never believe you needed lessons. You seem so expert."

"Excellent riposte!" Jeanjean turned on his magnificent smile, and said to Maia, *"En garde."*

Maia smiled back at Eve. "Thursday then?" She put out her hand.

Eve took it. "Thursday." Over her shoulder, as Eve slipped sideways into Jeanjean's low car, she asked Mac, "Will you pick me up at the office? Call the Embassy, they'll tell you where."

"Sure," Mac said, watching her arrange herself prettily in the small cockpit of the Ferrari. She certainly had very nice legs; it was a pity she kept things at a higher level.

"Good-by, Signor Cellini," Eve called to Russo.

Russo's eye corners crinkled a little, and he bowed very slightly with an old-fashioned flavor of dignity in his work clothes. He had not said a single word until then, and he had the cool objective look of a blind man at a prizefight.

Jeanjean high-stepped into the Ferrari without opening the driver's door, and slid down behind the wheel. He started the engine with a roar that made every taxi driver and pedestrian and chauffeur on the Place turn around, even all the way over to the Ritz side. He looked around for a moment, tasting all the attention, revving the engine up and down, then shot into traffic like a rocket for the moon.

Maia watched the red bullet go. "I doubt the lady expected to risk her neck to make her point." She turned toward Mac as if about to add something, but stopped when she saw his face as he watched the red car accelerate into the stream of traffic. "Let's go," she said gently. "I'm impossibly late for my appointment."

Their big car moved sedately through the crowded streets of midtown Paris. Maia sat in the back seat with Mac. Russo sat sideways on the folding seat in front of Mac, glancing now and then at the paper parcel beside him on the second folding seat. They rode in silence.

Maia put her hand over Mac's. "I'm glad to see you," she said. "It seems like such a long time. There's so much to talk about, isn't there?"

He swung away from the window and looked at her expectant face. "It all depends," he said. There were moments when her eyes became so expressive that her obvious good looks became remarkably lovely; this was one of those moments, and, as always, her beauty with its trace of far-off sadness touched something inside him. He had been staring out the window unseeingly, sensing that the calm of the last two weeks was broken now; he felt angry with a complex variety of angers he could hardly sift apart. If he had been an observer a moment ago, while they had been exchanging their remarks in a kind of free-for-all, a primitive slugging match disguised as words, it would have been more interesting; but he was no longer an observer, the cool trained analytic observer. He was as much a participant in the whole tumbling broiling business of work and love as anyone passing by on the street. He realized for the first time how far behind he had left the ivory towers of Greenwich and New Haven, how completely he was enmeshed in a new world which required jungle strengths and reflexes. He understood, too, why the new statue of Maia was so different from anything he had ever done before, full of feeling. That was the key—*feeling*. After thirty-odd years of protecting himself against feeling, and pretending his self-protectiveness was somehow a scientific triumph of rationality, he realized that to be a fine sculptor was the same thing as becoming a truly mature man—that thought and feeling must go together, neither at the expense of the other, both parallel and strong.

"Signor Russo," Maia said in French, "you keep watching those gold bars like the father of an infant."

"I don't have gold to work with every day," Russo said slowly.

"It's been a long time. I like to go over things in my mind before we melt this down."

"I have an eight-year-old son, Signor Russo. Would you allow him to come and watch you while you work? He would be fascinated."

"I would like to have him, Principessa. But it is the doctor's statue," he added in his special dignified way.

"Thanks for the courtesy," Mac said gravely, appreciating Russo more than ever. It was a small but significant thing, his deference to Mac's wishes in the matter of inviting a guest to the foundry; his respect for creativity and good artists was so unassuming, so unfashionably simple and not complicated by the babble which usually passed for discussion in the arts, that Mac admired him as much as he did those remarkably able craftsmen, the scrub nurses who assisted surgeons in the operating room. For a moment he wondered what Miss Perkins was doing now back there in New Haven; briskly terrorizing some apprentice scrub nurse no doubt, or, equally likely, being as patient and explanatory as any other good teacher—and then the thought was gone with Maia speaking beside him.

"Henri won't be underfoot," she was saying. "I'd really like him to see men doing something technical and skillful. He's growing up so isolated"—she smiled a trifle, but with a trace of defeat— "he thinks money is something which comes in bundles and is always added up on counters—and he really has no father at home to model himself after—"

"Sure," Mac said. "Please bring him." Her voice had a suggestion of resignation in it which made him realize how strongly she must love her son. This was another of the many Maias.

"You're so thoughtful today, Mac," Maia said.

"Sure," he said.

"Did anyone ever tell you that you say 'sure' very often?"

"No," he said. "I never thought of it. Maybe I try too hard to be agreeable, the way I was raised."

"I enjoy it," she said. "The town is filled with gay *caballeros, toreros, bon vivants, boulevardiers*. An agreeable man with a skill at something other than making money is very relaxing."

"Please," he said. "You make me sound as homey as an old flannel bathrobe."

293

"Maybe that's what I need, now that I'm growing old, Mac."

"Would you like me to reassure you?"

"Of course, darling. But please don't say the obvious American things about silver threads et cetera."

"I won't."

"There," she said, "that's even worse. I mean, when you begin to sound clinical."

"I didn't mean to, Maia."

"You make me feel like a patient instead of a person."

He took her hand. "You couldn't be more mistaken, Madame Obenpharo." He grinned. "Some of my patients were awfully discouraging, but I always tried."

She turned her hand within his, letting it lie on the seat between them. He liked the firm slender feel of it. "And you don't miss it, Mac?" she asked. "The surgery, the problems of diagnosis, the patients, all that?"

"No," he said, "I never even think about it." That wasn't strictly accurate, now that he considered it, but it was as close to the truth as one ordinarily approached without walking barefoot over broken glass.

"Why did Dr. Desmond call you that unusual name?"

"Maccabeus?"

"Yes, yes, that's it. Is it something special between you?"

"Well," he said, "it's a long story."

"We have time. And I refuse to drop it politely."

He looked at her, searching her eyes. "So much curiosity, Maia?"

"Yes." Her eyes moved from one to the other of his, as if each had separate answers. "So much, and more. You would be amazed at how much curiosity I have about everything about you."

"Please," he smiled, "I've had enough amazement. There are so many Maias. Maia of the coiffures and the remarkable working clothes. Maia, the river goddess—"

"—no goddess nonsense—"

"—river mermaid. Better?"

"Better."

"Then," he said, "most amazing is Maia the banker."

"I confess," she said. "I tried to impress you."

"You did. I'm like Eve. I could never balance my own checkbook. You scared the hell out of me," he added, saying it in English because it was that kind of statement.

She threw her head back and laughed with the free spontaneous enjoyment he liked so much in her. "Oh, Mac," she laughed, "Mac, Mac, Mac." She stopped, then added, "Maccabeus. Is the special name Eve's private property, or may I use it, too?"

"Use it. It's from the Bible."

"Oh," she said. "I thought it was of those special things between Americans. Like understanding the game of baseball. Or calling Woolworth's the five-and-ten, a store with a special meaning."

"I thought that bothered you, Maia. Eve wasn't trying to push you aside with American colloquialisms. She just happened to say it."

"You think very much of her, don't you, Mac?"

"Do you mean very much, or very highly?"

"This way you have of answering a question with a question. Is that a doctor's way, or just a personal one?"

"I never gave it any thought, Maia."

"You keep surprising me," she said, "so I'd best keep amazing you."

"Maybe the most amazing," Mac said, "is Maia the mother, with a son she cares for very much."

"Amazing?" she said. "A mother loves her son. That's as ordinary as the air we breathe."

"Sure," he said, then grinned. "I mean, yes. Many things are ordinary. The American who runs to Paris to dabble in the arts is ordinary, too—"

She interrupted quickly. "Dabble! Mac, you're not dabbling. Signor Russo, to the rescue. Is he a dabbler?"

"Definitely not, Principessa." Russo sounded as if he preferred them to pretend he wasn't there.

"That's going to cost me a higher foundry fee," Mac said. "Anyway, the American who strolls along the Seine with his Parisian girl friend, that's very ordinary too, you know."

"But I live right there on Ile St. Louis, darling! Where else could we walk?"

"I'm not debating it, Maia. I just want to tell you that it's not

295

ordinary at all for a Parisienne to bring her son along to see a statue being cast by a friend who is a sculptor." She was beginning to frown, and he hurried to explain. "I mean, I think it's a healthy thing, to want to open up a boy's world. I mean, I'm glad you feel Signor Russo and I have something to offer him."

"You do. That's the whole idea."

"I respect you for it."

"Whatever is between us, that is something else. It cannot harm my son."

"I respect you for that, too."

"Ah," she said, gripping his fingers tightly, "the respect. That's harder for a woman to get than some other things."

He could see she was touched.

"I've just decided on another confession," she said.

"The confession box is closed for now, madame."

"I'm serious, Mac."

"If you insist."

"I do. For a selfish reason. It's good for my soul."

"For selfish reasons, I'll take it."

"Twice last week, I drove out to your houseboat. I detest women who chase men, but I decided the usual rules were no use this time. Not after what happened that afternoon on the boat—" He looked warningly at the back of Russo's head, but she ignored him. "Not after I didn't hear from you, day after day. I thought"—now she glanced at Russo, too— "well, I told you on the phone this morning what I thought."

"Why didn't you come down the steps to the boat and say hello?"

He noticed that her hand in his had begun to feel cold and tense. "It was dark each time I came," she said. "All the other houseboats had lights on. But yours was dark each time." Her voice changed. "I thought you had gone away—" she began to say, and stopped.

When he heard the new sound in her voice, and looked at her face, he lifted her fingers and kissed the back of her hand very lightly. "Child," he said, "they all have electricity from wires up on the street. All except my boat. I have no electric lights at all."

She tried a cautious smile. "Honestly?"

"Sure. Two of them have television sets. I use old oil lamps."

296

She opened her purse with her free hand and took out a small handkerchief. "How silly," she said, "my thinking you had gone away—" She turned her face away. "Television. On a houseboat."

Their car turned a corner, and there was the great gray-white Corinthian temple of the Paris Bourse, with its tall stone columns and glassed-in roof. Maia looked up at it and said, "Of all times to arrive for an appointment." She sat up straighter and put the handkerchief back into the purse. "Bank business is the last thing in the world I want to think about now." As the car drove up to the main entrance, she smiled faintly at him. "I'd like to leave my hand, Mac, but it's hardly possible."

He released her fingers. As he began to speak, the chauffeur opened the door beside her and she turned to step out. She was already looking out past the driver, looking up the wide stone steps to a small knot of men in dark business suits. One of them waved to her as she got out of the car into the sunshine, and she waved back. She turned back to the car and bent to look inside. "I hate to run off like this, Mac," she said.

He decided to reach out for humor. He did an imitation of the vaudeville Frenchman, hunching his shoulders and spreading his hands outward philosophically. *"C'est la vie,* madame," he said, rolling his eyes toward an understanding heaven. He was trying hard.

"C'est la guerre, you mean." She nodded over her shoulder. "Do you see that little group up there? They're the men who set the black market rates in foreign currency, you know, what the government calls the parallel market. Every day they meet out there unofficially and fix the exchange rates of the dollar, the pound sterling, and the Swiss franc. It's very hush-hush, but the Ministry of Finance must know their rates, so you see that policeman there?—he's taking a little slip of paper with the rates scribbled on it, and he'll telephone the Ministry."

She went on explaining it like a guide trying to make a dull visit interesting, but she had become the banker again, quick-speaking, with a brittle competence. He hardly listened. The other Maia of a few moments ago was better.

He held out his hand again. *"Au 'voir,* Principessa."

She sensed his meaning, and took his hand, speaking more softly

297

now. *"Au 'voir,* Maccabeus," she said. She smiled faintly at him. "So you never went away, after all."

"No, I was there all the time."

He watched her walk lightly up the brightly sunlit steps of the Corinthian temple, straight-backed and priestess-like under her torch of hair.

(3)

"So you're the lucky man!" Dr. Allenby boomed. "I've been trying to get Eve to one of these French style tête-à-tête lunches for weeks. And now, here you walk in on her last day in Paris!" He shook his head, wrinkling his eyes with laughter on the borderline of annoyance. "There ain't no justice, Dr. Adams."

"You're right," Mac said, "there ain't."

Dr. Allenby was a U.S. Public Health Service medical officer on the American Embassy staff, and, as Eve's nominal chief, he was in the business of being right. He was a short pumpkin of a man, straw-haired and red-skinned, and, Mac decided, full to the brim with good living, heartiness, and hypertension. Humpty-Dumpty in a Harris tweed suit, with the correct desk-top symbols of status—the double pen set and the thermos water carafe.

"Did you have any trouble finding our office, Doctor?" Allenby said. "Cité du Retiro isn't exactly a main drag."

"No trouble at all," Mac said. He wondered how much longer Eve would have to be in her office, because Maia had asked them over to her house for between twelve and twelve-thirty; now that he was back in the world of clocks he had regained the habit of using them. "Eve gave me very exact directions about getting here—right up to your office door," he said.

"What a girl, what a girl!" Allenby exclaimed. "First time Washington sent her over, we were all set to give her a hard time. You know how it is. You expect one of those lady doctors built like the side of a brick privy and twice as hard, and in walks Eve like a dream girl on Paris high heels, with the head of a professor of medicine."

298

His round face wrinkled into a pumpkin clown's smile and he boomed, "What a girl! I'll never forget it. The World Health crowd in Geneva was beating my brains out at the time. Memos, plans, amendments, a real paper snowstorm. So I wrote orders for Eve to waltz down there with me as a technical advisor on pediatric pulmonary disease" —he dropped his voice and grinned— "but actually just to see if she was real. Or maybe wearing psychological falsies, ha ha!—and damn, if she didn't have Señor this and Monsieur that and Dr. Soandso eating out of her lily-white hand in a week!" He stopped short, as if he realized his interest in Eve sounded more than fatherly, then shot out, "You and Eve kissin' cousins?"

"Old friends," Mac said. "Classmates." Dr Allenby was wasting no time. At this rate, Mac thought, he'll soon be asking me to fill out a government form with five carbon copies, and take a Wassermann test.

"You sure had my staff in a lather back there a couple months ago, just before you got to Paris," Dr. Allenby said. "Blew up a real storm."

"Oh?" Mac looked non-committally at the large-scale color map on the wall beside Dr. Allenby's desk. A couple of months ago was a century ago.

"Embassy started calling me one afternoon. Boss, Ross, whatever their public relations chief high muckamuck is called."

"Warren Ross."

"That's it. Big operator named Dr. Malcolm Adams arriving, he said. Could we whip up a *curriculum vitae* for the Paris newspapers, look the doctor up in the index of specialists, list his research work"— he snapped his fingers— "everything except your fingerprints and a damn glamour photo." The booming stopped short again, an effective technique, because the sudden silence caught the ear. "Doctor, you've sure had a busy life. Clinical practice, government consultant, research"—he paused, making it clear he was pausing diplomatically— "and all the rest."

"Well," Mac said, "that's all mostly behind me." He had been a different man in a different world. It all seemed so far away now.

Allenby shook his head. "When I read about your sculpture work in the Paris *Trib,* well, don't get me wrong, Dr. Adams, but if you don't mind, my first reaction was: A humdinger of a surgeon like that—a *sculptor?* Why, that's like hauling vegetables in a Cadillac." His eyes were still wrinkled in a smile as he watched Mac, but he was not smiling.

"Well," Mac said, "at least you can eat vegetables."

"To be honest-to-God frank, Dr. Adams," Allenby said, "I really got myself a little worried about Eve. After all you know, she is Embassy, and she isn't Bohemian, if you see my point."

"Absolutely," Mac said. He glanced at his watch. It was past twelve already, and Maia had said that she and Jeanjean would put on a fencing bout if he and Eve came early enough before lunch; also this doctor was becoming tiresome.

Allenby moved his hand in a little circle to include Mac and himself. "We doctors know how off-beat people really are. But doctors themselves, that's a different story. They've got to be solid." He paused, giving the impression he was granting Mac the opportunity to profess his solidness, but Mac said nothing, thinking: This kind of inquisitorial solid one always insists on his own personal definition of what's orthodox, always beginning with an air of reasonable restriction and always ending with the nailed cross, the lethal forgiveness, and the heap of burning faggots.

Allenby suddenly smiled. "Now that we've met, Dr. Adams, I'm reassured about Eve's friends. You don't seem like a long-haired artist at all."

The door opposite Dr. Allenby's desk opened and Eve came striding in quickly, going directly to Mac. "I thought that long-distance smorgasbord on the phone would never end! That was Copenhagen on the line," she threw over her shoulder to Allenby. "State Serum Institute. They'll co-operate." She turned back to Mac. "Am I forgiven?"

Mac could see Allenby watching, so he leaned forward and kissed her lightly. "Sure," he said, "Dr. Allenby and I were having a fine fatherly talk about you."

Eve put one hand on his arm and smiled at Allenby. "Mac and I are old friends from way back," she said.

"I know," Allenby said, frowning a little, "classmates."

"More like checkmates," Eve said.

Allenby's thin frown deepened. "Before you run off with Dr. Adams, Eve, two items. One, do you want me to handle the Geneva call for you this afternoon?"

"Thanks," Eve said, "but there are so many details maybe I'd better take it at the Obenpharo's. Do you happen to know Maia's number, Mac?"

He saw the trap, but life was too short for pretenses with honest people like Eve. "Sure," he said, "Odéon 11-12."

As Allenby scribbled Maia's telephone number on his desk calendar, Eve said coolly, "Aren't Paris numbers sensible? So easy to remember."

"Sure," Mac said. "Your number here is Anjou 81-70." She smiled, recognizing his maneuver.

"Funny thing," she said, "Odéon 11-12 is the number Jeanjean gave me."

"The Obenpharos have a big house," Mac said. "Maybe he's a guest there. Or trying to impress you. Sure it was 11-12?"

"Well, it's so easy to remember, after all, 11-12. You don't even need one of those little black booklets with the little gold pencils. Which reminds me, how goes the new gold statue?"

"We're pouring it first thing tomorrow." So, he thought, Jeanjean hasn't wasted a minute.

She shook her head. "Wish I could be there, Mac. Almost like launching a ship."

Mac smiled. "Adams' Folly."

"I'd love to see Adams' golden Folly. If only I weren't leaving."

Allenby cleared his throat to interrupt them. "Item two," he said as soon as Eve turned toward him, "is that letter from the Pasteur Institute."

"About their new plague research?" Eve said. "The one that—?"

"Yes. I left it on your desk."

"Plague?" Mac said. "Bubonic plague?" He had believed tuberculosis was the subject of her assignment, and plague was one of those diseases which belonged in the Middle Ages.

"Not only bubonic," Eve said, "but also the pneumonic form."

"I thought T.B. was your specialty."

"Actually," she said, "the whole range of pulmonary diseases.

301

From pneumonia to silicosis. If it's in the lungs and it hits kids, just call good ol' Doc Eve Desmond. Naturally, T.B. is near the top of the list. But I've never seen a case of plague hit the lungs, and when that short-wave report Dr. Allenby got from North Africa came in"— she turned to Allenby—"where were those cases reported?"

Allenby looked at the large wall map beside his desk, and traced a little row of colored map pins to the Atlantic side of the North African coast. He took heavy horn-rim glasses from the desk and put them on, leaning toward the map. "Agadir," he said. "It's a town fairly close to Casablanca, where they had an outbreak of plague in '44 and an epidemic in '45. And we have a big naval base at Port Lyautey, just up the coast."

"When I get to Algiers," Eve said, "I can get a connecting plane to Casa without losing any time. Or maybe I can persuade a Navy pilot to drop me off at Port Lyautey."

"Shouldn't be too hard," Mac said. "Navy pilots are highly susceptible to persuasion."

"I wish you'd drop the idea, Eve," Allenby said. "Scientific research is one thing, but with all that lead poisoning in those Arab countries right now—"

"Oh, nobody would shoot me."

"Well, there's other ways of getting hurt," Allenby said.

Eve grinned. "You mean fates worse than death?"

"It's no joke. Last week the rebels stopped the train east of Oran and raped the four European women on it. Then they disemboweled them." Allenby turned to Mac. "See what I mean about our mutual friend, here? Insubordination. Always giving the boss a hard time."

"Maybe I can take your problem off your hands right now," Mac said. "You in the mood for lunch, Eve?"

Eve stared out of the taxi window at the Gothic courage and despair of Notre Dame's piercing towers as they rounded the curve of Quai d'Orleans on Ile St. Louis. "Just one more block to Maia's?"

"Yes."

"Mind if we stop and walk? It's too lovely out to be riding."

"Sure," he said. He told the driver to stop, and they got out of the taxi.

"I've always liked islands in general and this one in particular," Eve said. "Paris is so busy nowadays. But it's all over there, on the other bank. Here, on this side, on the island, it's as restful as a pause in music."

Mac looked at her in surprise. There was an undertone of feeling which she rarely allowed to show.

She slipped her arm through his as they walked beneath the tall trees which grew upward from the stone pavement of the quai, old leaf-crowned giants. They were elms, and for a moment they reminded Mac of Connecticut and home and something else—elms? What else do elms remind me of?—something about cutting them down?—then the thought was gone. The Seine moved slowly beneath them, green-gray, a smoky mirror to the clouds, timeless. The sidewalk was empty except for one small man in a loose white Arab *djellaba* and skullcap who hurried by them. The narrow old houses across the street were shuttered against the sun, or shadowed beneath wide orange and yellow and blue canvas awnings offered to the sky like broad domesticated flags. Eve's heels made a slow pleasant strolling sound in the quiet street. Like an event in a dream, the moment felt as if it had no beginning, no ending.

After a silence, Mac said, "Did I tell you you're looking very ultra today, Eve?" Her deeply black hair made her skin seem very fair, with the unexpectedly blue eyes which were always so clear-eyed blue, so fine-eyed blue.

"I hope you mean what I think you mean."

"That's just what I mean."

"My last day in Paris, with two or three months of trains and jeeps and skirts and slacks and nylon blouses ahead of me. I thought I'd live a little, even if these high heels cripple me." Then she added, "Besides, think of all that competition at lunch."

"Oh, Maia usually takes it easy daytimes."

"Uh-huh. Just a little old three-hundred-dollar sheath, with that body inside and that hair on top."

"If you insist," he said, "you've convinced me."

She stopped for a moment and leaned her elbows on the stone parapet, looking down thoughtfully at the river. Below them, at each side of stone steps which descended into the water, two thin-hulled

one-man racing shells moved lightly above their brightly colored reflections. Eve looked sideways at Mac.

"You know," she said, "I'm in one of those moods of confession
and absolution." She paused, but he said nothing. Only a day or two
back Maia had said something to him about confession—what was it?
I confess. I tried to impress you.

"I can't tell," Eve was saying, "whether it's the effect of all that
huge Notre Dame symbolism, or the way the river just keeps going
by, or whether it's because it's my last day in town and Heaven only
knows when I'll see you again—" She sounded elegiac and a trifle
sad. It was a mood he mistrusted, because people made decisions at
such times about which they were always sorry, later.

"Now, Eve. Now, now, now."

"Don't now me, Mac. I'll be bouncing over half of Europe and
clear across North Africa, then I'll come back to Paris just long
enough to write my report. Then back home."

"I'll see you when you come back here, Eve."

She shook her head a little. "I don't know, Mac. I really don't."
She took his arm again and they walked on silently until they crossed
over to Quai de Bethune. Eve shaded her eyes with one hand and
looked up. "Is that Maia's house with all those monogrammed awnings?"

"Yes."

She squinted at the elaborately carved cornerstone of the house,
then asked, "You have 20-20 vision, don't you?"

"Yes." He shrugged. "You see? Hopelessly normal. Even my neu-
roses are normal."

She smiled fleetingly. "Stop boasting. Maybe that's your big attraction."

"I thought women cared only for professional tough guys, sadists,
and baby faces."

"Girls do. Not women. Women prefer men."

"Thank you, Dr. Desmond."

"All right, my normal smarty pants. Read it. What's all the carved
lettering in the cornerstone?"

"The original architect, and the builder, and the history, and the
dates. Under the modern remodeling, it's a very old house."

"Old as Adams Farm?"

304

"Older."

She lowered her hand from her brow and looked directly at him. "And Adams' golden Folly?"

"Take it easy, Eve."

"I warned you. Confession and absolution."

"They don't always go together, Eve."

Something was wrong. She had gone back to her original theme.

"I'm not sure that I care," she said. "Confession is an investment in a clear conscience, I suppose. Absolution is just an extra dividend. Houses like Maia's take nice normal Americans like you and chew them up without spitting out the bones."

He laughed. "My God, Eve, don't tell me you're worried about me." Everything about her, he realized, was a little heightened today; her eyes, the pink in her skin, the way she talked. It was as if she had a slight fever.

"I just wish you'd never met her." She smiled a little crookedly. "Forgive the possessive sound. I don't like it myself. It's just that I wish she'd folded her little Arab tent and quietly stolen away."

"She isn't Arab."

"I know, I know."

"But your friend, Eve, what's his name, the Spanish hotrod polo player, he's plenty Arab."

"Don't you really remember his name?"

Suddenly he did. "Jeanjean. Like the name of a candy bar, spelled backward."

Eve's eyes held his for a moment. "How's Maia in bed, Mac?"

"Do you want a scientific summary? Or just a blow-by-blow description?"

"Either way. Jeanjean says she's a sad sack."

He was beginning to feel the conversation turn within his blood. Now he realized how serious she was when she used words like confession and absolution, and he tried to turn away from the naked realities she was mentioning with such an air of deceptive simplicity. "Eve," he said, "you sound like one of those French plays where the husband comes into the bedroom while the lover hides under the bed while the wife locks the young maid in the closet because she knows the husband—"

"Stop it, Mac."

305

"You asked for it, Eve."

"People never get around to talking to each other, really, do they? I know it's unforgivable, but I thought for once in my life I'd try."

"All right. How's Jeanjean's hotrod in the hay?"

Her face and throat were very faintly pink now, making her eyes seem even more blue. "I tried, but we never even got there."

"Spasm of your New England upbringing?"

"No, damn you."

"Me? Why damn me?"

"Because I realized I was only trying to punish you. And doing the wrong thing for the wrong reasons suddenly stuck in my throat."

"If you're so smart, ma'am, why ain't you rich?"

Her lips tightened angrily. "Your vulgarity isn't helping anything, Mac."

"You started this, Eve."

"But I haven't made any stupid wisecracks. Why are you acting like a dirty boy? Because I've made you uncomfortable? Because I ask you to take a look at yourself?"

"Maybe. Maybe so. I apologize for the stupid part. But if we're going to be honest, why pretend your hurt feelings are really concern for my immortal soul?"

"I'm not pretending about my feelings. You think it's easy for me to talk like this? I'm not pretending about my concern for you, either."

"Why, Eve?"

"Because at the very least we could be very good friends. Companions on the long lonesome journey. At the most—"

"Lovers."

"You've thought it, too."

"Of course." They faced one another directly now, unaware of the street around them, ringed in their painful intimacy. "Is it brutal," he said, "for me to say this year is sort of last chance for both of us?"

"Yes, Mac. That is brutal. But I'd rather have you say it than just think it."

"It's true, isn't it?"

"How do you mean, last chance?" Eve asked. "You make us both seem in our nineties."

"That would be simple," he said. "Second childhood. But we're in our thirties, and that's second adolescence."

306

"I don't have the slightest idea what you're talking about, Mac. I was talking about us."

"So am I. I saw this second adolescence in my patients—being a pediatrician, you couldn't see it in yours—what I mean is"—he paused; how to say it and still make sense?—"men and women in their thirties who thought they'd finally reached places in life they had always wanted—you know, the job, the status, the children, the money, the whatever—and then all of a sudden, without any obvious warning, all of a sudden they face the crisis of not being sure. The housewife says she should have been a singer. The banker decides he should have been a surgeon. The actress knows she should have had kids and a house in the suburbs." His lips tightened. "The surgeon who tries to be a sculptor."

She was frowning deeply. "What's the crisis? Everybody gets these feelings, off and on. Why call it second adolescence?"

"Because they—or we—or maybe not you, because you're solid, but maybe this applies to me—it's as if all the running around and storms of adolescence to find ourselves, to find a mountain worth climbing, or a path worth following, it's as if all that searching hadn't succeeded at all. And now, in our thirties, we start to look around for a new identity, this time for keeps. It's a crisis because a lot of us never find the answer, and feel it, and keep running around in circles, unhappy as hell."

"That doesn't apply to me. I know what I'm doing, and I want to do it. I don't have everything I might want, but the idea doesn't bother me very much—"

"Except sometimes, alone, late at night."

"Even then, not too much, Mac. And as for you, you had an identity better than most. Except for your reverend grandfather, you come from a long line of doctors. As a surgeon, you rank with the best. Now that you've opened the closet door and rattled the skeleton inside, I can see you had a beautifully tailor-made inherited identity you're trying to throw away like a man walking off the edge of a bridge with his eyes open. A quiet suicide. Self-punishment for God only knows what."

"Maybe I don't want a tailor-made inherited identity," he said. "Maybe I want to make one by myself."

"That does sound a trifle adolescent."

307

He said quietly, "Dr. Allenby remarked my being a sculptor was like using a Cadillac to haul vegetables. Is that your idea?"

"Of course not. That's a stupid comment, even though he's not a stupid man. But you'll admit ninety-nine out of a hundred doctors would say the same thing."

"Maybe that's the root of my gripe about medicine. The technical side of the surgery is so good, and the laboratory work is so clever, we've begun to treat the test tubes and the X-rays, and the money questions in good medical care are so fouled up with special angles and downright lying—hell's bells, Eve, you know as well as I the human margin in medicine shrinks a little every year. My coming here isn't suicide. It's a breath of life."

"Is this why you're here, doing what you're doing? Because medicine has some tough problems to solve?"

"Could you please take your thumbs out of my eyes?"

"I'm not gouging you, Mac."

"You damn well are, Eve. I've made my contributions to medicine. Time, research, organization, money, and sweat, all of that. I didn't duck it, or go off fishing. But everything I'm doing comes from a point of view—I can see now all my difficulties with Laura weren't the little things we disagreed about, but actually because we had two different ideas about how to live."

"Now we're back talking about the same thing."

"Meaning Maia?"

"Yes, among all the rest, Maia too."

"What about Maia?"

"Is she part of this second adolescence, this search for a new identity?"

"I don't know. I can't be that objective about myself."

"I can, Mac."

"For this and that reason."

"Yes, my dear. For this and that reason."

"I said before: last chance, Eve."

"That isn't true, Mac. Damn you, it's just not true."

He waved a hand. "All right, all right. I know if you wanted, you could lay 'em in the aisles."

"I'll accept the implied compliment and ignore the crude delivery."

"I'm eating lots of crude bread these days. Lots of vitamins."

"But the primitive Mediterranean approach won't keep body and soul together in the long run, Mac."

"Soul. There's our mutual New England background coming out."

"You're not going to say the usual trite things about New England, now, are you, Mac?"

"Aren't you going to serve up all the usual corn about the cold-blooded Northerner who's frazzled by the hot-blooded Mediterranean?"

She made a small fist and held it to her brow, shaking her head. "I'm a bit sorry I started all this. You've tied me all up in moral philosophy. I always do better talking about people, not ideas." She put her hand down, and began to smile. "I've always thought it was a bad sign when a man and a woman pretended to be talking about ideas, when they were really talking about themselves."

He smiled back at her. "As Maia would say: How American. You prefer action to talk."

"Not always. But at the moment, yes."

He took her arm firmly. "All right. Off your high horse, and up to lunch we go."

"How lovely you look, Dr. Desmond," Maia said as she greeted Eve and Mac. She wore an unusual plaid poncho over her fencing costume, a woolen oblong without sides or sleeves, only caught around the waist with a wide belt, and medieval-looking.

"Thank you," Eve said. "I'm sorry we're late. I held Mac up at the office, and then again right outside on your doorstep."

"That's what doorsteps are for," Maia said. "And no one notices the time here, anyway. And lunch won't be until later because we have to wait for the Rosses—you know Cindy and Warren?—oh, of course you do—and remember, we promised you a fencing exhibition."

"Well," Mac said, "Eve and I just had our own pleasant little duel. It'll be relaxing to be a spectator this time."

Maia looked quickly from one to the other, then smiled a little. "And I thought that look you both had when you came in was hunger." She skipped on. "Shall we go up to the terrace? Jeanjean

309

has put out all the equipment. Today we're using those new Italian foils with electric buttons at the tip. You know the type? A scoring touch flashes a little light."

A toy-size brown French poodle ran into the foyer, yapping excitedly with toy-size barks, dancing around Eve. "Ah, my little Tabac," Maia said. "See how he loves you at first sight, Dr. Desmond?"

Eve bent to pat Tabac, who turned to lick at her fingers immediately. "Little Tabac," she said, "little peanut pie Tabac." She glanced up at Maia. "He's darling. We're obviously meant for each other."

"He's yours, my dear."

Eve stood up quickly. "Oh no, really, I didn't mean—"

"We got him only yesterday, for my son. They aren't attached yet, and we can get him another."

"You're very kind, really. But I travel much too much."

"Too bad," Maia said, "love at first sight doesn't come often." She rang for the maid, and when the girl came, Maia said, "Marie, bring Tabac to Henri and tell him to take the dog for a walk in the park." She turned back to Eve. "We should form a ladies' traveling club. Awful, isn't it?"

They walked together through the tall paneled foyer, past several large paintings, to the little elevator being held open by an Arab servant whose name, Mac remembered, was Yacoub. The elevator had been built into the central space left by the turns of the large staircase, and, as its little plush wrought-iron cage hummed upward, they stood very close together. Mac caught the very faint difference in perfume each of the women was wearing, and realized that the variation in choice might very well say a good deal about each woman if only he knew the esoteric language perfumes were supposed to speak. Confession, Eve had said. Absolution was an extra dividend. He might as well confess to himself that there was a special kind of excitement in being with both these women at the same time, the pagan and the pilgrim.

"It must be very convenient," Eve said casually, "having Jeanjean living here."

Maia glanced at her quickly, and then across the short space at Mac. He thought he was able to keep his expression from changing.

310

"He doesn't," Maia said. "Sometimes he uses our telephone number, for snob appeal, like a child. But he's a wonderful sports coach, and he's often my guest." She paused, then added with a casualness equal to Eve's, "He said he enjoyed seeing you last night, Dr. Desmond."

"Please call me Eve, won't you? I always think of you as Maia."

"Thank you, Eve. He said you're the first American woman he's met who's very much like a Frenchwoman, meaning it completely as a compliment."

"That's nice," Eve said. "But I doubt I'd make one of his better athletic pupils."

Maia's laugh rang out heartily as the elevator stopped at the top floor. "I'm sure you'd do any sport well, once you decided, Eve," she said as they crossed the hallway, "any sport, outdoor or indoor."

What a pair, Mac thought. Actually they respected one another, each gifted enough to feel no real envy of the other, and it occurred to him that there actually were passing virtues to the three-cornered arrangement the French called *ménage à trois*. Then he realized that he would have been incapable of having such an idea occur to him six months ago, and that he must be changing faster and more completely than he recognized. He had always known there were men and women with clearly thought-out points of view about how they wanted to live, so clearly thought out and so strongly held that their ideas amounted to a kind of moral passion. Ethics was not a fashionable subject, except when the word was used to mean the regulations of a profession; as a pattern for living, no one would use such a word, even if it occurred to them, even if they wanted to use it in the ancient sense which crossed his mind: a pattern which would include an honorable relationship with two women. The Moslems and the Chinese had worked it out—but then, he thought with a trace of amusement and impatience with himself—not even Maia was Moslem, and none of them was Chinese. We each believe we're individuals, he thought. I suppose we're unique enough not to be types, yet we're actually whatever our worlds made of us, sculptured and molded into inherited images we never chose in childhood, patterned as we grew. And now the molds and patterns of our fathers are going, going, gone. The old paternal gods brood over empty altars, and Eve chooses to-

311

day to raise the uncomfortable questions which we pretend don't exist by keeping ourselves busy at games and pitching pennies.

Maia had thrown open the tall double doors to the room which led out to the glassed-in roof terrace. "We go through my room," she said as they entered it.

Mac stopped to admire the opposite wall. Above a small fireplace the entire expanse of wall was carved paneling in the center of which, set directly into the wood, was a small foot-square painting of a little girl. In effect, the entire wall had been made into a massive picture frame so that, by contrast in size, the fragile open innocence of the child in the painting seemed even more tiny and delicate.

"You like it?" Maia asked, sounding pleased.

"Very much," he said, and, as he looked over his shoulder to answer her, he saw the faint surprise on Eve's face. He realized she must have assumed that he would be familiar with Maia's rooftop apartment.

From behind them, Jeanjean's voice said in French, "At last! Where have you all been?"

As always, he managed to be a little larger than life, ballet style, standing silhouetted in the open square of sky formed by the folded-back doors to the terrace. In the near distance beyond Jeanjean, Mac could see the tops of Notre Dame's towers and one of the statuesque rooftop medieval angels blowing an exultant trumpet upward toward the great blue bell of heaven.

"Dr. Desmond!" Jeanjean was saying to Eve as he came toward them in his faultless fencing costume, "you look more beautiful than ever today, if that's possible." Eve began to smile at the exaggeration, but as Jeanjean bent over her hand, she saw Mac watching Jeanjean's movement to kiss her hand, and her smile faded as Mac's eyes then met hers.

Maia missed none of this, and smiled wickedly, enjoying it all. "Shall we begin, little ones? I asked Warren and Cindy Ross to come"—her smile widened—"as neutral observers, you might say, but Warren called to say they'd be along later. He said—" now her voice began to bubble with amusement and she changed to English, "he was in bed with the Ambassador on a very hot problem and couldn't leave." She had already unbuckled her belt and was lifting

312

the woolen poncho over her head. "Let's go outside and begin. Yacoub will bring up a tray while my opponent and I prepare for combat."

They stood erectly, Maia and Jeanjean, their bodies in profile to one another, their heads turned toward the adversary. Before crossing blades, they gave each other the formal salute with the thin foil, then repeated the salute to Eve and Mac. It was all done very precisely and with some attempt at seriousness.

They slipped the meshwork masks over their faces, stiffened into the *en garde* position, their knees flexed into a balanced crouch, and the bout began. Maia was the attacker from the beginning. She moved with a beautifully co-ordinated smoothness from advance to lunge to recovery, then a swift advance lunge, with Jeanjean engaging the blades in the middle distance, parrying, then counterparrying swiftly with the point of his foil flashing in a circle. He began to return; a quick riposte with a lunge, forcing Maia back, then back again, their blades clashing until she retreated defensively out of his foil's distance. Suddenly she renewed the attack with a progressive one-two-three, engaging and disengaging the foils in opposite directions, using a beat attack against the middle of Jeanjean's blade, forcing a retreat, her feet moving with ballet precision, forward, forward, forward again, then a lightning balestro done with a catlike forward jump and simultaneous lunge which put her point precisely at the center of his torso, a scoring touch. The signal light on the little box on the floor behind her flashed. Mac called it *"Touché!"* while Eve applauded.

Jeanjean raised his face mask, and wiped the sweat from his eyes. "Very nice," he said angrily to Maia, "very nice, but watch the left foot in the lunge position. It must be anchored." He demonstrated by falling fluidly into position, advancing in a lunge with flawless precision, keeping his left foot anchored.

Maia raised her mask and laughed. "You do it so beautifully when there is no opponent!"

"The idea is to do it correctly," Jeanjean said. "This is sport, not a combat." He looked annoyed, and wiped his forehead again.

"The idea is to win," Maia said. Mac could see her smiling faintly

313

with triumph beneath the strange metallic shadow of the meshwork mask.

Jeanjean turned to Eve and spread his arms slightly. "You see? Always the pupil knows more than the teacher. Always."

He faced Maia again. "Ready, Madame Champion?"

They dropped their masks over their faces and began again, this time omitting the polite salute to the spectators, plunging immediately into battle. There was a new tension in their postures; now each had become an attacker. Jeanjean began simply, with a straight thrust before the blades engaged, finishing the opening of his attack in opposition, in a high line, so that Maia could not attack simultaneously in the same line. He shifted immediately to a cutover, passing his blade over the point of Maia's, and swiftly made a thrust on the other side. Maia feinted, as if in a real thrust, and as Jeanjean closed the line of feint, she neatly swung to a new opening, attacking his blade, appearing to advance to the short distance. He parried defensively, using a fine counterparry to protect a larger area of his torso, followed by a quickly executed compound riposte, binding her blade. She danced back out of blade distance, then returned immediately. The only sounds were the quick tappings of their feet, the metallic clash of the blades, and through it all the panting passionate sound of their breathing.

Mac and Eve looked at one another. "Clinically interesting," she whispered, "isn't it?" He nodded. The artificial air of a dancing lesson was gone now, and the jungle had crept in.

Jeanjean muttered hoarsely within his mask and renewed the attack. A thrust, disengagement, cutover, a feint with a disengagement, as Maia replied with a parry of counter sixth, then he beat her blade and lunged, missing her by a fraction because she handled her body so quickly. She gave ground, held, gave ground again as he threw himself against her weapon until she suddenly spoke sharply in Arabic and used a stop thrust counterattack, taking on new speed, faster, the blade gleaming. Both she and Jeanjean were gasping an occasional hoarse word, until he fell back a step, and another, followed by her blade, followed, threatened, attacked, lunge, almost a kill, again, again, attack, attack, Maia lunged. . . . *"Touché!"* she cried.

He threw his mask up furiously. The sweat was streaming down his

314

face. "I try"—he gasped—"to teach you—and you change—a lesson —into an Olympic bout!"

She lifted her mask completely off her head, shaking her hair loose and wiping her forehead within the crook of her elbow. "I won!" she said, sounding so delighted Mac stared at her. She and Jeanjean had gone far beyond fencing, he realized, and she must have badly needed to win for some hidden reason. Their combat had had such an aggressive quality that many little things began to become clear.

Jeanjean stared at Maia unblinkingly, then whipped his mask off and threw it on the floor, dropping his foil on top of it. He looked at Eve and said, "*Dispenseme,* excuse me," and walked quickly off the terrace into the house.

Maia looked pleased. "How pleasant revenge is! This is the first time I've ever scored against him twice." She raised her foil and sighted along it with one eye, as if it were a rifle barrel. "How wonderful it must have been in the olden days, when there were really sharp points on these, and swordplay was not for play." She dropped her weapon. "Now safe little electric lights go on, and all we can say is *touché.*"

"Off with their heads," Mac quoted. "The Queen of Hearts herself."

"That would make Eve Alice in Wonderland, wouldn't it?" Maia laughed. "And you're the Mad Hatter."

"That's truer than you think," Eve said. "I know I'll wake up any minute, now."

"Eve," Maia said, coming toward them, "you have a look of hidden sadness. The way people do when they should be weeping."

"Maia," Mac said quickly, "the fencing match is over."

"No, Mac," Eve said. "She's right, and we all know it."

"I like you very much, Eve," Maia said. "If I didn't respect you, I wouldn't say it."

"If I weren't going away tomorrow," Eve said, "you wouldn't say it."

"Very clever. Very true," Maia said.

"And," Eve added, "I've learned to respect you, Maia."

Maia shrugged. "That's not the same as liking."

315

"What a day," Mac said. "Everyone's heart worn on everyone's sleeve."

Eve ignored him. "Why the sudden liking, Maia?"

"Because I always feel for the loser," Maia answered quickly.

Eve's lips parted, but she said nothing.

"Maia," Mac said. "Maybe you'd better put something on before you chill."

"I'm quite warm, thank you. Maybe it's because I've never beaten Jeanjean before that I talk this way. You see, I'm always the loser."

"But you have everything." Eve made a small gesture with one hand, taking in Maia, her apartment, her special world, the wide horizon of Paris in a great circle below their rooftop. "All this? And you think you're a loser?"

"You forget," Maia said. "You're Alice, and everything on my side of the looking glass looks upside down."

"Let's not carry the idea too far," Mac said. "Maybe we ought to do something sensible, like having lunch."

"As soon as Cindy and Warren arrive," Maia said. She smiled at Eve. "Yes, I like you now more than ever. I thought you were armor-plated and invulnerable. But you're not. Losing hurts you as much as it does me. If you were European, we could be very good friends."

Eve smiled unevenly. "There's been less pretending today than anytime I remember. Tomorrow I'll be sorry. I know I will. But today I feel just like you. *Touché* and all that." She paused and looked at her hands. "As we came in, Mac said I felt so strongly because I knew this was my last chance."

"Ah, how cruel," Maia said. "And I believed he was the first never cruel man I had ever met."

"Both of you are lunatics," Mac said. "You go through this emotional hara-kiri and then blame me. I'm just an innocent bystander."

"Not any more," Eve said. "Nobody is. Not even the rich Americans."

"Maia," Mac said, "you're shivering."

"Yes. Suddenly I'm cold."

"I'll get something for you."

"In my room, darling. I left that woolen poncho on the chair beside the bed." As he went off the terrace Maia said to Eve, "What can we do? He and I. You and I. What can we do?"

316

"I don't know, Maia."

Maia came to Eve and put her arms around her, and, after a moment, Eve embraced her lightly, too. Maia stepped back and said, "You were the one who looked sad. Now I'm the one who does the weeping."

"Yes."

"Because I'm really still a loser. You're stronger than I am."

"Yes."

Maia slipped her arm through Eve's as Mac came back carrying the woolen plaid poncho. "Let's not wait any longer for lunch," she said. "I'll shower later. Eve, let's you and I swim through barrels of champagne."

"Here's your blanket," Mac said.

"Thank you," Maia said, "but I'm warmer now."

"I'm sorry we missed the fencing," Cindy Ross said across the lunch table. "Mm. This champagne is so light and cold." She smiled in her bright birdlike way. "Or is it the saddle of lamb that's so warm?"

"Do you like it this way?" asked Maia. "Roasted with rosemary, and with new peas?"

Warren Ross laughed. He had been drinking in a steady deliberate way since he had arrived and his laughter came easily. "You know Cindy, Maia. Just as long as she doesn't have to bend over a hot stove herself—except in this case, she's a hundred per cent right."

"Where's Jeanjean?" Cindy asked. "My dream man."

"Probably sulking," Maia said. "He'll smoke some *kif* and—"

"What's *kif*?" Cindy asked.

"I don't know the English word—"

"It's like hashish or marijuana—" Eve said.

"That's it," Maia said. "Then he'll go out and drive his red racing car like an airplane until he feels better. Actually, I was very unfair to him. He expected a light exhibition match, with Eve and you applauding his gracefulness, and Warren and Mac envious. Instead I attacked him like a fury."

"Gosh," Warren said, "I'm really sorry we came too late to see the show."

"We heard," Eve said. "You were in bed with the Ambassador."

317

Warren glanced shrewdly at Maia, raising his eyebrows questioningly, then took a long drink of champagne.

Maia said, "I wasn't gossiping, Warren, so please don't look at me that way. After all, American slang still baffles me all the time. And this one was as bad as the other one I heard at the bank this week: kick the bucket. What an expression."

"Warren's favorite," Cindy said, with a spot of pink over each cheek from the champagne, "is the idea that's as hot as a two-dollar pistol."

"Now there," Maia said. "That's one I don't understand at all." She looked surprised when all the others began to laugh.

The maid came into the room. "Yes, Marie?" Maia said impatiently. "What is it?"

"Telephone, madame."

"Take the message, please."

"This is from Tangier, madame."

"Oh." Maia glanced around the circle, and put her napkin firmly on the table. "Excuse me, please," she said, standing. "I'll take it in the *petit salon,* Marie."

After she had walked out, Warren lowered his voice and said, "All hell's busted loose in North Africa. More than the usual bombings and assassination this time. Organized, simultaneous uprisings, like a military operation. The Arabs overran a small coastal town and butchered every European they caught. The dispatch the Ambassador got said the brutality was overwhelming. Women disemboweled. Kids' throats cut."

"Warren," Cindy whispered.

"Honey," he said, "they're doctors."

"But I'm not," she said. "I can't bear such talk."

"That's always the first step to evading the matter," Warren said. "The United States has to take a stand on all this. I hear the North Africans are planning a big demonstration on the Champs-Elysées tomorrow. That means more trouble, because the Algerians want to fight, and the Paris cops can get awful tough with street mobs. Mac, you haven't said a word for the last half hour. What do you think?"

"Well," Mac said slowly, "moral indignation comes so easily with this kind of news. It's harder to find out the underlying causes." He

318

was silent a moment, thinking: I suppose it's just as easy to wish I were back on the houseboat working away and concentrating on something enjoyable, but in the long run turning my back on the world won't work either. He drummed his fingers on the tablecloth. "I don't know, Warren. You're trained for this kind of problem, and I'm not. I can see the air bases, and the Middle East oil, and the Suez Canal, and the Communist infiltration, but on the other side is the whole African and Asian glacier edging toward a new kind of independence. If you're asking me just to get yourself an American man-in-the-street sort of viewpoint, I'm not in the street because I'm temporarily not working for a living."

"I can tell you what the French think," Warren said, then lowered his voice again. "Especially about Roger Obenpharo. They say he's one of the top brains directing this. To them, he's a criminal who has to be caught, tried, and sentenced."

"Warren," Cindy said quickly, "we both adore Maia, but should we be lunching here?"

"I told the boss, and you know what he said? He said, 'Wangle me an invitation next time.'" Warren laughed. "I didn't know the old boy could still get a—"

"Warren!" Cindy cut in. She moved his champagne glass out of his reach with an exaggerated comic gesture.

They began talking small talk in English while the maid served coffee, and then Maia came back. "I'm sorry I had to be gone so long," she said as she sat down. She looked a little troubled, and they all drank their coffee quietly.

Eve put her cup down. "Will you forgive me if I run? I have a million little things to do before I leave, Maia, and I'm sure you want to salvage the rest of the day."

"As a matter of fact," Maia said, "I'll have to dash down to the bank." Her voice changed. "There are a number of things happening overseas which affect our position."

"Not trouble, I hope," Cindy said.

Maia shrugged noncommittally. "There's always something. Most Moslem politicians keep themselves in power by making trouble."

Warren stood up. "If you're going back to your office, Eve, take my Embassy car and give Cindy a lift. I'll tell the driver."

"Aren't you coming with us, honey?" Cindy asked quickly.

319

"Uh-uh. No, I want to stay and talk to Mac." Warren looked at her, and everyone understood he wanted her to go so he could talk to Mac alone. "If you aren't tied up—?" Warren began to say to Mac, as they all began to move toward the door.

"If you don't mind walking," Mac said. "I'm going over to Notre Dame."

"To make faces at the gargoyles? There are a few who need plastic surgery badly."

Mac would have preferred to walk alone, there was much he wanted to think over, but it was clear Warren meant to speak to him.

Maia took Mac's arm and held him back as the others went into the foyer. "Come upstairs, darling, and talk to me while I shower."

He smiled, "And then rush off to the Banque Obenpharo?" He shook his head. "No, but I'll see you tomorrow afternoon at the foundry when Russo and I pour you in gold, Principessa."

She lowered her voice. "That call was from Tangier. Papa says things are breaking up faster every day. He wants me in Tangier next week." She glanced sideways at him. "That doesn't leave us much time."

"You'll be back here soon, won't you?"

"I have a strange feeling. I feel this may have to be a long stay. Papa is not well, and the whole political and financial situation"—she put her hand on his arm—"things have a way of crowding in, don't they?"

"As soon as the statue is poured," he said, "can you get away for a few days?"

She brightened. "I was hoping you'd say that."

"Mac?" Warren's voice called from the hall.

"In a minute," Mac answered. He turned back to Maia. "I'll arrange something. Something easy and relaxed and primitive. Maybe a slow sleepy boat trip up the river and through the canals. We'll live on omelets and French bread and drink barrels of Dutch beer."

"I have a better idea—if it's gluttony and the good life you want—"

"They come second," he said. "Let's keep first things first, Maia."

She made a little kiss in the air toward him. "I know where we can live on *foie gras* from Périgord and Chamonix honey and snipe on toast done on a spit over a vine shoot fire—"

320

"You're the glutton, you. Where's all this?"

"Aïn Salah."

"What's that?"

"It's a little country house we have. It means The Good Well. In the Seine-et-Oise. Small. Isolated. Very old, with creaky parquet floors and fireplaces you can stand in without stooping. A little lake in back, and a duck pond, and rows of hedges."

"Sounds like Adams Farm," he said, "but with an Arab name and a French accent."

"Isn't that the sign on your houseboat door? Adams Farm?"

"Yes. But the sign came from my home in the States. A place a little like your Aïn Salah. Is it really a well?"

"It was. Papa's father bought it long ago and had it made over, as a plush hunting lodge actually. There's a whole forest of wild duck and garganeys and snipe." She took a deep pleased breath. "We'll eat ham smoked for almost a year from the neighbors' farms, and butter out of frozen jars. We'll drink all of Papa's prize Chambolle-Musigny '37."

"Sounds too good to be true."

She smiled. "I feel much better now. I was feeling all alone again. You didn't want to come upstairs because you were afraid I was using you something like Jeanjean, eh? What the French call a *cavalier servant.*"

"Partly," he said. "And partly I just feel like walking along the river toward Notre Dame. I'm going to pay my respects to the Young Virgin of the North Portal."

"You sound like a Catholic."

"Well," he said, "the sculptors who carved the Young Virgin knew what they believed, and what beauty should look like. I'm no scholar, but I'm impressed by it."

"Complicated people are always attracted to big simple ideas."

"There's nothing complicated, Maia. I'm just going for a walk."

"Eve did this to you?"

"Partly."

"You feel deeply about her, don't you?"

"Partly."

"And I would partly dislike you if you didn't. I like her tremen-

321

dously. She has a little bit of the Young Virgin of the North Portal."

"I'll figure that out while I walk along the river," he said. He bent and began to kiss her lips lightly, but she put her hand behind his head and made it close and deep. "Darling," she said against his mouth.

"Maybe," he said, "I'll come upstairs after all."

She gave him a small push toward the hall. "*Va-t'en,* you cathedral gargoyle worshiper. We always seem to meet in foundries or bank offices."

She came with him to the foyer and took both Eve's hands. "Good-by, Eve. Pleasant journeys and please come see me when you return."

"Thank you." Eve sounded withdrawn now. She was cool and poised, again well guarded.

"If you pass by Tangier, please come to Villa Obenpharo. Papa would adore you and Mamma believes your kind of emancipated intellectual woman is the peak of creation."

"Sounds a bit frightening to me," Eve said. "Aren't peaks awfully icy? Actually, it's hardly likely. I'll probably go directly from Algiers to Casablanca."

Cindy looked at her tiny jeweled wristwatch. "Come on, you emancipated woman, if you're going to give me a lift. Bye-bye, Maia. Please invite me to lunch tomorrow, and the next day, and forever after."

Outside, the afternoon sun was oblique and warm. Maia waved to them from the great door, looking very small within the massive entry of double oblongs beneath a stone-edged owl's-eye window.

Cindy was in the Embassy car already, waiting for Eve to join her. She turned her window down and said brightly to Warren, "Warren, sugar, will I be taking advantage of your official car if I do some shopping on a bypath on the way back?"

"Just so long as the path isn't in Rome or Madrid, honey," Warren said. "Just sort of keep it within bounds, if you dig me right, angel."

Cindy grinned at Eve. "Isn't he the sweetest? Aren't you coming?" she added, as Eve turned back to Mac.

Warren frowned at her. "Of course she is. Give the girl a chance to catch her breath."

"Well, Mac," Eve said. She put out her hand. He took it, but held it to one side so that he could lean forward to kiss her brow.

322

"Don't," she said. "You don't know what a child I can be. I'll begin weeping in a minute."

"I'll see you when you come back, Eve."

She shook her head a little, trying to smile, and said nothing.

"I should have planned your last day better," he said. "I'm sorry if I gave you a hard time."

"You didn't, Mac." She looked past him at the river flowing by, then at Notre Dame, then back at him. "We had a little walk, a little talk."

"You still feel we came, we saw, and we're conquered?"

"Not me," she said. "You make me remember the first few lines of a poem that goes something like:

> The wise commit the errors,
> The good commit the sins,
> The brave are full of terrors,
> Only the loser wins. . . ."

He kissed her then, feeling her lips quiver a little under his. She turned quickly and got into the car beside Cindy. As they drove off, Mac watched them go. Eve did not turn, and he wondered if she was right about their not seeing one another again.

Warren fell into step beside him as Mac began to walk toward Quai d'Orléans. He gave himself a cigarette and held the pack toward Mac. Mac took one. Warren lighted his own and Mac's with one of his endless supply of wooden kitchen matches. Through the smoke he said, "You don't smoke much, do you, Mac?"

"No. But right now, yes."

"Everybody I know smokes like a chimney. How do you avoid it?"

Mac shrugged. "I don't know. I smoked a lot in medical school, if I remember. Pipes." He laughed. "Heavy collegiate pipes. You know the kind. But during my surgical residency there wasn't much chance, we were so busy with patients all the time, and some of the older men gave me the idea smoking never helped a surgeon. Some such old wives' tale."

"Odd," Warren said. "I never realized how many big and little disciplines are imposed on doctors in their training. In some ways it's like military training at West Point or Annapolis, but with more study, more years, less sleep, and less pay."

Mac realized Warren was approaching something in a roundabout casual way, and it was the kind of afternoon on which he was willing to drift a little while with the current. It hardly seemed a few hours since he and Eve had walked this same street toward Maia's house and she had spoken to him as she never had before, and never would again, probably.

"Well," he said to Warren, "if I had a son"—he realized as soon as he had said this that he was testing himself to see whether he could at last openly handle so painful an idea—"I'd be perfectly happy to see him choose something other than medicine."

"I thought all doctors wanted their sons to be doctors."

"Lots do. Maybe most. My father did." He tried not to think of Stan while he spoke, but it was impossible. Again he saw the small narrow body beneath the surgical drapes, again he stabbed himself with pain.

"What would you want your son to be?"

"Anything that kept him happy at work, happy in love."

Warren shook his head. "Man, you make it sound like one and one makes two." He drew deeply on his cigarette, then said, "You're a lucky dog."

Mac looked surprised. "Why?"

"Do I have to draw pictures?"

"Eve?"

"And Maia. And the way you live. Even Cindy has a crush on you."

"I'm secretly in love with her, too, but don't ever tell her."

Warren blew out some smoke and half laughed, half coughed. "I won't. She says it's your old-fashioned otherworldliness that gets 'em, but I tell her anybody who can retire young with money in the bank sure as hell isn't otherworldly. What's the real secret, Mac?"

Mac remembered Monsieur Obenpharo saying: *I'll tell you my secret. I'm wound with a golden key.* And when Mac had answered that he had no secret, no golden key, the huge old man had said: *What a pity.* "Warren," he said, "there isn't any secret. Cindy's just kidding you. File it under ye olde battle between the sexes."

324

"For a while, Mac, I thought you were using ye olde reverse English. Namely, as we bureaucrats say, every time they talk about"—and Warren paused to spell out each letter—"l-o-v-e, you start talking about astronomy or Confucious. But it can't be that simple, because these girls are too smart."

"Good God," Mac said, "do I seem as awful as that? First, you have me not smoking. Now I don't chew tobacco or spit. What do you want? A Sunday school kid? A poor pale boy with a slow sad song? Actually, if we're going to talk about me—and all day today everybody's been casually talking about me—"

"See what I mean? You're a character. A refugee from the Renaissance."

"Hell's bells, Warren, I'm no more a monk or an ascetic than you are."

"Then what's all this Notre Dame stuff?"

"Millions of tourists come to see Notre Dame. If I had a camera I'd be just another one."

"That's what I mean. This put-on humility of yours."

"Warren, old man, I'll be glad to punch your goddam nose. Are you lonesome for a fight or something?"

"I guess so. Maybe I'm anti-doctorish today. Today your filthy virtues make me very aggressive for some reason."

"Because you don't know my beautiful vices."

"There," Warren said. "There you go again. I can't even fight you. You turn your goddam other cheek."

"All right," Mac said. "I won't. Hold out your left eye and I'll spit in it."

"What's the idea, Doctor?" Warren said. "Just what the hell is your basic idea, my dear Dr. Faustus? What's this feeling you give out, all these little vibrations, that you've gotten hold of something that makes guys like me look like peanut peddlers at a circus?"

"As one peddler to another," Mac said, "I guess that's just about the name for what I was doing, too. Selling a special brand of peanuts called plastic surgery. Well, now I've stopped for a little while to catch my breath and to make sense out of the circus. Eve and I were just talking about how that's what people do in their thirties. Maybe that's what bothers you. You're still the daring young man on the

325

flying trapeze. One of the success boys, always on the make."

"That isn't so hard to understand. Even for a success boy."

"You asked me, so I told you."

"Well, what's the real answer? What's the score? Is there any sense to the whole three-ring show?"

Mac pointed his cigarette at the great Cathedral hanging massively above them in the gray-blue sky of France. "There's one answer that worked for a long time."

"Not for me. Not any more."

"Not for almost everybody any more. Even the ones who pray the most and pretend the most. But what have you got in its place?"

Warren walked beside him quietly. "The American Embassy, I guess," he said, "now that I think about it."

"Understandable for you and me—or anybody else about whatever home country they come from—but with that idea we might as well be two of Caesar's legionnaires in Egypt, talking at the foot of the Sphinx about imperial Rome. We'll never survive the next wave of Vandals any more than Rome did."

"So that's what you're looking for. A new religion."

"No. Not if you mean a formal pattern with a hierarchy and all the theatricals."

Warren stopped and flipped his cigarette stub in a long arc into the river down below them. Mac noticed the two little brightly painted racing shells still moored at the stone steps exactly as they had been when he and Eve had come this way; they swam lightly in the summer sun exactly as if nothing between Eve and him had changed on this day of duels. No blows given and taken, no love offered and rejected. Here was what the river spoke of: the cosmic indifference. It washed away no wounds; it simply ignored them until they healed.

"Judas priest," Warren said, "if the watchdogs in the Department heard me talk like this they'd toss me right the hell out on my ear. I know one or two Bible-happy Southerners who'd gladly burn me at the stake."

They had crossed the ugly little metal framework bridge between the islands and were on the Notre Dame side now, with the twin towers which looked so alike, but were not alike, soaring high above them with their extraordinarily massive weightlessness, the stone

326

miracle of tension and balance. Beneath them, Mac thought, were layers of religious faith like geologic strata. The arched Roman temples, the Gauls' sanctuaries of wood, the Merovingian basilicas of the Dark Ages. They walked in the great cool shadow of the Cathedral, a world of stone angels and demoniac gargoyles, carven submissive queens and prayerful kings on their humble knees.

In the little park beneath the trees, a few women sat watching their children play on the swings in the deep shade. Several knitted, but the others chatted quietly, everyone ignoring the Cathedral which was as much a daily part of their lives as the river and the sky. In any case, few of them believed what it said. The children played quietly near their mothers, the older ones darting in and out between the swings like hummingbirds. Two Arabs walked by, each wearing a red fez, the taller in European clothes, the shorter a dark-bearded man in a brown *djellaba* talking constantly and waving his arms angrily. Occasionally a quick nervous spurt of traffic ran by them across the Pont de L'Archevêché, and then the quiet flowed back in, with the bells striking the hour so high above them that even the bronze hammer strokes were only a soft intrusion. This was why, Mac realized suddenly, every road from the furthest corner of France to Paris was measured from the bronze plaque in the plaza before the Cathedral; there was no state religion, yet it was clearly here that the ancient heart of France had beat through every devastation and every plague. Here was a passion beyond flesh, a concept now as forgotten as the names of the original workmen. This idea had first occurred to him after the liberation of Paris in 1944, when de Gaulle had come to Notre Dame, and now he understood far better why such a visit transcended all the ceremonials and the uniformed military show. Despite his different childhood's faith, here was the Church Triumphant, the tower beyond time, the target of his ancient ancestors' fear and hatred so deeply burning that Christianity had never become whole again, after the Reformation, never become a universal daily way of life again. Now, as always, there was still the search for final and single answers, the single final answers of the ancient religious prophets with their One God above all others. And wasn't his own research work back home the same kind of monotheistic search? His pursuit of its ultimate mysteries was much like

327

his grandfather's stern and mystic pursuit of the ultimate Father.

He had talked only a little while back with Eve about the need for identity, and now he was grateful to her for having begun the talk. He had lost his fear of abstract thought, of critical reasoning. The wisps of memory which had drifted so faintly through his mind, the disconnected bits and pieces of himself, were coming together now into an understandable pattern which went further back than childhood, as far back as the Capitall Lawes of New England which had regulated his ancestors' lives by the authority of the Old Testament, rather than the common law of England.

Here was why Obenpharo had impressed him as having such granite strength, for Obenpharo saw himself in a long, long Mediterranean perspective which funneled back through centuries. At first Mac had believed it was faintly comic, like the snobbish posturings of ancestor worship of the beribboned D.A.R. and Colonial Dames in the States, but now he saw Obenpharo's sense of time and origin for what it was, a taproot of strength.

Warren had seated himself on a park bench and was smoking another cigarette in quick puffs. He looked up at Mac's withdrawn and thoughtful face and wisecracked, "Don't just say something. Stand there."

Mac sat down beside him. "Warren," he said, "what is it? What's the trouble?"

Warren blew out a long stream of smoke and said quietly, "I think I've got syphilis." Suddenly his forehead was covered with tiny sweat drops.

Now Mac was on familiar ground. "What makes you think so?"

"Last week I went in for my monthly blood checkup and the report came in this morning. It's been eating my guts out all day."

"Mind if I ask some questions?"

Warren laughed with a nervous bark. "Judas, don't pick now to be polite! I'm talking to you not just because you're a friend I can trust. I expect medical questions."

"What's the monthly blood checkup for, Warren?"

"Well, it started with a mild chronic anemia. On my last trip home I went in for one of those three day superexaminations at Columbia and they found a slowly bleeding duodenal ulcer."

328

"And they said that caused the anemia?"

"Yes. And when we got the ulcer all nicely healed, the anemia was gone. What they called secondary anemia, I think."

"Sounds right. So that's why the monthly laboratory check on your blood now?"

"No. Now I'm on one of those anti high blood-pressure drugs, and my doctor says I need a monthly check on the white blood cells this time." He tried to grin. "Sounds complicated and it isn't exactly inexpensive."

"Wait a minute, Warren. A white cell count has nothing to do with a Wassermann test for syphilis."

"That's the hell of it. The doctor wrote 'complete analysis' or something on the label of the blood sample, and a brand-new technician at the lab just automatically did a Wassermann." He lighted another cigarette from the glowing stub of his last one. "Can you imagine discovering something like that by accident?"

"When you had your three-day examination at Columbia they must have done a routine serological test on your blood. You didn't have a positive test then, right?"

"Right. I didn't." He looked sideways at Mac. "And you're wondering whether I picked up the disease since then. Or about Cindy— or why we don't have children—"

"No," Mac said. "I was only wondering whether you knew that there can be quite a difference between a positive Wassermann test and having syphilis."

"Well, my doctor said something about a false positive and doing some more tests."

"Sure. You ought to do it. Co-operate with him."

"I was so fouled up when I heard all this I thought he was soft-soaping me and I went stomping out to the nearest bar." He gave his short laugh again. "Then I remembered my meeting with the Ambassador coming up, so I settled for a quick little *espresso*. Maybe you noticed the way I hit Maia's champagne at lunch."

"No," Mac said. He had, of course. "Warren," he said, "if you have syphilis, there's every chance you can cure it and take care of Cindy, too."

"For the love of God, Mac, how the hell can I go to her with such a thing?"

329

"If the other tests check out positive, how the hell can you consider not going to her?"

"Cindy would never take it," Warren said slowly.

Mac said nothing. He had learned that husbands and wives knew very little about one another, and would do whatever they would do. No doctor could change their fundamental conduct with a few words. Suddenly he remembered something.

"Warren," he said, "just before I left the States some hospitals had discovered false positive Wassermann tests in patients taking some of these so-called high blood-pressure drugs."

Warren looked up from the ground. "You mean just a drug—?"

"Sure, in a very few cases. I don't want to give you a phony crutch to lean on, but you might be one of the rare cases."

"Oh, I'm rare all right," Warren said. "So much so, I'm bloody."

"Good afternoon, Monsieur Ross," a small formal voice said behind the park bench. Warren turned quickly in his seat, startled. Henri Obenpharo stood behind them leading the toy French poodle, Tabac, on a long braided leather leash. The little dog kept circling the boy, and, as he spoke, Henri stepped in and out of the leather circle around his ankles.

"Well, Henri!" Warren said. "Taking your dog for a walk?"

"We've just bought him," Henri said. "I'm trying to train him, but he keeps tying up the leash."

"Henri, you haven't met Dr. Adams, have you?"

"No, sir." Henri unsmilingly stuck his hand out toward Mac. "How do you do, Dr. Adams."

Mac found himself being equally formal as they shook hands stiffly. "How do you do, Henri."

"You look very much alone, Henri," Warren said. "Aren't there any boys your age around here?"

"A few." Henri shrugged. "They run around and act like babies."

As Henri talked to Warren, Mac watched his slender face, formed like Maia's but with dark eyes, and bronze hair with gold in it when a thin shaft of the overhead sun speared between the trees and touched it. The boy must feel very much separated from any of the usual tribal life of boys his age in the neighborhood, Mac thought. Even his clothes must be a barrier, because most French kids wore very short

330

shorts and sandals with ankle socks, but Henri wore shorts in the British style, to the knee, with high calf-length ribbed socks and spotlessly white summer shoes. He held himself erectly when he spoke, with the kind of self-sufficient quality children who are very much alone develop. It occurred to Mac that Stan, his own boy, had had a little of the same quality even though the kind of world Stan had lived in had encouraged group activities much more strongly—and Stan had had a father, and there had been no training for inheriting an empire. Yet there was the faintly lonely air of the only child about Henri which reminded Mac very strongly of Stan.

"Henri," Warren said to Mac, "is the Obenpharo family expert on gold coins. Aren't you, Henri?"

"I collect them," Henri said seriously. "Last week I got a British Maundy money sovereign."

"He collects gold coins," Warren said, "the way I used to collect stamps."

"I collect stamps, too, Monsieur Ross. Our bank gets letters from all over the world."

"And how is your work at the bank progressing, Henri?" Warren asked, sounding much too hearty.

"He's stretching it, isn't he, Henri?" Mac said as the boy began to frown a little. "But, after all, don't you go to the office often? Doesn't your mother take you?"

"Yes," Henri said firmly. "She's supposed to take me this afternoon. The trouble at home means lots of extra work at the bank."

"The trouble at home?" Warren asked carefully.

"Yes. It's in all the papers. The North African trouble."

Warren's eyes met Mac's briefly. "No sign of Tom Sawyer or Huckleberry Finn, would you say?"

"Who were they, Monsieur Ross?"

"Two American boys in a story. They played tricks on everybody. Very"—he searched for the word—"active."

"Why?"

"Mac," Warren said, "you've had fatherly experience. You explain it."

"Is your family in Paris?" Henri asked Mac politely. He was having a difficult time with Tabac now, changing the leash from one hand to the next and sidestepping being entangled by the leather thong, but he never dropped his levelly courteous adult manner.

"No," Mac said. "What Monsieur Ross means is that I had a son your age, Henri. Would you care to have me hold Tabac's leash a minute?"

"No, thank you. At home I have a much quieter pet. A little fawn about this high."

"Seriously?" Warren asked. "A real live fawn?"

"Yes. My mother bought it in Tangier."

"Well," Warren said, "I've heard you can buy anything in Tangier, but this is the first time—"

"What do you call the fawn?" Mac asked. "Bambi?"

"Yes. How did you know?"

"I just guessed, Henri."

A timeless bell high above struck the half hour, and Warren looked at his wristwatch. "Judas, how tempus fugits."

"That means time flies," Henri said.

"Henri," Warren said, "don't tell me you know Latin, too."

"Not very much. My father has a room full of Latin books at home, and Grandpapa says I should know Latin, too."

Warren looked helplessly at Mac. "So long, chum," he said in English. "Got to get back to the pine-paneled salt mines. Thanks for the curbstone consultation."

"Let me know how it all works out," Mac said. He turned to Henri. "Monsieur Ross has to leave, but I'd like you to join me in an *apéritif,* Henri."

"Thank you. May I have Coca-Cola?"

"Certainly. Maybe we'll find a place to sell us a bar of soap, and I'll carve you a soap Bambi."

Henri smiled widely for the first time.

"That did it," Warren said. He shook hands with Henri. "I've got to catch a taxi. Nice to see you again, Henri. Give my regards to your fa—" he quickly corrected himself, "—your grandfather."

"Thank you," Henri said as they shook hands.

An hour later, when Yacoub drove Maia to the little park beneath the shade trees beside the Cathedral to pick up Henri, Maia saw him sitting beside Mac on one of the park benches, Tabac was

332

sleeping with his head between his paws at their feet, and Mac and Henri were bent over a small white cube which Mac seemed to be cutting with a penknife, like an apple. Neither the man nor the boy saw the car stopping at the curb, and Maia sat for a moment watching them there together. Henri was talking very fast, looking directly into Mac's face and smiling, using gestures which seemed to involve the carving process. Mac was nodding slowly from time to time, quite seriously explaining and pointing out details with a different set of gestures.

That is how a father and son should be, Maia thought suddenly, and for the first time she wondered about the idea of marrying Mac.

BOOK IV

Pilgrims and Pagans

(1)

"FROM way up here," Bud Williams, the American pilot of Monsieur Obenpharo's plane said, "Spain looks pretty nice down there, doesn't it?"

"It does," Mac said.

"On the ground," Bud said, "it's nothing but crud."

Bud Williams had invited Mac to come forward into the pilot's cockpit as they began their approach to the Straits of Gibraltar. After weighing the pilot's limited conversation against getting a new view of the Straits and Tangier from the air, Mac had accepted the seat beside Bud Williams which the co-pilot offered him. From the glassed-in cockpit in the plane's nose, Mac was able to see from horizon to horizon, the entire sweep of the eye taking in the classic Mediterranean vision of blue depths beyond blue beyond darker distant blue, all under a calm golden downpour of tropical light. There was only an occasional cloud far beneath them to give a toy perspective to the tan tumble of Spanish landscape. Many miles starboard Mac could make out the steel-gray slant of a local rainstorm with cubes of village houses and tiny trees seen hazily through the water vapor like outlines in a Chinese silk screen painting.

The overwhelming sense of space in every direction suited Mac perfectly. He had been sitting in Obenpharo's plane, letting waves of memory wash over him, recalling the weeks in Paris which had opened up his view of himself and his understanding of Maia and his future work, sensing a new feeling of freedom. It was an experience he had never had before, this kind of living with the idea that his personal frontiers were open, the old boundary lines gone, the range of his experience dependent only on his courage and self-discipline and intelligence.

"We'll be touching down at Boukhalf Airport real soon," Williams said, "and you'll get your first smell of Tangier. I'd ask you to an American steak dinner tonight, except I've got a big deal cookin' at the Carnivale." Bud closed one eyelid in an exaggerated wink and rubbed his thumb and forefinger together to suggest the exchange of money, then added, "But I'll show you the sights any other time you holler."

"Thanks," Mac said. All this was probably a boastful hint about smuggling, and Mac let it go at that.

Suddenly Bud Williams jabbed a finger skyward. "Hey! Look at those babies go!"

Far overhead, at about twenty thousand feet, a V-shaped squadron of jet pursuit planes was flashing south, toward North Africa. Each plane was a small arrowhead on a mile-long shaft of vapor contrails which hung parallel in the great height like smoky celestial skywriting. Bud Williams squinted at them. "Look like Mystères," he said. "Very pretty ships the French put out."

"Jets?" Mac was surprised. "In Africa?"

Bud Williams grunted. "Of course. Before all this trouble is over, they'll need everything they've got. Especially in Africa." He made a gesture toward Spain below. "Hell, what about us? I hear tell we're negotiating for bases in Morón de la Frontera, San Pablo, and Torrejon. And a radar station on Mallorca, they say."

"What about Tangier?" Mac asked.

Bud pushed his cap back a little. "Beats me. I can't figure out how those Arab wogs think. But I've heard old man Obenpharo say Tangier will be an International Zone only as long as the Moroccans want to use it that way. After that," the pilot said, holding out his hand, "they'll take it like this." His fingers closed into a fist. He shook it and held it higher, a clenched salute. "And this is Roger Obenpharo. The iron hand in the iron glove. A real piss-cutter, that guy. He's got this new get-up he wears all the time now, blue Tuareg desert clothes, with his face bandages covered by the blue veil. You've got to see it to believe it, the way he gets up in front of a native crowd in wool nightshirts and drives them wild."

He turned to Mac. "Think you'll be able to fix his face?"

"I'll do my best." He knew he sounded pompous, but he didn't want to talk about it.

"I get a funny feeling just thinking about cutting a guy's face. Even an open Boy Scout knife bothers me. How do you do it?"

"One step at a time," Mac said.

As Bud went on talking about Roger Obenpharo and his power with Arab crowds, Mac remembered the North African political demonstration he had seen in Paris the day after Eve had left town, the day after they had had lunch at Maia's house. Warren Ross had mentioned there would be a demonstration, but Mac had forgotten all about it.

Actually, now that he thought about it, that demonstration had changed his own direction. Not his goal, but certainly the direction he had been following with Maia, because he had been forced by it to return to surgery. The Mediterranean world and all its arabesque designs of intrigue and violence had always seemed remote and unreal to him, like a motion-picture newsreel of a faraway fire. But now he knew better; he could feel the heat of the flames, and he knew he was going to risk being burned.

. . . That day in Paris had begun very pleasantly, because Maia had come to the Thodier Foundry to see Mac and Russo pour the gold statue of herself, and she had brought Henri with her.

When Russo had lifted the cover from the oven in which the gold was being heated, a bright pillar of fire had leaped toward the high roof of the foundry, flaring so brilliantly the remainder of the space seemed darkly shadowed around him and Mac, and Maia and Henri. Mac and Russo had been stripped to their waists, shining with sweat in the reflected golden glare. The mold of the statue they were about to cast stood near the oven, tightly clamped and bolted within iron frames, raised up on a platform between sawhorses.

Mac walked over to where Maia and Henri stood, and took his towel off a hook to wipe his forehead. "You know," he said to Henri, "most young bankers like you never see how gold is melted or poured."

"My grandfather knows about it," Henri said, in his serious grown-up way. "He knows all about gold."

Maia smiled at Mac over Henri's head, but said nothing. She was dressed *à l'anglaise,* low-heeled British shoes, a blue linen skirt, and white linen blouse with a convent girl's collar; with her hair up she looked forever seventeen.

"I'm sure your grandfather does know all about gold," Mac said.

"The golden rule," Maia added.

"Maybe the other way around," Mac said.

She raised her eyebrows. "The rule of gold, you mean?"

"Yes."

"That's probably more accurate," she said. "Everyone always says it, of course. Maybe it's one of those slogans everybody believes and accidentally happens to be true."

Mac looked at her. "With your hair up like that, maybe we ought to mint a few ancient-looking coins with your profile. Very Grecian. We could put a signature on the coin: *Aphrodite*."

"That's the most flattering idea I've heard in years."

"You look strong," Henri said to Mac. "Do Americans lift heavy things every morning for exercise?"

"Well, Henri, lately I've been carrying a few heavy ideas." He tapped his head. "Builds strong muscles up here."

"Ideas don't weigh anything." Henri looked offended, as if he were being talked down to.

"You'd be surprised, Henri. Some of them are hard to carry."

Russo came over to them, wiping his streaming face in the bend of his elbow. *"Aie, ragazzo mio,"* he said to Mac, then added in French, "Let's go. She's just right." He went to a tub of chipped ice and took out a bottle of wine which he uncorked and held out dripping to Mac. "Lacrima Christi, from my brothers in Firenze," he said, "in honor of your statue of the golden Principessa."

Mac noticed that Russo referred to Maia as golden, not the statue, and he remembered how Maia had seemed to him the first time he had met her. He took the wine and said, "A thousand thanks, maestro. The toast should begin with our guest of honor." He held the bottle toward Henri.

"For me?" Henri was startled, and sounded pleased.

"Yes," Mac said. "You're a fine young man, and you're our guest."

"Go ahead, darling," Maia said. She smiled intimately at Mac, grateful for his gesture of making the boy a member of the group.

Henri took the bottle with both hands and took a deep manly

swig. He swallowed hard and tried to speak, but for a moment no word came. They did not laugh at him. He held the bottle toward Mac and said chokily, "A thousand thanks."

Mac nodded gravely, and offered the bottle to Maia. She took it and wound one elbow across his, so that their arms were linked. "An honor," she said, and took a deep drink.

Mac offered the wine to Russo, who bowed his head slightly, with dignity, and said, "After you."

"No," Mac said, "we both come after the gods." He winked one eye at Henri so the boy would not take the event too seriously and poured a small libation on the ground. "Under the protection of Aphrodite," he said, "I name this statue 'La Nymphe au Coeur Fidèle.' "

Russo and Henri clapped lightly, but Maia stood with her hands clasped tightly together. She had come prepared to be pleased by the whole event, and she knew the various shades of meaning for the word *Nymph;* yet it was Mac's addition of the *Constant Heart* which touched her most deeply. It was a new idea, a romantic and foolish idea, she decided—but pleasant at this moment. I wonder, she thought, could I ever be constant? This Mac would be worth it. I'll never meet another like him.

Mac and Russo passed the bottle between them, drinking the cold wine thirstily with their heads back, until it was empty and Russo tossed it into the nearest open brick oven with a fine christening crash. "Let's pour your statue," he said.

He and Mac wrapped leggings and aprons made of carpet around themselves while Russo sloshed the woven material with water. They put on asbestos mittens and dark-tinted protective eye goggles and then approached the blazing crucible. Russo pushed the overhead crane along its track until it was above the oven, then he and Mac lowered the arms of the crane until the metal tongs held the heated crucible of molten gold. Slowly they raised the heavy crucible from the oven, feeling great waves of heat strike them. Their goggles fogged and sweat ran in streams down into their trousers and leggings. "Easy easy easy . . ." Russo kept saying softly. By guiding the crane they were able to bring the loaded crucible directly over the bolted framework of the mold into which they were about to pour. Together they

341

locked forked iron bars which looked like bicycle handlebars into each side of the crucible. These would be used to tip the crucible forward to pour, the final moment.

Maia bent over Henri. He was watching Russo and Mac so intently he did not notice her. "Henri," she said quietly, "do you see how much hard work goes into gold, away from banks?"

Henri nodded, but did not take his eyes off the men. They looked heroic, silhouetted against the glare. Russo and Mac were on opposite sides of the crucible now, each grasping the double-handled iron bars. Russo raised his head questioningly at Mac, wasting no energy in speech. "Ready," Mac said between his teeth, and Russo grunted, then nodded, and the pour of molten metal began. The incandescent gold was brighter than staring at the sun, so bright that both Maia and Henri stepped back and shielded their eyes. As the men tilted the crucible further, the mold beneath the pouring lip filled rapidly until, with a quick expert gesture, Russo pulled the plug from the mold and the liquid gold ran down into the wax figure of the statue, locked and buried in fine sand. When the metal began to overflow the top, showing that every carefully made channel leading to the space between the core and the mold had been filled without leaving any air spaces, Russo signaled Mac. They leveled the crucible and moved it within the metal sling of the crane back out of the way.

"Bene, bene," Russo said happily. "Nice job."

Mac came toward Maia and Henri, stripping off his asbestos gloves and pushing up the dark goggles.

"That was wonderful!" Henri said. His enthusiasm was so different from his usual controlled politeness that Mac walked directly to him.

"Would you like to try on the goggles and the gloves?" Mac asked Henri. Solemnly, while Maia watched them with a little smile, Mac put the goggles over Henri's head, then down over his eyes. Henri held up his hands and Mac slid the heavy gloves over them. For a moment Henri stood still, then he took a step forward and put his arms around Mac's waist. Mac put his hands on the boy's shoulders gently and stood still, saying nothing, and when he looked up at Maia he saw she had turned her head away.

342

Later, they sat in the shade at Le Rond Point while Mac gave their order to the waiter. They had come there because the little outdoor puppet theater was across the street, and Maia had promised Henri they would see the play. "Vermouth cassis for Madame—" Mac said to the waiter, then turned to Henri. "Will you share a *citron pressé* with me? With ice in it?"

"Can I have Coca-Cola?" Henri asked.

Mac looked up at the waiter. "Do you have it?"

"Of course," the waiter said unhappily. "With ice, if necessary."

"And a *citron pressé* for the chauffeur of our car there."

"The blue Mercedes, monsieur?"

"No. The next, the black English car."

"The Moslem chauffeur, with a red fez?"

"Yes," Mac said.

"*Oui,* monsieur." The waiter managed to convey the barest suggestion of a shrug, a patient man willing to adapt himself to nonsense.

After the waiter left, Maia said, "Such a lovely day. I can hardly remember anything so nice in a long time." She looked around with pleasure. "Did you know La Paeva once had a magnificent mansion here at Rond Point?" Her smile came to him and rested like a touch. "Do you mind if we speak French?"

"The way I feel right now," Mac said, "French is just the language." He was tranquil because the work with Russo had gone so well, and because Maia and Henri had enjoyed his having made it a kind of an event. And the city was at its best, not too hot; leafy and spacious, with a before-vacation mood.

"I like French the best," Henri said. "English makes me feel stiff, and Arabic is hard to say."

Maia looked across the table at her son with a trace of a smile in the corners of her lips. "*Ya, habibi,*" she said, "today is a good day for you." She put her hand over Mac's on the table and added, "That in Arabic means darling. It means beloved one."

"Why wouldn't Monsieur Russo come with us?" Henri asked Mac.

"He didn't want to wash up and change, then go back to finish the work," Mac said.

"I thought it was finished," Henri said.

"No," Mac said. "After the metal cools, the sand has to be shaken

343

out, and the metal core removed and cleaned in acid, and the little air tubes attached to the statue have to come off. There's still much to do."

"You should be there now, helping him, shouldn't you?" Maia asked.

"Yes. But I also should be here with you. Russo understood."

She tightened her hand over his. "I never knew there was so much work in it. For one small statue."

"Ya, habibi," he said, with just enough lightness in his tone so that even Henri smiled.

The waiter brought their drinks, and, while he was placing them, he said quietly, "The boss refuses to allow service to your chauffeur, monsieur."

"Why? A man needs a drink on a warm day."

"Of course, monsieur, but even if the man comes to your table he will still be refused service. The boss has hard feelings about North Africa. His brother and his wife and two children—" The waiter paused and glanced sideways at Henri. He leaned toward Mac and said very quietly, "In Meknes. The Arabs. With knives, a massacre. Too horrible to describe."

What is right, Mac thought swiftly, and what is wrong? Yacoub was no cutthroat, and the boss was probably a decent enough guy. Meknes was in Morocco, and Yacoub was Moroccan. If ever there had been simple answers, certainly there were none now. He got up. "Bring me another glass, please. I'll take this one out to the car." The drink had taken on the diplomatic stature of a principle, now. It was a trifle foolish, but this was no time for retreat.

The people in the front rows of the crowded terrace watched him curiously as he carried the drink across the street to where Yacoub had parked Maia's car in the shade. Yacoub saw him coming and got out of the car quickly. "Monsieur," he said, "this is not necessary."

"No," Mac said, giving him the glass, "but it's a hot day."

"Thank you, monsieur." As Mac turned to go, Yacoub said, "Monsieur—"

"Yes?"

"Do you know about the demonstration today?" Yacoub motioned with one hand at the Champs-Elysées nearby.

344

"What demonstration?"

"For the independence of the North African French colonies and Algeria."

Mac noted the fine distinction; Morocco and Tunisia were colonies, but Algeria was legally part of France. "Oh yes," he said, "I remember now. I heard something about it. But I don't see anything."

"Monsieur, look over there. The big police van. And look down there past the trees." Yacoub pointed toward the Jardin des Champs-Elysées where the pointed roof of the puppet theater showed above a tall screen of hedges. "See the little black car with the radio pole in the air? Believe me, this will be a big thing. They say the Citroën plant is closing today because of no workers."

Mac looked around. Well-dressed people were strolling by, the café terraces were crowded prosperously, the horse-pulled carriage with the famous lady guide wearing riding clothes and a bowler hat was filling with a family of German tourists, traffic was running normally, and directly behind the police radio car a thin boy with a black ducktail haircut and zoot-suit clothes was kissing his girl good-by with a long-drawn expert lingering. It was a Sunday painter's water color scene, with no threat in it.

"You've been hearing scare stories," Mac said. "Every week there's a new one." It was true. Parisians had become so jumpy that each week they blamed the change in the weather on those terrible atom bomb tests of those terrible Americans.

"Political demonstrations take time and organization," Mac added. "They don't jump out of the ground."

"There are many ways to carry water to the market, monsieur. They will find a way to jump out of the ground."

Mac found himself shrugging slightly, not as a comic gesture, not in irony, but genuinely shrugging with a mixture of disbelief and unconcern. "We can't run around in circles because of rumors. Especially on a pleasant day like this. Madame Obenpharo has promised her son to see the puppet show. We should return inside the hour," he told Yacoub. "If you're afraid, take off for home. We'll catch a taxi."

Yacoub nodded his head once, a small fatalistic bow. "No, monsieur. I will be here, *insha' Allah.*"

345

A puppet dressed as a clown poked his head between the curtains of the outdoor puppet theater and looked around the audience with bright quickness. "Ha ha!" he shouted, then the curtains opened. He wore baggy pantaloons, and had rouged cheeks and a long tasseled stocking cap hanging down, which kept getting in the way of his gesturing little hands. He threw his arms out. "*Bonjour,* my little pigeons!" his doll's voice cried. "Welcome to *Le Petit Guignolet!*"

"*Bonjour,*" one five-year-old boy answered. He was wearing an American cowboy hat and a belt holster containing a pistol so cleverly copied in plastic that it looked real. His mother pulled his sleeve, but he refused to sit down.

The puppet opened his arms more widely. "*Bonjour,* my little strawberries!"

"*Bonjour,*" several children answered, more joining in.

"*Bonjour,* my little elephants!"

"*Bonjour!*" More of the children were standing up now, and they were all answering together. "*Bonjour! Bonjour!*" Even Henri, seated on the wooden bench between Maia and Mac, had jumped to his feet.

"Are you really little pigeons?"

"No!" the children cried. The link between actor and audience had closed.

"Little strawberries?"

"No! No!"

"You're all little elephants, then?"

"No!" they shouted. "No! No!"

"What are you?"

"*Children!*" they shrieked. The little five-year-old cowboy ran up to the stage and tried to reach up to grasp the puppet. The puppet leaned far over the little footlights to shake hands with him, and everyone clapped. Suddenly a rubber mouse ran up behind the clown and all the children cried warningly, "A mouse! A mouse!" The mouse vanished. The puppet held up a hand, and they all became silent.

"Today, children," he said, "we have a Punch and Judy show for you." They all clapped again, but stopped when he leaned forward intimately and said, "But first, if you would like to see it, we have a special show for your parents and friends—because they're children at heart, aren't they?"

The children were quiet until he added, "Don't you want to see the grownups' program, too?"

"Yes! Yes!" they called out.

The puppet put one hand over his heart, and pulled off his cap with his other. "It is the story of Héloïse and Abélard, from the olden times when France had kings and Paris was the light of the world." There was a little recorded flourish of horns, and some cardboard scenery of steep-roofed medieval houses slid onto the stage from the wings. The puppet dropped his stocking cap and ran offstage, only to reappear suddenly on the opposite side wearing a long dark cloak and a flat velvet medieval hat. In a new and dignified storyteller's voice he announced, "It is the year of our Lord 1117, on the Ile de la Cité. The Cathedral of Notre Dame is the center of the life of the island, which is the center of Paris, which is the center of the world." More cardboard scenery, this time the lower levels of Notre Dame, appeared on the stage to tower above the cardboard houses. A stern old tall marionette, dressed in black completely, with a fur collar on his cloak, walked slowly on the stage with his hands crossed behind his back. The storytelling puppet came closer to the little footlights and leaned confidentially toward the audience. He nodded toward the old man striding in deep thought before the Cathedral's portals. "The Canon of Notre Dame, Fulbert by name, a man of power. He is the uncle and guardian of Héloïse." He stepped back quickly into the wings as the Canon Fulbert came downstage.

"Is he the villain?" Henri whispered to Maia.

"Let's wait and see," she whispered back.

Fulbert walked along the apron of the stage, delivering his soliloquy. His niece Héloïse was the fairest flower in the land, filled with grace in form and thought, and the time had come for her higher education to begin. Her teaching must be worthy of the niece of the Canon of the Cathedral. Ah, but where to find a tutor of fineness equal to this fair pupil? A tutor well versed in theology and Latin, learned and well spoken?

In the background, a new marionette, Abélard, appeared onstage from behind the Cathedral of Notre Dame. He was tall and handsome, a prince among men, dressed in a plain monk's cloak and carrying a thick manuscript.

347

Ah, Fulbert told the audience, here was the man. The finest intellect in France, a future priest fluent in the arts, simple and clear in language. He would arrange for Abélard to tutor his niece; he would arrange their lives so that all would benefit. He would arrange everything.

Maia's eye caught Mac over Henri's head. She had been leaning forward a little, as deeply interested as Henri, and now her lips formed a soundless single word when Fulbert explained how he would arrange the lives of Abélard and Héloïse. "Obenpharo," she said.

The recorded flourish of horns was repeated as the cardboard scenery changed. The narrator puppet reappeared to explain the scene was now the outer chamber of the apartment of Héloïse in the house of her Uncle Fulbert, on the Rue des Chantres on Ile de la Cité. "That's near where we live!" Henri said excitedly to Mac, and turned back to the stage. Mac recalled the story of Héloïse and Abélard hardly at all, but he could see that the older children in the audience and their parents watched it with the same interest a similar American group would have watched a dramatically costumed and clever puppet play of Abe Lincoln and Mary Todd.

The story on the stage marched ahead, filled with the pageantry of cloaks and cloistered chambers and the bright lilting medieval gestures of the time. Héloïse was the fairest of the fair, gentle and swan-necked. As Abélard's passion mounted, as he set aside his lute and ballads and spoke of undying love, she turned and rose like a bird caught not only in a web of feeling, but within a medieval cage of power and customs which forbade such love.

The narrator puppet returned like a miniature Greek chorus, speaking a kind of elevated prose so that the audience could share his omnipotent view of the pain and terror in human life. "Woe!" the puppet said. "Woe unto the lovers! Woe unto France! Within the next generation the intellectual, Amaury of Chartres, was uncovered from his grave in the cemetery of the Holy Innocents for the sin of unorthodoxy. Ten of his students were burned at the stake because they had studied the natural philosophy of Aristotle. Any man in whose home the *Pater Noster* was found translated into French was stamped a heretic. Abélard, like Amaury, was a man out of his time, and the times were perilous. There was war on every side, the

348

Four Horsemen were abroad, and everyone knew the Day of Wrath was near. Plague broke out and swept the land. Serfs, with ears cropped to show ownership, became cannibals in the agonies of famine. The world of Héloïse and Abélard spoke of humility and charity, but practiced cruelty and power." The puppet bowed his head.

Mac noticed Maia listening intensely, and as he looked around slowly, so was the entire audience. It was in the tradition of a morality play, and the audience recognized the modern parallels. They had lived through war and chaos and fear, and they knew Héloïse and Abélard were doomed. When Héloïse fled to Brittany to bear Abélard's child, the next scene presented her sitting in a wooden chair beside a country fireplace to answer Abélard's offer of marriage.

In the distance outside the puppet show were the noises of the world of Champs-Elysées, but within the theater's screening circle of hedges the audience hushed as Héloïse read the letter she wrote to Abélard: "Nothing have I ever, God wot, required of thee save thyself, desiring thee purely, not what was thine. . . . I call God to witness, if Augustus ruling over the whole world were to deem me worthy of marriage, and to confirm the whole world to me, to be ruled by me for ever, dearer to me and of greater dignity would it seem to be called thy strumpet than his empress."

Maia's eyes were filled with tears. Mac reached behind Henri and touched her shoulder, but she shook her head impatiently. She did not want to be reminded she was watching a puppet play; she was in the twelfth century, alone and with child, filled with pride beyond shame, knowing Fulbert's furious wrath.

When Fulbert plotted with hooded villains, each with a dagger to his belt, the audience hissed. Then Abélard appeared, praying with humility and repentance in his monk's cell as the Cathedral bells tolled. The audience became very still as the villains crept in on him; then the leaping frenzy, the overturned candles, the darkness with daggers rising and falling, and only those who knew the story remembering the mutilation Fulbert had ordered for Abélard so that Abélard's manhood was gone.

The narrator came onstage again while the scene changed, and then, finally, Héloïse and Abélard stood before the convent she was to enter. It was their last meeting. Her jeweled slippers and silk

349

sleeves had been put away, and now there was only the plain habit of poverty and service to deny her beauty. Abélard, foremost of the monastic intellects, now stood crushed with humiliation, but Héloïse spoke as always when the final convent gates opened: "So sweet to me were our days they will not pass from my memory." They embraced for the last time. The gates swung shut slowly behind her and the curtain closed.

The Punch and Judy show which followed was all confusion, laughter, and jumping jacks popping up to add to the comic delirium. The children enjoyed it noisily, and the adults with them welcomed the bright clownishness after the Gothic shadow of the first play.

Mac hardly noticed the puppets because in some subtle way his talk with Eve yesterday, his visit to Notre Dame, and the medieval puppet play somehow came together into a meaningful pattern for him. He had read of the experiences of mystics to whom deep convictions suddenly occurred, but he considered himself a modern scientifically trained skeptic who could fairly easily explain the inner distortions which made certain kinds of individuals mystics. To grasp at truth by a leap of faith into the outer darkness was completely alien to him. Yet, sitting here now on a wooden bench, with Henri jumping up beside him to shout "Watch out!" as a jumping jack came suddenly to life behind another marionette, sitting here now the thought came that he had turned a corner in his sculpture. One moment he had nothing more in mind than watching the little stage, and in the next the entire thought was clear. Just as sculptors rose from copying objects in nature and began to carve men and women in stone, the next step—it seemed so obvious to him now—was to go beyond, to begin to capture lasting ideas in lasting stone. How to do this without creating more of the naïve and slipshod abstract nonsense which filled the galleries already would be partly a technical problem, partly a problem of ideas, partly risking being pretentious— and then he realized Maia was saying his name.

"Mac," she whispered, then a bit more loudly, "Mac." She was leaning toward him behind Henri, who was glued to the Punch and Judy show.

He bent toward her. "Yes?"

"Do you hear shouting out there?" She nodded in the direction of the Champs-Elysées.

350

He listened. It was difficult to hear, because the puppets on the stage were busily swatting each other and running in circles shouting "Ooh!" and "Ah!" but occasionally a sound like that of chanting voices came through the encircling screen of hedges.

"Yacoub told me there was going to be a demonstration," Maia said quietly. "Do you think we ought to leave? Our car will be stuck in all the traffic."

He glanced at Henri, who was so fascinated by the puppets he did not notice his mother and Mac whispering behind him. Mac shook his head to Maia, indicating Henri, and she sat back in her seat with a faint frown.

Within ten minutes, more people had noticed the increasing sound of shouting, and a few adults who did not have children with them got up to leave. Suddenly the approaching sounds took on a new timbre. The shouting became high-pitched and broken, and through it cut the brass scream of sirens. The audience jumped up and the puppets onstage froze with their paper hands in the air. In a moment the narrow exit from the little outdoor theater was jammed, while the loud-speakers behind the small stage began to play recorded march music and one of the puppets waved good-by, shouting, "*Au 'voir,* little elephants! *Au 'voir,* little strawberries!"

"Let's wait here," Mac said quickly. "We can't get out of the gate and we can't go through the hedges."

The noise was all around them, confused and angry. Another siren sounded in the distance, with the mechanical scratch-throated noise of klaxons joining it. At the gate a child fell and began to scream on the ground within a forest of legs. The head of a bearded young man appeared within the proscenium arch of the puppet stage, looking obscenely huge among the stringed dolls. "Hey!" he called, "what's going on?"

Mac put one arm around Henri, the other around Maia. He thought they both looked frightened, so he said, "Let's talk to the maestro puppeteer until all this blows over. He looks like an interesting guy."

"What's going on?" the bearded puppeteer repeated as they came up the aisle toward him. "Bastille Day celebration early?"

"A political demonstration," Mac said. "Congratulations on an excellent performance."

351

"It was wonderful!" Henri said excitedly. "Especially when the tall puppet didn't see the short one crawling away with the bag of gold."

The tall limp puppet on the stage came to life and bowed to Henri. "Thank you, monsieur," he said with his hinged mouth, opening and closing his lifelike eyes. He put out his little hand politely. Henri shook it, laughing. Somewhere nearby several shots were fired.

"Would you perform at a private party?" Maia asked the puppeteer. "That beautiful story of Héloïse and Abélard?"

"Ah, you and your family liked that one?"

"Very much. Very very much. I almost wept." She was smiling because he had said *family*.

The bearded man mistook her smile and smiled back appreciatively, managing at the same time to look her over admiringly. "We rehearsed that one a long time," he said. "The costumes are all authentic of the period. It is very tragic, but every audience loves it."

"Do you give private performances, monsieur?"

"Sometimes."

"I'm giving a Bastille Day party and—"

"Ah, madame, such short notice." His eyes covered her again while he shook his head. He clearly regretted more than the short notice.

"You can't?"

"Impossible. Next year, perhaps?"

"Perhaps," Maia said.

The tall puppet stood up and bowed to her across his arm, then to Mac and Henri. "Many thanks," the puppet voice said. "Please come back to *Le Petit Guignolet*."

The exit was clear now and they left the circular theater easily. Crowds of people stood clotted around trees, shifting, occasionally running as something unseen happened further along the avenue. Police whistles blew; the shouting rose and fell.

Mac put one hand on Henri's shoulder. "Stay close to me until we get to the car." Henri nodded. Beside them, a woman shouted at a running man, "Where you running, rabbit? The Métro exits are all blocked by the cops!"

A hundred yards away, over the heads of the crowd, Mac could

352

see large placards bobbing along. They were written in French and in curlicued Arabic script.

Independence for Algeria!
Return the Sultan to the Moroccan throne!
Hail Bourguiba of Tunisia!
Liberty, Equality, Fraternity!
Down with Colonialism! Down with Faure and Grandval!
Accept Obenpharo Ten Point Plan for Morocco!
Remember *La Date Fatidique*!
Remember our heroic dead!

A long straggling parade of thousands of men was pushing its way forward. Many wore coarse *djellabas;* a few were Frenchmen. Most were in ordinary working clothes. A line of march was impossible, because the helmeted riot police were everywhere. The police officers wore jaunty kepis, and deployed their men with the speed and precision of years of experience with street demonstrations. Hundreds of the marchers were singing Arabic songs, thrusting up their right hands with forefinger extended in the Algerian nationalist salute. Here and there the *garde mobile* would cut into the marchers after a man who was shouting and waving a stiletto or swinging tire chains like a gladiator, and a fight would begin. Again the whistles and the hoarse klaxon bark of the great blue police vans, with furious demonstrators pounding against the police. Small groups on the sidewalk began detaching themselves from the onlookers and joining the marchers, a strategy of appearing suddenly where there was little police coverage. A photographer knelt in the gutter to take some pictures, but a demonstrator carrying a sign brought the wooden handle down over the man's shoulder like a whip.

As Mac and Maia and Henri edged slowly toward their car, Mac could see a crowd of demonstrators around it. One man was trying to drag Yacoub out to join them, shouting angrily in Arabic. Yacoub clung desperately to the steering wheel while a second man grabbed the red Moslem fez from Yacoub's head and jammed it into his face. Then Mac lost sight of the car because the crowd shifted sideways. He plunged between anonymous bodies, pushing people aside, using his shoulders and completely unaware that he kept repeating, "Pardon . . . pardon. . . ." When he was only ten yards away he saw a thin bearded young man wearing a brown *djellaba* approach Yacoub. The man was screaming with a foam of spittle and suddenly black-jacked Yacoub with the handgrip of a pistol. Yacoub's head struck the horn ring of the steering wheel and lay there. The horn began blowing with a steadily insane monotone.

Mac tore people aside to reach the car. As he came up beside Yacoub he hit the two nearest men as hard as he could, and immediately he was the center of a boiling mass of hands, arms, curses, blows. Something struck him like stone between the shoulder blades and he fell forward, just managing to catch a handle on the car to keep himself off his knees. Dimly he heard Maia close by screaming in Arabic. The only word he could understand was ". . . *Oben-pharo!* . . ." then a blow on his head sent him pitching forward into the metal and down on his knees. Bright spots swam across his eyes. He sensed an oncoming primitive death of knees and kicking feet and forced himself up with one huge heaving effort. He hit the nearest face with all his strength, feeling a stab of pain up into his elbow.

A file of *garde mobile* police was chopping into the mob now, while one of them pushed open little spaces as a path for Maia and Henri. Maia had her arms around the boy and her face was twisted with fury. The Parisienne was gone; her hair was down over her shoulders and she shouted in quick Arabic spurts at the nearest demonstrators. One spat obscenities back at her. She swung her open hand and caught his face with full force. Mac managed to pull open the rear door of the car, keeping it open with the policeman's help while Maia pushed Henri into the car ahead of her. Just as the boy sat down, a marcher jumped up outside the car beside him and swung a tangle of tire chains against the closed window. The glass shattered inward, showering Henri. He threw his hands up toward his face, which suddenly seemed to bleed everywhere at once, and began screaming with pain and fear.

BENARI OBENPHARO stood looking down at the Bay of Tangier from his green-glass walled office at the top of Banque Obenpharo, staring stone-faced at the Straits beyond, looking out in his mind over the linked Atlantic and Mediterranean worlds. In his mind he scanned the great harbors and markets of the globe; London, Brussels, Paris, New York, Antwerp, Cairo, Calcutta, Rio, and Hong Kong. They had been weeks apart when he had joined his father in the bank fifty years ago. Now they were within several hours of his office. Without conscious effort, like a chess champion playing a dozen games at once, he weighed and balanced Banque Obenpharo's position in each major market. He worked out patterns of commodities and raw materials, transportation and money exchange, forecasting the decisive political weather in each gambit of his mind.

The blue string of smoke rising from the cigar in his hand made little shaky knots in the air. That meant the fingers and thumb of his right hand had begun their odd tremor again. Dr. Carre, his physician in Paris, had called it a Parkinsonian tremor, a kind of sabotage of certain brain cells, and had given him pills which might or might not help a disease about which very little was known. There were other pills for the coronary arteries of his heart. Pills and pills. Obenpharo never took them. He put the cigar into his mouth and hid his tremorous hand from himself in his pocket.

How much longer will I live, he wondered. If my son were here, instead of Nathan who stands nearby so quietly and understandingly and whom I respect greatly but who after all is not my son, if Roger were beside me, I would still have the strength I always had. I would grasp the world of men and politics and wrestle for all the trophies and rewards of commercial combat. If my son were here —my lost living dying son. The handsome boy with his mother's eyes—how had he become a fanatic revolutionary? At the Sorbonne? In the endless talk of Paris salons? Who could have foreseen it? What crisis in the mind of a successful young man of thirty could bend him so sharply toward a whole new way of life?

Now if I can live long enough to see Henri come of age, Obenpharo thought, I will be willing to step down and die like a man.

For a moment he saw himself being buried standing upright, as was the custom of some ancient kings, and somehow this amused him grimly.

Again he stared down across the rooftops of Tangier at the bay below the city. "Have you noticed, Nathan?" he growled to his bank manager. "Look down at the harbor. Empty. People are staying away from trouble. Have you noticed fewer Mediterranean cruise ships coming by?"

Nathan came over to stand beside him. "That white ship is no cruise ship, Benari. It's chartered to carry Hebrew refugees from Morocco to Israel." When Obenpharo looked surprised and took the cigar out of his mouth, Nathan added, "Now don't tell me I don't keep you informed. But I don't like to bother you with little items of misery not connected with business."

Obenpharo turned to look down at the chartered ship lying whitely in the great blue circle of the harbor. He puffed his cigar once or twice, then said between his teeth, "Refugees. It's like fever in a sick man. It's a bad sign."

"Benari, stick to banking. Let the rest of us worry about the refugees. After all, for two thousand years, three times a day, we've been praying: Blow the great trumpet for our freedom and raise the banner for the ingathering of the exiles and gather us together from the four corners of the earth, and may our eyes behold the return to Zion in mercy."

Obenpharo growled and turned away from the glass, then swung back. "I'm worried about more than refugees. Banking is a form of civilization, and I'm worried about banking. Every day the Arab pipedreamers drain some water out of the Mediterranean and pour in more gunpowder. My fanatic son and his fanatic followers. Any day they can seal the whole powder keg with a big cork at Suez."

"When I think out loud like that," Nathan said, "I'll put a cork in my mouth."

"Add two and two," Obenpharo said impatiently. "Use your head, Nathan. It's not hard. Commercial atomic power is twenty years in the future. Until then, we run half our world mostly on Arabian oil carried in our friend Theologos' tankers." He closed one of his big fists. "They have us by the testicles, Nathan."

356

"And we have them by the throat, Benari."

"A Stone Age deadlock. Except that now we have atoms instead of clubs."

Nathan smiled thinly. "What nightmares. You need more sleep. Mecca and Moscow can't mix in the long run. Don't worry—Theologos' tankers won't sink and the Arabian oil will go on flowing. Suez Canal shares have always been like having stock in"—he gestured with one hand—"in I don't know what. What's the most solid thing in the world?"

Obenpharo gave his lion's bark. "Nothing. Not gold. Not governments. Not even our own molecules. Nothing. Not a damn thing is solid any more."

In Copenhagen, Eve sat with a dozen other physicians of the World Health Organization, listening to the report of their British colleague. She tried to be alert and interested because he was describing the important British experimental attack on tuberculosis using *Mycobacterium muris* vaccine, but somehow her attention kept wandering. She understood herself well enough to know that this kind of daydreaming meant she wanted to be elsewhere, doing something else.

She stared at the back of the head of the doctor sitting in front of her. He was Norwegian, and as soon as the Englishman sat down, he would surely stand up and patiently and logically review the evidence in favor of BCG vaccination against tuberculosis. Her eyes moved downward until they reached her legs. Her ankles were crossed. They looked relaxed and pleasantly slender. Neat but not gaudy, as the current phrase put it. I ought to cultivate a more open sensuality, Eve thought. I look too healthy and neat and dull. I ought to wear sheer nylons instead of the service weight. Earrings. A little more lipstick. Less neat, yet not gaudy. Are my instincts wrong, or is it the hard self-judgment that always follows? Why do I always feel safer when I can think first and respond later?

Mac, she thought, what are you doing now? We met so well, and never reached completion. She stared at her ankles and, without thinking, uncrossed them. Mac, what was it? Are we too much like brother and sister, too close, too much from the same cool, careful

357

home? Or is this only a temporary war for you, with some kind of inner armistice and peacefulness ahead? I can understand about Maia. Anybody can understand about Maia. But not everybody, not anybody, understands that only her unhappiness needs you, and there's nothing in that for you.

The quiet voice of the English doctor broke in. "In London, Birmingham, and Manchester," he was saying very precisely, "over fifty thousand school children between fourteen and fifteen years of age are taking part in this test. Thirteen thousand of them reacted negative to the tuberculin test and were left unvaccinated as controls—"

Eve's eyes moved lazily to the walls of the conference room. Epidemiology intelligence maps hung side by side: Schistosomiasis in Egypt, trachoma in Turkey, poliomyelitis in the United States, plague in North Africa.

North Africa. She looked forward to her trip to Algiers and Tunis. Somehow she always liked the sudden change from the stone streets of Europe to the clear hard sunlight of Africa. She had no tourist poster illusions about the diseased and poverty-stricken world it actually was, and she shared little of the respect for Islamic customs which so many European intellectuals had. She had only impatience with the medieval Moslem social system which was democratic in religion, but in politics had become a few strong men and many serfs. Even though it was very colorful for the tourists and their cameras, even though the fatalistic philosophy of Islam was very restful for wearily complicated Parisians, she would prefer a solid middle class able to read and write and vote for fewer infant deaths, fewer flies, and clean water.

Yet there was a vitality on the Mediterranean shore of Africa which she always felt as soon as she stepped off the plane into the strong vertical sun. Sitting now in cool, scrubbed Copenhagen, she remembered the hot white streets of Algiers and its nearby nighttime sound of tambourines and tomtoms, the crying flutes of Arab music in its forever dissonant minor key. Perhaps the attraction for her was that these sunlit people experienced their world directly without filtering it through a meshwork of ideas. They felt first and let abstract thinking take the hindmost.

Eve noticed the world map of North African plague had several clustered rows of red pins connecting Casablanca and Agadir; one thin red row aimed inland like an arrow toward the Saharan caravan routes. The French public health people would have the plague under control by the time she reached Algiers, although she might be able to track down a case or two in some isolation hospital if her tuberculosis survey work gave her any free time. Plague would be worth seeing, academically speaking, because a case near Los Angeles had just been reported and at a big medical center like her own in New York she might be called on to make such an unusual diagnosis. Hardly likely, but possible. All things were possible.

New York. Would Mac ever go back there? She knew so many Americans who never went home again. There was even a slogan for people like Mac: *You can't go home again.* Ever since Ulysses, men had lost their way in the Mediterranean. She smiled slightly to herself because her daydream was becoming fantastic.

Eve looked down at her nice ankles and crossed them again and leaned back trying very hard to concentrate on the important British medical report.

"You speak French better than I do," Jeanjean Rasa said to the young American girl with the long blond hair.

"Oh no," she said, "you're like everybody else in Paris. You're just flattering me."

Jeanjean stretched his brown hand across the little café table and put it over hers for a moment. "I never flatter," he said. "In my home, in Spain, there is no Paris chi-chi. A gentleman tells only the truth. But maybe in a way that sounds like flattery to an American schoolgirl." He said it so well he almost convinced himself.

She let her hand rest beneath his, obviously liking it, while she used her free hand to lift her glass of Cinzano. "You know," she said, "that's the third time you've said schoolgirl. I'm not. Just because I'm starting at the Sorbonne in September doesn't mean I'm still a schoolgirl."

"Books," he said, taking his hand back. "That makes you a schoolgirl. You should be sitting here drinking Coca-Cola with a nice French boy, not me."

"Oh no," she said too quickly and eagerly, then stopped. She had heard about these Spanish aristocrats, their pride and fierceness and ability as lovers, and when his warm brown hand had covered hers she had felt a sudden hollowness deep in her body.

Clearly, she was wealthy, Jeanjean thought. It was in her clothes, her expensive little camera, her casualness and confidence. They shared a small terrace table at Le Jockey, across the street from the Square Viviani, the little park where Jeanjean had picked her up. Hakim, who was supposed to bring him his share of the money from the last collection, was going to be late, and Jeanjean could not resist filling the time with this pretty girl with an unpronounceable name.

Jeanjean and his friend Hakim had set up a headquarters to collect contributions from the hundred thousand Algerians and Tunisians and Moroccans living in Paris. To those who looked to Cairo for guidance, Jeanjean said he gave their collections of cash to the Cairo-directed Liberation Front. To the rival supporters of Hadj Messali he said their money went directly to the National Movement. It was all very patriotic, he said. It was also very underground, especially the bulk of collections which went to Jeanjean and his friends.

Jeanjean preferred very young American women like this one across the table, with money, not because of the money—Hakim and their business of making patriotic collections from the North African shopkeepers was going well—but because rich young American girls were so vulnerable and grateful. Their sense of sin gave them a quivering unsure intensity in bed which none of his Moroccan girls could match. To an Arab girl it was only a part of living, not an event. They were like the plump mice he fed his falcon, unquestioning, mutely accepting the patterns of nature, the claws, the beak, and the beating of hawk wings. But these other girls, rich and young and readers of books, these gave him a new excitement because when he changed with them from the usual pleasures to several delicate cruelties they always fought back. He felt that to subdue them until they lay exhausted, panting and helpless and hardly able to speak, was as good as scoring a winning touch with foils or driving a field goal in a polo match at full gallop.

He remembered one girl, much like the blonde girl across the table from him now, who had fought him longer than most, making him work too hard for real pleasure so that he had to hit her a few times.

360

Then she had suddenly surrendered. Later, she had put her fashionable American clothes on in complete silence, keeping her back turned to him, and had gone out the door without looking at him. From the window, he had seen her cross the street below him, walking in a slow dreamlike way, walking slower and slower, then stopping to lean against the wall. Suddenly her knees had bent beneath her and she had fallen to the sidewalk. He had known how she felt because he had been rather tired himself.

Some of these girls even came back to him a second time, changed and submissive, anxious to please. At this point, he always made it clear he was no longer interested, and they began to grasp at anything he offered. A really intimate Moroccan party? Would smoking a little genuine *kif* be an interesting experience? If they agreed, he knew they were ready to be turned over to his friends, for play or profit, or both.

He had discovered that they considered him incredibly handsome. "Didn't I see you in a French movie?" they always asked. His velvet eyes, his athletic body, his never-failing act as a Spanish aristocrat, his completely simple and direct approach to what they had always hidden, even from themselves, was irresistible.

He smiled across the table at the blonde girl, letting her have all the whiteness of his teeth, the tanned skin, the deeply expressive dramatic eyes. "How did you say to say your name?"

"Just call me Bev," she said. "Beverly is too hard to say in the romance languages."

"Bev," he said softly. He could tell by her quick pleased look that she found his accent charming. He put his hand over hers again, managing to expose his wristwatch with the gesture, and repeated, "Bev."

"Maybe," she said, "I'll begin to study Spanish this fall term."

"Oh no, no," he laughed—his wristwatch showed that Hakim was seriously late, now—"I can teach you all the Spanish you need." Softly he said a few lewd phrases in Spanish, saying them slowly and with enjoyment.

"I don't understand," she said in French, and began to add something, but then only touched her lips with the tip of her tongue and took another drink.

"You see?" he said in French. "You understand the language al-

361

ready." With another part of his mind he thought: That pig Hakim will have to learn some European punctuality. After all the arrests the French cops had made this afternoon during the big political demonstration, our collections should double, even triple. Maybe, he thought, they'll be sore at the French and there will be less need to persuade middle-of-the-road North African shopkeepers to contribute to a patriotic revolutionary cause. Too many North Africans in Paris did not want to take sides, so the methods of persuasion Hakim and the others used had to become less comic and more serious now. A cola bottle, properly applied to the body openings, could be very funny, except that some of the older shopkeepers became seriously hurt from broken glass in the intestine and died while they were being persuaded to contribute.

"I'm so glad," Bev was saying, "that you were nice enough to stop and help me persuade those French kids to pose with Notre Dame in the background."

"What?" he asked. He had almost forgotten her. "What are you talking about?" Where the devil was Hakim? He sensed that something serious was happening, and the feeling of not knowing made him nervous.

She nodded across the street, at the great Cathedral standing in the sky. "Notre Dame," she said. "I'm going to take a course in medieval architecture—"

"What the hell are you talking about?" His irritable voice surprised him. Name of a name, where was Hakim?

A fragmentary fright crossed her eyes, then she smiled. He was undoubtedly being very sophisticated, and everyone knew that Spanish aristocrats were really very earthy. What'll I do, she thought, if he runs one of those strong brown hands up my leg?—and she got the hollow feeling in her stomach again.

Jeanjean watched two Paris police cars come racing around the corner. They turned into the one-way traffic toward Quai St. Michel. Now he looked at his wristwatch openly. Something serious was going on, and if Hakim did not come very soon it would be necessary to go himself directly to that room upstairs over the Moroccan nightclub. The club was undoubtedly watched by the police, *tant pis,* but he would risk it.

The girl saw him frowning a little at his watch, and said quickly, "I hope I'm not boring you. I mean, talking about the university courses I'm going to take." She looked at him directly. "I'm going to move over here to the Left Bank, but I certainly don't expect to study all the time."

Another police car went by, and two men at a corner table stood up and crossed the street and leaned on the stone parapet above the Seine. Something happening up the river interested them. Jeanjean felt an unknown danger and jumped up quickly. "I'm sorry, Bev. I have to hurry."

She stared at him. His moods changed so quickly! How had she bored him so completely, when only a minute ago he made her feel she was his only interest? She stood up beside him. "Give me a lift to the Métro. We can talk on the way."

Jeanjean had heard the far-off sound of a police klaxon and was hardly listening to her. "What? The Métro?"

She smiled brightly, and, she hoped, enchantingly. "Oh, I've learned the Métro stations. I never use taxis because I want to get to know the real people of Paris."

He threw a folded bill on the table and took her elbow. "Let's go."

As they crossed the street toward his red Ferrari, she said, "You know, I love to drive sport cars. When I saw you drive up in this one, I thought: If only I could meet him." She looked up to see if he accepted the flattery, ready to wrinkle her nose cutely if he smiled down at her. But he seemed not to hear her, and walked directly around to the driver's side of the car without opening the passenger door for her, so that she had to hurry to get in by herself.

The Ferrari came alive like an airplane, a roar of pistons, and zoomed into the street. Jeanjean swung the low car into the road which ran along the river, shifting gears expertly to pick up speed. He threaded between the lanes of traffic very skillfully, revving his engine up and down to warn cyclists to get out of his way. Suddenly he slammed on his brakes and cursed in Arabic as the wheels locked and squealed on the cobblestones.

The American girl threw up her hands in time to keep herself from being thrown against the windshield. "What happened?" she cried.

"Road block," Jeanjean said between his teeth. A solid mass of cars had stopped ahead of them. He shifted gears again, to reverse the car, but a warning horn blew directly behind him and he braked the car again. More and more traffic crowded in behind them, boxing them in, and drivers were getting out of their cars and mounting the sidewalk to see what was happening at the head of the line. Jeanjean shut off his engine and leaned back with annoyance. He and the American girl glanced at each other, but she saw that he was not even thinking about her. He stood up in the car, holding the rim of the windshield, and tried to see over the stalled traffic.

A police truck was turned sideways in the road, and a crowd had collected on the sidewalk. Everyone was looking over the stone parapet down at the Seine below them. A boy climbed a lamppost nearby, and Jeanjean shouted up to him, "Hey! You on the lamppost! What's going on?"

The boy turned his head. "What?"

"What's going on down there?"

The boy grinned. "The police. It's a nice day, so they go fishing in the river."

"What did he say?" Bev asked. "Just when I think I know the language, Paris slang fools me."

Jeanjean was not listening to her. He stepped out of the car and began pushing through the crowd on the sidewalk.

Down below, on the cobblestone embankment along the river, a group of police had set up a lifting crane whose grappling hooks were being guided into the water by a police crew in a launch. There were shouts and confusing hand signals on the deck of the launch as the steel hoist chain tightened under the river with some invisible load and began to lift slowly. Up out of the water, strangely naked, rose the feet, the ankles, the legs, hips, shoulders of a drowned man. His hands had been tied behind his back, and the wire which bound his ankles together was attached to a lead pipe. Something shiny and glassy protruded obscenely between his buttocks. Several photographers knelt swiftly at the edge of the quay as the upside-down body twisted limply and swung inboard. One man ran upstream with his camera, then turned to catch the drowned figure silhouetted against the twin towers of Notre Dame in the near distance. The police launch

364

began edging inshore slowly as lines cast to it from the quay were shortened.

Jeanjean noticed a stir in the crowd along the parapet. Several policemen were politely asking anyone who looked North African for identification papers and making notations of each. He turned quickly and saw more police coming slowly from the opposite end of the block. Immediately, he began to work his way through the crowd back to his car.

The American girl was just finishing putting on fresh lipstick as he reached her side. He saw that she had decided to become very casual, much less eager, because she did not turn her head but only tilted the compact in her hand so that he had to talk over her shoulder to her reflection in the mirror.

Without having to think about it, now that he needed her, he let his face relax and the fine white automatic smile begin. At that, her face in the mirror changed hopefully.

"Bev—" he said softly.

When she heard his warm change of voice, she turned her head to look up at him directly. "What's going on?"

He shrugged. In her world there were no bound ankles, no lead pipes, no cola bottles forced into bodies. "Some kind of stupid accident," he answered casually. He put his hand on her smooth blond arm, stroking his fingers slightly on it. "Bev, you will please forgive my rudeness, but I am very late for an appointment."

"Oh, I can walk to the Métro."

He made a princely gesture. "My friends do not walk. They do not go by Métro. Can you drive a sport car like this?"

"I've driven Jaguars and M.G.'s—"

"Then you can drive this." She stared at him. He smiled more broadly. "You're afraid. Too much power?"

"No. No, it's just—I mean—I'm surprised, I mean."

He put his hand over hers. "Please," he said, looking directly into her eyes, "if you could meet me for dinner."

"Well, first I'll have to—"

"Whatever you must do, Bev, please do it. We had hardly a chance to talk. Eight o'clock? You will? Good! I will feed you the best. We meet first at the Crillon bar at eight."

"How shall I dress? Left Bank or Right?"

"Very Right Bank. Very chi-chi, eh? Come prepared to swim in champagne."

She was smiling very prettily now, the open athletic smile they all had. "Don't worry about your car. I'll have it at the Crillon in one piece. Just don't report me to the police if I'm a little bit late."

He glanced over his shoulder at the crowd. Two policemen were quite close. He turned to her and lifted her hand gently toward his lips. "Eight o'clock, Bev. I have to hurry now."

Quickly he threaded his way between the packed cars and motorcycles and little Citroën trucks, until he reached the opposite sidewalk. He walked the half block toward Boul' Mich', walking not too rapidly, then turned into a small Algerian bar. The very fat black-haired woman at the zinc counter inside was wiping glasses.

"Ah!" she exclaimed when she saw him. "I paid! I paid your friend Hakim this morning!" she said quickly in Arabic. "If he told you no, he's holding back on you!"

"Slow down, Poupée," Jeanjean said in French. "Slow down. I only want to use your back door."

She frowned and said nothing as he walked by, only allowing her eyes to swivel with him.

Ten minutes later he hurried into one of the narrow turning streets near Boul' Mich'. He stopped in front of a door shaped as an acorn-pointed Moorish arch under a tall sign: SAFARI. On each side of the door were framed photographs presenting Arab dancing girls in their working clothes. He rapped the brass hand of Fatima on the door. It opened a crack, then swung open. A dwarf with hennaed red hair and a black turtleneck sweater stood there laughing.

"Another hero!" he laughed, sounding like a maniacal child. "*Le gros légume.* The big vegetable himself, running for cover. I told them you'd be here," he said in Arabic, and laughed again. "How's Bébé, my little falcon friend?"

Jeanjean grinned and rubbed his hand through the little man's red hair. "She needs some fresh meat, like you." He walked past the little man through the darkened bar, past all the stacked chairs, and pushed aside the curtain of beaded thongs which led to the nightclub. Low divans and leather hassocks, with brass trays on short legs as tables, ran around the edge of the room to the stage. At this time of

366

day the place was empty of patrons and looked very long. Several musicians were sitting cross-legged on the floor with tambourines, a drum, and several flutes, playing idly for the couple rehearsing a dance in the middle of the floor.

Jeanjean paused automatically to look at the girl. She was about fifteen, Spanish or Berber, cream-skinned, with long black hair and a curved too-young body. Her partner was a giant muscular Sudanese wearing only leopard-skin trunks, and his part in the dance was the traditional one of enacting the chase, the capture, and the subjection of the girl. She was dressed now; but at night, for the nightclub customers, she wore only a black strip of lace tied off-side in a large bow over one hip which she could move separately from the rest of her body for emphasis. The lace strip also provided a place into which customers could stuff their tips after her dance, while only the drum beat and she moved her hips in rhythm as she went from one divan to the next.

Jeanjean began crossing the empty room through the center of the dance floor. The tall Sudanese suddenly saw him and, while he held his long arms in the air for the dance, he waved both hands in greeting. He nodded his head as a signal toward the girl, who was circling him, and, when Jeanjean was close enough, plunged his hand down between her legs. Jeanjean caught it skillfully and they shook hands beneath her, pump-handle fashion. The music stopped as the musicians began to laugh loudly because the girl looked so funny hopping from one leg to the other as Jeanjean shook hands with her partner higher and higher. The girl swore in Arabic, clutching at them to keep her balance while they raised her until only her toes could touch the floor. Suddenly they pulled their hands apart and her heels came down hard.

"*Olé!*" shouted one of the musicians. "A little higher and she would be pregnant."

The girl bared her teeth at him. "You should pray for the balls to do it yourself, pig."

"You should make that part of the dance," Jeanjean said.

Out of sight, on the floor above, a man began shouting. They all looked up at the ceiling. The man's voice changed to a blubbering scream and suddenly stopped.

The big Sudanese dancer nodded toward the steps at the back of the musicians' stage. "Katim and Ibrim and Abid have a fat Algerian upstairs. A wine importer. He says he's a French citizen and he should not take sides."

"He'll take sides," Jeanjean said. "He sounds like a man ready to take sides."

The curtain of thongs parted and the red-haired dwarf came in. He carried a bottle of cola in each hand. As he walked bandy-legged toward them he raised the bottles overhead to the musicians. "Anybody need a purge?" he called to them. "A good soda enema?" He shook the bottles to make the fluid foam, then lifted his thumb from the mouth of one bottle to let the gas pressure shoot out a thin stream.

Some of the musicians laughed. "The little cleanser," the drummer called out. "The little bowel boy."

"Two bottles, curved to fit," the dwarf called back. "One at each end."

"Get upstairs," Jeanjean said to the dwarf. "You talk too much, you flea bite."

The dwarf shook one of the bottles at him, pretending to squirt it, and Jeanjean ducked instinctively. The dwarf giggled and turned to run; the giant Sudanese caught him and held him up in the air wriggling. He turned his head sideways fiercely and tried to bite the giant's arm.

"Look," the Sudanese said. "It bites. A little biting louse."

The dwarf saw Jeanjean coming toward him and shut his eyes tightly. "Everybody is talking too much," Jeanjean said in Arabic. "Now you come with jokes." He slapped the dwarf's face. "Can you remember to be quiet?"

The dwarf kept his eyes and mouth closed tightly. Jeanjean slapped him again, very hard. "Well?"

"Enough," the girl dancer said. "Enough hitting."

Jeanjean looked her over with a deliberate obscene slowness. "I'm a little disturbed today," he said. "Today I don't like the way things disturb me."

"I never disturb you, Jeanjean," she said.

"No," he said. "But I like to disturb you." He turned to the tall Sudanese. "Take him upstairs. Tell Katim to be more quiet."

"The music helps cover the noise, Jeanjean."

"Yes," Jeanjean said. He called to the musicians. "Play, play! What are you paid for?" As they picked up their instruments and fell into a slow thumping Arabic rhythm, he turned back to the girl. "Dance by yourself, now. I like to watch you."

On the Old Mountain Road, which ran from the edge of the city of Tangier along the Straits, overlooking the ancient water from a sloping height, the Villa Obenpharo was a low white castle under the hot sun. In the largest of the balcony bedrooms Mutirra Obenpharo stirred restlessly against the pile of pillows in her bed. Ruqayya stood up quickly from her cross-legged position on a large leather hassock. "Madame? Another pillow?"

"Maka'een bas," Madame Obenpharo said in Arabic. "If only I could lie down instead of always sitting up."

Ruqayya looked horrified. "Madame, you know how hard the breathing comes when you lie down."

"I know. I know. I know all about the breathing. And the heart failure. And the swollen ankles. And all the rest."

"Ah, my poor little Madame."

"My poor little birds, you should say." Mutirra looked up at the large wicker birdcage which hung from the lofty beamed ceiling like a chandelier. It was open on all sides so that the birds could come and go freely. She could hear the canaries and lovebirds chirping inside, and only Lilli, the completely white dove, clung with her little talons to the edge of the open cage, bobbing her head beneath one wing. "You forgot to remind me to feed them, Ruqayya. Bring some of that Ceuta bird seed and some sugar water."

Ruqayya stopped short at the door and stepped aside to let Monsieur Obenpharo enter.

"Ah, Benari!" Mutirra was very pleased. The afternoon came alive now. She was no longer caged in her silk bed, because her husband was here now, and he always brought the outside world in with him.

Obenpharo bent from his great height and kissed her. "I brought you a present, my dear." He held up a delicately made golden birdcage and wound the clockwork built into its base. Immediately the little toy bird inside began to sing, turning and posturing and open-

369

ing its tiny beak realistically. "It's Swiss," Obenpharo said. "Those are real feathers. Clever, eh? Isn't it remarkable how it looks so alive?"

"Yes," she said.

"What's the matter? You love birds. I thought you'd find it charming."

"I do, *chéri*. You were sweet to think of it." She took the golden toy from him.

He looked up as Lilli suddenly left her perch on the big open wicker birdcage and sailed across the room to land and strut plumply along the windowsill. "At least this Swiss one sings when you wind it and won't leave droppings. Your pure-white Lilli stooled on me yesterday." He gave his closed smile. "Not even sultans would offend me, but your Lilli lets me know where I stand these days."

"I like to see them fly around the room, Benari. The window is wide open, and I like the way they all stay with me."

"Because the birdseed is here, inside, not outside."

"I don't care about the reasons. They're alive and free. And they stay." She set the toy birdcage on the floor beside her bed, thinking: I don't like this present. It reminds me of me. He had said: *Isn't it remarkable how it looks so alive?* It reminds me too much of myself. Droppings or not, I prefer my own living birds. She made an effort to change the subject. "What's the news in the city, Benari?"

He knew she meant news of Roger, because inevitably Roger and the Istiqlal party made the real news, but he said, "The usual. The building boom is all over. The Contessa Marty has a new boyfriend, an English musician this time. A refugee ship is in the harbor. A new dig at Cotta has turned up a Phoenician vase I would like to buy if I can, or steal if I can't." She smiled, her mood lightened, as he went on mixing the serious with the social. "The Americans are talking about raising their Legation to Embassy status, if the Sultan comes back, and moving it to Rabat. The Club Diplomatique announces a new series of polo matches, beginning with the Egyptian team. They want me to referee."

"Then Roger must be in Tangier, if the Egyptians are coming. One of them is surely an underground contact between him and Cairo."

Obenpharo barked softly. "Roger is in contact with everyone, just

370

like a son of a banker. Except that he also is in direct touch with the Prophet of Allah." He had failed with all his chatter. She always came back to Roger.

One of the lovebirds left the open platform of the wicker cage and flew to Mutirra's shoulder. She brightened again, and turned to make little kissing sounds to it. Obenpharo watched her affectionately, thinking to himself: That about the gift of the Swiss mechanical bird, that was a bad mistake. I need to be more careful, because everything reminds her she is helpless. Everything reminds her that Roger suffers every day like a holy ascetic with a torn face, and that Maia and Henri are far away in Paris.

"What does Henri call that little fawn of his?" he asked.

"Bambi."

"I saw her when we came up the drive to the house. Growing nicely. Henri will be very pleased when he sees her." Obenpharo noticed that she had begun to smile a little at the mention of anything connected with Henri, and he went on trying to make her more than a bedridden onlooker, a useful participant. "You must remind Ruqayya to keep after the servants about leaving enough water out for Bambi."

"I will, Benari."

"It's important in this summer weather."

"You always surprise me. After forty years, *chéri,* it's wonderful how you always surprise me. You come in like a wounded lion, then you become concerned about small animals."

"Please. Don't give me credit I don't deserve. Small animals, polo games, what's the difference? I need to concern myself with something these days."

She recognized the tone. "Things are going badly at Banque Obenpharo?"

"No," he lied. "Too well. Nathan here, Maia in Paris, the bank doesn't need me."

"I need you."

"Thank you, *chérie.*"

"The way I feed the birds, Benari. That's how you feed me and keep me alive. I'm really the one who is useless."

"Beauty is never useless, Irra." He took her hand.

371

She smiled at him with all of herself in her great dark eyes, feeling like crying. He was the last of the noble kingly men she remembered from her girlhood, and he deserved more than a crumbling world, an enemy son, and a dying wife. She smiled at him with love and gratitude, and only her free hand shook a little above the silken sheets.

The soft sound of loose sandals approached, and Ruqayya came into the room. In broken French she said, "Monsieur Obenpharo, one says the telephone below calls from Paris."

"Tell them to tell Mademoiselle Obenpharo in Paris I will call her back in an hour."

"It is not Mademoiselle Obenpharo, monsieur. One says it is an American doctor, Monsieur Wah-dahm."

Mutirra frowned at her husband. "Who is that, Benari?"

Suddenly Obenpharo's face changed. "Adams! Of course, of course!" He stood up immediately. The old man was gone, the warrior was back.

"Mac," Maia said, "I don't understand." Her voice was low, and she was trying very hard to control herself. The nurse had just wheeled Henri into the small operating room. The bleeding from his many face cuts had stopped, a patchwork of clots lay on his forehead and cheeks and chin, but Mac had put him face downward to make sure no bleeding from inside his mouth would run into his throat.

"It's hard to explain, Maia," Mac said.

"Mademoiselle Obenpharo," Dr. Carre said very soothingly, "there is nothing unusual when Dr. Adams refuses. Doctors prefer not to operate on people very close to them."

"But it's so senseless!" she said. "Why should he refuse? Dr. Adams is a first-class plastic surgeon, and my boy is in there with his face all cut. Mac, I don't understand."

Dr. Carre and Mac glanced at each other. Maia had brought Henri to Dr. Carre's private clinic because he was the Paris physician for the Obenpharo family, and his clinic included an operating suite and rooms for a dozen patients.

"Maia," Mac said patiently, "I know it seems crazy. I want to help Henri the way I would my own son"—his voice thickened faintly as the significance of what he was saying struck him—"but, I mean, legally speaking, I have no license to practice in France. It's against the law."

"You're a famous visitor. You've been asked to do surgery in Paris, Mac. I know you have."

"I've always refused."

"For other reasons. Not the legal ones." She took his hand. "What is it, Mac? This is all so incredible! The boy means something to you, doesn't he?"

"Yes. Very much."

"And you know what he means to me—"

"Yes."

"This is unbelievable for me. For you to be cruel. I can't believe it."

"Maia, I would if I could—"

"But what stops you? Nothing. It's so simple. Help the boy. Help me."

Dr. Carre said very formally, "Please forgive me. We shouldn't delay too long. I'll get into my surgical gown and wait for you, Dr. Adams." She's right, he thought. This American is fantastically stubborn in his own quiet way. Adams as a surgeon was supposed to be in the first rank, and this surgery on the Obenpharo boy's face was not at all complicated. Mostly deep cuts. It required great nicety and control and a knowledge of face structures, but nothing really complicated. Yet, as he and Mac had taken off their street clothes and put on the loose surgical scrub suits which were like pajamas, he had seen Adams' hands trembling. A drinker, he had thought angrily. Not a single surgical death in my clinic during the last six months, and now a drinker comes here to operate. He had seen them before, these surgeons who slipped into drinking and ended with their hands shaking. He had complete contempt for such men. But the Obenpharos always got what they wanted, and if Madame Obenpharo wanted the invisible magical skill of a well-known American surgeon with visibly shaking hands, that was her privilege.

Dr. Carre tipped his head slightly in a miniature formal bow to Mac. "If the law troubles you, I will be happy to be the legally responsible surgeon. Technically, even though you do the surgery, you

373

will be," he paused "—let us say you will be a renowned visiting assistant." He could see tears beginning in Madame Obenpharo's eyes. *Sacristoche,* what a shame, he thought. Such a superlative woman. An exotic beauty. Why did they always destroy themselves with fakes like this American? How had this Adams ever built such a reputation as a surgeon? By bribing journalists, no doubt. The man was not only uncivilized, but not even handsome.

Dr. Carre nodded curtly. He wanted to leave them quickly to settle their argument themselves, and went through the door of the scrub room next to the operating suite.

As soon as Dr. Carre was gone, Maia said, "Oh, Mac, Mac, why are you punishing me like this?"

"Maia, believe me—"

"Mac, did I hurt you so much that day on the boat? I apologize a thousand times."

"That has nothing to do with this—"

"The boy needs you. Mac, please, you're always so, so thoughtful, so reasonable, why are you so unreasonable now? Is this one more time when I destroy your peace of mind?"

"Maia, it's too hard to explain." He held up his hands to her. They were shaking. She stared at his hands, then at him. "You see?" he said. "It's not so simple."

She took his hands quickly and pressed them out of sight between hers. "Mac," she said, "*bon Dieu,* this is not something I did to you."

"No. It started before I ever met you." He remembered so clearly. Stan lying there on the operating table, the thin rim of blood around his naked brain, dying. Again the familiar blade stabbed him.

"You control so much about yourself, Mac. You can't control this?"

"I don't know."

"Tell me what happened, Mac."

"Sometime. Not now."

"No. Not now. Now you need to help Henri. If Dr. Carre does his face it will be good, but not as good as your work."

"Let's not take chances, Maia. I'll assist Dr. Carre."

"No, Mac. You do it. He'll assist you." She was trembling a little. "I know that underneath I'm only a superstitious Berber girl. Don't

374

you see the omens in all this? First, Roger's face hurt by the French. Now, his own son's face hurt by his own followers."

"By God, that's really superstitious."

"I told you. But I think this way. Don't shake your head. I believe these things. Now you are like a father to him. You will heal him so he will never be ashamed of his face. Help him, Mac."

Mac took a deep breath. "Maia, my own son died while I operated on him." He had expected pain when he said it, but there was only the dull bottomless sense of something with no name.

She pressed tightly on his hands, still holding them between her own, then, as she began to weep very quietly, she raised his hands to her lips. "I thought it was that—" she whispered against his fingers. "And I made such a nuisance."

"No, no. Don't say that, Maia."

"You can do it, Mac. Your hands can still do it."

"Why take chances?"

"This is different. What happened in America, happened."

"I don't want it to happen again."

"See? See how still and steady your hands are now?"

"It comes and it goes."

"But now it's gone. Oh, Mac, please, don't make me beg you— for your sake as well as Henri's—you can't be one of those men whose hands shake—"

Sooner or later, he thought swiftly, sooner or later I'll need to face this again. Maybe she's right. I can't turn my back on my whole life of training and surgery. I can't be half a man, because this is the way my life was put together, and I can't turn my back on half of it.

She looked up at him, then bent her head forward slowly until it rested on his chest. He gently pulled his hands out of hers and put them on her shoulders. They stood quietly together, not speaking. She felt patient and unmoving under his hands, the hands that were steadier now, if only they would stay steady. Her silence waited for him to decide.

Finally he said, "If you'll take the gamble on me, then I'll gamble on myself, too."

"No gamble," she said, muffled against him. "When you decide

375

what you have to do, you will be fine." She stepped back. "I'll telephone Papa Obenpharo in Tangier while you're in there."

"No, Maia. Wait until I'm finished. Then maybe I ought to tell him myself. You know, more exact details."

"More exact details. That's better, darling. That's exactly how you should sound."

They looked at one another briefly. Then he turned to go into the clinically shining scrub room.

(3)

AT THEIR height, overlooking the lights of Paris from Maia's sixth-floor terrace on Quai de Bethune, there was a pleasant coolness in the nighttime summer air. It was the evening of Bastille Day, and, since morning, there had been the military reviews, the holiday crowds and flags everywhere, and street dancing. Now, great golden fireworks splashed skyward in the dark.

"It's a little like an old-fashioned Fourth of July back home," Mac said to Maia.

"You're thinking of home, Mac? Are you lonely?"

"No." It was true. He had just come up here to this airy rooftop platform from downstairs. He had been giving instructions to Henri's nurse after he had changed the surgical dressings on Henri's face himself. Now that Henri was back from the hospital, it was difficult to keep him in bed, so Mac had introduced a favorite American sick-room remedy for children, a television set. The sound of fireworks, a boy watching TV—somehow it had all reminded him of home.

As he had left Henri's bedroom, he had remembered Maia's joke about using Bastille Day as her birthday, and he had called downstairs for a bottle of champagne and two glasses. He had come back up in the little elevator, and when he had carried the tray onto the terrace off Maia's bedroom he had found her leaning on the parapet watching the fireworks. She turned and he held up the cold bottle.

"Happy birthday."

Her face was a pale oval in the dimness. "You remembered! The man of surprises."

She came toward him, and he kissed her gently. Since their argument in the corridor outside Dr. Carre's operating room yesterday there was a new gentleness between them. While he filled their glasses, she said, "His face doesn't hurt too much?"

"It hurts, but he's more interested in the television programs."

"Dr. Carre was very nice to loan us a nurse."

"Dr. Carre even spoke with less formality to me after the surgery," Mac said. "Until then, I'm sure he was sure that I was a bum." He realized with surprise how much they sounded like parents; that same mixture of affection, frankness, and administrative detail. He gave her a champagne glass and lifted his own. "To my prophetic superstitious Berber girl—"

She interrupted. "No, not that. Not even as a joke. You don't need primitives. You need a modern European woman."

"But it's your birthday. What do you need?"

"You."

Yes, he thought, we've become parents. We each think first of what the other needs. When he said nothing, Maia added, "Tonight I feel very much that you are the best gift for me."

"Now you've made it my birthday, too."

She lifted her glass toward him. "To our birthday."

They emptied their glasses and set them down. They looked at one another in the cool half darkness, then he took her into his arms. Somewhere below, on the narrow medieval streets which ran inland from the river toward the center of the island, a group of men and women were singing and clapping, with the sound of an accordion coming through pauses in the noise of celebration.

As they stood together she moved slightly against him, coming even closer. "Don't say anything," she said. "Let's just stand here."

High over them, an airplane coming into Paris threw ahead twin shafts of landing lights, the red and green points at its wingtips going on and off like heartbeats. Lower, a glowing fireworks star streaked toward the moon, riding a high-curving rocket trail, and burst hugely over the Eiffel Tower. It was a night for holidays, the faint silver and blue in the sky making everything just light enough to see, the shadows deep plum color.

Maia moved away a small step. "I never knew how pleasant it could be. Just standing together."

"Don't think about it. Just come back here."

She came back. "It was never before like this. For me a man was always a fight, a duel. You know what I mean?"

"I think so." She sounded so experienced that he found himself disliking the idea.

"You don't like it when I talk about men."

"Well," he said, "yes and no. I really want to know all about you."

She shook her head a little. "You wouldn't like it. There is a whole world you can't even imagine."

"I could try."

"No, it would not go so well to try." She looked off into the distance, as if Morocco and her home village of the Aït Attiq lay along the horizon, then back at him. "I haven't always lived like this—a big house on a Paris island, with the moon shining over everything."

"Even if it's only a midsummer night's dream, Maia, take it." She's right, he thought. That's how she protects herself. She lives on islands. Here. The Villa Obenpharo in Tangier. The Banque Obenpharo. All islands. She can be reached only by certain bridges.

"I won't spoil anything, darling," she said. "That's why I won't tell you all about myself. You know too much already about the Berber girl down from the hills, pretending to be a Frenchwoman."

"Too much? Are we still supposed to have illusions about each other, Maia?"

She laughed. "A few, don't you think? It took me so many years of trying so hard. And now I have the habit. I always try too hard in Paris. I'm always afraid somebody will come up to me at a party, or in the bank, and say: 'Take off all those expensive things. We know who you really are.'"

"And who are you, really?" He put out both his hands to take her face between them, without realizing it was the same kind of protective gesture she had made yesterday outside the operating room when she had covered his hands with hers.

She paused before answering him. "I suppose I don't know who I am. I play any part people give me. In Tangier, I am of the Obenpharo family. It's a little like royalty. People stand at arm's length. In Paris, I am very chic. I enjoy everybody's surprise because I can

378

work in a bank and be so elegant at the same time." She sounded like a young girl telling secrets. "I enjoyed surprising you."

"Why me?"

"Because everybody I know tries so hard to be gay. They think it's vulgar to be serious or intelligent about something. You don't."

"You didn't surprise me at all at the bank, you know."

She laughed. "That's a lie. I did."

"You didn't. You just bowled me over. The country boy and the queen."

She laughed again. "I know. The elegance. The hair. It never fails. You see how I tell you all my secrets?"

"Which Maia is telling me?"

"The real one, darling. Not the hair. Not the elegance. Certainly not the Banque Obenpharo."

"We're talking too much," he said in English. "Maybe we need a little in the liquid department." He began to refill their glasses.

"We're not talking too much," she said. "And why do you speak English? What does that mean about the liquid? Oh"—she nodded as he held up the bottle to explain—"one of those American jokes I can never understand." In her accented English she said, "Do you want me to talk English?"

"No," he said.

"Why not? We can pretend this is the Fourth of July and we're in New York. All those lights out there will be New York. We'll be in your world, not mine. I'll be glad to talk English, darling."

"No," he said, "it will just get in the way. I don't want anything to get in the way."

"I love you when you talk like that, Mac. Until now I thought: There's so much fun and excitement in being all those other things I told you about. Elegant. Or very businesslike and clever by repeating Papa's banking ideas. I thought: But this is more satisfying, because with him there is none of the foolish kind of excitement. A new feeling I never had, so I don't know the name for it. No trying or pretending. You know what I mean?"

"Yes," he said, "but I don't agree. For me, the excitement is still here. Not the foolish kind." He made a primitive gesture. "This kind."

"I know, darling."

379

"All the time you've been talking, Maia—"

"—I know, I know—"

"—I've been wanting—"

"—don't stop me talking, Mac. I may never get another birthday like this."

"The superstition again? Judgment Day? More omens?"

"That Arab parade yesterday did it to me. Twenty years disappeared when I became angry. Twenty years, poof! Gone. I spit and screamed the way I did in my village in the hills. I amazed myself, and yet I couldn't stop."

"And then I hurt you again at Dr. Carre's clinic."

"I'm glad. I feel so much closer to you now. I told you before, darling. Always a fight with the others. Never this peacefulness. I don't know what to do with this new feeling." She made a puzzled little humming sound, then drank her glass completely and held it up, examining it. "It can't be all bubbles," she said in a small voice. "Can it? I want this to be real."

"It is."

"You don't know how often I wonder. You see? I analyze myself. Maybe I can develop an inner eye, like your intelligent lady doctor." She opened her arms half comically. "Look at me! At last I'm really beginning to feel and think like a Frenchwoman."

"Maia, you're still trying too hard. Let's just accept what we have."

"Ah," she said, "should I laugh or cry? That's something from you. Accept. But no, you wanted to look inside of me and yourself and figure everything out."

"I was foolish. But I'm learning, too. Maybe I'm becoming Moslem."

"So now you say: accept. And now I'm the one who talks so much, like a French girl from the university. That puppet play," she said suddenly. "I understand it now. *Rather thy strumpet than his empress*—wasn't that wonderful?"

"It was."

"You sound as if you don't agree. To you it seems too, what's the word, too romantic? It was a real letter. She really wrote that."

"I know. But the age of chivalry is gone."

"Oh, Mac. You always try to be so sensible. The age of chivalry

380

is still here. After all, there's Notre Dame still standing over there, and here you are."

"Don't make a medieval monk out of me," he laughed. "This is one night when I definitely don't want to be a monk."

"You want to make love—"

"No," he said, "it never occurred to me."

"I've never made love by talking," she said. "This is the very first time. I enjoy it. Give me my chance, darling. I feel a little drunk on it. And you're so nice. You look as if you're listening to everything I say."

"I am. I'll listen all night if you want me to."

"Now I understand so much I never did before. I understand the Europeans now. I can understand how people fall in love with music, with ideas, with sculpture. Why they fight for politics, like Roger. Now I understand what you meant on the boat that day, that first a man and a woman must be friends or there is really nothing there."

"It's nothing to cry about, Maia—"

She turned and walked away from him to stand beside the parapet looking out over the darkened breathing city. When he came up behind her and put his arms around her she leaned back against him. He opened the neck of her dress and cupped his hand over one breast, feeling the nipple stand erectly against his fingers and the slow beginning movement of her roundness against his legs. He bent and kissed the warm curve of her neck.

"Ya habibi," she said quietly, "that's very sensitive, there." She stirred under his hands. "Do you want me to turn around?"

"Yes," he said against her skin.

"Like this?"

"Yes," he said.

"And this. You like this?"

Her hands felt cool. "Yes," he said. "Is this sensitive, here?"

"Yes, yes. Your mouth is so warm. Don't stop, don't stop."

"I won't."

Against his mouth she said softly, "My birth day"—making two words of it—"for the first time it really is."

There was no hurry now, none of the frenzy of the first time on the boat. Now they were sure, with a steady mounting sureness that

381

went up, then higher, then higher still, locked sensually in a single warm searching world. There was no wild pursuit, no wilder capture, but only giving and giving again without any holding back. Only at the climax she arched her back shiveringly and gripped him as if the room were spinning, then fell back into the fan of her hair across the pillow.

When they awakened later, there was little sense of time passing because the room was still in the same summer half darkness, and in the distance the searchlight beams still lighted up the winged stone angels climbing Notre Dame's high roof to blow their stone trumpets toward heaven.

She curled against him, then kissed his eyes, his chin, his forehead, with warm dry lips. Then he did the same to her. *"Ya, habibi,"* he said.

"No jokes. Please."

"I'm not joking. I'm serious."

"You'll never know. You'll never never know."

"What? Never know what?"

"Darling, you'll never know what it was like."

"As long as you know, Maia."

"You'll never know. The first time. My head is still turning."

"Really, Maia? The first time?"

"The first. I always knew something was wrong before, but the doctors never helped me. Some women are like that, they said. Some women just can't."

"Maia—"

"You'll never know. Maybe that's why I tried so hard that day on the boat."

"Now you don't have to worry any more."

She put her arms around his neck and pulled his head down to rest on her breast. "I can't believe it," she said. "I can't believe tonight really happened."

"It really happened." He lifted his head and kissed her very completely. "You believe it now?"

"Yes. I believe it now."

"Do you believe this?" She moved under his lips, but did not answer him. "This," he said, "do you believe this?"

"Yes. Yes." She bit his lower lip gently.

382

"And this one is a good one to believe."

Again she did not answer, responding intimately now, reaching and moving, making small sensuous sounds of abandonment. The whole great wheel of the world turned again for them.

In the morning, they had breakfast on the terrace, each knowing without asking that they did not yet want to leave the airborne rooftop. The sun was slanting, without heat yet, and Mac decided after careful inspection that the stone angels on the Cathedral had not moved and the river still slid between the stone embankments. Somehow, something significant should have changed.

Yacoub came and went silently with the breakfast things, saying nothing, understanding not even to bring the morning papers.

"It seems as if just a little while ago," Maia said, "I sat out here one morning reading about you in the newspaper and looking at your picture."

Mac rubbed his chin with the back of his hand. "Back then, I probably had a shave."

Her eyes lengthened, smiling over her coffee cup. She set it down and said, "I've heard every man has a secret wish to grow a beard."

"I can see myself with one. Really going native."

"Please, Mac, I know how foolish I sound, but I'm still sensitive about comments about Moroccans."

"Maia," he said, "I was talking about Parisians. The natives of the Left Bank."

"Pardon. A thousand pardons, my native, my sculptor. My bearded maestro."

"That reminds me," he said. "Russo should bring the gold statue today."

"So soon? Really? How nice."

"He said it would be on his mind all through his vacation, so he stayed in town an extra day to finish the work."

"I like him," Maia said.

"So do I. You know, in English we say about men like him: He says what he means and means what he says."

"I like you, too, darling. You mean what you say. You do understand, don't you?"

"How do you mean? Understand what?"

"How silly I can be." She shrugged. "You know, about that *native*."

"Now I do, yes. It's less than nothing."

"I need to forget all my foolishness now. A new beginning. Reborn, like who is it—the Hindus?"

He stood up and came over to her side of the table and kissed her. It began lightly, then she tilted her head toward him and put her hands up to hold his face. Their mouths began searching, until it became so fierce their teeth clashed.

"Maia," he said against her, "in the cold light of day, with coffee and without champagne, and while I still look sleepy and need a shave—"

"I know, Mac. I know what you're going to say."

"You can't. I just thought of it."

"I thought of it last week, Mac."

He looked at her blankly. "Marriage?"

She began to smile, then pointed at his face and threw back her head for complete and open laughter. "Look at you! Just look at a man when he discovers she thought of it first!"

"Now you'll have to tell me—"

"Last week, darling, when you were sitting near Notre Dame with Henri, and I came by to pick him up in the car. How very good it would be, I thought."

"For Henri?"

"Of course. For me, first, naturally. But also for Henri. It's all part of the same feeling."

"It would work, Maia. We could make it go very well."

"In the cold light of day?" she asked, making a small comic face. "While I'm still sleepy?"

"But you don't need a shave," he said. "That's very impressive."

They laughed out loud together. "Oh, Mac," she said, "is this one of those ideas you need to invite in to sit down in the corner? You know, you have to say: Sit over there where I can look at you."

"Look it over, Maia. There's no hurry."

"I'm so glad you're so sensible."

"I'm not. That's just part of the illusion, like your red hair. I'm all for getting married this afternoon."

384

"Papa Obenpharo, very much the grandfather of Henri, arrives this afternoon. Let's pick a better time, darling."

"You think he'd object?"

She thought about it. "One never knows with Papa," she said slowly. "He says he's the last of the true Mediterraneans. He sees the world in a way that would never occur to me."

"The first time we met he talked about you."

"Really? Are you serious?"

"At the time, I thought he was using you as bait on his hook."

She frowned. "Terrible word. We've been over that. *Finito.* I thought we finished all that. What did Papa say?"

"I can't remember exactly. Something poetic about the three beauties, and your having one of them."

"You see what I mean? Papa is full of talk like that."

"He offered me a great deal of money to do the plastic surgery for Roger."

"I know about that part, because he had the bank ready to pay you in dollars, or francs, or gold, or whatever you wanted. I'm so glad you said no."

"Maia, Maia, my three poetic beauties, which one of you is talking now? A few weeks ago you wanted me to go to Tangier."

"I did. But you see how wise the Moslems are? It's all written. *Mektoub,* my mother used to say: What is written on your forehead you cannot change. You had to stay in Paris and I had to stay, and so here we are."

"Yes, but you have to leave for Tangier soon, didn't you tell me at lunch the other day?"

She dismissed it with a gesture. "Only for a little while. A week or two. Just long enough to make Papa ship gold out of our vaults before a sudden Moroccan coup can grab it."

"In just a week or two?"

"I always come back, darling, and this time quicker than ever before. It's really very important, or I wouldn't go." She smiled gently. "I'll come back, and then, while we're still sleepy, and if you still need a shave, we'll see a lawyer—"

"Good God, what for?"

"Because I have only a Moslem divorce, not a French legal one."

385

"Then let's just have a Moslem marriage."

"You see? Can't you see how fast you're becoming Moslem? First you talk about how we must accept. Now you talk about a religious marriage."

He grinned. "I know they'd consider me a heathen."

"*Roumi,*" she said. "My *roumi habibi.* I'll be a heathen, too."

"What if I went to Tangier?"

"Mac, are you serious?"

"Of course."

"It's very flattering for you to pursue me, but truly, Mac, I'll come back very soon."

"That's not soon enough," he said. "What if I went there to do the surgery? Fix Roger's face. Restore the Obenpharo family. Earn a very exaggerated fee."

She was staring at him. "Darling, if you need money—"

"—no, no—"

"—this talk of fees—"

"—only because Obenpharo thinks that way. I'll gladly do it free."

"Seriously?"

"Yes. I'm not rich. Certainly not by Banque Obenpharo standards, but—"

"Darling, when we talk to Obenpharo about marrying, he'll be very European and ask you about this. Money, and where you stand and all that."

"I doubt that he gives a damn about money."

"He doesn't. He takes it for granted because there's always so much of it there. He only takes care to conserve the principal."

"Maia, it just occurred to me: you mean he'll think I'm thinking about your money?"

"How American, darling. You're sensitive about it?"

"In a way. The way you are about *native,* that's how I am about a rich wife."

"But I'm not rich, Mac." She made a little outward gesture with both hands, indicating everything around them. "All Papa's. My income from the bank could never pay for all this."

"Fine. So that will be clear to Obenpharo with very little discussion." He looked at her directly, and added gently, "You're of age,

386

Maia. Do you really want me to go to him with some formality?"

"Yes. Please. Be European just this one time, please. He has so much dignity, and for you and me I like the idea of being dignified. Mutirra would like the idea."

"If that's the thought, then I like the idea, too."

"You see why I love you?"

"And I love you because you're a rich redhead."

"Come here, you unshaven native."

"No, I'm having a very dignified European discussion."

"I will have to learn about this. How to tell when you're joking."

"I'm not joking about going to Tangier. I'm willing to go, and I'm willing to do the surgery."

"Since yesterday you became willing?"

"Yes." He held up his hands. They were steady. "See?"

"But you said it comes and it goes. Is it gone?"

"I believe it is. I'd like to make sure."

"And drop the sculpture?"

"No. Certainly not. But each in turn."

"You understand me about Roger, darling? I want you to understand about Roger. Surgery or not, I don't care any more."

"Maia, doesn't Mutirra feel for him the way you felt yesterday for Henri?"

"Yes!" she said fiercely. "But Roger destroys her. He destroys his father. Maybe his world will destroy our world."

"This sounds close to hatred, Maia."

"Then let it! I loved him once, the way young girls do. Now I suppose I hate him, but not only because of the simple reason you might think."

"You prefer for me not to operate on his face?"

"Do it. Do it. But please know it is not for me. It is for Papa and Mutirra. It is for yourself." She looked at him very seriously. "We need to be very clear about this, darling."

"All right. And you still have to go to Tangier?"

"For a little while. I explained. Then back to you."

"Then, later, a little while again? Then again? Back and forth?" She stood up. "What are you saying, Mac?"

"I think I'm saying we should stay together."

387

She looked directly into his eyes. "The first time for me," she said quietly. "No one has ever wanted me like this. You have no idea how much I love you."

"In the cold light of day," he said. "Sleepy and unshaven?"

Later, they went downstairs to have lunch with Henri in his room. Like all children, he immediately sensed their happiness and tried to smile, but the stitched cuts and gauze bandages on his face made it a sideways grimace. Now that his grandfather was flying to Paris especially to see him, Henri was more grown up than ever, except when Yacoub came in and he giggled behind his hand.

"What is it, *chéri?*" Maia asked Henri. "Yacoub, what is he giggling about? This looks like some kind of secret between you two demons."

"Wait until you see it, Mamma. Yacoub says it's in the foyer."

She looked at him, then at Yacoub, then at Mac. She stood up slowly. "No, I don't believe it—"

Henri giggled again. "You'll see. Just wait and see!"

"Why wait?" she said excitedly, and ran out. Mac followed her down the steps to the large foyer. There, on a simple wood base near the door where Yacoub had placed it purposely, stood the statue of the river nymph of the constant heart.

Good man that Russo, Mac thought as he went downstairs. He always means what he says. Holiday or not, he had promised it would be finished, and here it was. As Mac came closer he could see there was no letter, no bill, just the beautifully finished statue with her secret golden smile and her gold hair free in the wind.

Maia turned to him. "Oh, Mac, Mac, it's wonderful! So *alive!*"

He nodded, looking from her to the statue and back, feeling very strongly that everything had come out the way he wanted it to, at last.

BOOK V

Homecoming

(1)

TANGIER curved in great rising steps, terrace mounting above terrace, a white amphitheater of hills overlooking the choppy crosstides of the Straits of Gibraltar. The city lay in the uppermost corner of North Africa, facing two oceans, two worlds: the lighthouse at Cap Spartel flashed toward the Atlantic above the pitted Phoenician ruins of Cotta and the underground Caves of Hercules; on the Mediterranean side, the light at Cap Malabata winked its great eye toward the low-lying shores of Spain across the Straits.

Between the two great maritime lights the city rose steeply from the wide beaches and the harbor and the warehouses and the railroad station, climbing a pitched slope up to the Boulevard Pasteur and the Place de France. The city dipped to the Medina on one side; on the other, the streets rose gradually to the Marshan and out to the new suburb called California. Here the modern houses overlooked a valley on whose far side the Sultan's representative of the Cherifian Empire was building a new mud-colored castle. The castle was not yet completed, because of time there was an eternity, *insha' Allah,* and only several years of work had thus far gone into it. Also, the Sultan's representative, the Mendoub, was already housed in a large villa on the Rue Shakespeare much nearer to the center of the business section of Tangier. Perhaps this location was wiser than the suburban castle, for it was necessary for the Mendoub to make it clear to the ten nations who administered Tangier—nine, actually, because the Soviets had refused to sit down with the Spanish on the Committee of Control—it was necessary to remind them that the International Zone of Tangier was still technically a part of the Sultan's Cherifian Empire.

391

The Mendoub's Friday ceremonial helped as a reminder that the many Europeans and few Americans were newcomers, and that the Moors were not. Friday was the Moslem Sabbath, and each Friday the Mendoub left his villa to attend religious services at the Mosque. Like a Western leader, he rode in a long black Cadillac. Near the Mosque he would have his limousine stop so that he could walk slowly for a distance between two lines of white-robed Faithful, backed by a mounted troop of uniformed Mokhaznis who sat erectly at attention in their saddles. Most of them were tall desert men with blue cloaks flaring out in the constant wind off the Bay of Tangier, tall with their red fezzes and weapons, proud beneath the lifted saber of the officer's salute and the flapping streamers of the color guard topped by the five-pointed Star of the Cherifian Empire. In the nearby gardens of the Mendoubia, facing the sea, were the forty cannons for the forty months of siege the seventeenth-century British redcoats had suffered before Sultan Moulay Ismail's armies finally cut off their water supplies. Christian prisoners had been roped across the mouths of the loaded cannons then, the usual slower methods of killing having been judged not adequate for the situation. Also, in this way each cannon shot could carry a higher meaning of mercy to the unbelievers.

If it were not for the Mendoub's Cadillac, the Friday ceremony and the mounted warriors would have been very much like the times when the helmeted Crusaders had leaped across the Straits from Europe and fought their way inland until their French king had died in his tent of plague, the Black Death. Plague still lingered in Morocco, but the Cross had returned to Europe. The Islamic Crescent still faced Mecca five times each day, but now with a Cadillac parked nearby.

Even the Tangier street names taken from the Romans of the first century would be changed if the Istiqlal revolutionaries gained Moroccan independence, people said. The wide coastal Boulevard Antée, named for Anteus who had first built Tangier for his wife and had called it Tingis in her honor, would probably be renamed Boulevard Mohammed V when the true Sultan, Mohammed ben Youssef, returned to his throne. True, he was still an *éloigné*, a distant one, as the French delicately termed their political exiles. The French still refused to bring him back to Morocco with his veiled wives and his twenty-two concubines and his proud sons and his emancipated daughters and his dignified advisors and his feudal servants. But Roger Obenpharo's Istiqlal party was more powerful than ever now. The fighting in the streets of Fez and Casablanca and Meknes still went on, and there had been two assassination attempts on the French-appointed substitute Sultan. The stubborn inevitable rape and disemboweling of women still occurred, the burnings of French farmers and their farms and their time-nurtured citrus trees, and the classic method begun by Caesar's legionnaires of smashing of infant heads against the nearest wall. Each time the Moroccans attacked, the French struck back with harshness, imposing curfews, blocking roads, organizing the *ratissage,* the type of mass roundup called rat-trapping. In these operations every male Arab was forced behind barbed-wire enclosures for search at gun point. There was much face-slapping and teeth-slugging and bayonet-sticking and iron-handed searching for weapons while the veiled women crouched below the city walls wailing for their husbands and sons.

The French had publicly invited Roger Obenpharo to a meeting, but he had not even answered. They concluded he was holding out for the true Sultan's return to Morocco, or he was dying. Either way, he was silent. One shrill newspaper reported he had been seen in Cairo with Hadj Messali and the old warrior of the Riff days, Abd-el-Krim. Informers said he was hiding in the French zone, in Fez, then Rabat, then Casablanca. They said he moved openly through the Spanish zone, where the Spanish police somehow had great difficulty in finding any anti-French leaders or arms. Later, the informers were found with their throats slashed open, and the traditional severed penis jammed traditionally between the teeth.

In Tangier, the international comers and goers who met at Raïssa's Carnivale between bedtimes began to invent all sorts of stories about Roger Obenpharo. The theme was usually the same, that he was a new kind of combination of Mahatma Gandhi and Robin Hood. The stories made much of the famous broken face, the desert warrior clothing, the Sorbonne legal education, and the conversion to Islam.

Now it was summer, the month of Aid-el-Kebir, when each family should slaughter a sheep in ceremonial commemoration of the sacrifice of Abraham. This month was the second anniversary of the

393

exile of the Sultan by the French, *La Date Fatidique,* the fateful date, and the Istiqlal had passed the word: Boycott the ancient religious festival. Spare the ritual sheep. Turn this year's ceremonial slaughter against the French.

Bud Williams piloted Monsieur Obenpharo's personal plane in a wide circle over Tangier so that he could show Mac the Villa Obenpharo from the air. As the plane tilted and the city wheeled by, Mac looked down at the tall white city buildings marching uphill from the sea. He felt a tap of memory. Tangier's apartment houses and hotels had the white boxy concrete and glass appearance which he had heard called low-grade chronic Florida modern. Seen from an airplane Tangier looked like Miami.

"You should have been with us last week," Bud Williams said. "Old man Obenpharo told me to take this approach over the bank and then over the villa so that Henri could see everything from up high. The Banque Obenpharo is that tall building with the green glass penthouse."

"Henri must have liked that," Mac said.

"He couldn't sit still. For a kid who used to be so quiet and serious, he's sure changed. Acts his age now, more natural." He glanced at Mac. "You sure did a nice job on his face, Doc."

"Well," Mac said, "actually he didn't have much more than a few deep cuts." Maybe I've become too paternal with Henri too quickly, he thought, but I like the way the boy is easing up on himself. Obenpharo has been treating him as a crown prince for so long that Henri forgot he was a boy.

Bud Williams was still talking. "The old man was wild when he got your call about Henri being hurt. My God, you should have seen him on the trip to Paris. They say he's practically all set to teach that kid the whole damn banking business, starting from the top down."

Mac said nothing. He thought the pilot had a quality seen in many Americans who disliked being employees so much that they continually discussed their employers with an intimate derogatory half-joking manner; as if talking about harmlessly foolish friends.

Bud Williams looked at him. "I heard Mademoiselle Obenpharo tell the old man she wished you could have flown down here with them."

394

Mac decided to stop any rumors before they started. "I had to stay in Paris to buy surgical equipment," he said. "It took more time than I thought it would."

"You should have told me sooner," Bud said. "I could have flown you over to Germany. I've got a big wheeler-dealer there who could have got the stuff for you whoesale, plus ten per cent."

"With another ten per cent to you?"

"Of course. That's how the frogs and the krauts do business." Bud Williams pointed below. "There's the Villa Obenpharo. See that white line along the cliffs?"

Mac looked down at the jumble of crowded box-shaped houses along the shore. "No."

"Look. At the edge of the modern part of the city. See it? The white line is a road going along the cliff. Gets higher all the time. See it?"

"With lots of trees?"

"Yes. That's it. The Old Mountain Road. At the top is Villa Obenpharo."

Of course, Mac thought. The Obenpharos would build no place else except at the top. The penthouse on top of the bank; the villa above the cliffs.

"During the war," Bud went on, "they say the old man had high-power binoculars and telescopes all over the place so he could spot German and Italian sea and air movements. The Spanish kept trying to scare him and once in a while somebody would shoot at him. But the old fox kept slipping military intelligence to Gibraltar, and after the war the British Minister gave him the O.B.E. Veddy pukka sahib, and all that sort, y'know."

"Why be sarcastic?" Mac said. "Not everybody with that much to lose would have had the guts."

"*Merde,*" Bud said pleasantly. "If you look quick, here's a close look at the Villa Obenpharo."

Below, swiftly approaching them, was a large square within a square of white buildings, a Moorish castle with checkerboard-tiled inner courtyards and arched balconies. A colorful formal garden was spread between the main buildings and the edge of the cliffs which dropped straight into the sea. Acres of trees surrounded the white

395

villa, and, outside them, ran a high wall with watchtowers at the corners.

Looking down at the lush greenery, the hot whites and the bright specks of garden colors, Mac thought how different all this was from the Obenpharos' gray formal house on the quiet island beside the Seine. The many different contradictory Maias were easier to understand now. Places had a way of changing people. This Moorish villa rushing beneath the plane was only several hours away from Paris, yet an astronomical distance in Maia's way of living.

Mac looked down at the Villa Obenpharo on its mountainous stone shelf overlooking the crosstides of the Straits, and experienced a brief airborne omnipotence in seeing how the conflicting histories of North Africa and Europe expressed themselves within Maia in ways of which she herself had no idea. Am I exaggerating, he wondered. No, probably not, because I'm convinced that much of what I am was shaped by my father's fathers.

This is going to be fine, he thought. Really good. That feeling I had when we started out from Paris, that vague sense of flying toward unknown complexities, all that is gone now. The self-questioning is gone. Everything looks fine down there in that clear hard sunlight. The Villa Obenpharo looks just remote enough, close to the city of Tangier and the hospital, yet far enough away. Roger's surgery will be a complex sort of flesh and bone sculpture, he thought, and it's good that I'm thinking of it in terms of sculpture. I'd gone dry in my surgery. Too skillful and too mechanically dexterous. I needed to get away from it, and now this is a fine way to come back. With a steady hand. A fresh eye.

A valley flashed by beneath him, with tiny white-domed marabouts of Moslem saints on the crests of hills and the little figures of two polo teams dashing over a long green field like mounted toys; then some lower hills, then a flatter terrain, and then the sound of their engines changed as they entered their downward glide path toward Boukhalf Airport and the ancient sun-drenched ground of Africa rushed upward toward him.

Maia hugged him, then held him at arm's length. "Let me look at you."

396

"No," he said, "at you. Everybody here is looking at you, and I always go along with the crowd."

The umbrella-covered terrace outside the airport's restaurant-bar was filled with people, most of whom had decided it was more interesting to watch Maia than each other or the airplane arrivals. Several tables were taken by a group of French military pilots who still wore their flying coveralls while their jet planes were being serviced at the far end of the airport. They were all young and filled with good cheer, more like vacationers than supersonic fighter pilots, and their enthusiasm for Maia was very clear. They admired her in the open European café fashion, frankly, obviously, neither polite nor impolite, but merely making it clear that she was being admired without restraint.

Maia was ignoring it, or not even noticing. "Don't worry about your surgical *bagages,* darling," she said. "Yacoub will have it through customs very soon."

"I'm not worried, Maia. Really. I'm in tune with the world. Walking on air."

She gave him her smile. "Such talk. I detect an overtone, Mac. Or should I say undertone?"

He grinned. "Over, under, in between. What's the difference? I had a bad attack of my old disease on the way down here—"

"Disease?"

"You know, thinking, thinking, thinking—"

"Will the patient live, Doctor?"

He took her arm. "Happily forever after."

"Now I know why they say Americans exaggerate. But I like it."

"No exaggeration. On the plane I remembered lots of things, mostly on the dark side. Then to step out into this bright golden light and find bright golden you—" He paused.

"Don't stop, darling. You have no idea how exaggerated and how nice you sound."

"You have no idea how nice you look. Have you ever been kissed very completely and scientifically on the terrace of the Tangier airport?"

As always, she managed to look striking as well as beautiful. She was bare-armed, and wore a blue silk dress draped in folds like an Indian sari, with a length of cloth carried up over her hair against the

397

sun. He had never seen her look more elegant and Parisian, and yet, at the same time, oriental and exotic.

"You," she said, "why do you look like that? What are you thinking?"

"I'm thinking how nice it is your intelligence makes up for all your plain looks."

She laughed and put one hand on his arm. "You don't know how good it is to hear you talk nonsense again." She looked around. "I wonder what's taking customs so long."

"Bud Williams, probably. He's the kind of guy customs men enjoy."

The loud-speakers overhead announced the arrival of the Air France plane from Algiers, and a small group of men left one of the tables on the terrace to crowd together around the metal fence at the edge of the runway. Mac noticed that they all looked alike; dark-haired, tight suits nipped in at the waist, all wearing red fezzes and large-framed opaque sunglasses. When the Algiers plane rolled up to the debarkation point they all stopped talking and watched the airline people push the wheeled metal steps to the plane's door. If their dark glasses had not made them so anonymously blank-eyed and serious, they would have given the impression of a welcoming committee.

The first passenger who stepped out of the shadowy interior of the plane into the sunlight was Jeanjean. Even this exit from the cabin was handled as if it were a stage entrance. He stood for a moment on the top step, looking around as if acknowledging applause, looking taller than usual because he wore a red fez, then he turned back to say something to the airplane hostess in the doorway which made her smile widely. Mac could see people behind Jeanjean who were waiting to leave the plane, but Jeanjean stood on the top step surveying the terrace onlookers until he found the pocket which contained his sunglasses and put them on slowly and ceremonially and stared at the welcoming committee wearing glasses like his. He saw Maia suddenly and waved to her.

Maia turned her back. "Of all people," she said to Mac. "And wearing a Moslem fez."

Jeanjean paused at the metal fence just long enough to speak to

398

the little group of dark-haired men, then came down opposite Maia. "Maia," he said in Arabic, ignoring Mac, "you are more beautiful. And so good to come meet me."

Maia kept her back turned and said quietly in English to Mac, "Don't notice him. He loves acting when there's a crowd."

"Ah, Doctor!" Jeanjean said in French. "I did not see you there. Maia dazzled me. Are you coming to Tangier, or just leaving us?"

"Coming," Mac said. That *us* was clever. Jeanjean was expert at suggesting intimacies. "Tangier is now my second home."

"Very good, Doctor. Mine also. I saw your beautiful lady doctor friend in Algiers, at a distance."

"Eve? How is she?"

"Beautiful teeth. American dental work is the best. But her smile was not like in Paris." He laughed pleasantly. "Very quick, the lady doctor, very efficient now. An American executive. No time for fun. I had no idea she was such a big vegetable in international medicine."

"She is," Mac said. "In America, in Washington, she sees the President every day on medical consultation."

"Truly!" Jeanjean was impressed until, a moment later, he realized he sounded like a fool. As always when he was insulted, he smiled with all his magnificent teeth. "It would be very generous," he said. "I will clear customs in one moment, I mean generous to give me a lift into Tangier. You no doubt have the magnificent Obenpharo car."

"Unfortunately," Mac said, "the car will be occupied with some magnificent privacy."

The shining smile widened. "Another time then, perhaps."

"Perhaps." Then, before he could stop the impulse, Mac asked, "What brings you to Tangier, señor?"

Jeanjean tapped his red fez. "Patriotism." He nodded toward the group of dark-haired men waiting for him near the doorway to customs. "My friends invite me to come from Algiers. I cannot refuse."

"But I thought you were Spanish."

"Ah. So. Yes. Well, we are all Moorish peoples, you know. Also the Tangier championship polo matches. The Egyptian team is coming."

Maia swung around furiously. "The Egyptian saboteurs, you mean!

399

The Cairo gunmen with military instructions!" Mac was surprised by her intensity.

In Arabic, Jeanjean said, "Ah, still life in that body? Another pretty piece for Coca-Colonization?"

In Arabic she said, "Thou filth. Thou filth of filths."

"Thou beauty. But what ugliness when angry."

"Killer. Blackmailer. Pimp."

"Patriot. I raise money for the revolutionary party. Now I am on thy husband's side."

"I am free, filth. I spit on thy party, and there is no husband."

"There is. Me. I am the only one for a proud Berber."

Mac stepped forward and said in French, *"Va-t'en.* Beat it. I don't know what you're saying, but beat it."

"If not, what? Fists? American fighting, like savages? Like the cowboy films?"

Several of the dark-haired men had moved down the fence toward Jeanjean. One of them spoke sharply to him, and when Jeanjean did not answer, rapped out a command. Maia swung to them angrily. "All of you, you should all be in jail."

The first man, the man who had spoken to Jeanjean, bowed slightly to her and said very seriously in Arabic, "Tangier is a free zone, madame. The jails are over in the French zone."

"Yes," she said, "and also the dead women and children, and the men covered with gasoline and burned alive."

Very politely, the man said, "It is a war, madame. These things happen." Deliberately, he added, "Even an *evoluée* like you should sympathize."

"You are savages. Drug addicts. Algerian thugs adding to Moroccan troubles."

"No. We have waited a long time, and some of our people become desperate." The short dark-haired man turned to Jeanjean and again bit off an Arabic phrase in a tone of command. Jeanjean frowned at him, bowed slightly to Mac and Maia as if they had had a friendly talk, then moved down the fence parallel with his friends, toward the customs entrance.

One of the French pilots came over and said, "Monsieur, madame, pardon. Those *salesarabes* make some difficulty? Is there some assistance my friends and I can give?"

"Thank you," Maia said. She was still trembling a little. "Thank you, no."

"After yesterday," the pilot said, "it would give my friends and me pleasure to make a small intervention here."

"Thanks," Mac said. "Everything is under control. Thanks."

"Nothing, monsieur. Madame." The pilot went back to the group of umbrella-covered tables where his friends sat watching him. They had become quiet and watchful.

Mac looked at Maia. Her face had changed. The sun was bright, the white-coated waiters brought iced drinks to the terrace tables, but the day had changed. "Yesterday?" he said. "What happened yesterday? Why were you so angry?" He found himself amazed now, because he would have preferred her to have been indifferent to Jeanjean. Something complex and intangible and North African had just happened, he did not understand it, and the whole bright sunlit illusion of his arrival was gone.

"Didn't you hear what happened yesterday?" Maia sat beside him in Obenpharo's car. Her fingers smoothed a fold in her dress over and over again. "Didn't you see any morning papers in Paris before you left?"

He put his hand over her nervous fingers. "No," he said. "It's just a habit I have, ignoring newspapers. I'm not a banker, and I don't need that daily diet of news."

"Mac, please, no joking. Not this time."

"I wasn't. I—"

"I know it's an American habit to pretend to take serious things in a joking way. But this is a bad time." She looked out the window at the sparse Moroccan *bled* their car was traveling through so smoothly. They were passing a field in which an Arab farmer was plowing with a wooden tool whose design must have been at least a thousand years old. Mac saw the small swift arrowhead shapes of the French jet planes taking off steeply from the airport, and the contrast between the farmer and the fighter ships was too obvious even to mention to Maia. Yet, there it was.

She said quietly, "Yesterday the real North African revolution began. *La Date Fatidique*. Not just cutting down telephone poles or smashing street lamps or throwing grenades into bars. Yesterday it

401

was planned and co-ordinated military action. All across Algeria and Morocco, all at the same time, fire and killing. In Khouribga, near Casablanca, the Arabs went wild, but always under the control of some kind of leadership. And in Oued Zem—" She stopped, then said, "You heard none of this in Paris?"

"Nothing," he said. "Last-minute packing and all the rest. What happened in Oued Zem? I never heard of it."

"It's just a small Moroccan town on the Tadla plain near Casablanca. A small sleepy town where the French have lived for years. A town hall. A school. Like any town."

"What happened?"

"This time it was the Berbers. From the mountains—perhaps the Smaala, or the Ouled Aissim." She shrugged. "Usually they side with the French against the city Arabs, but not this time. The *caids* turned their tribesmen loose like hawks. They came riding into town from the hills and took it for six hours. After those six hours, not one European was alive. Mothers had to watch their children being butchered. Then there was the cutting off of noses and tongues and burning alive with gasoline. Every patient in the hospital was killed. The atrocities were unbelievable."

"But that's mob murder, not military."

"It was military at first. You should see the reports coming in from our branch banks. Many of the attackers wore uniforms. There was strict leadership. There was the timing, co-ordinated with attacks on dozens of French villages all across the Constantine Department of Algeria." She touched his face lightly. "My poor Mac. You looked so happy when you came off the plane."

"I still feel fine. I've missed you very much since you left last week. I've missed Henri."

"There's enough of you for both of us, isn't there, darling?"

"Yes."

She kissed him lightly, then leaned back in the seat. "It's so good having you here. You can't imagine the coming and going at the bank. The cables and radiograms and telephone calls. Papa hasn't left his office on top of the bank since yesterday. He sent his apologies for not meeting you at the airport."

"Thank you."

"Please don't sound so formal. He really wanted to meet you. He

402

likes you very much, darling. Papa is not a simple man, darling, and when he likes you that's better than a medal."

"I consider myself decorated. Actually I'm happy you came to the airport without him. You ought to dress like this all the time."

"Exotique?"

"Yes. Now that you're going to marry a doctor, you should know that you create very basic biological changes."

"That's a joke, isn't it, darling?"

"Half and half."

"It must be told with a straight face, no?"

"Yes."

"Isn't it terrible how I'm never sure?"

"You'll learn. I'll learn. We have all the time in the world."

"Happily forever after?"

"Yes."

"The world won't push in and break our auto windows with chains and destroy us?"

"Of course not."

"Forgive me, but don't Americans always say of course not when the rest of us worry about trouble?"

"It never occurred to me—"

"It occurs to everyone else all the time. Oh, Mac, don't you know there are twenty thousand Americans on Moroccan air bases? Would you believe most of them think all this terrible fighting is like a small carnival sideshow?"

"I'm talking about you and me, Maia. I'm trying to say you're so close to the whole revolution, you and the Obenpharos, that you forget that there've always been noises in the background."

"But the Obenpharos are always in the middle of every big change. Without us, all the threads begin to come apart."

"Maia, you've lived on your islands long enough. Obenpharo is big, but not the beginning and end of the world."

"I hope you're right, darling."

"Of course I am. Someday you'll stop being an Obenpharo—"

"Impossible! I owe them my whole life!"

"But you don't have to pay with your life. Only with your gratitude and your affection, not this Moslem servitude."

She stared at him, shocked.

"Maia," he said quickly, "this is a hell of a way for me to arrive."

"Darling," she said in a low voice, "this is how it will always be."

"Don't misunderstand. You love the Obenpharos. I respect them—"

"Mac, don't ask me to leave them. They're dying. The whole world knows their son is one of the top men behind the revolution here. It kills them exactly the way a knife does."

"I'm not asking you to leave them." He nodded over his shoulder at the rear window, at the boxes of surgical equipment strapped to the luggage rack of the Rolls so high that the rear view was blocked. "Does all that look as if we're leaving? I'll stay in Tangier as long as you do. I told you in Paris, I've come to join you."

"And I told you in Paris I have never seen a man give this before. Take, yes. But they never give." She took his face between her hands. "Have you ever been so thoroughly kissed in the back of a car driving into Tangier?"

"Mrs. Adams," he began to say, grinning, "you ask too many—" but he never finished because she was kissing him.

They rode through the bright Mediterranean landscape holding one another tightly, back on their island.

(2)

A SMALL bent-over very old man who wore a Moslem skullcap stepped out of the gatekeeper's hut as the big car rolled to a stop before the massive double gates of the Villa Obenpharo. He made a considerable ceremony of the opening of the two copper-studded gates, first one, then the other. Even though he was clearly very old and feeble, neither the chauffeur nor Yacoub got out of the front seat to help him. The gates were the gatekeeper's, his work to do and his dignity as a doer, so there was no reason to help him. He raised his hand in half salute and smiled toothlessly at Maia as the car moved past him.

"Even he likes you," Mac said.

"He remembers when I came here. He remembers a shy Berber

girl in her first Western clothes. He remembers Papa's marriage to Mutirra. He remembers the day Roger was born." She looked at him. "You see how they are? Time means nothing. Last year or ten years, it's all the same."

The curving drive, bordered by sentinel royal palms, turned through acres of pine and eucalyptus trees until they approached the villa which rose sharply outlined in the sculptural burning sunlight. They came to a stone-paved inner courtyard with walls almost as high as the outer ones at the gate. A low building along one side must have been a large stable many years ago. Now it was a multiple garage. On the far side of this stone yard the drive curved again, winding around to the arched front doors of the villa.

Despite its size, the villa looked light and gracefully suspended among slender columns and pointed Moorish arches. Like the finest Islamic architecture, the building gave a feeling of a freedom from clutter and a dignity of balanced proportions. There were subtle perspectives, one arch framing another some distance behind it, and the great simplicity of unbroken surfaces contrasted with the most complex tile mosaics and elaborate arabesques in wrought iron. Giant wisteria trees and mimosa threw traceries of shadow everywhere.

Several servants were waiting for them, and began to move together down the broad steps as their car stopped. Maia leaned forward toward the front seat and gave Yacoub some rapid instructions in Arabic, then turned to Mac.

"I hope Henri is back from his swim," Maia said. "He's been waiting every day to see you."

Inside the villa, Mutirra was wheeled forward in her aluminum chair to meet them as they came through the doorway. Within the tall tiled room, beneath the intricately carved beamed ceiling with the double staircase rising off to each side and a soaring Moorish arch which outlined an outer fountain courtyard—within all this Mutirra looked tiny and lost. She wore an old-fashioned floral chiffon and an elaborate coiffure, like a hostess from a garden party of the past.

She held out both hands to Mac. "At last, at last, Dr. Adams!" she said in accented English. "I heard the airplane pass overhead and it seemed so long before you finally came. How nice you're here at last."

405

"You're very kind, madame," Mac said in French. "To take me in while I stay in Tangier was very kind."

"Maia," Mutirra cried, recognizing his courtesy and now speaking French also, "listen to him! Is he always so formal, like the old-fashioned French?"

"He's old-fashioned," Maia said, "but only in the nicest ways."

Mutirra turned her small head back to him. "You're almost in the family, you know, not just a visiting doctor. Henri talks about you day and night. He is not back from swimming—did you see our beach when you flew over?—it's a long climb up here from that little beach. But he'll be here soon, and so will his grandfather, I hope." It was as if she could not stop talking. "Benari's been at the bank for two days running now—I'm sure you heard all about our terrible political troubles in Paris—but he called to say he'd be here very soon. I—"

Maia interrupted her gently. "Mother, Mac will be here a long time. You'll tire yourself if you try to tell him everything at one time."

Mutirra took one of Mac's hands and said in English, "Please, forgive me but I must ask—and by the way, please do not speak French because most of the servants understand it"—she nodded her head upward—"they listen behind the *moucharabiah*—"

Mac glanced up at two balcony-like structures suspended above each staircase. He suddenly realized that their carved wooden scrollwork of designs-within-designs was actually a pierced screen through which visitors could not see, but from behind which came faint whispers of invisible onlookers.

Maia saw his glance. "Accept it, darling," she said quietly in English. "Every step we take, the servants know it. An old Moorish custom."

"Maia," Mutirra said, "may I ask him—"

"About Roger?" Mac said in English. As soon as she had mentioned political troubles he knew why her nervous flow of talking kept on. He saw her very large dark eyes become even larger and more luminous.

From outside there was the sound of a car approaching, and a servant crossed the foyer slowly toward the front doorway.

"That must be Benari coming now," Mutirra said quickly. "He'll

say I'm nagging you, to tell me what you think before he comes."
She held her hands clasped tightly together, staring at him tensely.
"Tell me."

"Madame," Mac said, knowing as all doctors do that every ques-
tioner has an answer which they want the doctor to give, "I wish I
could give you a quick and favorable answer. But I haven't examined
your son yet. The sooner I do, the better. My only information comes
from a set of X-ray films your husband brought me, with a one-page
report from a doctor here."

"I realize," she broke in. "I understand that. But does it all look
hopeful to you?"

"Even the clinical report is several months old now. Hasn't your
son been under the doctor's care all that time?"

She began to close her eyes with the leaden look of fatigue, then
opened them heavily and looked straight at him. "No. That's why
I'm so worried." Her voice dropped. "I can't imagine how Roger
lives. He has very great will power, but after all, with that terrible
open wound in his face—" She reached out to grasp his hand again.
"Forgive me for not welcoming you better than this—"

"I understand how you feel, madame."

"—it's all been bottled up inside me so long—"

"—of course, of course," he said. "I'll do everything I can to help
Roger."

"Doctor, you'll never know how grateful I am—"

"Please. Don't be. You probably know that I really came for Maia
and Henri and myself."

"I'm grateful for that too. Waiting to see them happy again keeps
me alive. For me, Henri is Roger all over again." She smiled sideways
at Maia. "Except for his red hair."

Maia bent over Mutirra and kissed her cheek. "Mother," she said,
"just leave everything to Mac. Don't worry and don't stay up too
long for comfort."

The tall front doorway burst open, and suddenly there was a running boy shouting, "Mac! Mac!" and a toy French poodle barking
noisily and a servant carrying a wicker beach basket and another
with a briefcase, all followed by Monsieur Obenpharo and another
equally tall man. Henri ran toward Mac while Mutirra said, "What's

this? What's this? What's all this barking and running and shouting?"

Henri stopped short. "Pardon, Grandma." He became a miniature grownup immediately and put out his hand. "I'm glad to see you, Mac."

"Hell's bells," Mac said, "that's no way to say hello." He put his arms around Henri and gave him a bear hug, and he felt the boy's arms tighten around him. He saw Monsieur Obenpharo standing aside and watching silently, with dignity. "Let me look at you," he said to Henri, holding him off. "You're my only patient, you know, so I have to watch you." The thin red lines still ran through the skin of Henri's face, but they were very thin and cleanly healed.

"My face doesn't hurt any more, Mac, but the scars are there."

"They're new," Mac said. "In six months you'll hardly see them. In a year," he added lightly, "people will say: Who's that fencing champion?"

"The servants say it came from Allah," Henri said. "To be like my father."

Mutirra drew her breath in sharply, and in the dead silence Obenpharo stepped forward. "I hope you've forgiven my not meeting you," he said as they shook hands. "Our bank has turned into a street brawl. I couldn't leave, and I knew our Paris manager was coming to the airport to meet you."

"She came," Mac said. "She saw. She conquered."

The tall thin silver-haired man behind Obenpharo came toward him with his hand out. "Caesar's propaganda," he said with a slow deep welcoming smile. "Benari must have sold you his usual line of classical Mediterranean pots and pans."

"Monsieur Nathan Cohen," Obenpharo said, as Mac and the tall thin man shook hands. "He's the best bank manager in Tangier, but the world's worst chauffeur. Why do the tallest men drive the smallest English cars?" He turned to the tiny toy French poodle at his feet. "Stop yapping, Tabac! Henri, call off your man-eating hunting dog." He bent and kissed Mutirra, murmuring, "Sorry to be late. Irra—" Then he kissed Maia lightly and said, "You surpass yourself in that blue silk, my dear."

"Henri," Mutirra said, "take your Tabac out and be so kind as to wash the salt water out of your hair and comb it and dress decently. We'll have tea soon." She smiled at Mac. "Pardon. Cocktails."

"Never touch them," Mac said. "Alcohol dissolves the bones."

Mutirra looked blank, and Maia said, "Mother, that's an American kind of joking. Like the cowboys in the cinema." Then she added reassuringly, "Sometimes it *is* funny," and they all laughed.

"Nathan," Mutirra said, "you'll please stay?"

"No," Nathan said, "my feelings about my driving ability are hurt. I'm leaving." They laughed again. Nathan swung to Mac, "That was American, no? What is called poker-face joking?"

"Mac," Henri said, "was that our plane that came down low over the villa?"

"I think so," Mac said. He glanced at Obenpharo. "It's a very impressive view."

Nathan held up a long bony hand. "Stop, Doctor. That kind of talk only invites long speeches from Benari about his Phoenician ancestors and the mighty sailing ships of Sidon and Carthage."

"And the Hebrews," Obenpharo said. "King Solomon and his *nouveau riche.*"

Mac saw that the two old men, who were really very dignified friends, were trying hard to act like their idea of informal humorous American executives. They want me to feel welcome and at home, he thought, but they don't quite know how to do it.

Mutirra said, "How terrible we are! Dr. Adams hasn't even had a chance to sit down. Henri, off to your bath with your little barking monster. Benari, why don't you show Dr. Adams his apartment—"

"Mac," Henri said, "did you see Bambi when you drove in?"

"Tabac and Bambi," Maia said to Mac. "He's always surrounded by little animals who eat from his hands. Like somebody in one of those Walter Disney films they show in Paris."

Obenpharo took charge. "Maia, Henri's grandmother obviously can't command your son. Perhaps you can march him off, and then show Dr. Adams where his rooms are and then—" He took out a massive gold watch, which, Mac remembered, gave the time in all the world's financial capitals. "Is an hour to tea time too soon? Nathan, not at my invitation, but at my wife's, you'll stay?"

Mac saw Nathan's eyes meet Obenpharo's. The old man doesn't want to see me alone, Mac sensed. I don't know why, but he doesn't. He wants someone from outside the family so we can all keep up this parlor game of half joking and pretending we have no troubles lying in our throats waiting to be said as abruptly as Mutirra had asked about Roger.

Maia put her arm through his. "Come along, Maccabeus. I'll show you the grand tour on the way."

Nathan looked at Mac. Not a muscle in his lean face moved, yet something in his expression changed. "Maccabeus?" he repeated. "Is that your name, Dr. Adams?"

"It's a kind of family nickname, monsieur."

"But it's a Hebrew name. From the Apocrypha."

"My grandfather's middle name was Maccabee."

"Ah. A Hebrew grandfather."

"No. He was a Protestant minister in the part of the United States called New England."

"I don't understand the connection."

"Well," Mac said, now that he saw that Nathan was clearing up some kind of point for himself which he considered significant, "in those days, Hebrew and Greek and Latin were the languages of the universities. My grandfather went to Yale—"

"Ah, yes. The University of Yale. My son Joseph wanted to go there."

"All theological students learned Hebrew at Yale."

"Because it was the language of the Bible?"

"Of the Old Testament, yes. Even the motto on the Yale seal is in Hebrew."

"I see. So you have your minister grandfather's name. To carry a family name, that's an old Hebrew custom too." He nodded approvingly.

"Now," Obenpharo growled, "who's boasting about ancestors? All we need is the Queen of Sheba, and the party will be complete."

"Actually," Mac said, trying not to smile, "my name is Malcolm."

Nathan shook his head a little. "Just when I understand Americans, this happens. Actually, Doctor, Maccabeus was a great biblical hero who fought for his God against impossible odds."

"Explain it, darling," Maia said. "I've always wondered, myself."

"It's not mysterious," Mac said. "My friends thought it was a sort of joking family name to give me when I went at things very hard. Like—well, it would be like hearing Henri refuse to go take his bath and saying: We bow to your wish, great Pharaoh."

410

Benari Obenpharo laughed aloud for the first time. "Not Pharaoh. Obenpharo."

"I surrender," Nathan said, raising both hands. "I'll stay for tea."

Mac turned in a slow exploratory circle around his room, then came back to where Maia watched him with her little smile. "The bathroom most of all," he said. "The gold swans for bathtub faucets. I'm beginning to feel like Ali Baba and the Forty Thieves."

"Only Ali Baba," she said. "The forty thieves stay down at the bank."

"This is all so different from your Paris house."

"Of course, darling. Two different worlds, two different houses."

"And you," he said. "Two different women."

She put her arms around him. "That's not so clever. I told you my secret myself."

"But now I really understand it. Don't be surprised if I come downstairs to tea wearing a red fez and yellow leather slippers."

She laughed. "You know," she said, tightening her arms, "we can stay up here, if you want. We don't have to go downstairs."

He kissed her throat gently. "That's a wonderful primitive idea."

"I'm a primitive girl, remember? Since you stepped out of the plane I wanted to tell you so."

"And when I saw you at the airport—"

She loosened his tie skillfully. "Now that you've arrived I feel especially happy."

"And especially fantastically beautiful." He kissed her right cheek, then her left cheek.

"That's because I feel that way." She started to kiss him, but caught his lower lip gently between her teeth. "Really," she said, muffled against him, "we should go down soon—"

"Soon enough," he said. He ran his hands along her warm arms. "But a man needs a personal welcome in a strange city."

"This is personal, darling. Just for you." Her legs parted and she caught one of his between them. She slid one hand through his shirt and ran her fingernails cunningly down his side.

"And this is how to be welcomed in Tangier? Standing up and talking?"

411

Her thighs tightened. "Yes. Standing and talking."

"No," he said. "Like this."

"If you take that off me, I'll take this off you."

"Off it goes."

"If we're not going to stand," she said, kicking off one shoe, then the other, so that they sailed under the bed, "I won't need these."

This time it was different, half comedy because somehow they had begun comically, tumbling and rolling like athletic newlyweds. Once or twice she took the lead away from him, but they knew each other so well now that under the pretense of pagan struggle and voluptuous pursuit there was a swelling tenderness. Her skin was more tanned than in Paris, and with the warm flush in it now she was as smoothly golden as the statue of the river nymph. Then the comedy was gone and there was only an urgent mounting seriousness, the long wave running into shore, mounting, until she lifted very hard and clung to him for a taut drawn-out moment, then dropped back.

After a long silence, so long he thought she had fallen asleep, she said in a small voice, "This is what you meant, darling. This is how it should be."

"Yes."

"You don't like me to talk about it so much, do you?" Her voice sounded far away and sleepy, as if she were talking to herself. "I only want to keep reminding myself—" She stretched her body along his luxuriously and yawned. "If I fall asleep . . . you won't go away?"

"No. I'll stay right here."

"Mmm—" she murmured, and a minute later she was asleep.

He kissed her softly, but she did not even stir. Stay awake, he warned himself. Hold on to all this. Everything here may be new to you, but she must have a whole web of memories of this room, of Roger, of the time Henri was born, of her arrival at the gate and her girlhood here and trying to hurry herself into being European. He looked at her vulnerable sleeping eyes, seeing beyond the lovely open face, beginning to understand the slow smile, really understand it, and feeling a new depth of tenderness. This is how it should be, he thought. We still have some distance to go, but we're on the way and this is how it should be.

He looked at her completely relaxed face with its tiny secret smile, and the faintest suggestion of upturnings at the outer corners of her eyes. The entire façade of the chic European woman executive was gone, and now the polished slope of her body was curled against him the way a child seeks comfort and warmth.

This, he thought, and her sleepy question about his not leaving, this was really Maia. Her fear of abandonment by the one she loved. That may be too simple, he thought. But she has always been abandoned by each person she deeply needed, and now, without realizing it, she probably believes that to give love brings betrayal. To avoid betrayal, I suppose, and all the relived pain of each new betrayal, she must have feared and avoided truly loving. Remember all this, he told himself. This is important to remember, because you may not have this kind of balanced, clear-sighted, revealing moment again for a long time. This is a unique day because you've just arrived and see the contrasts. Remember that she must be learning to trust you the way a small child does, testing each thin-ice step as she goes. Logic has nothing to do with all this, because it goes far back. Just hold on to this idea, because you think you're too excited to sleep, you think you're being thoughtful and penetrating, but if you fall asleep you'll wake up later wondering what it was that struck you to the heart.

He slid out of bed quietly and padded barefooted across the cool tile floor to his leather traveling bag to take out his shaving things and a shirt. Wrapped in pajama trousers at the bottom of the bag was a small wooden sign he had packed away several weeks ago and forgotten. He had taken it off the half-size swinging door which led from the street down to the houseboat because he had decided that he did not know if he would come back to the boat, and because he, too, had a childlike taproot which needed a fragment of his native earth, some kind of symbol of origin and permanence.

On the bedside table near Maia, where she would see it first when she awakened, he propped up the small wood board. As he went toward the bathroom he glanced back briefly at the narrow white-painted New England sign, pale, clearly printed, very simple in contrast with the tiled and carven arabesque of this regal Moorish bedroom. It looked odd, but very simple and real: ADAMS FARM.

He smiled to himself, feeling relaxed and friendly enough toward

413

himself to permit this kind of gesture, and went in to shave before Maia awakened.

"Our American guest is a little late coming down," Monsieur Obenpharo said to Nathan. "Have another glass of this sherry."

Nathan held out his glass. "I never touch alcohol," he said, sounding as if he were smiling inside. "It dissolves the bones."

Mutirra put her cup of tea down beside her. "Even if it's American humor and impossible to understand, it's very pleasant to have someone willing to joke here." She tilted her small head toward her husband. "And I'm glad he's late coming down. He and Maia needed a chance to talk together. And did you notice how he and Henri were? Like father and son. None of our foolish formality. I think—"

"Chérie," Obenpharo interrupted gently, "it's you who insists on formality."

"Because I'm a different generation. We were raised by French governesses to be ladies from the age of two. White gloves, chin up, straight back, clear speech. We never spoke unless an adult spoke to us first. Henri's joy to see Dr. Adams would have horrified those Frenchwomen."

"Chérie," Obenpharo said, "you're nervous and you're talking too fast. I wasn't criticizing Dr. Adams for being late. I only wanted him to see our little surprise before the sun went down and spoiled the whole effect."

The surprise was mounted in the center of the inner terrace on which they were sitting. The carved fountain and the tiny manicured trees, the designs of gladioli and roses and Iris Tingitana, the little stone mosaic walks between the pools of light and shade, all were out of a Persian miniature. In the center, reflecting the setting sun, almost too bright to look at where its surfaces threw back the light, was Mac's golden statue.

Nathan followed Obenpharo's glance at the statue. Only he knew how much difficulty Obenpharo had gone to in order to arrange this for the American doctor, because Obenpharo had asked him to make certain, personally, that it was done perfectly and quickly in a city in which mechanical undertakings were rarely quick and never perfect. "Nymph of the Constant Heart," Nathan said as he rotated the stem of his sherry glass thoughtfully between two fingers. "You know, to meet him for the first time and to hear his cowboy jokes, one would not expect such a name, or"—he motioned his glass toward the statue—"such a remarkable piece of work."

"He's a closed man," Obenpharo said.

"Oh no!" Mutirra said. "He's very open."

"Open or closed," Nathan said, "what's the difference?"

"Stop pretending to be a tough cowboy yourself," Obenpharo growled. "You know there's a world of difference."

"Don't bark at me, Benari," Nathan said calmly. "After a terrible time at the bank, I'm feeling very mellow in a sherry sort of way for the first time in days. It's very pleasant to sit by your nice wife and contemplate that very fine statue. Your barking is bothersome."

"I apologize, monsieur," Obenpharo said.

"Apology refused, monsieur. You accuse Mutirra of being nervous, but you're the one."

Obenpharo turned to his wife. "My avenging Fury. Mellow, he says. I think he's a little bit drunk."

"If I am, Benari, it's the first time in fifty-eight years. What did he charge you for that golden statue?"

Obenpharo's stone face cracked into a small smile, then he laughed. "You banker," he said. "You mercenary money-changer. Can't you imagine something too costly to have a price tag?"

"Benari, if you're being so soulfully artistic, he must have charged you a mint of gold."

"You two," Mutirra said, "both of you. Stop it. It was a gift, Nathan. To Maia."

"Didn't you notice them together?" Obenpharo asked. "Do you think Maia dresses like that to interest the passing Tangerois?"

Nathan put his glass down. "I noticed. I noticed. But I've seen Maia looking very beautiful at other times and other places."

Very quickly Mutirra said, "Nathan, l'affaire Jeanjean is finished and over. This American doctor is not for amusement. This is marriage."

Nathan rubbed his chin with the back of his hand and said nothing. Then he picked up his sherry glass between two fingers and went to walk around the golden statue, pausing every few steps to examine it carefully while he sipped his glass. Obenpharo and Mutirra watched him silently as he walked back toward them.

"It's alive," Nathan said quietly. "It's completely first class."

"Jackson wrote me," Obenpharo said, then added to Mutirra, "—he's our correspondent at Chase National in New York—he wrote that Adams had a very fine exhibit of his sculpture, at the best gallery, about a year ago. And his ability as a surgeon is as good as gold."

"He must have been very much taken by her when he did the work."

"Oh, Nathan," Mutirra said, "stop pretending to be a hardheaded banker at the Bourse, and stop selling her short! She's as much a first-class person as he is."

"The ancient war cry of mothers-in-law," Nathan said. "I don't criticize her." He spread his hands. "Maia is Maia."

"For the love of heaven," Mutirra said, pounding her flat hand on the arm of her wheelchair, "why are we all avoiding the thing that worries us?"

"Irra, Irra, we're not avoiding it. We can't make miracles in a day, especially after the last few days of explosion. It may seem quiet here, but over the border people are being killed right now."

"You have sources of information, Benari. You can find out where he is."

"Irra, when Roger disappears, his disciples will gladly cut the throat of any man who reveals his position. The French secret police have every trick in the book, and even they don't know."

She sighed and leaned back in her chair, exhausted.

"All afternoon," Nathan said softly, "I've been wondering what we will tell Dr. Adams. Thank you for coming, but your patient has vanished? What do we say, Benari?"

"Nothing. You can delay him. Take him to the American Legation and then to the Service d'Hygiène to register for the practice of medicine. Show him Dr. Moore's clinic facilities where he will operate. Let him assemble his equipment. Let him go swimming with Henri at the beach. I'll invite him to play polo at the Diplomatique. I'll show him the Phoenician ruins."

"Benari," Nathan said patiently, "don't make yourself sound like a Phoenician ruin. You think you can fool a man like this? Already he guessed something in the air was wrong."

"Not fool, Nathan. Just delay. A little honest delay. If Calypso could keep Ulysses amused for seven years on our shore, Maia can do it for seven days."

"Don't drag Maia in," Mutirra said with her eyes closed. "Please leave her out of all this."

"She's in it, Irra. The whole world is in this mess, and you want her to be out?"

"Both of you," Mutirra said, opening her eyes slowly, "you both have the sensitivity of stones. Roger was once her husband, her child's father. And this is the man she will marry." She leaned forward, pleading with her husband. "You wanted him here. He's here. Leave Maia alone."

"It's impossible," Obenpharo said. "When I met him in Paris he told me there was no key to him. He was wrong." He turned to his bank manager. "Nathan, do you think you can begin the arrangements tomorrow?"

(3)

"WHAT is your preference?" Nathan asked Mac courteously from across the low Moroccan brass tray which was their lunch table. "The Tio Pepe is good, but they have Dry Sack or Oloroso if you prefer."

"I'll stick to the Karrouba, thanks," Mac said. He was beginning to feel that Nathan was treating him like an out-of-town client. "With everything you've organized for me this afternoon, I'll do better with a little less wine and a little more efficiency."

"Admirable, Doctor. Very American, very admirable." Nathan had taken Mac to lunch in the restaurant within the Mehdi el Menebhi palace. They sat on low leather hassocks and ate *couscous* and drank mint tea while the small orchestra on a raised corner platform wailed and beat its way through dissonant Arab rhythms. A barefoot dancing boy was performing in the center of the floor, turning with the light hollow-boned delicacy of a bird and looking spiritually aloof from the sensuality he was acting out.

Nathan nodded toward the dancer. "You notice he's dressed as a girl? The silk kaftan and *t'fin* and the scarf around the hips?"

"Yes." He wondered why Nathan insisted on acting like a guide. He's avoiding something, Mac thought, but what is it?

"This boy is one of *les petits amis* of the American pilot who flew you here."

Maia had told him that everyone knew everyone else's affairs in Tangier, or tried to find out if they didn't know, and Nathan's comment about Bud Williams fitted. He decided to fall in with Nathan's casual-sounding conversation. If Nathan wanted to move forward by going sideways, like an Arab trader, he would follow.

"Where are all the famous harem dancing girls?"

"The Moslem authorities here won't permit dancing girls. Morocco is the strictest of the North African countries, so in places like this they have boys who act like girls instead."

"Before Maia canceled her Bastille Day party in Paris she said she had dancing girls coming. Weren't they Moroccan?"

"Technically, no. They're from the east, inland hill and desert country, Kabyle, Berber country. Maia's home ground. Berber girls are not usually veiled, and the best dancers are the Ouled Naïls, from places like Ghardaïa. They set up oasis camps for the Chaamba, the camel drivers, at caravan crossroads."

"They sound like the dollar-a-dance girls in California saloons during the old gold-rush days."

"Not exactly. These dancers are not whores, not in the European Christian sense. They're more in the ancient pagan Mediterranean tradition, the cult of holy prostitution. The girls are raised in it, and there is no stigma. It is vaguely like the Indian temple dancers, not quite like geisha girls. Benari can tell you all about it."

"You know a good deal about North Africa, too, don't you?"

Nathan shrugged. "My family has been here for some time. Most of them are buried in the Israelite cemetery in the center of Tangier. We don't boast, like Benari, of two thousand years. We've been here only since 1492."

"In America we teach the kids that's when Columbus discovered the New World."

"Here, among the Israelites, we teach them that was the year we were driven out of Spain by the Inquisition. My family fled from

Toledo with only the clothes on their backs." He smiled faintly at Mac's expression and held up one hand briefly. "Stop. Don't let all the antiquity choke you. You're in a different world completely, even with all the modern trimmings. I've heard our American clients say in the bank: Stop, look, and listen. Slow down and let things happen."

"Monsieur, is your idea of slowing down our flying visit to the American Legation this morning?"

"Ah. That's different, Doctor." He raised three fingers. "One, it is courteous for you to call on your own people, not so?"

"Yes. Of course." But, Mac thought quickly, why the hurry?

"Two, and this should appeal to your practical side, your Legation must affirm your professional status so that we can ask the Service d'Hygiène to license you to practice surgery in Tangier. Three, I find it amusing to visit the local headquarters of American diplomacy inside what used to be a house of pleasure."

"And after lunch," Mac said, "we have an appointment with the Director of the Service d'Hygiène?"

"Yes," Nathan said. "Then to the Club Diplomatique to join Maia and Benari for the polo practice."

"And Benari has asked me to slow down, too. By playing polo, even though I explained I'm as rusty as an old iron hinge."

"No matter. A little exercise. My son Joseph will be on the practice team with you. Your only purpose is to warm up our first team for their match with the Egyptians tomorrow."

Mac poured a long drink of his iced Moroccan spring water, the bottled Karrouba, thinking all this over. He put his glass down. The time had come to make a few things clear, Mac thought. "You must be a very successful banker," he said. "So persuasive."

Nathan raised his eyebrows slightly, but his thin bony face did not show any other expression.

Mac held up three fingers. "One," he said, imitating Nathan's tone, "you tell me to slow down in a slow country. Two, you keep me very busy. Three, I find it amusing that nobody has even mentioned Roger Obenpharo."

"Ah. Yes." Nathan's eyes swiveled away, and he motioned to the waiter for the bill. "Shall we go? They'll be waiting for us at the Service d'Hygiène."

419

Tangier's health department, the Service d'Hygiène, was in a narrow sloping street in the Moorish quarter, the Medina. Nathan had to park his car at the base of the Kasbah, the great crumbling fortress walls, and he and Mac entered the Medina through the Tannery Gate.

At the Service d'Hygiène a young Spanish health department official in a white laboratory coat was waiting for them. He seemed excited, and could hardly wait to begin talking very quickly in Spanish as soon as Nathan had finished introducing Mac. Nathan answered in Spanish. It went back and forth, a dialogue between instruments in a musical tongue, the official's violin pizzicato, and Nathan's slow dignified cello.

"Señor the sanitation engineer of the health department says," Nathan explained, "that a health matter of the utmost gravity has unfortunately called away the Director to the administration headquarters. Many regrets are expressed."

"Is this," Mac said in English, beginning to feel manipulated, as he had with Nathan at the restaurant, "is this what the Spanish call the moment of truth?"

"Yes, so to speak. It sounds actually serious."

The Spanish sanitation engineer began to speak very rapidly, using his hands now, sounding anxious to be convincing.

"He says," Nathan translated, "that he regrets greatly if you will take offense. He asks if you are willing to come see the problem for yourself. Perhaps you can help."

"The situation calls for a co-operative yes answer, don't you think?"

Nathan nodded. "I would advise so. There is your license still to be approved."

"What does he want me to do?"

"He asks, have you done medical work in the field of—I don't know the English word—"

"Bacteriology? Public Health?"

Nathan talked back and forth with the Spanish sanitation engineer, then said, "Can you do a scientific cutting up and analysis of the human body?"

"An autopsy?"

"*Sí, sí,*" the Spanish engineer said. "Autopsy."

"Tell him," Mac said, "I'm not a pathologist—"

420

"*Sí, sí,*" the Spanish engineer broke in. "Pat'ologist."

Mac shook his head and tried French. "*Chirurgien.* Surgeon."

"Ah," the Spaniard said, then added something.

"Señor the engineer says he will be grateful for your surgical help. His training is only in public health sanitation work and not in—what did you call the cutting up—?"

"Autopsy."

"Yes. He asks us to follow him."

They went through several laboratories. None of the technicians handling the scientific glassware and microscopes turned around; all of them seemed too quiet and too busy. They reached a small back room in which the bodies of two men were stretched out stiffly on stone autopsy tables. One of them was being dissected by a man who wore not only a gown and rubber gloves, like any pathologist doing an autopsy, but also a cap and mask, like a surgeon taking sterile precautions during surgery on a living body. The gowned man turned when they came in and nodded to Nathan.

"Hello, Nathan. What brings you to this bloody little pesthole?"

Nathan peered at him. "Alec? I didn't recognize you under all that. This is Dr. Adams. Dr. Alec Moore."

"Moore with an *e* on it," the doctor said. "How do you do, Dr. Adams. Don't dare shake hands in all this muck."

British, Mac thought, and relaxed. Not one of the cool remote ones.

"Have they sucked you in, too?" Dr. Moore asked him. "I haven't done a proper autopsy since the good Lord only knows when, and now there's this emergency call from the Service d'Hygiène for doctors and deadhouse surgery."

The Spanish engineer called into one of the neighboring laboratories, and, after a moment, an assistant came in with several sterile cotton-plugged bacteriology culture tubes. Dr. Moore said, "Here we go," and began to heat a metal spatula in a Bunsen burner flame.

Mac noticed that he was swift and skillful. He might even be a pathologist, despite the remark about not doing autopsies. One never knew with the British, he thought, because they are raised to underplay everything, even their exaggerations.

"What's that for?" Nathan asked Dr. Moore. "Looks ghastly."

421

"I'm just sterilizing the skin," the British doctor said as he pressed the heated spatula over a swelling in the groin of the corpse. The sizzling hiss and smell of burned flesh spread in the room. Dr. Moore talked as he worked deftly. "This sterile hypodermic needle goes through the skin to get a blood sample from inside the swelling, the bubo. This bright-eyed lad at my side will grow the sample on culture media so they can find out what kind of germs were inside that swelling."

The Spanish engineer gave them gowns, gloves, caps, and masks. While they were getting into the protective clothing, Nathan said quietly, "This is very interesting. I mean his bringing us in here, and asking you to help dissect. With the Director gone in a hurry, something big must be bothering them."

Mac began to lay the cap and mask aside; after all, the cadaver hardly required precautions against surgical wound infection, and beneath all the excited talk everything seemed a bit casual.

"No, no no!" the Spanish engineer said, shaking his head and motioning him to put on the cap and gloves. He pointed to the lemon-size swelling in the groin of the first cadaver. "Bubo." He turned and explained in Spanish to Nathan.

"He says we will please wear caps and masks," Nathan translated. "The first corpse was a friend of the second. He thinks the first that Dr. Moore is dissecting had some kind of disease which is dangerous and they wish to know if the second died of a communication of the same disease."

Beside them, the Spanish official was putting on a surgical gown. The lab assistant walked out with the discolored blood samples. Dr. Moore straightened above his autopsy table and looked over his shoulder at Mac.

"If the first had a bubo in his groin—" Mac began to say, questioningly.

Dr. Moore interrupted. "Smell a rat, Doctor? This sudden health department enthusiasm for full dress autopsies? And all the fancy lab work?"

Mac suddenly remembered having met Eve in the office of Dr. Allenby in Paris, and having seen the map of North Africa with color pins pointing to a disease focus around Casablanca. "Ask him," Mac said to Nathan, "if the first death is due to bubonic plague."

Above the level of his mask, Nathan's eyes looked as if he had been struck. Dr. Moore said nothing.

"Ask him," Mac said. "I doubt that he'll be sure until the lab work and blood samples show the bacillus, but I'll bet he's willing to guess."

Nathan turned stiffly. He waited until the Spanish official finished forcing his hands in the rubber surgical gloves and had put on cap and mask, then he said softly and questioningly in Spanish, "The plague?"

Mac expected another rush of language, but the Spanish official looked back and forth between him and Nathan, then shrugged a little and said in Spanish, "I think so."

An hour later they left the health department with many expressions of mutual thanks and esteem. Mac had his license to practice medicine in Tangier, and the Spaniard had a neatly dissected autopsy completed before the unrefrigerated cadavers became noisome.

Dr. Alec Moore looked as bulky in his tropical suit as he had in his surgical gown, a rumpled casual-sounding man. "Knew there was something off-color right off," he said. "Dr. Hamana—he's the Director of Service d'Hygiène—doesn't call every day for the fine art of autopsy."

"Are you a pathologist?" Mac asked.

Both Moore and Nathan smiled. "Shall I tell him?" Moore asked Nathan, and turned to Mac. "I'm the Obenpharos' family doctor here. My esteemed colleague and stuffed shirt, Dr. Carre, don't glower at me Nathan you old goat because he damn well is stuffy, he takes care of them in Paris. I was in on the plot to shanghai you into coming to Tangier." He laughed. "Don't look so surprised, Dr. Adams. They'd heard you were in Paris, and the old man wanted to know what medical channels to follow in looking you up in the States and asked my advice." He clapped Nathan on the back. "Cheer up and confess to the man, Nathan!"

"Well," Mac said, "here I am."

"Damn poor timing, too, I'd say. This plague muck. They'll try to hush it up. Scare off the tourist trade, and close the bloody banks, you know. Mustn't have any of that."

"Two cases—if they're proven—hardly make a real problem."

"Wish I shared your optimism. Didn't one of your cities—New

423

York, was it?—vaccinate half a million people after a smallpox case arrived from Mexico? The real reason Dr. Hamana wasn't there to greet you is because he's up at the Administrator's office right now to ask for World Health Organization assistance."

"Our beloved brilliant Administrator," Nathan said. "See nothing, say nothing, do nothing. A political genius."

"That's the word," Moore said. "And they'll boot this beloved little problem up to the Committee of Control. And the rules of said beloved Committee require unanimous agreement among all the member nations before action occurs. Did you ever see nine nations agree on anything?"

"Are you saying nothing will happen?"

"Don't be blunt, Doctor. Graceful or poetic or any damn thing, but don't be blunt in Morocco."

"Oh no," Mac said, stopping in the middle of the narrow street. "Let's be blunt. Your cadaver had buboes—"

"Right. Both sides of the groin. Necrotic as hell."

"Mine didn't. But mine may have had plague without bubo formation."

"Bluntly," Moore said, "he may have the septicemic or pneumonic form of plague. The damn *Bacillus pestis* kills them so fast, the swellings never have time to become visible buboes."

"Alec," Nathan said, "are you threatening us with an epidemic?"

Moore snorted. "I'm not. The good Lord is. Roger Obenpharo's friends and followers have disorganized the whole country, and that includes health department services. Plague thrives on uncollected garbage, because rats do. The rats carry the bug and die, and their bloody little fleas hop onto people and pass along the plague." He ran his hand over the top of his head, looking at Nathan. "If that second mucker had plague in his lungs, we've had it. The pneumonic form travels from person to person like a common cold." He grinned at Mac. "Bad timing, Doctor. Saw plague in Dakar in '44. Terrible stuff. Well, I'm off to L'Institut Pasteur to see if I can beg, borrow, or steal some vaccine against the bloody disease for my patients."

"Can't you stop for a drink?"

"Wish I could. Too many house calls I'm late for, including the good Madame Mutirra Obenpharo. Like to discuss her case with you,

424

Doctor. Problem of diuretics. Fresh viewpoint always helps."

"Any time," Mac said.

"And let me show you my clinic. Nice little surgery. You'll be using it to work on Roger, y'know." Dr. Moore turned to Nathan. *"Salaam aleikum,"* he said, and turned off into a side street waving his hand cheerfully.

Nathan said nothing while he and Mac continued to walk through the noisy alley-streets and down the worn stone steps through the old fortress gate of the walled Medina. After Moore's macabre cheerfulness was gone, they did not discuss the plague. As they got into his small British car, Nathan said, "We have some time before the polo. Would you like to see something interesting?"

This tourist guide efficiency is becoming tiresome, Mac thought. "Well," he said, "maybe we ought to get to the polo so that I can try on the gear and see the pony Obenpharo has for me—"

"Ah, my son Joseph will do all that. He's your size, or one of the others will be. Joseph is there now, getting everything ready for you."

"He must be almost as successful a banker as you, Monsieur Nathan."

"He's a good son."

"I envy you," Mac said.

"Soon you'll have Henri. The boy has sensitivity, intelligence, control. I'll envy you, Doctor."

"Many thanks."

"Do you mind if I speak frankly, Doctor?"

"Please," Mac said. This should be interesting.

"Did I detect a critical note a moment ago, Doctor? That remark about successful sons?"

"No. Admiration. You and Joseph are so organized. You're surrounding me with activity, and I wonder why."

Nathan started the engine of the car. "May I," he said, "wait until we see Obenpharo after the polo to explain?"

"Sure," Mac said in English. "I mean, yes."

Nathan drove along the base of the towering fortress walls toward the center of Tangier. He stopped the car at a group of wooden shacks, and unfolded his long legs out from under the steering wheel. A half-dozen Arab youngsters came running out of one shack like

425

scrawny puppies. Nathan gave them all peseta coins and appointed senior and junior watchmen for the car. In English he said to Mac, "They've learned to dislike us from their fathers. Since the political independence troubles, they have become tough. If you don't pay this blackmail, you come back and find your tires slashed."

"Isn't that the system the Arab countries with oil use on European pipelines?"

"Exactly the same." Nathan said nothing more until they walked on. "This way, Doctor." They walked through the open iron gates of a sloping downhill cemetery. Very few gravestones stood erectly. Most were oblong stone or marble set into the grass, like oversize tile steppingstones. A rim of thin cypress and pine trees stood at the far edge, tilted sideways from the constant inshore wind coming from the Bay of Tangier at the foot of the steep hill.

Nathan swept his hand in a small half circle over the gravestones. "All of them," he said, "my family, or relatives. The little stones are the children. From childhood on, I have been here more than a hundred times." He looked sharply at Mac. "Are you thinking that I am odd?"

"No, not at all. At my home in America—I mean, my former home —we had a family cemetery in a meadow some distance from our house. It went back before the American Revolutionary War, but it wasn't as big as this."

"Your family did not have the ghetto and the intermarriage." Nathan stopped before a row of tombstones set close together, and read off the Hebrew inscriptions in translation. "Yamila, Shalom, Ysaac, Salomon, Mesodi, Shemaya, Judah. All of one family. You notice the inscription is in Spanish?" He read it sonorously, accomplishing something for himself with this little singsong ritual which Mac could only guess at. *"Y Jehova velerá por ti siempre en las sequias hartará tu alma y enfortescerá tus huesos y serás como huerta de riego, como manadero de aguas que nunca faltan."* He stood silently when he finished.

Mac said nothing. He had not understood a word of the Spanish, other than Jehova, but he understood that Nathan was doing something subtle, with meanings within meanings. Family, he thought. The Hebrew secret of survival. The secret my Old Testament grandfather's fathers knew.

426

Nathan spoke suddenly. "Have you ever noticed the unusual gold ring Benari wears?"

"No."

"He didn't tell you the story?"

"No."

"His father got the ring from his father, and so on, far back. Some years ago several Italian archeologists were digging around Thymakerion, a very very old buried Phoenician village founded by Hanno before Roman rule, and they found the skeleton of a tall man embracing that of a woman. On his finger was a ring just like Benari's."

"I see." He did not see. Just follow his lead, Mac thought. Don't interrupt him. He'll come to the point later, if not sooner. Apparently this is a country where you move forward by going in circles.

"*Alors,*" Nathan said, "we must not be late for the polo. The practice team is counting on you."

They walked back between the stones which lay half buried in the ground, back to the iron gate. Nathan gravely inspected his car, then paid additional peseta coins to the entire circle of children. There was no exchange of smiles or thanks. It was a business transaction.

As they drove off, Nathan nodded over his shoulder toward the ancient cemetery. "That whole family, so close together. The year my great-great-grandfather was Consul-General of Tangier there was an epidemic of plague. They all died within a week of one another."

The white polo ball went rolling diagonally across his pony's path with just enough speed and hop to it to make a proper stroke very difficult. His smart pony swung nimbly, hoofs of the opposing team pounded nearby as he lifted his mallet and shifted far over in the saddle for the awkward backhanded off-angle swing. A confused shouting around him. *Ride it, man! It's yours!* Then, as he brought his arm swinging down for the stroke, the sudden clatter of hooked sticks and pain nailed his shoulder back so hard that he tore at his reins to keep from falling. Whoever had fouled his stroke had done it thoroughly.

The big alarm clock on the sidelines rang tinnily. The Arab timekeeper immediately pulled the rope handle of the brass bell, and the chukker ended. Three down, one more chukker to go.

Mac straightened sweatily in his saddle and looked around to see who had hooked his mallet so hard. His shoulder ached. Jeanjean rode toward him out of a bunched group of his team-mates, a picture postcard polo player in a blue jersey and cream poplin jodphurs on a deep-chested beautiful pony. All during the third chukker of the practice match Mac had watched Jeanjean's fluid horsemanship that was all invisible skill and smooth handling, no rein-pumping, no giddy-yapping knees and legs. Jeanjean had been Mac's opposing number one, and had neatly beaten him every single time Obenpharo, the umpire, had thrown in the ball.

Now there was an exaggerated look of apology on Jeanjean's face, but in the shadow of the rim of his helmet his eyes were narrowed. "Very sorry about that," he said in French to Mac. "My pony. Very bad behavior."

Joseph, Nathan's son, rode up angrily. He was captain of the scratch team on which Mac was playing. "You fouled him, Rasa," he said intensely to Jeanjean, without raising his voice. "You reached across his pony."

"Balls, Joseph. I just apologized."

"Save the dirty tricks for the Egyptian match tomorrow. We all know the doctor hasn't played in years." He turned in his saddle to Mac. "Want to stay in for the last chukker?"

"Of course." He ached all over as they dismounted and began to follow the other players toward the grouped stableboys who held their fresh ponies. He felt the tap of memory, remembering playing on Porter Bradford's team at Westbury years ago before the usual Long Island crowd. Damn few aches in those, because they were all young and immortal. Now the too-tight jersey shirt Joseph had loaned him was sweated through, and he knew the pain in his shoulder would be worse later.

It would be only sensible to stop now, except that Maia was sitting on the rail at the sidelines with all the other spectators, with Obenpharo nearby on a handsome Palomino and looking as aloof as an umpire should. Mac knew that, for Obenpharo and Maia, he was obliquely on display before their Tangier friends, a kind of athletic debut. Somehow there was the need for him to be slightly larger than life, like the college athlete in the Big Game with his girl friend visit-

428

ing in the stands, yet he only felt ridiculous and hot and foolish and furious enough to want to punch Jeanjean in the face. It's a boy's game, he thought, and I'm acting like a boy. Take it easy. No childish performances. He did not look toward Maia. Obenpharo had ridden to the sidelines, mid-field, to lean down from his horse to speak with the timekeeper.

"How's your shoulder?" Joseph said, walking beside him. "I see you rub it."

Mac dropped his hand. "A little pull." His head was drumming with heat and fatigue and anger and annoyance with himself. I should be among the spectators, he thought. Sitting next to Maia, cool, with a long drink, enjoying the good shots. This game is like long-distance swimming or competition tennis. You don't just pick up where you left off years ago, and you should have had the plain common horse sense not to have tried. What gave you the boyish idea that Maia would applaud a muscular performance like this? Why don't you save your heroic displays for the operating room, where you've had some practice and know your way around?

"It will help," Joseph said, in step beside him, "if you can finish the last chukker. Our only substitute has a pulled tendon."

So have I, Mac thought. "I'll finish," he said.

"Watch Rasa. He's really champion caliber, and you see how he loves to play the big vegetable."

"I'll watch him."

"I notice your mallet is too short for your size. In English measuring, the length is only"—Joseph did the arithmetic in his head—"fifty-one inches."

"Good enough. Don't worry about me."

"Want me to take number one?" Joseph asked politely. "I have more practice, and I think I can handle Rasa for the last chukker."

"Thanks. It's not necessary."

They changed ponies and rode onto the field into their positions as Obenpharo took the umpire's post. He held the ball, ready for the underhand toss between the opposing players. Mac saw Jeanjean's eyes rake him across the distance between them, and he tensed in his saddle, focusing completely on the ball as if it had real importance.

429

The toss. He broke fast and caught the ball a split second before Jeanjean, passing it to Joseph and hearing a faint cheer from the spectators. The underdog, he realized as the ground raced by, it's always the underdog they cheer. An opposing back in a blue jersey crossed and swung, capturing the ball and passing it neatly with a forehand cut to Jeanjean, who smacked it goalward, pounded toward it, tapped it in a short dribble to line it up—*now! ride him off now!* His team-mates shouted at him. *Go to him!*—and Mac pounded in at a quarter angle and broke Jeanjean's drive. Jeanjean's face swung, brown and surprised, then his white teeth showed in a wide grin. The joy of combat.

The blue-jerseyed players on Jeanjean's side spread skillfully. A fellow from the British West Africa Bank in a white jersey, Mac's own team, had luckily taken the ball, tap-tapping it up the field. Joseph's scratch team was putting up a good fight now, a few of the spectators were standing and applauding as a very nice forehand drive by number two on Mac's side put the ball into the blue goal. The teams changed ends, and now Joseph's white-jerseyed team half faced the late afternoon sun. They were excited now, giving the first team some real competition, and they kept calling encouraging instructions back and forth.

Time became a gallop, shouting, pounding down the field while the crows sailed overhead and rose in the hilltop updraft over the sainted Moslem tomb nearby, and several of the stableboys squatted to watch the game which had suddenly become a match.

Joseph's team felt the invisible underdog thrust toward victory, and the blue jerseys with Jeanjean began to fight for their honor as the first team. "One more goal!" Joseph shouted. "Let's beat them!"

The sun stopped, time stopped, there was no sweat-drenched thirst, no aching arm, the pony became part of him now, only the sidelines racing past him, the ball rolling and bouncing across the center of the field. He had it now, *turn on it!*, swing left?—no, right, pass to Joseph with a nearside backshot?—no, take it, that's it, take it, *watch it now!* down the field, offside fore shot, crack it again, shouting all around him, the goal lined up at an angle, easy does it, ready for the scoring smack. . . .

A darkness and bright spots rolled past him, and his head and neck hurt. The ground had come up and hit him like concrete. Arms were helping him up off the grass. He stood swaying, with the tape sling of the mallet still looped around his wrist. Jeanjean was walking toward him through a blur of voices with that same incredible smile, as if to help support him, saying, "Sorry. Sorry. Didn't mean to ride you off so hard." Without thinking, Mac pulled the loop off his wrist and swung his fist as hard as he could in Jeanjean's face. Jeanjean fell sprawling, there was a tangle of restraining arms and hands clutching him, then Jeanjean was up, snarling now, and Mac hit him again. He tried to go after him, but both teams were dismounted and had them apart now while Jeanjean thrashed around, and Mac heard himself saying oddly in English, "Okay. Okay. Let go. I'll stop. Let go."

The lightheaded washed-clear joyful simplicity of fighting. It was as if he had always wanted to do exactly this, from far back in his intelligent courteous boyhood, and at last the time had come.

(4)

THE Old Mountain Road twisted and dropped downhill toward the city beneath their small two-seater car. Maia drove expertly between the scrub cactus and high walls of the estates bordering the road, skillfully swinging past overloaded donkeys and barefoot children. At the bottom of the hill they sped through a group of hovels called Drideb, Suicide Village, because of the number of accidents there. Nothing had ever been done about them because, *insha' Allah,* what was the use? Outside the scabby little café, a radio speech was screeching loudly to a group of Riffs and city Arabs squatting in the doorway. They watched impassively as Maia and Mac drove by, as if there were no one passing, only a movement of air. The radio harangue was punctuated with roaring crowd responses, like the *Sieg Heils* during Hitler's passionate speeches of another time.

Maia nodded toward the hoarsely shouting sound of the radio. "Cairo propaganda. They can't read, so they listen all day. Drive out the bloodsucking colonial powers. So on, and so on." She turned a corner expertly, but too fast.

431

"Would you like me to drive?"

"No. I feel a little tense, and I like to drive. I promised Henri I'd come back as soon as I dropped you off at the bank."

"Going riding?"

"No. It's too hot. We're going swimming at that little beach at the bottom of the cliff. Henri wants to try out that underwater snorkel equipment you brought him." She looked sideways at him. "When you finish seeing Papa, come down and join us, Mac."

"I'll try. I promised Alec Moore to review Muttirra's case with him this afternoon."

"Irra adores you, did you know? You're the strong stranger on the white horse, solving all our family problems. Her health, and Papa's. And Henri is changing for the better."

"And Roger," he said, because he was on his way to see Benari Obenpharo about Roger, because he wanted to stop the constant evasion about Roger. "Let's not forget that particular family problem."

"And me. You're even taking me off their hands." She drove the car to the side of the road and stopped. They were in the Marshan area now, with modern apartments all around them and a partly constructed new church across the street without a single workman in sight.

"Stopping?" he said, as she shut off the engine. "I'll be late for my appointment with Benari."

"That's what I want to talk about, Mac. This efficiency. Something is changing in you. This week you began those very nice clay figures of Henri and his animals, but you're going at it so hard. Today, you call up Benari and insist on an appointment. Why are you pushing yourself and him so hard?"

"I never see Benari at home, Maia. I think he's avoiding me. I think he's avoiding any mention of Roger."

She shrugged. "Perhaps so. Let him. Also, I think maybe you're a little angry with me since the polo last week."

"No, no," he lied. "Forgot all about it."

"But you haven't, darling. I'm sorry I sounded so annoyed with you—"

"—Maia, don't be the little loyal girl friend. You disagreed and you said so—"

432

"—Mac, you must admit you behaved badly—"

"Hell's bells!" he said in English, then, "I don't see that, Maia. Jeanjean kept fouling me, so I hit him."

"—but this is Morocco, darling, not the U.S.A. You know as well as I do, a gentleman doesn't hit people in the face."

"Alec Moore told me last week: Be graceful, be anything, but don't be blunt."

She ignored the sarcasm. "Exactly. Beat him at polo, or driving, or cards, or fencing—"

"Damn it, I don't play those games that well!"

"You see how it looked to everyone else. You are the cowboy American with the fists, he is the better performer at games, so you choose unfair weapons he does not have: the fists. Even Benari thought you made a mistake. At the Carnivale they invented a calypso song about your fight."

"To hell with Benari and the Carnivale crowd. Only you count. Maybe you made the right diagnosis." He looked at her. "Jeanjean is a better performer."

Her face changed. She looked away, then back, and when she saw him still watching her intensely, she looked away again. "We were talking about the hitting. Do we have to talk about this?"

"Sooner or later."

She turned back. "Yes. Maybe that's why I stopped without realizing. I think all this week I wanted to talk to you. Even in bed you were different."

"Shall we analyze it? Chemically, biologically—"

"Ah, Mac, Mac, look at us, look what's happened to us. First you were the thinker, only I had the quick feelings. Now you do what you feel, and I'm the one who thinks and thinks until I have a headache." She put her hand over his. "Do you think I need a doctor?"

"Maia, do we talk about this or don't we?"

"Mac, you turn away from unpleasantness all the time—"

"The hell I do!"

"You do, you do, but you don't know it. Why shouldn't I? You convinced me in Paris, you showed the beginning of a new way to live. We were both going to drop everthing in the past. *Finito*." Then she added quickly, when he snapped his fingers and made a throwing-away gesture, "Yes, just like that. Throw the past away."

She leaned toward him intensely. "Or are you still so unsure of yourself that you fear him?" When she saw his hands clench and his knuckles whiten, she leaned back. "The hands again? Everything with the hands? The sculpture and the surgery and the hitting?"

His mouth was so dry he could hardly speak. Two Spanish girls in dark convent smocks and ribboned pigtails rode by on bicycles with small briefcases strapped to their handlebars. He waited until they passed, and said, "I never thought I could be so angry with you."

"Enough to hit?"

"Not to do it, but to feel it."

"Maybe to do it would be better for us both. The new Mediterranean man and his Berber girl."

"Jesus, let's not go over that again!"

"Why not? I have been hit before. By the English painter I lived with when I was twelve. By Jeanjean. Now your turn." She spoke harshly, with tears beginning to shine in her eyes. "You were the new beginning. A new beginning. But no, you have to carry all this anger inside like a jealous boy, and hit people in front of half of Tangier society."

"Muck Tangier society!"

"You could have stayed in Paris. Life was so much simpler on your houseboat."

"Damn right. And I know all the rest. That you wanted to come here alone. That I insisted on coming—"

"So you came. Alec Moore told Mutirra you did beautiful surgery yesterday in his clinic on a tumor in an old man's face. Beautiful delicate work. Your hand did not shake, did it?"

"No. It was a very good job, for the patient and for me."

She spoke quickly, trying to make a point. "And your gold statue sitting in the garden, isn't that good to see? At last you have two kinds of work you love, with steady hands in both. Work, play, and love, you tell me, and now you have all three. Then why the anger inside?"

He took his cigarettes out and lighted two and gave her one. Over her shoulder, in the delivery driveway of an apartment house he saw a man stop to unbutton his trousers and urinate on a wall bearing a printed sign: DEFENSE DE URINER. A white-helmeted motorcycle policeman rode by slowly, rubbing the sweat from his face. The little daily biologies of the world, minute mockery of private pain.

Gently now, without the harshness, Maia said, "Actually, darling, Jeanjean is a first-class sportsman. He does everything well, with a style that nobody except bullfighters and actors have any more. You must admit that has attractions. Don't look at me like that. Even your intelligent lady doctor was attracted. I can understand why men all dislike him. But you, you're the thinking man, the balanced man—"

"But no style," he said, knowing he sounded faintly childish. "Not an actor. Not a bullfighter. No heroic playing at dangerous games because I have no romantic notions about death. I've seen too much of it, and it's ugly."

"Mac," she said, "five years ago I would not see in you what I do now. No acting style on the outside, but inside: the man, the feeling and the thoughtfulness, the good sculptor and surgeon, the affection for a lonely boy with no father."

She said it very simply and he felt deeply moved. She had been wise to stop. This was their first big fight, one which had to come.

"Look," he said, "let's have one thing clear. Don't make me too simple. I admit the part you say. I acted like a jealous stupid kid, and I'm sorry. I'll even apologize to the handsome slob. But there's more," He motioned toward the world around them. "It's the vagueness of everything. It's the Mexican *mañana* and Italian *dolce far niente* multiplied by a thousand. I used to believe: Think first, then act. Then, with you in Paris I changed to: Act as you feel, think later. As you say, the Mediterranean man. Well, that doesn't work either."

"Something in between, darling. You'll strike the balance. We both will. But first we must trust each other."

They looked deeply at one another, then leaned forward and touched lips lightly. She closed her eyes.

"Where did I ever find you?" he said quietly.

"Your gift from the gods, darling. Don't ask too many questions." She flipped her cigarette into the street and turned the ignition key.

He put one hand on her shoulder, then slid it up until the curve of his palm rested on the nape of her neck, where the little curls were and the skin was warm. The tender, sensory bridge across which they

435

joined one another, the fragile pathway from the island of oneself to the world, the gift from the gods. She's right, he thought, as Maia aimed the small car toward the Boulevard Pasteur: don't ask too many questions.

Obenpharo sat stiffly behind the great desk in his glassed-in penthouse office, searching through his Moroccan leather cigar box for the precise cigar he wanted. It was a little ritual of delay he had used so many times he no longer realized he did it. When there was a question he could not answer, the cigar box and the choice of the cigar and the removal of the wrapper and the tip-cutting and tip-wetting and cigar rotation during a prolonged lighting and the early deep puffs, all gave him one of the few commodities he could not buy: time. An American lawyer had once told him that time always worked for the defendant, and at the moment, with Mac sitting across the room and Maia standing there looking down at the harbor, he felt faintly defensive.

"All right," he said, "I admit it. To ask you to come here for plastic surgery and then to ignore the matter must seem very contradictory."

"I'm ready to begin," Mac said. "The sooner the better, because I'd like to go back to Paris with Maia." They exchanged glances, weighing the idea. Obenpharo looked at Maia, but she did not turn around. "Alec Moore has a good clinic here," Mac went on. "He's invited me to use all his facilities. Tomorrow, or any time."

"I know, I know," Obenpharo said. "I'm paying him to do just that. The only thing I don't know is, where is Roger?"

Mac leaned forward abruptly. "Do you mean you don't *know*?" Now the delays and the feeling of evasiveness he had sensed became clearer.

Maia turned into the room from the glass wall. "I have to run off to pick up Henri," she said, moving toward the elevator.

"Don't go," Obenpharo said. "This concerns you, too. It's become a family matter, now that Mac is coming into the Obenpharo family. We're all involved."

Maia stopped. "This is one time I must contradict you, Papa. This time I'll be a Swiss banker, a stubborn neutral."

"Impossible," Obenpharo growled. "Roger's political storm is pouring in the streets. We'll all get wet."

"Not me, Papa. I can't live being torn in so many directions. I'll work for you in Paris, if Mac is willing and because I like it, but I agree with Mac. Back to Paris, for both of us, and Henri."

Obenpharo's eyes were invisible now in his great stone face, with cigar smoke rising before it.

"Maia means," Mac said, "that you wanted surgery, so I came—"

"—for other reasons."

"Admitted, Benari. For other reasons. But here I am. I want to start the surgery, then take Maia and Henri back to Paris. I can fly down every few weeks, and count on Dr. Moore's clinic to handle the nursing care for Roger."

Obenpharo clenched the fist with the cigar jutting out of it and set it on the desk like a weight. "So. How to find the location of Roger."

"You must have sources, Benari. You have a hundred strings."

"And I've pulled every one since the day you arrived. The Istiqlal party is close to success. The whole illusion of independence in a country with no money, no technology. Moroccans are jumping on their bandwagon. The French leaders had called a sort of *syndicat des anciens* at Aix-le-Bain this week to debate the return of the Sultan. They've even invited me to join—because they believe I can deliver Roger into their arms. And you want me to deliver him to you. The simple truth is that I cannot do either."

"Have you asked Nathan to pass along the word, Papa? He knows everybody in the Medina, every little alley. Someone will tell him where Roger is."

"No. The terror branch of the Istiqlal would happily cut his throat if they believed he learned Roger's location. Nathan has a bank to run and a family to raise in Tangier, no Paris house to run off to. Let's not involve Nathan."

"Benari," Mac said, "you just said we're all involved. We'll all get wet. Let Nathan decide for himself."

"Would you ask a friend you knew since childhood to risk his life? If the hoodlums in the Party thought Nathan knew nothing, but needed a warning, they might kill his son Joseph, or Joseph's wife. Your Western mind has no idea of the cruelty under the surface beauties of this civilization. I have seen young men in a café tie a dog's legs, and while it is still alive skin it."

"One way or another," Mac said, "everyone of us has his life in

437

this. Will they skin me alive if something wrong happens to Roger during the first operation, or the second, or the third?"

"Ask Nathan, Papa," Maia said. "All you have to do is call downstairs and ask him."

"Ah, the Swiss banker, the neutral. I thought you disliked Nathan."

"Only because he dislikes me. I know what he thinks—I'm an Arab tart. But he's honest and intelligent and I respect him."

"Do you want me to ask him?" Mac said. "I respect him as much as Maia, but I happen to like him."

"Do I look so old," Obenpharo growled, "that I can't do my own deciding? Ask him or not, I'll decide."

Maia smiled at Mac. "When he quarrels with you like this, you're really in the family." She pressed the elevator button. A moment later the doors opened and she stepped into the elevator. As the doors began to close, she raised both hands lightly to her lips and threw a small kiss to each of them, but her face was very serious.

The room was changed after Maia left. There was an echo, a vacancy.

Obenpharo sat back in his leather chair smoking his long cigar slowly. "Do you think," he said after a moment, "I'm too paternal and possessive about Maia? What the Americans call too bossy?"

"Yes," Mac said. "But it's understandable."

"I dislike having my sins forgiven. It's so Christian. Stop being your own grandfather."

"All right, Benari. Your paternal bossiness is detestable."

"Better. We'll make an honest pagan of you, yet." He picked up one of his telephones and asked for Monsieur Nathan. Then, after a moment, he said into the phone, "Nathan? Mac is here and if you have two minutes—yes, yes—thanks." He put back the phone and got up. "In a few minutes," he said as he walked past Mac to stand where Maia had stood, near the wide green glass wall overlooking the great circle of the city and the harbor. From Mac's view, Obenpharo was in silhouette against a limitless sky, white-haired and statuesque; yet, from the faint shoulder droop and head tilt and ponderous movement, weary and defeated, Obenpharo was a warrior fighting a rear-guard action in a lost battle.

Obenpharo spoke through cigar smoke to the window. "You've talked with Dr. Moore. What's Mutirra's real condition?"

438

"Her heart muscles aren't as strong as they should be. She's been getting along on digitalis, but now she isn't responding to the drug. Alec and I are seeing her this afternoon. I'm going to suggest one or two new drugs which should help her."

"Surgery can't help?"

"Not in Mutirra's case, no."

Obenpharo puffed slowly, then said, "Did Dr. Carre in Paris tell you about me?"

"No."

Obenpharo half turned to look at him. "Coronary insufficiency, whatever that means, and early Parkinsonism, whatever that is. Hadn't you noticed?" He held his left arm forward. There was a very faint pincer movement of thumb and fingers suggestive of pill-rolling, but nothing else. "It's not quite so noticeable today," Obenpharo said. "You really didn't notice it?"

"Well," Mac said, "I had a hand tremor, on and off, myself, so I might have seen it and shut my eyes to it."

"And Roger's face," Obenpharo said. "You'll consider it a difficult surgical problem, I'm sure. To me it is one of the most terrible sights of my life."

Mac said nothing, because there was nothing to say to a man such as Obenpharo about a son such as Roger.

"And Maia," the old man said. "Trying so hard, doing so well at being a big French girl in a big city. And only wanting to be a little Berber girl with a man she can trust. And Henri, a lonely little boy rattling around a big lonely house, with an old grandfather and a bedridden grandmother, and a small menagerie for affection." He gestured with one hand. "You see? Every one of us. We all need you."

"If you're feeling tired and discouraged—" Mac began, but Obenpharo interrupted him.

"No. Now that you're here, I feel fine." He came toward Mac and put his hand on Mac's shoulder for a moment, then went to sit heavily in his chair. "There are several thousand years' difference between us, you know, but now that you're here I feel hopeful about the Obenpharos for the first time. Best of all, I didn't buy you. You came yourself."

At last, Mac thought, the wheels-within-wheels, the whole compli-

439

cated arabesque pattern of motives behind motives, is clearing into something cleaner and simpler. "Did I ever tell you, Benari," he said, "that you remind me sometimes of my grandfather?"

"The Protestant minister? Really? The Maccabean? Is that possible?"

"Yes." Mac got up and grinned. He leaned across the desk and put his hand out. "Welcome to the Adams family."

"As they say in New York," Obenpharo said, taking Mac's hand, "it's a deal. Welcome to the Obenpharo family."

The elevator doors opened and Nathan came in. " 'Allo, Mac," he said. "Shaking hands? Has Benari just sold you some Mediterranean pots and pans?"

Obenpharo swung in his chair. "Ah, the chronic disbeliever. It's the other way around, for a change. Mac just sold me a piece of the New World."

Nathan stopped midway. "And for this circus you gave me a hurry-up call?" He started back toward the elevator.

"Sit down, Nathan. Don't pretend to be so energetic. I want to ask your help about finding Roger."

Nathan came back and sat down. "That makes my day complete. Two of our biggest accounts pulled out for Geneva today," he said. "And now you with this Roger business. None of the French secret police have found him and they have a hundred informers."

"But they don't have your special sources, Nathan," Mac said.

Nathan shrugged. "He's probably in the Spanish zone, near the border. This morning Joseph told me of an Istiqlal group near Talamrhecht."

"Can you find out for sure?" Mac asked.

Nathan shrugged again. "You don't realize. This is not New York or Washington. Here there is a certain amount of risk." He ran one finger across his throat.

"Benari told me about the risk. He didn't want to ask you. The asking is my idea."

"Why? What is the hurry?"

"It seems the Moroccan independence movement looks bigger every day," Mac said. "If I don't start operating on Roger soon, how much chance is there for later?"

"Also, you would like to go back to Paris?"

"Also that, yes. Sooner, not later."

One of the desk phones rang. Obenpharo answered it, then looked up at Mac. "This is Hadj Hassani, our doorman," he said. "Dr. Alec Moore is downstairs for you in his car."

"I'll be down in a minute," Mac said.

While Obenpharo spoke into the telephone, Nathan stood up and signaled to him. Obenpharo stopped speaking and put his hand over the telephone mouthpiece. "What is it, Nathan?"

Quietly Nathan said, "Hadj Hassani? Tell him to come up here."

Obenpharo frowned. "Here? What do we need Hassani here for?"

"You know our dignified doorman who writes classical Arabic poetry is also a big Istiqlal man? A possible pipeline to Roger?"

Obenpharo's face took on the stone look Mac had seen before. "Hadj Hassani," he said evenly into the phone, "Dr. Adams will descend very soon. Ask Dr. Moore to wait. In the meantime, come into the bank and take the elevator to my office. Yes. My office. Take the elevator up. Yes. Now."

The old bent gatekeeper shuffled out of his little hut and slowly opened the tall Villa Obenpharo gates for Alec Moore's car. As they drove by him he saluted Mac as he always did Maia.

"Chaps like us," Alec Moore said, as he accelerated up the curving drive, "we're babes in the wood on this public health epidemiology stuff. The Service d'Hygiène thinks of the whole city the way you and I think of one patient. That's what the Director's meeting was about."

"If the Director called all the doctors in Tangier, why didn't he call me?"

"He did. Told me so himself. He phoned you himself. They told him you were meeting with Monsieur Obenpharo. In Tangier, that's like being with the Sultan, y'know, so he dropped it. He particularly wanted you to take the medical responsibility of the kiddos in the American School."

"Practice pediatrics?" Mac said. "In my old age? My ignorance of pediatric medicine could fill books."

"That's true of most of us, Malcolm. There isn't one really specialized pediatrician in town. But all the Director wants is your ex-

441

amining the children and then giving one shot of plague vaccine to the lot of them and their families. You simply set up a health station at the American School."

Mac visualized crowded corridors, lines of children, the bared upper arm muscle and the quick hypodermic needle, the crying. The whole assembly line of mass preventive medicine. I'll need a thousand lollipops, he thought. But where would I find them in this town? For a moment he thought of Eve in Algiers, or, more probably, Casablanca by this time. Eve would be amused to see him drafted as a public health doctor. He could hear her voice: Serves you right, you overspecialized surgeon, you. Forgotten all you ever knew about bellyaches and runny noses! High time you learned to prevent disease, instead of waiting and then trying to cure it.

"Why so quiet?" Alec Moore asked. "Afraid of a bloody plague epidemic? I know I am."

"The Director of Service d'Hygiène expects to inoculate the whole damn city?" Mac asked. "Children, adults, Moors, Spanish, French, British, Americans? Two hundred thousand people?"

"Yes indeed. L'Institut Pasteur is working night and day on the vaccine supplies, the one shot EV strain. Cabled Paris today for more. The Director asked the Administrator to request formal World Health assistance, but the bloody Committee of Control said no. Ten or fifteen deaths don't make an epidemic, they said. Things are bad now, they said, but if people are frightened by plague and there's a quarantine, it'll cost the city millions. Their pocketbook nerve registered intense pain."

"There've been ten or fifteen deaths already?" Mac was surprised.

"Ten proven plague. Saw the lab reports myself. Five cases so-so, but almost surely plague. Widespread patchy hemorrhages in their lungs."

"Sounds like pneumonic plague. That's bad."

"Bad? Terrible! Raises my hackles! Can you imagine autopsy evidence of pneumonic plague, and our administrative buddies tiptoeing away from it? By God, I told 'em at the meeting, here's a disease that kills faster than almost any other in the world. Faster than beta hemolytic strep, which is bad enough. On top of that, if we see the pneumonic type develop and spread person to person by droplet in-

442

fection"—Alec Moore paused then said—"Lord have mercy on our souls, Malcolm." He brought his car to the foot of the steps of the Villa Obenpharo, but he did not get out. "Well," he said finally, "within a day or two the Security Police are going to put a *cordon sanitaire* around the entire Medina. Half a loaf control, but it should help."

"A *cordon sanitaire?* A really tough one?"

"Damn right. The whole Moorish quarter divided into eight sections, Gueznaia, Alcazaba, Dar-el-Barud, and so on down the whole bloody list. Road blocks, fences, police, searchlights, really strict street patrols. Nobody comes, nobody goes, unless they have a health department certificate to prove they've been inoculated with plague vaccine. Is that tough enough?"

"Sounds like a big compulsory sanitation concentration camp." He wondered if there were political implications in the *cordon sanitaire* around the Medina.

"Well, the police are there, of course, but so are the health department crews at inoculation stations, and the crews to trap rats and the crews to DDT the damn little fleas. And you and I, with our charming bedside manner, being heroic in the pestilence and sweating through the inoculations."

"But police control won't block pneumonic-type plague, Alec. That's like asking them to control person-to-person spread of the common cold."

Moore smiled thinly. "Nightmare in broad daylight, eh? And those posh fat bastards refuse to call Geneva for World Health help. Wasn't it an American who said the only trouble with people was they had so much human nature?" He opened his door and jackknifed himself up out of the driver's bucket seat. "Let's go see Mutirra and her little bird friends and discuss low sodium diets and these new diuretic programs you've been suggesting." He paused on the steps and shaded his eyes against the sun. "Has she mentioned Roger to you?"

Mac remembered how Mutirra had greeted him the afternoon when he first arrived. The small figure in the wheelchair, the bravery of an old-fashioned flowery dress. Somehow that seemed very long ago. "Hardly at all," he said.

"Y'know," Alec Moore said as they went up the steps, "the ironic

443

hook in this plague business is that the filthy disease thrives on revolutions, wars, and social disorder. And if there's one item Roger and his chaps specialize in, it's disorder. You couldn't have picked a worse time to come."

"Well," Mac said, "the Obenpharos are practically my family now. Isn't trouble the traditional time the clan pulls together?"

Moore clapped him on the back. "A brave sentiment, Malcolm. You sound like a bloody Highlander, I swear." The great front doors of the villa swung open, and a servant greeted them in Arabic. Moore stepped aside and motioned for Mac to precede him through the tall doorway. "After you, sir. Age before beauty."

Maia was stretched out in the shade of the candy-striped beach umbrella Yacoub had set up, and this was where Mac found her late in the afternoon when he came down to the little beach at the foot of the cliffs. Henri was crawling on his hands and knees in shallow water near the shore, wearing his underwater snorkel equipment, only the little periscope of his air tube marking his submarine progress. Behind him, Yacoub stood bare-legged in the water, holding his loose Moslem knickers up and following Henri's periscope.

Maia sat up cross-legged when she heard Mac's beach sandals coming across the sand. They smiled at one another across the short distance as he approached, because she knew what he thought about how she looked in a Bikini bathing suit. As he ducked beneath the edge of the umbrella, she smoothed a patch of sand with her hand. "Have a chair, sir," she said.

"American poker-face jokes," he said. "I don't think they're funny," and they both laughed.

"I thought you were never coming, darling." She said it lightly, trying to wash away the tiny bitter aftertaste of their angry talk in the car.

"Alec Moore and I had to spend some time with Mutirra. Before that, the time with Benari. After that, a call to the Director of Service d'Hygiène. Then I realized it was this late."

"Service d'Hygiène? You?"

"There's a health problem in the city and I've offered to help out, with all the other doctors. And then"—he took a folded letter out of

444

the pocket of his terrycloth beach robe—"a letter just came from Warren Ross." He opened the letter and scanned it for the second time. Warren had typed three pages himself, a slam-bang letter.

"Just hello, or something special?"

"Both. Cindy Ross has begun to call us the lotus-eaters, he says. Paris is very worried about North Africa, he says, but in the meantime fifty million Frenchmen have gone on vacation."

"Of course. Philosophers. The troubles will still be waiting when they come back." She glanced at the letter. "It looks long. Anything else?"

He sensed she was not as casual as she sounded. "Here, read it."

She was too grateful for his open offer to accept it. "No," she said quickly. "I'm too sleepy and half blind from the sun. Tell me."

"Well, an American friend of mine came through Paris, a psychiatrist named Harry Scott. He was on the faculty of Yale when I was there, and he asked Warren to say hello for him."

She glanced sideways at him. "Just hello?"

"Well, he said some flattering things. How good it would be if I came back to New Haven."

"Where is that?"

"In Connecticut."

Her eyes crinkled. "Your home ground."

"Yes."

"You miss it? Feel exiled?"

"Not really. It just seems very far away."

"A year ago, if somebody in New Haven said Tangier to you—"

"I'd say: 'It seems very far away.' " He picked up a handful of sand and let it pour through the funnel of his closed hand. "They're really very close, aren't they?"

Henri suddenly appeared upright above the water to adjust the glass window of his face mask. He saw Mac and waved.

"Has Henri been underwater all this time, Maia?"

"Yes. Now he's a marine scientist. Soon his menagerie will be filled with little fishes." She put her warm hand on his arm. "The luck is, he will have a scientist who is a sculptor for a father."

"I'll buy an encyclopedia secretly," Mac said. "I'll be able to answer any question."

"American jokes," she said, smiling. "I never laugh at them."

He brushed the sand off his hands. It had been a full day: their argument, the revealing talk with Obenpharo—*I didn't buy you. You came yourself*—and Alec Moore's worry about the creeping stink of epidemic. Now the subsurface echoes in memory begun by Warren's letter. "I think I'll take a quick swim," he said.

"That's all Warren wrote?"

The breeze flapped Warren's letter over, and Mac smoothed it flat again on his knee. "There's more. An American newspaperman in Tangier, a man who worked with Warren during the war, might give me a ring. Telephone, I mean."

"Warren, Warren. Mr. Public Relations. What's this newspaperman's name?"

"Walker. Ned Walker. Know him?"

"No. Benari might. Are you interested?"

"Not at all."

She shrugged. "Warren certainly writes long letters."

"That's not all. My friend Harry Scott saw my former wife, Laura, in New York. She asked about me."

"Laura? Was that her name? You never talk about her."

"No."

"Poor Mac. A circle of women. Surrounded."

He grinned at her easily. "Only by you."

"When you look at me like that, I know it's the Bikini."

He held out his hand. "Come on in. Get your Bikini wet."

"Swim?" she asked incredulously.

He laughed out loud and got up and strolled toward the water.

Maia watched him go, thinking: We're so close, so far apart, all those people he mentioned so gently, invisible lines running from him to a world across the Atlantic, his restlessness in the slow days at the villa. He has stopped his sculpture and now he is more and more busy in medicine. I knew he should have stayed in Paris, peaceful and working on that funny little houseboat. He will keep busy here, he will help us all because his whole life has been trained for helping, but in the end he will burn quietly in exile.

She thought of her cool tiny Arab house, hidden in the Medina. I must take him there. He says I live on islands, but this is one island

446

he will love. I'll have to open up the house again and clean it completely, like a ritual, so there's no dirt anywhere, no Jeanjean, no past, only the clean future because his being there will wipe out the past, and one day I'll take him through the Medina, pretending we're shopping. He'll crouch coming through the hidden archway in the stone fortress walls, wondering where I'm taking him, and then—she smiled to herself, seeing herself opening the copper-studded door with the hand of Fatima on it and leading him into the small foyer with the open garden beyond. I'll do it soon, she decided. I'll have the house made ready from top to bottom, a religious cleansing, then surprise him. He'll enjoy it. Even in Tangier, an island of our own.

Mac walked into the water slowly. It felt cold, but pleasant, after the heated hurrying he had been doing all day. Yacoub came wading up to him and pointed toward the sky. "Monsieur," he said, "you saw it?"

Mac shaded his eyes with one hand and followed the direction of Yacoub's arm. "No," he said. "Saw what?"

"A hawk."

Mac spotted a winged dot high above the cliffs, wheeling upward to greater and greater heights. Suddenly it turned and dove, plunging down an invisible shaft of air at great speed.

"A hawk for hunting along the cliffs," Yacoub said. He lowered his arm and pointed to the far-off figure of a man on the edge of the cliff about a half mile away. "They fly them from their fists," Yacoub said. "From here, that one looks like Jeanjean Rasa. Once, he flew his hawk along here every day."

His eyes met Mac's blankly as he lowered his arm, and slid off out to sea without a change of expression.

Mac decided no comment was needed. He watched the hawk plummet earthward, vanish during an invisible strike at an invisible target, then sail upward into sight again to wheel in a tight circle and dive again. He lowered his hand from his eyes, thinking: A busy day. This and that and now the naked flesh hunt of a hawk.

He tensed his body and plunged smoothly into the cold water. Icy fire struck his heated skin, then eased into a deep healing coolness. He swam underwater through the shimmering sandy spaciousness of the shallows, watching his liquid shadow ripple silkily over the sea bottom. Suddenly a wave of heightened sensation washed through him, an overwhelming awareness of the vast elemental ocean which cradled him, the saline nirvana. As he let himself sink into the numbing silence, a euphoric illusion like the drunken ecstasy of mystics trickled through the recesses of his mind: release from human bondage lay only in completing the great circle, returning not to dust but to the dark sleep of the sea. Surrender after all the lost battles, the cut-down green elms of home, the lifeless heart of his son within his helpless hand, the half-mast flags of memory in a world drowned beyond grief.

With his last strength he stroked his arms back strongly and surfaced, gasping for raw air.

A nearby splashing, a warm hand on his chilled arm, Maia's urgent voice. "Mac! You were under so long!"

He tried to rub the sting of salt water out of his eyes and open them in the dazzling sunblaze. "Don't worry," he said, and tapped his head. "Solid cork." The bottomless sensation of the death wish was with him still, and when his vision began to focus he saw a strange expression on her face as she looked up at him. He put one arm around her, holding her strongly, holding life, warmth, laughter, struggle, and together they walked up the sloping primeval shore.

(5)

A FEW days later, after Mac had forgotten the details in Warren Ross's letter, the American newspaperman named Walker telephoned him.

"I'm staying at the Velasquez," Walker said. "How about meeting me for a drink?"

"Thanks," Mac said into the telephone, "but this particular week there's a lot of high-pressure health department work and I'm in it—"

"You mean all this scuttlebutt I've been hearing about plague is true?"

"Well, I don't know where your information came from—" Mac began when Walker interrupted again.

"Relax, Dr. Adams," he said. "You're among friends. Warren warned me you were gun-shy with reporters. I really called you about something else."

A medical problem, Mac thought. The old familiar story. "I'll be glad to help if I can," he said professionally.

"I've called to help *you*," Walker said dryly. "Do you know the doorman at Banque Obenpharo? Name of Hadj Hassani?"

A silence hummed briefly in the telephone lines between them. So Walker knew about Hadj Hassani; which of course meant he knew something about the Istiqlal connection to Roger, and the plastic surgery. Before answering Walker's question, Mac remembered the little glass telephone switchboard booth in the Velasquez lobby, the pretty dark-haired Spanish operator inside, who might or might not be listening in on the call. Tangier was a city which acted only on inside information. "Yes," he said, keeping his voice flat, "I know Hassani."

"Good. He's raised an interesting item that affects a book I'm writing, and I thought you might be interested." Walker's voice was level, too level.

"Yes, I'm interested," Mac said. The entire conversation had changed, now. "Very much. You know, you're just visiting, but I'm practically one of the Tangerois, and you're a friend of Warren Ross, so let me buy you the drink."

"You're twisting my arm, Doctor. Can we make it tonight? Nine o'clock-ish?"

"Sure. Where'd you like to go, Mr. Walker?"

"Well, d'you know the Carnivale?"

"Yes." Maia had taken him there only once, but it was the sort of place you remembered. "It might be crowded. How will I know you?"

"No need to, Doctor. I know you."

Another silence, then Mac said. "Nine o'clock. See you there."

Walker's voice said, *"Muchas gracias,* Doctor," and the phone clicked.

The Carnivale was more crowded than usual. The mirrored pillar in the center of the bar rotated, flashing little lights around the room

449

and shining on the display of women's shoes. There were very few tourists to hear Raïssa's stories about the Downward Steps and her particular version of the phallic significance of the erect glassy pillar. Everyone was very gay and drinking steadily, like a bar during an air-raid blackout during a war. Outside the Carnivale many streets were actually dimmed-out because, even in the few streets with lamp poles, the bulbs had been smashed methodically during the political excitement of the past few weeks.

Raïssa saw Mac come in and hurried toward him, weaving between the close tables. He looked at her blankly while she greeted him like a brother. "Dr. Adams! Welcome, welcome. Any friend of the Obenpharos, bless them all, is a friend of mine. I'm Raïssa, the poor working girl who runs this snake pit, you don't know me, Maia didn't introduce us last time you were here, how *is* that gorgeous creature? Abdul, Abdul," she screeched at a passing Arab boy carrying a tray of drinks, "set up a corner table for the doctor and his friend." She turned back. "Mr. Walker said to take very good care of you."

So, Mac thought, this peroxide-blonde harpy with a man's haircut is part of the arrangement. Mr. Walker was thorough. First the note from Warren Ross, undoubtedly so that Mac would know that Walker was bona fide in Tangier, where bona fides were more important than passports, and now his honored-guest-your-host-will-be-here-in-a-minute treatment. He ordered a Scotch and soda and sat down facing the room. Wealthy French and Spanish younger sons, dark-haired and on the prowl for the girls and boys who specialized in wealthy younger sons; two British couples trying hard to be wicked; some bored junior American Legation people entertaining a few Air Force colonels surrounded by the usual retinue of captains and the girls the captains had arranged for in the limited time available.

He had told Maia he was going into town just before he had left Villa Obenpharo. "This time of evening?" she had said, surprised. "More plague inoculations?"

She knew he had spent the afternoon at the American School with lines of children, making sure that Henri was in line to be inoculated with all the other youngsters. The priority list, until more vaccine came from L'Institut Pasteur, was school children first, then doctors,

450

nurses, health department sanitation teams, government employees, then the people of the Medina. The modern quarter of Tangier and the suburbs, where Villa Obenpharo was, were to be last.

"No," Mac had said to Maia, "no more inoculations until tomorrow. Now I know why pediatricians look so tired. When more vaccine arrives, I'll have to inoculate you and Mutirra and Benari."

"Those awful shiny needles," Maia said. "But if you take one, I will, too."

"I've already had mine along with all the other doctors. But I still have to go into town."

"A brunette or a blonde?"

"Don't know yet. It's a secret."

"Well," she smiled, "I have a secret for you, too. A big one."

"I hope it's more pleasant than mine."

"Mine is very nice, darling. Wait until you see it."

"I may not be back until quite late, Maia. And I'll be at the American School all day tomorrow." He leaned forward and kissed her. "If I'm not back by tomorrow evening, don't worry. I'll be back sooner or later."

"Mac," she said very seriously. "I've been thinking. You were right about coming to Tangier. But now let's finish what we have to do here and go back to Paris."

"Back to our island?"

"Don't make fun. I'm serious."

"Afraid of the plague?"

"No, not that. That's an old story in Morocco. The health people always make it bigger than it is, because disease is all they see." Somehow she thought of Yacoub pointing at Jeanjean's hawk circling over the cliffs. It had seemed a bad omen to her, but it was impossible to say such a thing to a rational man like Mac. She would go down to her hidden little Arab house in the Medina, make it ready, a ritual of cleansing, and later surprise him completely, while in the meantime he reached Roger one way or another to begin the surgery. Then back they would go to the timeless island in the center of the Seine. Somehow the hawk had been an omen of some vaguely threatening unexpected attack.

451

"Dr. Adams? I'm Ned Walker."

Mac looked up at the sudden voice. He had been thinking about Maia, ignoring the noisy crowded clientele of the Carnivale, purposely not thinking about how this meeting with Walker might or might not turn out. He had managed to put Walker out of his mind.

"Sorry to be late," Walker explained as he sat down. "I was hung up waiting for a phone call from our mutual buddy—"

"Roger Obenpharo?" Mac said, too fast.

"No, Hadj Hassani," Walker laughed, and signaled the waiter. Then he said, "Let's go a little slower and a little more carefully, Doctor. This whole thing is being handled too much like cops and robbers for my taste, except that these Istiqlal boys carry guns and knives and take certain things very seriously." He stopped as the waiter came up. "A half bottle of Chaudsoleil, *glacée*," he said, then, as he saw the questioning look on Mac's face, added, "I don't know how long we'll have to sit here. Anything can happen tonight."

He and Mac measured one another across the table. It was clearly a question of dependability both ways. Walker grinned crookedly. "Isn't this the time you're supposed to ask: How did a nice clean kid like you get mixed up in this?"

"Are you asking me, Mr. Walker?"

"Make it Ned, will you? No, I was asking me, for you."

"Well," Mac said, "if Warren Ross hadn't written—"

"Let me sketch it in fast, Mac. You don't mind my calling you Mac? Look, we have to trust each other, or we can get ourselves hurt. I know about you—"

"Of course. My newspaper friends made me the greatest little open book since the Bible. This is about you—"

"Temper, temper."

"Temper, hell. I've just learned to say what I think."

"Good. We'll save time that way." He looked at his wristwatch and scanned the room. "Obenpharo told me to be ready to be met here between nine and ten."

Mac was amazed. "Benari?"

"No. Roger. Ah, here's the wine. God, I'm thirsty."

Mac waited until the waiter left, then said quietly, "Are you in the Istiqlal?"

452

Walker set his glass down. "No, nothing like that. But I'm doing a book about Roger Obenpharo. I came here a year ago to do a financial newspaper series on international banking and gold traffic, because Tangier is an open magnifying glass for the whole closed system. Then Morocco and the American air bases and the Mediterranean oil tanker lifeline and the Sahara desert oil and uranium discoveries and the geopolitics and the African revolution got me. And then I figured it was like India years ago—to focus it, you need Mahatma Gandhi."

"Roger Obenpharo is the Moroccan Gandhi?"

"More than you think. You've just about taken his place in the Obenpharo family, so your perspective is distorted. Turn the telescope around. I've seen him big. I've seen the crowds in almost religious worship, trying to kiss his sleeve. I've traveled with him, and hidden out with him, and played chess with him, and watched his Spanish nurse change the dressings on that God-awful face of his."

"Then you've seen the killing and the terror—"

"—yes—"

"—but you haven't seen his family at the small end of the telescope, and what he did to every one of them."

"—hold on, Mac. Leaders always hurt their families—"

"And," Mac said, "you still think he's Gandhi?"

"Okay, okay. I surrender. Half Gandhi. Half Nehru, with Nehru's toughness and stubbornness. Wait a minute! Let me finish. You've got to understand Roger—you've even got to understand why his father gave him a name like Roger—you've got to understand one of the few leaders in Africa who'll build a bridge between Africa and the Atlantic world, yes damn it, don't frown, in the end he will, you'll see—you damn well better see, because it's men like Roger, men we can talk to, who'll decide the shape of the rest of the century."

"Do me a favor," Mac said. "Don't make speeches at me. I'm in the Obenpharo family now, and I see your Moroccan Mahatma Gandhi from the bottom looking up."

"You're supposed to be a physician. A balanced scientific rational man. You're not supposed to draw moral judgments about your patients."

"I do about this one. To me, he's a piece of anatomical work and

453

I'm the muscle mechanic to fix him. The sooner I finish the job, the better."

"You're trying too hard to sound tough, Mac."

"No, it's just that people like Roger and you always forget the individual pain. You're so busy with the big picture that you don't see people the way I do—one at a time, hurt, and not sounding like an editorial in the *Times*."

"I sound like that?"

"Damn right. Roger's hypnotized you right along with the rest of the population."

Ned Walker moved his wineglass in little circles over a wet spot on the table. Mac decided to use his Scotch and soda, and leaned back sipping it.

A burst of laughter from the next table made him turn his head. There was a party of eight, with one man holding a small box overhead like an auctioneer while the others at the table clowned at shouting bids. The girl next to the man pulled him sideways and kissed him in the smacking style of grand opera until he brought his fist down like a gavel and, with much applause from the others, presented her with the box.

"Penicillin," Ned Walker said to Mac. "You know those little blackboards outside the sidewalk *cambios?* The ones with the daily money-changing quotations? Well, the bottom item they chalk in now is the quotation on penicillin, at black market prices."

"Why?" Mac asked. "What for?"

Walker stared at him. "Are you serious? For this plague, of course."

"But penicillin is no good for plague."

"Is that straight? I thought penicillin came close to being the great white magic."

"Sure. Close. But not close enough. The plague bug is one of the toughest little killers you ever saw, and penicillin doesn't touch it."

Walker burst out laughing. "And I've been gulping tablets every day the way some people say prayers!"

Mac shrugged. "The great white magic."

Walker leaned across the table. "And how about the rumor there's an Israelite factory named Haffkine selling salt water for vaccine, and cleaning up fortunes?"

Mac set his glass down hard. It had been a long tiring day. The liquor was making him a little sleepy as he had been afraid it would, and now this about Haffkine with the final crazy Tangier touch. "Haffkine," he said slowly, "was a great research bacteriologist, like Pasteur. Died long ago. During the early 1900's he did a beautiful research job developing the first good plague vaccine, and incidentally he was Jewish, and there's a Haffkine Institute in India."

Walker leaned back and laughed again. "God almighty, I love it! The penicillin they trust and sell at black market rates is no damn good. And the vaccine they don't trust is really great." He grinned at Mac. "So you'd say stay off penicillin and get the vaccine?"

"Of course. I've been inoculated myself."

"How about the rest of us in town?"

"As soon as more vaccine is flown in."

"Did you know that plane flights are at a premium now, too? Black market Air France tickets to Europe double and triple in price every day. Are you staying here?"

Mac nodded and took another drink. It had not even occurred to him to leave until he had begun the surgery Roger needed. Until now the plague was just as Maia had sensibly said—an old Moroccan story, and the daytime nightmare Alec Moore had talked about, the pneumonic form of plague spreading person to person in a medieval Black Death, was very unlikely. *A disease of social disorder,* Alec had said, *and Roger Obenpharo knows all about disorder.*

Ned Walker looked at his watch again and then around the room. At the end of the circle his eyes met Mac's. "I don't know," he said. "Anything might have happened. All I was supposed to do was identify you and ask your word not to tell anyone where you meet Roger."

"Of course," Mac said.

"Y'know," Walker said, "he's really a fantastic guy. Two days ago we were riding in the back of a closed car near Xauen and talking about you and Maia Obenpharo and this plague, all mixed up, and damned if he doesn't pull this out of his briefcase." Walker took a thin leather bound book out of his pocket and put it on the table in front of Mac. There were unfamiliar alphabet letters stamped in gold into the cover, spelling a title Mac could not read. He opened

455

the pages and saw the same lettering, in dialogue form, throughout the little book, with occasional lines underlined and French translation handwritten between the lines.

"Is this a Greek play?" he asked Walker. "The letters look Greek."

"Sophocles' *Oedipus the King*. Notice the lines he translated for me?"

Mac turned to the first few pages and held up the book to catch enough light to read the fine handwriting. Roger had written:

PRIEST OF ZEUS: Oedipus, ruler of my land
  you see our generations at the altar—
  —Our city—you yourself have seen!—
  can no more lift prow out of the wave of death,
  —The god who carries fire through the land,
  the ferocious plague, swoops down to empty the house of Cadmus
  while the grave grows more opulent with our weeping.

CHORUS: By such unnumbered death the great town perishes;
  unpitied her children lie upon the ground, spreading pestilence . . .
  Prayer to God the Healer rises
  but intermingled with lament.
  O golden Daughter of Zeus,
  send bright-faced deliverance.

Mac put the book down slowly. He wondered if this was the kind of elaborate scholarly joke he had heard Roger enjoyed, touching on plague as the gods' punishment of pride. Would Roger deliberately cast himself as Oedipus? Maia the golden Daughter of Zeus? The Healer, bright-faced deliverance—an intellectual uppercut for Mac?

Walker sipped his wine, watching Mac across the rim of his glass. "Believe me now? Know anybody else in this town, in his position, from his family, who'd even dream of quoting Sophocles at this particular time? Winston Churchill, maybe, but who else? Do you get the size of the man you're going to operate on?"

"All right," Mac said. "You've convinced me. Now I see why he sent an American to do this little messenger job on me, because you've really convinced me." Either I've overcomplicated Roger, Mac thought, or else Walker allowed Roger to impress him blindly.

456

But the references in the play seemed so obvious. Why else would Roger choose this particular one?

Raïssa's abrasive voice broke in above him. "How cozy you two boys look! Heads together, holding hands, it's a shame for me to break it up, but there's a gooney bird outside dressed in an Arab nightshirt and he wants the great Monsieur Walker."

Walker finished his glass and stood up. "Thanks, Raïssa."

She lowered her voice. "Don't go out the front door. Take the corridor past the men's room. We'll leave your glasses on your table."

"Okay," Walker said. He turned to Mac. "You'll follow in a minute or two?"

"Yes," Mac said. The corridor past the men's room, he thought, a heroic passageway to Oedipus the King.

(6)

AFTER Mac left the Villa Obenpharo, Maia crossed the inner courtyard toward her apartment. She stopped to look at the golden statue of the river nymph gleaming with a faint metallic sheen in the clear half-luminous night. This too? This is an omen, too? I must be what they say of me in town, Maia thought, an *evoluée* whose French veneer comes off as easily as the Paris clothes. I've begun to see too many omens. In Tangier the superstitious Berber girl always comes back. Yet, how to explain this vaguely pressing feeling, shapes of formless fears. Mac understands what Tangier does to me. He must. Why else was he pushing so hard to begin Roger's surgery so we can go back to Paris?

She walked slowly toward the gold statue until she came close enough to touch it. With one finger she traced the lips, feeling the living smile captured in metal. Oh, Mac, she thought, feeling a rush of warmth and gratitude.

Lights flickered, reflected on the statue from behind her. She turned and saw Yacoub shuffling along the colonnade beneath the balcony with a tray of lighted candles.

"Yacoub," she said quietly, suddenly reminded of her plan for the

457

hidden little Arab house in the Medina. He stopped, then came toward her.

"Madame?"

She spoke in Arabic, as she always did when she was alone with Yacoub. "Candles?" If Mac were here, she thought, he'd say: Hell's bells, those damn hand-blown Belgian lamps again? Benari needs a new electrical system, maybe a new many things.

Yacoub said levelly, "No lights, no telephone, no water until tomorrow, madame."

"Yacoub," she said, "when you finish this of the candles, come to my apartment. We are going to the little house in the Medina."

His face, lighted from below by the tray of candles, showed no surprise. It was as if he had expected this. "Madame, if you will dress as a *fatima* to go into the city. Especially the *haik*."

She frowned at him. Especially a face veil? And the hooded ankle-length cloak of an Arab woman? This was the final omen, but she trusted him.

"So it is," Maia said. "I will walk beside you as a wife walks beside her husband."

In the flicker of candlelight she could not be sure, but did a smile touch the corners of his mouth?

An hour later, as Maia and Yacoub crossed the Petit Socco, they saw a file of trucks being unloaded in the bright circle of light cast by the headlights of a ring of Security Police jeeps. It looked military. Rolls of barbed wire, metal mesh fences, and crates of a size and weight to contain weapons. A crowd of Moroccan men and boys circled at a distance, while helmeted police stood at spaced intervals to make sure they kept away.

"What is it?" Maia whispered beneath her veil to Yacoub. "The *ratissage?* With so many police it must be a big dragnet."

"This *ratissage* is not for political rats, madame," Yacoub whispered. "They say they block the streets to catch real rats. A *cordon sanitaire,* for fighting the black disease."

I don't believe it, Maia thought, as they hurried down a sloping side alley to avoid the crowd and the police. I don't believe the plaque is one-hundredth as bad as they pretend. They must be using

458

it for political purposes, throwing a ring of police around each *quartier* and using sanitation as an excuse to search through each house.

It was then she saw a squad of men wearing coveralls and boots and gloves and masked helmets carrying a long thickly rolled straw rug out of one of the Arab row houses. Yacoub stopped short and they flattened themselves back against the opposite wall. Maia noticed that the straw rug sagged heavily with one of the strangely dressed masked men at each end of it while two others opened a coffin-shaped wooden box and quickly shoveled spadefuls of white powder into it from a large sack labeled LIME. An Arab woman and a young girl came to the doorway, wailing in the traditional high-pitched way, weeping and tearing at their hair.

From where Maia stood she could see into the windowless front room of the house. A great iron pot with steam rising from it stood on a bed of coals in the crude fireplace. A heap of wire cages was piled near the boiling cauldron, filled with trapped rats scrambling within them like frantic squirrels. Another masked man was methodically throwing the cages one by one into the pot. The rats made a high squeaking panicky sound while they cooked and died. The thin rodent screeching came so clearly through the women's wailing that Maia began to shiver, feeling the hair rise on her arms.

A Security Police jeep carrying a dazzling searchlight turned into the base of the alley. It stopped because the rising steps from house to house were too steep to maneuver, even with four-wheeled drive. The lights of the jeep caught Maia and Yacoub squarely. Maia felt blinded. A booted helmeted policeman who wore a hospital-gauze face mask came heavily up the stone alley steps. "Are you the plague family?" he asked Yacoub harshly in Arabic. "What are you doing out in the street? You were ordered to wait for the *camion* to the isolation hospital."

"We are only passing," Maia said angrily in Arabic.

The policeman's eyes frowned above his mask. "You," he said to Yacoub, "does your woman always speak like this for you?"

"The plague family, sir, I beg your pardon," Yacoub said quickly, "they are across the street. We are only passing to our house, sir." Yacoub bowed humbly. Maia bit her lip beneath her face veil. *I'm an Obenpharo!* she wanted to shout, but knew that would only complicate matters for hours while the policeman checked up, and probably anger Papa Obenpharo beyond reason.

"Then get to your house and stay there," the policeman said. "The curfew just began. Hurry up."

"Thank you, sir, thank you."

"And lock your house to everybody. All the thieves of the Medina are trapped like rats, and they bite just as bad."

"Yes, sir. Yes, sir." Yacoub took Maia's elbow and pushed, indicating that they should turn back the way they came. She sensed instantly that he wanted to escape the sealed *quartier* before the curfew became efficient, or some wild gang caught them in the streets and robbed them. He was right. Her little house and the surprise for Mac would have to wait.

"You!" The policeman had turned. "Come back here! Not that way! That way is closed."

"Sir," Yacoub said meekly, "we want to go back toward the European section."

"So does every scum around here. We have a *cordon sanitaire*. Nobody passes." He hooked his thumb over his pistol holster. "Go back."

Maia took her purse out from beneath the layered folds of her cloak. She was perspiring with fear and anger under the headband of her hood and her face veil. In the brightness of the headlights she saw the policeman's eyes swing down to her purse. "Sir," she said in French, "we have urgent business in the city. We must go back to the European section." She opened her purse. "Please, sir, let us pass."

"Ah," the policeman said in street Spanish, "you speak educated French? I knew from the perfume and the way you walked on your high heels you were rich. And the bold talking to men. One of the special girls of the *quartier,* eh?"

She groped blindly in her purse and pulled out a fistful of peseta banknotes, trying to control the trapped feeling. The policeman walked to her and turned his back to the jeep's headlights, so that Maia stood in shadow between him and the wall of the house. He held out his hand, and, as soon as he took the money, he grasped her wrist with his other hand.

"Let go, fool!" she said furiously in Arabic.

460

"A little pimp and a rich French-speaking whore? Urgent business in the European section?" He twisted her wrist lightly as she tried to pull free. "One of the fancy expensive ones?"

"Sir"—Yacoub began—"please, sir!"

"You. You won't do any business in Tangier tonight. Nobody passes. Only in daylight, and only with a health certificate."

A man's voice called out in Spanish from within the plague house. "Pedro? Is that you out there? Where the hell have you been? Get these damned screaming crazy women down to the isolation center! Pronto! Pronto!"

The policeman dropped Maia's arm, laughing now, and tried to pinch her. She twisted free and ran up the alley with Yacoub's slippers clattering loudly behind her, followed by the laughter of the policeman and the thin Arabic wailing, trying desperately to skirt the eerily masked burial squad by pressing against the opposite wall, stumbling against the sack of lime and falling back against Yacoub, feeling a horror churn like vomit within her.

At the top of the alley, where it branched into a dim fork, she stopped, sagging and gasping for air and tearing the suffocating veil down from her nose and mouth. Her heart pounded in her throat. A hundred feet back down the slope there was new screaming as the police tried to force the Arab women toward the jeep at the bottom of the alley. A choking rush of memory struck Maia, all the carefully buried recollections of being native and at the bottom, the whole world of rags and hunger, of women like pack animals and men like dogs who wanted only another pipe of hashish and another passive unresisting sweetmeat body; the world where an eleven-year-old girl was brought down from the hills by her vengeful mother to the market of M'Semrir to be sold to the traffic bound for Saudi Arabia where the prices for girls rose higher each year because of the oil wealth. She trembled uncontrollably.

"Madame," Yacoub whispered urgently, "the curfew. They will beat us. Oh, madame, your purse!—did he get your purse?"

She held the leather bag out to him, unable to speak.

"Praise to Allah!" he breathed. "The key to your little house." He leaned toward her. "You must be strong now, madame. If the empty house is not already looted by thieves, it is the only safe place for tonight. Tomorrow I will go to the officer at the barbed wire of the *cordon sanitaire*. Tomorrow we will somehow manage to get back into the city."

She made an effort to stand up straight. "A weakness. A weakness come over me."

Yacoub had opened her purse. "The key, madame! I cannot feel the key to the little house!" He sounded very frightened, and yet as if he were trying hard to be protective.

My hurt Arab brother, she thought swiftly; for the first time she felt a personal bond with Yacoub, whose childhood had also survived the bottom of the Moslem world, to live now, as she did, on the bright side of a modernized feudalism. "Allah bless thy loyalty, Yacoub," she said in Arabic. "I will not forget thee and thy courage this night."

"Madame," he said, half crying and holding her purse toward her with shaking hands, "the house key—it is not here."

She rammed her hand frantically into the leather bag. Their only sanctuary in this dark jungle was her little hidden house. She combed inside the purse with her fingers touching lipstick case, cigarettes, lighter, handkerchief, *keys*!—no, only car keys—the handkerchief again, tangling her fingers, then suddenly deep in the corner the hard thin old-fashioned iron key. "I have it, Yacoub. The key is here." She tried very hard to control her voice, because it was important for them both to act with courage, and survive.

They hurried through the narrow winding alleys. Every one was empty, thin strips of whiteness of reflected moonlight, with silent shuttered houses. Once they crouched in a urine-smelling doorway as an armed two-man patrol clattered by them. Once they heard a woman screaming in the dark, then several shots, and they ran in the opposite direction. The rat maze of the Medina was doubly labyrinthine in the dark without even the usual dim street lamps. Both Yacoub and Maia guided themselves by instinct, knowing they must ascend one alley after another until they reached the ancient Portuguese fortress, then follow it to the low tunnel which pierced the massive stone wall and led to Maia's hidden house. In the Street of the Devil, which was no street but only a passageway of donkey width, the houses were so close that no moonlight could pierce the narrow cleft. By going single file and touching the houses on each side they felt their way along. From behind the closed doors of a café came the steady thump of drums, tambourines rattling in frenzy over the crying *rhaita* horns, gaiety on the edge of a precipice.

Maia was exhausted when they reached the entrance of the tunnel which led to her house, but she felt only relief as she stooped behind Yacoub and felt her way through the damp closed air. At the far side of the tunnel fresh air touched her face and she straightened gratefully. Yacoub was a dim shadow ahead of her, not wasting a moment, already rattling the iron key in the lock. He grunted with effort, forcing the key clumsily.

"What's wrong, Yacoub?" She whispered without realizing it, even though no one could hear them beyond the great stone walls even if they shouted. She knew by the sound the key was making within the lock that his hand was trembling badly. "Here," she said, "I know the trick of it. Let me open the door."

He stepped back without a word. She had the lock open in a moment, and swung the heavy mahogany door inward, then stopped in amazement.

Candles were burning within the small foyer, and at the bottom step of the staircase, wearing an Arab *djellaba* and pointing a gun at the door, was Jeanjean. He stared at her unbelievingly, then a huge grin split his face and he sat down on the steps and began to laugh. He called up the stairs between spasms of laughter, "Abid! Katim! Kif-kif! Saved by Allah! Come down! Come down!" He turned to Maia and Yacoub. "Close the door, Yacoub, you fool. The goddam Security Police are crawling tonight." He stood up, smiling his best smile. "Of all people. Maia Obenpharo. And dressed as a *fatima*."

Maia stood still. She had completely forgotten he had his own house key. All her omens of warning had been right, especially the hawk hunting high above the cliffs. But there was an edge of hysteria in Jeanjean she had never seen, this great long-lost friendliness which meant he needed something badly. She remembered the last time he had violated her in this house, and then recognition of his eyes and his laughing manner struck her. He was cloudy with smoking *kif,* more than she had ever seen before, which meant he could be drunkenly friendly one moment and brutal with narcotic craziness

463

the next, needing gentle handling and firmness to keep the smile smiling and the teeth from biting.

"I'm so glad you're here, Jeanjean," she said as pleasantly as she could. She pushed back her hood and began to unfasten her veil; both gestures meant she was within her own home.

Two Moroccans came down the steps cautiously, each holding a toy-size automatic. Jeanjean burst into laughter. "Revolutionary heroes! Tiptoe, tiptoe, heroes. First you let me come down alone. Now with a woman and a eunuch to fight, the heroes come down on tiptoes."

"Tell them to put the pistols away," Maia said in French. The two Moroccans were drunk on drugs, she could tell. Their eyes had that look of drugged men. Now I remember them. They had met Jeanjean at the airport.

"Who is she? One of your whores, without a veil?" one of them asked Jeanjean in Arabic. "Who is the man? Is this one of your Paris tricks?"

Jeanjean doubled over with laughter. "Paris trick," he wheezed drunkenly. "A Paris trick. Maia, did you hear little Kif-kif call you a Paris trick?" He looked up the steps at the shorter of the two Moroccans, a broad-shouldered chunky fistful of a man. "Kif-kif, Allah sent a messenger to get us out of this pesthole. This is Maia Obenpharo. Her family will get us out."

"The same woman who was at the airport?"

"Yes. The same. You want to be on the Air France plane to Paris tomorrow? Then listen. Maia's lover is a doctor. He can sign the health certificates to get us out." Jeanjean leaned forward and shook the arm of the second Moroccan who was staring with a kind of unseeing fixity at Maia. *"Aie,* Abid, wake up, man. You shouted I paid a fortune for black market plane tickets. Now, see? We'll get out. See how you must trust Jeanjean?"

"I'll trust you, Jeanjean," Abid said flatly, not threatening but merely stating his position half sleepily, "when you're dead or when you pay our share of the political collections."

Maia noticed that both Abid and Kif-kif spoke with Algerian accents. It was bad that they were not Moroccans, because Algerian city types believed in nothing, not even Islam.

464

Jeanjean came across the foyer and kissed her smackingly on the forehead. Maia felt no edge of warmth in it, only a smoky-brained narcotic clownishness, and for the first time she began to feel she could outsmart them all. They were drugged with smoking *kif,* and she felt sharply awake now.

"Tomorrow night you can all be in Paris," she said lightly. "You have the tickets. All you need is the health certificate to pass through the police *cordon sanitaire,* and my doctor will give you his signature on the papers in the morning."

"You see?" Jeanjean said. "I told you."

"Why?" asked Kif-kif. "Why should her doctor give us the official papers?"

Jeanjean raised his arms to call heavenly witness of his patience with fools. "Maia, you see why we call him Kif-kif? A little too much in the pipesmoke and his head becomes *toute bouleversée.*" He turned back to Kif-kif. "Stop staring at me like that. Your eyeballs will fall out."

"I don't like you, Jeanjean. I don't like your tricks."

"Fool! Where is the trick? This is a miracle."

"Kif-kif is right," Abid said slowly. "Why should the doctor sign the paper for us to get out?"

Jeanjean pointed at Maia. "For her. We take good care of what is his. He takes good care of what is ours."

"Ours," Kif-kif said. "Only remember it. Ours. No more tricks of disappearing money in Paris."

From upstairs a man's voice called suddenly, "Water! For the love of Allah! Abid! Kif-kif!"

Kif-kif nodded at Yacoub, "You. Eunuch. Get water. Don't try to run away."

"Where can I run tonight?" Yacoub said boldly. As he walked toward the kitchen he said over his shoulder, "I will bring water, if there is water to bring."

"You of the red hair," Kif-kif said. "You. Jeanjean's messenger from Allah."

"I am Madame Obenpharo. The name is not hard to remember." No, she thought, that is the wrong tone. They have been smoking *kif* and are only half in this world. The other half, the drugged half, is all

465

fantasy where anything can happen. Watch your tone. Let nothing fantastic happen.

"She needs to be hit," Abid said. "When a woman talks like that she needs hitting."

"Water!" the voice upstairs called. "Water!"

"You," Kif-kif said. "Do you have the medicine for fever? Ah-spirin?"

"Aspirin? Yes. In my medicine cabinet in the bedroom upstairs."

"Good," Jeanjean said hurriedly. Maia sensed he was on her side against the others, as subtly threatened as she, and as much in need of an ally. "Good," he said, "give it to Katim. You remember Katim from Paris? No? Ah, yes, the airport. You met him at the airport. He has a headache upstairs from too much *kif*."

"Poor Katim," Maia said, smiling carefully. "He can have all the medicines in the house."

"Ah-spirin," Kif-kif said. "Get it, messenger of Jeanjean."

"She is not my messenger," Jeanjean said. He was not smiling now. "Tomorrow she will be a messenger for us all, for the official paper." He jerked his head toward the stairs. "Maia. Get Katim the medicine."

She walked toward the steps slowly, feeling weakly jointed in her knees, as if she might tip over in any direction. Neither Abid nor Kif-kif moved, and she barely brushed by them on the steps. She could smell the drug in the air they exhaled and the rose water pomade in their curly black hair. She heard them follow behind her on the steps, and she made herself move slowly, with dignity, but with an emptiness inside her as if two cobras were behind her who might or might not strike, completely without reason, striking or not, entirely on impulse in their drugged state of half fantasy.

In her bedroom a small dark-haired man who must be the one called Katim lay stretched on his back in her silk bed. He had torn open his shirt. His face and chest shone with sweat. His eyes glittered brightly while he kept running his tongue over his lips. "Water," he said hoarsely as they came into the bedroom. "The thirst is killing me." The bed was surrounded by *kif* pipes, and the room stank of it.

Kif-kif nodded toward Maia. "This one is a messenger from Jeanjean. She has medicine for you, Katim."

466

Katim raised himself weakly on his elbows. "Medicine? Who needs it? I smoked too much. I need only a little water."

Maia took one of the candles on a brass tray and walked into the mirrored bathroom. She was shocked to see her face in the flickering light, and, when she took the bottle of aspirin tablets out of the medicine cabinet her hand shook so badly the bottle dropped and shattered in the basin. She bit her lip very hard to keep herself from crying out hysterically, and forced herself to pick up several tablets methodically. Bchind her, in the bedroom, she heard the men's voices take on an Arabic snarl. Eight or ten hours, she told herself. Just hold on for eight or ten hours. With horror she suddenly remembered Mac had said he would be busy all the next day and would not see her until evening. He may not even miss me! she thought in agony. No, no, Yacoub is here. And for some reason, Jeanjean is on our side because there is some kind of struggle between them, and he is using their critical need for health certificates in several ways. If I do not lose my head, she thought, and if Yacoub is careful and if Jeanjean can sleep off the drug smoke, if if if and all the rest, then all will come out. This nightmare will end. Hold on until daylight.

She walked more steadily back into the bedroom. Abid confronted her. "What was that noise?" His eyes were heavy-lidded.

"I dropped the medicine bottle."

"Let me see the medicine." He stared at the white tablets in her open palm, then picked one up carefully and touched it to his tongue. He nodded. "Give them to Katim."

"Love of Allah. I need water. Only water!"

"Here," Maia said soothingly, hoping desperately that she sounded like a considerate nurse. "Here. These pills will take away the headache."

There was a cautious knock on the door. Kif-kif immediately stepped behind it and tugged at his small automatic pistol. Yacoub opened the door slowly and put his head into the room so carefully that Jeanjean began to laugh drunkenly again. Yacoub's eyes scanned the candlelighted room: the bare-chested man on the bed with Maia standing beside him, the *kif* pipes littering the floor, the tense crouching chunky man behind the door holding an automatic. "No water," Yacoub croaked, sounding completely dry-mouthed.

467

Katim, on the bed, tried to raise himself on one elbow. "No water?" His eyes were shining with fever.

"Did you try every spigot?" Kif-kif said grimly.

"Yes, sir." Yacoub's eyes kept flicking toward the blunt little blue-steel gun.

"The rain barrel?"

"Yes, sir."

"Nothing? No water?"

"Nothing, sir."

"Here's something," Kif-kif said, and swung his gun hard against Yacoub's head. Maia cried out as Yacoub fell limply to the floor and lay still. Blood poured over his face. She started toward him, but Kif-kif said sharply, "Stay there."

"Let me stop the bleeding," Maia said desperately. "Please. Please."

"He truly bleeds," Abid said. "I never believed this kind had so much blood."

"He can't hurt anyone," Maia begged. "He can only help us all."

"She's right," Jeanjean said. "That was stupid. We need him. If he dies from so much bleeding, he helps nobody."

"One more dead nobody in a dead town." Kif-kif moved his head toward Maia. "Give Katim the medicine pills."

Katim tried to take the aspirin tablets shakily from Maia's hand, and she supported his raised head in the bend of her arm so that he could swallow more easily. She wanted to run to Yacoub's body, but she stood frozen, trembling. Katim coughed strongly.

"Swallow the pills!" Kif-kif commanded.

"Too—too dry—" Katim said chokingly. "I need water. I feel on fire."

Kif-kif glanced at Maia bending over Katim. "Maybe a good sweat with a woman will cool you," he said. Maia dropped Katim's head to the bed and stood up stiffly.

"Don't be crazy," Jeanjean said. "We need her for the papers tomorrow."

"A good sweat for Katim will not hurt the papers. A good sweat for all of us."

"Don't be crazy," Jeanjean said. "And don't point the stupid gun this way. The Air France tickets are held at the city office in my name, you fool."

Good, Maia thought as Kif-kif lowered his little automatic. Jean-jean sounds less smoke-clouded now. But little spasms of trembling struck her again. Abid leaned against the wall, picking his nose slowly and thoroughly.

"Jeanjean," Kif-kif said, "go find Katim some water. Maybe he has the black disease. He should get what he needs."

"Don't talk crazy," Jeanjean said. He held his hands carefully by his sides, not moving them.

"Then let your messenger from Paris give him a good sweat. I have seen a man feel better by morning that way."

Jeanjean glanced at Maia and shrugged. "I only want the health papers to get out of the Medina and get out of Tangier. I don't care what she does."

Kif-kif gestured to Maia. "Take off your *kaftan*."

"No," she said. "I have more medicine for him."

"He needs water to swallow it," Kif-kif said, with a drunken-sounding logic. "Jeanjean, go find some water."

Jeanjean looked at Maia, and shrugged again.

Her pounding heart choked her. "Jeanjean," she said, "don't go."

"Katim needs relief from his fever," he said. "I'll see you later."

"Jeanjean—!" she cried out.

"I'll get some water, somewhere," Jeanjean said, then, as he turned toward the door, Kif-kif raised his gun casually and shot him in the back.

(7)

"So," Roger said, "you are the American surgeon who came so far to help me."

"No," Mac said, "I came to Tangier for personal reasons."

"Ah."

"But if surgery will help you—"

"Ah," Roger interrupted. "Who will pay your fee?"

"No one. I'm a guest in your father's house."

"The whole city knows that. And that you will marry my former wife."

"Under French law, still your wife," Mac said.

"I do not recognize French law."

Silence. "I would prefer either to sit down or to leave," Mac said stiffly.

"Please, please be seated. Pardon. Your frankness about why you came to Tangier caught me, and I forgot." Roger leaned his head back against the pile of pillows.

He had been sitting on a very large hassock, legs crossed tailor fashion, when the Istiqlal guide had brought Mac and Ned Walker into the room. At the outside doorway to the street, Mac and Ned had passed several Riffs crouched on their heels over a small teapot on a bed of charcoal. Mac had assumed they were actually bodyguards, not men of the streets, when they spoke to the guide. Then, when he and Walker had been led into the hallway, several additional men leaning against the wall near a closed door had straightened quickly. Walker had spoken to them in pidgin Arabic, and had nodded to Mac. "Go right in that door. We're expected."

That was how Mac had first seen Roger, for as he had stood beside Walker with his arms partly lifted so the hallway bodyguards could tap his clothes for concealed weapons, he had seen Roger across the room enthroned by Moroccan leather pillows like a Buddha. Beside him sat a woman in a white nurse's uniform, and two more bodyguards. Roger and the inside guards wore turbans, but only Roger had the indigo-blue Tuareg face veil which Bud Williams, the American pilot, had described to Mac.

"Dr. Adams," Walker had said formally beside him, "let me introduce Sidi Mohammed."

Roger had nodded across the room. "You will confuse Dr. Adams, Ned. He knows me as Roger Obenpharo."

"He has agreed to respect your wishes for secrecy," Walker had said.

"I thank you for your bona fides," Roger said.

Walker had turned to Mac. He held out his hand and said in English, "So long, for now. Happy landings."

"I'll see you around town," Mac said.

"That depends," Walker said. "I'm getting an exclusive story here, and I have to follow it all over the map."

"Come, come, Ned," Roger said from across the room, "we don't move around so very much."

"Whither thou goest, and all that," Ned Walker said to Roger, grinning faintly. He shook Mac's hand, and Mac could see this quick departure must have been planned, as all the details tonight had been planned.

Walker had left the room and Mac had turned toward Roger.

Now, as he sat down for the first time, Mac saw Roger staring at him with his single uncovered burning eye. This must be something he does all the time, Mac thought. The eye to nail you, and a lawyer's directly attacking questions to cut you down. Just focus on that single eye. Think of the head you could model in clay on that half-covered face, the nose like a prow with the skin drawn tightly over jaw and cheekbone, the ageless Mediterranean face.

"I interest you, Dr. Adams?"

"Yes."

"As a patient? As an interesting technical problem?"

"Partly."

"Only partly? You mean, also as a revolutionary? A hidden outlaw? A nomad politician? One thousand and one Arabian nights, with dancing girls and the Foreign Legion in the background?"

"That's your description, not mine."

"Ah. You're a good lawyer, Dr. Adams."

"So are you, I've heard."

"I took a doctorate in the Sorbonne. *Faculté de droit.* You speak French well. Was that your university?"

"No. Yale."

"Only one school?"

"No. Two. The second gave no diploma."

"What was that?"

"The war. The Second World War."

"Ah. You expect a third."

"Only if men like you make it inevitable."

471

Roger's eye burned, and Mac saw the muscle bunch under the tight-leather skin, then ease, then bunch again. Roger closed his Cyclopean eye.

The Spanish nurse beside him said in broken French, "Please, Doctor, not to exhaust him. He should not speak too long."

"How do you feed him?" Mac asked, as if Roger were not there. "With a tube?"

"Sometimes. But mostly with a spoon. The type for premature infant feeding, with curved-in sides like a little funnel. It goes, but slow."

"How does he get his proteins?"

"Meat soups. I make it myself. The glucose I add, or he drinks sweet *thé à la menthe*."

"Any fats? *Mantequilla?*"

"Very little."

"Is there a problem of infection?"

"Only local infection now. The scar tissue is thin and breaks open. Then there is some inflammation."

"And then more scar tissue," he added.

"Yes," she said quietly. "Not good."

"He speaks very well."

"Yes."

"I did not expect such clear speech after seeing the bone damage in the X-ray pictures."

"The tongue," she said. "It is because the tongue and most of the roof of the mouth are good."

"That helps. It also helps reconstructive surgery."

"And the power of the will," she said. "X-ray cannot show that."

"No. But I see the will power now. It helps the surgery."

"I pray for your hands, Doctor. I pray each night for him to the Holy Mother."

"His mother prays, too," Mac said.

Roger opened his eye. "Be careful. This *enfermera* was trained by nuns. She will not approve the irony of your comparing mothers. She believes in a carpenter who became a God, while I follow a camel driver who was only a prophet."

"I thought you were a religious leader, too, because Islam does not separate religion from politics."

472

"Doctor," Roger said, "do you have any idea of how naïve you sound in these matters? You remind me of the American military men who run the air bases the French granted you, without consulting Moroccans. You remind me of the diplomats Washington sends here to deal with what they call the native politicians."

"All?" Mac asked. "All Americans are naïve?"

"Incredibly. They give foreign aid like money prizes in a popularity contest." Roger turned to both his bodyguards and spoke in Arabic. The nearest man immediately went to a corner armoire and took out a circular tray bearing a large brass teakettle. "So much speech," Roger said, "I must watch my fluids, you agree? You will accept mint tea?"

Mac recognized that Roger had decided to drop being a magistrate examining a hostile witness. Now he was going to play host à la Marocaine.

"Yes," Mac said.

"Perhaps you prefer whisky soda?"

I do, Mac thought, but it's the wrong symbol of this particular moment. It's a sahib drink, and the sahibs in the colonies had been badly wrong, and now whisky soda was the wrong drink. "No thanks," Mac said. "Mint tea will be fine."

"You like the sweetness? Most Americans do."

"Yes," Mac said. He noticed that the second bodyguard had set up what looked like a phonograph on a low taboret nearby. The men brought Roger several thin plastic circles which Mac recognized as reels of tape recordings. Roger shuffled through the reels until he found the one he wanted, and he handed it to the bodyguard.

While the man was arranging the tape recorder, the first bodyguard had used a bellows to brighten a little charcoal blaze under the brass kettle. Now he began the ritual of shredding the mint stalks and breaking chunks off a cone of sugar with a small copper hammer.

"You," Roger said, "you look around and see the fighting—"

"The terrorism—"

"No, Doctor. Mostly fighting. The terrorism stands out because it is a cruel answer to cruelty from the French. But the *Harakat el Mokahwamah* of the Istiqlal is an army—"

"Underground—"

473

"Above, now. But an army. With staff and line. How clse to resist in a country where the French caused a protectorate in 1912 and have ruled with martial law since that time? Since that time no freedom of movement, no freedom of expression, no freedom of assembly. Ah," he added as the bodyguard brought the tray with steaming glasses. He waited until Mac lifted a glass, then took one himself. "Your family settled in America when?"

Mac stopped the glass halfway to his mouth. "1638."

"Ah. So." Roger raised his glass. "To the Boston Tea Party." His single eye wrinkled in a strange smile.

"The British are now our best ally in the Atlantic world," Mac said. "The tea party is over."

"And if you were not naïve, Doctor, you would see that we are your best link with the Mediterranean world. In Arabic, Morocco is *El Magreb el Aksa,* The Land Furthest West."

"But praying east."

"We have two hands. East and West."

"Two hands? Or two faces?"

Roger put his glass down very slowly, then nodded to the man who stood beside the tape recorder. "This," he said to Mac, "is a part of the record of our last Central Committee meeting with a liaison group to France. No one else has even heard it."

"Why play it now? The newspaperman is gone, and I'm not an American diplomat."

"No, but your people went to a new world in 1638. And when you marry an Obenpharo, your Legation will want your opinion of me." He nodded to the man at the tape recorder. There was a click as the plastic reels of tape began to spool off smoothly, and Roger's voice spoke in French, disembodied and close, from the machine.

". . . they will say we are feudalistic. Tell them that the French created most of it. The French built up the mountain Berber tribes against the city Arabs. The French civilian official in every region is a feudal lord, with life and death powers. The French build up certain pashas and caids and tribal chiefs, like the Glaoui in Marrakech, by giving them fantastic privileges. Why? To serve as agents against the true Sultan. They will say to you that the religion of Islam is medieval and will block the creation of a modern Morocco. Tell

474

them that Islam has no clergy, no hierarchy. The teachers and students in the Islamic universities, the Karaouyine in Fez and the Ben Youssef in Marrakech, all want modern reforms. When they say the Koran and the *Hadith* go beyond religion, into personal and civic life, tell them there is an interpretation called the *Ijtihad* which allows us to adapt the Koran to the modern world. Remember the example of Jamal el-Din el-Afghani for reform and spiritual unification. When they say we are the Atlantic anchor of the Cairo axis, tell them we are in the West, a bridge between two civilizations. Our heroic struggles and sacrifices—"

The voice stopped suddenly as Roger held up his hand for the machine to stop. Quietly he said to Mac, "I will spare you the part about the heroes and the dying." Suddenly, surprisingly, he stretched his thin long arm across the table and tapped Mac's knee with two fingers, a kind of telegraphy of trying to establish personal contact, understanding. "Do you begin to see new sides to the matter, Dr. Adams?"

"Yes. And I can see much which can be debated."

"Debated?"

"Yes. Not only the cruelties, but the Communist penetration. The more than a drift toward dictatorship." Mac raised his voice because he saw Roger was about to speak. "But I didn't come for debate. I don't expect to be your convert."

"And I," Roger said, "do not expect to be your patient."

Mac was amazed. He had never doubted that Roger was anxious for him to begin the reconstructive surgery of his torn face. He had never met anyone with a badly injured face who did not want it sculptured again to what it was originally. For so many months now Roger's need for facial repair had been so obvious, so unquestionably obvious, that it had never occurred to Mac even to doubt that the entire weighty decision of leaving Paris for Tangier for just this purpose would end in refusal by the patient himself.

"I surprise you, Doctor?"

"Completely." Even now, he could hardly believe it.

"How typical of Christianity," Roger said. "God and the Devil. Good and Evil. Health and Disease. All the simple dualisms, and the Christian need for good works to enter heaven. Don't you know there

475

are millions of people so desperate to find just one mouthful of food each day that they don't care if they have tuberculosis or malaria or leprosy or hurt faces?"

"But you're not desperately hungry."

"No, but desperately trying to win a revolution. Within this month or next month, we will win it and the French will be forced to return the Sultan and we will be independent. Do you think it makes sense for me to lie chained to Dr. Moore's clinic bed for weeks at a time? One operation. Then another and another. Six months. A year, two years, who knows? I doubt even you know exactly how long it would take, am I right?"

"Yes. But your mother and father, and Maia—"

"Yes. So. My mother and father and Maia. My mother wants her son back, the son she gave all the love she could never give the father because the father was living in a romantic dream of ancient Mediterranean empire with money for soldiers. That is the mother."

"Walker showed me the Greek play," Mac said. "I got your point, but maybe you're oversimplifying your father."

"I do not oversimplify anything. I only see him clearly. He wanted a crown prince, a proconsul for his empire." He leaned forward and held out both hands. "When he holds out one hand, open like this, watch out for the other. It is a fist."

Mac shook his head. "You do oversimplify. You make him a simple villain."

"Oh no. No, not that. Only a man who likes to play God from the top of Banque Obenpharo." He leaned forward again, intensely. "Even with French Legionnaires against us, paratroopers and tanks, the Istiqlal revolution was built up from nothing to the edge of success. Now Obenpharo can dynamite us with one man."

This was too incredible to believe. "Surely, not me," Mac said.

"Yes, surely you. With your surgical knives and bandages you can confine the top Istiqlal leader to bed for months. And all disguised as Christian good works. A father's concern for his unfortunate son." He leaned back on his pillows and closed his uncovered eye, saying something softly in Spanish to his nurse. She went to a leather doctor's bag in the corner and returned with a drinking tube which she put into his tea glass. Without opening his eye, Roger

476

allowed her to lift the edge of his face veil and put the tube into his mouth. The level of the tea in the glass fell soundlessly until it sucked empty air at the bottom.

They sat in silence together until Roger said quietly, "You say nothing. I am only being honest."

"Yes," Mac said, "and also using me. Your Morocco will want American dollars and technical assistance, and Ned Walker and I are the beginning of the persuasion."

"I admit it. You can both be important people to us. Why should you sound so angry?"

"Because to you, your own family is not important."

"How naïve," Roger said. "You have much intelligence and much naïveté at the same time." He began to get up off his pillows, and, when the nurse tried to restrain him, he pushed her arm away. When he stood, finally, he was tall, as tall as Mac, almost as tall as Benari Obenpharo. "Listen," he said to Mac, "you are doing what the Americans always do. You turn your back on the dirty hungry mobs because they stink. You did it everywhere you went after the last war."

"That's a lie."

"A lie? That you always went where there was soap and water, good manners and clothes and good looks? The singing and the gold?"

Mac got to his feet now, too, with a feeling of anger rising swiftly. "Are you talking about Maia now?"

"If you interpret me so. I left her out completely to spare your romantic American feelings."

"You're sparing nothing tonight. Why spare me or Maia?"

"Because my father used her to comand you, the way he first tried with me."

"I know all about that. You've got it all twisted in your head."

"I? I am the twisted one?" Roger clapped his fingers over his eye, then dropped his hand. "How blind can you be? You're a scientifically trained man, trained to see people objectively, aren't you? Think of her. Think of her origins, when all her basic ideas were formed. As a doctor, think of her as a doctor. As a doctor what would you think if someone told you about a girl who tended sheep until she was raped by her father and would have been sold by her mother if a passing

477

missionary priest had not found her. And was mistress to an English painter, all before the age of thirteen."

"But she's changed. Matured. She's a European woman, now."

"Is she? In English don't you have a saying: Acts speak more than words? The man she kept, here and in Paris, was Jeanjean Rasa. Have you seen him?"

"Yes."

"Good. You agree he's only some genitals parading as a man? Have you ever seen his toys—the polo ponies and the racing cars and the little Arab girls and the hawk he flies from his fist out over the Charf? You don't answer, and I don't blame you. Inside his head, his feelings, he is as far away from the realities of modern living as she is. Ah, you think perhaps this is a—a kind of intellectual jealousy? Then look at an English lover of hers in Paris, a poet and painter they say, Laurance something or other. Did you know the man committed suicide this month with one of those farewell notes which included her name? Ask yourself—I mean as a doctor, we are discussing an illness here I believe—what kind of a woman chooses such men over and over again? I know you are not a psychiatrist, but surely you know more than only surgery of the face. Do you know the disease of beautiful women who can never come to a partnership with one man? They want men, but they fear them, they fight them, they always drift downhill into the arms of monsters. Haven't you ever seen the classic pair, the beautiful woman with the ugly man, the cruel man, the money-crazy rich man who has her as a possession?"

"There is your mistake," Mac said quietly. "She is beautiful, but I am none of those." He had gone beyond anger and surprise now, into an even elevated quietness where there was only this strange intense turbaned man weaving a political empire in his mind exactly as his father had fitted together a financial empire, both trying to use Maia and him, Mac, as an ally and a weapon. "I hope you won't fight her French divorce."

"Contrary. I welcome it. For a Moroccan leader, she is poison."

"Good. For me, she is not."

"But what will happen when you see reality? Has she ever told you about the little Arab house built into the Kasbah walls where she hides herself periodically? Ah, that strikes you. Ask Yacoub. He's the only one who knows."

Mac felt the earlier anger stab him again. "I'll ask Maia. She is more honest than you know."

Roger shook his head. "You have a lifetime of her honesty ahead of you."

"And you," Mac said, with cold deliberate anger, staring at the hidden torn face, "what kind of lifetime do you think you have ahead?"

"Ah, you still wish to begin the surgery, Doctor?"

"No. Now I could not consider it. I'll take Maia back to Paris, and you can take your face into the revolution."

"Don't play Jehovah, like my father. You sound as if you are pronouncing a death sentence."

"Yes. More or less slow. But if the nurse is right, and living as you do, it will be sure."

"Do you read the Latin poets? The line in Catullus: 'I am not really anxious for your approval, Caesar. I do not care.' "

Mac held out his hand. "We're even now. Good-by, Sidi Mohammed."

Roger took Mac's hand and shook it firmly. "No valedictory, please. We will meet again."

"I will avoid it."

"Impossible. Morocco is part of Adams Farm for the rest of our lives, don't you think?"

So Roger even knows about my little painted wooden sign, Mac thought. Eyes behind carved screens, bribed servants, the whole charade of medieval intrigue, all rushing toward the twentieth century like a furious child.

"The man who brought you," Roger said, "will guide you back. Within two or three months we will meet openly, because within that time the French will be forced to return the true Sultan to Morocco."

"*Pax vobiscum,*" Mac said, on impulse. "Or should I say, *Allah anik?*"

"Peace unto you, also," Roger said gravely, in Arabic, "and the grace of God."

(8)

THE two telephone calls came the next day. Dr. Alec Moore called first, early in the morning. Mac would always remember that the second call, from Benari Obenpharo, did not come until late in the day.

A servant had awakened him at Villa Obenpharo by knocking at his bedroom door repeatedly until he had sat up, startled and groggy, half drowned in the deep sleep which had overwhelmed him as soon as Roger's guide had brought him home at midnight in a closed car. He had fallen into his bed like stone, with a profound exhaustion, and now, when he answered the door and heard Dr. Moore was on the telephone for him, he needed a moment to rediscover where he was. During that moment at the door, he could not remember. Then, still not completely awake, he slipped his feet into the Moroccan slippers Maia had given him, put on his robe hurriedly, and followed the servant out to the colonnaded balcony.

It was not yet morning, he realized, but still the hushed drawn-out white dawn before the sun came up. As they shuffled across the inner courtyard toward the library telephone, he awakened enough to enjoy the statue of the golden nymph, looking cool and washed with light.

On the telephone, Alec Moore's voice was apologetic and forceful by turns. "Malcolm? Awfully sorry and all that for rocking you out of the hay at this ungodly hour. Hell's broken loose with the bloody plague. Could you lend a professional hand? Strictly volunteer. This isn't your show, really."

Mac combed his hair with his fingers and yawned enormously.

"Are you there?" Alec Moore's voice crackled in the receiver.

"Yes. I had to yawn."

"Well I'll be a son of a bitch! You won't do much yawning when you see these buggers pouring into the isolation hospital. The filthy plague is really explosive now."

Mac felt himself come awake. "The pneumonic form?"

"Most of them. That's why I said volunteer. We'll have to examine several hundred people while trying to breathe under face masks and a pile of protective drapery. Delighted that I inoculated you myself."

Alec's Falstaff chuckle came over the wire. "That'll give you a fifty-fifty chance of survival."

"What about drugs?" Mac asked. "Isn't streptomycin our best bet?"

"It's being flown in from Paris and Geneva today."

"Geneva!"

"Yes, indeed. Our Director of the Service d'Hygiène had an all-night all-out session with the fat-assed Committee of Control and got approval to radio World Health headquarters."

"Fine." Mac remembered Dr. Allenby of the U.S. Public Health Service in Paris, in the office next door to Eve's. "Will World Health send epidemic control teams?"

"Never thought to ask. I'm following orders, phoning all the English-speaking doctors in town. All that private soldiers like us need to worry about is getting the right dosage of the right stuff into these poor bastards—we'll use sulfas until the antibiotics come in—and watch their fluid balance because they're as dehydrated as the Sahara."

"Okay," Mac said. "I'll be down there."

"We thank you, Malcolm. Come along to my clinic, will you?"

"Will I have enough time for a cup of coffee, Alec?"

Alec laughed again. "The condemned man ate a hearty meal. See you soon, Doctor."

The second telephone call, from Benari Obenpharo, came late in the afternoon to the isolation hospital where Mac was working.

The day had seemed very long to Mac before Obenpharo's call came—a sweating heat and truckloads of people, the families and contacts of plague patients, all of whom had to be stripped, decontaminated, bathed, and examined. With Alec Moore as his tutor, Mac quickly began to diagnose accurately which ones had to be separated from the group, for individual isolation. "The eyes," Alec Moore kept saying. "The eyes get that feverish shine. Temperature, forty, centigrade. When you see that around here, you can bet a shilling to a pound it's plague."

Mac pulled on a coverall suit and boots and rubber gloves.

"Don't forget your face mask and helmet," Alec Moore said. "Just don't become casual or brave. And don't let one of the sick ones cough at you. Tuberculosis is playful as kittens compared with pneumonic plague. The inoculation you got last week will give you some protection, but no one knows quite how much."

Booted, masked, gloved, Mac faced him for inspection. "We'll die of heat stroke in this outfit," Mac said. "How can you examine a patient properly when you're dressed like a deep-sea diver?"

"You'll manage, Malcolm. No full-dress university workups here, y'know. Use your stethoscope a good deal. When you listen to their lungs and you hear coarse sandpapery râles, you can make the clinical diagnosis. It's pneumonic plague. Let the laboratory lads button up the bacteriology later."

So the long steam bath of a day had gone before Benari Obenpharo's call came. Mac's section of the hospital was a casualty clearing station in an invisible war. People lay on straw mats, men to one side, women to the other, rolling and tossing as their body temperatures rose rapidly from fever to high fever, then, incredibly for Mac who had never seen such a disease before, they went into a final agonal blaze. In the short span of hours he saw patients who had dismounted from the trucks with only a mild fever begin to burn with the terrible biological fire of overwhelming plague infection. He gave them drugs and fluid, and more fluid, fluid by mouth, by vein, by skin, by rectum, seeing the sickly shining eyes, hearing the sandpaper scraping sound in their lungs, watching them die swiftly, and his body became drenched under his coveralls with the sweat of fatigue and a fearful understanding of why Alec Moore had been talking so much last week about nightmares in broad daylight. Men wounded in combat and lying in medical aid stations never had this terrible quick dying from invisible inner enemies.

A British volunteer nurse, completely covered and masked as he was, hurried down the aisle toward him. He was on his knees beside an old Frenchman, trying to place a hypodermic syringe needle into a vein to begin intravenous fluids. The old man's arms were thin as chicken legs, the vein under the atrophic skin kept shifting away from the inadequately sharpened needle, and his gloved hands became clumsier with each attempt.

"Doctor," the old man said feebly. "Don't bother. Let me die."

482

"Hold still, *mon vieux*," Mac said. The vein slid sideways under the thin aged skin, again.

"My wife. Last night. Died. Terrible."

Mac looked up as the British nurse came toward him. "Will you hold this man's arm steady, please, Sister?"

"Doctor," she said, "there's a telephone call for you in the front office."

He controlled a maniacal impulse to laugh out loud. Telephones. Here, at the bottom of the pit, with human protoplasm at its least dignified dying in pools of coughed-up lung hemorrhage and vomit, a telephone call seemed completely ridiculous.

"It's from Monsieur Obenpharo," the British nurse added.

"Sleep," the old Frenchman said. "Sleep. Sleep." Suddenly he screamed, "Water!" He had just lost bladder control.

"Ask them to tell Obenpharo," Mac said between his teeth, "that I cannot play polo today."

"They said it was urgent, Doctor."

"Damn it, I can't run out there with all this infected clothing on. And I can't keep changing. Please have him call tonight or tomorrow."

Under the mica window of her helmet, he saw her eyes try to smile at him. "All this is quite dreadful, isn't it?" she said, in a controlled friendly voice. "Have you had your inoculation, Doctor?"

"Yes," he said. Finally he felt the little tug of the vein wall giving as the tip of the needle entered, and a split second later he saw the little gush of venous blood. Without being asked, the nurse adjusted the drip rate of the liter bottle of plasma suspended above the old man's arm.

"D'you suppose," she said casually, as she worked beside him, "more vaccine has come in from Paris or Geneva? I'm not working at nursing full time, you see, so I missed getting my shot last week."

He stood up off his aching knees. No plague inoculation. And working here. And that easy controlled voice. Only a British woman could carry it off. "I'll mention it to Dr. Moore first thing," he said. "I'll remember."

"Thank you very much. I'd best hurry along with your telephone

483

message, shall I? They'll think I've suddenly died of plague." She walked off quickly. Twelve hours later she was dead.

Soon after the nurse, Alec Moore came into Mac's wing of the hospital. He threaded his way between the patients in the aisle, looking hunchbacked with fatigue.

"Fresh shift," he said to Mac. "Take a break, Malcolm. I'll take over, here."

Mac looked at the bulky figure in the coveralls, Falstaff gone completely now, leaving only a heavy brave man sagging with exhaustion.

"I'm all right," Mac said. "Everything is about as much under control as we'll ever be."

"Benari Obenpharo is outside, in his car." He added, as Mac stood up quickly, "I believe you'd best hurry off. I'm afraid Maia's in some difficulty."

"Difficulty? Maia?"

"I don't know. I couldn't talk to Obenpharo directly, of course. They told me that's what he said. He's outside, in a car."

"Maybe I can telephone her," Mac said. "Maybe that will clear up whatever it is, and I can come right back."

"Treat her like a bloody doctor's wife some other time, Malcolm. Not today. Hurry along with you."

Yacoub sat in the back seat of the car, between Obenpharo and Mac, swaying limply between them as the big Rolls took the street corners fast, trying to keep up with the Security Police jeep which guided them. On the little folding seats in the back of the Rolls, Nathan and his son Joseph sat beside each other, occasionally exchanging a quiet word in Spanish. Once or twice Nathan leaned forward to question the Spanish police officer who sat in the front seat, beside Obenpharo's driver.

The police officer had been called to the barbed-wire barriers of the *cordon sanitaire* around the Medina soon after the noon Angelus bells had rung, and it was he who had taken the responsibility of letting Yacoub come through the wire while he made a telephone call to headquarters. It was impossible that there should be a connection between Monsieur Benari Obenpharo and this staggering *indigène*

484

named Yacoub with a blood-soaked head and a blue swollen eye. When the officer had seen the man's hands clench convulsively on the barbed wires, tearing the skin carelessly while he begged to come through, he decided it was worth one telephone call. Now, inside Obenpharo's car, he kept turning his head to answer Nathan's quiet questions, interrupting himself only long enough to give the driver street directions.

"Do not blame me, monsieur," Yacoub kept repeating to Obenpharo. "They were crazy with smoking *kif*. From the blood they must have thought I was dead. I did not dare to move, even after my head became clear."

"Both of them, Moors?"

"No, monsieur. Algerian thugs, I believe."

The Spanish officer said, from the front seat, "We have a man at each airline office, if they appear."

"Nathan," Obenpharo said, like the chairman of a confidential business group, meeting to salvage what they could from disaster, "is Air France flying today?"

Nathan exchanged glances with his son Joseph and turned sideways in the folding seat to face Obenpharo. "No. Grounded by quarantine regulations. The final plane left last night."

"You know this for a fact?"

"Joseph just came back from the airport, Benari."

"Good. I want my plane gassed and ready to leave at once, Joseph. You spoke to Bud Williams?"

"No," Joseph said. He looked at his father.

Obenpharo stared at him. "I said, specifically, Joseph, tell Bud Williams—"

"—Benari," Nathan interrupted, "Bud Williams is gone. He sold space on your plane at a thousand dollars a head, and took off for Europe last night."

Obenpharo leaned back against the seat and closed his eyes. "Mac," he said.

Mac did not answer. His clothing was drenched with sweat, and he shivered occasionally. His hands were fists, his fingers bent so tightly that his hands had become numb. Over and over again, Yacoub's report of what had happened to Maia tore through him.

485

"Mac," Obenpharo said more loudly, without opening his eyes, "did Henri receive a plague inoculation?"

Mac turned his head slowly. "What?"

"Henri. Inoculated?"

"Yes."

"How do you know?"

"I did it myself. At the American School."

"Good." He opened his eyes narrowly. "And Mutirra?"

"No. The chances of her being in contact with an infected person were practically zero. She was at the bottom of the priority list."

"And Maia? You inoculated her, yourself?"

"No. For the same reason as Mutirra."

Obenpharo swiveled his eyes to Yacoub. In Arabic, he said, "Answer me with great clearness and no fear, Yacoub. You failed to protect your mistress, but you did what you could. Honorably. We understand."

"Yes, monsieur."

"Answer me this, now. Madame Obenpharo, my daughter, she was alive when you left her?"

"Yes, monsieur."

"You said she was hurt, with cruelty. How do you know for certain she was alive?"

"What's all this?" Mac asked. "What's going on in Arabic?"

"One moment," Obenpharo said, then told Yacoub, "Answer me in French. Only what you know to be a truth."

"She was alive, monsieur, because she spoke to me. She could not move, but she could speak. She said: Find the doctor. Hurry. Find him."

Obenpharo's eyes looked into Mac's. "You heard him?"

"Yes," Mac said, in agony. "Yes. Yes."

After they had followed the police jeep through the barbed wire and had driven as far as the narrowing streets would allow autos to go, they got out and mounted the steep alleys on foot toward the great fortress walls. Obenpharo sagged back against a doorway, clenching his fist on his chest over his heart, his face white with pain. "Mac," he said, breathing with his mouth held open, "I can't. I'll wait in the car."

486

"Call Dr. Moore," Mac said. "Tell him. Also say I will need all the streptomycin he can spare."

"Joseph," Nathan said, "go with Mac and Yacoub. I'll stay with Benari."

The Spanish police officer turned around. "You will understand, please," he said in French. "From this man Yacoub's story, there may be plague in the lady's house. There are very strict laws now about quarantine and such. The house must be sealed until the health authorities come."

"I will be responsible," Mac said quickly, controlling his voice. "As a physician deputized by the Service d'Hygiène."

"Ah, good. A deputized physician may enter the house," the Spanish police officer said. "You understand my position, señor."

"Yes," Mac said. The dignity, the vest-pocket official dignity, always and forever, with the world burning down. "I understand your position. I respect it. Only hurry now. Time is of the greatest importance now." He swung to Yacoub. "Go first, Yacoub. We follow. Only hurry."

They continued to mount the alley steps, Yacoub leading, then Mac and the police officer, with Joseph last. The tiny boxy houses were all tightly shuttered, but once Mac looked up and saw veiled women, on one of the flat roofs, peering down at them. From inside a closed café he heard a radio announcer's voice booming in Arabic anger. Cairo again, he thought, and then remembered the day Maia had driven past the scabby little café in Drideb at the foot of the Old Mountain Road. That was the day they had had their first serious argument. Let her live to have many more, he wished fiercely. Let Yacoub's story be exaggerated, a hurt and fearful man's exaggeration. But the details about his finding Jeanjean on the floor, shot in the back, could hardly have been invented. The part about the small dark-haired man with the fever and the great thirst for water was probably more or less accurate. Less, I hope. Let it be less accurate. Let there be only the typical *kif*-smoking and drugged hallucinations. Let the part about the fever be untrue. Or if it is true, let the fever be any one of a dozen other diseases, not plague. Not the plague. Anything other than the plague I have seen all day. *A disease of social disorder,* Alec Moore had said. And that phrase he kept remembering from the Greek play Roger had translated. *O golden Daughter of Zeus, send bright-faced deliverance.* Let there be no delays of the drug shipment from Paris, or the epidemic control team from Geneva, and no official red tape at Boukhalf Airport, but only a swift bright-faced deliverance of streptomycin. And plasma. Physiological saline. Ten per cent glucose in water. She may need them all. The fluids, the energy, the proteins, the antibiotics. If I could hold off death for strangers in the isolation hospital, let me hold off whatever needs to be held off now.

He was thinking so intensely to himself that he walked into Yacoub, who had stopped suddenly. Their alley was blocked by several Moors who were dressed in mourning sackcloth and carrying a long structure which looked like a low wooden camp bed. They were shouting and waving their arms furiously at two masked coveralled health department burial squad men who were trying to carry a body out of an Arab house. The body had been sewn into a long cylinder of straw matting, and the burial squad men wanted to place it in the crude wooden coffin sprinkled with lime. The mourners wanted to lift it on their traditional wooden carrying platform, and kept tugging at the straw matting and shouting. Together, they blocked the alley completely.

"Hurry," Mac said between his teeth to Yacoub. "Force your way past them."

One of the health department men saw the Spanish police officer and waved frantically to him for help. The officer began shouting in Arabic, pushing by Mac and Yacoub. The mourners gave the straw matting a great tug, tearing it open, and the corpse rolled onto the pavement. Everything became arms, legs, shouting, fury. The officer drew his pistol.

Desperately, Mac clawed his way through them, shouting to Yacoub to follow. A burial squad man blocked his way, and Mac threw him sideways against the wall so strongly the man slumped to the ground. He stepped over the corpse and landed hard on a mourner's bare foot. The man screamed and spit into his face, but Mac beat his way by. Behind him Yacoub was shouting, "It's through the tunnel, the tunnel straight ahead!"

Someone grabbed his shirt, but he swung his body hard and heard the cloth rip off, leaving him free. Behind him, the officer fired into the air, and the report boomed in the narrow alleyway. Mac saw an opening in the thick stone walls ahead of him, a low tunnel deeply shadowed. He ran and plunged into it, head and body crouched low, smelling the smell of centuries from the stone and blinded by the change from light to dark. He groped forward with his hands, rapping his head against the stone painfully, falling to his knees, stumbling toward the light at the end of the tunnel until the dimness brightened on the far side and he could straighen himself in the open.

The mahogany copper-studded door in front of him was open, and, as he ran through, a large rat scuttled sideways and out of sight.

"Maia!" he shouted. "Maia!"

He began to run out into the little fountain courtyard, then remembered what Yacoub had said about the bedroom upstairs. He ran up the stone steps, shouting, "Maia! Maia!"

At the entrance to the bedroom he saw her lying flat across the bed, her head and eyes turned sideways, watching the doorway. Jeanjean's body lay on the floor, and in the door to the bathroom a small dark-haired man was crumpled in a heap like laundry.

Only her eyes moved with him as he came into the room. She edged her head painfully around and tried to speak, but there was no sound. He fell on his knees beside her, recognizing the terrible glitter in the eyes. Most of her clothes had been torn off, and he was able to put his ear directly against her chest while he felt her pulse at the same time. It was bounding, the racing pulse of high fever, and within her chest he could hear the crackling sandpaper rubbing sound of lungs desperate for oxygen.

Her lips moved, then she managed to whisper, "Mac—"

He smoothed back the tangle of hair from her face, and when she said his name, he broke inside and kissed her dry cracked lips, then realized they were caked with blood.

"Maia," he said, "help is coming. Can you hear me? Can you hear what I say?"

Her eyelids moved. She rubbed the tip of her tongue over her lips. *"Habibi—"* she whispered. Her eyes closed and she seemed to lose consciousness for a moment, then she opened them again.

"In a minute," he begged her. "Hold on for a minute. They will be here in a minute. We will bring the medicine here. I will heal you. Can you hear me? You understand?"

Her head nodded slightly. She said something faintly in Arabic.

"Yes," he said. "Yes. Yes. Don't talk. Rest now."

Her lips moved again, and he lowered his ear directly over them. "All—day"—she said, and stopped to touch her lips with her tongue —"I—remembered—you—"

"I'm here now. I'm here. Only hold on." Her skin under his hands was incredibly hot.

"—Paris—remember—"

"Yes, Maia. Yes. I remember."

"—the boat—the—gold—"

"The gold statue is home. When you are better you can sit and watch it. I'll make a new one for you."

She tried to smile, but only her eyelids moved, "—Yacoub—"

"Yes, Yacoub told me. He explained. Forget everything. In an hour, you will feel better. Don't worry. Only hold on."

"—Henri—your son—"

"Your son and mine," he said. Her lips formed words and he bent his ear close to her mouth, but the words were the Arabic of her childhood.

The wall of language.

He heard voices downstairs, the police officer shouting something, and feet clattering up the steps. Joseph came in followed by Yacoub, both exhausted and sweating. They stopped in the doorway. He turned to them. "Joseph, can you find your way back?" His voice cracked. He began again. "Tell Obenpharo to beg all he can get from Dr. Moore at the hospital."

The Spanish police officer came huffing behind Joseph. His hat was gone, and his eyes looked wild. "You cannot enter a plague house!" he shouted. "Get out! Get out!"

Joseph turned on him furiously. "For the love of God, shut up! Can't you see she's in there dying!"

The officer stared fearfully at Maia and crossed himself. Yacoub crept in the room, bent over, and fell at Maia's feet. He wept without sounds, his bruised face twitching and weeping.

From the doorway, Joseph said quickly, "The officer can lead me back to the car, Mac. I can be back very fast."

Mac hardly heard him because Maia's lips were moving again. "—Habibi—" she breathed. Her eyes closed.

490

"No more than an hour, Mac," Joseph said. "Tell me the name of anything special you need. Mac, you hear me?"

Mac did not answer because Maia's pulse had stopped, and he forced his ear over her chest to catch the heartbeat. There was none, because she was dead. He could not believe it, but he knew she was, and when the knowing reached him so that he believed it, he put his shaking hands over his face.

(9)

ONCE again they sat on the deck of the houseboat named *Sequana* for the Roman goddess of the river Seine, and once again the slanting morning sun of France shone past the twin towers of Notre Dame in the sky above them. The sun burned strangely, shadowlessly, and there was a circle of hushed silence instead of the traffic roar.

Maia sat on the gently moving deck and, as she tried to comb her hair, she laughed helplessly to herself because the wind whipped it into loose strands across her face.

"You know, Mac, I've watched the river from the terrace of my house so many times, but I never thought I'd sail on it like this."

"This is fine," he said. He turned to follow her gaze at the great Cathedral standing so weighlessly above its island. The shadowless sun seemed spaceless, unreal.

"I love islands," Maia said, "but I know the mainland is always just across the way." She held out her arms stiffly, imitating a puppet's gesture, and said, " 'Dearer to me and of greater dignity would it seem to be called thy strumpet than his empress.' " She dropped her arms. "Remember? Didn't you like it?"

"Yes," Mac said, feeling a rush of tenderness for her play-acting toward herself and the world.

"I even love you when you sound so calm and American and, well, I don't know what to call it. So sensible. You see everything so clearly, darling."

"Not everything. And not really very clearly."

"You'll be sensible about Henri, I'm sure."

491

"He's my son now, because he's your son."

"Wherever Adams Farm is, he'll enjoy living there with you.'

"Of course, Maia."

"But you will both miss me, won't you?"

"You don't know how much."

"If he cries sometimes, you will remember he is still a little boy."

"I know, Maia, I know."

"But you," she said, "you won't because you will need to be stronger."

"Sometimes, when I see the golden statue, I think I'll feel just like Henri."

"And you'll come back to the Mediterranean with him, won't you?"

"Of course."

She stood up, keeping her feet apart in steady balance on the deck, raising both her hands to her temples to brush back the wind-whipped hair from her face. He shielded his eyes with one hand against the downpour of sunlight to watch her, a barefooted river nymph, bright-faced, the golden daughter of Zeus, seraphic in the bridge-arched perspective of the slow silver river. Maia! he wanted to cry out, companion for the journey no one of us can make alone, stay here with me.

"You," she said, "why do you look at me like that?" She took a deep breath. "The sun is so warm and pleasant. I think I'll enjoy lying in the sun a long time." She gave him her small secret smile.

He tried to smile back, but she was gone.

In his fever, the oceanic darkness thundered toward him in great rolling waves. He swung out into space, airborne, freely falling now, falling falling, then swinging high again, with his fevered blood pounding inside his head and nothing real, nothing solid, but only his great floating disembodied nothingness. Once or twice he thought quite clearly: I have the plague, but then the thought slipped away and endless empty space wheeled around him.

He viewed himself and his world and everyone he had known with a great all-seeing astronomic eye, a processional stretching back to the far horizon line of time, seeing himself with the simple clarity of the dying. Once again he saw himself back in the States, with Laura

492

lost between the twin clay gods of success and eternal youth and plundered by the private pain of all idol worshipers; once again he bent in agony over Stan on the operating table, holding his son's stopped heart while the small bloodless face closed shut; once again he broke himself on the rack of memory.

A few times he seemed to himself to be dreaming that Alec Moore was beside him, putting intravenous fluid needles into his arm, which hurt, but which he did not mind because there was nothing he minded now. "That's better, Malcolm," he thought Alec said, and he saw Alec's mouth forming other words, but he did not care to listen.

In one of his dreams, Eve Desmond came in with Alec Moore and a portly looming man who must have been Dr. Allenby of the Public Health Service. Allenby went away, and Eve sat on the edge of his bed and said, "How are you now, Maccabeus?"

"Much better. It's good to see you, Eve."

"Dr. Allenby and Warren Ross have an Embassy plane, Mac. We'll get you out of here. We'll get you home." When he said nothing, she added quietly, "You want to go home, don't you? Or are you still running away from home, Mac?"

"No," he said. "You've got me all wrong, Eve. I never ran away."

She put her hand on his arm gently. "But you've become another one who believes you can't go home again?"

"No," he said. "That's nonsense. I can go home." He pushed the pillow away from his head so he could look up. "As a matter of fact," he said, "I have to go home again. Everybody does."

She tried to smile. "You've gone the long way around, haven't you? They used to say that's the shortest way home."

"Eve," he said, now that he realized she did not understand, "this is home, too. I see it all now. It doesn't matter what I do. It only matters what I believe."

"Every time you talk like this, I lose you," she said softly.

"Of course," he said. "Because you've been raised to respect what a man does. But I guess a long line of belief has to come first. From your family, your grandfather." He made a large, shaky gesture. "From Notre Dame, and Obenpharo's Greeks and Phoenicians. And Nathan's Hebrews lost in the desert. And Abraham who knocked the heads off the idols."

493

"What in the world are you talking about?" she asked, taking her hand off his arm.

"We never really thought about how much we'd lost, did we, Eve?"

"What's this all about?" she asked again. "The faith of our fathers and all that?"

"Yes," he said, "in a special way."

"You've been lying in bed with fever and mumbling for days." She sighed. "Is this what you were talking about?"

"I suppose so. Don't look so scared, Eve. I haven't lost my mind."

"Well," she said, "I suppose it's one of those ideas. You see it or you don't." Once again she tried to smile. "If you could only hear yourself, Mac." She shook her head helplessly. "You sound like an old man."

He laughed, weakly, for the first time. "Of course. Six thousand years old."

Later, an hour later, or a day, or a week, Eve came back again. This time Alec Moore was with her, and Warren Ross, and the American newspaperman, what was his name, yes, Ned Walker. They all sat in a half circle around his bed. He felt more lucid and able to talk, but he kept his eyes closed. Maybe they weren't there at all, and this was another intensely real dream. It was hard to know, now, what was real.

"He looks better today," Eve said in her calm warm voice.

"Easy does it," Alec Moore said. "He's on the downslope of the fever, but his fluid balance is still worrying me."

Eve stood up and came to the foot of the bed. "Mac," she said quietly, "you've opened your eyes twice. Why don't you just try keeping them open?"

He opened them with an effort. "Hello, Eve." He looked at Warren and Ned, who were standing now, too, smiling the way people do at the very sick.

"Well," Alec said, "welcome to the land of the living."

"I feel as if I've been away," Mac said.

"You have been," Alec said. "Doctors are terrible patients, and now that you're well, I'll be glad to be rid of you."

"How's Cindy?" Mac asked Warren.

494

"Just dandy, Mac, and she sent her love. She wanted to fly down this week with us, but the Navy plane could carry only three passengers."

"Three?" Mac looked at Eve.

"Yes," she smiled. "Warren and me and Dr. Allenby. Remember my boss? He's temporarily head man of the World Health team in Tangier now."

"And you?" he asked. "His strong right arm?"

She laughed. "Left. I'm your strong right arm."

Ned Walker spoke for the first time. "Adam's rib."

Eve groaned. "You see, Mac? The same old jokes we've always heard."

Mac looked at Ned Walker. "How's Roger?"

Ned Walker glanced out the window, then back. "Dead," he said. "He didn't even live to see the Sultan come back to Morocco. He missed the whole independence deal."

Mac closed his eyes. No one spoke. Far off, faint in the distance beyond the open windows, there was the murmurous sound of the sea. He opened his eyes after a moment and said to Alec, "How long have I been like this?"

"Weeks, Malcolm. A massive infection. I'm convinced that only whatever degree of immunity the vaccine gave you saved you."

"That," Eve said, "and Dr. Moore."

Alec bowed his head slightly toward her. "I only treat the sick, as Paré used to say. God cures them."

"The Obenpharos?" Mac asked.

"Never touched by the plague," Alec said. "This villa is so nicely isolated, y'know. But Mutirra just sits and stares and keeps the shutters closed. Benari the same."

"How's Henri?"

"He'll be in to see you right after lunch."

Mac put out his hand. Alec Moore took it, and said lightly, "If Benari were here, I'm sure he'd say you owe a cock to Aesculapius. Or one of the Mediterranean gods."

"I owe a case of Scotch," Mac said, "to Alec Moore."

Alec gave his rumbling laugh. "I'm going to have myself my first bloody drink in a month. Would you just send along one bottle right away, Malcolm?"

495

Benari Obenpharo came in after lunch with Henri, who ran across the room to where Mac sat beside an open shaded window above the courtyard. When Mac placed an arm around his shoulders, Henri put his face against Mac, crying. Benari stood silently, watching his grandson and Mac. He looked bent and deeply aged. All his conquests, glories, spoils, were behind him now.

"As soon as I can walk better," Mac said, "I'd like to go see Mutirra."

"Yes," Obenpharo said. "Irra would like that. Did Dr. Moore tell you how ill you were?"

"Yes."

Obenpharo shook his white lion's mane slightly. "How vengeful the gods are. Two old sick people like Irra and me, we lived through it, while the young and the useful were thrown down."

"They told me about Roger," Mac said. "I finally met him, you know. You had a fine son, Benari."

Obenpharo hunched slightly, the way a man bends when struck by a deep pain. "Yes," he said. "I always knew it. They stood in the streets for miles to say good-by to him."

"Isn't that what he wanted? To bring them all together?"

"Yes. Certainly. But now they'll do with him as they did with the other rich man's son, Buddha. They'll ignore his warnings against idol worship and make an idol of him. Face and all." He stopped, and made a helpless gesture.

"Mac," he said, "tell me, why are we bound to a wheel of fire like this? Is there any meaning to so much suffering?"

"I don't know, Benari."

"This is no time to be gentle or evasive, Mac. We're naked now."

"Benari," Mac said, feeling a profound compassion for the old man, for the boy in his arms, for Maia and himself, for all the mortal search for meaning, "don't ask me for magic." He raised his voice in a kind of sorrowful anger. "And don't ask me to take your hopes or your guilt, or mine, and everyone's, and make a new theology out of it. If you want easy answers, the world is filled with them. But they're for frightened children, and you're a man."

"Don't ask me for that kind of courage, Mac. I don't need it any more."

496

"But I do," Mac said. "I'm only talking to myself."

They looked at one another deeply, both dwellers on the harsh mainland, both having left all the comfortable islands of illusion forever, saying nothing because there was no need to speak. Mac turned to look down at the golden statue of Maia, hearing in the sunlit murmurous distance the great global crosstides of the Straits below the cliff, where the living waters of the Mediterranean and Atlantic met.

Set in Linotype Times Roman
Format by Marguerite Swanton
Manufactured by The Haddon Craftsmen, Inc.
Published by HARPER & BROTHERS, *New York*